The first thing I heard, ever, was a grunt. A snort of some sort - that's what woke me up.

Like someone clearing the back of their throat - too lazy to put any real effort into it - the sound was so repulsive that I couldn't help but take notice. Which is disappointing, retrospectively: it could've been something interesting like the slow, wailing howl of the far depths of Hell or the indistinguishable rumbling of beasts and creatures never before classified - or screams! Scary things, frightening things, any... things.

But no, nothing unique like that, just a grunt that startled me a little.

I opened my eyes - figuratively. My eyes were plenty open already. Consciousness set me adrift staring at the slats in someone's ribcage, jiggling around in front of me like a macabre Halloween prop. When I realized that this wasn't actually a decoration, that the bones and vertebrae were physically connected and moving about, it became pretty clear I wasn't okay.

I shuddered with a dose of surprise as bones closer to my view suddenly shifted back - my eyes instantly locked to them. There quivered a pair of arm bones connected to my wrist bones, 'hands' locked tightly to a pair of handcuffs linked to the 'people' both in front of and behind me in one giant chain. It drifted through their backs; their ribcages tapered off to just vertebrae before fading out to nothing at all. The tiniest bit more concerned for my situation, I saw that I suffered the same fate.

Something screeched in my ear as a loose, leathery wing nearly scraped the top of my head. The creature gave a sort of unnecessary bob to its flight; dull, lifeless eyes rolling about in its head while the beast charged up the side of what appeared to be a massive cavern. My eyes lingered for a second before slowly crawling up the walls of this Hellish pit, really getting a sense of how big this place was. Half-wrecked pillars propped the ceiling of the cavern up, detail faded nearly everywhere. Lines and lines of skele-folk wandered though cut archways, patrolled by these dopey-eyed demons lazily flapping about.

Farther down, the mist grew thicker, with lines of people crossing endless rooms down a chasm headed to the center of the earth. Something swam among them, large and dark, its body meticulously black. Its green, soulless green eyes glided behind a pillar and out of view, curling around the adjoining room and watching its surroundings carefully. The sight of the beast sealed any lingering doubts that this wasn't Hell, that my very real death hadn't taken place, and that I wasn't in the depths of a nightmare.

I had no memories of my life, aside from very basic things that even babies know: eating and sleeping, day and night; life in general; going to the movies alone was embarrassing, and culture defined who we were. But as for a personal life, I drew a blank. I had no memories of myself, no ideas where I might've lived, how I'd lived my life, if I had kids, or if I'd nursed sick cats back to health for a living. The only thing I did remember - a tiny blip of a memory - was a pair of blue eyes. They owned no body; there was no face with them, just a pair of Godforsaken eyes staring at me from the side, bugged-out and terrified.

I had no idea where they came from, if they were my own or belonged to someone else. They were just there, rolling in my head as I tilted this way and that. The rest of my mind was sickeningly clean. I had no idea of anything: what I truly looked like, how old I was before I died or what gender I was - I didn't even have a name! The handcuffs were probably rented.

I was Me, and that's all I knew. Me... and those eyes.

Pulled about as if on some motorized walkway, I tried saying something, to maybe try and give a quick "howdy" to the demons screeching around. Nothing. My skeletal jawbone snapped back into place, clicking my teeth together as I just floated past instead. Realizing that at least I could hear, I clicked to a beat and sort of looked around like a bored child. Behind me was uniform: each skele-folk kept their glare straight ahead, wrists out and stiff as ever. When I looked to the other lines, they were the same - I seemed to be the only one moving around.

Something darted beneath my vertebrae, swimming to the next pillar and leaving just a few centipedal legs showing, face locked onto someone else. Peering over, trying to see just what this thing was, I suddenly bumped into the neighbor behind me, and then into his friend behind him. Like slowly falling down a pair of horizontal stairs, I tumbled out of position; frightened, arms flailing, and hit by each successive skele-half behind me.

Scrambling to get a grip on something or someone beneath me,

I shoved myself away from the line. They all passed by at the same pace, skulls still facing forward as my spot marched farther and farther away. Frantically, I looked down at my wrists, back to the spot, then back to the rest of these loose-faced demons flapping around. One made a half-assed beep at me before flying off, continuing on his path. No big alarm. No one seemed really worried, no one cared - nothing happened. All they seemed to do was lazily move out of the way, giving me a wide berth, and continue with their jobs. I half-expected to fight my way out of there, snatch a pair of their wings and flap my way to an exit.

Chest bones quickly rising and falling like I had to catch my breath, something changed direction beneath me. The massive black something-or-other shot directly under my last dangling spine-bit as it wheeled around like a little helicopter, hundreds of claws and hands gripping onto the nearest pillar a ways down. Frozen, holding my not-breath, I saw its beady green eyes snap suddenly upwards and focus on me, narrowing. Hele-spine stopped.

"No... no, no!" I clicked. The gape of its maw lit up neon green, mouth extending farther and farther back like it was crudely stitched together. The green lights dotted the cave, back end of the monster lighting up places I couldn't see before. In a flash, it darted to the next pillar, higher up, eyes still on me. My fictitious blood went cold.

"NO! Nononononono!" My jaws clicked furiously together as I struggled to swim, arms wheeling around like a paddle boat, trying to get away. The creature let out a snarl, crashing from pillar to pillar as if it were drunk, barely coordinating itself. Spinning my hele-spine as fast as I could, I drifted at the pace of a fast walk, scrambling for the top. I didn't know where I was going or where I could even hide from something this big. Frustrated, I changed tactics, scooping at the air as fast as I could to move the tiniest bit faster. I kept gazing back and seeing that monster lurching forward, filling more and more of my field of vision.

The air suddenly rang around me as the demon howled, crashing into the nearest pillar. Large chunks of Hell dropped from the ceiling and I was sure it'd be crushed, offering me a fair chance to at least gain some distance. I expected some sort of satisfying crunch, but the ceiling only dropped a few inches before slowly healing itself back to the top, solidifying once again as the monster perched there, trying to find me with its impressively tiny eyes. I huffed though my collarbones.

"Aww, come on!" I cried through nonexistent lips, apparently so fond of talking that I was going to keep on doing it, despite that no one could possibly hear me and I certainly wasn't saying anything.

The demon located me again, gnashing its teeth as the green mist seeped everywhere. Like some hopeless idiot, I kept swimming away, making absolutely no difference in my chance of escape. I guess I just didn't want to drift there and give up so easily. I'd rather hang on to an impossible wager than keel lightly to the side, disappointed with myself. This was my barely counting, hardly-human life!

Its mouth stretched wider, secondary and tertiary mouths opening from various other places on the beast. With my head pretty much facing backwards, each arm swinging around as fast as my little shoulders would allow, the creature launched from that last pillar. It took about half a second of motion for it to catch up, mouth opening wider and wider as the two of us were pointed vertically. This wasn't fair! Here I was, stuck being some sort of soul-snack for a giant, pissed off demon crocodile centipede - that's what my life totaled to. Other people could become musicians, doctors, accountants - anything - and the best I'd be known for was some stupid skeleton half that got so pathetically nowhere that the demon didn't even have to try hard. Even in the four-and-a-half minutes I'd been awake, I knew that was pretty screwed up.

With a sudden rush of adrenaline, the monster sped up, using every bit of its power to snap onto those very last links of spine, my arms suddenly pinned down by my sides as I rocketed around the cavern at a breakneck speed. Clicking in silent, petrified screams, I saw the demon crash into the next wall, senses dislodged for a second as we started shooting to the other side. Hell seemed almost small. Thrown about, the pressure suddenly dropped from my bones, I spun, barely conscious and alone. Swinging my head around, trying to understand what had just happened, I realized that the demon was playing with its food. I could see it take a victory lap to the side, zipping about like a bolt as it shot to the bottom of the pit, eyes still keen on me and giving me a few seconds to mill over my long, fulfilling life.

"D...daammit..." I spun, just aware enough to realize what was about to happen, but not conscious enough to say anything or think anything important. Distantly, that beast screeched, charging forward as fast as it could go. "H... Hate this world. Hate you... stupid looking... demons."

I tried pointing at the lazily flapping demon closest to me and realized that I didn't even have any arm bones left. Whimpering pitifully, I tried to sob without any tear ducts. My body slowly rotated so I could face back down and watch my own death come up to meet me.

It darted from side to side, straight from the ground, and bathed the caverns in an awful, puke-yellowish green light. Details faded out like I was about to get hit by a speeding train. All I could do was float there and watch it happen, whining and moaning that life was terribly unfair. The demon pushed off that last pillar, tiny eyes frenzied and nearly split open like a demonic banana. I suddenly got mad. It wasn't enough to just think this was bullshit, it was bullshit. Why did my life have to be trivialized down to the first bad decision I made? What was I supposed to do, sit and stare like some brain-dead monkey as Hell carted me around for the scenic tour?

"C'mon!" I clicked silently at the nuisance, more than frustrated. "C'mon, idiot!"

My bones rattled in anger as the demon's teeth were all but a lunge away, shouting at its tonsils as they came up to meet me.

"DO IT!" I clattered together, challenging this monster as we erupted out of Hell. I was instantly knocked out. I remember hitting the ceiling hard, being thrown back into the void of its mouth, and instantly dissolving to nothing.

Being nothing is a lot like being a blemish on someone's skin; I was not linked with anyone or anything, I wasn't aware of anything. I was, at best, the last few seconds of my life cobbled together into one last, lingering thought.

"How..." The thought started, "...about...that?" How about it? How was that?

I didn't care about anything else. "How...about that?" My thoughts began to drift apart from each other, mind trying to find peace in its own existence, trying to give that light, silent nod and be happy about what I'd learned.

Happy...
    About...

    That.

2

Wait.

About that? Was I happy about that?

No. No, I was not happy about that. Give me five minutes of life and try to instill some sense of fulfillment? Ha! Not happy. Not fulfilled.

I felt myself begin to seep through those thoughts, sinking in as my annoyance gave me a voice again.

"How about... the demon?" The tired, mostly-dead part of me rambled on as I felt myself slowly pulse back to life, slowly realize that I couldn't just let this be done. I didn't like the demon. I wasn't happy about the demon. It was more than a little ridiculous that some stupid, fat-headed demon thought it could just shove me around and take what it wanted. Anger, frustration gave me a very basic mental form, gave power back to my actions. It almost felt like I hadn't been brunch. As I looked around for some demon to strangle, the world suddenly went pitch black.

It felt like I was somewhere again. I looked around in this completely dark world before I saw it: a light. Pure white, it seemed to zigzag around in the sky, burning through the world as it tore it apart. I followed it, watched it as - just like the demon - it seemed to notice me. The light went absolutely nuts, darting left and right all over the sky before finally stopping above my head. Worried something like before would happen again, I tried to take a few steps away. The light followed.

"I wonder what-" The light suddenly rocketed down, slamming around me like a column of water and catching me in it, screaming out in pain. It felt like little knives were paring me apart, disintegrating me once again as I tried to escape, walls of light solid and impassible. Thrashing back and forth, my fading body suddenly locked up, unmovable. A pressure sat on my chest, squeezing the life out of me as my breath became choppy and pained, giving me less and less room to breathe. I swore that'd be the end to this all.

Then, without reason, it let go.

Pupils rattling in my head, my body desperately tried to explain what was going on. Something trickled down my hand: a droplet of water. My eyes darted to my other hand, dripping wet as well. I was entirely soaked, head to soul.

Splatters of color began to apply themselves to the environment around me as it took form, defining the corners of a large room. It was a house, a living room bursting forth from the white light and nothingness. As if watching a negative slowly develop, my eyes darted to the details as they became dark enough to see.

I was… alive?

"What, round two? Haven't we had enough fun yet?" Someone asked tensely, voice low like they were insulted and exhausted - it sounded like a man. My eyes tried to lock onto the figure that spoke up, nothing but a ball of wisps and curves, mostly hollow. A larger man stood behind him, looking vaguely in my direction while he talked with a mother and her child. I pushed my body to make a move, to investigate what they were saying, to try and get a bearing on what had just happened. I was locked in position, immovable. I cringed: the water made it feel like my whole body was on fire.

My jaw was locked tight, unable to move, unable to turn my head or body any position other than how I awoke. I could feel the water on my face and did my best to twitch my head and shake it off. The first voice spoke again, laughing.

"Aww, does that hurt? It does? Well, good." Struggling to breathe as the man chuckled, I could barely tell he was dancing around like a proud dolt in front of me." That's exactly what you deserve for attacking these people here. Demons like you deserve nothing but agony above ground, where you're not wanted."

He laughed, stepping close to my face before delivering a quick, arrogant slap. Confused, frustrated, I coughed out a wheeze of pain - I hadn't done anything. There must've been some mix-up, some…mistake. I began to grow more frustrated, confused and angry. I could see the environment around me now: the couch, the pale sunlight from the windows, what looked to be early morning outside as it stretched across the floor - everything. The only thing left was this violent little ball of annoyance.

"Can…" My voice surprised me, shocked that I was actually able to talk, that I must at least have a throat enough to communicate. I just wasn't expecting it to be this loud, or this low. Before I could finish my thought, the end of a pole bashed into my teeth, knocking my head back. I whimpered, unable to move, struggling against whatever held me back. Wincing hard, I tried to speak again. "Help… Please…"

"After fighting you for a good hour, I'll be dammed if I let you breathe a single word painlessly." I didn't do anything! What was going on? It was right in my face, the bare depressions of eye holes, or something like them just inches away. Satisfied with this round of torturing, it strode away before turning back to me quickly, something sharp against my throat. My breathing picked up, enduring the lasting pain. The man laughed cruelly again and used the flat of his blade against the side of my face, pressing with just enough force to turn my head. I only breathed harder, mad.

"How does it feel, demon? How's the wrath of the Heavens feel on your ragged little soul?" He laughed heartily, pushing my head around and taunting me. If I could groan and roll my eyes at his haughty way of speaking, I would've.

"Not…. me!" I spat out helplessly, boiling with anger and feeling it course through the rest of my body as he teased the blade across my throat. With each new pulse of rage, the man took greater form, the shiny, almost-mocking armor adorning him; the pike he held. His eyes were wild and constricted, his stance distanced and ready for battle in various shades of blue and yellow. He was dressed in an ancient medley of attire, like some sort of spiritual warrior crossed with a quarterback with the mockingly bad touch that topped it all off; the feathered wings across his back. I heard the plates of his armor clink as he took a step back, finally, almost contemplating his options. It didn't last long.

The bastard lunged forward with his pike, stabbing it deep into my chest before I could speak again, laughing as he did it. I could feel it pierce through, surging the pain I was already in to new levels. Clearer and clearer he became with each pulse, until he was the same opacity as the people standing behind him, apparently unaware of the butchering taking place. A fighter…angel? I cried out just a bit, a high-pitched whine gurgled into a dull hiss; the sound audible in my ears and the man's as well. He lunged again, making another cut into my neck just below my head.

Push! Push! Something urged me on, nagging the edges of my thoughts.

"Your head will make a nice memento, don't you think so?" He laughed again, cutting the pike further into my neck as I could feel it exit behind me, the blade scalding hot. "Maybe I'll stuff it and use it to display my pike."

Internally I screamed out loud, thrashing against the cage this body kept me in. My gurgling became louder, before bubbling at a solid growl. I pushed the boundaries, pulling on my hands with all my might just to make them move; and, like molasses, they began to pull from their position. The weight shifted more to my legs as I grew taller in some respect, both hands shakily jerking up towards my face. My head pulled back farther and farther, lips pulling away to reveal my teeth. The hands in front of my face resembled a humans, though much more calloused and thicker. I watched the streaks of blood-red coloring run down my nose, miles in front of my face and felt the warmth of life reach down to my toes as I was truly born again, snapping back into my control.

The angel stood there, face puckering in concern while trying to take sly steps away. My lungs heaved; my body pulsed with energy, the searing pain of whatever liquid had been dumped on me evaporated away. I could feel my anger rise to the peak of what I had known and surge past it, driving me into insanity. How dare he? How dare he do this?! Wasn't he listening? My weight shifted back to something behind me, standing taller and taller, high above this insignificant waste of dust with his face held in fear, eyes widening as he got a better grasp on his weapon. My growling escalated, throwing my head back and bellowing out a shaking, earth-tearing roar that ensured everyone in a one-mile radius, dead or alive, heard it.

Throwing my weight to the ground, I leapt at the man, only to see the coward already running away from me. He looked over his shoulder and stretched out his gait, darting through the solid wall in front of us. With little second thought, I tore through it in hot pursuit, bursting the physical wall as well. Splinters of wood and drywall exploded in front of me into a bedroom, the angel darting through another wall as I followed him the same way. He skidded on the floor and made a hard right as my debris tumbled behind him, drywall and bits of a lamp crashing onto the wooden floor alongside. There was no one else in sight. I couldn't see the difference between a mother and a blender, all I knew was my need to tear apart this cocky angel who had the gall to try and sever my head for some stupid novelty.

All was rage as I lunged closer to him, reaching out and swatting the man off his footing with one hand. His clunky, medieval-period shoes scratched the surface of the floor up, stumbling and missing a step before he finally slammed to the ground shoulder-first, a tangle of metal and flesh as he rolled to a stop. I was atop the bastard in an instant, heart racing, seething with unbridled hatred. My two hands grabbed hold of his shoulder armor and pinned him down. I grinned and gripped him tighter, claws penetrating into his skin, denting his armor; he was my prey! I foamed and twitched in diabolical glee, breathing heavily. The angel turned to me, eyes wide in fear, two deep blue pools of terror I knew very well. Everything suddenly stopped, the floor beneath me seeming to drop out. Those eyes.

They were the only thing I knew very well.

They were blue. Plenty of people have blue eyes, but something lit up in my brain like 'Yes! There you go! You found them! Good job!'
The light bulb finally went on.

Cold, shaking, I coughed nothing but short heaves. No way. He continued to stare at me, eyes swirling with confusion after a moment as he looked to both of my arms pinning him down, then back to my face. I was suddenly very aware of my surroundings, very aware of what I had done, aware that I was not the only person here. The armor was shining, reflective, but a russet-colored stain in my direction tarnished its glow. As I moved, the stain moved with me, an unidentified mass of red and white. I looked to the two meaty hands grasping the angel; they were not mine.

I dropped the man instantly, scooting backwards until I suddenly hit a wall. Gasping for air that just wouldn't come, I accidentally knocked into a cabinet and ran into a fridge before wedging myself there, hands splayed out. Noticing they definitely weren't human, I turned one over, slowly flexing and grasping it. This was me. This was in my control. But what was I?

I shot back to the angel, just now slowly picking himself off the floor - he wasn't injured. He jumped back against the cabinets as I came close. Both of us froze for a moment, generally afraid of the other. Still mid-panic, I managed to reach out, grabbing his weapon half-embedded into a cabinet. My body awkwardly hopped to the wall and propped the pike up, backing away from it to see the best reflection of myself that I could. Strewn with my blood, the blade gave a distorted picture of a long, red-and-white reptilian face. Slowly, I pulled my lip up to expose the serrated teeth that lined my mouth and the horns jutting from the back of my jaw. My eyes, wild and green, were all but tiny things compared to the rest of me. Craning my head around, I could see the red-and-white sort of slinky body with a strip of hair along its spine, 'my' feet toddling to keep up the position I held now. The tail above twitched with extreme nervousness all on its own.

"Oh…God…" I froze in place, brows furrowed at this whole situation. The angel kept his position against the wall, looking to the other man - a Priest as I could see now - as he surveyed the damage I had done. The hallways behind me were practically dripping with bits of drywall, picture frames smashed and bent inward, floor covered in deep grooves. The only thing my mind could hold was a sputtering line of 'what did you do'. I had done this. ONLY I had done this. This was entirely my fault.

Staring in terror as reality hit me, I sat down heavily, utterly confused and overcome by everything. I wanted to apologize. I wanted to run away. I wanted to go back to being a drifting skeleton in the parade once more; anything but where I was, what I had done, and what I had become. With a glittering sound, the angel was behind me, hand just about reaching the pike, eyes fully intent on me. Our glances locked once more, another tremble by the exact blue eyes I had been looking for - the only ones I knew of. They obviously didn't know me. I looked away.

"Are you the police?" I rambled half-heartedly, looking to the

Priest and the mother slowly picking up bits of wall. "Can…can you tell them I'm sorry? I don't care if I leave or go back, I…oh…shit. I am so sorry." I tried to hold my head, feeling my arms were too short. The angel circled in front of me slowly, like he was catching a stray cat.

"I don't think I'm supposed to be here. I don't know how I got out. I don't know how I survived that…or what that was…or…" I vaguely tried to grab at my mouth in some sort of shock. What had I done?

I rocked shakily to my feet, taking a step towards the two people I assumed owned this house, trying to talk to the mother standing there. But her eyes were focused on the damage, and nothing else. Tracking, thinking. I was dead. I had to be dead. The Priest suddenly said a quick word to the angel, and him responding in kind, both very nervous. What an awful mess I made. A thought hit me.

"Please, if you can just tell them I'm sorr-"

"Shut up." He hissed at me very matter-of-factly as I shut my mouth." Can't you see you're not wanted here? Don't you stupid things understand doing shit like this is wrong?"

"I didn't mean anything; I'm not even sure why I'm here. You can talk to the Priest, ri—"

The pike leveled at my face, covered in some sort of golden powder along the whole blade.

"I told you to shut up. Don't you understand what I'm saying?" He leaned in closer, lip curling back "SHUT." He pantomimed closing a door, before giving me the middle finger and pointing to the ceiling.

"UP. Got it?" When I didn't reply to him, he continued on, "Humans here no like you. Demons bad."

He pointed to the mother and her child, then waved his finger in front of them. I lowered my head a little bit, ashamed. I wasn't sure my intentions were getting through to him. I had no issues with sitting quietly, gaze to the ground.

"God, you stupid monsters." He stood up again, frustrated with me. The angel took a few steps away, muttering to himself before holding a hand over the blade and chanting something foreign. I wasn't sure what he was going to do; I figured that he'd be chasing me back to Hell, back to where I apparently belonged in some hideous demon body I didn't own. I wasn't anywhere as big as that monstrosity, but I certainly wasn't small.

Looking to the mother, I noticed the child around her feet, staring directly at me. It wasn't staring past me, it wasn't looking out the window I sat in front of; it looked AT me. The child was all of four years old, five at the max, but the kid had a death grip stare on my face. I slowly moved my head to the left, watching her eyes follow, and repeated it to the right with the same results.

"Usually" The angel behind me spoke up, pike resting on his shoulder, "with demons that escape that realm, we send them back where they came from and call it a day. We don't eliminate masses of your numbers; you don't eliminate masses of ours. Keeps everything happy." I kept my head low, scolded. Fine.

"This has been so much fun. Not that I wouldn't love doing this again, but we're just going to clean everything up right now and make sure you're gone for good." He switched positions on the handle, raising it high over his head, stretching back and chanting again as it glowed a brilliant golden color.

"Waaait wait wait wait a second! I'm sorry, I'm sorry! I'll go back!" I stumbled, darting back into the living room and tripping over my new body awkwardly. Maybe I'd be able to find a hole, a portal, something to get me out of this. My reptilian/human hands grabbed at the carpet, a metal clanking duly resounding behind me. Before I had time to say something, to turn over and plead my case, the angel struck.

The pike tore through my body like I was made of glass, burning red hot on my shoulder down to the small of my back as I exploded into a cloud of black smoke. My remnants shot like a bullet downward, though the floorboards, through the basement ground and back towards the bowels of Hell.

3

"It's here; I know that damn thing is still here." The angel's voice strained with frustration; far away, swimming in echoes and muted through glass - I could hear it as my senses returned to me. I felt my body wedged into something solid, expecting brimstone and deviousness to be my environment now. Instead I opened my eyes to a world of wet, dark earth, but not Hell. Confused, I tried to turn over and get my bearings, finding myself completely encased in the ground like I was buried and laid to rest.

"So, we're NOT giving them peace of mind? Are you saying I'll be going back on my guarantee here, Raziel? They paid good money for that." A different voice, deeper - the Priest, probably. Guarantee? The ground knocked louder than the conversation before there was an annoyed grumble.

"I'm not saying that. But I wouldn't be surprised if we've got to make another house call here in a few months. We can blame another spirit then, for Christ's sake; they live next to a graveyard. That's something people believe, right?" The ground thumped much louder as if something was thrown against it before the angel complained again, " The Hell are you? I know you're in there!"

I tensed up a little, trying to keep extra still; not that I could move anyways. The Priest's tone rose quickly.

"If we're trying to convince them their house isn't haunted any longer, it'd be a good idea if you could stop banging on the walls like the damn demon!" There was softer, more muted talking as the angel rambled on his own.

"It's between right here..." I heard some sort of scratching mark, dulled by the earth, "and right... here."

Something shot into the soil not inches from the side of my face, retracted back out of the wall before I could even react. Breathing faster,

I prayed he wouldn't do that again. Might've been a little dull with his friendly banter, but he seemed to make a much better demon detector. The other man suddenly spoke up again, louder.

"Stop putting holes in the wall!" He muttered disappointedly like he was angry with a child as the other voice groaned, frustrated. "What failed us? You doubt my ability, or yours?"

"That… thing wasn't phased by my strongest attacks, or the seal. Egh… I mean, that's my high-class stuff there! Holy water made the damn thing change colors!" I could hear metal scraping the floor, the voice getting farther away. "Let them know the house has been purified, give them our number if they're terrified by anything else. I give it a month, max."

Softer mumbling before the sound left all together, heavy feet clomping up the stairs until the door finally shut - I let out a breath of gravel-y air. Twenty minutes passed before there was a slam of car doors above me, the rattle of some kind of engine before all was quiet.

Slowly, I tried wriggling around, going nowhere. Anxious and frustrated, I tried to flop around with no improvement. It didn't make any sense. If I was dead, and I was moderately certain that I was, why couldn't I drift easily through things as the angel - Raziel - apparently could?

I thought dead. Thought passable, thought light. My body shifted a few inches.

Slowly, tirelessly, I wormed my way in a dance-like shimmy through the soil until my nose hit the rough concrete wall of the house. With one last empty thought I broke through, getting an errant hand to the basement floor. With another ten minutes of shimmying and pulling, I flopped on the ground in beautiful freedom and took sweet, long, beautiful breaths.

I felt awful, slow, and lumbering. Hindered by muscle and size - with barely more than a second glance, I could tell I was still in the demon body. There was no other voice in my head, no driving panic to run away, or to figure out what was, was. I was very large. I was very uncoordinated. I was very burnt out by whatever-the-Hell that ordeal was earlier, and the last thing on my mind was to run around in glee. I sat and sulked instead.

I didn't want to be in Hell. It's not a place I dreamed of returning to; but it felt wrong to be here. Felt wrong to be 'alive', like I had been smuggled out of jail, like I had fallen out of an assembly line. I wanted to earn that freedom.

There was a dank ball cap lying on the floor in front of me, a pile of bluish clothes off to the left and various earthy colored garments off a distance in the dark. Light pierced into the basement in a few places; underneath the door jam and through the small windows at the top of the wall. My vision obscured; the giant ball of a nose in my view interrupted a moment of serene peace. My sight was nearly halved; the long reptilian-like nose still jutted from my face, each eye desperately trying to overlap one another in some decent vision. I huffed, tilting my head and snorting

in frustration as I whipped around in annoyance, like someone had put
an orange between my eyes. Behind me was a mark, a large triangular scar
burned into the wall. There were three outlying marks from each point of
it on the exact spot the angel shot me at to try and 'kill me off anyways'. My
lip curled at the thought of him.

I rocked to my feet, the unbalanced animalistic ankles instantly
crumpling off to the side. It took nothing to throw me back on my butt, my
tail whipping around and slapping against one of the wooden supports like
a drum. I froze, steps quickly rushing above me. I felt like I was in trouble;
the basement was penetrated by light, the door slamming open as a figure
stood in front of it.

"For God's sake, what now?!" She stomped down the stairs in a rush
to the basement. The woman from before, the mother, scanned the darkness
quickly before throwing on the lights. I scrambled to the other side of the
basement with a mix of front and back feet under the cover of darkness,
afraid to be seen. She stood at the bottom of the steps, young, black hair,
sweatpants; the look on her face said it all. She was unhappy, unnerved,
at wit's end. Waves of guilt hit me, ashamed of being such a burden and
trouble to these people. It wasn't their fault; it wasn't anyone's, really. But the
best thing for me to do would be leave and give them a little rest, let them
know I had my wits. That I wasn't going to hurt them. Maybe I could give
them that peace now.

I stepped slowly into the light in front of the mother, head hung
low. She instantly turned in my direction, squinting into the darkness and
took another step down, leaning against the rail cautiously.

"Hiuhhhh." I garbled, before clearing my throat and trying again,
"Hi."

She seemed to look expectantly at me, waiting for something. In a
rush, I managed to throw together an apology fairly quickly.

"I'm not sure if you can hear me, don't know if it matters." I
looked to my toes, all four sets of them, dragging a claw along the concrete
nervously. I hated this. I hated this all. The circumstances, the guilt, this
whole ghostly experience was surprisingly not a lot of fun. "I'm sorry if I
terrorized you; sorry if anyone got hurt. I made a mess of everything, and I
can apologize until I'm blue in the face, but-"

"EEEEHHHHHHHH!" The washing machine went off, sending
me into the air. I leapt, crashing down on a laundry basket that crumpled
under my weight, shooting it directly at the wall. The woman screamed,
making me scream, the two of us harmonizing for a second before we
simultaneously bolted up the stairs. Being the faster of the two I darted to
the top, all four legs splayed out in panic. Not a second later the woman
burst through me, through my body without any difficulty, shutting the
door which passed through as well. I grasped at my chest, feeling like my
spine had been pulled out and had danced around on its own when people

and doors passed through it.

"That was not alright." I spat out, trying to regain my composure and get a grasp on the situation. The woman scrambled about the house, picking up her daughter and grabbing the phone; business card in hand. I darted to the couch, sitting behind it as she stared angrily at the basement door, waiting for the person on the other end to pick up.

"Yeah. Hey. It's Katherine, from the house you just said was all purified and free of whatever the Hell just threw a laundry basket at my wall? Yeah? Mm-hmm?" The angel!No no no - anything but him. I don't think I could survive another visit. I panicked to intervene.

"Woah, hey! Hey!" I spoke calmly to the lady, resting my front portion on the couch. She ignored me altogether, so I spoke louder. "HEY! WAIT!"

She continued to look at the door and speak quickly to the Priest on the phone. I needed to get her attention somehow and prove I wasn't a problem anymore. At least so I wouldn't have to go through the pain and attempted decapitation like earlier. Next to her now, I spoke like you would to a deaf grandmother.

"HEY! YOU!" Even next to her ear, she didn't hear it. I tried for broke, yelling at the top of my lungs. "HEY!"

She stopped, eyes wide and bewildered, head thrashing side to side before cradling the phone in both hands. The child slipped down to the floor, grabbing onto her mother carefully. She stared at me and smiled, waving. I just stared back.

"Did you hear that!?" I could hear the Priest babbling something on the other end. No doubt the angel was probably there as well." I just heard something, like a squeak."

She looked around some more, looking down at the kid, still waving at me.

"Yes, hi honey."

I leaned back on my haunches, confused. A squeak? It was pretty obvious that she didn't get my apology; that the stares, the looks, the ironic placement of herself looking in my direction meant that she couldn't see me, and unless I went around screaming like a spoiled brat, she couldn't hear me either.

"Here, let me put the phone to the air, see if you can hear it too." She put the receiver far in front of her, looking around paranoid in the meantime. Anxiously I ran up to it, putting my reptilian ear to the phone.

"Listen you little shit!" It was the angel's voice on the other end, the sound of the phone changing hands. "I know you can hear me! I know it's you!"

"What kind of sick asshole tries to cut someone's head off?" I gave a furious sneer at the receiver, still angry, unsure how to accurately describe what happened. "I would've gone back myself if I only kne-" The angel cut me off.

"Don't you dare think this is over!" His tone cut up sharply, I could tell he was wringing the phone in his fussy little mits as I only squinted, insulted that I couldn't even get a word in. "Don't think you've won!"

"W-Won? What could I possibly win? Surviving? Why, what are you going to do? Come back and dump some more soda on me?" The woman pulled the phone away, not hearing any more sound from the living room. She began talking to the Priest about ways to keep me trapped in the basement. I wasn't through with the angel, though.

"You annoying... angel... man! I don't even know what to call any of this!" I threw up my giant, meaty hands as I could hear some sort of angry response on his end, the mother stopping her conversation suddenly.

"Do you have a static problem on your end or something?" I laughed as she said it, sitting down in front of her." I need you to come out here and stick to your guarantee and ACTUALLY get this thing out of my house."

I cringed a little bit, breaking my good mood. I was still squatting in this house, and I was still scaring the Hell out of innocent people. Amidst the game of death, I had forgotten about that for a moment.

"What do you mean!? I'm not paying another 1300 dollars for you to do the job you should've done in the first place! You promised no ghosts, spirits, or whatever the Hell has been haunting my laundry machine for at least six months, and it's only been a week since you 'exorcised' it. Best in town my ass!" She got quiet, rubbing her temples, placing the receiver on her cheek as she took some deep breaths. I took a slow step backwards, resting back like a true animal, ashamed that she might as well be yelling at me.

"Is there anything I can do that's cheap? Mmhmm…mmhmm." She jotted down a few things; something about candles, salt, incense before I grew annoyed and looked away. I picked myself off the floor and walked on all fours towards the wall.

A week. Something that felt like 5 minutes was a week. I grumbled, disgusted with the exorcist combo. If my spotty, Swiss cheese-of-a-memory served me correctly the way a broken puzzle could, a cleansing or blessing on a house was supposed to be provided by the church if you baked them some food or something in return. Not give them a ridiculous amount like 1300 dollars. The mother's voice escalated again over the phone before she slammed the receiver down. I looked back on the family, knowing plainly that I wasn't welcome here as the woman stormed away, frumping down on the couch with a dissatisfied huff.

"Thank you for having me, but I'll be on my way." I pulled together something of a smile, my teeth jutting out from various spots on my lips while the tongue in my mouth, without purpose, dangled out the front; it was a terrible smile. Fortunately, no one could see it. Though the little girl continued to wave at me every time I made eye contact, questioning if I was really invisible to everyone. Bereft of it all, I turned to the outside wall.

"Bunch of weird people here." I muttered under my breath, shaking my head.

I slowly merged to and through the living room wall to the outside world. The skies burst forth in a beautiful sunshine, birds chirping, gravestones… sitting there, an expansive sprawl of land that if turned the right direction away from the graveyards, was incredible. I closed my eyes and took in a deep breath of air, choking on it for a moment. Something was very wrong here. Standing perfectly still I took in the environment, my heart sagging as it hit me.

The wind; I couldn't feel it. The sun? I could see it, but not feel the warmth. The smell was the same as the house as it was in the ground. The senses I could see, but couldn't interact with. Taking a few steps, my enthusiasm began to dwindle as I moved no grass, and made no footsteps.

Yet here I was busting through walls and jumping on laundry baskets. None of it made a lick of sense.

My head drooped; I didn't seem to have a difficult time with the fact I was dead; more than that, people couldn't see and hear me, save the other supernatural beings on my same level. I felt crushed, lifeless, almost that the world didn't exist with me. I could hear the birds and I could see the wind, but it felt like I sat inside a glass cube, unable to feel the world. It scared me more than anything.

Something ruptured in me for a moment, a slip of panic. I ran full tilt the way a four-legged animal/demon/dinosaur thing should, stretching out farther and farther to get away from the house. The adrenaline, the power, the wild feeling of freedom almost compensated for the lack of connection I had to the world. I looked to the sky, beautiful as it had ever been, clouds skating across a new morning, the world spinning and twirling like it came to greet me.

I began to grin, finally enjoying myself when I slapped hard against the ground in a dead stop.

Dazed, looking around for the person or thing that interrupted my attempt at tranquility, I found no one in sight. Slowly, confused, I tried to take another step away, my left back ankle snagging in mid-air with a sickening jolt. I turned to it, finding my ankles both chained, a link coming out between my Achilles heel and the bones in my foot.

"Ohhh no." I tried taking another desperate step, seeing the links rise up, coasting back towards the house like I had been roped and staked down. "No no nononono."

I pulled harder, more frantic, throwing myself at the barrier that pushed me to the ground again and again. I dug into the dirt, angrier and angrier with my situation, tearing up the grass at the edge of my range, throwing myself against the links. I was stuck here? For some reason, the thought never crossed my mind. I just figured I'd walk out and wander around, experience things, not getting trapped here. Not getting tied to this house.

"Dammit!" I shouted, pulling to the left and making a large arc; chains whirring as they swept over the top of the grass. I put all my force into it, madly intent on either pulling away from the house, or pulling off my feet and being unable to walk any longer. Gritting hard, I pulled and wept for inches of gain, wept for any movement at all before the chains snapped me back, still tethered like any other wandering spirit. No!

With unbridled frustration I yelled to the air. The call swept out in a low, haunting sound.

4

I spent that day outside, broken, disheartened, a heaping pile in the field. Did my best to ignore the massive graveyard next to me and the mound of dirt with the grass seeds sprinkled over it where some big, dumb idiot of a demon came bursting out of the ground. I didn't look around much, mostly cringed at how long my nose was, cringed at the stubbyness of my demonic fingers. Stupid, vain things like that; made it easier to ignore the big questions.

There was a gratuitous amount of sulking involved, self-loathing at what I was forced to be, self-regret for being stuck with the people I hurt. I could tell it was a stupid thing to do, that of all things to care about, worrying about what I had no control of was pointless. But it still sat on the back of my mind.

I could fix it; the thought rang in my head and pulled my shredded will together enough to sit up and drag myself off the ground. The sun was low in the sky, the tall trees on the rim of the forest casting shadows across the field like loose, poignant prison bars. I could fix it. All was not lost, yet. I could at least try.

With an annoyed groan I got to my feet, watching my arms and legs move in a somewhat rhythmic manner. I began to walk slowly around the yard, my tail flopping about, my body bulky and tense. It felt like I was walking on my hands and knees, like I was scooting about the field, only faster, more natural. Getting the hang of movement, I began a trot, before breaking into a run, consciously aware of how I was doing it instead of relying on panic and intuition. This form was apparently here to stay, and if nothing else, I should be comfortable in it. I loped closer to the house until the graveyard was practically underneath me, feeling awkward and unwanted in my natural environment as I immediately stopped. It was an expansive thing, headstones dotting the hill, a few people walking solemnly through it on the far side. The rising shadows behind me began to pull over the graveyard, wind briskly howling through the trees.

With a slow, melodic walk, I started into the graveyard, eyes to the pile of loose dirt in the middle. It was between four graves, dirt scattered farther than the mound, like something explosive happened there. It made no sense in my head, nothing did. How did I manage to gain control of this form, when I was sure that there was nothing left to hold onto? The eyes, the angel's blue eyes, had been the only thing on my mind, while all remnants of me were dissolving away. Why was that angel the only thing I could remember? He obviously didn't know me from anywhere, unless a shower of burning pain was his way of saying Hello. I felt less panicked; with more memories taking up space, I was more at ease. Worst come to worst, I guess I could find the angel and ask questions another time.

The mound of dirt was spread before me, orange netting covering the whole thing. There were also a few tiny yellow flags to the sides of it, sprouting like menacing weeds in the cemetery. I spread the dirt around with one of my oversized fingers, no call from the mound. There was no Hell, no pull to go back, no sense from it whatsoever, no voice screaming at me to dive underground. Calculating where I'd be least likely to disturb the dead, I drove one hand into the dirt, reaching around like I could snag the top of those caverns. Nothing. It was a mound. It was partially covered in new grass. There was nothing else.

"Suppose there's no going back." I spoke to no one, looking around for some clues. The grave closest to the pile read, 'Anthony P. Settigan' and his wife, 'Susan', with the opposite marker being, 'Samuel Robinton' and his wife 'Rebecca'. None of them were me. I didn't know me, but I feel I'd know myself, given the chance. But these four people, none of them were me. I snorted, frustrated, watching the sun slip below the horizon. The last group of people packed up, their car driving past the mound and me, heading out towards the cemetery's exit. Overwhelmed by the loneliness of the now vacant graveyard, I sauntered back towards the house, thinking empty thoughts and slipped inside.

It was a bizarre sight. Salt was poured over the threshold; red candles lit around the house and placed along gashes in the wall like little shrines. Or like the power was out. Some kind of weird plant hung in each room and the whole place stunk. I could actually smell it.

"What…the…" I walked delicately through the kitchen, careful not to step on anything placed around the room. The whole house was slightly misty, almost murky, like something was burning in sacrifice. The smell made my eyes water, and made the air sickly and uncomfortable. Light flickered across the linoleum, the shadows from the candles danced along the broken walls. Salt line after salt line seasoned each room, leading to the mother and her child, jumbled and paranoid on the couch, cross in hand. I stopped, guilt-stricken. They were trying to ward me away, trying to keep me out of the house. With all the wall-busting and laundry-hopping, I didn't blame them. Looking at the salt line I batted it with my hand, scattering their decoration across the kitchen floor. They both looked up, the child fussing to pull herself from the mother's grip as she spotted my approach.

"We don't want you in here!" The mother shouted at the corners of the room, like she was chewing out the TV for doing nothing productive. "You've caused us enough trouble!" The mother looked around for any sign of me, readjusting her grip on the child. She hissed out something urgent as the kid rolled and struggled to get away.

"Yes Sweetie, I know you're fussy, but your nighties are downstairs in the dryer and mommy wasn't thinking when she went to the store earlier." She spoke back up for me to hear, tone harsh.

"We just want to you to leave. Please." Her voice turned joking, almost sarcastic, "I bet the exorcism probably didn't feel too great. If you leave, then we won't make the Priest come back and hurt you." I walked farther into the room, salt tumbling along my path as I noticed something on the coffee table. A box, its tiny wheels moving inside recorded our conversation; with a start she reached across the table and slapped it off, rewinding and playing it. It was a tape of empty air, of slight sounds, of the kid bubbling with spit and gentle rustling. They were trying to listen for me.

They were absolutely petrified. The way I had acted; at least the parts I could actually be conscious for; it made sense. To them, it would make sense to take all precautions, to do everything in your own power. But I was harmless, essentially. There was no part of me boiling in revenge, no part that wished anything but to just sit around peacefully; not drive a poor woman and her kid over the edge. I certainly didn't need the Priest and his angel pal back around here, not right away. I had to make this right. I wanted to have a place to stay. I didn't care if we were best friends, I just didn't want them to be afraid of me anymore. I wanted to convince them that I wasn't evil.

Determined, I loped through the basement door and down the stairs, grabbing the laundry hamper and dragging it behind me. Stopping in front of the dryer, I fumbled to open the door, grinning and ready to try and take back my reputation. I was not a bad person... err, spirit, and I was Hell-bent on proving that.

Twenty minutes later, I knocked on the top of the stairs door. Softly at first; I didn't want to scare them.

The woman screamed anyways. I persistently kept knocking, slowly getting louder and louder and probably making it worse. I had no clue how to peacefully introduce the idea of some nonphysical ghost helping out with chores. There's no manual for that.

"Go away! Oh, please, just go away!" Her high-pitched wailing began to escalate. I poked my head through the door to see her completely paralyzed in fear. She was curled up into a ball on the couch, her child wedged at a weird angle as she screamed into the couch cushions.

Frustrated and scared myself, I opened the door, shoved the laundry basket full of folded clothes through it, and slammed it shut. The mom screamed; louder than before, the wailing began to get softer and softer as she peeked an eye out from her hair.

The screaming stopped abruptly; the woman sat up quickly from the couch, confused, looking around like someone had played a joke on her. She whispered things to herself, too soft to hear, venturing closer to the basket of clothes, all nice and folded. Her face was drained of color, still held with fervent fear as she stood from the couch. The child slid from her grasp, immediately running over to me.

"Hello doggie!" She stood in front of me, arms over her head like she wanted me to pick her up. I looked back and forth; maybe I had been sitting in front of a dog picture, maybe I was in front of her favorite game, but no, there was nothing else. The woman seemed more capable than teaching her child that the door was called doggie.

"Doggie? Honey, what are you…" She trailed off, reaching to the pile of clothes and quickly filing through them, starting to get a grasp on the situation. I sat there, extremely awkward. "Did… uh… Doggie… fold these clothes?" Cautiously, the mother also looked in my direction. I remained silent, feeling the panic rising in my stomach, reassuring myself that they were trying to explain things, to just stick around. The toddler kept her hands lifted up, hopping around on the floor over the salt lines.

"Mmmm hmm!" She hopped over to the clothes, pulling a few out and throwing them behind her until she got to a specific outfit she wanted. The mother reached out and grabbed her daughter by the hand, keeping her close.

"Did you fold these clothes?" She spoke loudly to the house again. There was a very long, drawn out pause, waiting for the house to answer back.

I couldn't answer - so I sat there and felt stupid.

"C-Could you fold those clothes there?" She pointed to the clothes on the ground in front of me, the ones that the kid threw behind her. It was a pair of shorts and a shirt. I eased off my haunches and sat next to the coffee table, folding the pair of shorts easily and scooting them in the mother's direction. She picked them up gingerly, wiggling them like they were possessed by the Devil himself, like they'd get up and dance around.

Something unexpected happened - she giggled. She laughed, or more accurately, gagged on air. I relaxed too, letting out a deep sigh.

"Are… uh… are you a good ghost?" She kept her eyes fixated on the shorts while I folded the shirt. I pushed them to her side of the table. The woman jumped, seeing the folded shirt and began to laugh more in disbelief. "I take that as a yes. Good God, my house is possessed with the spirit of a maid!"

She rocked to her feet, abandoning her kid to stand by the table alone, kicking line after line of salt away as she trudged into the kitchen.

"I need a drink… or… a lobotomy. Maybe I'll just slam my head in the car door a few times." She pulled something from the cabinet over the fridge, suddenly shouting my direction. "Good ghosts don't bust holes in my new house, you son of a bitch!"

She laughed as she said it, like it was all one big joke - something like 'Ohhh hoho, you crazy demon!' I sighed and hung my head low, some mix of guilt and relief. The kid was at my feet, looking up at me, continuously waving.

"What's wrong Doggie?" She tilted her head and smiled as she caught my attention. I frowned, a little bewildered.

"You can't honestly see me, can you? Did your mom drop you on your head as a baby or something?" I joked, leaning farther away from her. The kid kept staring straight at me, suddenly throwing her head back and yelling to her mother.

"Moooooom, did you ever drop me on my head?!" I froze in terror. The kid giggled as her mother emerged with a red-hot glare from the other side of the partition to the kitchen. She suddenly began stomping in my direction while I tried to gather that I actually had a person who could relay messages. Sure, she was some four to five years old, but apparently I was accepted, understood, by a five year old. I just assumed I couldn't speak to anyone.

"Tell your mom that Doggie was joking!" I nudged the kid as she kept her eyes to her mother. "You know, ha-ha, funny joke?"

"Ha-ha!" The kid repeated, probably the most pointless part of the message. The mother was back in the living room now, pinning me backwards with an impressive amount of blind accuracy. I wasn't in the mood to have my soul danced around in; it sure didn't feel like fun the first time.

"I… uh… I'm sorry!" The mother kept coming, footsteps pushing closer. I forgot I needed to crank my volume to twelve to be heard. "SORRY!" I belted out, back against the wall. The mother stopped dead in her tracks, glass of wine in her hands. She looked up to the corners of the wall, then back to the kid, then back where I essentially 'was'.

"Says sorry." The toddler spoke out, rummaging through the clothes. The mother nodded her head slightly, completely confused.

"Yeah…" She seemed to withdraw into herself a bit, turning back to the couch. With haste, she snatched up the recorder on the table, rewinding it back in a sense of awe. "I heard it too, Sweetie." I remained hunched down, body braced for impact; staring back and forth for a conclusion of some sort to be reached. The mother pressed the recorder to her ear intently. The sound of the previous conversation came through, remarking about the ghost-maid and the slow trailing words that the mother needed medical help.

I leaned forward and listened with them, suddenly feeling the full weight of what was going on here. I was dead. Very dead. That, for some reason, still hadn't hit me, but hearing my own distorted, distant shout sound nothing but a scratchy whisper really drove it home. It was odd, seeing people trying to connect with me, that I wasn't in their same existence, that I was on some other level. It all just hit me.

I sat very hard, heart heavily sinking in my chest. My hands began to shake as I couldn't support myself anymore, slumping to the ground. The kid came up next to me and sat by my head, stroking my imaginary hair like she meant it. Pity from a five-year-old. I closed my eyes and wished I could disappear, too lazy to push her away.

"What's wrong, honey?" The mom stopped the tape recorder and set it on the table.

"It's sad." She kept stroking my 'hair', her hand passing through me in fairly uncomfortable waves.

"Why is it sad?" The mom came over to my side of the table; I opened my eyes to see her looking over me as well. Pity, pity, pity. I groaned and closed myself off again.

"I dunno." The kid kept petting me the way any child pets an annoyed animal; with a lot of unnecessary force. A thump; the mom placed something next to my head, wood floors creaking as she eased back and sat on her feet.

"You're the talkative one, you tell us." She spoke directly at me, where her daughters hand was. I stared up at the woman from the floor; her look actually seemed to be on me, not on the table, not on the couch, not distantly far away in paranoia. On me. I switched to the tape recorder in front of me, blowing some air at it. "C'mon, what happened, lost your nerve? I'm not hearing anything, Doggie."

There was the tail-end of a sneer, trying to goad me on. Considering the circumstances it made me smile, or grin at least. This woman was quick to overcome her screaming, tearful paranoia to challenge me straight on. It was refreshingly ballsy.

"Why am I sad?" I spoke with my lips to the recorder, tone not shy of someone yelling at a deaf old man. "I'm stuck. I can't leave."

The mother snatched up the recorder in a heartbeat, already rewinding it back and boosting the sound as she walked to the couch. I pulled myself from the floor, walking calmly to her side to try and hear it as well. The tape crackled with static, with the drastically loud thump of being set on the ground. A few seconds of shuffling, before my voice spoke through, so softly.

"...sad?" It sounded garbled, like I'd eaten the thing and spit it out before finishing my answer, "…stuck. I can't leave." They were clear. Feminine too, not like I sounded to myself at all. It was soft like a person muttering it from a house and a half away, but I could hear them; I wasn't that close to the recorder. The mother stared at the machine in her hands and almost dropped it onto the coffee table, setting it down and pressing the record button.

"Are you just tricking us? Are you that same… thing… that attacked us before?" She stared at the spot I had been on the floor.

"No. Not exactly - I don't think." I stopped, worried that my garbled sentence was going to come out wrong, "If I was, I'm good now. No more of that." I laughed nervously before the mother grabbed the recorder again, listening to the chunks of words able to get through. 'Not exactly', and 'I'm good now', with an evil, foreboding laugh attached to the end of it. I groaned, frustrated.

"Good now? And we find you folding laundry. What am I supposed to make of this?" She posed the question without the tape recorder on. I shrugged regardless of documented sound as the mother put her recorder on the table. She receded back into herself, sitting farther away on couch. "Well. So now we have a laundry folding ghost in our new house. I guess we were asking for it, living next to a cemetery." She laughed and rubbed the bridge of her nose.

I eyed the tape recorder, figuring I could make this work better. I smacked the red record button, startling the mother and her kid, pulling it closer to me so I could shout from a more comfortable distance.

"I'm sorry. I don't know what I'm doing, or why I'm here." I stopped, pushing myself to annunciate the best I could with a long, pebbly demon mouth, "What's your name?"

Shutting the recorder off, I rewound it and tilted it towards them. This time, my voice came out at something of a normal tone, like a regular whisper. But it all came out; every word. The mother slowly tucked her legs back underneath her in a sort of bemusement/bewilderment combo, looking to the little girl, then back to the recorder.

"It… its Katherine. Katherine Faegel." She laughed after she said it, leaning to her daughter, "This is Amber… um… what's your name?" She began nervously scratching a part on her leg with a sense of urgency and fear. I turned the recorder back to me.

"I don't have one." I had to work hard to push anything; but I was starting to get a hang of it. It seemed like things around the house only moved at my touch if I was angry, passionate, determined, or any other emotion as far as I could tell now. But lazy, relaxed, or resting actually made things more difficult. With our conversation growing more comfortable, pushing down on the recorder got harder and harder.

Katherine nodded and pulled her child closer, spitting out the real point of this conversation. "Is there anyway we can make you leave? Say a prayer or something?" My stomach dropped again, regret wearing down on me.

"I've been trying to leave all morning. I'm sorry for disturbing you." I turned from the living room to go into the kitchen as my voice spoke from the recorder, more distorted and garbled, like how the interrogation started. I was exhausted. It was near midnight now and I had no more energy to play telephone. I needed rest. I wasn't going anywhere. Things would get sorted out another day.

I walked throughout the house, slowly, things faintly familiar, hazy memories from the demon. I felt stupid and ashamed. What had I done to these people to have them resort to such an expensive exorcism? They seemed level-headed enough, not the type who'd run out and buy such a service on a whim.

Maybe it'd been years. Maybe hundreds of years. Maybe I've been haunting this same plot of land for lifetimes upon lifetimes. If five minutes felt like a week, there was no sense of time to me, at least right now. Everything was uncertain. Unknown. Above all things, I didn't have a name; all I knew about my life was a fight where I chased an angel through some walls, then got my ass handed to me, and blue eyes. Now I could add bargaining with terrified people to my short list of life experiences. Oddly, this didn't seem to help things all that much. I still felt terribly empty, unfulfilled, and being chained to a house wasn't helping much either.

Leaning against the wall, enveloped in shadows from the lightless room, I stared out at the stars in the sky. Familiar. Skewed in some way, but familiar. It was a reassuring sight, calming, silencing. I closed my eyes and imagined feeling the cool wind blow past me, and feeling the land resting.

"I have a proposition for you, ghost." I jumped, startled, finding the mother and her child behind me, the kid pointing exactly where I was like a little blonde bloodhound. "My... daughter will be pointing you out when I need you. But I have a proposition. If you will listen to it, knock on the wall or something."

I looked to the wall behind me, rapping my hand against it.

"Here's my proposition; you don't haunt us or attack us again, and we won't call any more Priests or exorcists here." She held up a hand, like she was instructing her invisible daughter." In turn, you also have to make sure that no other unwanted guests come in here: ghosts, burglars or solicitors. Otherwise I'll have to call a Priest and no one wants that."

I slowly began to smile, getting the gist of her intention. She was allowing me to stay on the condition I acted like a guard demon.

"Lastly, you answer to me. My first command is 'Don't come into my bedroom while I'm sleeping, because it's terrifying and I'm not real adjusted to this yet'. Second is to give me and my daughter some time to adapt to this. Sound okay?" She looked left of where I was sitting, off position from her bloodhound's point. "One knock for no, two knocks for yes."

I leaned back again, rapping twice on the wall. The woman smiled, muttering to her kid and leaving the room awkwardly after a moment of consideration, like she was surprised that I didn't put up more of a fight about her demands. I could hear them enter some other room, softly talking and laughing to one another. It was mostly the mom, Katherine, congratulating her child for doing such a good job. They were an odd family. Not bad, but a little odd.

I smiled a bit more, looking back to the stars and stretching out along the ground. Counting the constellations I could remember, I drifted off into a strangely peaceful sleep in a strange situation.

5

The next two weeks went by uneventfully. Katherine and Amber didn't communicate with me and I mostly kept to myself. Things greatly relaxed between us all; it became a kind of grace period in the household. The space gave me time to really take in my surroundings, to know the people I was 'guarding', and develop a sense of self all over again.

The house was perched on lifts, stilts almost, on the edge of the Juan Julio Cemetery. I had no idea who Juan Julio was, but he was important enough to get his own cemetery, that lucky dog. The Faegels - my landlords so to speak - lived in a practically uninhabited area. There was the cemetery, an abandoned house much farther down the road, and something like a fishing dock farther than that. That was the limit of my vision, the rest of the area was mostly obscured by trees.

I habituated a brown house, the very back end of the second level touched regular ground with the basement acting as the bottom level. The front was held up by thick supports, decoratively disguised to be like modern, sassy pillars so it didn't look like we lived in some shantytown. The garage was partially into the ground as well, a door leading straight into the basement. On the front of the house, overlooking the road, was a long, serene deck that I spent a lot of my time on. It was one of my favorite places to go, slumping around peacefully as I adjusted to my new life.

From time to time I'd patrol the perimeters, sit on the edge of the property alongside the road and watch the cars whiz past. I also got to know the names and dates of my silent audience in the graveyard. Maybe one of them had importance, I still felt like a fluke and if nothing else, but it kept my mind busy. I felt like I had places to be; restless, needing some sort of actual purpose instead of a implied, thrown-together one.

I grew more used to my form as well. It didn't feel nearly as awkward as it had when I started out. Still weird, but the sensation that I was scooting around on my hands and feet soon fell away. It had a lot of natural bounce to it; a lot of pep and lots of energy. I wasted time racing birds, lapping the yard and bowling over decorations with my house-chain if I could gather enough speed. I managed to keep myself busy in the simplest way, but it did the trick; I came to appreciate the tiniest bit of life I could still enjoy.

The Faegels were interesting people. Katherine left early each day, taking Amber with her to return at about six that evening. There was no husband, no boyfriend, not one that I had met. She was a woman of about thirty-five years old, a smoker; her skin the slightest tinge of gray on an otherwise youthful face. She had dark blonde hair dyed black, a thinner, taller woman, self-dependent. Very laid back, she was altogether a good mother in the most unusual times. Even pushed to the edge of her limits, she managed to bounce back quickly and only taking a few breaks now and then to glare at the house in disbelief, shaking her head.

Amber seemed to be almost five years old, tow-headed, at the age where she was a handful; I'd often see her bolting across the yard after a bug or bird of some sort, occasionally taking her time to stop and wave in my direction before bounding back to her mom. The girl kept an eye on me at all times, more silent as of late after her mother told her it would be best to leave the Doggie alone because it needed rest. I didn't mind a break from the fascinating world of ghost whispering, and neither did Katherine.

On the weekends she spent a lot of time gardening, maintaining a bed of flowers alongside the garage. Amber was always out there with her and they pretty much spent the days doing little things; cleaning, maybe watching a movie, playing outside. It wasn't a flashy life, there weren't box socials or midnight raves going on, just mundane family type of work. I'd just be there, more or less hanging around, bored out of my wits.

Finally, the vow of silence broke as Katherine talked with Amber at the edge of the yard. They both came towards me as I sprawled out on the grass, half-heartedly sunning myself. I heard them before I saw them, the little girl whispering 'Hi' with each step closer to me, finally stopping just short of where my spirit and the grass intersected. I yawned, stretching out before closing my tired eyes.

"Hello dinosaur!" Amber shouted practically in my ears as I winced in pain. Putting one hand to my head, I rolled away from them.

"I have a name for you." The mother said matter-of-factly, her daughter nodding in agreement. "I mean, only if you want one."

I quickly flopped back on my stomach, nodding rapidly in hopes that the little girl would repeat my answer; she did.

"Alright, good. I actually have a list of them, let's go back into the house and get you a name." She began walking without me as I scrambled to my feet, trotting behind her like I was an actual part of the conversation.

"I appreciate the time to relax, too. I'm not 100% on my house being haunted by maid-ghosts, but you're better than whatever that thing was before." She trailed off as we entered into the building. I couldn't help but feel guilt stricken.

Katherine put Amber down in the middle of the kitchen, quickly walking to the other room to get her name list.

"Watch her if you could, ghost." She said it nonchalantly, just like. 'Hey, Goddess of the wind, wash the dishes if you could, please'. I watched after the mom, becoming increasingly aware of the child at my feet.

"Your mother says some odd things. Things that even I find weird." I looked back to the girl, muttering under my breath, "Things that a dinosaur demon-person ghost finds weird, which I guess is an accomplishment." She stood beneath me, unamused, a look in her eyes that demanded I play with her, or she'd be tempted to drink the chemicals under the sink out of boredom.

"Uhh, wanna play Simon says? Kids like that, right?" The girl's frown turned immediately, jumping once in place before she took a few steps backwards, readying herself.

"I do." She swung her arms at her side, waiting for my first command; I gave a little laugh and stood on all fours, mirroring her. "You go first."

"Alright. Simon saysss… touch your nose!" I pulled my head closer to my stubby arms, touching my nose; the girl did the same, "Alright, good. Simon says pat your head." I lowered my head more to the ground, patting the top of it. I hit something hard, something that was not a part of my body; instantly I froze.

Feeling around the outside of it, I could tell it was a circle, with some sort of rubber strap connecting around my top jaw horn. Following it back to the circle, I felt a bridge over the top of my head, with a similar circle on the other side; it was in a natural dip in my skull, and felt like it was barely there at all.

"Goggles?" I wondered aloud, the mother came back into the room to find her daughter jumping around with her finger on her nose and hand on her head. She looked at us both and laughed, scooping Amber up to sit on her lap.

"I see you two had a game going on, eh? Well, maybe next time Doggie can teach you how to fold laundry, help mommy out with some cheap labor on her chores." She laughed and bounced the girl on her lap, ruffling through the papers scattered about the table. Grumbling slightly, I stood next to her, the kid pointing out exactly where I came to sit.

"Alright, so I was looking through a database of names, what they mean, and where they come from. If any of my suggestions sound good, knock on the table, let me know." She smiled oddly, warmly, like she was trying hard to make this commonplace and not obnoxiously weird. "You are a woman, I presume?"

I knocked on the table. Based on the recorder, I had to assume so.

She went through the names she liked, one by one, starting with Abigail, Abby, some odder names like A'la'a to names like Kristen, Kady, so on and so forth. Nothing struck me, everything rolled off as I sat there, playing with the goggles on my head. They didn't move. I tried jabbing my finger underneath it, using my tail to try and pry it off, but it held on tight as if it was glued down.

Katherine kept going through the list, the wear obvious in her tone as well. At least she was making an effort to bring me a little comfort, which for the last week I figured she was just hoping I'd leave.

"Nabeela, Nadeen, Nahara, Nao, Nella, Neri, N…"

Bells went off. Whistles, firecrackers, snap-pops; they all went off. It sounded so close, like it hit me over the head with familiarity. I knocked on the table like a drum. Neri. Neri hit a nerve. It was like a burst of light, of energy, of excitement. Agh, yes, there was hope after all!

"Which one, you damn woodpecker?" Katherine spat out. I stopped tapping on the table, prancing around it instead as she read the names off one at a time. When Neri came up again, I knocked on the table and sat, almost proud of myself. It wasn't my actual name, but it sure as Hell was close. Close was good.

"Neri." The mother tongued the word carefully deciding if it stuck or not. "Yeah, alright, I can live with that." She leaned over where I had sat before and patted the air.

"Means 'My Burning Light'. Fancy." She shuffled her papers as her daughter snickered and looked at me. She was trying, even if it was comforting the air. Katherine sat up in her chair, looking to the empty spot still, "My work is closing down on Thursdays and Fridays now, so we'll be keeping you company here at the house more often. I'm hiring a babysitter those first few weeks, so please don't scare the Hell out of her, okay? It's important for me to do my work here, so don't think we'll be playing and romping around all day, Neri."

I stared at the mother for a moment, before giving a knock on the table once more from the opposite side. Her glance switched to my side before looking to her daughter.

"Was mommy talking to nothing for a while, Amber?" She smiled as she said it, the girl giggling in response, before pointing me out. "Anyways, we also have a repair man coming in tomorrow to fix our walls, as well. So, you know, don't scare him either. Don't get me wrong; scare everyone else, but just not those people. Do your best to keep the Jehovah's Witnesses away from my doorstep while you're at it, they've come back with more energy this time." She got up from the table taking Amber with her, leaving me to sit alone in the middle of the kitchen as the glow of receiving a name slowly wore off.

I sat, perfectly still, hearing the fading footsteps, the barely audible birds outside, the house resting. That was it. There you go. This is all I had to look forward to. Silence. That was that; I had a name, that's all there was. My stomach began to slowly knot up, slowly churn on itself, rising to my heart as it began to beat harder. That was the only sound, like a sharp-ticking clock in silence, it only personified how vastly empty this house was; more specifically how alone I was. What more did I have? What more was left? The relaxation was nice, but it wasn't enough to keep me entertained, to keep me happy. The clotted, choking knot wound itself tighter.

This was it. The rest of my life. The rest of everything I had to interact with, a life devoid of conflict; trapped, stuck to this house. I looked around me, looked to my feet, looked at the rhythmic swaying of the branches against the wind as they too stopped. Everything went still. Nothing.

I gagged, suffocating on the silence.

Neri. Well, Neri was going to crack under pressure if something interesting didn't happen in the next ten minutes. I began to breath hard, searching for something to chew on, something to destroy in an inexpensive way. I left the house, strutting across the field, trying to figure why I felt like this. Maybe all the isolation was finally getting to me? Maybe this is why there were no nice ghosts around - they all just finally snap because they're too bored. It was starting to make sense why they haunted. I personally felt moved to scare the Hell out of someone, just for some entertainment. Just for something. Interaction, excitement, try and avoid figuring out why my soul had been sent to Hell, maybe. Try and ignore that crushing weight on my back.

Without thought, I loped to the trees, feeling that familiar pull on my ankles before I could get there. I growled, leaning against the chains to the point where they hurt. I could still feel that. I wasn't completely dead. I pulled for a while more.

It wasn't enough. Doubling back, I ran full-out to one of the posts supporting the house, trying to bang my head on it. I don't know what I was thinking; I think the finality of this all was driving me a little nutty. No use - my head kept going though the post, no matter how angry I was. I couldn't seem to hurt myself on the 'physical' things I could touch, just grab and manipulate them.

"This really is Hell!" I tried one last time, almost tripping down the hill as I passed through the beam once again. I stared angrily at the post before going back inside, looking around frantically for something to destroy. If only there was something here I could break, something on my level - like a pal ghost I could talk to...

Eyes wide, I slowly scanned over to the phone. I... could... call the angel. Not to go all buddy-buddy with him but, you know, maybe get some pointers on how to deal with all this unbearable free time. That wasn't too taboo, was it? I wasn't inviting him over for a drink; I just needed someone to validate my existence. My semi-existence.

"Yeah, yeah, keep telling that to yourself." I muttered under my breath, flipping through the cards on the table before I got to the only exorcism card in the bunch.

"Great Beyond. We go to the 'great beyond' of savings." I read flatly, feeling my hope fade already. "Not for 1300 dollars."

I knocked the receiver off the hook, the numbers on the front of the phone. I tried to dial the number on the card, finding my fingers hitting four buttons at once. Pushing it back onto its stand; I tried again, this time using a pencil. It hummed, warbling like static air. I kept what I thought my ear was to the end of it, even finding the dial tone relaxing in some way, before a man briskly picked up the phone - the Priest.

"Hello?" He said politely, like he had been waiting for this call. "Hello?" The lump in my throat wrapped around the back of my head, fighting to speak to something; someone.

"H... Hi! Hello! C-can I speak with the other guy? Your angel pal? Russle... I think?"

"Hello?" He sounded annoyed, juggling the phone in his hands, "Heellllllooooo? If this is a prank call, for the last time, this is a real business. Who is this?" I was going to lose them if I didn't do something quick. Panicking, I began to smack the phone on the counter and growled into the receiver before putting it back to my ear.

The Priest hesitated, laughing before there was a second voice in the background. The angel!

"Hey, I think your demon pal's on the phone." He chuckled, the phone being turned over to what anyone else would consider dead air.

"Hello?" He said, fairly calm and confused. I started to sweat a little bit; this was a stupid idea. Pulling the phone away from my head, I stared at the receiver, worried. What was I doing?

"H-Hi there." Was all I said, nicely as possible, considering the circumstances. It was all I had to say. He geared up to full crazy in no time flat.

"You have some nerve calling me again!" Barely a pause before he continued on without my response, "What? Call to brag about dragging your shamed soul around for another day? Think that since you managed to cower long enough underground that you've won, you spit?"

"No, no I—"

"If we weren't busy eliminating the rest of your friends, we'd be over there exterminating you from all levels of this planet!" He seethed at the end of his words, too angry to form another sentence and giving me enough time to get a word in.

"I'm not trying to pick a fight, I just want to talk." The growing feeling of guilt and frustration overwhelmed me, too heavy this early in the day. Yeah, it was a bad idea to call.

"And now you think you're such a smartass that you can call me here and hex me, or harass me, or whatever the Hell you're doing? God, its cases like yours that make my job all the more necessary, erasing stains like you off this plane of existence for good. God damn you!" The phone switched hands as I heard him storm off, the Priest muttering before the phone was hung up.

"Maybe it just wanted to be friends…" He laughed, the phone silencing with a click. I stayed where I sat, frozen still, the deafening silence again bearing down on me. Staring at the holes in the receiver like I could crawl inside and hide there, like something would scramble out, I took a shaky breath and sighed; stupid. Slumping forward, I rested my head on the counter broken, almost. Stupid.

"Wonder if you've got any tips for making the time pass." I muttered dead to the air. "Maybe some insight on how to deal with being something that everyone inherently hates. Or being dead. Not really settled with either." Sighing, I gently placed the phone back on the counter above my stupidly placed goggles with delicate, monster-sized claws.

Hearing the phone do nothing but growl its monotonous displeasure, I sat like that for some time. Eventually I exited out the back door again, walking silently, downtrodden until I was at the edge of the cemetery.

There I sat until the sun fell below the horizon, thinking everything over. Maybe I was damned to haunt this house, to be completely separated from everything around me. I didn't deserve any special calling, or anything different than any other ghost, I guess. Maybe I should just count my blessings that I can communicate with the two people I live with, stop being so demanding. Maybe that was my place in life.

It felt like I was waiting for something to happen, that I was waiting for excitement to come along. I think my imagination was stretching just a little too far. I didn't want my life to be about habitually fitting in. I wanted… something. Couldn't tell what that was, though.

Crickets chirped in the cemetery before me, the fog slowly rolling in from its northernmost edge. My exit lump of dirt was all but absorbed back into the earth, grass covering the bump like it never happened. Everywhere around me life was telling me that it was moving on while I sat in the same instance I left Hell with; confused, lonely, and frustrated. The graveyard unnerved me before, I never stayed out after dark for fear of whatever monsters had attacked before were just waiting for me. But now, I just hoped that a few other spirits might be around for some conversation.

"Is anyone out there?" I called out to the cemetery, sitting politely on the edge of it. "I'm not looking for a fight, just for some other bored spirit to talk to. There's plenty of you here, right?"

A whole lot of nothing answered back.

"I'm not as mean as I might look, I swear." I said a little quieter, feeling stupid. "I guess you guys don't have a lot of ghosts coming over here to chat, I mean, I don't blame you. If I saw some dinosaur-faced demon sitting and talking to me, the last thing I'd do would be strike up a conversation."

I listened for any sound, any voice. Everything was quiet.

"What am I supposed to do?" I hung my head low, frustrated. "The Hell am I doing here..."

Staring at my feet, I wiggled my claws, letting out a heavy breath. The graveyard was muted; it seemed to be filled with nothing but resting bodies, their souls long departed. I sighed again, extinguished and quiet.

"Maybe people are satisfied with little things, they're happy to find a place out of the way of everything else, where the tiny changes they make within their lives make them happy." I scratched the back of my head, flexing my bulbous fingernails out once and away like they disgusted me, "I'd give anything to have just... something happen."

The voice breeding now was young and meek, this spongy, downtrodden version of true emotion, more frustrated than sad.

"I don't think there's anyone here to talk to. Nothing here but a lot of empty bodies."

Slumping to the ground, I put my hands back over my head, shutting the world out.

"You can tell me things." I jumped, scanning for the voice, only to find it coming out of Amber standing ten feet behind me. Her mother was farther up the hill, arms crossed.

"She won't go to bed until you go to bed " Katherine smiled, "Neri."

" Why don't you tell me stuff?" The girl squatted closer to me, sitting side by side. I was a little awestruck, taken back, babbling on my words out of shock.

"I'm not aiming to burden children." I grinned haphazardly, really hoping I could find another spirit in the middle of a graveyard, of all places as she squinted a little, not getting what I was saying. "You're too little."

"Nuh uh, I'm almost..." She held up one hand, fingers splayed out before double checking manually. "Five."

I smiled and nodded politely, looking back to the graveyard.

"Why are you sad? Do you miss your family?" The girl asked honestly, sitting a little closer to me. "Cause I miss my dad sometimes." Head snapping back around to the kid, I frowned, somewhat surprised. I could hear the mother shifting her weight a little, letting out a sigh. Thinking, mulling it over, I readjusted my answers to keep things from going further into the depression pit.

"I do." I lied, I didn't have any idea if I had a family or not. I started to say something more as Amber scooted until she was practically rubbing elbows with me.

"You're very warm" The girl looked up at me, happy and oblivious in the glazed over way that kids use. They don't care about the big things, they live entirely in that moment. Very blunt, very honest. I smirked.

"Uhh... thanks. That's very kind of you to say." I was a little confused, but let it slide. "What happened to your dad, if you don't mind me asking?"

"He got sick. He's with the angels now. That's what my mom says." She looked over the graveyard with me. "But Mom says that death is a in-ev-it-ab-le part of life, that we can't be scared of it." She said it carefully, like she'd rehearsed it in front of a mirror, stumbling over the words. Katherine spoke up from the porch of the house, distantly.

"Well Mom, and Mom's therapist say that." She muttered sarcastically as I gave a quick grin, turning back to Amber.

"I suppose that's very true." I responded, considering the notion. The girl smiled.

"Are you with the angels too, then?"

"No, I don't think so." I looked back to Katherine, who was busy picking some dirt off the side of her house. "I'm not sure."

"Is that why you and the angel were fighting?" She started picking the blades of grass alongside her before looking up at me.

"You could see him too, eh?" I laughed a little, more tired than anything. "I think we were both just very confused."

"Is that why you're sad?" Because you're confused?" She was hitting these questions with a creepy amount of accuracy for someone her age. Her mom was staring right at her as well; she must know how observant her child was.

"I think I'm a little overwhelmed, while also being a little underwhelmed." I looked back to Amber as she frowned and stumbled on what I meant. I cleared my throat and started again. "It's a term adults use when they're confused, so you're right, I'm confused." It was just easier to go this way. She suddenly grinned.

"Maybe you and the angel can be friends?"

I laughed out loud at that one, hushing myself so I wasn't belittling the kid.

"No, I don't think that's going to happen. He's not interested in being friends."

"Why were you were calling his number then?" She giggled back, knowing she had me cornered. I could feel my eyes bug out of my head, at least a little bit. "Did he want to be friends? What did he say?"

"You know, I'm not really sure myself, he seemed pretty mad." I smiled a little, looking back to the star-filled sky. "And no, he was pretty clear on that one."

I watched the child shiver like mad for a second, doing her best not to let that dampen her good time, sitting out near midnight by the cemetery. Shaking my head, I motioned back towards the door.

"I think it's time to go back inside" I grinned, getting up from my spot. We trudged back up the hill, Amber relaying what our conversation had been about while I lumbered alongside, shaking my head. I called because I wanted help, that's why.

"Neri, stay alongside me here." Katherine said quieter, then louder for her daughter. "Go on ahead inside honey, mommy's gotta talk with Neri." Amber looked at both of us, opening the back screen door by herself and going inside.

"I know you can't talk back to me, so just listen." The mother spoke tersely. "I don't want you calling that Priest anymore, I mean, I thought that was your rule, and here I find you calling him yourself." Her scowl let up for a second, mumbling under her breath that she was talking absolute nonsense. After a moment, she put her hand on her head, pulling back her hair.

"If you're bored, or depressed, or whatever, let me know instead of calling and looking for trouble like that. When I said I was with you, I meant it; that man is nothing but a drain on my finances." Katherine said, "You're bored? I can understand that. I'll get you some puzzles or something in the morning. Sound good? I'll do my best to keep you entertained; you seem like an active thing." The woman laughed, starting to head inside.

"Boy, I guess it's good that my only neighbors are a bunch of dead bodies, I think I'd have child services called on me if people saw me talking to dead air in the backyard all the time." She waved a hand over her shoulder, "C'mon, it's time for bed."

I felt honored. At the very least, more accepted into the tiny family on the hill here, having people consider me like that. That night I curled up on the floor of Amber's bedroom, sleeping heartily with the rest of them like I belonged. Maybe other ghosts haunted because they were stubborn, that they didn't try to fit in. Maybe because they actually missed their families, longed for them, wished for that interaction. As I drifted off to sleep, I wondered what I had done differently.

Life was more comfortable after that. The next morning, I awoke to a stack of old puzzles lined up just outside the girl's door, everything from 500 to 5, 000 pieces. They were stupid pictures of puppies and three ducks and a ball, but it was entertainment. Eventually, we found other activities for me to do that would keep me entertained; play blocks, little square blocks that I could make spaceships, or castles, or whatever I wanted and finger painting. It was all kiddy stuff, but it was quick, cheap entertainment, and it kept me from feeling like I had to gnaw on the walls to be happy.

I watched over the house as requested and stayed away from the babysitter while she was over. Every now and then, I'd kick a chair just to keep her on her toes, which led to Katherine telling her eventually that the house was haunted by a friendly ghost. It didn't matter; it was the last we saw of her. We got a new babysitter after that, one who liked to rummage through the cabinets looking for money. She was kindly persuaded to leave after I made a doll float after her, judgingly. Our last babysitter was an older woman, Sabina, who even after we told her that the house was haunted with a nice ghost, stayed. She even insisted on leaving a small plate of food out for me at dinner, just so I felt included. Death was good for a while, things worked out, and everyone benefited. It stayed like that for three wonderful years.

Sabina sat in the padded chair, watching TV while Amber and I played with a mix of her Darby dolls and play blocks, what we dubbed 'The Grand Castle Siege on Hollywood'. I waggled the blonde doll at Amber's identical one, ushering a challenge of supreme despair.

"Come, Darby, I challenge thee to a duel! Your Caramel Macchiato against my Vanilla Espresso!" I laughed, shaking the tiny coffee cup in Amber's direction.

"I splash thee with fruity flavorings and a dash of my Claymore!" She posed the tiny sword in Darby's hands, smacking the coffee cup from mine.

"Vile fiend! You've ruined my fifteen hundred dollar purse! Thy lawyers shall be invol-" I shuddered to a stop, feeling the air around me ripple and distort, a large black mass pulsing in the corner. My vision snapped to it instantly as I dropped the doll.

I slowly got to my feet as the disturbance passed alongside the walls. It channeled through the TV, the screen flickered madly before turning off with a start. It then sharply shot to the farthest wall, leading into the kitchen.

"Neri, what is it?" Amber asked cautiously, still bent down low.

"I don't know. Get your mom, keep everyone in this room, okay?" I began to pace into the kitchen, the shadowy lump of energy hanging around that corner as well.

"Be careful!" Amber called, darting behind me to go get Katherine.

"I'm always careful." I said absentmindedly, glaring down the mass in the corner. It spiked out as I crept nearer to it, distorting and re-forming itself like it didn't know what to do. With a low, haunting sound, it began to laugh; the mass heaving and chuckling as a face came to surface in the black goo. A skull of some animal slowly pushed its way out of the wall, two yellow, pupil-less eyes rolled around to face me as the black, smoky mass dropped to the floor. Taller, taller it got until it towered over me, body forming into one I could barely remember, one that I had never seen myself, but was unmistakable.

"It's been such a long time, my good friend!" The demonic mass chided happily, its head skidding on the ceiling. The monster's eyes rolled around in two channels through its skull, balancing on two heavy front legs and a long, disorganized tail from behind. I started to shake my head back and forth. This… this wasn't possible! The demon seemed to pick up on my confusion. "Had fun on your little excursion out of Hell, huh? Confused? You thought that holy water had gotten rid of me, I get it. Please, I'm not that easy to kill."

I kicked up a quick smile trying to cover my confusion, taking a few steps away from it.

"You're the demon that tore me out of Hell, aren't you?" I spoke bluntly, a little mystified to say the least. Why didn't this thing attack back three years ago after it all happened? Why wait this long?

"Aww, you do remember me! I figure this has been more than enough time to sort your shit out. Ready to go back?" It laughed at my face, a mix of horror and confusion. "Yeah, you're all set; come my queen, it's time to go back now." It gave a royal little bow with its blackened, crumbled bones. I only shook my head harder.

"What? Whose queen?" I glared at the beast, pulling my lip back in a snarl, "I like it here, and I've got no interest in going back to Hell. I am not your queen." The demon gave what could be considered a frown, crouching down lower to the ground.

"You're not going to make this easy, are you?"

"No, I live for making life difficult." I grinned, spotting Amber and Katherine out of the corner of my eye." Stay over there!" I yelled to her, the girl stopping in her tracks. Too late; the demon spotted the two of them, charging in their direction as a broken mass of flesh zipped just by my face. I lunged, grabbing onto the trembling bits of its tail and pulling down hard. Amber screamed, pulling back on her mother as well as the demon's jaws snapped just short of the two women.

"Call the Priest!" I shouted through clenched teeth, gritting and tugging at the demon, "They're the only people that can help deal with something this big, even if the angel is an idiot!"

The demon whipped around with a jarring snarl, roaring out in a challenge as it gathered speed. Dropping the tail end of it, the monster charged straight into me, pressed tight against the wall. I couldn't go through it! More, more pressure as it tried to smother me, tried to encase me in that horrible black mass. Something cracked; a snap, the wall held as long as it could before the demon suddenly punched a giant hole out of the kitchen to the outside world.

I tumbled head over tail far into the field, hoping that the sunlight would kill the hulking black mass emerging from the house. It roared, lurching forward, doubling over with a second set of arms growing out where a set of legs should be. Scrambling to my feet I tried to face it, the two of us circling around one another, snarling. My thoughts were only of my terrified family inside.

6

"I see we're starting with a little song and dance this time!" The demon mocked me, the two of us bristling outside my house. It clicked and gurgled around on disjointed hands, lurching forward as swaths of black mist seeped through cracks in the ground. I'd been waiting for a real fight; practicing on being as fluid and graceful as a chunk-headed demon could be. The worst I scared away from the house were a few unwanted solicitors; nothing this serious. A large, black lumbering mass of half-exorcised demon was a whole different challenge. I didn't circle because I was looking for an open opportunity; I circled because I wasn't sure what to do.

Weren't we supposed to be on the same team?

The liquid monster weaved around my body as a sharp, biting pain took hold of my tail before I knew any better. My back legs scrambled, hoisted off the ground, my fingertips skipped and bounced in the grass as it pranced about. I could see the cemetery just over my shoulder, looking for the horizon to center myself.

"Wow, you're quite the fighter!" It laughed as I wheeled my arms around, twisting and looking for something to grab. "Time to go back now; cut this short before it gets out of hand." I flipped onto my back, spotting its happy little forelimbs popping out from this viscous black smoke before melding back in with each step. Growling, I latched onto its front legs as we locked in place; biting down on what I assumed was a leg-bone to show I meant business. The demon let out a reluctant, annoyed sigh mid-step, voice dropping all politeness.

"Why do you have to make this so difficult, my Queen?" The demon's bones in my mouth suddenly disappeared, jaws snapped shut on nothing, the liquid mass of black energy shifting around my grip. It threw its head to the side to flick me away from the house like I weighed nothing; I panicked, trying to spot the ground before I hit hard, rolling end over end. Flashes of green and blue confused my senses as I stopped, disoriented. Struggling back to my feet, my stance was wide and unstable. The demon scuttled happily.

"What do you want from me? Can't I just live here in peace?" I growled as it loomed closer.

"Don't you consider this fight just the tiniest bit of fun?" It laughed, towering far over my head. "You think you're kidding anyone, playing pretend? You think you can ignore where you belong?"

"I have a purpose here, which is to protect my family inside." I gripped the ground just a little tighter, tensing up. Anger, pure and thick gave me goosebumps, made my skin tingle and crawl. "I'm not going back." The demon rolled its eyes, pointing back to the house.

"You immediately called for help from an angel, even before we knocked out the kitchen wall! Where are your standards? Demons have one purpose. Protecting human beings isn't it." It laughed, its whole body shaking, neck back and throat exposed. Clenching my teeth hard, I lunged straight for the wispy, blackish veins before considering other options. I felt guilty, knowing it was right. This fight was already more engaging and exciting than anything else in the last three years here. I always knew that my time here was going to be temporary. That feeling of being out of place never fully went away, though it got desperately close at times.

The demon snatched me out of the air, grabbing me around the ribcage with its massive hands. It slammed me into the ground, pushing down with all its might. Ribs snapping, it felt like I would pop, gurgling out a cry of pain before it picked me back from the ground, throwing me far towards the woods. Half in and out of reality, I sailed through the air for a moment, ankles snapping taut as my house chain stopped me mid-flight, knocking me to the ground on the very edge of my ghostly limits. My ankles bled as I faded out of consciousness.

Coughing, gagging on air and grass, I snapped back to attention. Dizzy, chest still wracked in pain, the demon had vanished. No black mass in any part of this backyard, I stumbled drunkenly to my feet. I could feel my ribs re-joining, healing themselves and slowly taking the pain back to a numb existence as I wandered the yard, coughing hard, searching for where it ran off to. Shaking myself out, I stumbled back towards Amber.

There was a woman's scream from inside the house; I immediately bolted towards it. Steps from the blown out wall, I heard something slam in a rush from the driveway, my attention drawn back to the inside of the house as dishes, glasses, and kitchen chairs all floated about the room. A porcelain plate swooped low as I ducked, watching the silverware prance about in a line, just like the skeletal conga back in Hell. They attacked my family huddled together in the corner, plates smashing into the walls alongside them. A coffee cup nuzzled into the side of my head as I smacked it away; I wasn't sure what to do, baffled.

"I'm your target, not them!" I shouted to the ceiling, the faintest trace of the demon's shadow vanishing. The dishes all dropped from where they hovered, crashing to the ground in a great display as the worst possible thing happened. The Priest and his angel buddy came through the basement door as I stood among a mass of broken dishes and terrified people, scowling and snarling like it was entirely my fault. Slowly, serenely, I looked back at them, mouth frothing with anger, bits of grass still in my teeth.

And I thought the phone call was bad.

"Woah, no no no, wait, hold on a second, I-" I scrambled backwards, barely reading the utter fury in his eyes.

"You son of a bitch!" The angel roared out, punching me hard in the side of the head, the force flipped me over and sent me toppling into the next room. I could feel my eyes rolling around as he followed through, holding that curvy pike over my heart. I saw it for just a second.

"I should've done this the first time!" He yelled out, driving the weapon down at me as I could just see the lightning bolt of my red reflected in the side.

With a panicked little bay I clocked him clumsily upside the head with the side of my hand. Balance knocked off-center, he stabbed the ground next to my face, missing me by an inch at most. Sprawled, half jumbled over one another, I grabbed onto his armor with one errant hand and chucked him outside the wall behind me. Scrambling from the floor I braced for another attack. My face felt like it was on fire. He had been practicing.

"Is everyone alright?" I called back to them, not getting an answer. "You gotta tell Feathery McJackass here to fight the other demon!" Voice unanswered, I turned my head to see the whole group talking with the Priest, who was nodding his head solemnly. Thank God they'd be clearing my name, which maybe the Priest could get off his duff and call back his psycho little angel buddy.

There was a tiny 'poof' sound as the angel flapped straight back into the spot I kicked him out of, his weapon pointing straight in front of him in a charge.

"No... NO, STOP." I jumped to the side, the pike slicing into the wall that separated the kitchen from the living room and missing me by mere inches. He pulled back and tried again, grazing my face. It was a horrible mark, a very real pain that caught me off guard; my hand on the wound was covered in blood. "THERE'S ANOTHER DEMON, STOP."

The angel reared back with his pike to strike again as I hadn't figured out a plan. I just assumed he'd see the other demon and understand on his own.

"Cut it out! Leave her alone!" Amber shouted, leaning away from the wall towards us. The angel's face blanked in surprise, caught off guard by being spoken to directly.

"Her?" He cocked an eyebrow at me, squinting like there was a tiny name badge on the side of my face, confused by what was going on.

"Neri's a good ghost, don't hurt her!" Amber's voice was caught in worry. The angel frowned, shaking his head before looking back to me with a sullen, dark look on his face.

"It's a DEMON." He scoffed as Amber looked even more surprised, trying to find a way to explain my freedom. "You're not well. Stay clear."

"No, she's not, she's..." Looking between them both, I interrupted. I needed to focus.

"No, it's okay, I am a demon." I smirked, keeping my eyes on the angel as I struggled to catch my breath. "But I'm a good demon and still your friend no matter what, alright?" Amber nodded as the angel suddenly brought that pike up by my face, trying to protect himself with it. With an annoyed growl I knocked away the weapon, biting onto the wooden handle and locking my jaws tight on it. He grabbed the two sides not in my mouth, pulling back without much luck as his tiny wings flapped for extra power.

"That's a pretty stupid move, demon!" He suddenly reorganized his attack strategy, taking a much harder grip on his weapon. He began to mutter at the instrument, before his tone escalated to a final, "Ignis!"

The pike lit on fire from blade to end, burning upwards in a blue flame as I leaned back, surprised. He took a smug step away with his arms folded, waiting for it to drop out of my mouth as we both remained there. But the flames didn't hurt. They didn't even feel like anything but a rush of air and a bit of burning wood. Looking down at the pike through the fire I held on tight, watching his face melt in disappointment. They started to die down, pike handle no worse for wear as I huffed the remainder of the flames out with a single snort, pretty happy with myself. The angel on the other hand was not feeling as joyful as I was, looking at the weapon in disbelief like it chose to be weak.

"Drop itttt." He held out a hand like I was his faithful retriever, waiting for the stick to be thrown again. You had to be kidding me, how dumb did he think I was? I growled in response, tightening my lock on it. "Give it back, or I'll be forced to expel you from this house again."

"Yeerhh, und gew did suct a goot jog un ih the irst tine too!" I snorted again in his direction, taking a step forward as he took one back.

"You piece of filth! You can't threaten me with my own weapon!" He sounded undignified and outraged with an underlying tone of confusion. I sneered at him, biting down as hard as I could until the weapon snapped into three; the blade with a tiny bit of handle to it, the wooden handle in my mouth, and the remainder of it on the other side. The angel's eyes flared wide, hands grasping at nothing as he leaned over to pick up the weapon at my feet. "You... you... how dare you!" He glared at me, giving me just enough opportunity to give him a powerful headbutt square to the face. The angel went down, knocked senseless, the bits of weapon at his feet as he was finally silent for a moment.

With a growl, I spit out the rest next to his head, breathing hard. Feeling like a prized fighter and an acceptable guard demon, I turned back to my family happily. Katherine and Sabina remained aghast at the damage done to the house, effectively sucking out any pride or feeling of accomplishment, sunk into a pool of guilt. They picked at the dishes from the floor carefully, removing the largest bits that were still together. I looked to Amber who stayed next to the Priest, her eyes wary of everything around her. The walls began to heave, heavy with the black entity as it surfaced from the flower petal wallpaper itself, laughing.

"I think that went well! I could watch this all day!" The demon grinned, pearly white teeth made of rose stems and glue, "This is what you wanted, right? To call someone else and then knock them unconscious? Just how helpful IS this idiot?" It disappeared from one corner, resurfacing in the one closest to me.

"I'm telling you, you'll be saving a lot of time if you just come with me." It mocked, resting its head on one arm that appeared from the middle of the wall." If not, then it's going to be this long, drawn out thing that'll ultimately cause you more pain than it's worth."

"Why do you keep talking like you know what's going to happen?" I growled at it, the entity only replying with a laugh. There was suddenly a sharp, blinding pain in my thigh as I jumped a little, spinning around - the angel was breathing heavy against me, the end of pike plunged deep into my leg. He grinned like he had finally killed the grand monster of Hell as I shadowed him, that victorious glare flashing with recognition, looking back up half as threatening and determined. Frowning, I smacked his hand away, pulling the end of the pike out myself. I thought on it, smacking the angel on the head with his own weapon lightly before pointing to the corner with the real evil entity lounging nonchalantly, waving. The angel's face twisted about, dropping the facade for just a second.

"Oh." He said softly, eyes narrowing back on the pike from my hand as he snatched it, stabbing me with it again. I growled and gave him a swift kick in the shoulder and sending him skittering back outside once more. Pulling the pike from my leg a second time, the demon laughed yet again.

"He doesn't understand you, you know." It had both arms sticking through the wall now, resting almost comfortably, bored.

"I don't expect sympathy from him." I cringed as my leg wound began to heal itself, tossing the pike head to the ground.

"He is a simple idiot, that's for sure. But no, I mean you two can't physically communicate with one another. He's an angel. Their religious intolerance for any Hell spawn and mumbo jumbo like that keep demons and angels separate. It's a longstanding rule." The demon dropped to the ground, emerging from the wall." Everything you say sounds like gibberish."

"Why are you telling me this?" I struggled to try and fight back against that notion when the angel came back into the scene, beaten up, ready to fight. He saw the larger demon and myself next to one another chatting and lunged for the other; the demon grabbed his upper body easily while the angel writhed and began to grunt in pain.

"See, I can say, 'If you stop moving, I'll put you down' all I want to his face, but all he hears is something that sounds like old Latin verse, " The demon pulled him closer to its face, narrowing an eye as it squeezed tighter, trying to pop the angel like a spoiled can of corn. You could see him suddenly panic. "Best I can tell, at least. Unless you're a skilled arteest, like myself." The demon grinned as the man was starting to turn colors, hands shaking in terror. I frowned, annoyed.

"Put him down." I warned, snarling.

"What? No, I found him first!" The other demon shot back, twisting the angel upside down as he was turning blue. He looked over to me like he was about to cry, face wracked with pain and fear that didn't care where it sought help from. Giving an anxious whine, I hesitated before steeling myself.

"Put him down!" Teetering back onto my hind legs, I maneuvered around the angel and sunk my teeth into the demon's wrist.

If this all was one big misunderstanding, then it wasn't right for the two of us to fight, even if this blowhard was a big pain in my upper leg. He'd be useful if he could just get it through his head that I wasn't the enemy here. I had to stay with that hope, that if I just showed him enough times that I wasn't fighting against him, he'd have to see the light eventually. I twisted and shook my head like a dog with a pull toy, giving a garbled mutter.

"Let go! I need him for fighting you."

"Aww, how sweet! And dumb! But you're right. I say we get the real fun started!" The demon pulled back into the wall as the angel fell beside me, landing on his head. Unaware of the demon, it suddenly shot out elsewhere and latched onto Amber in a whirl of black smoke while it fumbled with its grip, dragging the poor girl. She screamed and kicked at the demon as it burst into the field with its front arms, tail bubbling with new activity; a whole new set of legs came sprouting forth and hit the ground with great force. The second set of arms began to elongate and spread wider and wider, the massive black demon growing a set of disjointed wings. It turned around and faced both of us, bringing the screaming child from the ground in its remaining front arms, hoisting it closer to its face. Amber screamed, petrified.

"I've got a prize for you, my Queen!" The demon cooed out over the terrified shrieking, "Now all you have to do is come and get it!" The spirit took two slow, enormous flaps.

"Amber!" Katherine shouted, darting from the house.

"No!" I felt glued to the floor, my body shaking as I watched her being lifted, higher and higher, out of my reach. Go! Do something! There's still time!

"So is this the big plan, huh demon?" I heard that voice behind me, dropping my frustration to new depths. He stood, arms folded, his eyes flat and accusing, " The two of you working together to go dismember some poor innocent child? You things make me sick." He gave this piddly smile as he said it, holding the tiny pike in his hands threateningly like he had the upper hand here, while we both listened to the sound of slow, melodic wing beats, the sound of us both just arguing instead. He might as well be wearing a dunce cap with a tiny sword toothpick while he was at it.

My patience snapped. I shoved my face purposely into his blade, inches from his face to show how weak he was.

"You were supposed to help! Do something!" I bared my teeth at him like a sick and delusional animal, pushing him backwards with little trouble until he hit a wall. "You're the Goddamn exorcist, go exorcise the demon!" He remained there, trying not to make eye contact like I was some sort of bear, trembling. My temper soured as I yanked the blade from my head, throwing it outside the crumbling wall, pointing to it.

"Do something! Help! Assist! Please!" He remained frozen, suddenly concerned, looking once back to the Priest as he was busy trying to console Katherine and Sabina. The gaze eventually looked back to me, worried like he was in trouble, unsure. Bellowing a monstrous growl with my one eye twitching, I grabbed onto the nape of his shirt and forcefully dragged him to the edge of the backyard. The angel squealed and screeched like a stuck pig. Propping him to stand like an adult, I let go, trudging into the backyard a bit to retrieve his shitty broken knob of a weapon, storming back up to him and staging it in his hands. The angel stopped his wailing, white as a sheet of paper as he looked incredulously down at the weapon, then back to me for a clue.

Looking around like I couldn't make it any more obvious, I leaned back on my haunches a bit, using both hands to give him a gentle shooing motion, a sort of 'Get on with it' sweep. The angel looked concerned, back to the weapon before back to me with a terrified frown. Snorting out my anguish I made fake stabbing motions to the sky, motioned him to get to it, and gave him a slight push out of the new breezy entryway of this house. He turned around to me in full panic.

"What?! I- I'm not qualified to deal with 100 ft tall living nightmares! Are you nuts?" My eyes went wider as I just stared at him, too angry to function. "I'm not even supposed to be dealing with demons as big as you!" The black molten demon screeched out into the air as I wish it popped the angel like a balloon when it had the chance. About to really give this idiot Hell, I heard Amber calling me back to important matters.

"Neri!" She wailed as I stopped, seething with rage.

"Literally useless!" I shoved him into the wall on my way out; I'd have to deal with this myself.

The demon wings grew massive, casting a great shadow onto most of the field; spines disconnected from the body itself, they grew to take up most of the demon's full size. I sprinted full out, trying to catch up with its tail as it still lapped at the ground, swinging back and forth to gain momentum and height. Amber's voice grew farther and farther away.

"Nerrriiiii!" She wailed as I stopped just below them, waiting for the tail to reach close to the ground. There was a rush of footsteps behind me, the angel racing desperately to catch up so he could feign being helpful at all.

"Put her down!" He yelled at the back of my head as I did my best to ignore the annoying threat of authority in his tone. I was done trying to put faith into that liability, that risk. Keeping my eyes to the demon, I looked for the right opportunity when the angel kicked me in the leg, shoving me to get my attention. I gave him a slow, deadpan stare as he jumped back, almost shocked. "Don't look at me like that, you can talk to it, you tell it to let her go!"

"Oh well, gee, I hadn't thought of that!" I sarcastically grumbled, craning my neck to the skies, "Hey! Let her go!" I said flatly. The demon looked just as sarcastically down at me, grinning.

"No!" It said once, gaining more height. I gave another glare to the angel, crouching down to wait for the tail to just swing low enough for me to snag it. The angel began to throw a fit, muttering under his breath as the tail arched high, ready to give its last pass before they'd be out of range.

"You stupid demon!" The angel yelled at me as I jumped for it, launching myself from the ground like an attacking crocodile. The massive black tail in front of me now, I bit down hard on the churning, shadowy blob, locking onto a bone of some sort, yanking the demon back down ten feet towards the ground. With all four limbs planted firmly again I held it there, the demon flapping and struggling to get free as I remained unmovable. It roared in anguish, jerking and twisting to get away. My one eye wandered to the angel with supreme gusto. I was looking for surprise, for confusion, but he stood there, hand on his chin, contemplating and not amused. With a snort, I began to pull back on the demon, readjusting my grip another foot up, and another foot after that. Frustrated that my unwilling cohort wasn't doing anything with the child just out of reach, I growled.

"Guh gurt hhh gurrl!" I motioned up as he ignored me. The demon whipped around and laughed at the two of us, yelling out in an earth-shaking, booming voice.

"Trying to bridge the great angelic divide, are we my queen?" It cackled at me, switching its tone to one still understandable, but thick under some kind of accent, "Together we will join to become the darkness that makes the blood of men scream!" It stopped struggling, giving me more slack, but flapping there proudly as I cocked an eye at it. The angel practically jumped out of his skin, eyes bulging from his head as he gave me a stare that could set me on fire.

"That's what you're doing?!" It yelled at me, picking up the pike head once again as I tried to register what the Hell was going on, shaking my head so quickly that I was afraid it would fall off.

"Hat hoesn't eegen make anee hence!" I yelped out, panicking.

"Impressed with my linguistic skills, eh?" The demon laughed, tone back to normal. I kept staring at the angel bewildered, grip remaining on the demons tail as he came after me again. It… that thing was able to talk to him, wasn't it? That heavier accent, that was the only thing the angel was allowed to understand. It was just screwing around with his head, now, dragging me under the bus with it. The angel tore the blade into my shoulder, cutting me deeply. I tried to kick him away.

"You are the worst help!" Whining, I dropped my grip on the demon to defend myself.

"I'll kill both of you before you succeed!" The angel tore straight at me again as the black tail clouded my vision, knocking him away easily. It continued around, swirling about my head until it snapped tight, a death grip of black smoke constricting like a noose. I dug into the earth, shaking my head back and forth to try and get the vice like grip off of me. Anywhere I dug my claws into wafted away like smoke, the only bit of pressure was just around my neck. The line cinched tighter, choking me so I could no longer speak. My back legs were pulled from the earth. The angel didn't help once.

"Real shame, you know" The demon soared higher into the sky, easily picking up distance." The angels always see us as the bad spirits, but it's really the other way around. What a notion!" It pulled me close to its face, now massively oversized and far more terrifying.

"There is no black and white, only gray!" It babbled on its own power trip, swinging me around for emphasis as it rambled on further, "Why should we be the ones stuck in the shadows, why were we not allowed in their perfect world? Why should the demons feel the wrath of a God that favors the stupid? We make things interesting again!" It craned its head back, laughing in a twisted, demented way. I gagged, struggling to keep a focus on this petty rant, looking back at the house to see it start to shrivel up, to fade away.

"Welcome to this world of unfair odds, my fair queen!" The demon shook me closer to Amber, " Why bother bridging the great angelic divide when we can dominate the living instead? Why waste your time with this pointless mission of rediscovery?"

"Neri!" She called out, shaking with fear. In the middle of beings strangled, I gave a gurgled smile.

"Iks guh-nuh be okh-keh!" I kicked at the line around my neck fruitlessly.

There was a whirring sound, the sound of chains cutting though the air as my restraints finally snapped tight. The demon almost lost its grip on me and began to flap in circles, keeping the tension on the chain unbearable. I could feel my spine being pulled apart, my legs tethered to earth while the demon pulled mercilessly. I bellowed out in pain, the locks on my ankles ripping flesh, bleeding profusely. The blood coursed down the links; the demon turned my head to see, just at the very bottom, the angel standing at the very base of my tether, weapon in his hand. He shouted something in our direction, too far away to hear what ignorant thing it was as he readied himself. The demon spoke quietly.

"This is my favorite part!" It hissed in a laugh, keeping the chain taut. The angel held the pike over his head, quickly burning that blue fire before he brought it down on the bottom-most link. The chain snapped. In that instant it felt like my insides evaporated, my heart, lungs and brain, erased themselves out of existence, disappeared as I slumped, unable to move. The demon gave a light toss back towards the house as I drifted, barely aware on my own. My body began to fall faster, blazing back to the ground. I began to recognize people, flashes of faces as they rose to meet me, closing one tired eye as I collided with the graveyard I once emerged from.

7

"What's that?" I asked Amber a few years ago, sitting against the wall as the child scribbled in her sketchpad on the ground. It was a fleshy looking thing, heavy strokes of black and red coming together to look like a spiky caterpillar; ominous in crayon. The face was sharp, dagger-like teeth, green eyes lined with a red raccoon mask, standing on two legs. I tilted my head to see around her body, reaching up with my back leg to scratch something under my chin.

"It's a surprise! Back up, I can't work like this." She laughed once, shielding the picture more. Her enthusiastic scribbling wrinkled on itself, watching her start something new lower on the page. I looked to the complete opposite direction out the window into the yard, watching the bird feeder. The sun was bright and warm, bugs and seeds drifting along the wind, hovering over the grass. Taking a content sigh I heard her knock away the rest of the crayons, holding up the picture for me to see. There were three figures, three amorphous blobs; the first was the black and red bug thing I had seen before, but the last two were a red and white thing, and a green and peach one. She pointed to the black blob and explained.

"This one is the monster that was here before you got rid of it." She changed her finger to the red and white, dog-like blob, "And this is you!"

I couldn't see what I looked like in a full sense, none of the mirrors in the house showed me anything but the wall behind me. I nodded. It looked like a diseased cow.

"That looks very nice - I'm surprised you remember back that far." I rose a finger to the paper, pointing to the green and peach, people-shaped blob." But who is that?" Amber laughed, bringing the paper closer to her and pointing at it herself.

"That's you too!" She smiled, catching me off guard." But only sometimes when it's nice and sunny out." I felt my hands freeze, my tail numb.

"Does that happen…a lot?" I felt almost bewildered, a rising sense of urgency. I forgot I was human at all.

Amber stared at me, taking my head in both of her hands and laughing.

"Don't worry, only once or twice" She smiled, plopping the drawing back on the ground. They hung that picture on the refrigerator for a while, slowly being devoured by the other illustrations that covered it. I spent hours there, trying to see myself through the thick, loose scribbles of a 6 year old, trying to remember my own face.

I felt something being poured on my head; it tickled like fresh water being splashed in my face, like someone trying to wake me up. The world around me crackled, slow washing machine sounds of a fluid being pushed back and forth. It was irregular, haphazard almost, before tightening into something much more dependent, stronger. The washing began to thunder in my ears, the beats getting faster, closer together before they broke apart, hitting my regular heartbeat.

The water continued to flow, making me feel tired, exhausted; it began to feel warmer, before skyrocketing in temperature, scalding hot. My heartbeat began to thunder in my ears, closer together again as everything inside me restarted. I could hear something flapping, my lungs desperate to open up, to live like it was supposed to, that gagging sensation welled in the pit of my stomach. I could feel myself twitching. My claws began to contract, lips began to snarl as a spark of energy hit, popping back to life, lunging from the depression in the earth and sucking in a huge, terrible breath that powered the rest of my body back to reality.

With just as much grace, I collapsed outside of my hole, breath shallow and rapid. The angel stood before me, angrily capping some holy water and tossing it off to the side as he stormed away from me, muttering something about being hard to kill. I groaned slightly, a disorganized mess of parts and thoughts, looking over the rest of my body. What I assumed were internal organs chased after me, collecting bits of Neri here and there to rejoin back with me as a whole. My legs and arms were broken in many places, bone fragments thrown about like confetti. They crawled back to join with me, sinking into parts of my tail which would then reform the bone part lost in my limb. I wearily looked above me, the demon still hovering in the sky, tiny in comparison to how big it really was. The angel was cursing at him, then at me, picking up whatever he had his hands on and throwing it at the sky for it only to plop right back down. Noticing that I was a bit more awake he stormed back to me, placing one dirty shoe over the top of my nose. I struggled to get it off, my hands unresponsive.

"What the Hell are you!?" He leaned down to grab at my eyes, poking hard to make sure I was still awake. "Why won't you just DIE?" The angel stomped on my nose, knocking my jaw around as it hung from one side of my face; it soon swung back into position, latching on and healing up. I shook my head, struggling to keep focus while half my body still remained in a crater. My eyes began to roll backwards, exhausted, which apparently was a problem, so the angel did me the favor of tossing more holy water in them. Immediately I jumped to my feet, trying to shake the water from my eyes as the red blur of a nose always in my vision, was gone. Replaced with a white one, I watched my own skin bleed coloration from the top, replenishing the red in just a few seconds. With a look relative of amusement, I glanced back to the angel who wagged the weapon in my face.

"I cut your damn tie to this house! You should be dead! Evaporated! How are you still here?"

I coughed, clearing my lungs of grave dirt. His glare narrowed as I shrugged my shoulders instead, the universal sign for 'I could not be more clueless, how the Hell would I know?'

"Great!" He ranted, pointing to the sky, "So Oh-Great-Healing-Demon that never seems to die, how do we get to the monster trying to eat the little child? Hmm? If my stuff doesn't work here, what's going to happen now?"

A little amused with watching him self-destruct, I shrugged my shoulders again. He stormed off, fussy as ever.

The rest of my legs and midsection were completing now, strength and vitality beginning to stream though my body once again. I pulled myself back on solid ground, shaking myself off and regarding the scene around me. Katherine, still by the house, called up to her daughter, hundreds of feet in the air. The Priest comforted Sabina as they too watched the skies for safety. The angel held his glare on the demon as well, face twitching in anger and frustration and muttering incoherently; he was grey-haired though his face was young, with darker eyebrows as thick as my demonic pinkie finger. His stance was rigid and angry, elbows and knees all at paranoid right angles; maybe all of six feet tall if he could find it in his will to stand up straight. The angel's eye slid to the side to catch me staring at him, stomping closer to shout at me from a more comfortable, in-your-face distance. He pointed to the sky, looking back and forth between the two of us and speaking five decibels too loud like I couldn't quite understand him.

"If I hold you hostage, will it come back down?" He obviously missed the grand, general point of this whole fight. I raised an eyebrow; shaking my head. I pulled at one of his wings, the tiny things flopping out barely past arm's reach. He smacked my hand, pulling back on his own wing like I had dipped the thing in butter and considered eating it.

"Why don't you go fly and get her?" I was getting more and more frustrated with him as he stared straight at me, eyes hollow and glazed

over. I repeated myself, this time using elaborate hand gestures, "You…
fly?" I spelled it out for him, the familiar blue eyes clicking suddenly.

"Oh! I can't." He looked away and didn't bother explaining, even as
I glared at him for an answer. A low grumble escaped my throat.

"Of course you can't. Who would expect something with wings to
fly."

The high-pitched, far away scream pulled my attention back to
important matters, of Amber and the demon hovering expectantly above
the cemetery bound house. Immediately, I felt my blood boil, lips pulling
back to shout Heavenwards.

"Get down here and fight me, you empty threat!" I snarled as
the demon only waved happily, pointing to the Amber and motioning
me to come up and join it like we were pals. I tried dodging around the
angel, finding it blocked with a splayed out hand. My growl escalated,
shoving a face full of teeth in his direction as he remained standing there,
contemplating and unafraid.

"Go ahead…" His flat, tired eyes slid my way, starting to figure out
my game. "Bite me." The angel flailed his hand against my nose, sneering
like a giddy child as my frown deepened more and more.

"You can't, can you?" The sneer pulled back into an even more
dramatic sneer than before.

"What's the matter? Go ahead, bite me, there's nothing stopping
you!" A slightly malicious delirium spread across the angel's face as my one
eye began to twitch. "Aaahh ha hah" The symbol of everything innately
good waggled both Goddamn hands in front of my face on a faulty
instinct.

With one more mild hand scumble, I bared all teeth at a moment's
notice, head darting straight for him and blowing a mass of air through
my nose. The angel immediately flinched, scrambling out and away as I
followed through on a snap, grazing a wing and yanking out a feather in
the process. Hopefully that would get the point across that I was merciful,
not stupid.

The angel looked in shock, entirely less confident and surprised I'd
reacted at all. Chewing the feather around, I spat it straight at him, head
down.

"Just…stay here." He put both hands up and slowly inched
forwards, back in my way. Why was I waiting for him? I was at least three
times his size! With a snarl, I shoved him forcefully aside, dashing past him
to find myself stuck, yet again. The angel had gotten a grasp on the end of
my tail, tucking it under his arm and gripping it tight with his boots braced
against the ground.

"You're staying here until I figure this out!" He held that
triumphant sneer over me, over-confident as always. Calculating his grasp
on my tail with how tall he was, I only raised it like a drawbridge a few feet

before his feet didn't even touch. "No, no! Put me back down!"

Enough of this.

"I have someone to save, whether you help me or not!" I tried shaking him loose, thrashing my tail side to side as the angel kept hold, finding myself stuck with a feathered ball and chain. Snorting stubbornly, I began to walk with him attached, hearing the clinking of his metal boots as my trudge became a jog, and my jog became a run. "It's my duty, my responsibility to these people here. If you want to be stubborn and stupid, keep your idiocy out of my way!" I pushed myself, getting faster and faster, anger and frustration fueling my actions.

Looking back, the angel struggled to keep hold, letting the hardened act drop for a few moments of panic as he tried to water-ski on dirt. I groaned out loud.

"Let go!" He frowned, composing himself, pretending that grabbing onto my tail wasn't a huge mistake. The ground began to whirl underneath me as I barreled full out, past the Priest, past the house, until I felt like I could fly. It was almost as I could feel my wings attaching, growing, becoming their own, pulling them straight out of a dream with each quick stride. Glancing to my side I could see the air ripple, the light distorted by something there, wing or not, far away from my sides. With a curious leap, I wondered if they'd respond; the barely visible air suddenly pushing down with phenomenal force, lifting my tiny leap up ten feet in the air.

Frightened, I looked back to the angel, just as shocked as I was. My body seemed to go on its own, wings working frantically, blurs beside my face as I broke away from the tethers of gravity and into the sky. We surged upwards towards the demon as it hovered there; laugh filtering through the world around it. I pumped my tail to gain more momentum; wings slowly began to shift to a red and white color next to me until they were solid things, healthy and reliable. I shook my head slightly out of disbelief, gritting my teeth hard to push myself faster. My determination became a force, an unbreakable thing. My body began to blur and my head began to swim, emotions boiling to the top as I put everything into it, into every wing stroke, every ounce of energy into gaining some hold on a ride that everyone else controlled. I was done letting this all pass me by. The demon didn't even see me coming.

Letting out a resonating screech I barreled into it, hitting the demon right in the back with every bit of force possible. The blow knocked Amber from the demon's grip, casting the petrified blonde into the blue skies, holding position for a second as she dropped like a stone. The grip released from my tail, the angel shooting out after the girl as the two of them fell back to the earth. With my claws dug into the demon's skin it whipped around, tearing the two wings from my back in one fluid motion. Its second set of hands grabbed me in sections, trying to crush my bones yet again. I went into frenzy, tearing at whatever solid flesh I could find; dripping in blood I lunged to the body section, going to work on bringing this monster back to the ground. Panicked, quick bites tore into the wing membrane, the monster bellowing out of pain as it tried to pull me away.

The demon grabbed me in its hands again, slowly losing altitude; it pointed me towards the falling Amber, the angel now latched onto her arms. The two of them floated back to the earth, his wings flapping like mad to try and keep both of them from hitting the ground too hard. The demon shook me at it, voice escalating.

"Traitor! How dare you dishonor your brothers and sisters relying on the enemy!" It tried to lecture me, face pained and body weak. I reared back, biting down on the hand and taking one of its fingers off in the process. The digit drifted off, smoke pulling away from it quickly to reveal three tiny, human-like bone fragments tumbling back to earth instead. Grip loosened I lunged back to the body, ripping and tearing holes anywhere I could find a solid mass among smoke.

The demon snarled painfully as those frantic, slashing arms grew slower and slower, the two of us dropping from the sky faster until its wings folded into a stark plummet. My arms seemed to pull away from my body, my legs shaking under my own weight as I began to drift away from the massive beast, pulled behind it by volume alone. I grabbed for a hold in demonic smoke with all my might as the ground swelled in size, spreading its embrace wide and accepting us back with a startling passion.

Crashing into the ground, we sloshed and tumbled in a confused mass. Hitting again we skidded hard, rolling side over side until we came to a stop far outside the house, resting in the yard of the abandoned house two plots down, far outside my original perimeters.

I stumbled from the mess with a manageable amount of broken bones, slowly staggering to the demons head as it too, remade itself. With tired, exhausted energy, I locked onto its neck, grabbing hold of a solid line of bones amidst the smoke. Heaving for breath I began to bite down harder, the demon spasming and thrashing around to slide its eye in my direction, glaring at me hotly.

"W…Well you've certainly proved yourself a formidable enemy. I suppose you're not completely useless." It gasped for air, trying to pull from my grasp weakly. My feet moved only slightly, splayed out and planted deep into the ground, cringing with the healing going on in my own body. "What do you think you'll gain, killing me like this?"

"I don't want anything."

"You're dooming yourself to a life full of trouble and despair, you know. I'm offering the easy way out, offering you to skip this pointless life and live the one you're supposed to." It struggled again to pull away, neck locked tight in my teeth.

"I don't want what you have. I don't want anything to do with demons." I choked on the demon's hazy body, in pain as it suddenly let out an enormous laugh.

"Such deep talk from someone so brainless! You think you know where you stand? You ARE a demon, my Queen. You're going to have to realize that." It's head shifted towards the house, eyes narrowing. "He's almost here, you know. You're not going to have another chance."

I warily looked over as well, seeing the angel running like a track star towards us, economy sized bucket of holy water in his grip. There was a limp, a noticeable favoritism to his step. I tightened just a bit, feeling the bones begin to bend under my bite.

"You can talk to him, can't you?" I tensed up, threatening the demon. It chuckled, arms snapping back into place.

"Want me to clear your name? Make everything right between you two?" It mocked me as a love-struck child. I shook the demons neck slightly, growling out of annoyance.

"No. I want you to repeat to him, in words HE understands, what I'm saying, okay? No funny shit."

The demon choked out a laugh, tossing its head a bit.

"Oh! I'm sorry, what reason do I have to comply with this request?" The angel was in front of us now, out of breath and setting down his bucket.

"Honor in defeat?" I garbled between hazy demonic smoke.

"You really think something like that exists between demons?"

"Please?" I smiled, antagonizing it.

"There is even less of that!" It hissed, eyes focused on my face in a furious growl. The orbs tired, letting out frustrated snarl of defeat, rolling its eyes and giving up. There was a pause before the demon shifted a little to face the angel directly.

"Angel!" The demon spoke on its own, voice distorted the same way it had been earlier on. He shuddered a little, looking at both of us with extreme skepticism. "What I say, I translate for the demon at my neck. Got it?" He didn't say anything, only raised an eyebrow. I figured that was enough.

"Ask him if Amber's okay." I huffed, struggling to keep my feet to the ground.

"She is saying, is the girl okay?" The demons tone was flat, bored with small, unimportant banter like this already. He looked a little bereft, looking back to the house before back to us.

"She's…injured."

"Is she still alive?" The demon translated for me, continuing on with its interpreting job.

"Yeah, I mean, she's alive, just injured, uh, scratched up, broken bones, that sort. They already called her an ambulance, she'll probably be okay." He relaxed the way he spoke for just a moment, before remembering exactly who he was and who he faced, bracing himself at the two demons once more. I let out a deep breath of relief around the demon's hazy skin.

"Tell him to kill us both." I said flatly, shivering just at the thought." I enjoyed my time here. I made new memories in lieu of old ones. But fact is fact, I don't belong here; no matter how much I like it. It's best that you and I are both gone."

"What? I'm not saying that!" It riled from its spot, legs pushing hard to move my grip from the ground- I pulled back best I could, feet skidding about. With another forceful chomp, we quieted again.

"Say it!" I bit down, cracking the bones. The demon grumbled unhappily, repeating just the first part.

"This isn't what I was throwing before." He babbled on his words, "I... I had to get permission to get this. It's 10, 000 times stronger than regular holy water." He held the economy-sized bucket of water in his hands, tilting it forward to show it was a brilliant blue color.

"Do it!" The demon talked for me, whipping its head around, "I don't think you'll survive this as well, my queen. If you let go, I'll stay still, I won't run away, promise!"

"You've hid away for three years; I don't put it beyond you to do it again."

"That hurts."

"So does death. Tell him to do it! Now!"

"I can't let you make this decision!" The demon thrashed to get away from me, my feet skidding against the ground as I was pulled off to the side. I glared at the angel, trying to speak with eyes alone, one that said 'if you don't throw that water right now, we're all done'. The demon's hazy skin began to seep between my teeth, the grip on the bones crumbling, dissolving. Glaring back to the angel I flared my eyes again, looking to the demons throat with a petty whine. Just do it already!

He crinkled his face, giving the lightest toss of the liquid in our direction, the barrel emanating light before it became a full out cannon of water. There was no delay. I felt it rip through me, felt every bit of the demon disintegrate in my grasp. It torn at my body, at my skin and flesh, ripping away all meat on my bones as they too were blasted away. The torrents of water burned brighter than the sun, wiping out all demonic energy, wiping the entire area clean to where thousands of tiny bone fragments were all that remained of myself or the demon.

Maybe now I could do this right.

I was told the area remained quiet for over five minutes. He stood there, picking at the bone shards and walking around, unsure what to do. The angel was conflicted to just leave, or to bury the fragments in the ground to keep my spirit at rest. He began picking up each shard, collecting them, noticing the bits starting to stick together, stubborn to rejoin and moving on their own accord. Dropping the fair-sized piece of bone to the ground, they began to roll together, collecting and re-forming with the other scattered bits to make up what eventually would be a human skull.

I felt like the faintest notions of humanity, a smudge of an existence as the rest of me began to collect together on its own. By the time I gained my awareness back, I was nothing but an empty assortment of bones. My head, neck, and top of my ribs were forming, quicker and quicker; I looked to my hand to find it skeletal, bending and flexing. I turned around, seeing the angel standing there with an over-abundant look of fear, eyes wide, pose stiff. I brought my hand over in his direction, finding it noticeably smaller than my demonic body's hands had been, and when the muscle finally began to sweep over my body, assured me that my hands were human, once again.

Coughing weakly, I rocked to my feet, stumbling forward and knocked back to the ground. With a huff I gathered on my two sturdy legs once again, shaking my head as the hair finally grew back over my eyes, finding muscles and nerves painfully stretching itself over my feet. It was dodgy around my ankles, the chain wounds torn into the meat behind the bone, stopped on the Achilles tendon. Before long I realize those wounds were suddenly wrapped up, both legs, noticing that I was now covered in regular, human skin and clothes. I kept flexing my hands, partially gloved, taking a few toddling foreign steps on the ground as I looked around me. The colors were more vibrant and warm. I could feel myself smiling honestly, walking just a little farther before hearing my own steps echoed. Whipping my head around, I caught the angel stalking me like prey, changing his grip on the weapon nervously.

I began to talk, chewing on my words incomprehensibly. I shook my head again, trying to remember what normal, regular speech was like when I didn't have to annunciate around two and a half feet of skull and teeth. Standing up as tall as I could, I found my height to be annoyingly short. Instead of coming eye to eye, we stood eye-to-chin. Be that as it was, it was still better than walking around as some demonic beast.

"You're a dedicated pain in my ass, aren't you?" I said softly, my voice feminine as it sounded in the recorder; I couldn't help but smile. He continued to inch closer, eyes very wary, very unsure of the whole situation. I held my hands out, palm up. "If you just let me be, we can pretend this whole thing never happened. I don't want to fight you."

A little louder, a little more authority this time; he was still the angel that tried cutting off my head some time ago, if anything he was unpredictable and brash.

His gaze locked to my feet, dragging me to them as well as small wafts of smoke began to course between my toes. I jumped away from it, the smoke only getting thicker, following where I landed and streaming after me with a mission. The demon! Why was it still alive? With leaps turning to a full on awkward dash, I ran from the smoke, body painfully slow in covering any real distance. The black energy grew thicker and thicker, a cloud of demon following wherever I went. I stopped, looking above me, finding the black cloud spinning slowly like I was inside a tornado; looking around for help; the angel was a safe distance away, eyes holding the extreme confusion they had before.

Waving my hands, trying to rid myself of this smoke it seemed to grow angrier, spinning faster and faster until everything around me was blotted out. With a final surge upwards it snapped shut, lifting me from the ground along with it. The smoke didn't hurt me; spinning me slowly inside of it until finally I was kicked out, booted from the whole mess. I opened my eyes to find that same red blob of a nose in my vision, hands clunky and demonic, the amateur artistic interpretation of a red and white, cow-like dog dinosaur thing. The tail swished in my vision, sealing that I was in the same body once again that I had been in for years, the same ugly, demonic beast. I frowned at my hands, still sitting in a very human-like way.

"Again?" I mumbled, noticing the angel slowly walking closer, coming up on me again like in a trance, his eyes fixated. I leaned away from him as his hands were suddenly on my back, the angel bracing himself up with his weapon as he lined the curvy pike head up to the very faint, yellow scar there. I stared at him as he stared at the mark, bringing the weapon high over his head like he intended to cut me in half with it. Before I had time to wiggle out of the way or smack him upside the head like earlier, he connected the two, the weapon blazing gold as it touched my skin gently, pressing down.

My back felt like twenty thousand burning arrows had just gone into that mark, like it removed all organs, bones, muscle, and even skin under it in a flash. It was blinding pain! Everything around me began to get smoky again as with another boot, I was shot out like a missile, thrown into the grass as I tumbled and rolled to a stop. Before I could get up and give my unrelenting attacker a piece of my mind he was behind me, grabbing me angrily by the arm. By instinct I leaned over and slashed at him, finding my human fingers dragging across his arm lamely. He pulled me like a spoiled child, dragging me without any respect or thought besides that I needed to be moved like a piece of furnitur--My human fingers?

"Wait, wait, wait! Just... I said wait!" I tried to get my feet under me; the pace the two of us walk/dragged was too fast and too erratic to do anything but hang there in a great deal of confusion and let stones pass through my back. I jammed my other hand to grab his knee while he walked, tripping the two of us up as I rolled out of his reach and back to my feet in a rather fluid motion. He jumped back into a ready position, both of us bristling at one another. The angel's gaze would occasionally go to my feet, looking for the same smoke as I scanned the skies for any approaching demonizing-cloud of trouble. No sign. I hoped it would last.

"Just...stop, okay? Can't we---" There was a shriek behind me, the sound of Amber crying out in pain. My head snapped to my own house where the paramedics were getting ready to take her away, helping her in the yard. It felt like she was my own child, bolting towards her without knowing, the angel behind me immediately; waving the weapon over his head and trying to slash at my back in the process. He was faster than I was; I dodged best I could, escaping the tirade with only a few wounds from it before I was back in my own yard. They rolled into her own house as I was quick to follow, hitting something solid in the doorway, throwing me back with vicious energy, stopping me cold.

"Demons have been exorcised from this house" He stated grandly before his tone lowered, "These people are finally free from you."

Hurt and bewildered I got back to my feet, pushing as hard as I could to try and get past the wall. No luck. There was a rough hand to the back of my wrist as he pinned me against the building, other arm pressing behind my neck to keep my face smushed against the outside wall, quickly tying up both arms like a pair of spiritual handcuffs. He laughed at me as I panicked, standing there so smug of his work, of the one time he managed to get something right, despite all the other times he failed so badly, this was the time he decided to boast his great achievements.

"You damn idiot!" I shouted at him, trying to pull my arms out of the rope as he obviously didn't think I was a threat anymore, letting me stand there on my own, "They were my family! Fam-aah- leee, you get that?"

"I'm sorry, I don't understand demon." He scratched the back of his head, laughing as he said it; you could tell he was slowly getting back on his mile-high horse. Something about him just infuriated me; that dumb, broken look on his face, how I had done 90% of the work, how we worked together and it meant nothing. I grit my teeth, trying to kick at him as he only stepped slightly out of the way.

"Hey! You should be thanking me; I saved you from those demons back there." He smiled a fake, shallow grin of an even faker savior, even as I reared back and slammed my head into his in the strongest head butt short of knocking myself out.

He stumbled back, the small trickle of blood on his hands from his nose. I grinned, blood in my teeth and down my own nose as well, head swooning, vision warbling with radiant black waves. I took the brunt of the damage; I didn't care. I'd show him who was really weak.

The smile quickly dropped, grabbing my arm again.

"Alright, enough of that, let's go." He dragged me along, using his other hand to wipe away the blood from his nose. I watched as my home slowly dwindled from view.

8

"Let's try this again." He started up once more, picking up the mini-pike and running a finger along the edge of the blade, like that'd be threatening enough for me to quit speaking non-English to him. I let out a sigh, more than fed up with this charade for hours now. My arms were tied to my ankles; a loop of some sort of blessed rope was around each wrist, my knees folded to where my feet almost touched the back of my head. There was a loop of rope around each ankle, tied together. We drove back to the Priest's house like that, wheeled inside and plopped on a chilling cold operation table like a slab of beef; not a wisp of black smoke to be seen. He suddenly stabbed the end of the pike just shy of my face into the table, "Who are you?!"

"You're gonna damage your pike like that." I looked at the side of the weapon, sliver of eye furrowing at the blade before looking back up the handle towards the angel leading this interrogation. "You got your feathers in a twist about me snapping the handle, how is it okay if you do it?"

"Who do you answer to?" He slammed his hands down onto the table, shaking it. He'd tried a lot of things, mostly threatening to injure or cut me in some way, without ever actually injuring or cutting me. About an hour in, I realized he was doing his best not to. Since then, it turned into more of a game of watching how he was trying to scare me, without ever actually doing anything. I didn't understand why. I don't understand much.

His hand was just shy of my nose as he leaned over, scowling, trying to really stare the fear into me, hearing this almost forced, labored breathing like it took all the strength in the world to hold himself back. Sneering, shaking my head a little, I stuck my tongue on his finger just to see how he'd react. The act dropped in a heartbeat like I thought it might.

"Aah!" He immediately backed off, rushing out to the other room for something, dousing his hand in what I had to guess was Holy water like it caught fire. I cracked up, wiping my head on my shoulder as the exorcist was none too happy. "Dammed treacherous demons! How dare you try to infect me!" Apparently Holy water didn't act to angels like it did to demons, spotting his hand not burned or seared in any way. Guess that was interesting on its own. My laugh settled, back to being tired and annoyed.

"I told you when I got in here that my name was Neri, that best I could tell I was from some sort of goofy skeletal conga line in Hell, and that I didn't answer to anyone. First time you asked. I have, at no point, tried to withhold any possible information. I know you can't understand me, but hey, that's out there." I kept on as he walked back into the room, checking his hand for... demonic lesions, I don't know.

"If you want me to answer forever, I can. But maybe it's worth pointing out..." I took a deep breath, starting with a light, airy laugh that morphed immediately to something so far past anger and disgust I only spat out fumes. "There's no point in you interrogating me if you can't understand me in the first place!" I snarled, rattling my binds and rocking around on the table.

"Why don't you just cut me free, then I'll do my best to tell you everything I know, since I neither know anything, or care about other demons, then you can let me go. How's that sound? How about we talk like Goddamn people for a change?" Seething, the angel leaned against the wall, unamused, eyes dark and tired. "Anything? Anything getting through? You're going to start up again, aren't you?"

He remained quiet, thinking, silent for a few moments as I waited for a response. I knew what it'd be. I knew exactly what he'd say.

"You feathered turd, don't you dare." Raising my eyebrows, goading him on, he only checked his fingernails for a moment before looking back up.

"Who are you?" The angel started up as I cut him off.

"Nope, okay, I'm leaving. I'd rather die. That's it." I rocked side to side, flipping sideways about to roll off the table. The angel scrambled, grabbing my binds and halting my escape before it even started.

"Hey! Don't do that, I don't have any more ties, knock that off!" He shoved me back onto the table as he spotted his arm next to my head again. "And don't lick me!" Closing my mouth, I rolled my eyes. Back away on the table, we both let out a frustrated sigh.

Things went quiet for a few minutes as we both didn't say anything, the angel checking to make sure I hadn't tried to infect him again. Letting his arms swing down, he muttered something.

"Why do I get the weirdest demons?" He grumbled as I smirked a little, shaking my head and looking away.

"I think that's the first human thing I've heard you say." The angel seemed almost offended I spoke at all.

"You think this is a joke, foul demon?" He whined. I gave a

sarcastic laugh.

"You kidding? I helped you take down a giant demon, and you cut me off from my family." I laughed hollowly again, eyes narrowed with a snarl the next instant. "I'm in stitches about the whole thing. But maybe that's because I've been in this interrogation for hours now!" About to raise his tone in this inevitable roller coaster of volume, I beat him to the punch.

"Just don't. You look like an idiot and it sounds like you're going hoarse." Putting my head back on the table, I heard him gear up again, "Shhh. You're noisy. Stop." The angel began emitting gurgling, furious sounds.

"Who the hell do you think you are, talking to me like that?" His head was just above mine now as I contemplated knocking his jaw into his teeth, jarring that smartass, overbearing grin just one more time. I didn't understand why he thought he deserved better than utter sarcasm.

"I am your big, bad demon, come here to inconvenience your life and make everything God-damn difficult! Feel the wrath of my inconvenience!" I did my best to meet his gaze, trying to show I was not the downed animal here. He suddenly took a step back, holding up the nub of a pike left like that'd protect him. I could only shake my head in disbelief.

"Really?" Trying to shift a little more onto my side to reach his gaze. "I go through a paragraph and a half of dialogue and you choose NOW to take it as a... you know what, I don't even care anymore." He only kept his face scrunched up, waiting for another solid minute as I thought the interrogation was finally over. Then, slowly, like nothing had happened, he began it again.

"Who ...are you?" I felt like tearing my hair out before a new voice spoke up instead.

"Neri." He said from the doorway, immediately catching my attention as we both jumped. Great. What now. "I assume that's who you're interrogating." Staring blankly at me for a moment more, the angel turned away.

"The family tell you that?" He walked away, coming up close to the Priest. I decompressed on the table, still breathing hard, still mad. The man nodded, roll of fat underneath his neck jiggling with acknowledgment.

"Apparently they were fond of your demon here." He said, looking in my direction before back to the angel. I could feel myself smiling, lowering my head again. I missed them dearly. "I don't believe it much myself, honestly. Demons are crafty." My smile evaporated; it shouldn't surprise me that the bigotry was strongest here.

"Now that they're out of its spell, they'll probably be okay; they'll come to their senses soon." He laughed something hollow and unconvincing. "We did a good job today, we should be proud."

"I don't know if I'd be able to live with myself if you two fatheads weren't proud of yourselves for doing little to nothing. I wanna thank YOU for standing in the doorway, and thank YOU for stabbing me repeatedly. Pats on the back all around!" I mocked, shooting as many visual icy daggers into them as mentally possible.

"Talkative one, hm?" The Priest gossiped to the angel as he shrugged.

"Maybe, I can't understand a word of it." Figuring this house existed in some sort of black hole of common sense, the Priest made a point.

"Then what are you doing?" He muttered as I immediately leaned upwards, nodding at the man.

"Yes! Exactly! Thank you!" I clapped with both hands bound up, as the angel only narrowed his glare, picking up on something before speaking up.

"The other demon found a way to get through, I figured this one could too." Surprised, I wish he'd said that three hours ago. Hell, I didn't know how it did it, I wasn't nearly that skilled. The Priest led the angel away into the stairwell, speaking to him privately.

The table was ice-cold, making my body shiver lightly as I tried to gain body heat. The way my body worked was different somehow now, more sensitive, touchier, I was actually able to feel the cold like I never had in the past. I picked up on some of the words between the two men.

"How long again did that demon live with them?" The angel asked quietly.

"Years." He chuckled like it was some big, hilarious joke. "The mom said it came back just after we left for the check-up, did chores for her and had been residing in the house since with no problem like family. Just started acting up weird today."

"We WERE a family, until you ruined everything." I muttered from the table, voice sad and laden with guilt. "And you're twisting words, Amber knows that wasn't my fault."

They both turned to me for a second before turning back away, continuing on with their little discussion, softer than before. I sighed. Everything had changed. Everything was so different. I just wanted what I had before; why did that demon have to come by and ruin it all for me?

I looked about the room since I had nothing better to do; there were two tall bookcases behind me, bottom shelves filled with strange, odd books that looked to be thousands of years old. The top had strange bottles, a miscellaneous assortment of holy things and not – so- holy things, pictures, glasses, remnants of people's lives. There was workout equipment in the far reach of the basement, small windows up top to the outside. Mostly, there was an abundance of things bearing a cross on them, including a large, wall mirror. I glanced at it, wondering if maybe that thing could show me my reflection at long last, what I'd been wondering for years and years. It didn't look like a regular mirror.

Next to the mirror was a TV, connected to a few smaller boxes with little controls hooked to those. Next to that was a music player of some sort, a big, boxy, un-blessed thing. The basement had two rooms to it, the larger surgery/entertainment room I was in now, and a little side room closet with what looked like a cot in it, a lamp, some books and a nightstand. Considering everything, it was kinda cozy. I guess I was expecting something extravagant from the people who charge over a thousand dollars a visit. I could hear the Priest leaving, their little whisper-fest over. He slowly waddled his way back.

"Neri, huh?" The angel spoke questioningly as the Priest went upstairs, unsure if that was my real name, or something I'd fooled the people into naming me; technically neither was the right answer. I turned to him in response, twitching my lip just a bit as I laid my head back on the table, away from him. He grumbled, pulling up a seat and sitting down, voice almost calm, but still bursting with doubt and suspicion, like he was one sassy answer away from screaming his head off again. Though we both seemed more tired now, more worn down.

"Fine." He leaned in his chair, making various uncomfortable noises of hostility and frustration. I kept my head turned away, intent on the ropes around my wrist- they shimmered differently, like faded strands of iridescence were woven in. Peculiar things. The angel cleared his throat and made hesitant, almost whiny small talk. "You were at that house for years, huh? Must've been boring when you weren't scheming." He spoke as I growled.

"You don't talk to many people, do you?"

"You know, you're the first thing I wasn't able to kill or exorcise." He prattled on, "And I've been doing this for a while. Fought the whole gambit, from the worst to the...pretty easy. I mean, they've all been easy but some... uh. They're more easy." The angel awkward-talked himself into a corner as he couldn't even keep up a conversation when he was the only person in it. He stopped for a second, awkwardness thick like he had no idea how to talk like a normal person. I'm surprised he had any other rhetoric besides 'vile demon' and" evil that needs to be cleansed'.

"Never fought anything like that other beast, though. I'll get um... chewed out tomorrow for not calling in for help, I know that now." The angel talked at the side of my head as I shuffled with my binds, more concerned about that instead. What was he trying to get from this? Though it was a bit more honest, but why was he even feigning being nice? Did he think if he stopped screeching I'd suddenly be able to speak up?

I thought on his ramblings, more annoyed. I could care less if he got a slap on the wrist.

"You don't care anything about the people you 'helped' today. All you care about is yourself, and your ends. You assumed what you think you know, and you've hurt an entire family in the process." I looked up a little, glaring at him, "But yeah. That's got to be so awful. My condolences."

The angel stopped talking, unsure what to do - I gave a sigh.

"If you're gonna kill me, just do it. Don't torture me with light conversation." I grumbled, moving my head farther from him as he started up again.

"Demons naturally try to infect other beings, it's just part of their nature. Your kind is born out of evil and negativity." He rambled on, brainless as ever, teaching the top of my head all about what I was supposed to be doing. Blah blah demons this, angels are better this way, etc. Starting to think he was trying to talk me to death. I tuned him out.

Unhindered dialogue about other demons, about accomplishments and how he was so keen and smart to get away from that battle with minor scratches and etcetera. I was tired of this. I may have wanted that excitement, that entertainment, but the only thing I wanted now was just to lay down, curl up and sleep for a few days, get my bearings on things and go about my way. The way he rambled on and on about himself seemed like a marathon to even listen to, crap I had no intention to remember, from a guy so full of himself that to relieve that hot air in his head, had to tell everything with ears all about it. I tried to shuffle myself farther from him, scooting just slightly away on the table. The angel went quiet.

For a couple moments it was just the two of us silent, pensive. I heard the chair scoot closer as he seemed to wait, uncomfortably stirring about by crossing and then uncrossing his legs and fiddling around anxiously.

"So, uh...do you miss them?" He said, almost with feeling, so quiet that I wasn't sure if it was something I had heard. I pulled my head from the table, giving him that flat, cold stare. He looked surprised for a moment before folded his arms and returning the glare; just as stubborn as I was. In fact, he was better at this than I was. Surprised, I glared harder, more frumped up, more bitter than him. Frowning, he doubled his efforts as well; we glared at one another until my will broke first, lowering my eyes and giving a solemn nod, head back to the table.

"You miss them because they're out of your curse?" I frowned, shaking my head no.

"What are you trying to do?" I muttered as he kept going.

"Did you put them in a spell?" I shook my head no again; a little intrigued where the conversation was going. It almost sounded like this was heartfelt, like it was as un-biased as I had gotten from him in the last 3 years. Furrowing my eyebrows I cocked one up, trying to show that this whole conversation was quite different than the three hour scream fest earlier. I didn't trust it for a moment.

"Why don't you just speak English?" He narrowed his eyes at me as I rolled mine.

"What do you think I've been speaking for years now? Doesn't it seem odd that my family understood me and you don't?" I held my tongue out of my mouth for emphasis, "I'm trying, alright? I don't seem to know how to speak it to you. Everyone else seems to get it but you and probably the Priest too." My head flopped back to the table as the angel leaned away, contemplating.

"The words don't match up, I mean, you can understand me, can't you?" I nodded as he suddenly scooted his chair closer, excited. He seem generally more interested in the conversation.

"Alright, what's one plus one?" I gave him a sort of lop-sided stare, looking around for some way to get out my answer with my arms tied behind my back. Grumbling a bit, I knocked my head on the table twice.

"Square root of 9?" I knocked three times.

"Nine times eight?" I squinted, mouthing 'Seventy Two'. He stared straight at me before scratching his head.

"I guess that is a tough one, I'd need a calculator too."

"It's not a 'tough one', it's seventy-fucking two. I helped quiz Amber with her times tables last Friday, you know, between schemes." I watched him lean away, getting back from the table. "If you paid a little more attention, this wouldn't be half as awful." I grumbled as he called over his back, heading away.

"You know I can't understand you, right?" He said as I sighed, putting my head back on the counter.

"Yeah. I figured. I'm crafty like that."

He wandered over to the other parts of the basement, taking off his headband; the hair still stuck up before he remembered himself and glared at me.

"Don't think I'm letting my guard down with you, you're still a demon. But at least you can understand me, right? That's something." I now felt like I had the energy to knock my head against the table seventy two times.

"I actually don't understand you, because you don't ever make any sense." I said with the least amount of joy possible. I sarcastically rattled my binds just a bit, struggling to pull a hand free. "Jesus, just let me gooo!" I rapped my binds on the table a few times, frustrated.

"I'm waiting for your smoky friend to come back. You also headbutt me when given any chance." I cracked a smile at that, laughing softly, stuck watching the angel de-armor himself. It was odd for some reason, it didn't cross my mind that he was anything but lame and armored. Every bit was an assortment of blue and gold, from the rounded shoulder caps with crosses on them, to the shining, obviously heavy metal boots gilded with gold. The chest-plate seemed to be steel, not silver, the stomach area lined with an old type of chain mail, shiny, almost new. Underneath it was simple clothing, like a common work shirt you buy at the department store. It was a mash of ancient looking armor, though some parts looked new or replaced.

Bored, I tried to twist my hands out of the ropes frivolously. The angel came closer to the table, setting one large rounded shoulder cap next to my head as I tried to hide my desperate escape.

"Didn't you or the smoky demon call this house some time ago?" I felt my blood go cold, eyes bugging from my head. There seemed to be some agenda to this conversation, even though it wandered pointlessly from one stupid subject to the other. He found out I could do math, now he was figuring why I was such a lonely idiot three years ago. "You did, didn't you?" With a snort I nodded, looking to the shoulder armor. It was pretty shiny, though covered in dust and mud where it gave no reflection.

"Did you call to threaten me?" His pulled the shoulder armor closer to him, hands brushing past the one edge. Though the haze I could see a faint peach color, with the very edges lined in green. Shaking my head no, I saw the reflection mimic me. Pushing my forehead to the table, I scooted myself a half inch closer, trying to make sense of it.

"Did you call for the Priest?" I shook my head no, not paying a lot of thought to the conversation, putting my head to the table and trying to rub the dirt off with my hair. "You called for me?" I nodded quickly, looking up to find the reflection slightly clearer. Definitely a human face staring back, but details were at best, unrecognizable. With a grumble I inched closer, pulling my head from the table to find him holding the shoulder armor up by his head out of my reach. I groaned out loud, smacking my head against the table out of frustration.

"What the Hell are you trying to do?" He peered at the spot I had been rubbing with my hair, staring back at me. "You're looking at the reflection? Why?" My best bet was to communicate with as many non-verbal and facial expressions I could. I mean, everyone could understand that, right? Thinking, I gave a sort of mongrel-esque whine, looking down and to the side. The angel stared for a second, looking back to the armor before the rest of the basement.

"How about this, you answer my questions, and I'll bring the mirror over for you to look at." I had to say, even if he was an idiot, he was pretty quick at figuring things out. I smiled slightly, nodding. It wasn't freedom, but it could answer some of my own questions that pestered me day and night. Plus, I didn't know shit about anything. I couldn't lose.

"Did you call me to tell me something important?" Raising my eyebrows slightly, I shook my head no. Even this far away from him finding out, I knew I'd never live this down.

"Did you call to complain?" Again, I shook my head no.

"Did you call to yell at me?" Feeling stupid, I averted my gaze and again, shook my head no." Why in the Hell did you call here, then?" I kept looking away, waiting for him to get it. I could hear him snickering, that feeling of regret and embarrassment rushed though me. He shouldn't be laughing, at the time he was the only other thing on my level I knew of, I just felt like I needed some sort of social contact. I could hear him cracking up, shuffling around and leaning to stare me straight in the eyes as most of my head was buried into my shoulder.

"I'm going to bite your nose if you lean any closer." I grumbled.

"Did you call because you were lonely?" He laughed as he said it, getting a great deal of kick out of belittling me. I squinted at him, mentally locking this moment away, the time the angel laughed at the demon trying to reach out for some sympathy; but I wanted to see that mirror, I'd do anything to finally find out what I looked like. With a deep breath I nodded slowly, placing my head face down on the cold, brushed steel table. There were more cracking sounds as he bust out laughing, running from the basement. "God I gotta tell the Priest that! Hey! Priest!" I could hear him bounding up the stairs, giddy.

"Featherbrained piece of shit!" I growled after him, nose smushed against the table as I had enough.

Shaking my head it was the first time I had been alone. Insulted, I pulled hard on my restraints, leaning forward to put as much tension on it. Before long I managed to slide one hand from the ropes, quickly undoing the remaining ties. I sat on the table, cracking my back and stretching out tall before getting to my feet. I toddled across the floor, bare feet smacking the tile quickly as I gathered to the mirror, excited and twitching with nervous energy to finally see what I looked like. Finally! Finally I'd be able to know, after three years of refrigerator art as my best guess. I took a deep breath, shaking.

I opened my eyes to find…nothing. Shifting my head from the mirror and back to it, this too showed me the wall behind me and nothing else. That little liar!

"God dammit!" I shoved the mirror, rocking it by the nail on the wall. My head fell against it, bringing up my arms to shield my face. It wasn't fair, he lied to me! I pounded a fist to the mirror, overcome with spitting anger. "Why does everything have to be so difficult?" I shoved myself from it. A sound from the steps made me jump.

"Hey!" There was a shout, the angel frozen, unsure what to do. "Don't bust my mirror!" He pointed at me, slowly edging closer as I stood there, already frustrated and embarrassed.

"Ohhh, I'm done with you." I griped, turning to the far wall and placing a hand against it. Thinking empty thoughts as I always had I leapt through it, scrambling my body from the dirt to walk in the night air, away from the building. Not knowing what to expect, I found myself sprawled out in suburbia, houses and fences all down the block. This house had a big backyard, not nearly as big as my old house, but big enough to warrant it a 'big backyard'. Looking around I began to walk through it, finding everything around me eerily quiet, almost comforting. Cool temperatures, a soft wind, the leaves of fall starting to turn colors and drop here. A small shed was in one corner, the grass a bit overgrown, but nothing atrocious. It was all just very normal looking. Again, not sure what I was expecting, but something a little more luxurious than this, maybe.

There was a sound behind me.

"Hey, where do you think you're going?" He barked; I turned to find him half-armored, one shoulder cap on, one boot, generally disorganized. That was a good question; what did I seriously think I'd be getting out of leaving here? I had no where else to go, no point in going elsewhere, with the only people who cared about me physically cut off from me. I let my hands fall at their sides.

"…I don't know." The angel continued to stare at me, a little more relaxed than before, picking up something at his feet. There was a chain coiled in his hands, illuminating down the links until it came to me, with a similar bind on my left foot; it didn't go through my heel as the last one had, but took on a more shackle-like appearance, wisps of spiritual energy smoking against my skin. The links of the chain weren't connected, but held in a perfectly regular line; apparently the two of us were linked together. As soon as he let go, they disappeared again.

"Yeah, hey, why not. Don't bother asking me if that's okay, go ahead and stick me with the angel that tried cutting off my head. Just… great." I sat hard on the grass, holding my hands over my face, muttering under my breath. The angel remained standing far away, shifting his armor to fit awkwardly. It was almost like he was waiting for me to go attacking him some more; I'd had to gravely disappoint him by taking the high road and working on things besides how hard I can head-butt the angel.

I brought my knees to my chest, resting my head on them as I stared at nothing, barely noticing that the angel went back inside, done with waiting for me. Sitting there in the cold, I tried to process where I was now. A rock and a hard place seemed balmy in comparison. Taking a few deep breaths, I put my head down farther, closing the world off as the wind blew.

The angel re-emerged from the back of the house, unarmored in the same regular garb from before. He didn't move aggressively or abrasively, it felt more like he was stalking prey. I gave a light scoff.

"I don't know if I should feel honored or insulted, are you unarmed out of trust or you feel I'm no real threat?" I knew the answer to that. He started walking my way, awkward as ever. I knew what he was doing. I growled like a cornered animal, waving a hand at him.

"Just go away." I peered an eye at him, finding him still coming closer, "I said go away! That's easy enough to understand, right? LEAVE! GO AWAY!" I waved both arms at him, the universal 'get out of here' signal that even babies understood. The angel kept creeping up.

"You don't see demons as anything but evil, soulless monsters, so let's keep that going!" Tears suddenly welled up in my eyes, putting one of my arms over my face to hide it. "Leave me alone! Just go away!" The angel stopped where he was. I put my head back to my knees, overwhelmed.

"I HATE you for what you did! Nothing gave you that right! I haven't done anything wrong!" My voice cracked, wiping my eyes furiously." I haven't... done..." Stumbling into silence I gave a few broken sobs, coughing and choking on my own frustration, head back to my knees.

Everything stopped being funny. Taking that bit of humor at my situation could only get me so far, and faced that I could never go back home, that I could never get away and that I'd have to face myself, it swallowed me whole. Having a goal to work for, like getting away, felt like a purpose. I realized how shallow that was.

Sniffling, I hadn't heard anything in a few minutes, face warm and clammy like a neurotic mess. I peered over my shoulder, finding the angel looking many more degrees of awkward than I thought possible, nervously wringing his hands straight down at his sides. There were so many things that rang out like he didn't actually enjoy doing about half the things he had, that there was regret and nervousness about doing his job. Then again, those were all equally balanced with extreme assholish like actions. I didn't get it, but seeing him pretend to care made me so much more aggravated.

"Here." I put my wrists together behind my back, like I was being arrested. "Here, tie me back up so God help you that you have to make a moral decision. C'mon. Making it easy for you now." I motioned over to it angrily as the angel only stood up taller, more worried. I wiped my eye with a shoulder, motioning to it again.

"What? You think this is a trap? What do you care? C'mon." Snarling, he stayed put. "C'mon, I committed the atrocious crime of maybe damaging the drywall inside, and escaping from a double looped rope. Devious shit right there. You think child murdering is heinous? Try light home repair, they'll put you away for years in Hell." Sitting up a little bit more, I turned around by a wider margin.

"What..." I put my hands down, chuckling, "Where's all that courage and high-horse shit now? You don't care. I know you don't care."

I sat cross legged instead, leaning back a bit as the look on his face went from nervous to full blown concern. My glare only narrowed.

"Why do you look like you do?" I went to lean back, head tilted The ground was growing warmer and warmer, an odd thing. I put another hand to it, finding wisps of smoke shooting from the ground where my fingers touched. Damn. Here I thought this was going to be a regular thing- being able to enjoy being human sized and functioning, instead of walking around as some hideous beast. The smoke grew thicker, twisting around me higher and higher until it snapped tight to smother me, same as before. I really didn't care anymore.

The smoke didn't feel so much as a different body, but one that protected me, like a larger, more elaborate box I was able to fit into, to control. The smoke began to dissipate, cascading to the ground and evaporating away to the grass, my vantage point much higher as it had always been on the surface world. I was back in the dinosaur/demon/dog body again, the red and white cow with the pointy teeth.

"You again!" The angel yelled out, tone back to harsh. He had to think the two of us were completely different demons. That had to be it. I snorted, keeping my head turned from him, body still in the same position.

"I'm tired of fighting you. Go away." I said softly, worn out. I didn't hear him leave, didn't hear anything but the two of us outside in the cold.

"You spit her out!" You could tell he was pulling this fight out from practically nowhere, neither of us really in the mood to duke it out again after such a long battle earlier. Gritting my teeth I spun around on my butt in a very serious, teaching sort of way.

"Alright, enough. I'm gonna make you understand this if it kills me." I found this body-box to be a lot less emotional, more straightforward; it kept me from crying anymore, at least. The angel continued to stare at me, arms partially out like he was going to lock me in a headlock and noogie the critter demon out of me. I held my hand out roughly what I thought my human height was. "Neri."

His eyes flickered, barely understanding.

"N... Neri, right?" He pointed at the empty space underneath my hand. I nodded excessively. Yes. Okay. We could understand that much. I brought the hands to my chest, repeating.

"Neri" Stayed like that for a moment before going back to abbreviating my human size again, repeating and bringing it back to my chest. It should be easy enough for even the simplest idiot to understand.

"You get it, right? Please tell me you get it." I was waiting for that identification in his eyes, that same flicker of understanding- there was none, at least nothing blatantly obvious about it. My explaining hands crept lower to the ground until I was just sitting there, glaring at him.

With a sigh I was on my feet, ambling slowly back towards the house. He side-stepped me as I got close, wary and confused as always. I looked to the house, a gray, split-level home with dark gray shingles, plain as all else.

"You're still Neri, aren't you?" He asked my back, unfurling my wings out that they reached past this yard on both sides. I craned my neck over my shoulder, bringing both of my front hands up to wiggle them in a very heartless patronizing way.

"Ta-dah" Enthusiasm drained and patience gone, I flapped my wings once to shoot to the roof. There I could be alone.

9

With tired, dragging steps, I found myself overlooking the neighborhood, still dark. Lights dotted the streets, the stars fading as the early dawn approached from a couple hours away. The roof was lit in subtle blues, darkest parts still almost indefinable. It was pretty, really.

I lay down on the roof, head draping over the peak, absorbing my new surroundings. It was exciting to see other part of the world besides a backyard sided up with a graveyard, and two lots next to it if I was lucky. This was an entirely different atmosphere, a bit closer to the city, less free roaming and more condensed down. But it wasn't bad. The streets lined up parallel to one another, a larger street at the end intersected it. The homes across the way were still closed up, lights off, people sleeping peacefully inside.

There was very little sound, very little disturbance, general peace. I lay there, practically catatonic, unmotivated and filled with regrets; it was my fault this had all happened; I knew at the bottom of everything, I was to blame. That demon tore up Katherine's and Ambers lives to isolate me, going on and on about me being its queen. I hoped it was a strange term of endearment; it'd ruin my little situation further if I was queen of…whatever the Hell that thing really was. No part of it added up, I still figured myself as that aware torso and head in Hell, who managed to get out of line and though many lucky, painful circumstances. There was a tiny, belittling voice in the back in the back of my head that sang my deepest frustration, that despite thinking myself a good person now, that I had been in Hell, that I had done something terribly wrong in my previous life to be put there, no matter how I "got out" of it. I sighed again, putting it out of my head. The best for me was to relax; all that could be figured out later.

Humming, slowly and softly, I began to feel all the exercise, all

74

the activity earlier pulling me, rocking me into that beautiful comfort
of sleep. The birds began to chirp, the wind whistled through the trees,
slight sounds of the world waking up again. The outside world was still as
peaceful and soft as it had ever been; stretching out comfortably on the
slats of the roof, I bubbled on the edge of sleep, thankful to let my tired
bones recuperate.

Thump.

Something beneath me knocked around, the room under my
body clattering for a moment, before something scratched and scrambled
towards me. I let out a very long, very annoyed breath, re-adjusting my
arms and nestling in comfortably in a way that shielded me from having
to see him. Muted, I heard him say something, sounds immediately louder
as I saw his head jut from the shingles themselves, from the room below.
The angel grunted, pulling himself through the roof behind me, grabbing
desperately on the shingles as he fell part of the way back down; I could
hear his wings flapping, trying for something, still fighting to get up. It was
a pretty pitiful sight. Without a lot of thought I flopped the end of my tail
just in front of him, tapping the thing on the roof. Watching with one wary
eye, he stared at it, then looked at me, debating the action for about five
minutes before reaching out gingerly; I hauled him through the roof with
effortless force.

"Thanks" He said softly. I didn't respond, closing my eyes back to
everything around me. I didn't want him up here- I needed some time to
myself. The angel scrambled up towards the top of the roof, sitting down
a little distance away. I waited for the stupid awkward conversation, the
annoying rambling of his greatest achievements, the various guilt-tripping
and other lines of conversation I was forced to listen to, but it never came.
No words came. He just sat there, silent, looking around the neighborhood;
after a while resting one hand on the chimney, watching the sky. He wasn't
wearing any armor.

We sat in complete silence, save for a few re-adjustments from both
of us at one point or the other, until the sun crept over the horizon, until
the people all began to wake in their homes, get ready and go off to work,
until kids were picked up for school. Still, the angel never made a sound; a
welcomed change. I dared to even call it respectful.

I found myself gawking at him more then I'd like to admit; still
strange to see him in somewhat normal clothes. It looked like his face was
built to constantly frown, eyes might as well of been hidden, they were
barely reflective, and barely blue. His hands looked sort of beaten up, like
he'd gotten them caught in enough car doors to toughen them up, even as
they were crossed over one of his knees. Barefooted on the roof, his foot
was at an odd position, ankle bruised and swollen. He had said Amber
had broken some bones in the process of them landing, was it possible he
was injured too? He had sacrificed his safety for her, diving after the girl

knowing that his little chicken stubs of wings wouldn't cut it.

Feeling guilty and generally feeling better for resting for a few hours, I picked my head from the roof, tucking my arms closer to my chest, arching my back and stretching my wings full out. They were curious things, when I wasn't using them and just had them folded alongside my back, they were practically invisible. Light distorted them, bent what you were looking at through the wing like it was underwater, but when they were working, they looked no different then the rest of my strange half and half color combination on this demon skin. As I settled back to my belly, I could feel him glaring at me. Still, the angel never said a word. The air was tense, swarming with uncertainty. Feeling a bit better, I figured it my duty to speak up.

"When I first stayed at the Faegel's home, they struggled to find me meaning." I said quietly, worn, "I needed it, for some reason, needed perspective. We both needed a good reason to be there at that house together, especially that first year, we scared each other." I grinned softly, remembering my time spent. He was turned to me, listening to words that made no sense.

"To die will be an awfully big adventure' is the best we found. I still think that shortchanges this situation on many levels." I sat up a little straighter, warming myself in the sun, now high enough. "I'm not going to claim to know what's going on. I can't say I'm much good at anything, stumbling through death is my best skill." I looked to him, a little weirded out that he'd flopped personalities so quickly.

"So thanks for the time to get my bearings. Keep this up and I guess you're not as bad as I thought you were." I swung my head a little, "You're still bad. It takes more then a few hours of quiet time to make me forgive what you did. But you're at least smart enough to realize when you shouldn't keep pushing things. Lots of people don't get so far." I sat up straight. He nodded, out of place, more evidence we couldn't ever talk to one another. I smirked, shaking my head.

"I don't know why I keep trying to talk to you." I took a long sigh, looking back out over the neighborhood, where I thought my house would be. I was clueless how far away I was from them both. "Thank you for helping out yesterday. I did most of the work, but you were at least helpful. Eventually." I got from where I sat, keeping my head low, taking slow, nonthreatening steps in his direction. You could see hims suddenly realize what I was doing, alarmed. Scooting closer I took a seat, placing my hands to my chest as he leaned away, worried.

"Neri" I said, watching his eyes flicker. He nodded, watching as I pointed out to him, "Razzl...e?" I guessed, hoping at least some part of that sounded like his name. I was close, that much was true, but the exact name of the angel, I'd only heard once, muffled and through a wall years ago. He looked alarmed, putting his hands to his chest.

"Raziel." He annunciated, confused. Nodding, I looked back to the world, unsure how to go about it; part of me still screamed for one-on-one interaction, on social bonds, on having something there that understood me. On the other hand, it was impossible- angels and demons don't hang out with each other. How I had gotten his far with my body not hacked to pieces was beyond me; then again, he wasn't trying to kill me now. Maybe there was hope for a little reconciliation, at least. A truce.

Biting my lip from fear of being let down, I stuck my hand out towards him in a handshake. He saw it, giving me an odd stare before looking at me in the eyes, then back to my awkwardly outstretched hand. The angel began to laugh.

"I can't do that" He giggled to himself as I slowly withdrew my hand, embarrassed. Raziel pointed upwards, lowering his voice. "I'd never live that down, and I already have a lot to make up for. You're only still here because I couldn't figure out how to kill you, that's it. Don't get comfortable." Shut down, I did my best not to show my tattered trust. Promptly, I had my back lined up to the arrogant angel, ignoring him once again. How stupid! How…what was the matter with me?

"Oh, c'mon, seriously?" He laughed, "Is that not something they teach you 'back home'? You and I, we don't mingle." He wiggled his two fingers in a mingling fashion for a moment as he scoffed.

"You should remember that." He bragged on, digging a deeper and deeper grave for himself. "But I guess I don't forget things as fast as you do, demon." I bust out in awkward laughter, menacing and murky.

"I'm at least trying! But don't worry, I won't be forgetting this for a long time." I growled out, tail twitching angrily. "You're a dirty stuck up liar, you know that? God, I can't believe I pegged you as anything but an irrational, thick-headed asshole!" My tail swiped around in loose actions, trying to push Raziel from the roof. I felt hurt, embarrassed, and vulnerable. Stupid, among other things. How I'd let my guard down, at a time like this. I was at a loss for words.

"Hey! I'm just doing my job!" The liar jumped out of the way, pushed tightly against the chimney. Aiming the best I could, he sunk into the house all of a sudden, to the room below my feet. Things knocked beneath me; I spun, trying to ready myself for his attack. Searching, searching for anything, two cold hands pressed on my back.

"And I've been doing this job for a very, very long time." He sneered, almost evil, smacking the flat side of the pike onto my scar, area erupting in pain.

"You arrogant little-" Everything swept into a musty darkness, launching my human-self from it and the roof, away from the house as my fingers strained through the black demon smoke for a hold. My body twisted, wheeling my arms around, desperately wishing for wings as the street came to meet me, hitting and taking out the mailbox in the process as I slammed into the road, knocked out cold. I saw the angel grinning the whole time.

"Ugghhh" My head ached some time later, feeling the cold, bitter steel pressed into my face as I stumbled back into life once again. Leaning around to stretch out, my hands and feet caught on themselves, opening one sore eye to find myself tied and thrown into the back of the van like before. I dropped my head back down to the floor, tugging tiredly at the binds as the van eased back into silence. This whole thing was starting to become a sad running joke. Something skidded over the metal chassis, my tether-chains brushed my face and lit up bright once more, then scooted away from it just as quickly, uncertain and meandering on their own. The chains blindly lead to the world outside this van; if we were tied together, the angel must've been walking around somewhere. I growled.

"That...son...of a bitch." Managing to sit myself upright, I took a look around. We were parked outside a store right in front of the van, lettered in straight, serious text, one that said it was a very serious place.

"The Christian Science Bookstore?" It had to be said out loud, I wasn't sure it was true, but that was the way the chains lead before disappearing once again.

I exited the van five minutes later, untied and decked out in some sort of spiritual hoodie, plain blue that I found crumpled in the back along with Raziel's armor. The hood was pulled over the top of my head, over the goggles, over the horns on the side of my face, pulling the drawstring tight enough that it wouldn't slip off. It was as normal as I could make myself based on what I felt around my face. Filled with a whole different sort of fire for revenge, I strolled up to the store, fists preemptively balled up, slipping inside like it was common news.

Immediately, the sound of machines working filled the air as I scanned for them. All I found was a small little shop, walls lined with books, cheap shelving. The far wall had hats and shirts pinned to the drywall like the people had been sucked right from them. There was a line of tables, four chairs to a set, inspirational posters, all topped with chicken-patterned drapes. It was an evil place.

I walked through the store, noting the one cashier at her post, one man scoping out the nonfiction section, with another older gentleman sitting down and reading something at the tables. It was normal, relaxed, no signs of angels, no sign of the machines that were working somewhere in this area. I followed the sound, hesitating before taking a step through the back wall to come across a small quaint workshop. Raziel was in the corner, working on some sort of lathe, carefully inspecting what I could only assume to be a new handle for his pike. He gave a quick glance over his shoulder, raising a hand up and mistaking me for someone completely different.

"Hey man" He said quickly, going back to shaping the wood. Raising my hand in response, I gave an over-emphasized nod, walking farther into the angel's blind spot. Perfect! How could I do this? An open opportunity for revenge, my target with his guard down and back to me in a shop full of pointy, dangerous things; I couldn't have asked for better circumstances, to be honest. I grinned manically, desperate. It was almost too easy!

The pike head laid next to me on the table, wood stripped from the metallic part embedded into it. Next to the pike were some metal rivets, a type of peg that held the whole thing together, looking fairly new. You could tell it was forged a long time ago, metal bent slightly, the very edges of it starting to rust and no longer terribly sharp; the sides blackened with patina, like it was rarely used. Picking it from the table, I twisted it in the light, inspecting it as the colors refracted through the blade like a jumbled and distorted rainbow.

"Nice, eh?" Raziel spoke to my back, "It's a classic; used it to catch this really nasty demon, got it tied up in the back of my host's van right now." He leaned low to the wood, inspecting it like he was going to take it to dinner, tapping the end of it on the ground to shake the loose material away and going straight into clearing some holes for the mount. Snorting, I rolled my eyes, dragging my finger over the edges. I remembered this exact edge being lanced into my neck. The pike had other marks, scratches, but I stopped on a bite mark, dragged across the blade; the spaces between the teeth were embarrassingly small. At best, the only action this blade saw was chopping down tiny, pointless demons. The angel gave a sort of happy smirk, swinging the thing around in one grand motion as he was apparently done. I could see the end of the pole from the edge of my vision, head and body still turned away.

"I've got Gauzier coming here soon, see if he can rid the little bastard from my sights. Here, toss it here." The angel motioned, tapping the sawdust from the weapon handle. It was right there, right in my hand, swing it around and get some sweet, well deserved revenge. Who cares if you think you know him? Did you want to know someone like this?

I tried to get that anger going, the emotion and determination to dole out what needed to be done. Right there! Do it! He's been trying to kill you for days now, make him feel what it's like to get his own treatment! He's never showed you an ounce of sympathy, why should you be the only one to suffer? You can do this! I grabbed onto the pike head harder, hands shaking, quickly turning to him. Ready. Ready as I'd ever be. I could do this!

I could...

I...

The pike head rattled in my hands, ready, knuckles red with the pressure as I watched it, like it was not my own. Pointed straight at the angel, I just had to lean forward a little bit to at least stick the bastard with it. But I couldn't move. The thought of doing that made me sick, no matter how awful he'd been, or how deserving he was. Staring at it, disgusted with myself, I suddenly felt like nothing. I was weak. I was pitiful. I couldn't even fight back against someone in the best circumstances, a prisoner in my own shortcomings.

...Dammit.

The will just wasn't there.

"I... I can't..." I took one last longing look at the glittering blade, admitting it to myself softly. I tilted it to see my eyes flash by, dismayed, sad in the gleam of the pike as I looked up, watching that smile evaporate immediately from Raziel's face. He looked once quickly down at the pike head again while you could see the cogs turning in his head that bragging about 'that little bastard' was probably not the best thing to do. Taking one wrist, I gently turned over his half-panicked claw of a hand and placed the blade delicately across his palm. "I'm not like you."

Surprised, he looked at the weapon once before back to me, shocked that he wasn't getting attacked with his own blade. Quickly in a panic, he slammed the pike head down on the table, far out of my reach as I stood there like a rejected fool, too attached to memories I didn't even know.

"Jesus! You can't, I mean, why are you in here, you're supposed to be in the car! If Gauzier finds you in here, we're both dead!" I almost laughed; raising my eyebrows like it was a challenge.

"You, maybe." He yanked the side of my hoodie, pulling me closer.

"It's not a joke! I can't be seen talking to a demon, or I'll get kicked out. You're my problem, I released you so I have to fix. Go back to the van. Just go ba-" Raziel's eyes shot to the wall behind me, cementing a smile so fake it was practically plastic, "If I don't...let him know that...you..." He wheezed into silence, rushing up to the angel behind me, bending and bowing a lot. This other one looked older; more weathered than Raziel, lines gathering in greater numbers on his face. He wore something relative of a business suit, professional looking, hinting at power with a stance that didn't take anything but the obvious truth. His wings were much larger, folded neatly in a bluish ensemble. I guessed it to be Raziel's boss; at least someone higher in power.

"Let him know... what? Who is this here?" The angel, Gauzier apparently, pointed over to me. For some reason I didn't figure myself a part of this conversation until then, watching Raziel's eyes widen in fear. There were a couple ways to play this: get everyone in trouble and watch the chaos unfold or humor this situation and try to play the better person. If I had a little more energy I'd probably resort to chaos, but I was still tired from among other things, being shot off of the roof into a mailbox. That still irked me.

Walking with slow, dedicated steps and watching Raziel's eyes the entire time, I bent low, bowing to the angel like he had done in a respectful manner. Raziel let out a disabled wheeze.

"They've given you an apprentice, huh Raziel?" Gauzier shook my hand quickly, genuinely happy. "It's been a while! What's your name, madam?" The man looked inquisitively to me as I panicked for a second, quickly looking over to Raziel. Surprised at Gauzier's words and unable to tell him my own, he nervously answered.

"….N-atalie?" The angel spit out, Gauzier turning to me with that overly expressive new-people face. The one where you don't want to offend someone because you know jack nothing about them, so you pretend every bit of new information is just gold. I could barely contain my surprised laughter.

"Natalie, huh? You have very pretty eyes, my dear." He bowed in return, taking my hand again. Keeping my composure, I smiled and nodded thankfully. Of course I couldn't help but stare at Raziel with that oh-so lovely look of 'do what I say, I've got this situation in a very tight, inappropriate grasp' as he kept alternating between the two of us, unsure how to interrupt this ruse. I looked back to Gauzier and smiled politely.

"So, what did you have to tell me about her?" Gauzier stood straight, hands in his pockets and attention turned to Raziel while I took a few steps back, out of view.

"It's uh…that…" He stumbled, eyes darting around the room for a hint, before glancing back over Gauzier, to slowly, like a sopping mess of disparity, resting on me for an answer. I rolled my eyes, pointing to myself and grabbing my throat. The angel frowned before he even started talking, like he was sickened by my help. "Natalie…has throat problems?" It ended on a strange, upward inflection as I shook my head slightly, crossing my fingers in an X and using my one hand to snap together like a surrogate mouth. His eyes lit up.

"She can't speak!" He spat out before recomposing himself in presence of his company.

"That's too bad, what happened?" Gauzier turned to me as I nodded sadly, back to Raziel for explanation. This time he looked immediately to me; I furrowed my brows- he owed me. That and I hated him. I curved my two pointer fingers and put them near my head, pointed outside, and wiggled my fingers spookily.

"...Demon... Outside... Curse?" He questioned again as I walked next to him, standing side by side. There was less of a snide smile after he spit out that lie, more of a giant gasp of terror, realizing what I was trying to do. That if he's my witness that some other demon got picked up yesterday instead of me, it only backed up my story of being some kind of wingless angel. That I was using his words to get out of being killed.

Hypothetically.

"Ah, that's right; you said that you had a particularly tough demon you captured, if I'm not mistaken. Must've been a Hell of a fight!" The angel laughed, far more relaxed and relatable. I could understand why he'd be in a higher position; they left the debatable psychos for low, maintenance work like stupid commercial exorcisms. "If you want, I can heal you from that, Miss Natalie." I raised my eyebrows and waved my hands at him, putting one arm comfortably on Raziel's shoulder and giving it a hearty and barely polite smack.

"I'm... healing her." He said with an incredible amount of distaste. He turned to me with the flattest, coldest pair of eyes as I continued to grin at him, walking back to the halves of the pike, still resting on the table. With an extreme amount of frilly prancing, I presented the two halves to him like they were cast out of sacred lambs, bowed before my great feathery overlords.

"Give me that..." He snatched the two parts with a growl, his superior critiquing his teaching style.

"Now Raziel, you've got to give them hope, reward them for doing good work. I know it's been a while, but you must still remember that." He turned to me like the eager, praise-withdrawn type; or someone stupid, "I'm sure you were a big help in the capture of the demon outside, weren't you?" All his condescending words needed was a tousle of the hair and a wink, I swear.

Gauzier did seem to be more on the ball with his trade, but already I was picking up that something was off with him too. I nodded, putting up both fists playfully, making the angel laugh. Behind his back Raziel kept the angry glare, fuming from just how easy it was for me to blend in amongst the rest of them.

"See, there you go. Now let's see what you've got outside this time." Gauzier led the way out back though the bookstore's lobby. Following nonchalantly, Raziel's face was practically stuck to me, trying to make eye contact; I ignored him, walking just a little faster. "Now, this was the demon you exorcised from the graveyard house on Euclid years ago, right?" Raziel looked back to his boss, nodding quickly before speaking.

"It was a class three specter at the time, yes." He gave me one last icy stare, walking more in-step with Gauzier like business associates. "Terrorized the family living there to where they were forced to hide in the closet for seven hours." My walking slowed just a bit, the wave of guilt hitting me like a strong tide. Raziel looked at me slightly, knowing how detrimental the information was. No, no, don't let him beat you like this; you know you had no control over what happened at that time. That demon wasn't you. I slowly smiled, reassuring myself. My best weapon right now was being the better spirit. It worked, the arrogant angel turned back to the other, frustrated.

"My host and I managed to dispel it from the premises."

"And it returned." Gauzier said, irritation plain to see on his face. "Obviously you failed at exorcising the demon. Again." His voice was bitter, worn down. I almost laughed, relishing in the chance to watch Raziel get bitched out. We walked through the outside door, towards the Priest's van as he hung his head a little lower.

"I threw everything I had at it, the demon just kept resurrecting each time; it defied explanation, it was very deceptive." Raziel brought his arms wide, one palm facing my direction; he was trying to point me out in a terribly obvious way. Thankfully, I didn't need to distract the situation one bit.

"Of course it was! It's a demon! They're always deceptive!" Gauzier's voice quickly rose, turning to Raziel. "You want an explanation? This demon was smarter than you, it was more powerful than you, and when you should've been calling for backup, you were too stubborn to ask for it. Raziel, this is how it's always been! You're assigned to class one and class two demons, ONLY. I'm starting to doubt you can even deal with the C2's now!"

"I can deal with much more than that, you know I have, give me a chance!" He pleaded, seeming to forget I was there.

"I have, Raziel, I have. I'm done giving you chances. Do some decent work for a change and we'll talk." The three of us stood at the back of the van, door still closed, "I don't need this thing to be open to know whatever it was, left. If it even existed." Gauzier, looked away, shaking his head; Raziel just about lost it.

"I'm telling you…" He pointed straight at me this time, teeth clenched, "The Damn. Thing. Is. Crafty. A trickster! It shifts forms! Screws with people's minds!" Gauzier followed his point and stared at me as I stood there for a second, before nodding in agreement. Raziel's familiar eyes constricted greatly as he slowly turned to me, absolutely brimming in anger; a far different person than when he sat there, contemplating things. Part of me actually felt bad for him; he seemed under a lot of pressure to not be such a screw-up, and in the process, screwed it up further. Raziel stomped his foot angrily. I only nodded more. Oh yes, this demon was quite crafty, I agree.

"I doubt your ability to train any other angelic exorcist, Raziel, if you're going to continue to act like a child." Gauzier spoke glumly, overall disappointed with the way he behaved. Raziel 's head snapped to him quickly, eyes dark before a very obvious realization, raising his head suddenly.

"Good, you can take her!" His whole mouth was open, the extreme revelation and happiness that if I managed to shove my apprentice off on the stronger angel, he'll find out who she is and finish her off for me, become some big hero. That's what I assumed, at least. I knew how to play this part. "She doesn't want to learn, and doesn't listen and... not good. Bad apprentice. DON'T MAKE THAT FACE AT ME." He screeched as I only gave an over-dramatic 'aww pal don't be that way' face. It was nice to catch a glimpse of full panic, instead of annoying facades of trust and calm.

I could sense a bit of uncertainty in the air from Gauzier, so I had to solidify my position as someone trying their darnedest to be the best darn angel apprentice.

Taking a deep breath, I lowered my head a little in feigned dejection, looking up through my eyebrows. With a sad, slow, meek little shake of my head no, I took big, dumb awkward steps closer to Raziel, giving him a great big hug. Every part of it sickened me. I could feel him tensing up to throw me off, so I locked my wrists and squeezed harder, hard enough to know it wasn't a friendly hug. I wanted that hug to say 'Turn me in, and I'll fuck this up so much worse than it is right now you won't know which way is Heaven or Hell.'

I was in a rather dark mood. Someone threw me off the roof earlier into a mailbox.

The angel growled under his breath.

"Don't... touch me, you piece of..." I used every bit of strength I had as he stopped, almost panicking that I was trying to snap him in half.

"She's quite affectionate, isn't she?" Gauzier lightened up a little, noticing my hug was if anything, over-dramatic. Raziel coughed once in surprise, struggling to move his arms.

"Affectionate? She's a monster!" He coughed again as I let go, putting both hands behind my back like I was energetic and ready to learn once again. Gauzier looked between us two, placing a hand on my shoulder with a disapproving frown.

"I think I need to have a talk with Natalie here, if you could give us a moment, Raziel?" He rubbed his arms gingerly, perking up immediately as he saw things starting to go his way.

"Take all the time you need. Really." He grinned evilly at me as Gauzier and I walked farther down the parking lot. I gave an over-dramatic, affectionate wave before turning my back to him. You could almost hear him curse from here.

"I don't know how you got here or how you managed to be assigned to Raziel, of all people." Gauzier started as I immediately relied on my dumb bashfulness to try and get me through another jam. This angel seemed to know what he was doing, seemed to have a better grasp on things; he was almost a better credit to my stance of angels. Still, if he apparently knew how to exorcise demons of my apparent rank, being a little more careful around him would be a smart move. "You should consider apprenticing with a more rounded exorcist to get your wings. Raziel's been, well, on the low end of things for a while. Not himself." I perked up for dirt, furrowing my brows.

"He's really just at this commercial work for some time off, to recuperate, get his direction again." We continued walking slowly, "Has he mentioned anything about his wife's 'falling'?" My jaw dropped a little as I shook my head no. Falling? Wait, this psycho had a WIFE? They couldn't be talking about actual falling; it had to be the religious type, the cast away, the 'out of the light into the darkness' type.

"It's not my place to gossip, but even though it's been a while, he's still unpredictable about it. He's already shown that he can't even protect his assistants." I nodded like a concerned parent as I looked over my shoulder, emanating nothing but pity. Raziel taunted until he saw my face, suddenly getting very concerned and serious, like he'd been shot. He knew something was up. "If you're serious about becoming an exorcist, it'd be best to train with someone in a better state of mental health." Despite the seriousness of the conversation, I laughed just a little, turning it into a loud cough instead. At least I wasn't alone in thinking he was a little off.

I smiled slowly, shaking my head no. Placing two hands over my heart, I interlaced my fingers, pulling it away. Gauzier looked at me uncertainly, looking back to Raziel as he paced relentlessly by the van. He too slowly began to smile, shaking his head as well.

"You knew something was wrong with him, didn't you?" He looked back to the angel, now incredibly paranoid about the two spirits talking shit about him just out of earshot. I nodded with a little more sentimental gusto; sure, whatever you want to believe. This didn't excuse him from what he had done earlier, it didn't change the way I hated him so, but it did give him a little more depth. I wouldn't call it dignified reason, but just the tiniest bit of depth on a very shallow opinion. It was also helpful that everyone else considered him just as much of a spaz.

"I appreciate you helping him out, though my offer still stands. If you feel you can't help any more, contact me and we'll set you up with a more helpful trainer. Raziel's stubborn like that." He nodded as I bowed in thanks, turning the two of us back around to rejoin Raziel, now thoroughly bewildered and paranoid. He patted my shoulder.

"You have a very respectful student here, Raziel. Treat her well." Gauzier had resumed being the nicer of the two angels. I raised my eyebrows and nodded. Raziel looked like he was at war with himself, to grab me and shake me by the throat, or just be blunter about it and punch me square in the face. "Maybe if you manage to teach her well, we could work out a better situation for you." Raziel's blue eyes flickered, anger lost.

"R-Really?" He questioned, looking back to me. I put my hands in the hoodie's pockets, looking around. Who was I to try and keep him from thinking I was helping him out? In a way, I suppose I was. On the other hand, this whole bunch of conversation had been one white lie over the other. I was no student, he was not teaching me, I was the demon and they were the angels. I was getting Raziel dragged in the dirt more than he already was and there was still a flicker of hope in his eyes, even though he knew all this. It confused me more than anything.

"You know, I'm due to exorcise a class four demon in just a few hours; would you and your student be interested in coming with? I know its stronger than what you normally face, but it might be a good experience for them to see some real exorcism work." Gauzier said with an air of supremacy. I was clearly able to hear him making fun of Raziel amidst it, but the angel leapt at the opportunity, insulted or not.

"Yeah, of course!" He said happily, hearing the Priest walking up to his car once again. "We'll follow right behind you, I have to let my host know" He bolted at the Priest, leaning and whispering straight into his ear. The clergyman nodded, smiling, waving in our general direction.

After the two host-Priests gabbed with one another and started traveling, I found myself in the back of the van once again, this time not restrained in any way. Raziel sat in the front seat, talking with the Priest excitedly, eyes wandering back to me as I sat there, looking out the window while their conversation died down.

"If I had more time, I'd tie you back up again; but I'm busy."

"Clearly." I pulled the hood from my head, bundling up in it. Gauzier traveled in his host's car far in front of us, out of range.

"I have to burn that now" He looked down at the hoodie I was wearing, apparently his. I rolled my eyes.

"Well jeez, make sure to stow crappier clothing next time when you're bringing someone in to be killed off. Sir." I muttered as Raziel kept staring at me, cringing as I moved about. Squinting, I made sure to snort obnoxiously through my nose, rubbing the sleeve on my face like I had a cold. That made the point obvious, the angel had a much more extreme frown, disgusted.

"What did he say to you?" Raziel leaned farther in his pilot chair, glaring at me from a lazy distance away. I did my best to put my pity-eyes back on, those deep, sorrowful looks, the 'oh my God, I'm so sorry' attitude. By the way his eyes widened, there was no real need to say anything. "Whatever it was, it's not true. Gauzier makes up stories."

"You poor, injured thing." I said softly, voice sopping with pity. "You're just misunderstoooood, aren't you?" Raziel sat up taller in his chair.

"It's not true!" He shouted, defensive.

"Raziel, please! I'm driving!" The Priest waved his hand around in some sort of pain, putting it back to the wheel and shaking his head. We drove in strange silence, soft music taking up the conversation.

"Pooooor bay-bee" I said softly, hissing it in the van. Raziel pulled something from the car's glove-box, chucking the user manual at me like a spoiled brat. "Ow!"

Laughing, I settled back down, spending the rest of the trip reading the manual and learning all about the Ford Transit.

<h1 style="text-align:center">10</h1>

God, what had I gotten myself into?

I felt like I was repenting for all my demonic transgressions, miserably hobbling by this smoldering clump of angelic death. It was Raziel's idea to prop me right next it, watch me writhe as I did my best not to cross my eyes and gag on the stench, of the aroma wafting through the large, expansive house. Holy incense.

"This should drive out our demon, don't you think?" Gauzier fanned the fire just next to me, happily grinning and completely oblivious to the torment I smiled through. It was a horrible smell, a mix of rotting bodies, sour cream, molded rat poison doused in sulfur; they told me it smelled like sage and lavender. The stench felt like it crept inside my body, randomly kicked around my nonexistent organs and held my lungs hostage; it made me feel like a big bowl of uncomfortable. Shakily I gave him a thumbs up and a smile, glaring at Raziel as soon as his boss's attention drifted away. Standing next to it now, I couldn't help but cough while my skin felt cold and clammy.

The house stood alone at the back of the plot, owned by an older couple with a lot of cats, alive and taxidermy. It was an older place, silent, quiet; their haunting had started some years ago, but only recently got more alarming; howling calls, gurgling, growling sounds from some of the rooms. It had been a problem house for a while; the demon hadn't claimed any angelic lives, but was generally a pest and impossible to eliminate. Lesser exorcists had come in here and failed, then informed Gauzier, the 'big guns' as Raziel had put it. If he was unable to defeat it, his boss would be informed, someone who they just referred to as 'that'. None of us seemed to want 'that' company; I could barely stand these two here.

They were all decked out in their ceremonial armor; Gauzier changed in his car. It was still a formal looking suit, but laden with deep scratches and dings in the metal, worn proudly. This angel had seen more battles, fought more wars, strolling around almost triumphantly in his dented up formal wear. Compensating, Raziel walked like his chin was tied to the ceiling, in his mish-mash of high school football pads and layered plating. By pitiful comparison, I stood in a baby blue hoodie, coughing, leaning against the wall like a disorganized slob. I was still exhausted from the day before, never really getting a proper bit of sleep. Napping, sure, that helped, but my body was running on empty, coughing up my lungs while standing alongside enemies. I was in sorry shape, the incense just added to my misery. Gauzier gave me a peculiar look as I coughed again.

"The demon curse is still negatively affecting her, the smoke can't be helping" Raziel mumbled. "Go stand by the door." At this point, if I were to be found out, he'd get in trouble for associating with me, for lying to his superior, numerous other offenses. Beyond that, if he managed to show off in front of his boss, he could earn serious accolades, respect. Best of all, he'd be earning that without having my head on his newly re-assembled pike. Everyone benefits. But just because I had managed to weasel him into a job he wasn't qualified for, just because I wasn't hog-tied like a barnyard animal in the van on the way over, did not ease my residual hatred of the guy. It didn't keep me from arrogantly glaring at him with every chance, antagonize him sarcastically when the time came. But I was far too exhausted now; I nodded at his words, moving a little closer to the door. The air from outside helped immediately and my cough settled, resting my head on the door frame; I could feel my eyes slipping down, searching for sleep.

"Raziel, pay attention." Gauzier spoke up as my eyes snapped back open, "We'll give this another few minutes and then start our search of this place. It's a big plot of land, so how about I take the top floor, you get the ground floor, and Natalie, if you're up to it, can search the basement."

I managed to nod enthusiastically. Before any work started, he lectured me for forty minutes about how to go about exorcising a demon correctly directly in front of Raziel, took another leisurely hour talking with his Priest, not to mention the two awkward hours driving here. The sun had set hours ago, making me nervous and worried, uneasy. The last time I was forced into the demon's body was late at night, near the early hours of the morning. It was 11 o'clock right now. My eyelids began to slip over my vision once again, head knocking into the wall as I nodded backwards. Snapping back awake, I jumped as Gauzier laid a hand on my shoulder.

"If you're not feeling up to it, you can sit this one out. You can rest a little while we search for this demon, it should take a few hours." He said with concern. I shook my head no, pumping one of my arms and nodding tiredly. I was curious. I wanted to see what these other demons were like. The angel looked back to Raziel, nodding in approval. "You've got a real fighter here, that's a good attribute." He actually cracked a smile.

"Oh, no need to tell me that. I swear she's impossible to kill."

"Well, good! We'll need that. You don't happen to have any spare weapons for your apprentice, do you Raziel?" Gauzier went into that sort of mocking, 'doing my best to make fun of this person and they don't even know it' voice as the angel seemed to panic for a second.

"No! I mean... Uh. Not... with me." Raziel fumbled as Gauzier looked disappointed with his job teaching an assistant. Sighing and gearing up for more mocking verbal abuse, Raziel tried to patch the holes in his logic. "We haven't covered that yet." He muttered, looking back to me once as I only rolled my eyes.

"Nonsense! She must've covered that in training!" Gauzier turned back to me as I grinned through another miserable smile helped by the stupid way he said 'nonsense'. "I've got something in the car that'll help." Gauzier returned the overly polite laugh and gave me a nod, leaving the doorway to saunter on out to his van as Raziel called after him.

"Don't get anything too-" It was obvious his superior wasn't listening to him as he dabbled on the rest of his sentence, "-useful." There were audible, annoying clanking sounds like he drove the entire armory to each visit as the angel turned back to me, disgusted.

"You try anything with what he gives you, and I'll end you right here and now" Raziel spit out, eyes narrow and distrustful.

"Hmmf! Nonsense! Poppycock!" I parroted, taking in too much incense air as it felt like my insides were drying out. Coughing, I slumped against the wall, turning to Raziel and shaking my head. Please don't make me do things.

"What, you're not excited?" He chided arrogantly, half of it almost gagging out like a joke. I didn't get it. I kept shaking my head no before sliding to the floor, head on my knees. I could sleep right here. The incense wafted directly over me as I nudged that pan away with my foot, pushing it towards Raziel. I slumped back into a comfortable, weary ball.

"Not a fan of the incense, Natalie? Get up." The nerve. Curling a lip at him, I remained exactly as I was, unmoved by his persuasive argument. I wasn't sure I even had bones anymore. "Get up or I'll exorcise you."

"That's not a valid threat. Stop being dramatic." I grumbled, hearing Gauzier shut his van. Raziel's eyes lingered on the doorway, voice suddenly more frantic.

"If he sees you like that, it's gonna raise questions." My eyes popped back open slyly. I got it now. If Gauzier sees Raziel's student napping in a depressed ball on the ground, that negatively affects him; takes the good-faith tally away from his name. That makes sense.

I held my hand out, asking for him to help me back to my feet. Raziel made a movement towards it like it was second nature, before stopping halfway like he'd been shocked, fist down by his side.

"I'm not sullying my hands; you have all the energy, get up!"
Sighing, I slid my one knee to the ground and slowly rolled onto my feet
with a hand to the floor. My eyes were still closed.

"Oh, tracking the demon, are we Natalie?" Gauzier turned to
Raziel enthusiastically, "I didn't even know you were teaching that, Raz,
good work!" I gave a thumbs up to the two of them, standing back on my
feet and beaming like an idiot, trying to hide that my eyelids felt like they
were made of lead.

"Here Natalie, you can take some of my old gear annnnd…"
Gauzier shoved a helmet and a large, expensive looking sword in my
face. You could sense Raziel panicking without even looking at the guy.
"The DESTRUCTOR. It's a little dull, but it'll still chop up anything that
gets close enough." The giant, somewhat confused grin on my face was
interrupted.

"NO. Not that. That's… um… too advanced." Raziel stepped around
his boss to try and slide it from my hands, confident for only that first step
towards me. Taking a half shuffle forward and huffing out a bit of air, his
hands retreated, petrified.

"It's just a sword Raz. How is it too advanced?" He gave a pedantic
explanation, intentionally being the most petty person around. "This side?
That's for stabbing. This other side you can hold. Sound okay?" Gauzier
gave me a thumbs up as I shuffled my handling of the gear for second,
returning the thumbs up and a smile. I switched to Raziel as he only
narrowed his eyes, lips pursed so much they might become a singularity.

Gauzier kept talking as I looked over my haul. The helmet looked
dinged up and dingy, like it was shoved under a mattress in a leaky
basement for ages. The sword was actually pretty shiny; I took it in my
hands, tilting the blade to see the best refection I could muster, which still
made me look like either the top half or the bottom of my face was crushed
by a passing car. With a snort, I swung it by my side, taking the helmet
under my arm; when neither angel was looking, I slipped my hoodie from
my face and put the helmet on my head. It covered the back of my head,
lined with some sort of animal fur. The vision on it was good; it had a
large window for my eyes and nose, keeping my mouth, head, and most
importantly, my horns out of view. I looked damn ridiculous wearing that
thing in a hoodie.

"That should be enough time, call when you find it, it's supposed
to be quite fierce." I nodded in agreement, watching Gauzier flap once to
shoot through the ceiling. Raziel stayed behind with me, looking around
suspiciously. Neither knew what to say to one another, I was too tired to
sass anyone about anything, and he was stuck between pretending to be my
teacher and hating me.

Looking down to the sword under my arm, I grabbed the handle
as the angel immediately had the pike just inches away from my face. I

watched his weapon, saw sheen on the metal shaking and weave with the lights and looked back to his face. The angel was shaking.

Slowly, I reached over with my other hand, grabbing the sword gingerly by the blade, careful not to cut myself on it as the pike pulled away a little bit. Putting it out a little farther, I offered the handle to him, wagging the weapon at his face as he just stood there, confused.

"I don't want your crappy sword. Take it back if you're so concerned I'm gonna attack you with it." I spoke low in case Gauzier was still within earshot. The angel didn't react, so I nudged him repeatedly with the butt of the sword. "C'mon, take it. I didn't scheme with it or anything." Finally reacting, he smacked the end of the handle away.

"It's to protect yourself with." He explained like he wasn't sure he had to, unsure. I stopped, let out an annoyed sign and flipped the handle back to my hand, slamming the sword down on the hallway table and left it there. I didn't need a sword to fight demons. I wasn't here to attack them.

Heading towards the basement, I punted the incense out the front door on the way. Raziel made some sound of disagreement, but by then I'd already dropped through the floor.

There was a pool table there, a laundry room, ominous hallway and a TV den with gratuitous closets and cheap clay things lining the walls. Sad faced children stared at me as I walked through happily, knowing from our first tour that the TV den held a nice, long, comfortable couch. Ideally I'd be able to get some rest, they can fight the demon, bond, pat each other's backs and give a series of jobs well done and I stand there, feign adoration and call it a day before anything happened. Ideally.

The couch was as beautiful as it looked the first time around. Standard, beige, TV magazines over the arm of it with a few overstuffed pillows. With little hesitation, I jumped onto the far end of it, dropping peacefully across the cushions and kicking up my feet, stretching out comfortably. My stocky helmet cricked my neck at a horrible angle, so I put it just on my forehead, the metal part sticking out farther than the couch.

I got maybe two relaxed, comforted breathes of peace out before things started to happen. There was a long, low, sinister hiss; it started softly, growing immensely in volume as I swore the demon was right behind me. Sitting up and looking around I found one of the family's many cats, orange and white, walking into the room to glare at me lying down on its couch. I took a sigh of relief.

"Sorry cat, find somewhere else to sleep." It remained there, yowling again while its tail twitched faster. I leaned from the couch cushions, hissing loudly, driving the cat from the room. With a laugh I settled back down, stretching out once again to think about how lovely a nice, quiet nap would be. That's about as far as I got.

The hiss returned, louder than ever, dropping its tone to be a flat growl, deep and dark. I raised my voice, confronting the menacing tones.

"Shut up! Go pester the angels upstairs!" I yelled out tiredly, rolling over to face the back cushions. The hissing cut short.

"Why? I've got just what I'm looking for right here." Something said, the whole room dimming and draining with energy like a power surge. Without warning my head snapped back, helmet ripped from the couch, realizing the demon had charged into it. Scrambling from the edge the demon hunkered there, chewing and grinding down on the metal, enjoying the rush of the kill. I froze in terror.

My first impression, it was a cat. The second impression was it was a huge cat, face devoid of eyes and replaced with vents, nose flaring constantly, muscles bunched in a ridge along it's spine like the skin had peeled back, taking up the majority of the room so quickly. It was a dark, almost black reddish color with just a few areas of highlight; there was a red glow to the bottom of it's belly as it seeped blood, a never ending wound slashed from throat to tail; it had the body of a very large, very mutated tiger, even bigger than I was as the red and white cow.

"You've managed to evade me" It growled loosely, voice echoing from all parts of the room. I remained plastered to the couch, watching the four yellowish vents of its eyes open up, scanning me. It seemed like a good time to make friends.

"I…I'm sorry, you want the couch, you can have it." I babbled, scooting off the sofa to drop to the floor, looking for a survivable exit. "I didn't mean to intrude, I was just really tired, and… antagonizing you was a poor idea." The black ebbed from its body, traveling across the floor in a heavy mist. The cat lurched forwards, looping around to follow my retreat out the other side. The horns on it's shoulders bobbed and swayed threateningly.

"Who are you, exactly?" I could hear the confusion in its tone, walking faster to keep up with my backpedaling. Those vented eyes kept opening and closing, scanning me down. Idiot! That was the answer!

"I'm a demon, like you!" I said happily, pointing to my goggles and horns. "We're brethren! Can't kill brethren, right?"

"I can kill whomever I please, demons are not bound by laws." It said with a grin. We now retreated to the pool table, backed against it. "Why are you here?"

"I'm uhm, in a weird situation." It shoved it's head at me, teeth partially revealed as I squealed a little in terror. "I'm with the angels upstairs! But they're oblivious me being a demon. One of them, at least." I forced a laugh, hoping to break the tension. I barely came up to its nose, hair being sucked to and from the nostrils themselves. Panicked, I spouted whatever I thought would extend my life longer than the next few seconds.

"I'm the Queen!" I felt stupid immediately after saying it. The demon laughed.

"Oh? Have you been cursed by the angels upstairs?" Cursed? Why did everyone jump to a curse?

"I'm…not cursed, I'm fine. I stink like incense, but I'm of sound mind and body." There was hardly more than words in my tone, wanting to scream and throw myself out a window. There was an odd noise, the growling from before, interrupted quickly to make a loud hum. It took me a few seconds to realize the demon in front of me was purring. With surprising form, it bowed at my feet as I sat on the edge of the pool table, my proverbial throne.

"Then I'm at your service, my Queen."

I responded intelligently.

"Ah…crap."

We had a serious discussion, woman and beast. The demon was the spirit of many cats, a patchwork communal entity that adored living at this home for their entire lives. It's arms bore a deep scar like they'd been stuffed and mounted, the line coming up under the chin to the other side, down the length of the body like a fur rug stitched back together. It was the joint effort and ambition of a slew of fat, happy animals, so it's main goal now was the same. Lay about, hang out with their owners, jump and attack birds it could never catch, prowl a territory. Though recently it'd gotten larger, less coordinated, accidentally knocking over things and not quite keeping to itself. It longed for interaction, companionship from it's previous masters. I related. It showed growing uneasiness of angels constantly appearing here and trying to kill it with no real reason; again, I could relate.

Somewhere in-between discussing how to kill the time in a non-destructive fashion and how to evade attacks, an idea popped into my head. With a little acting, we could make this work for all parties present; save the cat-demon, give Raziel a popularity boost with Gauzier, and I could keep my head. We bounced ideas off one another, the demon and I, until I thought we had a fantastic plan. Simple, effective, minimal acting. All Raziel had to do was not kill the cat demon, and be dramatic about it, and he was pretty good at that.

We just needed the blue and yellow feathered cog to be in on it. As far as I knew, he was still stalking around the floor above, looking for this demon.

"Do you think he'll be interested?" The cat's ears flicked around, trying to find the angel without having to go after him. I stretched back on the pool table, arms hanging off the side.

"I don't know. If he's willing to put up with me for the possibility of a promotion, then I figure you're a shoo-in." Scratching my head, I prepared myself for having to moderate this situation. "Then again, I can't pin the guy down. I guess if the worst happens, we can beat him up and run away. Sound good?" The demon cat gave a grin, vent eyes closing happily.

Looking around, I gave a tired sigh.

"Stairs are all the way over there." My eyes lit up as the cat perked to attention, "Could you give me a lift through the floor?" The demon nodded as I hopped down from the table, gingerly stepping on the cat's face with my one foot, careful to avoid any eyes. Like a performing porpoise, he shot me through the ground, landing delicately on the wooden floor like a gymnastic dismount. Pulling my hoodie back over the back part of my head, I put my face next to the floor quietly.

"Thanks! Stay right there!"

Searching for Raziel I loped down the hallway, tracking for any sound of him. It was dead silent, no trace of the clinking metal shoes, nothing but dead air. My pace picked up, jogging down the hall, peeking quickly in each room. Sewing room, library, window with two chairs for looking outside, sewing room. Something shot in front of me quickly, clotheslining my neck as I flipped on my back, head cracking the floor hard. Groggily, I rolled to see the pike stuck into the wall at least three full inches, blade end purposely turned the other way, right at my neck height. Shithead. Raziel peeked out from the adjoining room.

"Oh. It's you." The angel said like he didn't intentionally do this, pulling the pike from the wall and daintily inspecting the blade with very little care for my well-being. I rolled around and gagged in pain, struggling with my collapsed throat, little white stars dancing around my vision. Wheezing out obnoxiously I rolled to my feet, standing up and rubbing my neck gingerly.

"Why I'm helping you, I'll never know." I grumbled, snapping for his attention and pointing down the hall.

"Did you find it?" He asked, spinning the pike back around to put it away. I nodded. "Did you kill it?" Giving him an odd stare, I shook my head no. He sighed, looking into the room once more before gathering himself up, heading down the hall, shoulders slumped.

"Let's get this done with. I'll go get Gauzier." Giving up, already.

"Keep going this way, and you won't ever be anything but a stupid exorcist!" I huffed, grabbing hold of his wrist and leading him back to the room above where the demon waited for us.

"Hey! Wait! I'M the leader here!" He complained as I rolled my eyes.

"Of course you are." Navigating to the room, Raziel pulled and struggled, spouting out strange conclusions he jumped to.

"You're not ganging up on me with that demon, are you?" There was fear. I swear to God there was fear in his tone. I stopped suddenly, leaning around to give him a light smack in the head.

"I haven't done shit to you, you're the one trying to kill me, remember?" Growling out, I pointed to the room below us, displaying it grandly like a dutiful wench. He looked skeptical as I pointed generally where the cat demon was, trying to be as transparent as possible by putting my finger-horns to my head, then pointing to the ground. "Right there. It's right there, okay?" The angel remained unmoved.

"Demon, right there. Got it?" I repeated as his eyes were wary and dark. Nothing. Waiting for some sort of confirmation that he understood, I gave up, dropping through the floor." Going to assume you get it. "He'd figure it out eventually.

The demon jumped back, startled as I hit the ground in a crouch, looking for Raziel to drop in.

"So is this… Raziel a nice angel?" It said curiously. There was no hesitation.

"No." There was a little whoosh sound as he dropped in from above, instantly jumping back and freaking out at the size of demon in front of him, swiping the pike in its direction. It responded defensively, letting loose a growl that rattled the walls, the two of them bristling at one another. Raziel scrambled back to his feet, pike shaking.

"Hey! Shut up, both of you!" I stood between the two of them, hands splayed out and using myself as a bumper between two extremes. They both quieted down, Raziel sputtering out a usual line of holier than thou crap I grew used to hearing.

"This thing is a sick animal, it needs to be extinguished!" Rushing a step forward, he jabbed the pike out around me, trying to hit the demon at my back in a cheap shot. I grabbed it mid-swing, the demon pulling away, hissing out loud to fill the room with noise.

"Shut up and sit down or I'll break this goddamn thing all over again!" I stared dead at those familiar eyes, not afraid of him this time. That dumb, arrogant look held as he refused to back down, looking up once to the demon cat before back to me. My eyes narrowed, moving my thumb to the side to apply some pressure to the handle. "You know I can, Raziel."

His face lit up with this sick, repulsed stare as soon as I said his name, lip curling higher to pout as he looked back to the demon again. The angel huffed out an angry breath, looking away as I let go of the pike, pointing to the pool table, surprised that not backing down actually worked. It was easier to deal with him when it felt like he had no cards to play either. Turning my back, the demon watched with slit eyes as the angel retreated and sat down as it was told.

"How long have you been traveling with him? It peered over my shoulder, curiously scanning over the angel as he only stared in frustration in front of him, immature and stubborn like a ten year old, refusing to look at either of us. I groaned quickly.

"Two days, but it feels like an eternity. I don't suggest it." Relaxing a little, I walked back towards the demon cat.

Our plan was to fake the whole exorcism, having Raziel use his dramatic talents to lead the acting. That way, the demon could continue to live here with its family, the angels would stop visiting and antagonizing the situation and Raziel could come off as some sort of big-shot, taking down a demon we all knew would kick his ass given the opportunity. It was a solid, well rounded plan. I just had the monumental task of trying to explain it to the key component through charades, to a person that couldn't put together the simplest things, it seemed.

He sat bored on the pool table, shooting glances as the two of us talked last minute strategy. High-fiving on a finalized idea, I hissed through a nervous breath; I was not looking forward to this. The angel watched us both, aware we were gearing up to come over and talk to him as he sat a little taller on the table, tensing up. I motioned back to the demon cat and snagged a chair on the way over, planting it dead in front of him. How could I do this?

I took a seat as he seemed unimpressed, folding his arms.

"Hey, this seems familiar, huh?" I snickered, looking at the table and remembering to just earlier this same morning. Raziel didn't move or act, looking 10 degrees more fed up instead.

"Alright, meathead. Let's gather all your brainpower to figure this out, okay?" I had a decent idea how to get most of the points across, hoping he'd be at least attentive to what I was trying to say this time. I pointed to my eye "I need you to fight demon." I ended my series of signs by pointing to the cat demon.

"Yeah? And?" He said unimpressed, looking away. "That's what I'm here for." I clapped my hands happily, making both the demon and the angel jump. Holding up two fingers, I started again.

"You no kill demon." The angel nodded suspiciously as I pointed over to it, "It wants to stay here. Need you to…geh. Fake it." I looked around to help explain, snagging the pike from his hands before he could say otherwise. Pointing to myself, then to him, then back to me I faked hitting the demon. The cat spasmed in pain on cue and flipped partially into the other room like a well rehearsed ballet. Raziel jumped to his feet, either not getting it or thinking it was real.

"See?" I held the pike over my head, stabbing it into the ground just in front of the demon, gurgling and moaning like it was dead. The angel came around the side of me to see, somewhat disappointed that I wasn't actually stabbing and killing anything.

"You want me to fake killing this demon?" He questioned skeptically. Delighted with his progress, I gave him a light smack on the shoulder, impressed. The angel instantly scowled at me as I put my hand down and away by my side. Got it. Touchy angel. Taking a step back, I nodded excessively, pointing at him.

"You 'kill' this demon, you can be the big hero." I strutted around the room with my arms flexed, stopping to pull back some of my hair to mimic his. The cat-demon got back to its feet, sitting happily alongside me as I tossed the pike back to Raziel. He stared at the lot of us, scratching his head and looking around.

"Do you think he understands what we're asking of him?" The cat questioned softly. I tilted my head a bit.

"More or less. I'm interested to see if he'll go along with it. I'm probably the last thing he trusts right now." I looked back to the cat, patting it on the head. It meant well, an honest spirit. "We're just deceitful demons to him, and he's just a spastic angel to us. Interesting to see if anything will come of that."

"Can I eat him if he disobeys?" The cat demon leaned over, resting its head on top of mine. Laughing, I scratched the giant pet's cheeks as it started nuzzling my face.

"Maybe." Looking about the room, the clock to read 2 am. My body was getting restless, no longer tired, jumbling with energy in a bad way that made me nervous. Last night about this time I felt the same, changing over to the demon form a short time later. I tapped the clock, holding out my hands for an answer as his dawdling was going to cost us.

"Hold on I'm thinking!" He barked out, looking back to us again. "Why would you two things would do this for me?" Giving an odd sort of nod, I looked back to the demon cat.

"That is a good point. Why are we trying to help him? He sure as Hell doesn't deserve it." Laughing a little, I shook my head. "I can't imagine other demons would smile on this type of thing." Considering how the first thing went ballistic that I even asked for help, I had to assume so.

"We've all got something to gain. We're using him." The demon cat shrugged. "I think if other demons knew that, they'd be fine with this. I don't know, I don't get a lot of visitors. I'm just a cat." Staring at the personification of evil and all that's wrong with the world, I only bit my lip.

"Hmm. True. Not enough charades in the world to explain that." I said as the angel kept looking at us for an answer he could actually understand. "I'm just gonna shrug. He keeps expecting answers from me, so that'll have to be good enough." I gave a giant, over-embellished shrug.

"Golly gee, I don't know why, Raziel." I said flatly as the cat rubbed against my face, snickering. I almost wished I could take this demon home with me. He continued to glare at us, puckering his lips fervently before putting both hands up and seceding.

"Fine. But if I think something's just slightly off, I'll kill it for real. Then I'll kill you." The demon cat rushed from my back, teeth just short of his out pointed finger as it was quickly withdrawn.

"I'd like to see you try." The beast hissed as I patted it back into submission.

"Don't worry, he's too weak to actually kill either of us." Shaking my head, I tried to keep the enthusiasm up. "So, alright! Ready to start?" Looking to both participating parties, they stared away from one another, neither interested in working together. The happy atmosphere collapsed as I dropped my shoulders, feeling like I was trying to herd cats.

"Well, tough, because we're gonna do this." I pointed to the demon cat, "Go ahead and hide in your spot, I'll bring king idiot upstairs down to watch you two fight, okay?" I shooed the angel away as the demon cat slunk into the wall.

"Go on and be a big man." I headed upstairs as Raziel followed. Letting out a loud whistle, I called for Gauzier, pointing for Raziel to go again as he stayed, staring at me uncertainly as I lowered my voice. "You wanna be the hotshot, go ahead!"

"I don't trust you." The angel said lowly, like that was some sort of new development.

I feigned surprise.

"Well, Raziel, then I'm just so sorry I lost your trust in the first place." I ushered him away again, rolling my eyes "Just go."

He pursed his mouth, setting off down the hall as the demon cat was due to emerge from the opposite wall. Both Priests were occupying the owners upstairs, talking with them as their minions did the real work; The angels called them their hosts, like parasites. I whistled again, tapping on the walls a bit to help him locate me. The floor above creaked slightly, cuing me to play my role of the new and easily terrified apprentice. Gauzier slammed into the ground just in front of me, eyes lit up and tiny, electrified.

"Found it?" He said with a slap to my shoulder. I nodded, pointing quickly down the hall, waving him on like I was far too fragile and weak to see some lil' ol demon be torn to shreds. Far too much for my girlish heart to bare! The plan was to hang back, stay out of the fight, sit in the car until I transformed back and do my best not to get caught, shot, stabbed, or mutilated in any other way. Gauzier wouldn't have any of it. Grabbing my wrist he practically flew me to the room, through the walls in a very straight, direct line before I even had a chance to say no.

"This is your chance, darling! We don't come across C4 demons often, you get to watch a real professional at work" We flew into the scene, the demon backed against the wall, limping with conviction. The four vents for its eyes flared as I entered, taking one growling, hissing step at Gauzier, who seemed to be doing me harm. I did my best to wave him it away, stick with the plan, the plan would work. The two of them would fight, try and keep Gauzier from the equation, Raziel does his little tune and the demon 'dies'/ hides away, hopefully convincing enough to keep Gauzier from investigating and doing any other real harm.

Already, I was beginning to see holes, starting to figure the demon cat knew more or less that this was not going to be an easy battle, and that at best, it could live here for just a while longer. If it was already having problems keeping itself concealed, drawing attention, a simple 'no, I won't cause any more of a fuss' was probably not going to work. As I stood there, watching the two angels and the demon bristle face to face, I began to see it as a truly terrible plan any way you looked at it. We relied on luck now, and I relied on getting out of here unnoticed to hide away. My bones were tingling, skin tense with electricity and energy, all very bad signs.

"Alright Raziel my boy, let's see if you've still got what it takes!"

Gauzier cheered him on as Raziel grinned, forgetting our plan that easily. Lurching forward to thrust the pike at the demon; it bellowed in pain. The sound was something very real, a spray of blood shooting out past both of them. Writhing, it focused directly at me, arms splayed out as it contemplated fighting back or not. Raziel pulled the pike out, only about 3-4 inches of it dipped in blood; it was a shallow wound, but looked like it hit something important. With a grin he turned to look at me as I glared back, shaking my head no furiously. Go off the plan and that thing will kill you, and you know it.

The demon panicked and screamed out loud, charging directly at both angels, claws swiping and drawn. It knocked Raziel over, darting through the wall behind us; Gauzier was first on its tail as just like that, the plan went haywire. There was a bloodcurdling yowl, definitely in real pain as my skin went cold.

"No!" I darted into the next room, finding the better angel with his two sword pushing right through the middle of the demon cat's body; it whipped around frantically, trying to reach its attacker in a mess of claws and arms as Gauzier took some steps away, surveying his work. Almost laughing, he looked back to the two of us, rubbing some holy water on his clawed up arms. The demon was pinned once in the neck, once just below the ribcage- it's thick, animalistic paws couldn't grab at the sword handles. Panting, struggling for breath, it only screeched louder and louder, crying out in pain.

Raziel appeared next to me, staring at it as well, unsure what to do. With a shove, I pointed at him, raising my hands up. This was all wrong, all out of order; I looked back to it, heart breaking. It didn't mean any harm, didn't mean to do anything but just lie around and enjoy what it'd always been doing; lazy cat stuff. Raziel looked to the wall; he didn't look excited or glad this happened. After a moment the angel took a step away and looked elsewhere.

"It's just a demon." Raziel muttered. The coward.

" My queen!" The demon cried out, this whole plan fraying at the seams as I couldn't stay on the sidelines any longer. A powerful, angry little tick snapped. Before I knew any better, I was stomping towards Gauzier like a protective mother; hands balled up and ready to fight. It was one thing to defeat your opponent through tactic and another to surprise it and stake it to the wall, watch it bleed out of existence and pat yourself on the back. I'd pull the boards from the floor to fight him; that whole angel ruse suddenly didn't matter to me, this flimsy, semi-crazy symbiosis I had with Raziel was a figment of a thought. He didn't care about demons, but I sure did.

Halfway across the room, Raziel grabbed my shoulders as I fought to push him away, pulling me back towards the grandfather clock, right as it began to chime 3 o'clock, the witching hour.

"Shut up and look at you feet!" He hissed in my ear, barely getting above the terrible cries of the cat-demon at the wall. The clock struck a second time. Sure enough they were already enveloped in the smoke, already twisting about my legs. "Go hide!" He yelled discreetly, shoving me at the floor as I slipped back to the pool room below and hitting the table hard.

I took off the blue hoodie, chucking it aside as the screams of the demon kept resonating through, shaking the house itself. Looking up towards it, the smoke overtook me, forming and hardening back into the demon body. Hide?

No, no, I wouldn't be doing that.

The black smoke began to fall away as I became the same red and white cow I've always been, with that same, almost delirious protective instinct. This cat demon had been nice, it asked before it attacked, it was nothing but civilized and polite.

With a growl, I surged into the battle room once again, wings flapping once to shoot myself directly at Gauzier, still pinning the demon, none the wiser. Hitting him hard with the flat edge of my face, the angel went spinning from the room, launching him outside as I snorted like a rogue bull. I was a lot more effective this way. Without thought I tore the swords from the wall, flinging it back to clatter on the hardwood of this room, the second library in the house. The demon moaned, falling to the floor in a collapsed heap, coughing out weakly. I was alongside it in a second, helping it up.

"If you can get away, run. I'm sorry for the bad plan." I nudged quickly, the cat baring its teeth in an odd grin before taking the hint and sinking into the room below us.

With one demon out of harms way I turned behind me, backed against the wall as Gauzier calmly walked back into the room, in no rush.

"Well well!" He said matter of factly, "I was starting to think, 'you know, this couldn't be the demon that my men had talked about, too slow and predictable'. But you!" His voice escalated as I began to crouch low, pacing from side to side.

"You're the fun kind of demon, aren't you? Why is it the colorful demons are always the fun ones?" He picked the swords from the ground, swiping it quickly in front of him to rid the blood from the demon cat before pointing it straight at me. My eyes darted nervously to Raziel, frowning and keeping his glance elsewhere. I watched his face carefully, looking for some sort of signal, some hint on his motives, what this fight really meant.

The moments passed on without a word; the angel kept his stance ready to fight. There was no other plan. It was two angels fighting against a demon, that's all this was and not a notion more.

Huffing out a discontented sigh, I tensed up for the battle. Fine; I pushed the hair along my spine straight up, flaring my wings through the ceiling as I took a wider stance. Chin practically touching the ground I let out a murky snarl, loud enough to let everyone in this neighborhood and the next one over know that I was in a very unfortunate mood.

II

The wind shook the windows, pushing and rattling the glass against the sills as the three of us were frozen. Gauzier with his smug, eager grin, ready to fight; Raziel with his somewhat surprised, mostly unhappy sneer, and me, with my head almost touching the ground, snarling like a wild animal. My heavy tail whipped back and forth, smacking little items and throwing them around the room. A book passed through Raziel as he seemed almost offended, watched it roll past the floor behind him before focusing back on me. His eyes were dark and empty.

Gauzier flipped the sword in his hand, re-adjusting his grip on the weapon as he leaned over to Raziel, excited.

"This is your demon from before, isn't it?" He nudged him playfully as the angel stood there, blank. "He's got your signature on the side, I can see it. Must've followed us from the workshop."

He looked over the scars on my back, how they mimicked the pike's shape perfectly just on the left side of my body. Realizing there wasn't any clear way to pretend I wasn't this infamous, disappearing demon, I snapped forwards, far away from either of them with a bellowing growl. Neither angel moved.

"Yeah, that's the one." Raziel's voice was flat and almost silent, looking back to the weapon once more before over to me. Hair bristled high, shoulders hunched as far as they'd go, I frowned, just the tiniest bit. Just the last little nudge, begging for that last chance to find out how I knew his eyes. I didn't want to fight him; I'd really appreciate the chance to not be cleaved to pieces by two exorcists. He caught the slip, frowning a lot more, just for a moment, before giving off a discouraging sneer. You could hear thunder rumble in the distance.

Giving a defeated sigh, I instantly covered it with a raucous growl, stamping forwards a few feet and readying myself for this fight.

From the confrontation with the demon cat I knew a few things about my main opponent; Gauzier didn't screw around, he didn't drag out a point; he killed what needed to be exterminated and did it by whatever means, honest or not. Raziel on the other hand, dawdled and had a knack for theatrics as he rolled the pike around, held nearly straight out at my face.

Who was I kidding, really? This is exactly what he wanted. Dust his hands off from some crazy shapeshifting trickster demon, call it a day, live to fail and screw up another time. Just an oddity from so long ago, nothing important at all. Why bother trying to figure out why the demon attacks its own kind, must just be defective, clearly. I'd love to really smack him around a little, knock some sense into his fat head, but thanks to those damn eyes, it wasn't in my heart to attack him.

Gauzier on the other hand, I had no problem fighting against.

Digging into the wood of the floor I rushed forward, wings sweeping over the entire room with terrifying speed; Gauzier dodged easily around my charge, swinging the sword quickly to sheer my right wing completely off. It thumped the ground hard, momentum of my charge still throwing it ahead of me like a large, fallen tree branch as it evaporated into a rush of black smoke. With a stump for a wing I jumped away from Gauzier, evading him as he rushed straight for me, trying to take my head off too. The sword sliced into the side of my face, across my one eye and onto my mouth. Reeling back, I fell through the wall behind me in just the same position, against another wall. Both angels walked casually into the room, followed by the cloud of smoke as it absorbed into my skin, wing quickly reforming, good as new. Gauzier propped the sword onto his shoulder, tilting his head with a little smirk as I panicked, hands covered in blood from my face.

"So it heals, eh? Makes sense why you're so hard to kill. That puts you at least at a class four. No wonder you couldn't exorcise it." He slapped Raziel's shoulder as he still withheld any sort of joy with finally being rid of me, only looking over once with contempt as Gauzier had already moved onto more mocking tone. "So, how DO we kill demons able to regenerate?" I placed my one foot farther back, readying myself and trying to push away the panic and fear.

"Destroy its core." Raziel said, taking a harder grasp on the pike. My eyes jumped to him before back to Gauzier, already darting straight for me. He planted one foot into the ground and brought the sword up to about waist-height, trying to take out my legs. Scrambling against the wall I pushed off of it, pulling my legs into the air as the sword only grazed my skin. Gauzier tried to turn around and strike at me again, forgetting about my tail. I whipped it hard into his side, sending him skittering along the floor before shooting outside. Sneering at him, I looked back ahead of me and realized I landed directly in front of Raziel.

We paused, both of us. He had a clear, open shot to stab me right in the heart if he wanted to and I could've easily bitten the little annoyance in half. He looked over to his weapon, then back up at me like he forgot how this was supposed to work out, frozen as I frowned, echoing his hesitation.

Realizing there was some figment of a chance, I spoke up.

"Please..." I whispered, hearing the muted wing beat of the other angel behind me, instantly back to playing the role. I opened up both wings, growling and snarling as I rose onto two feet, still essentially standing there. Raziel looked surprised, almost afraid as I didn't go any further than that, making a whole bunch of noise to cover I was begging for my life from the person who probably hated me the most. But he wasn't attacking me.

My wings separated the room in half, giving us privacy.

"Raziel?!" Gauzier called behind me as you could see him panic again, wing beats getting closer. Frowning, I reached out and gently pushed Raziel over with lone hand before spinning on my tail, ready to fight back against the greater angel. There was a bright speck of light before I could do anything, mind suddenly hazy and disconnected as I stumbled my charge, swooning off to the side and rolling on top of one of my own wings.

Things moved slow, life drunkenly swayed back and forth as I rolled one eye backwards, spotting the hilt of the sword coming out of my left temple, sword lodged right into my brain. Letting out a yelp of dismay, I floundered back into the first room where Gauzier had staked the demon cat to the wall, trying to shake the blade from my head, trying not to panic.

Heaving for breath I propped myself up in the middle as I spotted both angels on the far side, walking in, a little confused themselves. Gauzier looked disappointed that I was still on my feet, Raziel just still had the same overall bleh expression he'd been sporting for the last ten minutes. My legs wobbled as I got my head around the situation, brows furrowing as I reached a hand up, touching the end of the sword with a paranoid whine. Blinking, understanding I was pretty okay besides being a little dizzy, I quickly yanked the sword away, shaking my body out.

Growling, I grabbed a hold of the weapon, chucking it somewhere far away somewhere else in the house.

"Thumbs. Great." Gauzier complained, out of breath. He smacked Raziel in the arm, motioning over to me like two frat boys about to tip over a cow. "Thankfully I've got two swords!" He brandished the other sword like this was some sort of new development. Raziel frowned, looking elsewhere.

"I know." Dissatisfied with the comradery, Gauzier focused back on me.

"That didn't feel too great, did it demon? You must be the brightest little thing around!" Baring my teeth, I focused right on that arrogant face of his, wishing I had the resolve to live up to my name. I wish I picked an easier battle to fight.

Gauzier bolted at me, other sword by his side as he started rambling about some banal, showy fiction. I charged.

"You've been causing havoc for too long, demon!" The two of us barreled into one another as I got a sword in the neck immediately, removed and graciously replaced into my front flank, searing like a hot coal each time. "Today, you finally meet a worthy adversary!" Rearing back I threw my body at him again as he suddenly flipped me over, throwing me straight towards Raziel with my own momentum. I could see the whites of his eyes as we crashed into one another.

I smacked him hard the first time as we tumbled about, using the back side of my wing the second pass to scoop him against me as I slammed my head into the ground, keeping pressure off of rolling him over and crushing him that way. By the third rotation I flipped him out and away, laying on my own wing bent backwards as Gauzier laughed like a pompous ass, finally coming to a stop.

I gave a weak cough at the stale, lavender air, half conscious. In the next aware flash, there was a shadow moving alongside me, unsure if this was Gauzier or Raziel, thrashing back a little bit either way before my head slumped to the ground, unable to fight back.

"Woah, Raziel, did you survive that?" Something yelled farther behind me. "I didn't see you there, sorry!"

The shadow loomed next to my head as I began to collect myself more, voice quiet and barely a whisper.

"Be patient. He'll make stupid mistakes when he's desperate. Wait for them and dodge what he throws at you for now. Don't show any weakness." Raziel said, nodding a little awkwardly and throwing himself away from me. I watched after him, shocked as Gauzier rocketed back through the wall, sword held out to take off my head. I sunk partially into the ground, wings giving a healthy flap to push me back and away from the attack without any traded blows. Gauzier struggled to regain control, hovering in the upper corner, changing the sword to the other hand. The laughter and joy was gone from his face, snapping quickly to Raziel.

"Are you going to help, or are you a total coward?" He shouted angrily, dropping into another attack; he hit the ground hard, using the energy to launch himself at me again, sword pointed straight at my heart. Annoyed, I managed to dodge out of the way, hitting Gauzier with my hand and back outside once more; momentary peace as I huffed for breath.

Turning to Raziel who looked as freaked out as ever, I grinned. I don't know what little switch had flipped in his head, but at this moment, that was everything. Wiping the blood off my neck with a sort of exasperated laugh, I ran towards the opposite wall, flipping myself over and breaking the very physical table. I shimmied a bit to lay in a distorted, pained way across the room as Raziel's eyes were at max confusion.

Hopefully, when Gauzier flew back in…

"Good work, Raziel." Gauzier stopped alongside him, the angel looking to the other with silver dollar eyes, then to me, whole body hopping once he realized what I was doing.

"Oh! Yeah! Totally punched…that demon." He struggled for words, shaking an awkward fist in the air in my direction after a moment. Flipping back onto my feet I snarled at him, faking a heavy limp in my arm as we braced ourselves for another round. Already, I was beginning to tire, the exhaustion I had been in before transforming back to this demon was boring through the adrenaline of the fight. Gauzier raised the sword in my direction, slowly edging closer to me.

"That was just a taste of the pain to be brought down on your cursed head!" I raised the wings high over my head again, puffing up to bluff how big I was - many bored hours of TV at the Faegels' house taught me that. "Look Raz, its all wing and no demon!" He sneered.

I tucked my wings back by my side, back still arched high, stance wide and powerful. Bolting forward, I jumped high into the air all on my own as the angel swung the sword below me, sailing silently above him. My tail smacked him in the side of his head, taken off balance as my front two feet landed, muscles bunching up through my body, charged up and giving Gauzier a donkey like kick right in his back. The sword fell from his hands as he traveled across the room, rolling to a stop in a bundle of feathers and back to his feet in one motion. The man wobbled just a bit, disorientated, wings fluttering weakly to help keep him upright. Snarling, I picked up his sword, biting the thing in my teeth. With a flick of my head I spit it at the ceiling, metal sticking into the roof with just the tiniest bit of dust falling from the hole as he was finally out of weapons.

"Raziel, get it!" Gauzier shouted, pointing to the angel as I managed to see the pike over his head, ready to strike. Time froze.

Here it was, moment of truth. Keep fighting angel after angel, or earn some sort of reprieve from this? Something different. I turned around to face him as he was already in motion, already made his decision, too late to plead or beg for help. I held my breath as he thrust the weapon directly at me, eyes focused and bright. I winced, readying myself for the pain as I felt its warbled, bitten edge skip off my shoulder, blade sliding along my scales as it rested under the armpit of one wing and stayed there. He spared me.

There was just a split second of surprise when I smiled, honest and true, before overreacting to the wound, writhing in a frenzy on the ground. Dramatically, I fell through the floor and into the basement, darting through the wall to collapse alongside the pool table at the other end of the hall. I tried to recuperate, heaving tiredly for breath, one wing clanking against the row of pool cues. Faking a fight was one thing, but trying to fight an actual battle with one while faking another was much more of a hassle. This needed to be over soon.

"Here!" Gauzier's disembodied head yelled out, sticking out from the ceiling above me. Grumbling, I leapt at him, the sword slicing me clean from gut to gill as I passed through the floor. It seemed like a shallow cut, looking down I could see myself bleeding profusely from it. I wailed out, bringing my wings around to scoot me against the wall, stream of blood following. I sat quickly, one wing warily unorganized against the wall behind me. "See that, the thing can bleed!" He laughed out triumphantly.

Looking to Gauzier I spotted Raziel just behind him out of view, urging me to stand back up. Gauzier got frustrated quickly, he had said. I couldn't show pain, had to antagonize him into doing something stupid. Wincing, craning my head back with a jerk, I opened my jaws up wider then I ever had, letting out a deeply strange, disturbing laugh, mocking Gauzier. It felt good, felt strangely satisfying, given I had a lot to laugh about in retrospect. I breathed deep and laughed louder, letting my tongue flop from side to side. The trick worked; my wounds healed themselves, the annoying, chiding laughter from Gauzier stopped, only leaving the two angels to stare at me peculiarly. Quieting down I snapped my head back to them, standing up and shaking out, ready for round two. Raziel grinned; face quickly dropping as Gauzier turned around to talk strategy.

Before I knew it they broke apart, this time Raziel running slowly at me, while Gauzier took to the air, sword braced and ready. He flew for my face, dodging to the left to spin round me, trying to confuse and mix up my actions; fight the angel in the air, or fight the one at my feet. Thankfully the decision wasn't hard; lining up my strike I lunged, mouth open, biting down on the top half of his body and slamming back to the ground, shaking him just a bit. Raziel stood a little shocked as Gauzier's lesser half struggled around, wriggling almost comically. I held the angel in my mouth, feathers sticking out from all sides of my jaw. Gauzier's hands flopped from side to side, pinned to his hips, dropping the sword from his grasp. He tried barking out some command, wheezing nothing but air as I put just a little more pressure on the bastard.

"Hey… Put him down!" Raziel shouted at me, half joking. I growled out angrily, nothing but noise and a show, shaking the angel the tiniest bit. I was utterly exhausted. Shifting my one hand to take most of the pressure, I lifted the other by my face, pointing at the soft spot of my cheek. There. Hit me there.

Raziel furrowed his eyebrows, shaking his head a little bit, charging straight at me. He reared back; I closed my one eye, bracing for the impact. All I got was at best, a gentle slap, immediately I blasted myself out of the room, dropping the other angel and careening across the way, taking out one of the walls on purpose and crumpling like I was dead. If nothing else, it gave me the chance to rest, even if only for a moment.

"What the hell did you DO?" Gauzier said groggily; I could hear the exaggeration in his words.

"Oh, just something I picked up in my time fighting this demon."

"Hell of a demon, I'll give it that." Their steps got closer, voices clear as daytime.

"I think it'd be best to bury the thing, put it to rest." Raziel said with some sort of authority; Gauzier merely laughed.

"You're a stitch sometimes, Raz." I could hear the angel practically next to me now. "It's not dead, just stunned. I'm cutting off the head while we've got the chance."

"You're what?"

"Give me your pike." I tensed up, worried.

"Just bury the damn thing!" Almost a yelp of panic, "Hey, give that back!"

"Stop being a sentimental baby! One two, here we go!" Gauzier said it like he was jumping rope. Before I had time to get out of the way, before I was able to sink into the floor, he did it. He cut my head off, right across the neck. This, needless to say, was not part of the original plan.

Everything was dark; though I knew I was still laying there, still very much living and existing. Slowly my senses began to come back to me, getting back on my feet, I tried to look around, tried to see something through this black haze. The world around me suddenly began developing, going from ranges of gray to blue, to green, finally adding red into the mixture to give me back normal sight. I stood there in the same place, still in the demon's body, the smoke falling from my newly re-formed head.

The three of us just stood there, looking at one another, the same 'what the Hell just happened?' expression. Gauzier quickly gave the pike back to Raziel, stomping into the other room.

"Alright, this is too weird, even for me. I'm saying the St. Michaels."

"You're what?" Raziel almost dropped the weapon, turning halfway towards Gauzier. He pointed back to me as Raziel kept up his guard with his eyes pretty much pinned to his boss.

Gauzier rounded the corner.

I gave Raziel a sort of wide-eyed stare, leaning a little closer. The 'St. Michaels' sounded like a sort of dangerous, unhappy thing I should really know about.

"It's a prayer, very powerful prayer." He hissed under his breath, "Remember that extra-strength holy water from yesterday?" He was talking about the cannon of white water, the one that practically turned me to dust. Yeah, wasn't going to forget that anytime soon; I nodded flatly.

"Think that, plus a nuclear bomb, and every inch of this house. Nothing survives it. Even I get sick from it. All demonic energy is just gone." He leaned closer, "Especially you and the other demon downstairs."

"Are you talking with the demon?" Gauzier said with concern.

"Giving this cursed thing its last rights!"

"Oh, okay." He relaxed, putting his arms out, "Keep that demon right there and make sure it doesn't get away."

"Of course!"

Raziel shook the pike at me as Gauzier began the passage, which started with some bible verses at the beginning as I sat there awkwardly. Already, I wasn't feeling great, my hands grasping in pain, head beginning to drop low. They'd kill me some way or the other, or they'd make me wish I was dead.

"He'd stop the passage if you were to leave." The angel before me suddenly spoke up as I struggled to meet his gaze. He raised his eyebrows, turning the pike horizontally to hold one hand close to the blade, the other hand far down the handle. "But I have to make sure you don't get away." I tilted my head just a bit as he stared directly at me, eyes switching quickly to the big, empty area of wooden handle, and back to me. My lips slowly pulled into a smile as I put it together; that son of a bitch.

About to bite onto it, Raziel spoke up again.

"I only get an allowance of wood so just don't snap it again, okay?" He muttered as I nodded.

Taking a deep breath I roared out, wrapping my tongue around it and gently bit onto the empty section of handle. Fighting this way and that, I pulled it around before gathering my wings to shoot both of us into the next room. Raziel held on as apparently planned, making a series of 'oh no's and 'its loose' statements as we both rushed past Gauzier, disrupting whatever concentration he had going. In another wing beat we erupted outside, through the walls, into the rainstorm, sky still perpetually dark as the morning approached.

Not two seconds after we left, Gauzier was in hot pursuit and right after us. Like on cue, Raziel began weakly kicking at me, trying not to look like he had made this plan up himself. I begged my body for whatever ounce of energy and speed it had left. Swooping down low to the ground I pushed off of it, keeping low in the trees to try and lose the angel through the brush. He came up alongside me, weapon ready; tilting the angle of my feathers, I shot away from him, taking up into the sky. My wings were only a blur, pouring everything I had to try and get away; I wasn't sure where and wasn't sure why, but away from the prayer of a thousand burning waters was an ideal start.

"Raziel, fight the beast while you're in range!" Gauzier shouted to me as I quickly shot into a dive, straight for the ground. Wings blasted me like a bullet to the earth as I pivoted in an entirely new direction, pushing myself as hard as physically possible away from him. Again, he lined up alongside me as I took to the skies once more, pumping my wings into incredible height, above the trees, the buildings, and towards the clouds.

"Hey, jeez, hold on a second, I'm slip—" Raziel's hands twanged from the sides of the weapon as it rattled in my teeth, the angel tumbling straight out towards the ground in a free fall, confused by lightning and thunder. Spitting out the pike I doubled around, folding my wings into a dive after him; Gauzier was rushing up to catch him as well, both sides of the perpetual Heaven and Hell rushing to save the commonplace, pain in the ass angel. I couldn't for the life of me figure why I was so dead set on saving him. If I just left now, if I split, I'd have my freedom. The thought never crossed my mind.

I won- just a hairs breath closer I bit onto him as softly as possible, teeth locking onto the spaces between the armor, shooting past Gauzier as our eyes locked for just a moment. Squinting, I instantly flipped over and went for the ground, screaming into a dive. My body slowly curved around, level again as I blew by the ground, wingtips almost touching the grass. A burning blue ball of energy hit right beside me, blinding me for a second and I veered away, arcing heavily.

"Holyfire!" Raziel yelled out, head and half his shoulder peeking out from the side of my mouth; a name to associate with cannonballs of blue energy. Turning my head slightly, Gauzier geared up for another, whipping it at me as I juked right. Even from where I was, I could hear him yelling out angrily, determined to have my red and white colored hide posed and stuffed for his wall. A ball of energy suddenly landed on my hips, scalding and tearing away at my body like it was molten lava. Stumbling, I slammed the fire into one of the many trees I passed, thinking solid, heavy thoughts as the fire and oil that burned with it mostly scraped away, along with a sizable chunk of skin and muscle. Heavy on the ground I went back to breakneck speed, finally realizing that I'd never been given the chance to learn how to fly and considering this was my first real time, it seemed like something I knew how to do beforehand. No time for that now; faster faster faster, I told myself with each flap; Gauzier began to fade back.

"I'm at the end of my limits!" He shouted out to Raziel, pace slowing.

"Tell my host I'll be back soon, this demon will be no problem!" He reached up and punched next to my eye, making it tear up. Annoyed, I shook him a little bit, continuing to run full out as Gauzier faded away, out of view and seeping back into the dark, blurry forest.

We flew for about another half mile or so before there was a strange pull, like a net of resistance slowing us down. Peering down at the angel, he had a similar grimace, feeling it too. I could hear his breathes shorten, wincing in real pain as he tensed up, looking around in a panic for a moment.

"Ah, God, here we go." He muttered, tension higher and higher as I flew against it, my wings slowed like I was flying through syrup. About to ask if I should stop via charades, something snapped, something invisible, and everything was just as it had been before. Looking behind me, I couldn't see anything there.

"Of course. He's gone, let me out." His hand waved tiredly from the side of my mouth. Slowing a bit I opened up, flipping him from my mouth to bite the cloth behind his neck, surging back into the sky, desperate to put as much distance between us and Gauzier. Lightning crashed close by.

"I… apologize… for this now." He sounded drunk and out of breath, reaching up to flop his hand around like he was signaling for something on the side of my nose. As he finished, the area under his hands lit up a bright blue, ebbing away as immediately, my energy level zapped to nothing. My wings hung at my side, barely moving, my arms felt like heavy lead, my neck hurt from pulling around a hundred and eighty pound angel. I immediately flickered in and out of consciousness every few seconds. The two of us plummeted from the sky.

Desperately trying to judge distance, trying to make as good as an effort as I could seeing the ground in blacked out hiccups, I fought for that awareness. Frowning, concentrating hard, I spotted the ground suddenly about twenty feet away, dropping the angel out to hit and roll on his own without my monstery body crushing him. Giving one slow, worthless flap I hit the ground hard farther along, plowed into the soil face first as I tumbled and rolled to a stop, wings broken and backwards, but no longer moving. I blacked out again.

I heard the rain course down in heavy sheets, being grateful for one of the times when I could only see the weather, not experience it. There were footsteps behind me, labored and sluggish as I surfaced that unconscious muck, eyes rolling around in my head as I tried to focus. The angel was there in the next second suddenly, giving a light kick in my side like a lazy horse.

"Get up, we have to keep moving." I glared at him, letting out a busted cough and weakly trying to slide my heavy wings closer to my body. I couldn't move. Laying there, heaving for breath he lethargically trudged up next to me, giving me a light kick in the face. I gave a short, pitiful whine. You had to be kidding me. After all that…

"Shut up, I know you're tired. Still, we gotta move. Let's go." My whine cut short, trying hard to get to my feet. Shaking, my best efforts shifted me onto my side. This body was not moving another step, even if I wanted to. I was completely tapped on energy in every way imaginable. I yawned, exhausted, using the last bits of my energy to keep my eyes open. Raziel walked ahead a few more feet, looking to the skies before yawning himself, reacting like he just shot fire out of his nose.

"W-what are you doing?" He walked back to me, my eyes slowly glazing over. I wasn't going to be able to fight this awareness battle for much longer. "You're going to sleep? You're a demon! Demon's don't sleep!" Raising my eyebrows just a bit, I yawned again. Raziel yawned contagiously, still trying to make a point.

"Stop it!" He had a hand over his mouth "What's the matter with you?!"

I wheezed distastefully at him.

"I don't sleep!" He stated as I yawned again and he followed. He was strangely mimicking my own actions; the building feeling of exhaustion started to weigh heavily on me as my eyes began to close on their own, trying to watch on the angel. "Why the…*yawn* hell would a demon need rest." His voice got quiet as he tried to walk away, swaying hard side to side, feet stumbling over one another. The angel stopped, wobbling where he stood, stomping in place.

As I finally drifted off to sleep I saw him fall to his knees, slumping to the ground face first peacefully like he was dead.

12

My dream was filled with colored skies, of clouded spires, of flying. The sky was painted in hues of green as more color mixed in further up, clouds reaching high above me, ending only as they drifted out of sight. It was a perfectly endless sky as I walked beneath, taking tentative steps. The sun warm, the day calm; wind blew beautifully. It was something I missed, the wind. It was accepting and reassuring at the same time, showed you how you truly existed, how life was able to move around you as an actual thing. More then that, it was the essence of vitality, the force that never grew still; I pined for it dearly in my waking hours. But this was not reality.

With unbridled joy I began to run, feeling it all, the grass underneath my feet, the wind, the sun, the air of everything around me, so alive. My heart pounded out of my chest, eyes open as I ran, stretching my limits, passing and conquering each hills as I ran past it, darting faster as I reached my hands out wide, taking into the sky, sailing high up.

The earth tore apart, lightning striking just overhead and shaking me from my dream as I popped awake, hitting my head against the ground. Rain had picked up, blowing in torrential waves, the earth powerful and angry. Looking at my hands, the rain passed through them, hollow and dead, separated from life unfairly. I couldn't explain it, it felt like I was cheated from something, kept from enjoying the part of life I missed the most; so many times I dodged around what a regular demon was supposed to be, how I was supposed to react, and still I was wrong. Incomplete. Different, not a real part of anything. Before I knew better I curled a lip at the storm, slamming my hands down angrily. The wind picked up in response, blowing the trees effectively shaking the world around it, everything but me.

"What am I missing?" I shouted at nothing, head swiveled for an answer; the wind began to slow, the storm letting up as the world ignored me once again. "Why can't I…" I let my head fall, still tired, barely having the energy to pull myself from the ground even now. The sun was trying to break into the world, stifled with remnants of the storm overhead. I must be losing my mind, must be reaching for things that weren't available to me. My dreams were normally filled with parts from the day, recapping whatever I'd seen as it built into quite the little repertoire of memories. Those were my dreams, old memories, but this; it was almost startlingly new and peaceful. Apparently it was peaceful enough to make me angry with the way things were.

Yawning tiredly I looked around, finding the angel slumped over in the same place he had been three hours ago. I rolled to my feet, plodding tiredly in his direction as he lay there, like someone shot him in the back of the head, face down in the dirt with his hands under his body. It struck me he might be dead, muttering something about not sleeping before keeling over, but judging on the snorting, wheezing sound he was making with his face shoved into the ground, he survived yet again. Staring at him I shook my head; nothing made sense in this world, there were so many things left unexplained that I just had to assume that eventually, I'd find out. But things like breaking an invisible net, having all the energy practically sucked from me, glowing balls of holy oil, I mean, it was almost sad how none of it bothered me anymore. Little unexplained things worried the Hell out of me back when, but now, something really strange could happen, and immediately I'd chalk it up to what was unknowable. If Raziel suddenly burst into flames, I'd probably just sit there and go 'well, it was doomed to happen' knowing that I had no idea why it happened at all.

He looked pitiful laying there, scrunched up and heaped over himself with his butt up in the air. His wings were half opened out in front of him, like a sort of dead bird that collided against the glass thinking it was an enemy. Noting on it, it wasn't a too far fetched description of the guy. Better then generic things like a medium build, fairly muscular, scarily thick eyebrows, taller then me by quite a bit and shiny shoes. Not to mention the way his sideburns seemed to grow out insanely long, no, I think the bird who hit the glass a few too many times was almost perfect. I yawned again, still far too tired to do anything but note on the absurdities of my strange little half-life; but leaving him out like this in the rain seemed almost wrong.

Gingerly, I grabbed the part of the shirt I used to carry him before, delicately dragging his unconscious ass to the tree like a lion with a kill. Twenty or thirty feet away sat a large oak, rain tinkling off of the leaves as his feet skipped a little off the ground, setting him against it. It really didn't matter, neither of us were affected by this realm of life around us; he stirred a little as I set him down, re-arranging himself comfortably. Watching for a second more I snorted at the little monster, walking away to sit isolated in the storm. Worn down and relentlessly tired, I fell back asleep in the same spot I had been, listening to the sounds of the rain sink into the world peacefully. There were no more dreams that day.

My eyes fluttered awake many hours later, the sun already high in the sky and clear of any lingering storms. I yawned, stretching my limbs out far in front of me, gathering to my feet to do the same for my wings. I hadn't had the chance to really see where I had gone while trying to escape, just blindly chased into the darkness, rushing away from getting cut up or holy-blasted from the house. Hopefully the demon cat had managed to make it with all attention drawn to me and Raziel. It was a pretty bad shape and didn't seem to heal from its injuries. My stomach knotted.

Using one meaty hand, I picked some mud and burnt out holy fire crud from my eyes, trying to wake up a little more before attacking the day.

We had landed in a meadow, uninhabited scraps of forestland and trees were scattered here and there, mostly finding a large network of fields all around us. Rural living, there were a few buildings a little ways down, old, abandoned industrial buildings that probably held nothing but leagues of field mice in them now. The land was patterned and dotted with farms, crops, a few lone windmills and old, discarded stone fences. Wind was steady and constant, skies still recovering from the storms earlier. Pleasant, pretty and peaceful.

I shook myself out, yawning again as I looked around for a moment to the angel, still asleep under the tree. He had shifted sometime since I had gone back to sleep, face-down once again in the dirt; so much for that effort. But he hadn't gotten up and sauntered off, still laying there like a sack of bricks. Sure hope he didn't have anywhere important to be, he seemed pretty insistent about getting out of the area earlier.

"Hey, time to wake up. No more time for lolly gagging, you got a full day of being a weird indecisive asshole to get to, so get up." I spoke in his direction as he continued to sleep there, unmoved. It felt like I was yelling at a lazy, one hundred and eighty-some odd pound tree stump, no reaction like he even heard me. Groaning, I walked over to him, standing just over his exhausted body. "You dead? I think you're breathing but I'm not sure." Lowering an eye close to the ground, I could see his chest rise and fall, so he wasn't dead. But good lord was he just either so tired he wasn't listening, or deaf.

"HEY. SLEEPYFEATHERS. GET UP." I yelled directly at the back of his head. Nothing.

"You're gonna make me do this, aren't you? Lazy McAngel, wakey wakey, feathered bakey." I poked his back harshly as he grunted once, making this throaty, exhausted 'eEH' sound before settling back down. Still no response, I was starting to feel tired just standing by him. Angered, I poked him repeatedly as he repeated the same sound like a broken toy, over and over. Pausing for a second, I gave a smile, poking him three times in beat.

"Another one bites the dust..." I muttered, singing. I poked three more times "And another one bites the dust." I started laughing, tapping my tail on the ground in beat until I'd gotten through a surprisingly majority of the song before getting bored.

Alright, time to get serious.

Remembering the kick he had given me while I lay exhausted earlier this morning, I grabbed an arm and flipped him like a soggy pancake as the angel landed hard on his back.

Instantly, his eyes snapped open like a madman possessed; I etched back, a little horrified as the eyes darted in my direction, adding to the creepiness.

"You! What…the…" He struggled to his feet, balance shifted and uneven as he toppled off to one side, flapping his wings slightly just to regain equilibrium. The angel took a moment to rub part of his back, apparently the hard part he landed on with his wings, in pain. "What the hell was that? Sleeping? Demons don't sleep!" One hand braced on the tree for balance he glared at me, half-angrily rubbing the sleep from his eyes and half confused as Hell. He winced, reaching a hand back with a confused look on his face.

"God, this part of my back hurts like Hell." He rubbed at music section of his spine, looking once to me, shaking his head and genuinely unsure why it hurt so much. With a huff Raziel stretched back, yawning tiredly before catching himself, apparently ashamed. I turned away.

"I haven't slept in God damn ages" Raziel scratched the back of his neck, noticing he wasn't laying in the mud-pile like he had fallen into. "Literally, ages. Are you sure you're even really a demon?" The question was partially directed at me, more then that it just seemed to be for open discussion. I shrugged in all honesty, hardly sure on anything anymore. They did seem to be the side I was able to get along with easier, even if my only experiences from angels were the two exorcists.

The angel gave a sickly, weary grumble, standing up tall and looking around the tree. Spotting a low step of rocks that was probably a fence at some time he walked over to it, sitting down tiredly, hunched over with his back to me. I could relate. I was still pretty tired from our frantic escape, now faced with trying to figure out how to get back home through sign language and hand symbols. I sat down, stretching my wings out again to yawn, looking around me at the open landscape.

So what do we do now? Guess it's time to figure out just what his last minute flip-flopping was all about- he didn't seem very concerned about me, what I was doing, or trying to kill me. He was also unarmed, pike left somewhere in the forest. I stopped, suddenly remembering the odd string of events from last night. Storming up to him, I nudged him in the back, pointing to the spot on my face where he had placed the mark that completely sucked all my energy away. He looked at it for a second, turning away again.

"Sorry, that's official angelic business, not for demons or…demon-like things to know." I glared at his privacy curtain of wings; he had to know that was a pretty shallow answer. After a moment, I gave a more aggravated huff, the angel shuddering at the sound. Raziel reached back behind his head and took off the headband, turning the thing over in his hands and rubbing some of the dirt off. "It's a tether." He said with a dramatic sigh. I raised my eyebrow just a little bit, wanting to point out the closest building was probably over two miles away.

"Not for you, for me." He looked nervous, flipping the headband around as he continued on, "Like you were tied to the house, I've gotta be tied to something, or someone. On my own, I don't exist long. Usually, that's the Priest, my host." Well, that certainly explained a few things. Could've maybe mentioned that at any other point really. I sat alongside him, putting both hands in front of me and mimicked the pull from earlier as we were escaping. Raziel nodded.

"Yeah, that. Honestly, I wasn't sure either how this would work out. You were tied to me, and I was tied to the Priest. You seem to exist just fine on your own. I'm actually leeching off of you, now." He pointed to his own nose, the same spot where the blue glow had been. I turned my head just a bit, spitting out a laugh.

"It wasn't a joke." He sounded hurt. I chuckled emptily again.

"Pretty sure it's a joke." A grin, I got to my feet, looking around. "It's ridiculous at any rate."

Walking away from Raziel, I looked over the landscape, trying to find a landmark I might've seen on the way in. Nothing. The whole area was empty. Beautiful, but empty.

"I have no idea where we are." Rocking on my feet for a second, I managed to stand up on my back legs, looking higher over the area, spotting a few dirt roads and a radio tower some distance away, a bluish haze in a suspiciously straight line farther off from that. Huffing discontentedly, I dropped back to all fours. "I have no idea where anything is. Probably the road back…somewhere… Has to be a road around here somewhere. It's not like the house was twenty miles from the highway, there's got to be something around here." I muttered, thinking out loud.

Turning back to the angel, I found him looking incredibly disturbed, on the verge of terror with his hands bunched by his torso, staring at nothing like he was frozen in time. Leaning closer, I squinted.

"You okay? What's the matter? You having a stroke?" The angel seemed stranger, a little more easily scared and emotional even, staring vacantly. "Hey. Raziel." I gave a light nudge as he looked over towards me. I did my best to give alternating thumbs up and down motions. He didn't move or look more than that. What was this? There was something vastly wrong, something different. The angel finally shook himself out of whatever little trance sleep had put him in, ignoring my hand signals entirely.

"There's something very wrong with you." He said it as a whisper, finger wagging in my direction like it kept beat before he declared the rest broadly, without a lot of tact " I should get going." Raziel was suddenly on his feet and into the field, taking long, strange steps like a foreign dance as his wings bounced more than usual. I shrugged.

"Fine, but we both know I'm not the only one with problems." I declared just as open handedly; he suddenly wheeled around, glaring at me like he heard what I had said. There was no doubt, he opened his mouth to say something, shutting it quickly and turning back to the field ahead of him in a panic. It slowly began to dawn on me that maybe I wasn't too far from the truth. He's never done that any other time I've spoken, like he understood me.

I rushed up alongside him, leaning down close to look at his face. Warily both eyes stared at me, fearful and unnerved as they jilted straight back ahead of him. Something was definitely up as he seemed to be sweating. There was something definitely strange going on. I decided to be honest.

"You can't hear me, can you?" Raziel's eyes stayed ahead of him, walking even faster than before. I mean, if he could, he was doing his best to pretend he couldn't. I tried thinking of little devices that could confirm this for me, if he could understand me, there were quite a few less then pleasant things I had to say. An idea struck.

"Boy, that Gauzier, he really was a good fighter, wasn't he?" Raziel tensed up a little bit, I could see his walk go just a bit off-kilter, eyes shifting to me quickly before going back to the path in front of him. It wasn't conviction enough, so I continued going on pushing buttons, "I mean, you were easy to fight against, but he pretty much kicked the crap outta the demon cat in what, two seconds flat? An angel who can get the job done that quickly, he must be a Hell of a fighter!" The frustration and anger was easy to see on Raziel's face now, his lips tensed together to draw a straight line across as his eccentric jostling became more and more erratic. Just… crack. I needed him to crack.

"Who knows, maybe you could ask him for some tips on how to fight sometimes, he seems like a really smart…" I saw the angel wince as I aggressively chewed on the word, "…and down to earth guy, if you'll forgive the pun."

Nothing. Both of Raziel's eyes were squinting farther and farther closed in rage, though. Just a little more… I went for broke.

"I mean, I didn't really get that sense from YOU, but Gauzier seemed to really care about the people, you know?" One of Raziel's eyes began to twitch, lips curling into a snarl. "I could see why they've got him in a management position, real greatness like that really shows through. You can tell he's really earned it!"

He suddenly stomped his foot with a belligerent snort.

"EAT SHIT. He learned from ME!" Raziel spit out quickly, eyes going wide as he couldn't help but continue on, furious, "That arrogant little shit gets so much praise for getting someone else to do most of the work and act like he did, don't give me that bullshit like he cares...about..." He stared at me, struck with fear, putting both hands on his head in shame.

"Hey there starshine." I grinned, equally as aggravated as he was for different reasons.

"Oh God, I'm talking to the demons now." He said quickly, his walk changing to a strange jog. This was definitely a different sort of Raziel right now, much more relaxed and a bit of a pushover. He suddenly dropped his hands, bursting into more of a run, straight down the hill and towards an old barn.

A refreshing change; I loped to catch up.

"Maybe it's the tether?" I offered, feeling odd talking to him one on one.

"It's definitely the tether, but that's still a bad thing!" He said, pulling the hands from his face to run faster. "When did you start talking like this?" Gaining a smidgen of distance, I ladled on another ounce of speed. Damn he was a fast little bug.

"I've always talked like this! I'm not doing anything new, it's something wrong with you!" The angel sped around a tree, those barely upgraded chicken-wings flapping along like it'd help while his armor clanked pathetically. Growling, I easily caught up to him, nearly sprinting alongside. You could see the distress radiating off of him.

"Really?" He wheezed, out of air.

"Yes really! You think I spoke Latin to my family? You think a 6 year old knows that?" This game was starting to run it's course as my annoyance showed through. "For God's sake man, slow down, you're not going to out-run me!" I said as Raziel suddenly came to a stop, wheeling around to confront me face to face, white as a sheet. Opening my mouth to say something, he practically jabbed me in the nose before a word left.

"You...just stop talking, okay? You wanna help? Shut up for a while." He looked back and around him, taking a quick seat on rock, his leg twitching, nervous like he was about to break down. "I... I need to figure things out. This wasn't supposed to be like this." You could hear him breathe twenty times in a few seconds, near hyperventilating if he had any blood or lungs to go by. But he was still very stressed out, and continuing on being an asshole wouldn't help. Debating my options, I sat down quietly.

The angel kept wiping back the hair that fell into his eyes before switching to lean forwards, nearly in the fetal position without falling over. If stress was 1-10, he looked to be an easy 20, refusing to look up at me and muttering to himself. I felt bad staring at him so I looked elsewhere, ignoring the sounds of frantic suffering alongside me. I'd already checked out the area, we were just closer to the bottom of a hill, the old barn was sat next to was peeling and sun bleached, grass and nests built into the tops and open holes of the wood, back and sides fallen in years before. I began to feel awkward and more out of place then I had ever been; part of me wanted to bring up the frustrations he brought me all those years. Seemed like a poor time to announce it, though.

Something rose uneasily in my stomach, a nervousness and fear that came from nowhere; it was bitter, terrifying and angsty all at the same time, it made me want to run away, made me want to get out of this area. I did my best to push it away, trying to relax a little as I saw Raziel's leg stop shaking, relaxing too. Pushing harder, the other leg instantly stopped as well. I eased up, recoiling from the situation as he began to rock anxiously once again, pushing the fear away as the results repeated itself. It was starting to make sense, at least my interpretation of what was going on. When I slept, he slept too. When he was nervous, I felt it. This tether was screwing with the both of us, some kind of mutual empathy thing going on. He looked down before speaking up.

"Stop it." Okay, so he was clearly able to tell I was fiddling around with the tether.

"This isn't what you were expecting, was it?" I said softly, looking out onto the field, trying to relax. He glared at me like I was breaking the no-talking rule, face quickly giving up.

"No. It's not." He pulled his heads from his hands, running it through his hair, still jittery.

"Talking to demons is… bad?"

"Yeah! Yeah. Very." He said shortly as I nodded.

Leaving the house like that; I didn't know what he wanted. I didn't know what he suddenly understood, why he suddenly wanted to help me escape. It wasn't patterned, wasn't consistent. If there was one thing Raziel was consistent at, it was confusing the living Hell out of me. My head lowered a little bit about to speak up before getting an idea.

Standing up, the Angel flinched, hands up slightly to protect himself as I trotted away over to the barn, looking for something in particular. Spotting a small piece, I picked it up like a faithful pet, loping back over to drop it next to him on the fence. It was an old piece of barn wood, crumbling and paint bits curled all over the place, like touching it would eject the paint from the surface and crumble the wood to dirt. Raziel looked it over for a moment before looking up.

"Something to pick at." I suggested, motioning to it, "When I'm stressed it helps to destroy things - not - not in a property damaging or life threatening type of way." You could see a look of recognition for a moment as he looked back to it, at my very terrible peace offering. Just something, I needed something, the stress made me feel like I'd need to throw up, it was awful.

"N...no thanks." The angel put it down to the side, uninterested. It knocked the wind from my sails.

Maybe it was time to move on.

"There's a whole hierarchy with you guys, isn't there?" He barely looked over to me, furrowing his eyebrows.

"Demons are supposed to have it too." The angel shrugged, "That's what I've heard."

"Yeah, well, no one's come up to me with a syllabus yet, so I wouldn't know." I stretched out, "Your pal Gauzier is higher on that list, isn't he?"

"Not always. I used to be his superior." He said candidly, before realizing the degree of trust he had just let out. "We're not supposed to be talking with one another, it'll get us both in trouble." I laughed, taken back that this was the biggest issue right now.

"So what? Call it a curse like everyone else does and blame me for it, I honestly don't care. How many times have you tried to kill me now, and you're worrying about talking to me?" I could feel him glaring at me. "C'mon, give it up."

"Like you haven't been trying to kill me?" He said it with faint conviction, already knowing the answer. "I'm supposed to kill you."

"Name one time! Go ahead! You name one time where I've actually tried to kill you, and I'll go ahead and send myself back to Hell." I egged on, calling his bluff. "I've chased you around and you deserved every bit of that, but I've never tried to kill you." My anger was infectious, the argument heating up quickly.

"Why is that?" He demanded, skirting around that he came up with jack nothing on the times I've tried to kill him. "Why haven't you at least tried? Speaking of, why the Hell did you stop the first time in that house? What do you want from me?"

"Nothing! What do you want from me?" I laughed out sarcastically, coughing just a bit before clamming up. I didn't realize we were both awkwardly afraid of the other, especially since he's been nothing but arrogant and boastful most of the time. "How about this; if you tell me why you're stuck as some bargain basement exorcist right now, I'll tell you all that."

It seemed like a fair trade, more then that, I knew he'd never let an actual personal secret go; even though I was already deciphering why from the information I'd already gotten. It had something to do with his wife's falling, something with being a coward. I could fill in the spaces without a lot of trouble on my own.

"I don't make deals with demons." He snarled, pointing a finger at me and hopping from the ground. My eyes narrowed.

"Then there's nothing more to talk about." I said grimly, looking angrily at my rejected peace offering. "Give me that back if you don't want it." I went to snag it back as the angel put both hands on it protectively.

"No, it's mine. I need this." He muttered, shielding it like a confusing child and putting it under one arm. Tilting my head a little, he motioned ahead of him like I better get walking. Whatever. I stormed past the way we first headed. I assumed that'd be the way back to the Priest. I could hear him pick at the piece of wood all the way by me.

For hours we walked in silence, staggered at a distance; I was in front, even though I knew no idea where we were going; he stayed at least fifty yards behind me, refusing to come any closer. Bored and a little lonely I began to hum, trying to figure out a way to get my demon lips to whistle as well. It was a kind of trait I discovered back at the demon cat's house; I was pretty good at it, but that was my human form, one with actual lips. Here, I only seemed to shoot out air.

The sun was directly overhead; around three pm in the afternoon was my best guess, the hottest part of the day. I could see the ground sweltering, rising up in balloons of warm air into the sky; Thermals, the clouds were swelling and growing in size, white and welcoming. Before I knew it he had caught up to me, looking in the sky for just a second before walking past, scoffing. Looking down he continued on, glaring back at me, still angry. His hands were empty, piece of barn wood picked away to dust.

I could feel how angry and annoyed he was. It started to dawn on my how pointless this argument had become; I had a chance to talk with something on my plane of existence with some small degree of intelligence; and here I was, holding up little pre-teen antics. Oh boy, I was sure showing him what a badass I was by ignoring the chance to talk one on one. It was stupid. We were both being stupid. Furrowing my eyebrows I swallowed my pride, speaking up; I guess I'd have to be the adult here.

"It's because I thought I knew you." I said quickly, purposely avoiding eye contact once again as I could hear him stopping, looking back to me. "That's why I stopped."

"Knew me?" He seemed uncertain, worried.

"Your eyes at least. Come into this world knowing nothing, except your damn eyes. I couldn't kill my own lead on what was going on, but I couldn't ignore it." He sounded like he was about to laugh, before remaining serious.

"Why my eyes?" He muttered as I shrugged.

"I've no idea. But I recognized you, I swear." He looked around, unsure what to do.

"I don't recognize you, though." I rolled my eyes, grinning.

"I kinda figured that."

"How long have you been here?"

"Above ground? Over three years. You stabbing me in the neck is one of my first memories." I thought on, it, speaking up again, "Below ground, conscious, about a thirty minutes or so."

"Then you definitely don't know me." He laughed, turning away, "Not unless you're at least four hundred years old. You look like you're 17, you know, not like that."

"I wouldn't know." I grumbled, resuming my walk, looking at him expectantly. Raziel looked ahead, then to me, then back to straight ahead of us.

"Hey, you told that on your own, that wasn't part—"

"Yeah, yeah, I get it. Keep your precious secrets; see how that works out for you. I know better then to put any real faith in you anyways." Maybe the normalcy of the conversation was starting to weird me out a little bit, that just yesterday I was fighting for my life, while today I was talking to the enemy, essentially.

"Wait a minute!" He stopped walking, wagging a finger at me.

"I'd illustrate my point, but I'm lacking a roof and a mailbox to throw you at." Suddenly I flapped once to face him, hopping backwards and holding out my hand for a handshake, like I'd done yesterday. Raziel remained standing there, hands ready at his side, unsure what to say as I pulled the hand away, flapping once into the air into a spin, purposely crashing into the ground. "That was about right, wasn't it?"

"I said wait a minute!" He shouted again, a little closer now as I lay 'dead' in the grass. Trapped in between two odd moods, half happy to have someone to talk with, half stuck still resenting him. No amount of near death angel-racing could change that fact right now. Something stomped hard on my tail, trying to get my attention.

"I did what I was supposed to do, stuck with some damn shape-shifting demon like you!" He pointed directly at me, accusing, "I try everything those assholes let me do, and you brush it off like it's a joke every time, you're damn right I'd try and pass you off on someone else! You're the type of demon that ruins everything!" I pushed myself partly up, still resting in the grass, stunned as he poked me in the neck.

"You screw it up by dodging around the system like it doesn't apply to you, how things are supposed to be, by disrupting how everything works. It's demons like you who take down good angels who don't deserve it, and everyone suffers because of one stupid decision! So don't tell me you're frustrated with the system if you're the one screwing it up in the first place!" The angel stood there, seething, sides working overtime to try and calm down. He glared at the reeds next to my head as I remained motionless, staring at him in surprise, careful not to make any sudden movements for at least a full minute until his frustration and anger lowered to a reasonable amount. Even then I was pretty sure that if I did start moving around too fast, he'd be at my throat with whatever weapon-like item he could find, which my money would be on the metal shin guards. His breathing finally began to slow.

"Better?" Raziel's eyes darted around as he took his foot off my tail, falling into a sort of sit next to me in the grass.

"A little." I waited awkwardly as he calmed down further, looking around dubiously to the environment playing host to our strange little conversation. Rolling back on my forelimbs, I slowly sat up.

"I didn't know." Tone hushed, I moved the tiniest bit next to him. "I'm just trying to survive, I don't want to hurt anyone."

The angel didn't move a hair, eyes fixated downwards at a tuft of grass surrounded by dirt. Thinking, I looked back towards the sky. I couldn't air my grievances now, like this. Raziel was difficult to pin down, conflicted. Adding a heap of guilt onto the pile might misrepresent my demonic race; I thought through his words, finding those pieces all lining up.

"Was this person your wife?" I struggled to say it, knowing the secret was toxic, but the angel didn't even bother looking over at me, deadened by the conversation.

"Yeah. Kicked me from my rank and clipped me, told me I had a lucky break." His wings flashed up, turning them a little to show that something had brutally cut all flight feathers off and most of the others as he awkwardly let the truth go. "They pretend like I was fortunate to get away from it with my reputation unharmed, but they took everything from me. Rank, my duties, my friends... everything. Now I get to be 'Raziel, the exorcist that beats up on dead pets for a living'." He kicked at the grass, bitter.

"Stuck as some 'bargain basement exorcist', reporting to the student I once taught. What an afterlife I lead now." Shocked, I looked at the top of his head for a moment before staring elsewhere. I felt responsible, felt to blame forcing these frustrations to the surface. But something told me it was good; not fun, but good. Honest. It explained quite a bit too, why he couldn't fly, why he was an incomprehensible bastard from time to time; the guy was stuck in a place where he, and everyone else around him, knew that it sucked. Honestly, it reminded me of my own destructive tendencies when I was utterly bored, reckless and alone. Raziel probably didn't feel too different than that.

I wanted to ask the obvious question, why his student looked a good twenty years older than him, but it seemed like a bad time. Maybe later. It didn't bring me joy to emotionally kill people; angel or demon. I don't think he meant to reveal as much as he did, feeling this sort of choking, uneasy anxiety. It's hard to open up to people, and especially at the tail end of an angry rant about your life to something you hated 12 hours ago.

Thinking, I spoke slow.

"I called back then because I needed advice." Looking about, the angel stared for a moment before speaking up, hoarse.

"Advice?" I gave a jovial nod.

"They gave me a home and they gave me a name, but they didn't give me any idea what I was supposed to do." Raziel kept staring, unsure. "The silence got to me after a few weeks. I think I chewed a foundational beam."

"Even though..."

"Yeah, well, how lucky am I that the only other spirit I've met left a business card with their number, so it was a short list." Shrugging my very demonic lizard shoulders I kept on, "I figured if I could talk to you where you weren't able to take a stab at me, you might be able to give me some pointers at how to make time pass for incorporeal folks. I didn't call to harass you. I didn't even know I couldn't talk to you until just a few days ago." Raziel frowned before giving a distant shrug. Things were still shaky.

I scooted a bit closer, sitting alongside him more.

"Between you and me, I think Gauzier sucks as a fighter." A lone Raziel eye wandered in my direction. "Only been above ground for three years and I feel experienced enough to tell. Awfully confident of his 'superior' skills; He got one little re-growing decapitation, and he just gives up." The angel chuckled.

"So you don't think he's a great fighter?"

"Please, at best he's a dead ringer for a prick." He laughed a little more, "I didn't like him since sentence one. I could tell you didn't either. He's creepy." I grinned, nudging him with my shoulder, tension breaking between us as I looked back to the sky, wishing to take flight, pining to live out my recent dream. At least once. If I was thrown away and chased for my head for the rest of my days, I at least wanted to experience that freedom just once.

"Why…are you so happy with all of….this?" He spit out unexpectedly. Turning to look over his distraught self, his questioning antics, I answered without missing a beat.

"It's nice to talk to someone on your own plane of existence." I waved around my hands for a moment, trying to back myself up somehow, "Even if it's wrong, I don't care. I'll take the blame for it." He smirked a little, looking back to the world around us, quiet once again as I eyed the skies once more, seeing a plane far off in the distances, blazing a trail through the clouds. We sat in relatively good graces, enjoying the nice day.

"If you want to leave, just go." Raziel looked up as well, scanning over the clouds with a small smile." I've got things to think about."

"Do you want to come with?" I felt almost stupid asking it, the signs were clear as day, he must miss that feeling, that freedom. The whole thing was generally pretty awkward. I wanted to be nice. I didn't enjoy causing misery. Then again, I was offering a joyride to the guy who tried, time after time to kill me off for good. At least one of us must've been crazy. The angel shook his head.

"I don't want what I can't have, if that makes any sense."

"Sure, that makes sense." I said quickly, gathering to my feet, " Why enjoy what you miss, even if only for a short time?" Spreading my wings out wide, it was far beyond both of us.

"Why be happy for a little while when you can be miserable for all of it?" I grinned and shook my head a little, "I told you I wasn't the only one with problems."

With that I took off, pumping my wings to shoot straight into the air, flying directly up from where he was, into the sky, crisp and blue. The sun was beginning to get lower in the horizon, the very beginnings of a sunset striking the clouds closest to it. I flew purely for fun, not fright, not fear, it was all for enjoyment, for exhilaration. Something hit me. Leave? Was he trying to let me go? Escape and run away? Ha! Are you kidding me? Slowing down into a hover, I saw the angel below me, looking up and watching as I flew about. It wasn't right; I didn't care if he said no; nothing beyond words hinted that didn't enjoy a stupid, carefree flight for no reason.

Without a second thought I folded my wings, falling from the sky quickly, headed straight for the ground with a slight spin. The grass was quickly in view as I opened my wings again, swooping low to the ground, silent as ever as my prey came into view, the angel standing like a prized rat, looking for the hawk. With relative grace I dodged around, keeping my wing sound to a minimum until I was directly behind the prey, crashing down and grabbing onto each arm carefully. In another moment, both of us were in the air, my wings flapping hard to pull the two of us into the sky. Raziel struggled, trying to turn to face me.

"I didn't want to go!" I could barely hear him over the sound of the wind rushing past, wings flapping hard as we gained height quickly.

"Then it's an abduction!" I pushed myself harder, high above the ground now, clouds lowering to meet us. "It's a demon curse!" I laughed, my grip tight on each of his arms as I suddenly shot upwards, sun streaking from the cloud in front of us as I tilted my wings just a bit in a loose twirl. Looking down at Raziel, he kept his mouth shut, hands clenched tight.

"You're not afraid, are you?" I shouted, banking quickly to the left, still gaining height.

"W-why would I be afraid?" The worry practically ebbed from the guy.

"That's good!" I said, folding my wings mid-air, keeping them tight against my body as we suddenly dropped from the sky in complete free fall. I could hear a high-pitched whining sound, something like an eagle crossed with a car horn wailing out past us, finding out it was Raziel as he reached back, trying to grab onto whatever part of me that was possible.

The ground was opening up, taking up most our view, closer and closer to the earth.

"Why are you doing this!?" He yelled back, giving up on trying to be the unmovable brick. Laughing out into the air, I made sure to give the toothiest grin possible.

"Retribution!" I yelled out, pushing him more in front of me like he was my shield against gravity. "If I can't kill you, I'm still going get some sort of revenge for the dickery you've put me through!" The angel leaned back to say something, eyes growing wide in fear as the ground was practically next to us.

"Ah, jeez, fly already!" He tried curling himself from the ground as my wings opened up, skimming the trees as I took off back into the skies. Using my momentum we soared back up, using the thermals from the road below us to rocket us back amongst the clouds.

"You can't scare me!" He was out of breath, doing his best to pull himself onto a sturdier platform, namely me. Brushing him off I heaved him into the air, throwing him out and away from me into the sky.

"Well, if you're not scared, then this is a joyride!" I laughed, watching him flail for a second before drop, albeit a little slower thanks to his stubs of wings towards the ground. He fell farther away, looking back at me and screaming something undetectable. Happily I waved, flipping over onto my back to begin falling back down as well, flapping my wings just a bit to catch up with Raziel as he struggled to keep upright. Noticing I was a bit closer he yelled again, a mix of insults and damnations, generally angry and frustrated at being treated like an object. I veered away, doubling back to fly just beneath him, his feet hitting the top of my nose as I leveled off, carrying him on the top of my head.

"Oh, will you shut up and have some fun?" I cackled, pumping my wings to soar higher back in the sky, trying to balance the angel on my nose. The sun was beginning to lower now, sunset blisteringly beautiful as we soared above the sunset line, into the higher reaches and alongside the clouds. With some simple, lazy turns I circled them, gliding around peacefully, out of breath.

Raziel kept his hands out, surfing on the big red and white wave of my nose, grimace slowly disappearing as he looked around. Before I knew it, I managed to get a smile from him, surveying it all. I grinned, drawing his attention away. Instantly he turned back to a frown, peace and serenity left.

"I'm tied to you and your annoying girly emotions, I can't help it."

"Oh?" I squinted, suddenly flapping hard as I could, gaining speed faster and faster. His feet started to slide back on my nose, arms windmilling around, trying to balance as I swooped into a big, lazy barrel roll in the sky to turn myself upside down, wings full out, no longer flapping. I began to drop from the sky, completely upside down, the angel still trying to hold onto the back part of my neck while being underneath my falling body. Feeling his arms lock around my neck I pivoted forward, now pointed face first, directly at the ground into a dive. Adding to the terror I worked hard to fly directly at it, clouds blurring, sun streaking as the wind screamed by us.

Accompanied with the angel's cry of terror towards the end, the ground shook in my vision, right beneath my nose I opened my wings, skimming the tops of the long grasses at just a few feet above the ground, land, and sky and trees all blurring beside us as they slowly got more defined. My wingtips almost dragged on the ground, changing the pitch of the feathers as we went slower and slower, coasting like a balsa wood glider without a sound.

Just as we'd start sinking into the soil I put all four limbs out, doing a jaunty bounce before coming to a stop. Raziel kept going, sliding off my wing to flop in the grass, petrified.

Grinning, I turned back to our original direction.

"Well, I feel better." I said, proudly taking a few steps alongside the sunset. "Now we're even, Raziel."

13

It was hours before he'd talk to me again. We gained some distance, mostly walking along the highway we traveled on; it didn't really make a lot of sense why I didn't just fly the two of us back, but time outside of the exorcist's home and exploring everything around me was refreshing. Light had faded hours ago, our illumination came from the cars as they whizzed past, streaking far ahead of us along the roadway and disappearing from sight. I could feel myself wearing out, the massive expenditure of playtime earlier had really grated me down to a soupy pulp as my feet began to drag.

Raziel had remained quiet for a while, either ashamed of himself, of me, or something in between. I don't think he was exactly mad, we walked side by side; no avoiding, no snide comments. Even when there were a thousand important things to discuss, we just…didn't. The two of us obviously felt uneasy of one another, him more than me if I had to guess. He'd let go of a little bit of what I assumed was the truth, something I wasn't sure constituted as walking a bad path, but I really didn't know all sides of this situation; I grumbled. My energy was getting zapped a lot quicker in the day, with the continuous walking and having to provide energy for someone else. Since Raziel had been attached to me, he'd definitely been easier to talk to, he actually understood what I could say, and his mood was more human, more stable. Walking for hours on hours was also keeping us quiet, pensive, wrapped up in ourselves in neat little bundles.

I caught him staring at my legs, brows furrowed before realizing I was locked onto his actions, quickly looking away. Shrugging, I went back to looking ahead of us both; I could hear him nervously bring something up.

"So is it… weird….walking around?" He muttered it at first,

standing up tall as I gave him my full attention. Raziel coughed quickly and waved a very caring hand in a non-caring way. Unsure, he only waved his hand around again. "You know, like that?" I gave a glib smile, egging him on a bit.

"Like how? What do you mean?" I knew full well what he meant- the angel skipped a step as he only waved more hands at me, like I should know exactly what he was talking about with a few short words.

"Like, that body. It is a body, right? Or it's a..." He stopped, unsure, worried about saying something wrong with our newly established lines of communication. I grinned, feeding on his awkwardness with a snicker. "I mean, you are a person, right? Or a demon, I mean- humanoid person... ish?" I laughed a little, shaking my head.

"Or maybe I'm just this monster, and the human's my disguise." I lowered an eye, mischievous as he only took a few steps away, still walking.

"See, you can't say things like that to me. I don't know if you're lying or not." He squinted again, tossing his head around like he was scoping out my monstery mitts for ashtrays. I slowed down, walking more daintily.

"I'm pretty sure I was in Hell as a person, I only gained this ability-" I raised an arm up sarcastically. "-After that first demon you fought ate me whole with one bite and got me out of Hell. I don't really know what this is, though."

"You don't?" He looked genuinely interested as I was happy to discuss. I shook my head.

"Until you more or less burned this whole form away, I didn't even know I could get out of it. I thought I just was this thing." I thought a little, remembering back, "No coordination, couldn't even run at first. So yeah, it's weird walking around, but I'm used to it by now." He poked a finger into my side, thinking.

"But it's the same consciousness, right?" I almost laughed as he elaborated on "You're not like hungry for flesh or anything like this, are you?" This time, I did laugh- Raziel seemed slightly offended by my response, shaking his head and looking back towards the road as I kept my head down, whooping for breath.

"Isn't it about time for you to go to sleep, or something?" He said tiredly, energy reflecting off of me like a handy little sub-gauge. I snorted indignantly.

"I don't have to." Yawning, I betrayed my own words, "I don't need you to freak out more then need be from a little sleep." It was meant to be a joke, a little humorous jostling, even if the memory of his crazy looking eyes snapping at me earlier in the day was unsettling.

"It's just not...usual."

"I don't think I lead anything in the usual category, Raziel." Another car sped past us on the highway, red taillights trailing away like two bloodshot eyes in the night. I spoke again distantly. "It's got to be awful, being constantly awake"

"Why's that?" Raziel yawned, leaning back to stretch out his arms.

"Well, I don't know, one day continues from the next, which flows to the next. There's no start, no end, no real sunrise or sunset, just the earth rotating around the sun in constant orbit. Everything around you rests while you're stuck in perpetual awareness without a lot to do. Your mind never relaxes, your body never rests, and it's always movement." I shook my head a little, "It sounds terrible." He tried laughing it off, finding one laugh didn't quite cover it, continuing in strange little huff-laughs.

"You get a lot done."

"Well, oh boy, sign me up for the red-eye lifestyle, then." I scoffed a little, "Why worry about getting everything done if you've got eternity to do it? If you're working to get things done right away, then aren't you really just putting a lot of stress in your own life by constantly having new things to do?" Raziel stopped suddenly, hands in his pockets.

"Anyone ever say you talk too much?" He said it louder as I apparently struck a nerve.

"No, actually. I haven't had anyone to talk to who wasn't eight." There was emphasis on that, softening up with warm memories of my previous family, "I'd try to discuss life theories with her, but it brought down the whole playtime atmosphere so I avoided it." I turned back to the road, walking again with a laugh. After a few steps, I heard him continue walking too.

"You really didn't curse those people? After what you did to them?"

"Hey, that first thing wasn't ME." I said hotly, temper flaring. I was getting a little fed up with taking the blame of what I couldn't control, namely that whole event. "The first thing I remember, Mr. Exorcist, is you har-de-harring that damn pike into my heart and not much before it."

"Please, don't kid yourself." Raziel rolled his eyes, pace quickening. I realized I was walking a little fast, irritated and annoyed.

"I don't remember, couldn't understand, couldn't control and had no actual awareness of what had happened; when having no part of it makes it my fault, you let me know, okay?" Storming alongside the road, he struggled to keep up as I continued on, "If I had known what was going on, I would've NEVER hurt my family!"

"Whatever, fine, take it easy!" He said as I glared at him quickly, face jutting back to the road, keeping up my furious pace with an irritated growl. "C'mon, relax!"

Frowning back to the path laid before me I eased up just the tiniest bit, slowly falling back to normal, to something reasonable as I remained frustrated, scared. The angel scratched his head.

"I don't think you actually hurt anyone, just, you know, scared them. When I first got there, you were just standing in the middle of the room, wobbling around like you were drunk. Even for a demon, I thought there was something wrong with you, like you were sick. Or the 'other demon' was sick." My pace slowed to a stop, attention full to the angel as I tried to see through his words. Hardening my glare I peered closer, the exorcist leaning away from me warily. It didn't look like he had anything to gain from lying to me about this.

"Honest?" The angel gave me a dubious look, shrugging once like the idea he'd ever lie was as blasphemous as I was. "So what about 'seven hours terrorizing the family'?" Raziel's eyes popped open once, looking away and shrugging a lot.

"Might have been, a little… exaggerated."

"How exaggerated?" I frowned, dissecting this lie all the way through. Raziel shrugged another half dozen times.

"Moderately?"

Slowly pulling my head away, I looked back to the road, taking some deep breaths.

"Well, That's a relief." I gasped happily, clutching at my chest. Raziel mimicked me sarcastically.

"I know, I can feel it. You were going to make my heart drop out with worry."

About to just ignore it and move onto something else, I figured it was a good enough lead into asking some questions in some vain hope he'd answer them, if he was in a truth-telling mood.

"From the tether, right?" I asked as the angel nodded, not paying much attention. "How does that work?" I turned my head a little, doing my best in tone alone to be non threatening and curious because I know this wandered into personal territory. As expected, he seemed instantly wary. I tried again.

"I'm reasonably sure the other tether I had to the house wasn't super informative." I put a hand up. "Not trying to encroach on anything, I just want to you know that I am by all means, an idiot when it comes to knowing about anything. But if you need information of the Faegels day-to-day for about 3 years, and how many soap operas Katherine watched in sweeps week, I'm very helpful." I gave another smile as Raziel only stared at me blankly, unimpressed.

"Tethers differ." The angel seemed nervous, carefully constructing what he could say that was bland and vague enough. "My tether to the Priest tells him when I've died, that he should leave. That's all he needs to know. It's simple. He can be hard to read."

"And mine?" I pushed farther as Raziel shook his head more out of disbelief, walking on while still talking.

"Yours is like a giant glass billboard with neon lights." He said like that was supposed to be an insult, scoffing as I gave a hardly bothered chuckle anyways. So I was very surface with my feelings, why would that be a bad thing? "It might as well read 'I'm sleepy and tired' in giant letters."

"I am pretty sleepy and tired." Raziel's response was immediate.

"I KNOW." Still intending for it to be some sort of insult, I bust out laughing; again, infectiously it lifted Raziel's crabby mood. I caught the angel smiling, trying to keep it reigned back. I'm happy to make people laugh, but the sort of involuntary control the tether gave weirded me out.

I took a deep breath and turned back to the road as it winded on, lit up by some streetlights a few miles down. This road was endless, stretching through the darkness like a sinister, evil thing. The gentle curves and uneven sway reminded me of the enormous black carpet monster that busted me out of Hell, that started it all. Standing up a little taller I frowned, looking once over to Raziel before back to the road. Eventually, this little excursion would end. Eventually, we'd make it back to the Priest's home, something that had been on my mind since being tied up in the back of the Ford Transit, as I now knew it was called.

"What happens now?" Looking to the sky, I could see the stars spread out above me as another car blew past, interrupting the peace as I tucked my head back in, trying to shrug off the cold breeze that came with it.

"What do you mean?" He asked, looking around cautiously. "We keep walking."

"Not that. When we get back to the Priest's home, what happens?" It was a blatantly honest question, not wrapped in any amount of lies or deceit, not hidden behind stupid little exploratory statements. The thought rang on me, what would I want to happen? There were a lot of fuzzy leads, a lot of circumstantial decisions that seemed to stand on if I could make a friend out of my enemy. If I could ever trust him. If I was even allowed to stay anywhere in the first place. If the annoying kill-cycle would go on and on. There was a lot of annoying uncertainty that sat on my back. He instantly looked uncomfortable.

"That. Well. I don't really know." He stumbled, counting on his fingers like it helped put everything into perspective by labeling the events. "I can't kill you. My boss probably can't kill you. He might, but I'm not sure. You're stuck with me. You're also supposed to be my student, which, sorry, I'm not teaching you squat about exorcism."

"I'm not really looking to take it up as a career."

He ignored me and went on, shrugging. "I'm sorry, I don't know."

"You haven't made up your mind."

"That too."

"If this whole bout of emotions and normal-ness is due to you being tied to me, are you going to go back to being a complete ass when you're not?" He glared at me, suddenly laughing.

"Yeah, probably." He followed me as we diverted from the roadway, walking a little farther into the fields once again as the sky remained pitch black, stars shining brightly.

"Doesn't that bother you? Having your personality chosen by someone else?" I muttered as Raziel suddenly stopped walking. I didn't notice for the next two steps, suddenly realizing he wasn't following anymore. Turning back towards him he was focused on something else, almost like he was incredibly concerned about what I said. Considering the somewhat lighthearted antagonizing that we were both doing, it rang out unusually serious. "Raziel?"

"Should... it?" He glared at me for a moment like a true mark of oddity, frowning again. I was beyond baffled that it was something he had to ask me. Confused, I muttered on.

"Yeah. It...probably should." Pulling my head away a bit, I squinted at the angel with the giant, hollow eyes. "You're acting extremely weird right now." Muttering, he suddenly snapped back, shaking his head out for a moment, catching back up with me with a laugh. Before I could push any farther, Raziel spoke up again, voice wary.

"You're not going to change into something worse, are you? It's roughly 3 ish." I dropped the subject. Couldn't tell if that was actually true, if he was just humoring me, or if he was a bit off his rocker.

"This is as big as I get, sorry to disappoint. I stayed like this for three years without changing to or from something else, so yeah, this is the grand finale of changes." Things went quiet again, wind picking up softly, almost blowing us along to hurry us back to the Priest's home. The land was lit in soft colors, streaks of lights emanating across is as the different fields became shorter and shorter, getting into more common areas, away from the rural landscape. My steps became heavier, more labored as I wondered if I had a bone structure in this body. I could stand sturdily; I wasn't like I was a smoky mass of weird, segmented limbs walking about like the demon at my first home, with just little bits of bone segments. It felt whole, solid, real. Did angels have bones? Must have something, if he was able to bruise himself earlier. I wondered if being...God, what did he say, 400+ years old had a sort of aging effect, that sort of lumbering, achy, heaviness that Katherine had always complained about.

"400 years old, eh?" It was said out of the blue, rolling on from my internal thoughts. Raziel looked up, eyebrows raised, beaming a little, "You poor bastard." The beaming stopped.

"It... it's not a bad thing!" He complained, indignant.

"Prove it." I suddenly sat down, weary. Dawdling, he looked around, trying to find a good point to prove that this eternal life of his was worth the hassle, suddenly staring at me and grinning evilly.

"I've experienced and remembered more than you ever will." I shot daggers at him for a moment before turning away completely. "I take it you're still not tired?" He mocked me, sitting down too.

"I'm just aggravated. Plus yes, pardon me for getting tired

energizing two people at once. I'm not a factory. This is as good a place as any. We can keep following the road in the morning."

"Plus flying around a lot to scare the Hell out of me for revenge, that's got to count for something too." Raziel muttered as I glared over my back. He looked up, holding both hands out like I was welcome to fight him on that thought. I mean, he wasn't wrong. I let up on the aggravation a bit.

"Well... yeah." I looked out over the field, getting a bit spacey and out of it, ready to bed down and sleep. What an absolutely strange day. Fun, though.

I ran over our conversation a bit more, stomach knotting up anxiously, needing to say something.

"How are you okay with that, though?" I looked towards him as he was finding taller dandelions to kick the heads off of. The angel looked back. "I'm sorry, I know you probably don't want to talk about it, but seriously, how are you okay with...not having a personality or a soul?"

"What? Who says I don't?" He laughed incredulously, insulted.

"Well, if you swing from tether to tether like adapting their personality..." I trailed off for a moment, thinking harder. "You were human, right? What happened to that?"

"Who says I'm human?" His voice went lower, more insulted that I was apparently striking out over and over.

"We were all human, though." I looked back as he had his arms folded, unhappy. I mean I was mostly just worried and annoyed, and he didn't seem to be showing that so maybe he was just flat out lying about parts. Wouldn't be surprised, "I mean, maybe you're some collaboration of like...squirrel souls or whatever, I don't know. Like I said, I don't have any idea how you guys run things...I just-" I stopped, thinking carefully on how to explain myself as Raziel spoke up, aggravated.

"Drop it."

"How do I stop." I spit out louder. The angel tilted his head a little that he didn't quite understand what I was asking. "How do I stop influencing you, because it makes me feel like garbage to screw around with someone like this. How do I stop. Then I'll drop it, I promise."

Raziel only stared for a moment as I had my head low, more worried than before. He took a few steps away, sitting down with his back to me, still in a crappy mood.

"Goodnight." What?!

"What? No? That's not a helpful answer!" I barked out, worried and anxiety doubling that beyond him being horribly influenced by me like some Tupperware container full of spaghetti stains, he also wasn't going to give me any way to fix it. It only made my stomach roll and heave as I watched him suddenly start anxiously tapping his leg. The angel seemed shocked by it too, looking back to me with an even heavier slate of aggravation. I pointed to him. "See, you're going to have to tell me something or we're both going to have a shitty time here."

"Egh, this is the worst." He spit out, tapping both hands on the side of his legs like a spastic fish. I started to feel his aggravation through the tether myself as an uneducated tether navigator that he reeeaally didn't want to tell me anything, but he was running short of options between what he kept secret, and what he cared about keeping secret. Raziel put both hands over his eyes, wandering around, frustration escalating.

"FFFFINE! I'M LYING." He toddled around, eyes covered. "You can't do anything to fix it, because like the billboard, I can just not look at it. I'm lying. It doesn't really work like that. I am fully capable of having a personality and a soul, and in fact, do. Only extreme emotions can mess around with the other person. Jesus." My anxiety dropped as he let his hands fall, looking wrung out of all his devious tricks. I paused.

"Oh." I turned back around, laying down. "Fuck you for lying then. Goodnight."

He stood for a moment awkwardly, eventually muttering and kicked around in the thistles behind me, picking at some plants and tearing off the leaves, generally being bored. Before long, I felt something jab at me in my stomach, a finger poking at my supposed ribs. My tail whipped around, hanging over him in the air as the finger pulled away quickly, the angel rustling some more.

Relaxing, I was about to drift off to sleep.

"What… do you remember?" He asked in a voice I wasn't sure I heard, murky and drenched in subtlety. Picking my head from the ground I looked to the angel, eyes downcast, twiddling his thumbs. "Besides my so-called eyes." It was general curiosity, interest. Yawning once to look out around us, gazing vaguely at what I saw, my thoughts were already glazed over with sleep.

"Everything." I said softly, words barely tumbling from my lips, "And pretty much nothing."

"That's not very specific." He went back to kicking at the reeds, digging his heel into the ground to spray dirt around.

"I don't remember anything important, just stupid things."

"That's still not very helpful."

"Fff. I'm tired. Poetic answers some other time." I twinged a bit as he kicked dirt at my side.

"Do you remember the names for things, but no actual timeline with them? Like you know everything's name, know how they work, but don't know why?"

I looked back at him, a little spooked.

"Yeah" I shifted to my other side, curling in his direction instead of away from him.

"No personal timeline? You know, no memory of family or

anything like that?" He was in a thinking pose, looking up at me as I leaned closer, nodding my head.

"That's... yeah. What's that mean?"

"Well, I doubt it, but that'd be one part of a three-part soul, a Tresillo."

"Tre…sillo? Isn't that music?" My eyes were wide awake and very interested.

"I think it's three notes played together, but they're linked, I dunno, someone thought it was a clever way of explaining things. I don't know, just a thought." He rolled his hand, yawning suddenly and stretching out like he was about to kick off to sleep. I couldn't allow that now.

"Hey!" I shouted quickly, hushing back almost immediately as you could tell I was a little devoid of useful information on my behalf. The angel's eyes snapped back open, leaning away as the yawn snapped closed. "Sorry. Keep going." I apologized, urging him to continue on. He opened his mouth to retort, to protest, hushing himself for a moment before going on. You could see I was already pushing my luck with this talk

"I…I can't." He immediately looked elsewhere, suddenly flopping over like he was trying to go to sleep. I was on my feet in a second.

"Hey, wait wait wait wait, nuh-uh-" I latched onto the two cloth headband-straps with a careful hand, lifting his head from the ground as he scrambled in surprise. "So you're not going to tell me now? That's it? You started the conversation just to tease me or something?" He popped off the headband, twisting about in the reeds to face me, hair sticking straight up.

"I can't! This is the type of stuff I get in trouble for!" I almost dropped the headband out of frustration alone. I was essentially fuming now.

"Three years wandering around this realm in a damn haze, and the answer's withheld by the list of 'stuff I shouldn't do.' Are you kidding me?" I sat down in a huff as he looked away from me, distrustful and somewhat angry. "I mean, you do know you helped me escape, right? How high does that rank on that list? Why can't just you just tell me what apparently everyone but myself knows? I don't care about whatever stupid secrets you have, I am not a damn spy, I don't care. But a little information on common knowledge would be nice!" He snatched the headband from my fingers angrily and shoved it back onto his head, spinning around to have his back to me, grumbling something about all demons being the same. Snorting once I growled audibly, mirroring him to flop back unhappily onto the grass some distance away as life and sound died out to nothing. Dammit! Why did I even bother?

The air around me was cold, almost bitter; the first nips of fall creeping closer and closer still as I sat there, mulling it all over. From what I had seen, what I'd heard and experienced, there was a lot more anger, a lot more stress than I ever thought there would be amongst angels;

just figured it was all about fluffy white clouds and harps. A system of rules, regulations, specific classes and specializations; it was intricate and complicated. More then what I knew, what I understood. I wanted answers. I craved them. Desperation was ruling my life, my sanity; I was scrambling at just the hint of an answer. Lowering my head a little, I had to let go of that overdone need to know everything at my beck and call. I was still new to this world, still figuring it out. I didn't really know anything for certain, it was all based on theories and speculations. I sighed; if I actually had breath, I probably would've been able to see it, it was that chilly.

"I'm sorry." I muttered, regretful of the persistent ass I'd just become. Raziel didn't say anything, so I continued on.

"I don't know how this world works. I have idealized thoughts of how it should work, but I'm also aware that's probably not how things are. It's just been on my mind for years now. A lot of free time alone gives a person a lot of chances to drive themselves into desperation at any answer." I turned a little to see him still looking out and away, rubbing both arms rhythmically, "So, whatever. If it's common knowledge, I'll find out eventually, I guess. If that's your thing, then there's no need to push things farther then you're able to and drag you further… are you cold?"

I stopped, tilting my head to the side. The angel's hands were both instantly on the ground, sitting there like a rock still turned away from me. After about ten seconds of absolute silence I could feel something jarring up the back of my spine, a severe twinge of cold that rattled like an electric shock. I watched the angel shiver visually at the same exact time. I almost laughed.

"You're freezing!" Raziel immediately turned around back to me.

"I'm not 'freezing'- I'm fine." The angel turned back away, "You make it sound like I'm on the verge of death. I'm not." He coughed once, going back to rubbing his arms quickly, sitting out there away like a stubborn ass. I squinted a little. Out of this body, I had that same problem, not able to make my own body heat; but in this giant dog-dinosaur thing, that wasn't an issue. Even Amber had said how warm I was. Waiting a few minutes more I let out an annoyed breath, dragging myself to my feet and taking those couple extra steps, flopping down just behind the angel. He leaned away, confused.

"I'm not going to be able to get to sleep if you're going to be sending me death-chills every five minutes" I grumbled, turned away from him to the dark night around us. "I do this as a mutually beneficial thing, okay?" He continued leaning away, glaring at me for a little while as he looked back around him, then back to me. Frowning angrily, he suddenly got to his feet, taking his own few steps to go suffer back into the cold, his back to me once more in a huff. I scoffed.

"What? Seriously?" Before I could properly raise my voice at what a stupid childish baby he was being, the angel spoke first, mumbling something to the blank, open sky.

"There's… three types of souls in a Tresillo" He said to dead air, speaking out in front of him like a loon. I tilted my head a bit, straining to understand. "Praeteritum, Praesens, Postremo; or the Past, Present and Future."

"What the hell are you doing?" He continued on, ignoring me, speaking louder.

"Life has just the one soul, a collection of all that happens within that life, which after you die becomes the past soul." He went on, explaining to no one in front of him like he was teaching an invisible crowd. I tilted my head a little more, trying to figure him out as he continued on, "Most ghosts and spirits are lingering past souls, unwilling or unable to pass onto the next phase of life. Getting to Heaven earns you a present soul for existing and living on; if you do something after death, get a job, then you earn a future soul, making you a Tresillo." I kinda watched him, baffled for a moment as he stopped, still facing the great black universe while spilling all this apparently illegal information. Another chill ran down my spine via Raziel as he coughed again.

"So still not…" The angel suddenly twisted around with a spastic look in his eye.

"I'm only rehearsing my information. I can't be held responsible for anything that hears it. Neri." He over-emphasized 'thing' distastefully, like I was forcing it out of him. I gave a sort of half-smile, still more confused then anything else as the exorcist turned back away.

Rehearsing out loud, in the middle some field, in the presence of a demon. Yeah, that'd hold up well in a court of law. I grumbled softly as he remained sitting there, back to me. My eyes popped open as I suddenly realized he was waiting for something, for the questions I had.

"So, uh, you're a Tresillo Soul?"

"Anyone who does anything after death is, you can't just be a present soul if you're existing and doing other things outside of just death." He answered militantly. Rubbing his arms again he looked at me quickly, facing dead ahead once more like the stubborn son of a mule he was. As I was about to turn away, movement caught my eye, both of his arms ever so slowly extended behind his shamed back, scooting a foot closer to me. We were at least ten feet apart. "But they can be segmented away. It's a punishment, and a serious one at that." The angel scooted another foot closer as I didn't have to ask any questions.

"You seem more like a present soul. They understand the world around them in a practical, logical, planned kind of way. We don't really describe them as anything, they're usually just the left over part that's discarded away if a soul gets their past and future ripped out." I perked up, obviously interested as he scooted another foot closer.

"You can do that?" I almost felt like laughing, a little bewildered on the inside.

"Getting your future removed is called Falling. Getting your past removed is called 'Rebirth'. There is no term for getting your present removed, because it's not possible. It's like the other part of a soul that can't hold together on it's own. No one really knows about it." He moved one last time, sitting there tiredly. "But that's only how it works for angels, I don't think demons have the same system, I think it's just a dead or not. I don't know if you can tell, but our whole education on the demon systems a little…scarce."

I shook my head back and forth, a little more than surprised.

"Figured as much." I propped myself up a little taller. "Say for the sake of awkward conversation, I'm not a Demon…"

"But you are."

"Shut up and let me have a little hope here for a second." I growled, going back to thinking. "If I wasn't a demon…"

"You'd be a dead ringer for a PS soul, the present soul. But you'd be a lot more…I don't know, robot-like? Like I said, there's not a lot of fact of how these souls act on their own, just a lot of speculation. But you can't see the Present soul, hypothetically, so that's probably not it." He yawned again, stretching out above him as the spinal chills began to subside. "It's not a good thing to be one part of three, especially the odd middle part."

"Can they re-join?"

"I think so, but you're not a Tresillo soul. You'd have to be important, or at least doing something other than wandering around." The thoughts of the 'queen' talk suddenly hit, unnerving me. "If you've only been around 3 years, then that's not likely"

"It's still possible" I felt like I was grasping at whatever explanation I could see, desperate to be anything but what I was at this moment. Answers. Real answers. God how I wished to have them.

"It's not possible, just convenient." He let his head drop tiredly, propping it up with his one hand, sitting maybe all of six inches away from me. "Trust me, being just a Praesens soul is not a good thing."

"Why not?"

"Because that means there was a reason you were splintered up, and only the notoriously evil people get that treatment. The very worst." It felt like my heart dropped out of my chest, that the shivering night air swept all the warm, reassuring feelings right out of me. The worst of the worst. The bottom of the scum barrel. I wanted desperately to think it just a small chance, that as he said, I had to be doing something important. Maybe I was just painstakingly new? An oddball.

My hands grasped the ground a little more. An oddball stuck wandering Hell; stuck under watch, under guard. I had to be there for a reason, I must've done something horrible. No, no that couldn't be it. I had to be more then that. There had to be something more. I had to be something else.

"Is…is there a way to know, or find out for sure Raz—" Something hit my side, pressing and weighing against me. The frantic internal rambling stopped as I looked to him, finding the angel resting against my back, arms folded tiredly, already asleep. I watched for a second more, smirking quietly before taking a confused, frustrated breath. How I wished it would all just fit together, just make sense for me. How I wish I had those definitive answers. How I wish I knew.

Worst of the worst, at the stark end of the bad spectrum, if I was that evil, bad person, if I was only the odd middle section of three, did I still have hope? Could I redeem myself? If I worked to keep doing right, if I stayed 'good'… It felt like my train of thought stopped, stuck, wedged into a block of uncertainty and confusion. Stayed good. I didn't even know for certain if I had done something bad. But if that was all true, if I really was some horrible demon fragmented into slivers of a soul… Peering back to the angel sleeping peacefully next to me, I snorted. If I was so horrible and bad, then this wouldn't be happening. He's some billion of years old, he'd be able to pick up on a really bad spirit, not nap against it. Then again his judgment was as solid as a crumbled brick to start with, he made a poor evil-o-meter.

The angel made a sort of odd gurgling sound before shivering again. I let out an annoyed sigh.

"For God's sake…" Bringing my wing around I covered him with it, slowly dropping my head onto the grass, drifting off to sleep. There were no dreams that night.

The next morning was relatively normal, as normal as an angel and a demon waking up tied together in the middle of a field on the way back to an exorcist Priest's home could be. There was shuffling, yawning and restlessness on the very edges of my awareness as I leaned forward, nuzzling into the warm pocket I'd created with my body heat, drifting back asleep. The rustling continued, stopping, stepping, my head suddenly kicked at around 8 am, Raziel's foot poking into the crevices of my face, changing to kick at the horns behind my head.

"That still hurts, you know" I mumbled, writhing a little in the grass to roll over onto my back, stretching out. "What's the hurry?"

"They're going to start looking for me today, that's what." He cracked his knuckles, twisting around a little to try and stretch out his back. "Hypothetically, they're going to assume you killed me. Takes two days for a dead-angel to come back to this world, so I have to link back up with the Priest soon or they'll be coming by and investigating this whole thing, which is something neither you or I want."

I pulled my arms and legs closer to my body, giving him a cold stare. Wait. You or I?

"And…you didn't think it would be a good idea to bring this up yesterday?" Rolling to my feet, I shook myself out and looked back to the highway, at the few amount of cars trolling past it, guarding it.

"It was an off day. Maybe I didn't want to rush right back to the Priest, delay my workload a little bit." Well, that was almost a backhanded compliment. I raised my eyebrows, looking to him as he refused to look anywhere close to me, "Don't look too much into it."

I pulled my upper half of my body up, stretching my back legs out and yawning again. I wasn't entirely rested.

"Fine. Should we start running?" My jaws snapped shut as I felt his hands on my back, Raziel was trying to lift himself up to sit on my shoulders. I flipped a wing up, knocking him away easily, tail twitching angrily at the angel as he was sprawled into the grass. "What do you think you're doing?"

He dusted himself off, shooting me death glares and refusing to answer my question like it was too personal to mention. I didn't get this guy sometimes.

"You can fly, I can't. Flying is the fastest way to get back home, where we need to be. I'm not going to be carried like I was the last time." The angel pointed at his mouth, standing back up. "What's the big deal? You're pretty much horse-sized anyways."

"Because I don't want some 400 year old man riding on my apparently 17 year old back!" There was a lot of stern intention meant, but I couldn't help but laughing saying it out loud. The angel stood there like I'd punched him in the face, twitching a little with a loss of how to combat my very honest opinion. In all actuality, he didn't look to be over his mid-twenties. Still.

"I'm not old!"

"Old man, I consider 100 old, you're pushing ancient!"

"Are you serious?" He went back to my side, trying to jump onto my shoulders again as again, I smacked him away with my wing. "That's it, as the higher power here, I demand you fly me back home!" I started to laugh, wing hanging ominously out, ready to hit him away again.

"You can demand all you want, there's no senior citizen's discount on this one, it's not going to happen" He ran at me this time, trying to jump over the wing as I ducked out of the way, sending him sailing into the grass, "No!" I don't know why I couldn't stop laughing, even as I trotted a little farther away from him. With his armor jumbled and messed up, he glared at me, shuffling around.

"What do you want?"

"For carting your heavy ass all the way back home?"

"Y…yeah, for that." He ignored my insult as I sat down, contemplating. Having the upper hand; he needed to get back home, I didn't really need to, but as for a stable place to exist, that was probably a good idea. What could I bargain for? Civility? Honesty? Precious secrets? Treat me like I wasn't radioactive or poisonous? I came to a conclusion; the best I could really hope for and the most I was willing to take.

"That cot in the basement."

He stared at me, waiting for more things, eventually tilting his head a little.

"That's it?"

"Oh! That, and if you're going to be tearing me out of this body and back to the other one, just ask. That hurts like flaming battery acid, I'm sick of you doing that whenever you please." I wasn't just asking for these stupid, simple items, I was asking to stay. Asking the impossible, asking what everyone in this area knew was a lot. The moments passed intolerably slow.

"Fine, deal." He walked up as I looked away, hands bracing to my side like I was a damn horse as I tried not to laugh at our previous charades. "Even though I technically don't make deals with demons" He followed up, covering his legal bases.

"Mm-hmm" I responded sarcastically; my legs buckled a little as he jumped onto my back, pressure heavy on my limbs as I frowned, unsettled, weirded out. He grabbed onto the hair on the back of my shoulders to brace himself, sitting up straight like he was some hot-shot king. I looked around, glaring at him, then back to the highway, still frowning.

"It's like I'm playing airplane with a full grown man. It's still weird" I grumbled, taking flight into the sky.

We flew low to the ground, keeping out of sight best we could, back into the city. Raziel had some sort of tracking on the Priest, coupled with living in this area for a number of years he was afraid to tell me, said he could lead us straight back. I skirted the highway, using it as a guide to keep in line with, so I didn't go too far off course. Houses and barns flashed past us, an industrial district and something like a community pool and taller apartment buildings. We weaved in and out of the hills in the area, flying low in the backyards of the houses as they rushed up past us, flashes of colors and architecture. Just over the heads of unsuspecting people, we flitted between buildings and along paved roads before heading up higher, more out of the way.

It took about two hours before we were into a neighborhood even I could slightly remember, flying at different speeds and greatly avoiding any churches that came up beneath us for the possible Priests residing inside. Soon, everything around me was familiar, the homes I looked over just a few day ago, the house barely in view.

"Shit! Stop stop stop!" I pivoted down quickly, putting all four legs out in front of me, legs digging into the soil and knocking over a fence as we skidded to a stop, about a block away from the Priest's home. "He's there, Gauzier's there." Raziel's face drained of color, looking to me as I looked back to him, shrugging.

"That's bad, right?"

"Of course that's bad!"

"Is he just waiting for you to show up?" I leaned over a few feet to try and see the house myself, only managing a glimpse of part of the siding and a corner of window. We were still pretty far off. "You guys have any sort of radar so you can tell exactly where he is?"

"No, I can't see into the house. I don't have x-ray vision." Raziel weaved around a little to try and see something with an annoyed huff.

"How do you know he's there then?" I grumbled flatly.

"His host's car is in the driveway." I shrugged up my shoulders a little to give a slightly higher perspective as the angel still weaved around like he'd topple off. "Though if I had to guess, he's probably going through my shit, so he's in the basement."

"Does he always do that?"

"Usually."

"Sounds like your best friend Gauzier's just keeping tabs on you like a true pal." Raziel kicked me hard in the sides as I immediately wheezed in pain.

"This is serious!"

"I am serious!" He kicked me again as I laughed, stumbling around a little. Through the tether were all sorts of jabs that this wasn't really the time to make fun, the emotional detectors reading near the same amount of anxiety a day ago. Taking a deep breath, I cut my fun and composed myself. "I'll be serious. What do I have to do?"

"You're gonna help?" He paused in his panicking, almost glaring at me.

"No, I'm going to be an obstinate pain in the ass for the sake of nothing. Yes, I'm gonna help, what should I do?" I looked back at the yard, trying to see into the windows, trying to get a read on anyone or anything lurking about there. I couldn't. My eyesight wasn't really that much improved, if at all. Waiting for an answer, I turned back to Raziel as he looked back to the house, contemplating some more.

"Getting closer would be a good start" I put both wings out, quickly sizing up my options as his tone suddenly picked up speed, "But you can't be seen!" Before the last word, I was already off.

"Think empty thoughts!" I shouted, folding my wings to dart straight through the first house, through rooms, baby toys, carpet, keeping low to the ground. A brick fireplace breezed through the two of us, a sickening, terrible feeling as we shot into the next house, mostly empty, a few couches and a computer, bathroom, a husband and wife sitting down at some table outside. We emerged from the second house, flapping my wings again to shoot us through the third, bright colors and dolls littering everywhere, cats and an old woman reading the paper. I flew as fast as I could, gaining speed to break through that last brick wall into the fourth house, the one just across the yard from his. Inside the home I flared to a stop, crumpling a bit against the wall as Raziel tumbled in just behind me, hitting a potted plant and knocking it over. The room we flew into had two windows looking out behind it, the perfect vantage point, but painfully small. I took up most the space, huddled down and low on the ground. "Done. What now?" I gasped for breath, grinning.

"You could've just flown back a block, gone up four houses, then…. never mind. Don't ever do that again." He brushed himself off quickly, righting the plant and creeping next to the window like a stalker. This was probably not the shining moment of his career right now, hiding in some person's spare room, looking out the blinds like an angry old man. I stayed where I crashed, waiting orders, pestering cobwebs in the corners of the room with my wingtips, growing more and more bored and claustrophobic. The tether practically danced with growing panic as he mumbled under his breath, planning things out while running into fictitious dead end after end.

Smacking my lips a bit out of boredom, I brought my head right alongside, peering out with him.

"So how's it goooinnng?" Raziel's frantic mumbling stopped, eyes panning over to me and none too happy about it. "What type of plant you think this is?" I gleamed.

"It's impossible." He stood away from the blinds for a moment, defeated and propped against the wall. "I've gone through all the options, and there's no way to get there unseen, create a fake re-entry, manage to fool him somehow, and get out of this without blatantly being exposed." He knocked his head against the wall repeatedly, staring straight up at the ceiling in a tizz.

"How about I just fly really high up and drop you?" The angel didn't even look over at me.

"I think he's going to be suspicious if I crash through the ceiling all bruised and broken." Raziel rolled his head back and forth, frowning and looking down after a moment as he could tell I didn't have all the information to make helpful comments. "It's a process. You're not just shot out of a cannon from Heaven or something."

"Learning so much now." I muttered as his eyes were instantly on me, miffed.

"How opposed are you to the Holy water cannon again?"

"Very! How opposed are you to being burned alive and painfully re-assembled?"

He grumbled again, back to knocking his head against the wall.

"How about I just create a really loud, annoying distraction in the backyard while you sneak in the front?" I said tiredly, shifting my one arm to rest more comfortably on the ground. "I got some rest, I could fend him off for a little bit." His head-knocking stopped.

"That actually might work. It's not unheard of for some demons to track down an exorcist to their homes, even after they kill them to wait." Looking much happier, he was suddenly on his feet, "And it's a Christmas Cactus." He rambled as I rolled my eyes.

That's the plan we went with, even though I never really got a thank-you for saving his sanity on a simple, cheap and effective option, without bashing my head against the wall in stress. But I'd have to keep Gauzier distracted for a while; had to distance the times between when he magically popped up, already in the house, and when I made my appearance. To keep consistency just in case Gauzier did see me fly through the four houses across the street, I climbed onto the roof of this home. Wings spread out I waited, watching Raziel dart off behind the house to the next street, starting his trek. I turned back to the home in front of me; I hoped this did work out. I hoped that even if he tethered back to the Priest, he'd be the same person. These last two days were almost fun, nay, they actually were fun. I didn't want to lose that.

Taking a deep, swelling breath, I bellowed out loud, pushing myself to be louder and louder until I though my vocal chords might drop out. The air around me seemed to vibrate and shake, flipping out my wings and standing tall on the roof of the house, making sure my distraction was as loud and distracting as it could possibly be. Flapping my wings once I quickly dropped onto the backyard of Raziel's house, breathing deep again to screech out another time, puffed up and animalistic. Back and forth I walked the pace of the yard, screeching and screaming up a storm, with no results. Just as I nearly figured that maybe Gauzier left sometime mid-planning session at the neighbors, that slinky little monkey came hovering out of the house, weapon in hand. Looking up to the other windows, I could see the two Priests staring out like kids on Christmas morning. Good, everything was set.

"Why Hello again! Certainly the persistent one!" I snarled and roared at him, curling my neck up to make a vague slash in his general direction. I was exhausted. "Seems you came back just in time for Raziel's re-appearance, he should be popping up any moment now." He tilted the sword's blade down at me, running his hand along it.

"But you already knew that, didn't you?" I narrowed my eyes, trying to read through his words. Something in his tone rubbed me the wrong way; I ignored it and continued to hunch and snarl, breathing hard and throwing whatever energy I had left to look as well-rested as possible. "So, demon, you decided to make this attack personal, hmm? You're an interesting one, aren't you?"

I didn't like how he talked to me now, even though the words were slightly altered, but it was like he was expecting me to respond. Flattening my body out, I made one slow charge at the angel, driving him to sink back into the basement of the house. As he did I saw Raziel out of the corner of my eye, taking his sweet-ass time getting back to the house, practically tiptoeing at the end of the street. Flaring my nostrils at him in annoyance, a sword suddenly burst through the other side of my neck. I gargled out a cry of pain, stumbling back with a bloody trail. My communal energy began to drain out of nowhere.

"See, that's what I find interesting. I cut off your damn head and you don't bleed a drop. But anywhere closer to the body, and you're like some kind of blood fountain." I took a few steps back, roaring and screeching out with my newly healed larynx. "You're like a great dissection project" His smile spread like a nasty little infection, readying himself to attack again. I tore into the ground as he flew straight for me; sword pointing out ahead of him. I knew that. I was going to use my brainlessness to my advantage.

Mimicking his sword point, the two of us connected dead between my eyes, brain sputtering and confused for a moment to adjust to the flat piece of metal. Snapping my head quickly to the side I pulled it from his grip, flapping once to almost dance around the fence, holding my head up proudly, grinning. Gauzier looked to his hands, looking back to me with disbelief. After a second, his arrogance kicked back into play. The sword lodged between my eyes wiggled with each movement, even more bulky items to cloud up my depth of field. I laughed out murkily, blood trickling through my teeth. Gauzier did about the same.

"I guess that's one way to use that hollow space between your eyes for something." He scratched the side of his face, off-put by being weaponless like he left his spare attacking items at home. Shaking my head quick enough, the blade made a twanging sound. My energy suddenly began to drop dramatically; having a hard time standing up like something sucked it all away. "Guess we can be sure that you don't keep anything useful th—"

A sound; a great dish of light and radiance suddenly swept from the side of the house in the upper story of the house, a beam of light shot away straight into the clouds. Gauzier only grinned some more as I watched the show, dazzled. This must've been the fake re-entry, thank God it was nearly time for me to rest. Just as I sprawled down low to the ground once more, braced myself for more roaring and screeching, something pulled on that energy net so quickly, snapping away. It caught me off guard, accidentally falling to my belly for a moment as the sword tumbled from my head, snatched up by the angel before it had time to settle into the ground. I got back to my feet, hunching farther away with my wings out.

"Hate to put you already back into battle after you just healed like this, Raziel." Gauzier said lowly, grinning at me as the angel walked calmly from the side of the house, armored up and weapon in hand. "But your friend here seems to be pretty persistent at finishing our fight."

"I've had advice how to beat this monster from the master of all swords himself!" Raziel said, voice devoid of emotion and any sort of trust as it had been as I kept recycling the same growl, exhausted. "Didn't have enough the first time, beast?" He stormed forwards, swiping the pike out back and forth to push me even farther backwards from the house. I meant to jump back away energetically, but my legs crumpled under my body, the swipe cutting a clear and deep mark across my throat. Blood sprayed out onto the grass as I reared back, alarmed and confused, looking to his eyes for answers. They were like before, hardened and glazed over, immune to any sympathy as he wiped the pike of my blood with a smile.

Crap, he really was the same asshole.

I hissed out angrily, leaning forward to bite him around the chest, maybe shake him around a little to get some sense back into him; he jumped out of my way. Foot suddenly on my nose he launched from my face, pike held far over his head. I could just see it as he brought it down, pointed edge first, intending to stab me straight through. I'd been stupid. Trusting. Ignorant as always. But as he fell closer he suddenly switched his grip, more or less stab-smacking the flat part of the blade onto the scar with half the pike slicing into my back. That burning, terrible pain shot through my body, the world evaporating into smoke as I was launched from it, my human-esque body shot deep into the dirt of the ground just beneath me.

Finally, man, finally. I rolled my eyes tiredly, sinking a little farther into the dirt in relief.

Voices chimed above me, the two of them talking for a while, laughing and congratulating as I hid there, body wedged into the ground. After what seemed like forever the sound died out, and after another long while, I heard him above me again, stomping and yelling, voice muffled like he was gargling into a pile of clothes.

"I said you can come out!" He shouted at the grass directly above me as I slowly began to worm my way out, shimmying through the dirt. My one hand made it to the surface first, something suddenly grabbing it and yanking me clear from the ground like a pulled weed. Gagging and sputtering, I stumbled back to my feet.

"Hey, that's better!" Rubbing my neck, I coughed and tried to blow the dirt from my sinuses. "You had me worried that you forgot everything and reverted back to being a pain in the butt. I'm glad you're not." I quickly touched my neck, my back, my head; they healed up fine. Hands on my knees, I coughed again clearing it out so I could breathe without feeling like rocks were nestling in my lungs. Brushing the dirt from me, I looked up as he gave me an odd look down, remaining quiet.

"But you're uh...did you hear what I said?" I questioned, seeing no acknowledgment, no understanding, confused. A stupid little thought that this understanding would last, even back with the Priest, quickly died away. My hopes fell, looking at both eyes, desperate for anything, any response.

"You…can't understand me anymore, can you?" It came out sadly, withdrawn, back to being that misunderstood demon creature once again. His eyes were sad, though, empathetic, before snapping back to how he had been, rather cold and indifferent.

"Let's go inside, Neri." He muttered, turning back to the Priest's home and walking back through the wall. I stood outside and watched, looked around me for a moment at the neighborhood, quietly serene and normal. Taking a deep, reluctant breath, I followed him back inside.

14

My nail ran along the top of the cot as I stirred back awake for the fourth time in the last hour, stretching out and enjoying the lair-like feeling of the darkened utility room. The warmth and interaction of having a real bed, really made for people to sleep on instead of the hard, unforgiving ground felt amazing. I'd try to sleep, clearly tired and exhausted from our shenanigans of the last two days, but my brain was an active and frustrating trap. What do I do now? Where do we go from here? He hadn't said a word since we entered into the basement, giving a bit of a nod off to the room; I was more than happy to go lay down and recuperate.

I had to stop bothering myself with these rhetorical questions. It was best to take a step away, see how things unfolded and keep the card in my back pocket that if things got bad, I could always leave. I didn't want to, but I could. I wanted answers, I needed closure if I was some version of segmented Tresillo soul or if I was just a demon. I could always make a point to try and ask Raziel about it later, after things were more settled and the awkwardness cleared.

Other issues were more relevant; had Raziel reverted back to a complete ass? He didn't seem too different; then again, he'd been avoiding me or giving me ample time to settle in without a word. He was a stubborn soul, but I had learned some important things from him. Things that had to equate to some sort of trust.

Opening my eyes again, I saw the operating table right on the other side of the doorway, a flash of memory of myself tied there and desperately unhappy, struggling to get free. The threats, the interrogation, how severely I missed my family. I put both arms up around my face, re-adjusting as my face-horns dug into my arms. That was another thing, how he had promised to show me what I looked like, and never kept it. I had called him a liar many times after that, almost a bigger offense than the various times he tried to kill me. Things seemed to hinge on trust.

I could hear him watching TV in the next room, this little room darkened in my consideration. Sitting up, I saw a few things around me, a bible on the nightstand next to the cot and a regular book next to that. I reached for the bible, looking around like I was about to break some massive golden rule, like the book would shoot laser beams out from nowhere and keep me from touching it, but as my fingers slowly landed on the book, nothing happened. Scanning the darkness for holy ninjas of some sort I picked the book up with a little more gusto, plopping it straight into my lap. Continuing with the Praesens soul theory, I knew what was in it, I knew what it was about, I knew it was an important part of Christianity, among other things; but I couldn't recite any passages, couldn't tell you the difference between Peter and Job. My knowledge of it for a demon was pretty good, but for any other degree of afterlife-creature, it was shoddy at best. I opened it, flipping through it quickly, a lot of red text, lots of black text, paper so thin it was almost transparent, the edges dipped in gold. I put the bible aside, picking up the other book next to it on the nightstand, War and Peace. I'm sure there was a joke in there somewhere, but I was still too tired to find it.

Everything else was plain, a cross in the corner, a water heater next to that along with a furnace behind a door. For someone to reside in this space for a number of years, it looked like a sad existence of things pared down to their basics. I looked back to the bible, picking it up and thumbing though it some more, going to the beginning and reading a little. The beginning was always the best part anyways.

"I…don't even know what to call what you're doing right now." The angel said, leaning on something in the doorway. I jumped a little, looking to him, before looking back at the book and cockily turning another page. "You're supposed to you know, burst into flames reading it. You know what, I don't care." I smiled just a little, reading over the spiel about creation; it was interesting, a little wordy, but interesting, eventually shrugging.

"Sorry, don't know what to tell you." I closed the book, putting it back on the nightstand as he turned on the light. There braced against his leg was the mirror, reflecting a whole lot of nothing besides a bed and a weirdly moving bible on a nightstand. Grabbing the book again I swung it around, watching the bible float in midair from the mirror, darting around like it was sick. Putting it back down, I pointed to the mirror, then to myself, shrugging. "I already tried to see into it, doesn't work for me" I looked to Raziel as he continued to glare at me, words breezing right past him. Going back to sleep couldn't help these problems, but still, I'd rather sleep then stand in front of a mirror that showed my nonexistence.

"I know this is all weird right now, but I did make a promise." He seemed uneasy, like someone entertaining a guest by force, "This is MY mirror, it only responds to me." He looked away for a second back to the living room, giving the mirror a hardy smack and making the surface rippling like it was made of water.

For a moment I thought it was a recording, a video screen of some sort, a woman sitting and looking away, but as I turned to it, she turned towards me. My body went ice cold, hands trembling as I sat there, completely in terror of my own face. Something kicked like mad in the back of my head. Go! Look! Opportunity! What's the matter with you!? Shifting a leg, I saw my reflection do the same. The poor girl in the mirror looked utterly terrified, eyes bogging out a little, ashamed, scared, petrified. I laughed just a bit, almost a sobbing sound as I suddenly scooting myself to the floor, legs under me. I was there. I could see myself there. Weaving back and forth, I could actually see me weave back and forth, leaning closer to see details.

I was normal! Relatively, but as Raziel had said, I didn't look over my late teens. There were no giant blemishes, no boils, no stereotypical demon / witch crap on my face or anything like that. Curious, I lifted up my one section of hair, seeing the two horns underneath it, black and nasty looking that were practically out of view. It was the same for the other side, which noted what I could barely see out of the corner of my eye, a large, brownish scar running over my collarbone, over my shoulder and down my back, where these strange, pointed black spikes came out. They weren't attached, I had never felt them; even running my hand past them now they were only vapor, untouchable things that waived at the slightest bit of wind or pressure. They just seemed to hover there. I furrowed my brows, looking back at the mirror as I did, giggling a little and running over little details in my mind.

I don't know why it was so significant; I knew I existed, but never seeing myself almost left me that I was ghost and nothing more. But physically seeing myself move, react, and exist, be it on a different plane of existence was like Christmas day. I couldn't be happier. The girl in the mirror had vibrantly green eyes, almost etched in a sort of yellow, highlighting them. She wasn't very tall, squatting on the floor made her seem shorter, her demeanor was beaming and excited. I spotted the goggles on my head, putting pressure on them again to try and remove them, finding them looping behind the back of my head, stuck tight. They were blue. It didn't matter; really, she looked like an honest, eager and intelligent girl. I couldn't be happier, even as the girl in the mirror began to cry, tears dampening my pants. I didn't brush them away, turning this way and that, getting the full picture, learning little things that I had died to know for years and years now.

About that time I realized I had been glaring at myself for almost twenty minutes while the angel stood there patiently, tapping the mirror every now and then as the reflection would start to fade. I laughed again, more in disbelief and incredible happiness, using my arm to brush away the tears finally.

"I thought it was broken" I stuttered, laughing some more and rubbing my sore eyes. I gazed straight at him, smiling happily, "Thank you. Thank you so much."

"You're welcome." He answered, my eyes snapping to him that he perfectly replied. Could he— "It was a lucky guess." Raziel said before my hopes got too high. Ah, well, at least I was fulfilled in one way, looking back to the mirror as it began to fade out once more. Waving my hand, I let him know I was finished, sitting shakily on the bed and putting my head against the wall, brimming with an overflow of emotions. Normally in this body, they got on my nerves; I had spent so much time in the demon body that this rush of emotions was almost annoying, but at this moment, they just made everything bliss. Maybe life here wouldn't be so bad. Raziel seemed unchanged, just as almost normal as before; I heard him get up, lugging the mirror from the room.

"Enough of that." He said quickly, frowning and storming back into the other room, angry for some reason. I snapped from my stupor, watching him go, standing up and walking towards the other room. What was going on? My toes threatened to cross the threshold from this tiny, two-booked room. "Hey! Hey!" He yelled at me, pointing to my toes just over the line.

"You stay in there, you're… you should be happy you get that much, that's where you stay." He pointed at me a little frantically as I looked down with a laugh, then back to his face, disturbingly serious. Faintly, someone above me yelled. The angel turned to carefully hang the mirror back on the wall, twitching as he did so. Okay, maybe he wasn't quite as nice or as stable.

"You're joking, right?" I laughed again, unsure, putting my foot cautiously over the carpet of the other room like I was about to step on it. You could see the paranoia and anger exploding from his face.

"Hey! I'm not screwing around, you stay right… in there!" He came storming over, shoving me harshly back into the room. I didn't know what to say, in a complete state of shock; it all evaporated away, that easily, just like that. Part of me couldn't let go that it was still some sort of joke, a prank as I picked myself from the floor, dumbfounded. "You know, you only get the cot, I'm taking my things out of here." He stormed in, pulling the thin comforter the two books, and the entire nightstand from the room, leaving me a small, wire mesh glorified sling- and a water heater.

Raziel dragged his things from the room, glaring at me the entire time, expecting resistance (which I would be glad enough to give) or some sort of fight, but I only pulled myself out of his direction, standing against the wall, baffled. What happened? Why would this be such a major flip, from being nice to being even worse than before? There was a strange way he twitched, like he was fighting a mental war in his head. Maybe he was over-reacting because he felt like he had given out too much trust? Maybe the Priest was this bad of an influence? Maybe Gauzier had said something to him that shook the guy up? I shook my head a little as he left the room, taking the pike and posting it diagonally over the doorway, like a giant 'No' sign.

"They really screwed you up, didn't they?" I said softly as he came back to the doorway, hanging his hands on the frame. The look on his face was indescribable, angry, tormented, deeply disturbed.

"You stay in this room like you are, if you're that monster, you go outside. No exceptions." The angel turned from the doorway abruptly, walking back towards the couch. That irked me, that I was being forced outside like a bad dog for something I had no control over, and that out of his great, deep mercy, he'd bust me over the head to let me back inside for another 24 hours. Gathering my annoyance I stormed to the door, trying to grab onto the pike to push it away, finding the whole wall electrified; a barrier. I pulled back my hand, singed and burned, hearing him laugh from the other side as I desperately shook my burnt palms out.

"Good to know that one still works!" He propped his feet up happily, stretching out on the couch as it dawned on me I really should've bargained for more than six pieces of bent wire and glorified rabbit fencing. "You're lucky to be inside at all!" I held my hand tightly, feeling it burn and sizzle.

"Bastard." I growled out, running to the back of the cot frame and turning it on its side, aiming at the door. The angel stopped laughing; leaning over to watch as I ran it, full speed, at the weapon. It connected, sparking and pushing on the barrier before as I suddenly felt the charge through the metal, shocking my hands and body. The frame shot away from the pike, throwing me back and into the water heater, denting it. I wheezed, the metal bars right into my ribs, tiredly pushing it away as I hit the floor, gasping for air. He didn't laugh this time, slowly going back to watching TV.

Coughing, sputtering for air I got to my knees, senses dislodged. I was eternally grateful that at the least the floor wasn't charged like the rest of the walls, that it was still safe...wait. I struggled, getting back to my feet to dawdle over to the other walls, feeling the same electrical charge on both sides, and the wall farthest from it. But maybe the ceiling was unguarded as well? Looking around for something small, I found a marble, covered in crust and wedged into the corner of the room. Carefully prying it away, I gave it a light toss towards the wall closest to me, marble shooting from it energetically. Good, good, this would work; I turned to the ceiling, tossing the marble upwards. It hit and dropped down as it would any other time.

"You can keep that marble, too" Raziel antagonized from the other side of the wall, "That's a gift from me and whatever kid lived here before we did."

"That's so generous of you." I grumbled out, dragging the cot frame to the side of the room just out of sight from him. I flipped the frame to stand on its headboard to make wide, finger sized mesh pockets acting like a ladder straight to the ceiling.

"Wait, what are you doing?" He leaned over farther, seeing my homemade escaping device and myself already halfway up. I grinned evilly, scrambling up the rest of it and through the unguarded ceiling above me. "Shit!" I could hear him distantly downstairs as my head poked through what apparently was the kitchen floor. Without hesitation I pulled myself through the tile, running away into another room, confused and desperate for a place to hide. It was a house of biblical proportion, really, not by the size, but by the massive amount of biblical things in it. Sad-faced women were everywhere, coddling leagues of swaddled babies and tiny men were crucified all over each wall like the Priest hunted them for sport. I darted from room to room, trying to find a good place to escape, or at least hide where it wasn't electrically charged. I had never really met the Priest, figuring if there was one type of person to stay far away from, it'd be him. By what I saw now, it was strengthening my opinion that Raziel's tether to the Priest was definitely infecting the way he did things, made him more irrational, difficult, almost bipolar.

My head whipped around, looking desperately for a resting place, spotting a couch far to the left of me, situated in some sort of quiet sitting room. Raziel was just behind me, up the stairs and charging along the same networks of hallways as I dove into the couch, half-passing through it, half resting inside of the thing, trying to control my breathing to not give myself away. It was getting later in the evening, I could hear a television on somewhere, other than the one in the basement. Even as far away from it that I sat, I could hear ranting, angry shouting, at least two or three men screaming at one another in a heated debate.

"Where are you!?" Raziel shouted out, not unlike the television program as I kept in my little hiding space, the middle of some couch in a sitting room. The Priest had to be watching this program, if that tether was anything like mine, this might be the cause of this strange, angry raid. "C'mon, you'll pop out eventually, you come out here now and I'll let you keep the room inside. If you don't well, you can have fun staying outside all the time." He laughed as he said it, voice getting closer and closer to where I lay. I began trembling, working hard to control my breathing and stay silent. He tapped the pike on the floor, hollow thumping.

"One thing I probably should've mentioned." His sinister voice was just over me now, "Anything I've ever tethered to, even if we're not linked anymore, I can still tell exactly where they are." My eyes snapped wide open- that bastard was humoring me; he knew exactly where I was!

"Dammit!" I leapt out from the couch, back into the living room just past him, dodging as he swiped at me, missing me by just inches. The angel grumbled, dragging the pike along the floor to hit me upside the head with it, knocking me over and into the next room, a large, wood covered floor and walls full of books. A library. Why was it always a damn library? Leaping back he tried to hit me again, bringing the pike back by his side, watching me trying to get away, unnerved and scared.

"Yeah! That's right! Tackle those bastards!" The Priest yelled from his room, riling Raziel up with no real reason to attack me. We both looked to his room for a second as I looked back to the angel, his face twitching slightly, hands shaking.

"This would've been so much easier if you just stayed out of the way in the room!" Raziel gritted his teeth together as he said it, like it was something he had to force out; I kept backing away, reaching a wall. I didn't want to die here. Or at least get cleaved in half on a bad mood, only to come back and get chopped to bits again. Pointing down the hall, I tried to reason with him.

"You know you're getting affected by that, you gotta, I dunno." I backed into the corner as he came closer, "Take some deep breaths or something! Relax!" The angel readied himself, bringing the pike far behind his back and winding up to strike me down, all because he felt the need to. I got angry, frustrated, feeling like I was infinitely responsible for whatever happened; I didn't deserve this and I was sick of having it all pushed on me. The angel swung the pike high over his head, full strength, no holding back as I retaliated, reaching behind me purely out of instinct, on a notion that was nothing more but panicked response.

I heard the air cut before I saw it, notches biting onto the pike and ripping it clear from his hands in one swift motion and straight into the wall. Two hands grasping it, I wielded the thing, a weapon of some sort, huge, flat and wide like I had been practicing my entire life for it. It was incredibly light in my hands, what I could only describe as a giant black metal paddle, at least ten feet long. And for the life of me, I couldn't tell you how it got there, but it broke the tension in a heartbeat. I suddenly realized what I had done, mind blanking completely as I looked at it in my hands, perfect, well-taught grip that I had, a red, almost evil light seeping from the notches on it. Just as quickly as I had pulled it out of thin air, the weapon drifted away, swept with the wind and gone from existence.

Completely in shock, I remained standing like that, Raziel doing the same, even as there was no weapon in either of our hands. We stood there, too stupid to realize there was still a problem, too confused and bewildered to say anything. It was the Priest who broke the silence, his screaming down the hall cracking into my terror- if I wanted this barrage to end; the screaming had to be remedied first. The great weapon caper would be solved later, accept it, do what needed to be done. Looking back to the angel who looked at me once more with a slight snarl I leapt backwards, falling into the room just behind me, one room away from where the Priest screamed indiscriminately. Raziel followed me immediately as I rolled to my feet, darting past the last room and into the Priest's sleeping room, where lo and behold, he had a football game on.

"Football?" I gasped, hearing Raziel just behind me as I dove for the TV cord, yanking it from the wall. That wouldn't do, still powered and angered by earlier I pulled it from the TV as well, the box sparking and going dim. Right off the bat, it didn't sate the Priest's anger as he jumped from his bed, yelling at the TV. Raziel was in the doorway, still angry as I dropped the cord, willing myself to fall through the floor, away from whatever destruction was due on me next. By a lucky chance, I dropped straight onto the couch in the basement.

The footsteps above me were frantic, but I could hear the Priest quieting down, the mood getting just the tiniest bit lighter. I watched the ceiling, looking where he'd drop through, looking where he'd strike next. This wasn't over; it all couldn't be over just that easily. While looking to the ceiling something hissed at me, Raziel peeking over the staircase that led down to the basement, the door still wide open.

"Hey!" He said, voice normal, still angry, but more under control, "What the Hell was that?" He rounded the corner, coming down the stairs like nothing had happened, like I had just swung by to watch the game and he had to get drinks. There was no remorse. None. Apparently normal Raziel was back at the helm, which unfortunately did not make me feel any better. My nails dug into the couch as he recognized something was wrong and stopped, slowly putting the pike against the wall and walking towards me like I was going to burst into flames.

"I'm sorry about that, he gets riled up, I can't help it. This whole demon in the same area constantly thing's still not really sitting with me, I thought putting you in the room would keep it all under wraps" He started backtracking, "But getting rid of the TV, yeah, that was a pretty good idea. Expensive, but a good idea." No amount of apologies or sorry's were going to make this up, just like that. I continued to tense as he came closer, getting to my feet and backing away from him. There was nothing but distrust and bewilderment that I could manage to hide, to accept the situation was under control and just go with it. It sat in my stomach like a rock, and I didn't understand why.

"I'm not going to do anything, he's calmed down, I'm calmed down, it's all okay." He was just in front of me now, standing there like my reaction was completely out of the blue. "So, uh, yeah, what was that weapon? I've never seen anything like it before." His eyes showed interest, showed no longing resentment for just chasing me down with the intent to chop me into bits for the last twenty minutes, or that he cared that what he did was incredibly terrifying.

Gritting my teeth I leaned back, slapping him across the face with every amount of force I had. His eyes went wide, shocked; face moved a significant amount where I slapped him. Still, no resentment. Just as angrily, I slapped him again, leaning forward and grabbing onto his shirt to twirl him about and slam that thick, stupid head of his into the wall.

"I know you can't understand me and for your sake, that's probably best right now." I could see the fear in his eyes; see the same sort of terror I had to go through on his little excursion as my voice went ominous and low. "I don't care if you're an angel, the devil or anything in between, there's no excuse for you to go around and beat up on me, when I've done NOTHING to you. I am NOT -" I picked his head a little from the wall and slammed him back into it.

"- your punching bag, and I'm NOT going to deal with your little bitch spaz fits when it's convenient for you!" My hands were shaking, "If you've got this problem, grow up and take care of it! Go run outside if you're hopped up on the angry! Don't go assuming that what you just did was excusable by ANY means, you piece of shit!" I dropped him from my grasp, storming off to 'my room' and snagging the pike along the way, dragging it behind me. Before locking myself away I gave him the finger immaturely.

"How's this translate?" I made sure he saw it as I took both hands on the pike, pulling back as hard as I could in the doorway to wedge it so tight the drywall cracked. Storming to my bed I gave it a kick, the frame knocking about the room before coming to rest with all four pegs on the ground. For the rest of the night, I lay there in silence; the smoke came by at 3 am and I was back to the demon body once again. Still, stubbornly, I remained crammed tight in that room and no one dared to say a word about it.

15

Time slogged on, my days panned out to have a lot of free hours in them, squatting in that tiny room with my less than tiny demon body in protest. The bed had long been shoved to the side, my limbs and extremities folded over one another in a heap, head and neck propped against one corner as my tail hit another two walls. It was miserable.

At the end of the third day, I forgot exactly what I was protesting, mind washing over itself, unable to keep up that unbending anger and sinking down into a thick, pasty muck of depression and isolation. I knew my original purpose was to show I refused to be that punching bag, that I refused to ignore what he had done after he thought it was okay to chase me down to kill me and blame it on the Priest's strangely passionate obsession with football. More then that, how attacking me and blaming someone else and taking no responsibility for becoming a controlling asshole was not going to fly. I didn't care if he was a saint from here on out, the side I saw was frightening. It was unpredictable and unstable, put these thoughts of doubt and fear into my head that at the next slight mood, I'd be out on my butt after so much hard work finally talking to one another. Maybe I kept myself in here to keep away from him. Maybe I was afraid to face him.

Occasionally, he'd huff and puff, come over by the room and yell things at my back that ranged from half-assed apologies, to insults, taunting, dares, un-funny jokes, ridiculing and back to apologies. I stayed silent through them all, batting the tiny marble around in the room, mind running over what happened for hours and hours, sleeping a large part of each day. The hot topic on my mind, besides angels, was my phantom sword/bludgeoning paddle weapon. Best I could figure, it appeared in my hands somewhere along the side of me, right out of nothingness. I didn't… activate it to come around, I didn't chant the magical words; it just became

159

real at a more than crucial time. When no one was looking I tried over and over to get it again, always ending up like I was looking for something or scratching my side. After the second day I gave up, figuring it a one-time fluke. It didn't ease my paranoid thoughts of being something much worse, much more demonic than I currently stood when properly assembled.

Somewhere around the fourth or fifth day of that week Raziel came up outside of my room once more, standing next to the pike still wedged into the wall. Instantly, I hunkered up, grunting a little and making sure that the only thing that angel could see was my very demonic butt. I let an eye wander back, bubbling to just about the brim of time I could spend in this room and keep my sanity intact.

He stood there for a second, slowly reaching forward to touch the pike, looking at the wall and shaking his head. Like a sacred, precious artifact he pulled it from the drywall, gently placing it just outside. Frustrated that for some reason his own rules didn't apply anymore, I scooted closer to the doorway, jamming the thing full of butt and legs, my tail filling the gaps. It was torturous for me to be in here, but I was in no mood to just try and accept him again as anything but a dangerous and reckless idiot. I'd given him so many chances already, and time after time... he just couldn't be trusted. Maybe I stayed in here because I knew there was no other life for me, I'd been banned from my first and this second one turning out to be full of heartache and despair, just as the demon had said. Maybe I was terrified of the world on my own, scared that the life I had envisioned outside those walls was a far cry from reality; still, those annoying blue eyes rung in my head as something important, they kept me tied here.

There was shuffling outside of the room, his big, bobble-head like face coming through the side wall and taking me by surprise. I jumped a little, pulling away from the door to curl opposite from him on the far side of the room, something of a few more inches away. He sighed, scratching his head before stepping completely into the room, arms folded.

"I'm sorry, alright?" He said flat as ever, more annoyed that I was hunkering down in his space, taking up his precious air. There was no sorry in that. Lifting my head just a bit to look him in the eyes, I scoffed, the only response I'd given in days and days before laying my head back down. Raziel breathed heavily, arms far out from his side, "What, that doesn't count?

"Not when it doesn't mean anything" I let the words drop away, no longer caring what happened after all this. If I was forced to live in the world on my own, I could do it, I'd at least try. Raziel walked a little farther in the room next to my shoulders, putting his one hand up; instantly I jumped, shuddered, even before the angel did anything. He pulled his hand away, looking to it, then to me as I lay my head back down warily.

"C'mon, you're not really afraid of me, are you?" It sounded like a joke to start, dropping to a whisper as I curled a little tighter. Leaving was starting to sound like a good idea. If I managed to get out of here on my own, it'd be a lot less stress for everyone involved, demon or angel. There was the sound of metal boots clicking together as he took a deep breath. "Then, I guess this is really all I can offer you." He said to the stagnant air, as I continued to ignore him. You could hear that awkward hesitation, all the confidence that whatever he was pulling would be enough to patch everything up going straight out the window. Coughing nervously, he forcibly spoke up again.

"C'mon, you gotta look, saying this out loud ruins it." He sounded like he was holding a new puppy or a box of gold; something really precious and sentimental. Sighing, I turned over to see him standing there, hand out, re-offering the same handshake I had on the rooftop a week ago. It was a sentimental gesture, don't get me wrong, but my God, he couldn't have picked a worse time to do it. I looked to him, then to the hand, then back to him. He meant it, I could see that he meant it honestly, and I had options to respond. There was politely refuse, laugh at him and be a real ass about it, or shake it, signifying meeting? Equal ground? Did it even mean anything right now? Nodding sagely, I chose the best option.

Quickly, sarcastic and demeaning I guffawed like he had on the roof, idiot laughing like someone had cut off the bottom of my brain. He looked hurt, but thankfully, I covered his face with my hand to wipe that hurt right away, grabbing him by the head and shoulders, shoving the angel forcefully back into the other part of the basement, through the wall. Before he could have the chance to re-group, I blocked the entrance with my butt again, leaning against that wall, back to playing around with the marble.

"What do you want from me?!" Raziel's voice gave a warbled crack from the other room. After a few minutes, he stormed away, talking with the Priest upstairs; probably to have him exorcise me right out of existence and kicked from the house. At least I had a marble to play around with. Time began to pass slowly once more.

I began to doze off, unaware what time it was, what it was like outside, knowing that my weather in here was water heater, with a chance of beige-colored utility room. Just as my eyes began to droop, I heard new voices entering into the house, excited and energetic about something, the sound of heavy clopping down the stairs. Exorcists, they had to be the cavalry, the guys you call when a stubborn demon refuses to get it's ass out of the doorway. They began to gossip just behind me, laughing and joyful as that angry little hurt began to spread and fester. Snorting, I growled a bit, showing my displeasure at whatever was going on.

Fingers began to poke at my toes, sharp little nails jabbing into the soft part of my skin ruthlessly. I'd show these people a thing or two, rearing back my leg to give them a hefty kick in the head should calm them down a bit. Shifting my stance I pulled my leg back a little and wound up, foot stopped instantly by the flat side of the pike. Raziel laughed awkwardly.

"Woah woah woah. Sorry, she's a little angry right now, probably thinks you're someone else." I picked my head from the ground, hearing a voice I never thought I'd listen to again.

"Neri?" Amber called from the other side of my butt-barrier as I practically did a complete circle around the room by the time she finished my name. Face to face, I could see her standing there, crutches under each arm. My heart broke to see her injured, but generally I was overwhelmed and instantly feeling much better.

"Amber!" I cried out, scooping her up carefully in my arms, suddenly feeling how desperately tiny this room was in an instant. Putting her down carefully I grabbed the pike, smacking myself in the back and popping out of the demon mist like a great magic trick. "How are you feeling?" I leaned down, helping her walk over to the couch. From the wrap it looked like a broken leg, just one, no other major injuries besides one long scratch on one cheek.

"Good! You found your other body!" She said incredulously as I leaned down for a hug. She looked over her shoulder, "Mom, she got her body back!" Katherine smiled and nodded, feigning enthusiasm.

"Good! That's good, right?" Awkwardly smiling, she turned to the Priest. "I still really don't know what that all means." The Priest nodded in agreement, shrugging.

"I stopped trying to explain things a long time ago."

"So how's the house? Any bad people come there since I left?" I sat on the couch, only then really noticing that my master plan of sitting and sulking forever had been foiled. Glancing outside, it turned out to be roughly late morning. I rubbed the sleep from my eyes, stretching out my back and arms as it felt good to stand up and walk around.

"Not really, someone came by selling papers, but Mom chased them off." She said, picking at her cast, "It's been really quiet since you left, are you having fun here?"

I gave a sarcastic hoot, silencing myself to reassure her I wasn't laughing at her. Raziel stood over by Katherine and the Priest, turned slightly towards me and Amber as I replied, being nosy and listening in.

"I am. There's a lot to do and the angel does lots of stupid things that make me laugh constantly, I'm having a lot of fun here." It wasn't entirely true, but it wasn't a lie.

"I'm glad you like it, we really miss you." She leaned over, hugging me around the waist. Bending down, I hugged back properly. "I'm glad you're coming back with us today!" My heart crumbled.

"No, I - I'm staying here, Amber" I hugged her tighter, "You're all grown now, you'll do just fine without me. But don't worry, I won't forget about you."

"I won't forget you either." She buried her head tighter as I patted her shoulders.

"Good, that makes me happy." I smiled deeply, slowly pulling her away from me as we both sat on the floor. My eyes wandered to the angel who was staring at the two of us with a lot of unusual interest. Our eyes locked for a second as I quickly looked away; indignant- just because I was in a good mood now didn't mean I had forgotten everything that happened. Turning back to Amber I grinned, leaning back to sit down. "So, how did your mom know where to find me?"

"We didn't. They called us." She pointed at the Priest, then to the angel, whose only response being found out was to raise his eyebrows and turn away smugly.

"Bastard." I hissed under my breath, half meaning it. It was a much better apology than 'I'm sorry alright? Now get outta my room' was.

"They said you were sad and needed cheering up. Why were you sad?" Amber asked innocently. Play the angel as the bad-guy? Couldn't do that now. Anything but accolades for having fun here on a scale less than 'amusement park' would make me seem like the bad person. Bastard indeed. I jumped around in my words, trying to pick them carefully.

"I was sad, they're right." I relented, squinting a little, " The angel uh, Raziel, doesn't understand anything I say."

"I could translate for you like I did for mom."

"No, no, that's okay; we've got a system going." I could feel the angel watching me, trying to decipher what I was saying based on Amber's responses. "I had so much fun living with you two that it's been an adjustment to new things, which is stressful and makes me sad." I managed to make her nod, understanding a little part of the truth.

"We're thinking about getting a puppy to replace you" Amber said bluntly. I laughed, a tad insulted but really thinking on it, I was probably puppy-status anyways. "But we've gotta get our house fixed first." The laughing stopped. No amount of puppy-related jokes could stop this wave of guilt. Katherine interjected.

"You're going to make her feel bad, saying that." She smiled, turning back to the Priest, "Insurance will cover it, we managed to claim it as an exploded gas line and we're only paying a moderate deductible."

"I'm sure it's as much our fault too, we can split that in half, each pay a bit. We don't try and end our exorcisms with injuries and the house falling to bits" The Priest walked from the room, looking for checks or something along those lines, Katherine following. It left the two non-living forms and a small, wounded child. He stayed by the wall, trying to give a little privacy by not just outwardly gawking at the two of us. It looked stupid, like he was forcing himself to stand in a corner.

"Ask him if he wants to come over here." I said flatly, trying very hard to keep a positive spin on everything at the moment.

"What was his name again?" She leaned over, both of us looking in his direction like we were telling secrets.

"Raziel." I scooted back by the couch and leaned against it, folding my arms. That awkward semi-conversation before someone caves and apologizes; I hated that conversation. Amber called out for him as he turned around theatrically like it was completely unexpected, walking over to the two of us and sitting down.

"Do you live down here?" Amber went back to playing with her cast, fingers picking at the hardened plaster edges. He looked between the two of us, wary this was some sort of trap, some scheme. As he dawdled on his answer I re-adjusted my arms, folding them tighter and giving him an expectant glare.

"I do, yes."

"Why don't you live in Heaven?"

"I have to stick around here to…" He looked at me, then to Amber, frowning to re-arrange his answer. "Keep things in order." I raised my eyebrows. First answer must've been 'to exorcise demons' but saying that to a kid whose friend was a demon would not score brownie points. Crafty bugger. Amber looked back at me, then to him, laughing before she even asked her next question.

"Do you do stupid things that make Neri laugh?" She said, looking to me for a reaction as I tried to force back a smile. Man, I missed this kid. Raziel frowned at the both of us, looking to the window quickly before back in our direction.

"Yeah, I guess so."

"Like what?" She asked, full attention to him as he glared at me like I was asking these myself. I only raised my eyebrows again, shrugging a little. Those kids, you know, and a large part of TV land knows, say the darnedest things all on their own. Before he could answer, Katherine came back down the stairs, digging into her purse and getting her car keys.

"C'mon pumpkin, time to go, we've got errands to run." She turned back to the Priest as I helped Amber up and gave her the crutches. Taking a hand under her arm I began to lead towards the basement door before stopping for a second.

"Hey." I got Amber's attention, nodding towards Raziel with the most parental look I could. "You have anything to say to him?" Thinking for a moment, her eyes lit up as the angel was unsure of the devious trick I was playing.

"Thank you for helping me!" Amber said happily, trying to give the overly-proper curtsy I had taught her years back. Laughing, I pulled her back up before she toppled over, wobbling a bit as she stabilized herself.

"You're welcome." Raziel muttered, almost sad for some reason. I kept myself focused on my task, not wanting to give too much positive reinforcement that I wasn't still annoyed and upset at last week's shenanigans.

"C'mon, no one expects you do to that when you've got a broken leg, a thank you is good enough." Snickering, we hobbled towards the end of the basement.

"Thanks again for calling us, she hasn't let up about finding out what happened to our little guard ghost since the hospital."

Raziel scoffed.

"Guard ghost?" I tried to stare a hole in his face, turning back slowly to Amber as she crutched her way towards the exit, walking her the whole way. Walking like I was visible flesh and blood we went outside, the sky overcast and raining lightly. The girl stopped before she was about to get into the sedan.

"I'm really glad I was able to see you." She leaned over as we hugged one another, squeezing her tightly.

"Me too. Heal up and don't worry about me, there's all sorts of fun I have to have." I looked at her, smiling, before hugging her again, "Be good, kid." I lingered in the hug before letting go, standing back as she got into the car on her own. I missed having a family.

"Bye." I waved at her as she rolled the window, suddenly excited.

"There are no goodbyes, only see you laters!" She said quickly as the car backed up, Katherine opening the window just a bit.

"They taught her that in class. Bye!" She said quickly, pulling out of the driveway. The car lurched into gear as I waved, mother and child suddenly speeding away, out of view. I stood there in the rain, the noise of thunder picking up as the rain grew more steadily. Slowly, my eye crept behind me, looking to the house I knew I had to go back into, where I knew I'd have to deal with the problem that I avoided for days and days. Grumbling, running my hand through my hair I sighed over and over, turning back towards the door, back to the angel, back into the hornets nest of annoyance and temper.

I got so far as the second stair down into the basement before the barrage started.

"Was that a better apology?" Raziel said, leaning just outside of the wall of my room, the tiny windowless wonder with the beige accents. Taking a deep breath, I gave a nod, that yes, huzzah, that was a better apology; I tried to walk back into my room, his hand shooting out across the door frame in front of my face. It was kind of expected.

"No, that marathon of sulking is over, you stay out here." I could tell already he was getting frustrated.

"Fine." I turned away, flopping down on the couch and stretching out. "I can just bitch and moan all I want out here." I rubbed my head on the pillow, purposely trying to be invasive if 'this whole demon thing wasn't really sitting well with him'. Giving a thought, I grated my feet into the couch as well. The action felt hollow, like nothing. It was like I gave up trying to talk with him, relying on stupid childish antics. We couldn't communicate and it was growing to be a big problem if we were trying to be anything but stupid, bitter enemies. I sighed, rubbing the bridge of my nose and sighed all over again. I think we both at least communicated that frustration enough.

"I can't have a conversation with you. I don't know what your problem is." He said just as exasperated as I felt, suddenly storming towards me. I opened one eye, instantly pulling away on the couch and into the corner, even as he grabbed onto my wrist, dragging me behind him as he jumped through the wall. Well, this seemed oddly familiar; I managed to get my feet underneath me, getting pulled straight away from the house as the two of us walked quickly. What the Hell was he trying to prove? Was this is it? The big eviction into the world, the end of our jolly good try to understanding?

We continued to march away from the Priest's home, through other houses, past other streets, far away from my tiny dank little room. He didn't say a word, face frowning, fixated dead in front of him, determined. His hand had a strong, angry grip around my wrist, pace continually rushed and hurried as we walked in silence, storming away from the Priest. I kept quiet, afraid.

At least six blocks away our steps began to reverberate, began to rattle the ground around me as I started feeling that pull, that net wrapping around life beginning to fray. He felt it too, his pace immediately slowing down like we were traveling through a horrible blizzard; but step after step we moved forward, arrogantly braving the unraveling world. I knew what he was doing.

"Hey, wait a second!" I pulled my wrist from his grip as he continued on without me, one foot after the other in defiance. "I thought that was a one-time thing, won't you get in trouble for doing this on purpose?" I stood back a bit, genuinely worried.

"I… kind of …heard that." He said, gritting his teeth and taking more labored steps away, teetering on the edge of his field. Looking back at me for a second he took that last step, suddenly breaking through it, hopping on one foot and turning around quickly, eyes panicked like a fish out of water. I ran up alongside him as he slapped my hand, that same blue, glowy shit from the first time ebbing away into my skin. Just as instantly as before I felt a large part of my energy drop away, bringing me to my knees, gasping for air.

"Oh, you crazy…stupid…" I said warily, hands gripping the ground like I'd fall over. "Couldn't pick a time when I wasn't already tired?"

"There. Now. Go ahead." He too gasped for breath, the two of us kneeling there like idiots, breathing as asthmatics for a few minutes.

"What are you trying to do, take me to prom or something?" I wheezed for breath, shaking my head a little, "This wasn't necessary."

"I suck at charades and I'm not in the mood to figure out how to read lips." He threw his arms at me tiredly. "So, what's the matter with you?"

I looked around, more enthralled about dodging the conversation than confronting him and having to actually answer that question.

"How is this marsh so close to your house?" I said with despondent interest.

"What? What is it? Are you afraid of me after what happened?"

"Gosh, I don't want to get you in trouble for talking with demons now..." I said, still dodging the conversation; looking up at him to find him glaring like I've never seen anyone ever glare before. It practically kicked the truth out of me. "I'm not afraid of you. Not really, anyways. Caught me off-guard, scared the Hell out of me."

"So that's it?" He egged on.

"No, I know you can't really do anything to actually kill me." I crossed my arms, a little cold, getting a little more of a nerve. "But I'm not going to put up with…whatever the Hell you want to try and blame that on again. Go get a punching bag- an ACTUAL punching bag if you're rattled off your gourd."

"And that's why you stayed in the room for five days?"

"No. That's not why." I looked back at him, brimming on the truth, reluctant to trust him at all, no matter the somewhat kind somewhat thoughtful steps he had taken to make this happen. He came closer to me, the argument starting to feel like an old, bickering couple.

"What is it, why won't you just tell me?"

"Because I can't trust you!" I snapped at him, walking around a little, nervous, "I've tried. I've really… really tried to, but time after time, again and again, you show me that I can't. I'm tired, Raziel, I'm worn out from all of this."

"Tru...You think I can trust you?" He burst out in a mix of surprise and frustration, fueled by my own. "You think this is easy? You ever had the same text, the same saying beat into your head over hundreds and hundreds of years, that demons are only there to be killed, and especially not to be trusted. That they'll charm you right into damnation, pluck you straight from the sky and force you into their own services." My reeling mind stopped, forgetting that side of things.

"Now try having one in your home, who's not doing anything wrong, who was helpful when you needed it and you're stuck thinking 'Is this part of the trap? Is this the part where they kick me out for good? Is what I'm doing wrong?'" He let his hands hang down, tired. "If only you were easier to kill, none of this would've happened. I should not be caring as much as I do whether or not some demon sits around and sulks, tormented by what you call trust issues!"

"You literally tried to kill me seven times in a row!" I threw my hands up in exasperation, like I was the only person talking sense. "You were the first person I ever had contact with, and you instantly tried killing me over and over!"

Raziel was quick to snap back.

"You're a demon!" Something sharp and thorny stuck me from all sides, this tiny angry little lightning bolt lighting up that idea above my head. It hit a very agitated nerve. "What else am I supposed to do?"

"THAT." I snarled, getting a finger down on what I was actually mad about. "It's exactly THAT."

"Exactly what?" Raziel rolled his eyes, about two short snippy answers and three screeching sentences away from just storming off.

"I..." I looked around, trying to figure out best how to say it, how to dump the bucket of issues I had where they didn't go everywhere at once. The angel wasn't in a patient mood. "I just..."

"You just what?" He huffed with a sneer, pushing that final button that opened the giant doors on the big pile of fear and terror that had been clawing at my guts since day one.

"I didn't WANT this!" I screeched, making him take a step back. "I didn't ask for ANY of this!"

"I didn't ask to be a demon! I am the bad person here, and I don't even get to kno--" I choked on my words, tone warbling hard enough to catch myself off guard. "..I don't even get to know why!" I could feel miserable, worn tears start streaking down my face.

"I worked my ASS off to be the opposite of what people thought I'd be- I had to listen to years of the same story of the big terrifying demon that wrecked my host family's lives knowing full well that was some part my fault." I wiped my face once, voice ragged and distraught, "I am well aware of where I stand in this world, and I'm well aware I'm not welcome, okay? So you can cut that 'You're just a demon, I ought to be killing you' bullshit out right now, because trust me, I'm aware of it." I seethed, looking up the slightest bit to see he was no longer parading around his asshattery, surprised.

"So how am I supposed to act, then? I try my best, I get stabbed in the heart. I try to fight back, I get gutted like a fish." I sniffled, wiping my eyes again, "I can lie and pretend all I want that I'm not, pretend that it's all some sort of mistake, but the underlying thing is that I can never...beat... that. Bottom of the barrel. It doesn't matter how good, or nice I try to be, I'm screwed, regardless. So what's the point?"

Flopping my hands against my lap in exasperation, it all came bubbling out.

"What can I do, Raziel? Huh? How am I supposed to act?" I took a step forward, voice drowned in frustration as he only took a step to the side, but not away. "I had a decent life going, and you took the only good thing I had left--- you spoiled my heinous, insidious demon plot of trying to ignore I was a Goddamn demon in the first place!" Clenching my hands tightly, I looked away, furious.

"You've taken every good thing I had and left me with the reminder that no matter how nice, or how good I try to be, I am ALWAYS going to be the demon. You want to know the worst of it? Want to know what makes all of this so much more fun?" I faced him directly, snarling. "I AGREE with you!"

"I'm petrified wondering if it's in my natural programming to be the giant moral butthole of the universe! If you hired some other exorcist pals to come by and wipe me off of this earth today, I couldn't cared less." My tone broke, "I didn't want this! I didn't ask to be a demon! You think little miss goody-two shoes here wants to summon a giant, fuck-off weapon that looks like the gates of Hell? You think that helps things? You think I'm happy that exists? Without it, maybe I can assume something went wrong, but with that? With some crazy, stupid boat oar piece of shit weapon?"

I seethed angrily as he just stood there, shocked while the truth all flooded out. I couldn't keep it in if I wanted to.

"All the while, I get to deal with some familiar eyed dickhead who thinks bravado and deception is a better moral compass." I started out angry, tears suddenly racing down my face again. "Who doesn't have to try to be good. Who I trusted that maybe I could have something stable, something better, that there was some glimmer of hope. That I had an actual chance." I lowered my head, letting my tears fall down by themselves, tired.

"Then at the first hiccup, everything goes wrong, and I'm still just the demon."

Raziel made a sound like he was going to say something, closing his mouth as I brought my head up the tiniest bit. I felt stupid; vulnerable. How was he supposed to respond to that? Crumpling a bit more, I kept my eyes tight on the ground, watching the water wash beneath my feet.

"You don't know what it feels like to have everything taken from you, because that's what it's 'supposed' to be. You work so hard to prove people wrong, and it's never enough. Why bother being anything better? Why bother trying? Why not just fall into those stereotypes, if that's what I'm supposed to be doing?" A sick, grim smile appeared on my face, "What if other demons are right?"

My whole body felt cold and lifeless as I thought on it for a moment. Who the Hell was I kidding.

"I don't want to hurt anyone. I don't want to be that." Wiping my face one more time, I ran a shaky hand through my hair. "I can't expect you to know what it feels like to have everything you meet hate you, to have everything taken from -" I stopped, glancing back up with a thought.

Raziel looked as miserable as I felt, standing there, wings hanging out just enough to show the unnatural edge they had to the side, wings chopped to bits. He didn't say anything, he just had this worn, tragic look, like he'd lived that thought for a thousand years, drowned in those same fears years and years ago, leaving behind a desperate, empty soul. That he was probably well aware of what I was going through ten minutes ago. I felt like an idiot. Any snippet of arrogance that was once present in this conversation was long gone.

I stopped talking, only taking a dejected sigh and clearing the last of the tears from my face. I take it back. I think he did actually understand where I was coming from, maybe even better than I did. What a mess.

Everything inside me felt twisted and sick.

I kept my eyes to the ground, twisting, turning about to face away from him. The rain alongside us began to pick up a little as I slogged jaggedly towards a rock, emotionally dead.

My hands wouldn't stop shaking.

I sat down, running my hands through my hair nervously. Raziel remained standing there, head to the side, brows furrowed. What a day.

The sound of rain filled the silence for at least ten minutes as we stared opposite of one another awkwardly. My priorities and ambitions were everywhere. I knew I was a demon. I don't know why this surfaced now, of all places. I don't know why I thought telling him this would change anything. I mean, he probably understood in some regard I wasn't trying to be the absolute worst thing on this earth.

The real kicker to all of this is that no matter how much we wanted to parade around that we couldn't trust one another, we did. It's nice to think you still have boundaries when you say you don't trust the angel that spent 3 years figuring out best how to destroy you, but I trusted him enough that I wasn't afraid for my life right now. Same went for the inverse-he wasn't armored or protecting himself, and he was actively trying to fix a situation without the use of force. We probably trusted each other more than our own respective sides. What a frustrating thought.

"I wouldn't worry about what people think." He suddenly spoke up, sounding just as sad. I stopped, raising my head up a little, confused. Was he kidding? Lowering an eyebrow, he only looked away, "People are going to assume regardless. Words don't mean much." Not quite getting his intent, I raised my head up a little more, back towards him with my voice froggy and dry.

"What do you mean?" The angel only shrugged, just as indirect.

"It's not your job to change people's minds, that's what I mean." He sounded almost happy saying it, but the face he held was still concerned and depressed. Smiling at his surprisingly upbeat advice with the crook of my mouth, I gargled out my dour response.

"And what does that mean if I was a serial killer in a former life?" Raziel frowned, hands in his pockets as he slowly began to walk over towards me.

"I don't think you were a serial killer." Drowned in a pit of emotion and selfish wallowing, I was happy to turn back to sarcasm, covering up those mile-deep holes once again. I didn't pick up that he didn't think I was a bad person and mistook it for some sort of critical analysis.

"How can you tell?" I asked, unfolding myself a bit more. Raziel walked to the other side of the rock without a response, just a series of shrugging and indirect answers.

"Oh, I can't." He said quickly as I waited for more, latently disappointed in a sarcastic way.

"Thanks." I snapped again before realizing just how much I needed to get those issues off of my consciousness. I looked back to the ground, guilty at taking an unnecessary amount of time to face my personal demons. If I hadn't acted like such a brat, this situation wouldn't have gotten this bad. "I'm sorry, Raziel. Just about everything. This wasn't your fault."

"No, it is."

"Well okay, it is, but it's unfairly lumped in with a lot of other stuff you didn't cause."

"Pretty sure I caused those too." I gave a dry, dead huff, shaking my head.

"Maybe."

"Well, I'm sorry for chasing you around the house. Among other things." I gave a sideways smile, happy to at least have that. "I mean, it's not just the demon thing. I haven't had someone, you know, stay in the same place before."

I looked up, giving a blasé sort of stare as he reorganized his thoughts a bit.

"It's all just weird." His voice went low again." But what happens now?" He slowly took a seat opposite me on the other side of the rock; echoing the same confusion, the same want to know how this all played out; just as raw, as worn, as conflicted.

"I don't know." I whispered, rain rolling off the rock, rippling and reflecting this world around it. He was right- I was stuck where I sat- I was always going to be evil. That would always be inherent. I looked down to the warbling mirror beneath my feet showing only the grayed sky; the two of us remained bone dry, separate, hated, misunderstood, shunned and confused from life around us, both stuck playing into a fight with the other side.

There was an awkward hand suddenly patting my back like a mistake, repeating and landing once more in consolation. The touch was shaky. It almost felt like sarcasm, like 'it's okay- I think' but I smiled, just barely. Neither of us really had a clue. The hand pulled away as Raziel turned back to the outside world, quiet again.

"We really should've talked about actual things on the trip back here." I sniffled with a threadbare smile. The angel made a similar chuckle. "Would've cut the time sulking in half, at least."

"Probably, yeah."

"Thanks for calling my family." I smiled warmly, remembering them. "I didn't think I'd ever see them again."

"It's no problem. I could tell they really missed you." He snorted a little. "If that was a curse, it was a pretty convincing one."

"I couldn't curse anyone if I tried; I can barely make scrambled eggs." I laughed softly, grinning like a tired, stupid idiot. It was infectious, both of us laughing to a terrible joke, laughing out loud amongst the marshland, in the rain. Laughing like we missed it. Like we needed it.

I quieted down.

"Why do you think we can't understand one another normally?" The sky around us continued to storm, the whole area of marshland gloomy and overcast. "That first demon, the crazy flying one, called it something like an Angelic divide." The angel looked to me, nodding a little.

"I've actually heard that term before too. Though always from the crazy demi-angelic sects."

"Demi-angelic?" I raised an eyebrow, readjusting myself on the rock. He nodded.

"Fallen who manage to find one another, gather and protest outside some churches. It's written on their signs, though they're chanting in another language." He tilted his head a little, "Different than whatever you're speaking"

"Why was it such a shock that I was finally able to communicate with you when the giant mutating mist-monster could?" I turned around a little to look at him, giving the lightest dismissive shake of my head.

"Bigger demons like that tend to speak this interim slush-language, you hear both Latin and English at the same time. It's hard to listen to." Thankful he was being much more apparent than before, I gave a thoughtful harrumph.

"And right now, I don't?" I elaborated, rolling my hand. Raziel shook his head no.

I raised my head a little, bringing it back down on my knees, contemplating things, but altogether worn out. My arm was just in front of me as I watched the rain pass through, the earth ignoring me; looking to Raziel, it did the same thing, ignored by everything around us. Neither of us was actually a part of this world, just humoring ourselves by working alongside everyone else.

But in that same problem, we were equals. I practically put my head on the rock, exhausted.

"God, I'm drained." All the emotional fanfare earlier really zapped my extra energy. I could see Raziel nodding behind me.

“I know.”

Grinning, I tried to focus.

“So we can’t be friends.” I said flatly as he looked towards me, then to the ground and shaking his head no.

“That’s high on the list of things that would get me in trouble.”

I looked at him for a moment, trying very desperately to dredge up whatever rage I could, whatever hatred I could boil together, trying to see if there was anything left in me to keep me from what I think we were about to decide. Empty; shaking my head, I put my chin back to my knees.

“I don’t hate you. I keep trying to, but I think the ridiculousness compensates.” I chuckled a little saying it, echoed by Raziel as he laughed softly.

“And you’re not….so evil.” That actually came to me as a bit of a shock. “That I know of.” He meant it as a joke, a bit of a prod. I smiled happily, wiping my eyes and leaning back with a bit more energy, feeling better.

“There’s got to be a way to make this work- A sort of truce, since neither of us can really harm one another at the moment... right?” I questioned as he suddenly rolled his eyes, shaking his head with a groan.

“Yeah, they don't pay enough for that.” He rumbled out as I huffed out a laugh. So we both sat there, thinking a term that'd make us friends but still distant enough that from a literal standpoint, we weren’t really friends. Allies… it was close, allying with a demon was still something shunned, apparently. After a few more minutes of diligent, tired thinking we came to a viable answer.

“How about associates?” I chewed on the word as Raziel crinkled up his face.

“I’m definitely not supposed to be associating with d... you know.” The fact he wouldn't say it like it was taboo made me chuckle for second.

“Di-ssociates, then.” Raziel stopped, eyes flat and tired.

“I don't think that's even a real word.”

“That's what makes it one, a good pun, and two, a great word to use.” The angel stared far into the swamp as I explained, sigh slowly escaping like a shriveling balloon. “What are they going to do? I know for a fact they don't have a law against if it's a somewhat fake word in this context.”

“Also that's probably the best I’ve got, and it's all downhill from here.” He sighed again as I kept going. “You'd think sleeping in a room for five days would make you well rested but here we are.”

“I regret being able to understand you.” Raziel muttered. The unabashed smartassery cracked me up.

This felt honest, felt relaxed, unpreserved and real conversation, what I longed for dearly. Still, we knew it was wrong, we knew we were supposed to hate each other, communication was practically nothing, and we were still driven to try and be friends. We both had to be a little touched in the head.

"You think we're just humoring ourselves until this ends in a horrible blood bath?"

I meant it as a joke, I honestly did. Raziel looked around him, squinting, looking to the clouds and taking a lot of heavy, contemplative breaths.

"Probably."

"So we're not friends."

"No. Dissociates. I guess."

"Completely different."

"Yes." He tilted towards me a little, staring for a moment before hastily re-re-offering up the handshake. It was starting to seem like a bad punch line, now. "To not being friends." He stated, giving it an actual meaning, a purpose.

"I swear this Goddamn handshake is going to follow me forever." I grumbled under my breath with a smile, hesitating.

I looked to it as it became the culminating moment, that big, stupid decision to make or not to make. We weren't idiots, thinking this was going to work forever, that by miracle after miracle, this was going to seem okay to anyone else who'd manage to learn about it. This was a bad decision. It was selfish. But we could drop this act, drop this need to fulfill our designated roles, to give up on the combative hatred and just be two idiots stuck together. Looking back to the angel, I looked to the hand. Could I do this to myself?

To him?

With a huff, I shook that hand.

"My name is Neri, I'm from a skeletal conga line in Hell, and I don't answer to anyone." I grinned as Raziel frowned for a moment in concern. I slapped my other hand on the top of our handshake. "There. Now we're all caught up. That's my secret. I'm the most clueless, uninformed demon out there. That's everything I know." He paused before rolling his eyes.

'To die will be an awfully big adventure' I was determined to make that so. Continuing to shake his hand, we both had a look like our palms were made with live grenades as the handshake stopped; both of us looking distantly away, knowing full well what we had done.

"We're so dead." I said, frowning as happily as anyone could ever frown. I wanted to giggle, to laugh, be giddy; I had made a friend.

"We're already dead." He said, standing up from the rock, shaking his head a little. Gathering to my feet as well, I unknowingly mimicked him, shaking my head at a whole lot of nothing. We were so very doomed.

With a moment of hesitation, we set out back towards home.

16

"Get it! Kill it!"

I egged him on from the couch, trying to be encouraging. Another football game thundered upstairs, the Priest screaming at the new, much bigger, much more testosterone-aggravating TV in the quiet room. At least this time we were both well aware how to skirt this situation, to keep it as benign as an angel beating the shit out of a punching bag, pretty much envisioning my face on the front of it, could be. There'd been a buying excursion, purchasing a new TV, a punching bag, and a new mailbox, along with other little things along the way.

"C'mon, you call that punching? PUNCH, you baby!" I yelled at him as he stopped, resting against the bag with his glare panning my way. Not that he could understand anything, but you can tell an insult just by the gusto you put into it. As those over-drugged, angry eyes got to me, delivering the message he didn't appreciate being heckled by the lowly demon infesting his home, I sat up straight, pointing to the bag.

"Don't look at me like you're gonna rip my arms off, go beat up the bag if you're angry!" I panicked, sitting back properly on the couch, farther away. His glare switched back, throwing a set of rumbling punches before wobbling with exhaustion; another round of cheering and shouting escalated. He had brought friends. Football was a fandom more than one Priest shared, and now they were having an angry little pow-wow together upstairs. Thankfully, none of the other Priests were licensed exorcists or could see Raziel and I.

"Why do these games have to go on for…" He grit his teeth, punching the bag especially hard, "THREE HOURS." You could tell he was frazzled, that there was really nothing but a drive to beat the crap out of something, being manipulated on a simple level. It seemed like torture; I got from my seat, dashing upstairs to go check the score, go check why this was still going on and standing by the TV. Overtime. Team A and Team B were getting ready to kickoff for another round. This was still not over; shaking my head I walked over by the Priest's bedroom, falling through the floor halfway there, landing neatly back onto the couch in the basement.

"Overtime?" He said tiredly, leaning against the bag like a drunk. I nodded slowly, switching directions and shaking my head. He turned back to the bag and kept at it for a few more punches before altogether slumping against it, knees buckling. You couldn't help but feel bad, but still, it was a lot better than that being my face. Or getting chased around until TV cords were ripped out. He slowly looked over to me, not angry, just miserable as I got from the couch, pointing him towards where I sat.

"Here, c'mon, that's enough." I helped him to his feet, the angel looking to me for a moment with the tiniest hint of malice, like a tired, overworked circus bear looks at the handler that on a better day he'd think about acting out. But like this, it was the slightest notion immediately dismissed that doing something required energy that the bear just didn't have. Raziel gave a sort of worn out huff, climbing to the couch and breathing hard. Even if it meant I had to sit around with a paper bag on my head, this tactic had done well enough that I really didn't have to worry. I stood next to the bag now, eying it like an opponent before stopping.

"How do you get this much..." I went and grabbed my disguise hoodie, now returned, "...sweat on a bag when we're literally spirits. How is that even possible?" I used the hoodie to wipe off the punching bag as Raziel immediately grumbled.

"Mmmhhhh." He protested into the cushion, weak and disarmed like an over-swaddled infant, helpless to do anything as I ruined the sanctity of this dirty hoodie found crammed in the utility hatch of the Transit. I waved the hoodie at him.

"It's YOUR sweat!" Looking at it once more, I shook my head, "Somehow!"

Raziel looked tiredly miserable as I waited for a moment, offering him the hoodie.

"Why, you cold? The angel looked away a little more with an incredible amount of frump, making some sort of inhuman high-pitched whining, placing one hand over his face. "Don't be a tired baby." He stayed that way, jumbled in a pile like he fell asleep.

Smiling and sticking it to the side, I got back to business.

Hopping onto the balls of my feet I stood there, waiving and juking like the punching bag was an actual opponent, keeping my hand turned towards me, defensively. I could see him watching me do it, skeptical with my expert stance and technique.

"Take notes." I said professionally, shimmying around the bag and giving it a dead eye. With little care or knowledge of what I was doing a threw my punch, hearing my fingers crack over themselves. Pulling away,

I shook my hand by my side, pursing my lips like it was all intentional. I didn't have to look at Raziel to know he could see right through my bluffing. I continued on, throwing another punch, barely moving the bag at all. This form was so weak it was almost shameful. Snorting, I punched again and again, before growing so frustrated I tried headbutting the bag. It moved quite a bit more.

"No shock you're better at that than your crappy punches." He said tiredly from the couch, shaking his head at me before just laying face down. "You gotta turn your wrist before you hit, keep your arms up and guarded." I mimicked the actions as he said it, giving a little whistle to make him turn back and check.

"Yeah, like that."

I looked back to the bag, getting closer as I kept the same position that was apparently correct, tilting a little side to side as I gave it my all, hand and a few bones snapping painfully against the bag.

"FUCK!" I yelled, dancing around a little and cradling my hand as it healed itself, shaking the thing out once more until it was good as new. I could hear him laughing at me, face down into the couch to stifle it like that was any real help, wings flipping up and about like on a pair of tangled strings. Determined to keep on trying at the very least I went back to the bag eying it like it was someone I really hated. Gauzier came to mind, but I more hated him by association, Raziel I hated on occasion, but I had no real thing to personify my anger towards. I stopped, looking at the bag like a face would suddenly appear and drive me to throw an actual punch. Frowning hard enough to put wrinkles on a baby I gave up, kicking the bag once for good measure and walking away.

"Hold on, you're not far off." The angel shuffled to his feet, standing tiredly and showing both of his palms that he wasn't a threat, or jacked up on the crazy for the time being. I scooted out of the way as he took up the stance again.

"Put most of the pressure on your leading foot, keep your hands up, and just…" He glared at the bag, punching it once, hard enough to move the bag around on its chains. "See? Easy."

"Yeah, this from the guy who punched me across a room. You have an unfair advantage." I grumbled as he stood aside, staggering on his feet. The game upstairs was quieting down, Priests talking amongst themselves as the two announcers jabbered on and on; the game must've just ended.

"Oh thank God." Raziel said tiredly, jumping to the same conclusion as I set up my stance again, glaring hard at the bag as I focused, trying to remember it all. Dodging and weaving I committed myself, throwing a punch a hard as I could. It hit. It didn't bust my wrists in the process, no bones were broken; It just didn't move the bag an inch. Raziel bust out laughing, covering his hand with his mouth quickly like my dignity wasn't already spilled out onto the floor. I frowned once again, looking to him, hoping I did it wrong, that I really wasn't that horribly weak.

"I'm sorry, it was fine, that was exactly how you do it." He looked to me, fanning himself, "It's just... God damn, maybe you should just stick to fighting the other way?" Groaning, I lowered my head, frustrated and annoyed. That bad. I was that bad. Even my half-assed wrong painful punches got better results than an actual one. He wouldn't let up. He continued to laugh, hands on his knees as I just stood there, the fool.

Determined to prove myself one way or the other, I locked in my stance, glaring at him instead. Maybe proper motivation was needed. Real motivation. Punching a bag didn't make me feel like I accomplished anything, but punching something that really annoyed me... I let out a quick jab at him across the face, his head snapping to the side quickly as he fell straight down onto his ass, dazed.

"Oh ho ho, God, Raziel, I'm sorry!" I retched in horror, cackling the whole time. "I figured it'd be like a feather hitting a concrete slab, I didn't think it'd actually do anything!" He remained sitting, shaking his head out a little; the angel tried to pick himself back together.

"I'm sorry, Raziel. Genuinely sorry." Offering him a hand, I found I wasn't even strong enough to pull him from the floor. "I mean, I know I'm laughing but I am sorry."

A noise clopped down the stairs, the Priest looking around the doorway and shouting into the basement.

"Hey, time to go, we've got a call." He paced about above us, picking up a few things, keys jingling. There wasn't any time to dawdle; Raziel remained sitting on the ground, not only exhausted, but disoriented from getting punched straight in the face. By me. It still made me feel good.

"C'mon, you gotta get up." I went behind him, pushing at his back to put him into a crouch, in from that I pulled him into a stand. He looked at me, angry and spacey.

"That hurt like hell." He said, scrunching his face up, slowly wandering towards the door in strange, off center patterns. I watched him lean hard on the wall up the stairs, toddling straight into the other wall as he danced his way out the door. Halfway to the car, I noticed he was walking empty handed, dashing back into the house and snagging the pike from the wall as the three of us packed up to go. The house was around twenty minutes away, the Priest loosely talking in the van as he drove, turning onto the interstate highway.

"Fairly routine, Raziel." He stated loudly. I could see him stretching out, his eyes glaring at me angrily as they swiveled back to the Priest while he continued on. "Family's been hearing growling, children have been getting scratches across their backs, markings on the wall, all that. Probably the same one it always is. Shouldn't be too hard for you, right?"

"Easy work." He said tiredly, yawning and stretching out again. He didn't seem so appalled by the idea of a semi-physical thing sleeping any longer, though you'd find him just sitting there, eyes empty and hollow as he stared at the TV all night. Every time I noticeably woke up for one reason or the other around the middle of the night, he'd suddenly get up, start doing something like he was self-conscious about letting all the time go to waste. Sometimes, for kicks, I'd just move around in the bed a little bit, and instantly, you'd hear other things going off, the weight machine going, or now the new edition punching bag being worked on. None of it really proved that an insomniac's lifestyle was a pleasant one.

Pushing against the back seat I sat up straighter just a bit; I'd been in this body for a few days, when it got to be around 3 am that night, just re-seal my back, try to go about my day. It still felt like my insides were melting out of my spine, but I did enjoy the things I could do as a small, compact, tiny little normal human thing; picking up things, turning in a circle without knocking items over, being able to fit into a space without my neck cracked at a funny angle. But it was bony and hard to sit in for long periods of time, and the cold got to me like my clothes were made of paper.

The car traveled along, switching from highway to highway as we made our way to the house in question; the Transit hit a sort of shaking point going as fast as it's undersized wheels could that I noticed something. Lack of a certain noise; something big, something stupid, something painfully obvious that either my tittering or his lack of awareness should've told either one of us on a better day. Leaning over to see him confirmed it.

Bringing my leg back peacefully I kicked hard at the back of his chair, making the tired, groggy angel turn around like I lit the back of his head on fire.

"What? What is it?" He hissed at me, eyelids sliding over each eye so warily slow. I pointed to my shirt, pinched the fabric then pointed back as he squinted his eyes a little and shook that big, lopsided head of his. "Why? What's wrong with my-" Raziel grabbed at his own shirt, getting a handful of fabric before pushing himself farther away. There was no armor. None. We'd left it back at the house; if I hadn't grabbed the pike when I did, there'd be no weapon either.

"Dammit!" The words seethed between his teeth as he looked around desperately like a chest piece was hiding underneath the car's overhead mirrors. The rest of the car ride was spent scouring every inch for any segment of armor, something that wasn't so beck and call. Nothing.

The house was almost stereotypical. Old. Rustic. A long, winding curvy road up to the house, the jumbled, decrepit gate that was half torn down, half fallen over. It was the type of house you find in bad cartoon episodes, the only thing we missed was a convenient thunderstorm, maybe an old man sitting out in the front with a pitchfork. Thankfully the yard was a different story, three kids played soccer or some sort outside while the parents watched from the porch, an older grandfather sitting behind them and reading the newspaper in the afternoon light.

As we left the van they came running up, touching the tacky decals on the side of the Transit, little fingernails already digging into the paint job. Raziel motioned me off to the side, away from the rest of the commotion.

"I can't…" He seemed rushed, voice choppy and ashamed, nervous for anyone around to hear him say anything, "I can't exorcise this demon without that armor." Doing an extremely exaggerated 'why' motion, he looked over his shoulder before speaking again.

"Listen, it's not the same for me as it is for you. If I get my arm ripped off I bleed to death, it doesn't re-grow, nothing happens, it's just gone." Well. That made things quite a bit more serious. Staring at him and putting my arms out to the side, he turned away from me and stormed back towards the van.

"Well, if someone hadn't punched me in the damn face, and I will get you back, then this wouldn't be a problem." He hesitated, running his thumb over the handle of the pike, over the very slight teeth marks I'd left in it, frowning. Thinking for a moment, he turned the handle towards me, this flat, unhappy look in his eyes. I gave a dramatic shrug.

"Well I'm SORRY for having paring knives for teeth, Raziel." Waving my hands around, I got his attention away from the never ending blame train.

"I'll help, okay? I will be the punching bag for this one to the best of my ability." I pointed to myself, "Me. HELP" Raziel struggled to decipher my message, shaking his head no.

"You'll… what?" He was tired and aggravated, I was quickly joining him, so I turned to the van and used a fingernail to write 'help' in the lumpy paint job and pointed to it. You would've thought I'd written it in blood.

"Do you have any idea how much custom paint jobs cost?!" He tried smudging it out as I only pointed to the kids on the other side doing far more damage than I was. Raziel rolled his eyes, gathering the pike up. "Well I can't yell at them, can I?"

Letting out a disappointed huff, I banged on the side of the van; the kids instantly scattered.

After a pause and a few more sighs, the angel considered my last ditch effort to salvage this visit.

"You're going to help? How? Did you figure out how to use that giant sword thing? Or are you just going to prod the monster to death?" Thinking it over, I eventually shrugged. I was Neri, friend to some demons and able to talk with most. I figured I could just talk the demon into a resolution regardless. Raziel rubbed the back of his head, dragging the pike with him and heading towards the door, downtrodden and dragging his feet. "Good. Great. I'm not even wearing shoes."

"Hey now." I smacked his arm, pointing out I'd been barefoot since day one. The angel scoffed.

"Some of us have appearances to keep up, you know." I let him walk a little farther ahead of me, hunched and dragging his pike, the end skipping against the ground and sparking up. Raziel's wings were like two disorganized mops strapped to his back, out and everywhere at once. I shook my head.

I caught up with him, falling in tow.

"I've had problems with this demon before, it moves around this neighborhood, but it's always the same symptoms. Each time I exorcised it in the past, it just pops up somewhere else a few years later." The talking quieted down as we rushed through the threshold, into the house where its outsides reflected just how unstable and overused the place really was.

The rooms had a liveliness to them, there were drawings, report cards, soccer equipment and other paraphernalia thrown about the house; where it touched seemed more inviting already as the other corners were poorly lit, ancient lighting still in place. We walked into the atrium, looking around as the father, a balding man of forty or so, pointed out specific places they had trouble. Most of the darkened, unattended rooms were the problem ones, the second library upstairs, someone had gotten pushed into the wall, the study room downstairs is where the kids got their scratches from, along with little other isolated incidents. Unarmored, tired, and oddly understaffed, things were looking bleak.

An hour later, with the Priest and the family all out of the house, the two of us patrolled. I walked a few steps ahead of him as the clearly labeled bait/scapegoat, he kept a good distance behind me making sure we weren't being followed. We paced up one hallway, turning onto the next, ever vigilant, top of our game and not compromised in any way, shape or form. Turning to glance at Raziel, I saw him nearly run into a wall, yawning. With an annoyed grunt I shoved him in the shoulder, propping open my eyes to try and signal him to stay awake.

"Shuddup, it's your fault anyways." He said tiredly, the angel's eyelids hanging low. When I protested, he tried to back his statement up, "You're the one who says I should punch myself into exhaustion, who knocks me in the head, who… it's just your fault, okay?" Raziel stormed past me in real emotion, real annoyance, glancing into the next room like it'd be bursting with demons, turning around just as fast in a jittery state. He was right, not entirely right for blaming all of it on me, but still right in most senses of the word.

"I'm sorry about that, I really am. I don't mean to compromise your work here." I apologized, Raziel looking back to me quickly as the words hit the over-prided zealous look, dimming a little, trying to understand. There were far too many signs pointing that all of this was a very bad idea to be here in this condition.

Something caught my eye just over his head, two dark ovals moving along the wallpaper, suddenly blinking as they steadied, form obscured by reflections of light. It only took me a second to register that the demon had been looking for us, hunting us down the entire time. Remaining perfectly still, I twiddled my fingers at the side of me to get Raziel's attention.

"What are you doing? Keep going." I kept my eyes on the demon as it stopped moving, narrowing its eyes like it was gearing up to strike. 'Neri?"

"Down." I mouthed as clear as possible. He tilted his head a bit as the demon suddenly made his move, leaping from the wall, massive and monstrous as it was.

"DOWN!" I shouted as we both dropped to the floor, jaws snapping over the two of us as both massive arms slammed down alongside, scooting the tall, hunched-like body. In another second it seeped though the side of the hallway, quickly darting back into full view, stance wide. I jumped to my feet, pointing at it and trying to rationalize.

"Well it's a lot bigger this time." I heard Raziel murmur behind me, shocked.

"Hey! Wait! Wait! We just wanna talk. You should know me, right?" I stepped as close as I dared, which still amounted to at least twenty feet away from it's large, overhanging snapping jaws. The demon had horns all along its back, remnant of something like a spiky goat. The face was mostly teeth, two beady black eyes higher on its head, more like a spider with a big, deep chest. The beast raised up a little bit, tilting it's head at me before letting out a glass shattering scream, sounds slowly becoming words.

"Yyyyourrr skiiinn will become the floss of my teeth!" His fur bristled out in all directions, head slowly swooping back and forth as it stomped the ground.

"Yeah, I don't think you'll be able to talk to this one." Raziel was back on his feet, steadying the pike nervously. No, no, that couldn't be true, there had to be a way to work this out. I took a step closer, motioning for the angel to hang back.

"Listen, I'm not here to hurt you, I just want to see if we can work out a deal of some sort, where we can figure out a way for you to stay happy and for your family to stay happy."

"I live for no more then the pleasure of terror, for the pleasure of fear!" The beast hissed in excitement, taking a step closer to me; I could see the muscles rippling, anxious to fight, to tear up, to destroy. I wanted to help, I wished I could make a difference.

"Is there maybe something we can get for you to get you to leave?

Maybe a-" The demon suddenly charged straight for me, head hitting me hard as my thoughts blanked. It kept through as Raziel dodged out of the way, slamming me into the back wall with a bone-breaking crunch. There was no way to reason with it. What it wanted was destruction, and by keeping the family petrified in fear, it was happy. There was no pleasant middle ground.

Shaking my head a little I could see it again, how it relished the fight as I clung to its face, arms suddenly holding tight to the back of it's jaw. With a little toss it threw me from it, biting down hard onto my hand. Snapping to attention I grabbed onto its tongue, pulling it from the mouth as the monster opened wide, lunging at me as teeth suddenly bit down, shearing off my arm cleanly just below the shoulder.

"Irony!" Raziel shouted from behind me as I grasped at my arm nub, blood spraying everywhere. The monster suddenly looked over me, awkwardly hopping in the angel's loud mouthed direction with just a few galloping steps. I couldn't let him get to Raziel, I could regenerate, I could heal myself, I wasn't going to be responsible for his injuries too.

"That's not what irony means!" I bellowed back, lunging out to grab hold of whatever I could.

I latched onto the demon again and planted my feet into the ground, skidding behind him as it slowly noticed the tiny weight it dragged. The goat-beast began to kick, shaking me around and knocking me into the walls, annoyed. My arm began to regenerate slowly, black silty smoke falling down as my shoulder nub eased up on spraying blood everywhere, ever so slowly healing. If only I could re-surface, recall that weapon, the giant paddle notched thing. Maybe it was a 'thrill of battle' thing, a 'terror to save my life' kind of weapon; but with my one good hand latched onto the goat's ankle, I had nothing to try and summon it with. I stubbornly held on.

"Demons nary attack other demons, you ignorant fool!" The goat suddenly faced a little closer to me, addressing me directly, "Count that first attack as a warning to your traitorous self!" The monster suddenly jerked up right, blackish blood spraying from its throat as it whipped back around towards Raziel, holding the weapon out to the side, pike drenched in the goopy mess.

"We tried it your way, Neri. It's not interested in playing nice." Raziel taunted the demon, holding the weapon over his head, ready to strike. "You must be some black hearted son of a bitch to beat up a defenseless woman." Leaning to the side to catch this exchange, face pretty much resting on the demon's hocks, I gave an annoyed scoff.

"Hey! I'm not defenseless." I mumbled as the demons body arched, ready to tear Raziel apart; even as I tried to hold him in place. Something was telling me my involvement in this fight was a very small. I could hear fighting; I could hear sounds of frustration and anger, of excitement and danger. But all I could see was blackened demon butt. Taking a deep breath I let go, walking a little farther out to the side to see just the fight going on. This form was weak, it was pretty pointless. The best I could do would be a distraction; after fighting for my life time and time again, sitting one out felt stupid. Mr. Four Hundred Years of expertise here must know how to fight without getting a scratch on him, right?

The goat demon lunged forward as Raziel jammed the pike halfway down his throat, pushing a little forward like he was trying to jimmy a car door open with a coat-hanger. The demon roared out weakly, shaking about as the angel leapt to the side, holding on sturdily to the weapon as he ran up the side of the demon in pure momentum. Feeling like a small, womanly third wheel I looked to my arm, shaking out my hand as just the very ends of my fingertips were finishing up healing, using my new hand to cross my arms and lean against the wall, bored.

With the angel standing on the demon's back, pike hooked onto some part of the angry goat thing's throat he grinned as he looked over to me, quickly pulling back on the pike to snap the demon's head clear from its body. The exposed skull part tumbled onto the ground and rolled to my feet as its body staggered around, drunk, slumping down for his big dramatic dismount back next to me. I could see him beaming, see him incredibly proud of showing off what a bad-ass he could be fighting a giant goat thing that tore off my arm in one neat little slice. Raziel fiddled with something by the body.

"Hey. Need a hand?" He turned around, trying to hand me back my own arm. Giving a frightened look of disgust, the angel tossed it over by me as I hopped out of the way.

"Aeugh! Are you kidding? What is the matter with you?" I mean, if nothing else we could all appreciate what a clean job the demon's teeth did, but still. "What is it with you and the puns today?"

"See, that's how it's supposed to go, I don't need the armor!" He said jubilantly, swiping the pike off to the side to clear the black blood from the handle. Impressive as it was, there was still a lot of blood on it. I gave a humoring golf clap, looking away from my own appendages.

"Yes, good job." He kept nodding, looking around like there'd be something else to take down. "Fancy little dismount and everything." My sarcasm was nearly as clear as the outside light was beaming in, shining on the side of the goat's body. Beaten over the head with hints, he still didn't get it, bragging on.

"You can't just sweet talk everything, Neri. You know?" He smacked the side of the pike against the wall, trying to clean it off. "Sometimes you have to be brave and just go for the fight."

"Mmhmm. You're pushing it." I stopped clapping, looking around for the exit.

"See, they're supposed to disappear like that when you do it right."

He pointed to the carcass, something that was very much not disappeared.
It actually looked like the thing was beginning to move again, reviving
itself. The skull in front of me rocked back and forth, teeth wiggling
in place. Raziel began to turn away, waving his hand like some macho
superhero, " We should go, I'm exhausted." No… no no no, this was
definitely not right.

"Hey! Wait a second!" I shouted as he turned a little, waving a
hand at me.

"Yeah, yeah, you were a big help." He mocked, misinterpreting my
words. He couldn't see it. He couldn't see the goat in front of me as it slowly
began to move again, slowly began to pick itself together. Actually, the two
parts, the body and the head, seemed to be reviving individually. Maybe
something with being a fellow demon gave me the ability to see it, or that
he was cloaked from angels, it… dammit!

I put my fingers to my mouth, letting out a long whistle, trying to
get his attention. The body of the demon suddenly looked at me, tongue
flopping out, a nice clear view of the beast's insides as it gagged little
desperate sounds. Raziel managed to turn just a little as the demon's body
charged me, throwing me against the wall, bouncing off quickly in order to
shut me up.

"Wait, what the… where is it, I can't see it!" He shouted, grabbing
hold of his pike fearfully and holding it in front of him. It had been toying
with us, been fooling whatever stupid angel that came here, thinking it was
killed off, only hiding, managing to escape and keep wreaking the same
havoc elsewhere. It played out like an old movie, how the demon began
slowly loping towards Raziel, how his eyes were darting around, panicked,
shouting out for help I wasn't able to provide. He'd be injured or killed, I'd
be to blame, the regret, man, I couldn't even begin to think of the regret.
He wasn't far from me. He was fifteen feet in front of me, at best; I could
still do something, break the chain of events, fix things now. I could see the
demon's muscles bunching up, rearing back to take one fatal bite on the
angel, completely unaware, panicked, when I finally reacted.

Hoping for the best I reached at my side, grabbing hold of
something solid and swinging it in a short arc in front of me, the giant
paddle-weapon sailing across the room like a giant dart. It felt weightless to
me, but it impaled the demon into the wall next to Raziel, body flickering
back into all visible view as Raziel jumped back, not a two feet away from
getting hit/bitten himself. He glared at me with complete shock, just like
the first time this happened. Unnerved, furrowing my glare and puckering
my lips, I looked to the angel.

"I'm not defenseless." I spit out childishly, the weapon suddenly
evaporating like it had the first time, showing the carnage underneath it.
Bits of debris floated down, our big, awkward silence only getting more and
more awkward. Neither of us said a word about a giant weapon coming out

of thin air. Or how we just now caused more damage that this goat demon ever did; again, maybe ignorance on this whole subject was bliss.

Something scurried at my feet, the demon's skull now equipped with teeth-legs like a spiders, zipping around in terror as the tiny little eyes in the demon's nose glared at us, trying to terrorize. Snapping from my funk I grabbed the skull's protruding horns, picking this whole demon up all on its own as the legs worked furiously in the air. Behind me, Raziel began to work on actually ridding the demon's body, crumpled and stunned, destroyed by the 'Gates of Hell' weapon.

The skull began to shout insults at me from the tiny little mouth, squeaks of arrogance and frustration as I lifted it high in the air, walking over to the far wall to smack the demon against it repeatedly. If nothing else, it jumbled its thoughts and speech until the goat skull simply hung there, legs dangling tiredly at its side. When Raziel was done properly exorcising the demon's body, he held out a hand for the skull. I offered it first, before pulling back cockily. He glared at me, pushing one eyebrow higher as he shook his head a little.

"Alright, you were a big help." He relinquished, snagging the demon skull from my grasp. Grinning quickly I walked away from it, staring at my weapon-made hole. I'd have to harness that. Get good at it. Even in this weak little body, that weapon seemed like a real force of nature, helped me even the odds a little.

I let out a laugh, delighted and giddy.

17

"Are you done reading that yet?" I stuck my head half through the wall, arms swinging back and forth as I was trying to pry the immovable object from the place he always sat, always reading pretty much the same three books. Raziel ignored me, only flipping a page as slow as possible, thoroughly engrossed. Letting out a sigh of disgust, I rolled onto my back outside of the wall, head and arms still poking through. "What more are you gonna gleam from those same books? Come outside, we can practice fighting each other."

The angel frowned and rose the book up, blocking my face with it. Really?

Letting out my most pained groan I dragged my upper body through the wall back outside, sitting up straight.

Something had happened. We had a visit from Gauzier, something curt and short said in private that I was told to leave the room for. Then after that his boss leaves, and it'd been like this since. Quiet, aggravated, distanced. He wouldn't talk to me, he wouldn't entertain any pantomime I had, he just stood around for a little while, walked around the house randomly, then sat in the basement and picked up the same book he's read over and over.

Gauzier must've threatened him with something. Raziel and I had been doing regular visits, a few more between the wacky goat demon spider thing with good success. So there shouldn't have been any reason he got yelled at. I wondered if his performance review was coming up, something stressful. Sitting against the house now, I grabbed at handfuls of grass, ripping out whatever bits I could. Even tethered to the Priest, he was generally easy to talk to. I just wanted to know what was going on, if I had done something wrong.

Looking at my handful of grass, I got an idea. Sticking my head

187

and other arm through the wall to the basement, I unlocked the little window up top, tilting it gently and not making a sound. Then like an antsy two year old, I slowly began sprinkling handfuls of grass inside the basement like flurries of snow. Raziel kept the book blocking my face for a handful or two, before it slowly began to lower, confused. The angel looked off to the side, listening for something.

"What is that sound, what are you..." He spotted the grass at the bottom, unimpressed face slowly following the trails as I let the last handful slip between my fingers. "Really? Are you like a hyperactive dog or something? What's the matter with you?" I grinned.

"Hello Raziel. Glad to have your attention." Making an over-dramatic worried face, you could tell he knew I was prying about the visit by the roll in his eyes. "So, what happened? What's the matter?"

"Clean it up." He barked out authoritatively, putting the book to his nose and making it obvious my tactics were not working. Rolling over on my stomach a few times, I put myself just right over his head, looking into his book with him. Reading a quick passage about positioning of a battalion, he slammed the book down in his lap and glared over at me. "I'm not in the mood for this, Neri."

Giving my extreme worried face from before, I motioned for him to come outside a number of times. When his face didn't change I made talking-mouth pantomimes, trying to let him know he could talk to me about these things. Raziel's face scrunched up, getting the hint before leaning over, just plain angry.

"NO." He bellowed, book immediately back in his face as he moved to the far side of the couch. Aggravated and shot down, I began to pull myself back outside before I heard the Priest clomping down the stairs.

"Hey, Raziel, we've got a call." The angel lowered the book in surprise, giving me a scowl before looking back to the Priest. "We're heading out now, so pack up. Bring all your gear this time." He joked, rummaging around the house for something, looking for his keys.

"Yeah, I know. That won't happen again." Raziel gave me an icy stare, putting the book down and rummaging around for his gear. Hopping into the basement I stayed far out of the way, standing there nervously. He filled his arms with most of his gear, only a shiny pauldron and a shin guard left. About to keep up the same aggravated attitude he let it drop a little, motioning off to the two pieces. "Grab those and let's get going." Raziel said quietly, already heading outside. I pushed him too far and now we'd have to deal with a spoonful of awkwardness, which was never fun.

The job this time was a standard haunting. The Priest said that this house had "big problems" all the time, that usually every Friday they'd get a swell of activity. All other days of the week, nothing, but then on Friday a lot of their stuff would fly off the walls, things knocked over, trash strewn about the yard. This all seemed to revolve around a large, mostly abandoned barn at the back of the property. They thought kids were partying in there at first, but eventually figured out it was a demon or ghost of some sort. Raziel made a joke that maybe it was an angry cow. I wasn't sure if that was a jab at me.

The house wasn't terribly far away this time, just about twenty minutes of smaller, less traveled roads. With the days being colder, I kept myself bundled up in the spare hoodie, stretching out tiredly in the Transit as the two of them talked. While most of our calls were later at night, this one was right around dinnertime, even a bit earlier with the sun still just above the horizon. I watched it bob and sway amongst the trees, obscured as we passed telephone poles and street lights. Yawning, shuffling up against the window with a shoulder, I dosed off.

The sound of the side door opening made me jump, waking up groggy and disoriented as Raziel only ignored me, dragging his gear out and suiting up. The Priest made mention that he was going to head inside to talk with the people, see if they could give any more information before we got to work. Watching the man go, I stretched again, bundling up in the hoodie, protecting myself from the cold. Raziel was looking for his last pauldron hidden underneath the driver's seat from sliding there sometime during the ride. The angel looked back and forth before I leaned over, grabbing the edge of the pauldron with my toes and dragging it out like a new world monkey.

"That's gross, don't do that." Raziel muttered, wiping the pauldron off before putting it on. "Ready? This won't take long." Snapping on his last armor snap, he motioned outside. Glad to see he was in a better mood, I scrambled from the van.

We closed the door, propping the pike up on the side as he readjusted something for a moment, about to walk into the house. But as we stood there, I could hear something faint, like a radio being on far away. I looked around, trying to figure out just where it was coming from.

"We can go inside, get whatever information the Priest has, then check this place out. It's still early out so activity shouldn't be too..." Raziel stopped, frowning, locking onto the same thing. "You hear that?" He muttered as I nodded, walking a little ahead.

"Is that music?" We stuck to the shadows, trying to be stealthy. Raziel followed behind, armor clanking noisily with each step. I nodded before grimacing at the noise he was making; he stopped, rolling his eyes again. "I'm suited up to take damage, not sneak around, Neri." Holding up a hand, I motioned him to stay there before pointing over to where I thought the music was coming from.

"Stay here." I said for good measure. Raziel nodded, slinking farther back into the shadows best he could. I took off in a jog. Around the side of the house, towards the garage, the music only got louder and louder. At the back of the property was a large, somewhat unkempt looking barn. It was the most ghostly, frightening looking thing I've ever seen, but light seemed to pour from the windows. The music was loudest there, definitely coming from inside.

Why would this be out there? You can't tell me we had some sort of music-demon on our hands.

Edging closer inch by inch to the closest window, something slapped a hand on my back.

"Hey there!" A voice, someone I didn't know made me leap out of my skin, stumbling on my heels to turn around and face my enemy, fists up, ready to fight. There behind me stood another demon, a woman, two small horns coming from the middle of her head as she looked just as frightened as I was. After a moment of confusion, she laughed. "You're here for the party, right?"

Double checking her horns, her friendly manner of speaking, and the fact that I too had horns not hidden at this exact moment, I eased off my paranoia a little. A demon. She had to be a demon too. Was she the one haunting this place? I didn't want to tip her off I was some sort of angel lackey, so fell into immediate fibbing habits.

"I am! I heard there was a party or something for...demons....." I gauged her response as she nodded, excited. "Demons! Right! And I wanted to see what was going on, I'm new to the area!" The woman clapped her hands together.

"Fantastic! I had to admit, I didn't know if you were a demon too, you had me worried for a second!" We both laughed as I feigned giddiness. "There's this crazy looking car in the driveway with ghosts painted on the side, so I'm a little on edge." Giving a nervous chuckle, I tried to pass it off.

"Ah, yeah, I don't blame you. I was afraid I'd run into some big, nasty demons, so I was trying to be quiet." I said, honest as I could be as the other demon seemed to nod.

"Yeah, I've had to deal with my share of those demons as well, we try to keep everything cordial back here, so everyone can have fun." I nodded before realizing something.

"Everyone?" The woman clapped again.

"Yeah! We tend to have a pretty good crowd on Friday nights. This is our local base for the area, powered by a few Outlets so everyone can have fun and relax a little. Then on Fridays we invite everyone over to party!" Not entirely sure what an Outlet was, but figuring I'd spoil my cover if I asked, I nodded. Great. Not just one demon, but many demons.

"How many do you think you get here on a Friday?" I tried to dance around the obviously prodding question by making it about something else instead, "It's not too big of a place, seems like it could get crowded." She nodded.

"Sometimes. I think our biggest crowd was about thirty or forty demons and various demonkin. Most Fridays we tend to get about fifteen or twenty." She suddenly grabbed my shoulders, leading me forwards happily, " Here, let me show you around!"

Raziel and I were way out of our league. Twenty to forty demons? You kidding me? We had trouble with two the other day!

"So I'm Mia. I've lived around the area for a long time." Gosh she was forthcoming with information. Taken off-guard at the doorway of the demon dance party just in front of me, I didn't bother making something up.

"Neri. I've been around for only a few years." Mia suddenly stopped.

"You have? But you're so well spoken! You must've had a great teacher!" Okay, now I was confused. But again, not wanting to blow my cover, I went along with it.

"Yeah! I did, he's uh... unforgiving but fair." Off put thinking Raziel somehow taught me to talk at all, I shook my head, feet at the door of the barn as the music was shaking the old, wooden beams. Worried, I looked back to her, "I didn't bring anything for this party." Mia laughed, shoving me through the doors as the music suddenly blasted.

"Don't worry! Just have fun!" She yelled above the dull roar of about twenty to twenty five demons all dancing and partying around in the middle of a giant open room. Most of the barn was dedicated to the dance floor, the big open section with a few tables off to the side, a number of demons dancing around, having fun. I gave a sort of unsure grin, surprised.

On the other side was a few tables, some shadier areas populated by a couple larger, more animalistic demons hanging out, talking with each other. A few others danced in their seats, some stood along the sides, most were milling about having fun. At the far wall were a set of doors, closed off to everyone else.

"This is our main room for everyone else, then the rest of our local family stays in that backroom. But right now, everyone's out and having fun." She smacked my shoulders, going on ahead. "You should mingle, get to know these people, we're all good demons here. No monsters, I promise!" I nodded like I was excited to party before remembering I didn't come here alone, freezing up. He wouldn't wait in the shadows for long, I had to be tailing me into here. If he came inside and showed he was an angel to everyone here, they'd take him down on the spot. Mia saw my panic, confused.

"You okay?" She said like a concerned parent as I nodded quickly.

"I am! I may have lied to you a little bit. I didn't come here alone." I muttered as she slowly crossed her arms, worried, "I've got a friend back out in the yard, but he's terrified of crowds like this. I'd love to meet everyone, but I'd rather drag him in first so he's not standing alone all night, you know?"

"Oh! Right!" She nodded, going on ahead, "Take all the time you need, but be sure to say hi when you get in here, okay?"

"Absolutely! Sure, let me just..." I backed into the doorway, propping the door back for a hasty escape. "Snag him and we'll be right back." She nodded and turned around as I bolted from the doorway, back into the blackness of night. We had to get out of here. There was no way we could handle this on our own.

Slinking back into the shadows, I searched for him frantically. Couldn't hear anything, looking around like he might be behind a tree, inside the house, wherever. I called for him quiet as I could.

"Raziieeelll!" Hissing like a distressed snake, I scoured the yard. "Razzieeellll!" Darting to and from shadows, I suddenly stopped, hearing a light whistle. Searching for him, I caught sight of a hand waving at me from the other side of the yard. Scrambling over to him, he was hunkered back, practically invisible.

"The music is coming from the barn." He whispered like I didn't know. I gave an excessive nod. "I saw someone come out and take you inside, they didn't seem harmful. Is she the only one there?" I shook my head no dramatically. Raziel turned his head a little.

"How many are inside, then?" I flashed my hands up about three times, before pointing back to the Transit like we needed to leave. The angel only frowned at me. "Flashing what?" Sighing, I did a quick count on my fingers like I was numbering people, before showing my hands out three times to tell him there were thirty people inside, give or take a few. I could see his eyes go huge in the darkness.

"Thirty people inside!?" He gave a distraught screech as I motioned for him to keep quiet, pointing again to the Transit that we couldn't handle this. Raziel kept his gaze elsewhere, angrily thinking about something. After a minute or two, I pointed towards the Transit and pushed him again.

"We can't back out of this one." He said solemnly. Smacking his shoulder angrily for an explanation, he only repeated it, unusually stubborn. "We just can't, Neri. We can't just..give these demons a warning like we've done in the past. That's catching up to us." Thinking on it, I put it together on my own.

"Gauzier?" I muttered as Raziel nodded, looking away. I paused, regretful that we'd have to disappoint king asshole himself, but this was way too big for us. I motioned to Raziel, pretending to have a phone to my head, holding up four fingers, and backing up away from him. It took him a second, but he figured it out.

"I can't call for backup. We'll have to figure out a different way to tackle this, maybe take down the main person in charge and dismantle it that way." About to berate him for a stupid plan, it hit me. If we could talk to Mia, explain the situation like a group of calm adults, maybe this wasn't completely suicidal. I'm sure they could move their operations somewhere else, more remote, and there'd be no blood shed. I nodded, smacking his arm. "You have an idea?" Nodding again, I dragged him back by the Transit.

After an excessive amount of charades, I got him to understand the plan. We were going to do the opposite of what I had to do when meeting with Gauzier and have him pretend to be a demon by hiding his wings under the hoodie. Then we'd calmly go in, try to talk with her alone, make her aware of the situation and talk it out. Everyone was already relaxed in a fun atmosphere. Any other way, I'd never suggest this. But she seemed reasonable, she already knew me, and we could do this as pleasant as possible.

Raziel stood there, pulling at the armpits of the hoodie, cautiously walking out of the shadows, trying to be nonchalant. Hearing his fidgeting, I grumbled at him, stopping our march into the lion's den. The angel put his hands far out to the side.

"We're not going to fool anyone with this, Neri." He muttered, shuffling his wings around, "I look like some kind of hunched mutant, and I'm gonna get myself killed without any weapon."

"We can't walk into a party with a goddamn pike, Raziel. We have to trust everyone will be relaxed and not on edge." I poked one of the protruding feathers back into the hoodie, worried as well. "We're gonna be adults, talk this out, and run like hell if it doesn't work." We arrived at the door, waiting for a moment.

"Ready?" I looked behind me; he only grimaced like he was about to jump into a pool of lava. Bracing his shoulders up, I tried to prepare him best I could. "Let me handle talking, just keep quiet, it'll be fine."

"I have a really bad feeling about this." He muttered as we slipped inside.

Our first few moments were okay. A couple demons looked over at us, then right back away, uncaring. Giving a motion for Raziel to slide off to the right of me towards the shadows, I only caught the side of his face, eyes wide in horror. The angel looked to me, only mouthing 'oh my God' as I nodded, trying to find Mia.

"I told you there were a ton of people in here." I muttered, slinking off and away without seeing my new contact. Raziel inched up alongside a support beam, pushing back against it and trying to keep his wings as small as possible, eyes darting around like any one of these demons would catch a hint of his angel-ness and beat the tar out of him. One of the more monstery looking demons locked eyes on him, motioning off to it's friend as they both turned around, trying to figure Raziel out. Something tugged on my wrist suddenly.

"These demons know what I aaammmm." He hissed, panicked. Holding up both hands, I tried to tell him to calm down. Raziel's eyes only went wider, looking around at every single demon and making himself incredibly awkward about it. About to rework our plan entirely, I spotted Mia exiting out the back room, immediately waving to her and motioning her over. She waved back, heading in our direction as Raziel slunk into the shadows again.

"There you are! You got your friend this time too, huh?" She looked over my shoulder, trying to coax the angel out from the darkness like a bashful child. I could see Raziel only look over to me, trying to figure out what to do. I motioned to him myself.

"Yeah, he doesn't get out much. C'mon." I muttered as he frowned, nervously walking out from the dark. Grinning and looking back to Mia for any hint of trouble, I watched her face lock onto his, smile melting into disgust, before outright rage. I didn't have time to react.

"YOU!" She screeched at the top of her lungs, even above the music and the party. Mia suddenly took up a stance, chanting something quick and practiced, emitting some kind of strange glow with her hands straight at Raziel. Swinging her arms over her shoulder, she threw him without touching him into the opposite wall, through all the partying demons, breaking their spiritual boombox as I was surprised that didn't kill him outright. "YOU PIECE OF SHIT."

"Woah! Hey! Jesus Christ, what the Hell!?" I scrambled after Raziel as Mia had the crowds full attention.

"Restrain her! She's not thinking straight!" Someone tackled me to the ground as I fought to try and get free, pinned there. I was at least able to talk.

"Mia! What's going on? Why in the..." Spotting something moving in the heap of broken equipment, Raziel shoved a piece aside to collapse on top of the pile, bloodied and banged up pretty bad. "Raziel? You okay?" His eyes passed over me once before sitting back against the wall, half conscious.

"Neri, you've been under a spell by this monstrosity." She said quickly, chanting something again as the glow lit up around her hands, the words ending in "..and Mother give strength to my actions and make my words true." As she grabbed the air again, Raziel rising from the rubble, pinned against the back wall. With another little hand motion she pulled the hoodie away, showing every other demon our ruse. I heard an audible anger surface through them all boiled by the word 'angel'.

"A spell?" I struggled for breath as the person holding me down suddenly pulled me to my feet, arms locked behind my back. Raziel seemed to collect himself a little, in rough shape. "You guys know each other?" I saw Mia's hands grasp tighter as Raziel popped awake, looking down at himself and having a hard time breathing. I could hear him wheezing for air.

"Know him? I know him. I've been trying to find this self righteous abomination for fifteen years!" She snarled, seething with rage as she set Raziel down. He got a wild look in his eye for a second.

"It's a curse, Neri! Poltergieeesssh-!" He managed to eek out before Mia readjusted her stance, teeth clenched together.

"Don't you DARE try to poison the minds of any more demons. It's my WILL, you malignant growth!" She muttered her curses again as he suddenly locked up, immovable. "How about you stay right there and keep silent?" Raziel's eyes darted back and forth, trying to cough, or talk, or say anything at all, now voiceless. This wasn't good- I'd believe Raziel way before I'd think to believe random demon woman that I was pretty sure wasn't batshit crazy five minutes ago.

She glared at him for a moment more, snapping her fingers all of a sudden. Nothing happened. Looking around, I watched the demon walk to Raziel, lip curled up.

"I want you to hear this, I want you to hear every word I've got to say to you." You could see a bit of terror in his eyes, looking over to me before back to her, face locked in a grimace. Anger and surprise caught up to me, now understanding this situation a little more.

"Let him go, Mia! Let us go and we'll walk away, I promise!" Figuring that'd make her mad, she only turned back around towards me, somewhat upset.

"No, Neri, you've been put under a spell by this thing." She looked back to Raziel as he looked around, eyes narrowing a little in pain as he tried to move around and letting out a snort of air. "Angels can be terribly good at pretending to be decent people." Looking to the friend pinned against the wall, the damage and chaos around me, and the demons all chanting for blood, I frowned.

"You're not really acting like the better person here." She slowly sauntered up, glowing hand out towards me as I realized she wasn't going to convince me through casual conversation. "Wait, what are you doing?"

"Here, I can break it for you. Then you'll see what's really happening." After the magic tricks she pulled with Raziel? I wasn't going to sit still and let her curse me too. Raziel didn't have me under a spell; of course not. What sort of backwards, 'I'll do everything in my power to get rid of you' situation would that require? I wasn't under a spell. But if I kept siding with Raziel, that might put me in a position I couldn't do anything to stop this. I had to figure out a plan.

"I promise this'll fix everything." She said again as I tried to fight it. Could I be cursed too? She was powerful, I had no idea we were going up against someone so outgoing, friendly and also highly advanced curse master.

Kicking my feet, trying to pull away, she hovered that hand towards my face as I thrashed back and forth. Her words filled my head, blacking out she muttered something over my eyes. I felt my mind go blank. Time stopped and everything went silent.

We stayed like that for a second, stuck looking at her palm, eyes unmoving as she pulled her hand away, looking over at me. That was it? What happened? What did she do? Shuddering, snapping back to full awareness, I looked at the situation again. Had something changed? I didn't feel any different, beyond feeling like I had dosed off for a second.

I looked back to Raziel and felt nothing but worry and fear for his sake, looked back to Mia and felt only surprise and anger at this whole situation. Frowning a little, I shook my head. Yeah, no, not under a spell. Still perfectly fine. But if I let them know that, they'd beat the tar out of me too. I had to play pretend for a while.

"Oh...God, what happened? Where am I?" I stumbled around comically on my feet, let go by the demon holding me back on Mia's order. Bending over to my knees, I wiggled my head around a lot, trying to be as disoriented and recently freed demon as I could be. "You saved me! I've been stuck under that thing's control for a month now!" I pointed desperately at Raziel, over emphasizing all the shock and disgust I could. I heard him give a desperate whine as I went up to her, putting a hand on her shoulder.

"Thank you, so much. How can I ever repay you for saving my life?" The demon's eyes scoured over every inch of my face, trying to make sure I was telling the truth. I gave my best grin, my best sign of relief when my insides felt like bickering butterflies. I decided to elaborate, "It was like I was there, stuck behind glass, trapped. But I knew. Right off the bat that you might be able to help me. Thank you Mia." She seemed to enjoy protecting people, playing leader, so I tried to play up to that aspect. After another moment of uncertainty, she put a hand on my shoulder.

"You're welcome, Neri. Everything's going to be okay now, you have a new family." I grinned, wincing hard.

"Good, That makes me... happy."

I looked back to the situation, now able to actually do something. But Raziel's panic caught my eye, that sort of desperate plea for help you could spot just glancing at him. My stomach knotted up; I tried to give him as much of a reassuring look as possible. Mia began to talk again.

"Now that we have our threat neutralized, let me tell you all just who this monster is!" She was speaking to everyone else now as I slipped back into the crowd, strategizing.

"Do you remember who I am, Raziel? What you took from me?" I looked around the room, suddenly stopping as I realized what she was saying. "You remember fifteen years ago, of a specific child you happened to exorcise?" A chill ran down my spine, now looking back at Raziel in a new light. A child? The crowd of demons got noticeably angrier as I was a little off-put myself.

"You remember what you called her? A pest. She was only a child! She was my child!" Mia took a few steps closer as you could tell Raziel was at least aware of what was going on, grimace still plastered on his face. "It took me so long to find my own child after death, and you take her away from me like it's your God-given right! She did nothing to you!" Her voice cracked, shaken as the demons howled for blood, riotous and angry. My time was growing shorter. I couldn't just run in there and try to drag him away, I had no idea how curses worked. I turned my back for a second, looking around frantically.

"You want to see a pest? I'll show you a real pest!" More curse-chanting just as I turned around, catching just a glimpse of Raziel disappearing altogether, clothes ruffling down emptily, spotting the tiniest thing at the bottom as the demons all bellowed with laughter. Squinting, I could just barely read the shape as some sort of rat. A Ratziel, if you will.

"For fuck's sake, you can do that?" I gasped as the demon next to me nudged and pointed at him. A bigger, brutish fellow with a tiny head and tiny little demon horns and a tail, he suddenly raised a fist in the air, chanting himself. I had to keep looking back to the rat at the bottom of the pile, bewildered this could even happen at all.

"Smash him! Smash him!" The guy started, inciting the others a well as Mia started playing to the crowd, standing over the tiny figure. It suddenly hit me. They were going to kill him. They weren't going to just scare him away, they were actually about to kill him. The other demons start picking up the rant before the entire barn is shaking with those words and I found my options dwindling fast. "Smash him! Smash him! Smash him!"

"No... no..." My words were swallowed by the group as I pushed for the front, seeing Mia holding a foot over where he stood, frozen and helpless in mid-rat grimace.

"I know you're not going to stay dead." She bragged as I struggled to push past a few burlier demons at the edge of the circle around the two of them. No...c'mon, move, Raziel. Move!

"But maybe in that hole where your heart used to be, you can feel the tiniest bit of my pain!"

"Raziel! MOVE!" I screeched out, busting through and tackling Mia into the table next to her, breaking it in two. She looked at me with utter indignation and disgust, seeing where my loyalties stood. Scrambling back onto my feet in a daze, Mia shouted orders.

"Kill him! Now!"

"No!" I turned around to tackle more demons away as they were already stomping on top of him, the sound of bones snapping and breaking the next moment.

"NO!" I squealed, shoving them out of the way anyways to dig through his clothes. There, at the bottom was a smattering of dust and some sort of liquid spreading across the ground. A knot formed in my throat.

"Neri! Why did you-"

"Because he was my friend!" I roared back, turning around to see the demon behind me with their foot arched back. Oh.

Snarling in defiance it kicked me square across the face, head snapping backwards fast enough, hitting the wall hard.

My eyes were already open for a while as I slowly stirred back to life, heart heavy and sick. Some time had passed, night more dark and full, the sound of the party still happening on the other side of the doors. I was in the back area, away from everyone else with just a dim light in the corner to illuminate me. Whimpering something miserable, I rolled over to my side.

I didn't see the bars at first; my face was pressed up against them as I only saw the rooms outside of them; a cage. Something antique from the turn of the century that you'd parade lions around in for the circus. Up on wheels, I was at the corner of the room away from everything else, straw all over the bottom with a blanket covering the sides. An animal cage. Fitting.

He couldn't be dead. He had to be...elsewhere. Teleported away. Some various angel trick I didn't know about. He'd always been so paranoid about demon curses, brought it up all the time and I never figured it could be a real thing. I was a demon. I hadn't cursed anything. I hadn't been around other...proper demons, I guess, but it just seemed silly. A name you give to something you can't explain, that was it. But it was real.

I let out another pathetic whine, covering my head. He couldn't be dead.

"You're awake." A voice, startling for a second as I put my head back down, distressed. Mia. "I'm sorry we had to do that, but it's for your own good, Neri." I didn't meet her eye.

"Leave me alone." I grumbled painfully, flipping over to my side to have my back to her.

"He must've re-cursed you in the time I cleansed your soul, I'm sure we can fix this." Taking along, drawn out sigh, I hunched more.

"I'm not cursed. I know full well what I'm doing and it's stupid to think someone completely immobile and unable to speak could do anything like that."

"So you knew he was an angel." Her voice anguished just saying the word. I gave an annoyed scoff.

"Of course I knew. I've been traveling with him for a month and a half."

"You're an exorcist, then? Mia said incredulously, just as surprised as I would've been a couple months ago. "A ...demon exorcising demons?"

"No. I'm an advisor, at best. I needed a place to stay and Raziel took me in." I muttered as the leader scoffed." I do my best to talk with demons causing problems to get them to go elsewhere. Raziel exorcises the ones that are too violent."

"I doubt that." She took a few steps closer as I made sure to stay away from the sides. "Angels, and especially that angel whose dust is tracked all over that room now, don't tend to entertain alternative options, no matter what it is. They're soulless, remorseless puppets."

"And I'm telling you we came in here to talk before you tossed him into a wall and killed him." Raising my head up the tiniest bit, I snarled like a wild animal, "Hard to mill sympathy for you when that's your first reaction, if you want to talk about brainless puppets."

"If you've seen what he does to demons, you wouldn't think so!" She fought back as I pushed it farther.

"I've seen it! I was one of those demons!" I howled just as loud as she did. "I don't know what happened 15 years ago, and I don't doubt it's true. But humiliating someone and killing them off in grand fashion sure as Hell isn't going to break a person from their habits! You want to make a difference? Be the better person!"

"He MURDERED my child!" She screamed as I fought back.

"And WE came in here to warn your CURRENT family, instead of killing all of them off too!" Seething, she had her fists balled up like she'd try cursing me to death as well. "I'm not going to speak for him because I don't know what happened. If he exorcised your child, then yes, that's awful. But you can't ignore that you screwed up!" Bristling like a wild animal, I stared her down.

"He would've killed us all given the chance!" The demon shouted as I went quiet, shaking my head.

"And yet here we are, huh?"

She geared up to say something else before stopping, turning away with a huff. I huffed back, watching the door swing closed, alone again.

The soft, bleated mewling of the music from the other room quieted down, heavy bass thumping heavy in my heart. In pain, dejected and tired, I huddled in the corner of the cage, trying to get some sleep. What was going to happen? Without Raziel, who would even know I was here? Who else did I have?

Shivering, pulling in tighter, the wind began to croon and howl outside.

Someone would come for me, right?

18

I slept for a little while, too nervous to fall asleep completely, but too broken to stay awake. I could see the cold fall through the slats in the roof, gripping along the walls to swell and slosh around, slowly filling the barn. My arms were full of goosebumps, shivering into a tighter ball and thinking of better times. The wind kept a steady tone throughout the building, doors and windows whistling and the weather got worse, the night got colder, and time slowly passed. The adjoining room kept up with it's happy party beat, though I couldn't hear many people actually having fun.

Sniffling, blinking a couple times into the darkness, I put my head down more, forcing myself to get some sleep.

I thought of the open fields, thought of the warm, welcoming outdoors, the ambient crickets that chirped and whistled. Imagined the sun. Imagined the grass tickling my nose, the dream starting to seep in, to slip away. Concentrating harder, I dropped my surroundings and ran happy and free of my own will, sprawling out and enjoying the sunshine as Amber and Katherine worked in the garden. Specks of light and bugs flew over the grass, the sun just about to set in the temperate sky. A bug flew closer, zipping over my head to twirl and chase it's prey before speeding back towards me, landing on an outstretched claw. Giving a happy grin I pulled it closer, letting it crawl around my hand.

Piercing through my fantasy, I felt something crawl over my hand in real life, the dream and the reality sloshing together for a second. Half aware, I barely understood something was happening at all until the same feeling squirmed up the side of my face this time, tiny barb-like claws digging into my skin. Jumping in surprise, I thought it was a spider and let out a mumbled yelp, flopping over on the other side of my body and backhanding at the area where the spider was at.

I hit something at full strength; a black mass went shooting across the cage, twanging into one of the metal bars and dropping to the floor with a noisy thump. Gasping for breath I tried to collect myself, mystified and jumbled against the far wall. My heart was racing.

Peering at my hand and trying to figure it out, trying to identify the ghost spider waking me up, I realized the only thing it could possibly be. I scrambled after where he fell off the edge. Shoving my face against the cold steel bars I spotted the little blackish rat laying there on his side, half conscious and slowly blinking. The wave of relief almost brought me to tears.

"Hey!" I bit my tongue to keep quiet, reaching out to try and snag him with my hands. No luck. The cage rattled and creaked as I missed, swiping again and again with everything I had. Noise, movement outside, I panicked. Grabbing a length of straw I jabbed the unconscious Ratziel, trying to get him to wake up, to get him to at least hide for safety. Nothing. Putting my face against the bars and making sure he was still there, I stuck my leg out from the side of the circus cage, found his tail, and picked him up with my toes just as a demon came in from the outside room, hearing me move around.

"What are you doing?" He barked from the door as I scrambled to huddle around him. "Keep quiet in there!" The burly man from before gave a standard answer. I tried to feign sleep as Raziel slowly began to stir about, trying to stand up. Cupping my hand, I held him down.

"Shhh." I whispered as he suddenly panicked, teeth sinking into the side of my hand as I bit my lip. The little rat started to frenzy, scrambling back and forth to shove himself at any possible gap to escape, having a harder time keeping him quiet as he bit and scratched again and again, suddenly through my fingers. "Raziel, stop! STOP!" I hissed a little louder as it drew the guard's attention.

Raziel scrambled through my fingers and away from me, suddenly confused, looking around that I wasn't some random attacker that had managed to grab him and that he was back in the cage. He unfortunately put himself close to the edge of my confinements, the dumb little rat focusing too much on me as a hand surged from beyond the bars behind him. All I could do was make a panicked wheeze.

"It survived!" The burly guard muttered, snatching Raziel up in a few attempts, about to yank him back outside, to parade the downed angel around as they'd finally finish the job. The pain on my hand gave me an awful idea, looking once more to the rat before back to the size of the demon. With an angered huff, I sunk my teeth into the guard's wrist like a desperate animal, inspired by my surroundings.

"Let go!" He slammed my head against the side of the bars with all his might as my thoughts jumbled, jaw aching already as I refused to let go, one hand bracing on the bars, one hand trying to get Raziel free, one leg underneath me, and my last leg kicking the guy in the face. I could barely read the rat's look of utter terror.

Wham! Wham! Wham! Wham! The pain radiated through my body as I only bit harder, trying to inflict real, long-lasting damage, tears streaming from my eyes.

"You monster!" The man bellowed again, pulling as hard as he could against the bars, finding myself slowly getting closer to Raziel as the demon tore his own arm up. My weak human-ish teeth ripped open veins, causing a mess. Still I hung on.

Focusing, concentrating on trying to pry Raziel out, trying to concentrate about biting harder and harder, I had a new problem. Like a searing hot iron there was a blinding pain from my side, getting a glimpse of the demon's other first rearing back for another strike. I remember the attack coming towards me, but nothing two or three seconds before or after the hit, devastating and nothing like I'd ever experienced, at least as a human being. Nevertheless, I persisted, biting harder and harder. Focus on that. Don't let go.

"Drop him or you're losing a hand!" I garbled between blood, biting with everything I had. I could feel the space between my front teeth, a seam in my skull starting to bend apart from the force, kicking the guard a few more times as you could hear the indecision. After another few punches, I could feel him open his hand underneath my bite.

"Fine!" I dropped the demon's arm as it stumbled back, bleeding all over the place. It didn't stick around to monologue, scrambling from that back room to alert Mia off the bat as I only righted myself. Nothing seemed to work right, wobbling hard side to side, glaring at the door for a few seconds longer. My sense of self was like a slopped over pile of mashed potatoes, disorganized priorities and jumbled thoughts. Vaguely remembering what was happening, I looked to the critter and tried to give my best smile. Guessing by his terrified glare, I must've been in bad, bad shape.

"Ratziel. Get it?" I blew the liquid from my lips, wondering how I'd come to be soaked from the rain. Or something.

I found myself staring at the bottom of the cage, slowly tilting forward before I could gather enough braincells to figure out why. I blacked out cold before I hit the ground.

"Did you have to go THIS far?" A voice, angry, feminine.

"It's here. I didn't have time to ask for it politely while she was ripping up my arm." Movement, noise, worry. "It wont stop bleeding. I think I'm gonna die from this."

"I can heal you from it later, just hang back." A couple footsteps, people getting closer. "Where is it now?" Her head was turned, voice softer.

"I've been watching the cage since we got in here, I haven't seen anything." Someone else took a few steps closer, the sound arching around my head as the demon was checking different angles. "Wait, it might be..." The steps got closer as the cloth beneath the cage was lifted up. I didn't feel Raziel anywhere around me, tense for a moment that they'd find him there. The desperation and despondent huff of the demon reassured me he wasn't, though.

"Wait... come back here" Mia muttered quietly as the other demon stopped, about to say something as the demoness repeated herself. After a couple moments, she spoke loud and clear. "Did you enjoy your nap, Neri?"

Egh, dammit, she saw me move before- no point in pretending. Opening my eyes I did a quick scan under my body, finding nothing there.

"For such a loving demon family, you guys don't shy away from the merciless violence." My body was molten, still disheveled and hurt as I got to my knees. Where was he? If he wasn't under the curtain and he wasn't in here with me, he might be back in the walls, but that'd be the least secure place to hide.

"Where's the angel at, Neri? We know you had him in there with you. Somehow." Mia's voice was gritty and tired. Shaking my head and giving an incredulous huff, I went to sit back against the far wall of the cage, rotating my hips around to prop myself up. As I did I felt the swing of my pockets go especially far out, like I had a roll of nickles stashed away. When I sat down, it felt like I was sitting on top of a power cord under my one thigh. A slight pause was all I showed, leaning back against the wall and trying to not reveal my surprise that I was 99% sure Ratziel was hiding in my side pocket. He'd have to deal with me sitting on his tail for a few minutes if he wanted to get through this unscathed.

I shook my head, using the opportunity to look down the slightest bit, seeing my right pocket flap up, partially open. Closing it right now would be even more of a tell, so I put my hands to the side.

"If he's smart, he's back at the Transit." I readjusted my back a little more, giving a slight bit of room as instantly the 'power cord" pulled away. Okay, he's not dead. That's also good. "If he's dumb, he's probably just hiding outside, though." I gave a couple ragged coughs.

"Why would you spoil where he's at?" One of Mia's sub-demons piped up, suspicious.

"Because he's a black rat in the dead of night. You think you're going to find him either way?" Straightening my back, I brought my hands up towards my face. "You think I actually know? It's not the first time Raziel's left me to die." With a couple quick movements I fixed my busted nose, dropping my hands to my shorts and closing the pocket off. Good ol' misdirection.

"You've changed your tune from before." Mia took a couple steps closer, looking all around the cage. Tensing up a bit, I realized I was playing my dour card a bit too hard.

"Nothing's changed- I'm just as frustrated as you are that I've got to deal with this on my own." Looking around I sat up a bit straighter, crossing my legs. It'd cut the space for him to be in my pocket, but again, he's just going to have to learn to cope. "Imagine taking time to convince someone you can do this peacefully and then be responsible vouching for your stupid bullshit." I waved my hand at this whole setup, growling.

Mia crossed her arms, insulted like she had the room to think I was judging them too harshly.

"My terms are clear. We're not trying to bruise and batter our captives." She stood next to the cage, despite the gentle warning from her comrades. "You tell us where he is, we'll let you out. That's the end of it."

"You're expecting me to put a lot of faith into someone who curses people around her to get what she wants." I grumbled as Mia suddenly used both hands to grab onto the bars, pushing it a couple inches back towards the wall as I couldn't help but jump. This cage had to be hundreds and hundreds of pounds and she moved it like it was made of paper.

"It's my WILL, it's not a curse!" She leaned forwards, glaring in. Miffed, I returned the stare.

"My apologies. Someone who forcefully wills people to follow her commands." Being fairly indestructible, at least to angels made me needlessly cocky sometimes, I should've probably used a bit of tact, but I was getting pretty fed up with dancing around her delicate ego. "That soft enough for you? How about 'someone really good at convincing other people through fear?'" Making these deep, inhuman sounds she turned away, trying to calm down.

"What are you plans, Neri?" Mia beckoned a couple demons closer as I kept my eye on them, ready to act. "You're a demon, you're not meant to help angels." I growled.

"Who cares what I'm supposed to do?"

"When he inevitably abandons you, what are you going to do then? Do you see any other angels and demons here? You don't think there's a reason why that is?" Frowning, I only leaned over more. "I can't imagine angels think what you're doing is right, do they?" Her words cut deep as I didn't have anything to fight back with.

Same phrase, same thought. This wouldn't last forever. We were more or less using one another to either further our business standing, or using the other for cheap stability and living a life generally free of being stabbed.

"I think if you had time away, you'd realize you're being brainwashed." Mia turned back around, holding her arms up a bit to the side, sincere. The mood flip took me off guard. "There's places for demons to go, Neri, there's other places for you out there." The thought stayed with me for a moment before I crossed my arms, laying back against the cage.

"I'm happy where I am." I looked her square in the eye, ladling on that extra bit of malice that I was getting fed up. "You've already pranced me down your spotless path about how lovely your program is, before and after a kick to the face. Save it."

"You're honestly saying that haunting some KILLER'S house is better than your own kind?" She walked closer, looking quickly around the cage. She'd see the inconspicuous lump eventually- we had to end this interaction. "Do you hear yourself?"

Going at this gently didn't work, going at it glumly didn't help, I'd have to go way over the top to get them to finally leave.

"Do my own kind miss me that much? Because it SEEMS MUCH SAFER WITH THE BABY MURDERER!" I shrieked, instantly feeling awful after I said it- but it worked. Mia made a couple of incredibly shocked, flabbergasted faces before looking back to her crew, also just as off put and disgusted.

"YOU'RE JUST AS BAD AS THEY ARE!" Mia screeched, storming off and motioning her people to head outside and look for Raziel.

"WHY DO YOU THINK IT WORKS OUT SO WELL!?" I screamed after her, on my knees for a second as I ranted and raved like a banshee, shaking the bars. I gave some awful, horrible gurgling sounds as I shook the cage, making a racket until I could no longer hear any demon out by the door, or anywhere nearby. Slowly quieting down, I listened, making sure I couldn't hear anything but the obnoxious wubbing of the music. No foot scuffs, no walking, no mumbling. Silence.

Heaving a few quick breaths I slowly eased off and let my body shake and jitter. Demon or not, indestructible or not, she still scared me.

Taking a sigh of relief, I slowly sat back against the cage, undoing the flap on my pocket and peering in, seeing if he'd come out on his own- he didn't.

"If I didn't deserve going to Hell before, I sure do now." I gave a sort of worn, happy breath, staring at what looked like a pile of dirt at the bottom, curled into a tight ball. "Hey there. You okay?" He popped his head up, looking around in confusion before looking straight up.

"Hi. It should be safe now." I put my hand in there, giving him a tiny finger ledge to hop up on before pulling him out as again, he hesitated, looking to my hand before back outside.

"I promise, Demon's honor, she's outside looking for you." You could hear some audible clanging, some complaining and short, snippy words being tossed around, backing up my story. Ratziel looked back to my hand, tentatively putting a stubby rodent hand up as I pulled him out, setting him down on the cage floor. He looked, best as I could tell on my knowledge about rats and mice or whatever the Hell he was, extremely awkward. Eyes darting around, head lowered before looking right up at me, mystified.

"You alright?" Concerned, he only kept staring, tiny black, soulless eyes switching from side to side of my face. After about four or five seconds of awkward silence it started to get to me, recoiling back a little." "What is it?"

Raziel dropped his head, looking around the cage for a moment, before looking back up at me. I started to laugh nervously, off-put and creeped out.

"What IS it? Your tiny ass button eyes are freaking me out." I put one hand out covering his doofy rodent face from me so I couldn't see him just continuously staring. I saw him still sitting there, so after a moment or two I lowered the hand, and sure enough he was still glaring at me. "Ick! Stop! You're the worst!" I laughed, shaking my head and leaning forward to put the hand to the ground just in front of him. What was the matter with him? I didn't have a fear of rats or anything, but it was like being a part of a B rate horror movie.

Trying to keep my laughs as quiet as possible, something grabbed around my wrist all of a sudden. It made me jump, looking down I saw Raziel finally stop staring at me ; he stood next to my hand, tiny mammalian arms wrapped around my wrist in a hug. It stopped being so funny in an instant.

"Oh."

I crumpled a little, seeing a bit of what he'd been going through as he remained latched on. My heart twisted and tangled up with my stomach, feeling awful and appreciative all at once. I guess I thought he was enjoying this. I don't know why, but I figured in all he'd heard today and everything he'd gone through, this was some sort of wacky fun-time story, instead of walking down memory lane of him destroying people's lives. God knows just the places he'd been in trying to get over to my cage vs escaping the other room and what that had to be like. It was odd and goofy to me. But seeing someone who I thought was fairly incapable of showing any sort of gratitude or emotion desperately grasping onto my wrist like I was about to leave and abandon him really hit me hard. I didn't realize it was so bad.

"Heyyyy" I dropped down on my stomach, bringing an arm around to give him a much better hug. I gave the tiniest, reassuring pats with a pointer finger before burying him into my elbow against my face. "It'll be okay, man. Don't give up."

I thought for a moment, hugging harder.

"We'll find a way out of here, between your ratginuity and my unfailing social skill-." Raziel suddenly sat up, looking to the door and made five different ' shut up' motions in the span of a half second. Furrowing my brow, I heard it too- footsteps just beyond the door. Dropping my head to the ground I went silent as he went as flat as he could be, just a shadow in the negative space of my arm. Absolute silence.

The man silently opened the door, walked around a little bit, slowly coming up towards the cage as I could feel Raziel's heart humming like a motor. You could hear each tentative step, each slow scuff as it didn't seem like Mia or the other guy from before. Playing dead was the best option but if he got too close, I might have to act again. That'd be the worst case.

A step. Another. Louder and louder they got as the mental line I'd made in my brain was crossed, too close for comfort. I opened my eyes, turning slightly in his direction- a random demon grunt.

"You here to get a disfiguring scar too?" Huddling up a little bit more, I looked through my eyebrows and tried to be as fearsome as pretty much just a human being with stupid goggles could be. The grunt stopped. "Giving out free samples, today only."

His slitty demon eyes went wider, taking a couple steps back and raising up his hands with a shake of his head. Looks like he was checking up on me. The grunt only slowly backed farther and farther away, nervous, green, not entirely the same brand of ruthless as Mia.

Finally far enough back, I lowered back down, resting my head on my arm.

"Rad. I'm going back to sleep." I turned back towards Raziel as he was a little farther up, very cautiously watching the other demon as it milled and paced for a little bit. Whispering soft enough that I couldn't even hear it, I spoke to Ratziel. "Let me know when he's gone." I could feel him nod as I focused on pretending to be asleep so hard that I dosed off.

In what felt like about 10 minutes, something began angrily slapping the side of my nose with the tiniest hand; my eyes shot open as I had an arm up, ready to swat that bug away once more before remembering what had happened. Raziel gave an irritated look up to my hand before over to my face, appalled.

"Whoops, yeah, let's not go through that again." Raising my head up and trusting I wouldn't be woken up if he wasn't gone, I checked by the door. Nothing. I rubbed the sleep from my eyes, propping myself up. "Sorry about that, it's been a long day." Yawning and stretching out over my head, I flopped back down on my back, still tired and using my feet to step all over the top of the cage.

"How many times have you been a rat before?" I raised an eyebrow. His eyes scoured the floor, counting on his one hand the number of times. I scooped him up and put him on my stomach, try to at least talk eye to eye. Ish. He raised up three fingers.

"Is that counting this time?" I laughed a little, happy to have some brevity back in the conversation. He tiredly looked down, the same deadpan stare as he shook his head.

"So how do you get out of this, then?" Lowering the hand, he only drew a line across his neck. Death. Great. "You can't just...heal yourself?" Raziel shook his head no before his eyes lit up, pointing at me. I sat up straight.

"I'm not going to kill you, Raziel." He waved his hands around, only pointing at me, then wiggled his fingers. It took me a moment as he kept repeating the action. Pointing at me, wiggling his fingers. Seeing I wasn't figuring it out, he did something else. Put his fingers like little horns, pointed outside, and did the wiggly fingers thing. Oh!

"A curse?" Raziel nodded excessively as I mimicked him. The rat jumped to the ground to put on a show alongside me. He pointed to himself and went back into the same position he was at in the other room cursed to his eyeballs. He then pointed to me, did the curse motion, then pointed back to himself, suddenly moving. Raziel repeated the whole show a second time. "You're saying I cursed you to start movi- Wait, I can do it too?" My eyes lit up, remembering I gave a 'Raziel, Move!' command, right before tackling Mia into the tables.

"That's impossible! I didn't say any of the paragraph and a half Mia apparently has to, I just told you to move." Ratziel shrugged as had a tiny crisis of my own, "I've yelled plenty of things before, Jesus Christ I didn't know I could curse things too! I've never cursed anything else before, have I?" More worried and more loud than I should've been, Raziel only told me to be quieter, shaking his head. When did the curse work, and when was it random? Looking around I muttered to myself a bit before the rodent tapped my arms a few times, making some sort of 'we should leave' motion.

"Right. We can figure that out later, I guess. You've gotten to know this place, right?" He shrugged, giving an unsure nod. "So how do we get out of here?" I asked, eager. His tiny, blank expression fell, shrugging.

"You don't know?" Ratziel shook his head no. I scoffed.

"I know, given the current state and the number of demons outside looking for you this might seem like a bad idea, but why not go get the Priest's attention and call for help?" Checking his expression he suddenly looked much more annoyed, folding his arms. "You might be able to do it." I mumbled, unconvinced as his expression worsened.

Thinking on it and letting the idea stew, something crept up in my throat.

"I hate to mention this, but letting you die would've... probably... been the best way out of this, wouldn't it?" Expecting an angry response, his shoulders dropped a little, looking away. "Instead of whatever additionally screwed up thing she's got planned for you now." Jeez, I really did screw this up bad. Raziel gave a sort of sideways nod.

"Egh. I'm sorry about everything with this." Grumbling, he patted my knee before taking a seat next to me, leaning against my pocket. I gave a smile. It seemed like him dying would've probably been the quickest route out of here, but he seemed equally appreciative that he wasn't dead.

"You going to stick with me here?" I asked as his response was immediate, giving a stubborn nod. I lingered, a little frustrated that this situation would be infinitely more difficult with his fragile self here, but happy I wouldn't have to do it alone. Snorting, rocking myself back to a sit, I grinned. "Alright, let's figure something out then."

"So we can't call Gauzier because everyone here would be dead." I counted on my fingers, lingering as I thought it over a second time before moving on. "We can't call the Priest because apparently he'd probably just mercy-kill you off, never see you, or just call Gauzier." I could faintly see Raziel nod, going around checking the durability of the bars on the cage for a loose one.

"We could try un-cursing you by... cursing you again, but we don't know how that's going to work out, and we do somehow fix it, that'll leave you weapon-less and easily re-cursed/ mauled to death by many demons." I dropped my hands and stretched out tall, laying there like a dead fish. "We could try to barter with queen crazy, but she's pretty straightforward on what her terms are, and that'll more likely than not, lead you to be killed and my shitty demon-ness is probably gonna keep me captured. Good. Great. This is great. Any loose bars yet?" He frowned, shaking his head as I lay there, thinking. What could the dynamic duo of a woman and her rat really do? I stopped.

"Wait, you think the curse is transferable?" I looked down as he looked back, unsure. "I'm not anxious to be a rat, but it'd be a lot easier to get out of this place when you can just fit through the bars, you know?" Toddling back over, he tilted his head back and forth a little, considering it.

"Might be an option." I lower a hand towards him, extending out my pinkie finger. Raziel looked over it, before back up at me, face all squished up and disgusted before even trying anything. He refused, only pointing to the demons outside and the problem that'd still be there. "Well I'm not saying we'd just waltz out there, we could fuck up their walls and eat all their food first." Joking around, he looked back to the hand, contemplating it.

"We could make the great escape, keep to moving shadows, become the night, make friends with raccOEKC-" Jumping, I looked to the red mark on my pinkie finger, already bit. "Warn me next time!" Expecting some smarmy lording that he finally got to attack me back, I found him retching and dry heaving, both hands on his mouth with the same constipated grimace from before.

"Oh it can't be that bad, don't be such a Pup." I leaned over as he stopped retching, eyes aggravated and dead, "Little rat humor for you there. Get it? Baby rats are called Pups." Facade not changing, I watched his frown slowly infect the rest of his face. I brought my hand down.

"No go on the rat thing, by the way." I booped him on the head with my bit finger a couple times until he smacked it away, Chuckling, I laid back down. "Also, just remembered, you've already bitten me so we should've known that was a bad plan."

"Which that sucks, because then I could've added Rat to my repertoire of..." I stopped, gasping like a bolt of lightning shot through me. Oh shit...

Suddenly I was sitting back up. The way Raziel whipped his head around to stare at me told me we thought of the same thing at the same time, instantly both of us looking to the cage size and the much more instant issue we had at hand. After a month and a half being human all the time, I'd let it slip my mind. This cage was not nearly big enough to accommodate me when I transitioned back to the red and white lizard cow, and it wasn't far from 3 am. I could already feel my body starting to jumble with energy.

"It's not big enough. We don't have the pike and I'm not gonna fit in here soon. Uhh..." I looked to the little rat, reorganizing my priorities. "Okay. We have to make decisions and work quick. I vote for a de-cursing and threatening Mia, then if all that falls through, I'll hopefully bust out of here and not be cramped to death. We can find a way back home and figure out the curse thing then. Sound good?" Thinking for a second, looking around, he gave an enthusiastic nod.

"Alright! Let's give this a shot. First thing's first." I grabbed onto the bars with my hands, putting my feet through the opposite side against the cold wall and pushed with all my power. The heavy box shifted and scuffed on the ground for a moment, resting a second before shoving it another few inches or so away from the wall. Gasping for breath, I quickly sat back up, scooting Raziel in front of me towards the far end of the cage.

"I don't know what I'm doing. The thing before was a fluke- you know that, right?" He dusted himself off, nodding. "I can't guarantee this'll work at all, or that it won't horribly hurt or kill you in the process. But when that doesn't work, you run like hell and get somewhere safe, okay?" Frowning, he nodded again, ready.

"Okay uh..." I put both hands out, wiggling my fingers around a little bit." Uncurse!"

Looking around, we waited for something to happen. Nothing.

"Stop being a tiny rat! Un-Rat!" He lowered his hands a bit, glaring at me. "De-rat!" Thinking for a moment, I wiggled my fingers a little bit more. What the Hell was I doing.

Mia had this big, long windup of a sentence before she did anything, so maybe I had to be more detailed?

"Please, Mother give strength to my actions, clear all previous curses from this man." I looked up as nothing had changed, Raziel looking to me before back to each hand. "Clear his curses and make him impermeable to all outside forces. Give action to my words!"

I opened an eye to find everything as it was.

"Make things happen?" I added as an addendum. Raziel gave

a shrug as I wiggled my fingers to max wiggling distance. "Please? Do anything? Something?" All I saw were two idiots making up a whole lot of gibberish. Aggravated, I dropped my hands.

"I'm not good at this." Giving a despondent garble, Ratziel only gestured a few more times that just heaping on whatever I came up with was still a good idea.

A sound; the doors behind me suddenly opened up to a company of demons, all formed in a neat little squad with Mia leading the pack ahead of them, heading straight for my cage. Tensing up, I swiveled around to put my back to the outside, shielding him best I could.

"Big surprise, look where he's ended up." She muttered, disinterested with my problems like a fed up aunt taking care of a rambunctious child. "What are you doing?"

"Stop being odd! Fix the thing!" I wiggled my hands desperately. "CLEAR IT UP! UNCURSE! NON-CURSE! FIX IT!" I shouted, tapping him on the head as the rat fell back, tripping over his own tail and tumbling out the back of the cage and beneath it. I threw myself against the bars, trying to grab him but my hand was too big to fit in the space. Oh no. Ohhh nononono.

"Were you trying to lift my curse on him? You know that's impossible, right? Where is he?" She scoffed as I suddenly put both hands behind my back, like I was shielding something roughly rat shaped and rat sized. Okay. Plan B. Time to buy time for him to escape and just hope.

Smoke just started to waft up, roping out and starting to gather. Great! Great, only had a few minutes before this all became a lot more difficult.

"Nowhere. Listen, Mia, you have to let me out." The entire party of demons burst out laughing as I smiled along with them for a moment, nodding. "I know, funny, right? But seriously in a few minutes I'm going to either suffocate in here, or tear the whole thing apart. If you let me out, I'll count the kick in the face, the mind-squeedgie, and the repeated punches a wash, and just leave." The demoness walked a few paces closer, arrogant and bitter.

"I don't believe you." She sneered, eyes prying behind my back for some hint if Raziel really was there or not. I leaned more in front of her, smiling.

"Remember when I said I was one of those demons? I didn't look like this when Raziel and I were enemies. I was a whole lot bigger and nastier." A thick rope of smoke wafted up, catching everyone's attention. "I'm agreeable now. I'll be much less agreeable then, I promise." She stood up, taking a few steps away- I hope Raziel had managed to get away by now.

"Hey, it's fine. I'd like to see how authentic a demon you really are." Mia nodded to the side, "Because you'll either suffocate him in there with you, or bring the cage down and crush him. I know he's still under there, we've had our eyes set on it since we came in, and I know he's not in there with you." Letting out a disbelieving gasp, I lunged at the bars.

"Let me out!" I screeched, "We can solve this without any violence, I promise!" A thick bunch of smoke wafted around the cage with me for a moment as time was nearly up. The look on Mia's face changed, less cocky.

"Do you know what a class four demon looks like? Does that mean anything to you?" More smoke gathered around in the cage, ominous and evil. "Let me out, or you're about to! Please!"

Something gave the slightest, muffled thump beneath the curtains cage, like a pumpkin being kicked over as I sat up in surprise, trying to hide my reaction. That was a good sign, right?

"You're bluffing." She said, less convinced. Looking around anxiously to the other demons, she snapped back into her arrogant habits, motioning one demon towards the cage, "Get the rodent out, I'd rather kill him off personally than let this happen on accident." The smoke became a torrent, swirling around as I only rattled the bars fruitlessly.

"Mia! Please!" It poured in through the gaps in the cage sloshing from end to end as it suddenly snapped closed, out of time. "MIIIAAAAAA!" I suddenly slammed into one wall, body filling immediately into the other wall before it felt like everything in me was being crushed. Arms were tucked so far next to my body that I could feel my spine, head and neck was crunched up and spiraled around- I took up every single particle of space that cage with just barely the room to take in the tiniest breaths. Opening up my one eye facing the outside world, true to my word, I was instantly 500% less agreeable.

"You son of a bitch!" I snarled, getting a glimpse of myself packed in like a sausage in a casing. Though if it's any small consolation they didn't seem super happy what I said was true, panicking themselves. "AGghhh as soon as I get out of here I'll give you something to worry about!" I managed to shimmy around in the cage a bit, thrashing side to side with no result. This was bad, little white stars were starting to dance in my vision from lack of oxygen. I felt like a shark trapped in a bucket.

"Should we just kill it?" The one scrawnier demon from before rushed up, looking me over. Mia was more aware of things, though.

"You idiot, stay away from there!" She screeched as the demon was suddenly knocked down, laying flat on his back as he looked beneath me in a panic. After a moment he was dragged under the cage by his feet. I stopped thrashing for a moment, confused. What? How?

More thumps, more movement as suddenly the same demon was jettisoned from underneath the curtain, slamming into the far wall, knocked out cold. He didn't just fly a few feet, he went straight across the whole room. I knew that attack, suddenly grinning.

A couple moments passed before a voice rang out, smile heavy in his tone.

"FIRSTLY." Raziel's normal, uncursed human head popped up from underneath the curtain, back on his feet with a hand braced against the cage, a bit wobbly. "It was a mouse, not a goddamn rat."

Another demon charged forwards, sword coming down at Raziel's shoulder as he ducked back and let the blade hit the cage. With his right elbow he jammed it straight into the demon's left ear, following through with a punch from his left that sent the demon across the room, near to his friend.

"Secondly..." He joked, finally turning back to see the predicament I was in, jammed like sardine into the cage, "OH, Christ, you okay?"

"NAWP." I gurgled, pushing hard with my head and neck to get absolutely nowhere with these bars. "DYING."

"I don't even think opening the door is going to do anything anymore." He worried, spotting another demon rushing up, still holding the previous demons' weapon. Raziel squared off, dodging the first strike and driving his sword into the demon's shield. Lodged in he suddenly pulled back, yanking the shield from the monster's hands and into his. After dodging another strike he smashed the wooden shield across the demons face, sending it not as far as the others, but still a pretty admirable distance across the room. A couple more demons remained behind Mia as she took focus.

"That's enough!" She bellowed, hands all the way out, concentrating into something horrible and massive. "I don't know how you managed to nullify the effects temporarily, but some lesser demon isn't going to win out over an elder one!" You could feel this pulsing, radiating heat coming from her, watching her palms go brighter and brighter as she chanted the same curse over and over. Each time the effects doubled, building more and more as even her own people backed away, the two demons behind her rushed up and dragged the unconscious folks away from the action. If he started running now, he might be able to- I stopped, realizing something.

"What are you doing? Run!" I garbled out as Raziel didn't move from his spot, focused and thinking. "C'mon! Run!" The angel leaned over, dropping the one weapon and taking a few steps to the right, directly in front of me.

"Hopefully this'll open the cage." He turned back towards me for a second, giving a thumbs up. "You can probably heal from this, right?"

No...

"Don't you dare think about doing this!" I thrashed back and forth, pushing hard against one bar in particular as it bent away, just slightly. "Raziel, you better not! Run!" The wind in the barn began to swirl and draw from outside, pulling everything towards Mia as she had her arms far as she could go, heat sweltering. Wheezing, slamming myself side to side, I begged him.

"Run! Please!" I got both eyes facing towards him as he looked over his shoulder, confident. "PLEASE!" You stupid, showboating piece of shit!

"I'll see you at home in a couple days." He turned back around, putting both his arms and wings out as Mia was ready. My stomach dropped. She brought her arms side to side, swung them both back as far as she could go before leaning forwards and letting that curse loose as Raziel willingly sacrificed himself.

"RA-" A colossal surge of lava blew past the angel, through the bars on the cage- melted that- before into the wall of the barn, melting that too. I felt myself shoot out from the cage like a spring snake jammed into a can, pushing through and out the other side of the lava on the far side of the room, sputtering. The tide of lava was a block about ten feet tall, about fifteen feet wide, and about thirty feet long, burning in a massive glob mostly on the yard behind where the cage was, grass and parts of the building on fire. Raziel's place was empty.

My bones quickly fixed back together as I sputtered and coughed, dragging my tail from the lava to recuperate away from it. Why would... why did he... that grandiose, showboating shit wasn't even necessary, he could've...maybe gotten away. Might've survived...

The grief filled my stomach, welled up in my heart, seeped into my lungs as the demon form here compensated a little. I was a little less angry than I would've been as a person, a little less vengeful. Unfortunately I was so far off the deep end it didn't matter which scaling back it did. I was still 'very' of all those things, even now.

I looked back to the lava pile, seeing nothing there as it slowly spread out, seeping into the ground. I dropped my head to the floor.

"S...see? Eye for an eye, Neri. Uh..." I could hear her stop talking as I looked up, focusing on her like prey. "So you're, uh... You're free to go." I opened my mouth a little, snarling as I got back to my feet.

"Yeah?" Mia took a couple steps back, looking around for a place to escape to.

"Y... yeah! I, uh... I feel pretty... satisfied with my revenge, so... you know. Everything's fine."

"Is it now?" I brought my hair straight up, unfurling my wings to hang out and ominously, very slowly walking towards her.

"It's just..." She leaned back until she hit a wall as I stalked closer, growl escalating with each step. "It's just 'eye for an eye.'" She bumbled as I grabbed her by the torso, pinning her against the wall.

"Yeah? How about I rip out both those eyes, shove 'em up your ass and the we can see how good we feel then?!" Mia struggled back and forth a little, fairly worn out from giving the last curse her all. "You've done nothing but spit in my face over and over and over again, please, thrill me with the tales of your fantastic mercy! It's not 'eye for an eye', it's 'old grudge decides to destroy everyone's life!' Look at what you've done to your own compound! To your own people!" Pulling her from the wall I shoved her towards the door to the dance hall, now crammed full of demons both shocked and terrified of what she did. Mia looked over them, obviously regretful before looking back to the whole side of their living quarters barn, now removed. Her eyes locked on something behind me.

"If you only pulled your head out of your ass and thought about more than yourself, maybe anything you said tonight would've stuck." I was staring right at her as she slowly frowned more, looking over my back getting angrier at what I thought was her own situation. "So I hope your little self destruction tornado was worth it!"

"You have to be kidding me" She muttered, not paying attention, I shook her around a little bit.

"I could just break your damn spine, would that be better? Pay attention!" Mia looked around me, pointing over my back as I only scoffed. "Yeah, I'm not dumb enough to fall for that." Mia pointed again, aggravated.

"He's right there." She looked back to me, outraged.

"Oh, I'm sure he is." I gave a quick look over my back, seeing a figure laying out in the grass with his arms crossed, like he was taking a nap, still laying in a half foot of receding lava. About to turn back to Mia I stopped, instantly letting her go. "Wait...what the Hell?"
I rushed over there, pretty far out from the barn by twenty or thirty feet- he was in the very thickest part of the blob, arms crossed, looking very peaceful and asleep. There's...no way he was actually alive though, right?

"Raziel." I bellowed as he instantly woke up, somewhat tired and out of it before his eyebrows lowered farther and farther, head snapping around.

"...What..."

"That's a good start." I offered him a hand to pull him back to his feet, "'How' is a good one too." Using his lava-covered hand he grabbed for my claw as I flinched, readying myself for a burn, but...nothing. It wasn't terribly hot, it actually seemed pretty relaxing. I pointed down to his feet, still up to his ankles in lava.

"How am I..." Raziel leaned back down, running a hand through the lava and pulling a chunk of it up. "It's not hot." We both turned to glare at Mia for an answer on if this was supposed to be hot or not. Given how everything else burned out; the barn, the grass, everything, I think it might've just been us.

"ARE YOU KIDDING ME." Mia seethed. That was a pretty good question too. Raziel nudged my shoulder.

"Did you... uh... curse me with something that protects me from other curses?"

"Man, I said everything I thought would work." Smiling a little more and letting that happiness seep back in, "You were on my case about sleeping before, but how is it okay for you to take a catnap in 10 ft of lava?" I leaned over and nudged him as he pushed back.

"I thought I was dead." His words were distant, shocked. "The lava was so nice and warm, I assumed I was about to wake up in Heaven."

"I saw you get destroyed by lava. So, uh, so did I."

"NO. NO, NO!" Mia stormed over, careful not to step in any lava by her, but suddenly more interested in figuring out why her curses didn't work as opposed to destructive revenge anymore. She stopped right in front of us, leaning down and putting the tiniest bit of a pinkie finger into the nearly dissipated lava. By her response, you could tell that it was still scalding hot as she shook her finger out, desperately trying to get the lava from it. "WHAT DID YOU DO, Neri. HOW?"

"I dunno."

"How do you not know!?" She jabbed me in the nose, still really not getting the hint that I was not in the mood to play nice anymore, "Younger demons do not have the ability to negate older demon's curses. That is law. So WHAT DID YOU DO?" I squirmed a little more.

"I said, 'Hey, curses! Knock it off!' and it happened, I literally don't know." Mia suddenly pointed at me, then to Raziel and taking a few steps away as I turned towards him. "Now it's a curse and not 'her will'. Pfleh." Raziel grinned and shook his head.

"Wait, wait you negated the direct effect, didn't you? You knew I was going to cast lava and you protected you both that way. That's it, isn't it?" She suddenly assumed a new stance, arms pretty much all the way out to the side, but not quite. Mia seemed pretty tired. "So if I don't give you any clues, you'll have no idea!" The demoness rambled off as like her, we were also pretty tired.

"I mean, you cursed me, right?" Raziel muttered, trying to figure it out as well. I nodded. "I don't know why it's working so well, if what she says is true. What I don't get is why curses don't work against you on your own."

"Sure doesn't reinforce that young, mistaken demon thing, does it?" My heart sank a little, worried and barely paying attention to Mia as she was wrapping up with another curse, bringing her hands together once more. There was a quick, bellowing noise before nothing happened, silence. He and I looked around, wondering where this curse would take place, before shrugging and going back to discussing. Mia started fuming and stomping around in another rage.

"I mean, in terms with dealing with stuff like this, it's pretty handy." Turned most of the way out of the view from Mia, I was grinning, happy to survive something else terrible. Raziel returned the gesture.

"Oh, no doubt." He folded his arms and looking himself over, "I'm pretty happy at the number of times I haven't died toda-EGH" The angel gasped, leaping and scrambling against my wing in a panic.

"What, what is it?!" I looked around, spotting something off but not having it register to my brain.

"The ground! THE GROUND." Raziel scrambled to my back as looking down, I noticed the large, empty chasm beneath our feet, a perfectly round hole about thirty feet in diameter. Parts of the building slid down, bits of rock tumbled in from the side- moonlight struck the side of the hole, but nothing showed the bottom of this infinite crevasse. Looking under my own feet I could spot some select bits of ground- I picked one foot up careful and the ground remained- leaning a bit forwards and stepping somewhere new, the ground followed, giving me the sensation that the hole was merely painted on the grass, and everything felt normal and unchanged. Giggling nervously I tried a few more times as Raziel watched, slowly taking his own steps, in a never ending cycle of shaking his head in disbelief as he pranced around.

"HOooooowww!?" Mia wailed, beside herself. The demon stormed up to the edge of the hole and put one foot just over where the 'ground' would be. Leaning back she brought the foot down, sinking through and down into the hole. Stumbling away, she only stood outside of it, mad.

"We should probably wrap this up." Raziel came back over to me, suddenly serious. I gave a nod. "What's your judgment on this one?" Shocked that he was asking for my opinion on this very personalized visit from someone determined to torment and destroy his everything, I only shook my head no.

"I think my judgment is a bit biased at this point." Mia interrupted me, apparently trying something new.

"Lend me your great, mighty power, Excelsis! Strike down my foes and give action to my words!" She cursed us both this time, with millions of bees. They swarmed, crawled all over both us, angry and loud and irritated as she was. But they didn't sting us. Or if they did, it felt like a million tiny, gentle massages at once. Very pleasant.

Raziel looked over at me, mid-bees for a second, shaking his bee-covered head before back to Mia. Giving a similar scoff, I sat down, waiting for this curse to clear on it's own. After a few minutes of watching Mia scream and tantrum to the soundtrack of swarming bee sounds, we both shook ourselves off as the insects got bored and flew away.

"Anyways. My judgment is clouded by this whole ordeal. Curses, what have you. BEES." I leered at the demon before looking back to him. "This is your party, Raziel. You've gotten to know them more than I have - I'm fine with whatever you choose." Mia only glanced between us both like we'd doomed her already.

"Please... no, I help this entire area's demons, they need a place to go or things would be so much worse." She begged as I'm sure neither of us were really listening or coherent beyond being tired and wanting to be away from this assignment as soon as possible. "I'm sorry about everything, Neri." I snarled.

"I'm not the one you're trying to impress, here. Our interaction is done." I motioned back towards the angel as Mia realized I wasn't on her side anymore. I never was.

"I've made up my mind." He stopped her, eyes flat as he looked over to me, and back to the rest of the demons crammed in the door, watching this torrent of plagues unfold. Raziel walked closer to Mia as she cowered away, looking to me one last time for help. He knelt down and held out three fingers.

"In three days, there'll be another exorcist coming along to double check we did our work here. Some demon in your group has been causing problems for the main house, breaking dishes and harassing the owners." He said dutifully as I slowly grinned, folding my wings back up to stand there normally, watching Mia unwind herself. "Figure out who is causing the issues and deal with them. If you move out of this place for a week or two, then keep to yourself back here without interacting with the people in the house, you can probably stay here for a couple weeks more. Though with all the... holes and lava, might be a lot shorter than that. Afterwards, it's in your best interest to find somewhere else to stay. Got it?"

As he spoke, I loped over towards the other demons, a good amount of them recoiling and scrambling from the door. I spotted something particular, though.

"Hey, that hoodie, can I get that back?" I asked politely, pointing to this one young, gangly demon towards the back, clutching the hoodie like a security blanket. I lowered my head, trying to look less intimidating, "I'm not going to hurt anyone, it's ours, I just want it back."

The demon gave a cautious nod, slowly handing the hoodie to the demon in front of it, which passed it along towards me. After a couple moments, I had it in hand, giving an appreciative nod.

Turning back to the two of them, Mia was still shocked, slowly shaking her head.

"I don't get it, why aren't you..." Mia questioned as Raziel turned away, motioning over to me that it was time to go. I followed him towards the exit. The demon only got angrier. "You think I'm going to trust what you said? As the monster that murdered my child?"

Raziel stopped, eyes dark. He hesitated for a moment, twiddling his fingers.

"I'm sorry for your loss." The angel left, heading through the hole out the back of the barn. She didn't say anything more.

We tiredly trudged from the back yard towards the Transit.

"Honorable." I spoke with fabricated pomp, eying a few demons at the doorway, unsure what to do as we simply walked away. Raziel nodded.

"Mm-hm." We passed a few heavily shaded trees, falling into

darkness before popping up alongside the light of the moon.

"Heard some of that speech I gave the demon before, didn't you?" He nodded again.

"Mmmm-hmm."

"Bees, man." Letting out a sigh, I had no idea what to parse through first.

"Bees are a new one."

"Lava dome is ...standard?" I asked as he toddled side to side for a moment, shrugging.

"Fire is standard. Giant hole is new. Rodent is rare, and Lava dome is fancy, I guess. I don't know. I don't... I don't know." We laughed, both still blown away by the unadulterated bullshit of the last twenty minutes. Things grew quiet as I thought about the whole situation, curious myself. I didn't want to ask, I didn't really want to know the answer, but in terms of being honest and truthful, I had to know.

"I hate to ask this. Did you... um..." He looked farther ahead of himself, frowning a little. It took him a moment or two to answer, suddenly looking a lot older.

"They blend, after a point." He looked upset, plainly worried. "I used to assume not being a demon is a better existence for a kid. Nowadays I just call for backup." He looked over once at the end of his words before back in front of him. My stomach knotted more.

"That's got to be tough to live with." He didn't reply, keeping quiet. I left it at that.

Coming around the side of the house, he suddenly stopped, staring at something. I slowed down myself, double checking to see if there was some other demon ahead, some issue.

"Something wrong?" I said as Raziel looked down at his hands, around at his wings, before over to me.

"The...uh... Transit is gone." Snapping my head around, the spot where it sat was indeed empty. The oil on the ground looked like it had left somewhat recently, at least a half hour gone. "The Priest is gone and I'm... not tethered to anything." Eyes wide, I wasn't sure how to approach it.

"I didn't think that was a thing you could do, Raziel."

He shook his head.

"Neither did I. I've got maybe fifteen seconds on my own before I die, and I'm really aware that's happening when I'm not attached to anybody. Not to mention we're...you know... talking to each other." He looked over himself again, covered in a frown. "So what did you curse me with anyways?"

"Clear all previous curses and make you impervious to outside... forces." I smacked my head with my hand. "Meant to hold off against more curses, not every damn thing. Ugh, I'm sorry. You feel okay?" Raziel kept frowning, worried by something as he glanced back to me.

"Yeah, no, I feel great. Especially since I'm not getting covered in lava or bees anymore." He muttered. "I'm just not used to being on my own like this."

"That's right, you're not influenced by anything right now!" I smacked his back as he only appeared worried and unsure, "How's it feel to be yourself once again? No longer a slave to girly emotions and what have you?" I laughed a little, expecting him to join me in generic banter. But true to his word he stopped, only looking over himself quietly and not influenced by my moods. The angel surveyed around, turned back to the house, to the barn far behind us, contemplative. He seemed thoroughly spooked.

"Listen, Neri..." The seriousness of his tone instantly made me nervous. Apologizing to Mia made him fidget pretty badly, but he was wringing his hands at a record setting pace now. "You're... um..." He paused, having a hard time trying to get the words out. Anxious at what he was trying to say, I defaulted back to minor self loathing.

"I'm probably older than Mia? I know." Looking away, my stomach was an undulating knot of anxiety too. "Should've asked how old she was, that might've been helpful."

"No, not that. You're a..." He looked around, infinitely more anxious and making me infinitely more worried. What was he trying to say? "You're a..."

Nervousness made me blurt out stupid things, interrupting him again.

"I'm a...never going to dabble around in cursing people again? I can promise you that." I leaned away a little as Raziel finally spit it out, more angry than I think he intended.

"You're a true friend." Taken back in surprise, I was speechless, tensing up with all four hands and feet to grab onto the ground. Raziel looked doubly awkward, looking down and nervously kicking at the grass and weeds. "Y-you are. So thank you. For putting your neck on the line like this."

I started saying one thing, stopping, realizing that I didn't want to antagonize him for this, thinking of another thing to say before stopping and realizing that as he was apparently the most himself right now, that's what he felt he had to say. It left me sputtering for a couple seconds, gurgling and taken back. I was unsure what to do. All of my standard responses seemed mean spirited or inappropriate, like I couldn't physically understand what it was like to have someone appreciate me. To want me around. It was like the most expertly placed punch to the stomach in the best way. I only shuffled a little, sitting down. I had to say something.

"Thank... you." I garbled out, no hint of sass, no wordplay, nothing but unfiltered gratitude. I slowly put my head across his shoulder, shifting to my one side to hug him with my one arm, the best I could do that wasn't some manic double-armed bear hug. He hesitated for a moment, returning the gesture as we stood in the ghost of where the Transit stood, hugging. If I wasn't some massive monster, I don't doubt I would've been bawling like a baby.

About to say more, we both heard the barn-demons starting to head towards us, fists up and angry. Letting out an annoyed sigh we both headed out, able to fly home. We talked about unimportant things and didn't bring it up again.

I landed in the backyard of the Priest's home, lights dark in the place as he'd already gone to sleep. I waited for Raziel to get inside, attach back to his host, then come outside and smack me with the pike. But minutes began to tick by, tiredly rolling around in the back yard, watching the stars with a yawn. Raziel suddenly exited out the back, pike in hand, back to being angry and agitated at every little thing randomly; I assumed he was tethered once more. But that wasn't it.

"Neri! Your damn curse won't let me connect back to the Priest at all!" I flopped my hands around, busting out in a laugh.

"Oh, for God's sake."

"Is there a way you can...uncurse this curse?" I turned around, sitting there and making my seal more apparent.

"You mean with another curse? I don't think that's a great idea." Rolling my eyes, he stormed up to me and shot me out of the demon monster's body, tumbling a few times over in the grass before back up onto my feet, now well practiced in the art. "I tried my best, but I was also just saying a bit of everything because I didn't know what I was doing." I gave a curtsy.

"Mm hmm." Heaving a sigh, he looked around, unsure what do to." So I guess it's a waiting game then, huh?"

"Guess so, yeah."

"You want to play video games?" Squinting, I gave him a look.

"What's that?" Motioning me back towards the house, we ended up playing them for them for a while. We had about three more hours before the curse suddenly snapped away mid race, doing a quick scramble up the stairs to attach back to the Priest. Worried our game night would end there, he eventually made his way back down, picking up the controller again like nothing had changed.

"Ready?" I gave a slow grin, nodding. We played for a while more.

19

"Eh!" I grunted at Raziel, scouring the various crap around the room in complete boredom. He pretty much just gave up on trying to actively hide what things were about, what he did and didn't tell, as long as it didn't get personal. So I was free to point and grunt at what I wanted to know, and he'd tell me. This time, it was a small silver cross, about an inch high, with some sort of description on the bottom in a language I wasn't sure was real. Flipping it onto the back, I could see it was a pin of some sort. It looked old, even for spiritual fictitious metal.

"You get that for graduating and getting your wings." He sat on the couch, half aware, half zoned out, late on a Sunday night. I inspected it a little closer, confused about the only word I could read.

"Why does it say 'Powers" on it?" Flipping the pin over once again, I walked over to where he was, "Unless it means you've got some kind of super graduate powers."

Pointing to the word specifically on the metal, he took it from my hands.

"Oh. That's technically what this job is." He rubbed his finger across the word, shining it up. "Sort of the old fashioned way of talking about an exorcist - I'm glad we don't use this system much anymore or I'd be calling Gauzier his 'lordship' all the time." Cringing, he gave the metal back.

"Yeah that sounds pretty shitty."

I placed the item back on the shelf, looking around curiously at whatever else I could learn. In my time here, I'd pretty much scoured and learned everything I could.

Three months had passed since the Ratziel escapades and things were relaxed and good. Every now and then Raziel had to check in with Gauzier, what he'd exorcised, any problems he'd had, what he'd been teaching me. This forced him to actually teach me things, usually right before these meetings in an effort to keep up this whole ruse. Gauzier didn't ask a lot of questions about me and we were pretty keen on switching up the story on why I wasn't talking outright; we played the demon curse story for a month, then switched to I was taking a vow of silence, then to just generally being shy. He left it at that, still talking to me every now and then, but mostly keeping his business with Raziel.

Other than the time with Gauzier, or the time spent at the church, (which I sat outside for, that was a firm rule) it wasn't usual for frustrations to boil over now and then between Raziel and I. It never got to a point of trying to cleave my head in half, but it was never a terrifying time, he had certain ticks that would set him off and I did my best to accommodate them. We had disagreements, or I'd harass him into a boiling over point from time to time when we just needed a little space. Quarters here were fairly cramped.

When that happened, I'd duck out early, go roam about the rest of the house or take a walk outside, reassuring myself the entire time that my existence here was due to him, give or take. That frustration settled too and for most of my time here, I could confidently say we acted like equals.

The Priest (whom I found out was named Dave, though you'd never know it that both Raziel and I called him 'the Priest' uniformly) turned out to be a haplessly interesting guy. No wife, no kids of course, not as terrifying as once thought, dedicated to the church first and foremost, but he had a massive music collection. Katherine and Amber at the first house would turn on the radio from time to time, but didn't have an active collection of any sort. The Priest did; varied, hundreds of artists, years of music all stored in this small reading room at the far end of the house. The rest of his humble abode had typical Priest written all over it, but that music room was my sanctuary.

He remained dubious of pretty much anything in the house; one time I was running around with a vase for some reason or the other, right past him, and he barely batted an eye. Raziel and I were tolerated like spoiled kids, whatever broke was replaced, whatever caught fire was extinguished. He was usually calm about it. Of course, whenever a football game, or unfortunately, a hockey game as well would come on, that whole serenity would be right out the window. He wasn't angry, just incredibly passionate, which always threw Raziel into some kind of rage fit in response. Knowing how to successfully dodge those fits, I'd either help him train in the backyard, or just go off and listen to music while he beat the crap out of the punching bag in the basement. We had no more repeat events like before.

Early on my time there became routine, like an actual, living breathing life. I'd wake up, stretch out and wave Hello to Raziel, who'd be busy trying to look like he just got finished doing something and not just staring off into space like he actually was. From there I'd walk around a little outside, read a book or so, check out stuff on TV. Every now and then we'd all have to go on errands, sometimes to the shop/ bookstore, to church, groceries, go look at slacks, etc. It was a very simple life, very laid back, relaxed considering the circumstances, it was the kind of life that I actually enjoyed. I had someone to talk to or to at least grunt at, I had a place to live, I had stuff to do. It was a very good time.

But something began happening far more often; we'd have to go help exorcise a ghost or a demon somewhere. Their exorcism business had been doing so well that they began to earn a reputation; we began to be the team that was called when a particularly stubborn demon would come about. Go figure. That brought up a new batch of problems. Originally, there was a system. The three of us would go to a house, search around, find the demon. I'd give the thumbs up if it was a good demon I could talk to and convince to leave, thumbs down for a bad demon that needed to be exorcised. It felt like cheating, like deceiving my own side, but I had to accept that with each demon, it varied. Some called me a queen, some called me a slanderous bitch. Most of them ranged between that.

With more than one exorcism team around, our actions had to be carefully planned, mingling with other angels. They varied too, some were incredibly nice and a little regretful of their jobs, and some took it to a level that was the stuff of nightmares. But to them, demons were demons, no matter the case. The quickest route to getting fired or kicked was to not do your job, was to give the demon the time of day and let it 'corrupt your soul'. I couldn't judge a good or bad demon any longer; I just had to chop up whatever was there like the rest of them; and more then a few times, the demon in question was some variation of homesick animal refusing to leave its master. Watching angels bash that kind of demon's head in over and over again, it'd tear me apart, make me bitter and filled my dreams with miserable, recurring nightmares.

After a while, I had a hard time associating myself with any demon; it made the job easier to do, but it felt like part of me was slowly getting choked to death. I'd laugh with the others, I'd help pour the holy water over a screaming, dying soul; I began to lose touch with what was actually going on. It was only after I saw Raziel glaring at me as I laughed at some poor demon that I felt that guilt all of a sudden, stopping me cold. I didn't participate much in the exorcisms for a while, just hung out with the Priest and whomever he was interviewing. It killed a lot of my energy, a lot of my moxie. Soon after that, I found myself sitting through a few sleepless nights, staring off into nothing, same as Raziel. My mind was becoming a fateful little trap that wouldn't let a single thought go.

I remember one night especially, staring straight at the ceiling, mind racing as he came over by the doorway, arms crossed.

"There's stupid people everywhere, you know." I jumped a little, looking up and sitting to the side of the bed quickly, rubbing my hair with a grin trying to offset that I was existing in my own little Hell. "You don't have to kill the good demons just to fit in."

Furrowing my eyebrows, I cracked a small, dead laugh, how this talk seemed like one your parents tell you about how to deal with the annoying kids at school. How if they all jumped off a building, if you would too. I also laughed a little that now there was more then just bad demons to him, there were good ones too. If he said that to an exorcist, he'd be fired and kicked so many times over.

"I'm serious. I'm not telling you to go join up with the rest of the demon brethren or anything, but have some sympathy." The laughing stopped. I sat straight up, shooting him a sort of wide eyed 'who would say such a thing' glare. His frown didn't change. I could feel my eyes twitching a little, my appalled glance fading quickly. He was right; I knew he was right. Raziel nodded a little and looked around, sliding the pike from the wall.

"It's about that time." Ugh. 3 am. Raziel liked the duty about as much as I liked getting my skin peeled and melted from my back. Resting my head in my hands I waved him off. Maybe I needed a good dose of what things really were all over again. Maybe I needed to find my bearings on this world.

"Not tonight." I said faintly, getting up from the bed and walking through the basement.

"You going to be okay?" He called cautiously; it was the first night I had ever denied wanting to stay human, choosing my once thought grotesque form over humanity. I nodded a little, swaying my head back and forth. I didn't really know what I was. "You don't actually have to go outside if you don't want to." He muttered for my sake, even though it was a rule made in the middle of an argument, it did make sense. I'd barely be able to move around in here. Shrugging, I looked back outside.

My eye caught on the smoke by my feet, whisking up behind me, awkward to be out in the open for the first time in months. Parts of me missed this form, what it was capable of doing, what I kept sealed away each night. I originally thought of it as a horrible, grotesque demon face, but after some careful prodding, I managed to get some mirror-time in this form as well. It wasn't SO bad, it certainly wasn't human in any way, but if nothing else, it was a very expressive dinosaur-looking face. I could live with that.

Back in the brisk air and back to being a good seven feet tall I shot to the roof, spending the night watching the stars. I was alone for a few hours, time to think things over, to sort it out, settling my mind. Sitting peacefully, serenely, the light began to peek up from the horizon; Raziel joined me shortly after that to watch the sunrise.

"Hey! You awake?" He flicked me in the back of the head as I suddenly realized I was still standing in front of the cabinet, staring hollowly at the items on the shelf, reminiscing. Shaking my head out a little I laughed, awkward and embarrassed. Raziel shook his head at me in response, not actually angry but a little bereft of the wind that blew threw my ears sometimes. Since I had stopped exorcising my own kind, I was slowly getting back to what I'd consider normal, more relaxed, more curious on everything around me. It'd taken a while, but again it all became fascinating to me.

Raziel shook his head again, grinning a little. He really was a nice guy everyday but Sunday. He meant well; I was starting to see my whole exorcism as a series of massive misunderstandings on both our parts. Being resilient to being killed also helped that situation. We had a system, mostly a series of whistles, grunts, pointing and other little mouth-noises that weren't quite words. It wasn't the same as talking one on one, but it helped him understand a lot more of what I was saying, now that everything wasn't being taken as a threat or mistaken as a curse. And when I was really desperate to say something more complicated, I used paper. A no brainer-right? Well, trying to steady a piece of paper with a floating pencil's a lot harder then it seems, and trying to write with the thing was like dipping a toothpick in ink and calling it a writing utensil. I don't know how the poltergeists do it, it's hard. Eventually we got a small whiteboard; I don't like to use it.

We laughed a lot. More accurately, I laughed a lot at his expense, and he'd laugh at my overly-trusting nature with fellow demons. In all honesty, we had fun teaming up. The paddle-weapon made various returns into the world of exorcisms, only for one blow, or one parry. For the most part, though, he did most of the work, exorcised 90% of the demons pretty quickly, I helped when necessary. Most of my job was being the demon-o-meter. Made me feel important, choosing who lived and who died. Most of the time they lived. Every now and then, though, there'd be a really vile, dishonest evil thing to possess a house, and I'd have to think of the welfare of the people over what I regretted doing.

"Did you get that? Hello?" The end of the pike jabbed at me lightly in the head, snapping to reality once again as I realized I was staring at him, mind off on another tangent. He leaned closer, snapping his fingers in my face as I glared back, snapping fingers in his. "Oh, well then, what did I just say?" My mouth shut tight, looking side to side, regretfully bowing my head and submitting that yeah, okay, I wasn't listening. Raziel was suiting up.

"Alright, well, once more, there's another call." He slipped on his chest plate, adjusting the thing to fit like it wasn't a big, heavy annoying chest plate. I pointed to my wrist. "Yeah, it's late, but it's a pretty interesting call" I wandered back to the couch and sat on the arm of it, leaning against the back.

"What makes it interesting is that the reports are of some large, dinosaur-like demon terrorizing a house. Sound familiar?" I practically shot back to my feet. It couldn't be; this couldn't be the same damn me-demon that I fought with the first time. Raziel grinned, nodding his head a little, "See, it pays to actually listen to what I say. The real kicker is that it's right in the same neighborhood you came from."

My hands were frozen, my mind racing with a bag of questions. I flailed my arms around, looking back and forth like there was something I could do to hurry us along. The rest of the armor sat in a pile in the corner; I rushed over to it, grabbing a shoulder- plate and two pointy shin-guards, dashing across the room and up the stairs.

"Dammit, get back here, I need those!"

The Ford roared to life, backing from the driveway as the Priest ran over details like he had done a thousand times before.

"The mother called me in a panic, says that things have started haunting her house in just the last few weeks. Apparently she's in the middle of a new haunting right now." The Priest put the car in drive, snapping his head over to Raziel as he finished putting on his armor. "Is this related to what happened earlier this year?" I looked quickly to him, then to Raziel. The angel looked over his shoulder to me, who leaned forward with utmost anticipation. I had always wondered just how he managed to smooth my living in the house over with the Priest, especially if I assumed Raziel asked him to call my family to invite them over.

"Possibly."

"Is…that…associate of yours in this van right now?" The Priest looked a little more threatening in his direction. I always wonder what people in the next lane driving past think if they happen to see that.

"Yes." He let the secret escape, or what I assumed was a secret escape. The Priest grumbled some more, shaking his head and looking into the rear view mirror like I'd pop out of thin air. I shrunk down a little bit.

"I trust you know what you're doing." He said flatly.

"Yeah, me too." I glared at him, even though this was technically on my side. "You're on thin ice, pal." Raziel shot me a glare, pointing his finger at me that was generally the non-verbal rule of 'you shut up' as I cracked a laugh and buttoned my lip for the rest of the ride.

Walking up to the place, it certainly had the same sort of eeriness to it. The house was modern, a little strangely built, but pretty recent. There were no graveyards; it was close to my original house, but far enough away that I didn't recognize anything around me. Maybe this was just a new, similar demon; maybe it was actual brethren. I began to get excited; what if this demon was just like me? What if there were others out there?

"Don't get your hopes up." Raziel was behind me, leaning on the pike and inspecting the house from outside. Looking to him I gave him a little squint before just looking back to the house. He was getting good at reading expressions, advanced to a level that almost made it creepy. I wondered if he really couldn't understand me anymore, or if he was just screwing around with me in really elaborate, unnecessary way.

Leading the way like a sparkly band instructor we entered into the house, immediately recognizing the sound of screams coming from the second level. We both looked to the top of the stairs, seeing a woman suddenly darting across our view, a large, massive, familiar skeletal face and hazy black form in tow. Raziel was quick to race after it initially before hesitating, looking up towards the demon before back at me. I was half up the stairs myself.

"Isn't that…" He said, completely dumbstruck. My head nodded faintly.

It was the same demon. What I saw, same skull-shape, same… everything. It was impossible! I felt the house shudder; chill like the cold radiated from the walls. All the energy in the household rippled, that awareness, that recognition; I knew we had been spotted; I knew that this entire visit would be personalized, just for me. It was a trap. I instantly began to back away from Raziel, began to separate myself. Not this. Not again.

"This is a bad demon, right?" He said emptily as the cold began to focus.

"Of course it's bad!" I hissed back, leaping over the rail bar as my intuition was going nuts, a whole symphony of alarms and terror to chase my steps. Pushing myself farther away, I stood alone in the middle of the floor, hand hovering by my side. I motioned Raziel to stay where he was as I eyed the walls suspiciously. Where was it?

"Well, it's our little angel wannabe" The wallboards rattled with the disgusted, murky voice, coming from every darkened corner at the same time to rattle my fears. "Come to exorcise another demon, demon?" Where was it? My breath got short, scared.

"What did it say? What does it want?" Raziel hissed at me, holding the pike in a ready-attack position. Scattered and frantic, I pointed to myself repeatedly, feeling the jolt of energy suddenly rip through the air. The demon burst through the middle of the staircase, hands gripping onto the railing and scattering them at the touch.

"This ends now!" It shouted as I ripped the paddle weapon from thin air, throwing it straight for the hazy skull demon. There was a snarl, the weapon hit dead on, spikes into its face as it exploded into a plume of smoke. The demon screeched unhappily. "Oh, don't you dare!"

It surged through the black mist, unscathed, mouth over me like the serrated jaws of death. Before I could think to escape, it snapped me up tightly.

"Neri!" Raziel called as the beast landed hard on the floor. It turned, busting through a few more walls before leaping clear into the outside, running full out on disjointed limbs that were clear of fog. The house began to shrivel from view as my mind raced, panicked as huge, sickle-sized teeth pinned my arms to my side, a passenger to whatever this demon had planned. As we slowed back to a walk it became shrouded in shadows once more, spitting me arrogantly onto the grass as I flipped once to a stop. There was no other time where I wished I had my demon body handy. For just a few moments, we were alone, demon panting/growling in irritation, enraged. The haze around the demon sucked closer and farther away as it breathed, rushing out through the grass with it's long, angry drawl. The demon lowered its head, tiny beaded eyes furrowed tightly on me.

"I'm sick of this, alright? I've played your little game the first round, and now this little mission of yours has to stop. I mean, seriously, exorcising your own kind? What the Hell is wrong with you? Is that what you're so desperate to learn?" It waited for an answer, looking angrily in both my eyes as I couldn't help but gape, taken back and confused. Something inside me began to boil angrily as it's eyes narrowed closer, "Get your head out of your ass, you pathetic excuse for a—" The demon's mouth snapped closed, letting out a frustrated sigh as we both heard Raziel jogging after us, armor clinking, not far now. I couldn't even begin to gather myself to try and understand why this demon knew me as well as it did.

Raziel huffed and puffed to a stop, holding the pike out, the end rattling like mad.

"Hey! IF...if you want a fight, then I'm--" The shadowed mass suddenly bit onto the pike head itself. He grabbed the handle with both hands, trying to pull the weapon from its mouth as the demon snapped the pike off where the metal latched onto the wood. Biting onto the very edge of the metal blade, grinning with a warped and dented piece of metal jutting from its mouth, the demon threw it back into it's turbine of teeth. Chomping down again, it spat the hunk of scrap off to the side, twisting its body around proudly at doing so.

"Demon matters. Piss off for a few minutes, junior." The demon spat out in plain English, same thick accent. Glittering bits of metal fell from its teeth, gleaming. Raziel stood there in unabridged shock, glancing hollowly at his holy weapon, now just a frayed stick and a metallic jumble as the focus came back to just the monster and I.

"You... you're not the same demon from before, are you?"

"Aww, why would you say that?" Its voice suddenly jumped in octaves, clearly feminine. Clearly very close to my own. I took a step away;

looking around for some sort of help, some way out of this. There was more fight in me when I wasn't in a weak form like this, more anger, more vengeful as I'd always been, but I had nothing. The demon hissed at me, jabbing her head practically next to mine. "You're obviously still hiding, so let me talk to you like you're an idiot, then. You don't fit in here, you know it. Quit this stupid charade while you're ahead, save you, save him, cut all this bullshit that's in store and come with me."

"I don't know what you're talking about." I folded my arms before quickly un-folding and using it to point angrily, "Now, as your queen, I demand you show me your real form, not this half-baked in-between you've got here." I muttered the words like I knew what they meant. In-between? The demon laughed, raising an eyebrow.

"Well, there's still hope for you then, isn't there my queeeeen?" The demon bowed sarcastically, black shadows quickly dropping from its shoulders as she rose up from it, gaining height, gaining mass. The hazy demon was essentially a floating skull demon head, accompanied with insect-like legs that shot out from the middle/ but this…this actual form was a thousand times more terrifying. At least three times the size of the first form, it was massive. The body was a dull, darkened red a few steps from black, with a great row of spines/ horns coming up from behind it's head, tapering out onto the body, with one very large giant horn in the middle of its face.

The head was like mine, though the snout stumpier, tail shorter, the nose almost more pushed up with one loose ring hanging from it. Two massive teeth shot from the bottom lip that hung saggily from the corners of her mouth, but what was really noticeable was the white scar-like tick marks all over her body. Each one of its legs had two large protruding bone-spurs from the sides of it's ankles, back toes gathered up on one another to make a sort of jumbled peg. It's body and face was almost a horse, the legs were thinner, body overall less muscular or bulky as mine was, but standing at least twenty five feet tall it didn't matter. I used all my will to look over to Raziel, who had taken more then a few cautionary steps away, eyes flared wide in complete terror.

"There, how does that work for you?" The voice thundered from the sky as I wondered how embarrassing it would be to ask it to go back to the small, hazy looking skull monkey it had been. The demon eyed me with supreme annoyance, bending all the way back down by me to give me the same snarl as before, magnified. "Look at yourself! You call this an existence? Playing assistant to an exorcist? Have a little dignity!" I suddenly snapped from my awed trance.

"My existence here is my concern, not yours or any other demons, so butt out!"

The demon gave out a very girly, indignant gasp that almost broke my anger.

"You say that like I haven't…" She trailed off, biting on the own side of her mouth, "You stubborn brat. Why do I bother with you when you treat me like this." Her tone suddenly wavered with emotion, snapping back to the cold, heartless tone of the gigantic demonic beast before me.

"You're coming back with me. I'm not wasting anymore of my time playing babysitter to you!"

"Babysitter?!" I stomped forward, hands on my hips. The idea of a giant dinosaur horse demon thing was surprisingly comfortable; distantly familiar. "With all the destruction you've caused, all the torture you've put me through 'babysitting' me, I hate to see what you do to your enemies!" The demons head snapped quick to me in real anger, glaring with tiny, beady little red eyes.

"Whatever that life was, I don't want it anymore!" I yelled like I knew what I was talking about, guessing and assuming she wanted whatever got me into Hell in the first place. Wanted the worst of the worst. "I don't want to be a demon, I want to make my own choices. I don't have to listen to you!"

"So that's how its going to be." It grumbled low, shrinking a little in size to something a less massive and more dexterous. "You stupid, spoiled little brat. Always playing human!" She reached out and grabbed me, holding onto me tight. Quick on her heels she spun around, pointing me in Raziel's direction, which remained frozen in place.

"Has your little lover boy here seen all the tricks you can do?!" The demon began to laugh manically, thumb submerging into my spine, a feeling that felt nothing short of a thousand sewing needles going through my skin. It began to shake me, my body changing like someone was flipping TV channels, my perspective and features that I could see changing too. I suddenly became taller in one, shorter in the other, fatter with the next, vision full of long blonde hair after that, shorter once again before switching back to how it had first been, my regular human/demonic body. Tiredly looking up to Raziel he looked completely baffled, fading out as the demon brought me close to her face.

"This is your very last chance. Come back to Hell with me, or stay up here and suffer though more heartache and loneliness than anyone deserves." Her voice drew sympathetic, sad. It didn't switch back. Heaving for breath I curled my lip, glaring at her.

"I don't want to associate with you. I don't want to be a demon!" She glared at me for just a second longer, disappointed, before pointing me back in the angel's direction.

"How about one last trick." It said lowly, like someone forced it out of the demon. Her thumb jammed back into my spine before pulling out, dropping me hard onto the ground. Instantly, my senses began screaming at me. "Why don't we enjoy the real thing for a bit, remember how life actually feels!" — Real?

I felt the grass around me. Felt it. Little hairs tingled on my skin as the wind blew past. Looking at my hand I only saw solid flesh, no visibility behind it and no transparency. I was real, visible. It all would've been a gift any other time. I looked over to Raziel, seeing him, though faint like a ghost. He leaned over and swiped a hand right through my head, my body reacting like a cold chill as my eyes bugged from my sockets. I gave a pitiful cough.

My insides felt like they were full of needles, hands began to shake, jittery as I dropped to my knees. No, no I wanted this, wanted to feel everything like I pined for in my dreams, but my body wasn't stable. There was something missing in this, as a viewable apparition, but my soul was frayed, it couldn't handle the stress. Intelligent spirits knew how to do this, manifesting physically, but my soul was thrown into it without a clue. I felt myself begin to shut down, coughing into my hand and finding it covered in blood as it struggled to get back to the other realm, dying slowly and painfully in the human one.

"Isn't life wonderful" The demon growled at me, a slightly stronger view of it as it sat there, watching me suffer. My body began to shake, desperate for food, water; my thoughts began to cloud on themselves as I only propped myself up with my arms, blood dripping steadily from my eyes, nose, mouth and ears.

"Neri!" I could hear him faintly, clear, but soft and nestled in a bed of static, even though he was shouting. Heaving for breath I could barely bring myself to his gaze, vision quickly darkening. I heard him shout to the demon, panicked. "Stop doing this! Neri, are you okay? What do you want?" The demon only laughed as I kept my head low.

"Now you want to talk? Here, let's talk about demons killing off other demons, how about that?" It jabbed a frustrated claw hard at Raziel's armor, denting the shoulder piece. "You're nothing but the problem here, you little worm!" She angrily translated as Raziel seemed to ignore her, head down by me. He frowned, looking back up to the colossal beast.

"That doesn't give you the right to kill her!" The skull demon laughed.

"Kill? Please, we're like cockroaches. You on the other hand have no business addressing me with anything less than the utmost respect." Raziel was suddenly yanked out of view as the demon snapped him up, holding tightly onto the angel in her mouth.

"Stop!" I coughed out, voice echoing loudly around me, trying to get closer, trying hard to see through the black mist that was quickly overtaking me. A quick little shock from the demon brightened everything back up, setting back my body shutting down by another minute as I had to suffer through painfully dying again.

"You'll want to see this." The demon said evilly, biting down harder on Raziel. I could see him struggle in pain, eyes begin to widen in fear as I crawled to get closer. My heart was racing, blood oozing from my eyes and nose all at once.

"Stop! Don't…" I gasped for air, desperate for options; I couldn't let him die, couldn't be responsible for any more violence like this. "I'll… go with you… just don't hurt him. This is my fault, my responsibility, don't take it out on someone else!" Coughing again, the cold, icy stare of the red-eyed demon looked over me pitifully, no joy on its face, no pleasure in what it was about to do.

"I gave you nothing but those chances, and you spat in my face. I'm only doing as I was told to, by you. Welcome to the second phase of your master plan." The demon suddenly bit down with everything it had as Raziel screamed out in pain, body snapping in half and falling from the massive demon's jaws. Each half hit the ground with a sickening thud not feet from where I lay.

"Ra…Raziel!" I reached a hand out towards him, couldn't move, couldn't breath as he lay as two bloody lumps of angel, rolling a bit. His eyes were half open, gasping for air once or twice before quickly shutting, resting, the body letting out one last sigh. Raziel's eyes looked dull, flat. This couldn't be real, it had to be a trick as I saw him lay there, halved, very dead. Whimpering, I struggled forward another few inches, trying to help, trying to do…anything. "Ra--" As my fingers finally were able to brush the metal of his armor, the body began to blow away with the wind like condensed ash, disappearing to nothing.

Tears began to fall from my eyes, bloody red tears. I couldn't stare away from where he had laid, to even recognize that the demon had suddenly vanished, to see that I was not alone in the yard, to understand anything but devastating horror. My body made the decisions for me as I slowly slumped to the ground, collapsed over myself as my heart gave out, dying.

20

"Miss!"

The heartbeat was there; sloppy, lazy, crotchety and annoyed with all actual existence, but still there. Stirring back into consciousness the grass was beneath me, blades of it pricking into my nose. I was still alive, a real thing for the time being.

"Miss, are you okay?" My thoughts struggled to gather, to recognize who was screeching at me, breathing hard as my heart raced out of control. Wait. I knew that voice. Woah, woah woah, wait. I pushed myself from the ground, propping onto my elbows high enough for my head to turn to the side, finding the Priest standing over me. He wasn't looking past me, wasn't sensing some sort of ghostly disturbance somewhere else, it was me. Right at me. I flopped a hand to my jaw line, feeling the side of my face completely smooth, devoid of jaw-horns. Like a driving force to the back of my head I coughed up a lot more blood, coating both arms in the stuff. You could practically hear the Priest's blood pressure skyrocket.

"Oh my good Lord." He crouched closer to my face as I closed myself off, putting both hands over my head. I deserved nothing. No sympathy, no help; I didn't deserve the chance to be alive, not even for a second. That wasn't going to be a problem for much longer; my heartbeat began to get erratic, strange.

"Don't help." I hissed out, dropping off mid-sentence, heart throwing itself around wildly as the black mist clouded my vision quickly, knees buckling from under me, strength dying quickly. The mist doubled up with the actual black mist, the demonic-body mist as it began to shoot from the ground, covering me up slowly. "I'm so...sorry. I wasn't strong enough." I coughed out, looking quickly to the Priest as the mist covered over my body, expanding out, shipping me back to the demonic beast I

234

once loathed.

"Miss? MISS?" He shouted, looking around frantically as I disappeared from his view, pulled from the human world of the living, back to the one I belonged in, the transparent world where the best I did was watch alongside. After a moment I was spat out, good as new, body systems check, functional, right as rain except almost three times my height and half as adorable. This didn't alleviate my mood.

I slowly moved my body out of the way of his desperate search. He whipped his head around before yelling back to the house, the call of sirens not far away. The man sat, pulling a handkerchief from his pocket, wiping his forehead and muttering to himself as he looked around him, scanning the grounds carefully. I sat like a severely regretful monster not two feet away- the Priest could never see me, only finding out where I was through Raziel. I don't know why I was invisible to him. Probably something relating as nothing but an evil, conniving demon. I felt like utter dirt.

He slowly stopped, sitting back on his one ankle, knee to the ground as I fidgeted around, curling tighter into my self, head hanging low. With an unsure frown, he whispered into the early morning air, like he was afraid to talk to himself alone.

"You're still here, aren't you?" He said lowly, not mad, but only concerned. I nodded out of his vision anyway, conditioned well. The Priest didn't say anything for a few minutes, only rifling around in his pocket as I sat there, awkward. Out of nowhere, he suddenly dropped his handkerchief on the ground. Expecting him to pick it up, the Priest stared at the cloth, waiting for something from me.

It landed half inside my foot, half on the grass. A test; this had to be a test. What should I do? Give the old man some kind of reassurance that the half-dead woman on the ground was still sitting about, or ignore it and stop trying to give him any more hope, stop trying to force my existence, try and disappear. I had to stop pretending that I was a welcomed guest, that I was just misunderstood, that I could fit in. Looking to my body as it sat here, tail swishing about, wings hanging sadly from my back, the long running tuft of red hair along my spine and the four sets of nasty looking claws, I mean, who was I kidding?

Still.

The Priest looked at that handkerchief, looking back and forth a little more, running his fingers along the seam of his shirt. He knew something was up; if my detachment from Raziel was anything like his, it would definitely be something noticeable. Picking it up or not picking it up, damage had already been done. He knew it was me, he had to. He'd be trying to talk with anyone else, be trying some other way of communication.

Tired, morale low, I carefully stuck a claw under one end of the fabric, barely getting leverage as I slowly placed it into his open hands, handing it back to the Priest solemnly. The action said that yes, I was still here; even if everything in me felt like my presence was a huge bother, that I didn't deserve to be. The man looked vaguely in front of him, holding the napkin for a second before folding it, placing it quietly into his pocket. He seemed hardly shocked.

"Raziel is gone, hm?" The Priest turned back towards the house, hearing the sirens getting closer and closer, turning on a street that would eventually lead them here. Someone must've called them for me. My heart dropped a little; he knew what had happened. Taking a sigh, the Priest shrugged, "It happens. He'll be back in a few days, he always is." I knew this. In my mind, it didn't make things any better. I fucked up. Bad. Demons had a hierarchy too, he said. Now I knew it.

He stood from his spot, scanning for me one last time before walking back towards the house without a word. I watched him go, sat there like an oversized, unloved dog, unsure what to do. I had to look, my stomach fluttered with worry, with fear that I'd see half a disembodied angel, scrambling on the ground towards me in bloody hatred. But as I turned, as I looked, all I saw was the bits of the pike and an open field.

Nothing was there; no stains, no blood, no armor, remaining ashes, nothing. The pike head and the bit of handle were the only things laying about; I sat down with a groan, protectively shielding the wrecked weapon like my own young. What the Hell happened? My fight with the she-demon the first round was nothing like that. Was I being led on? I mean, that had to be it; I'd never willingly sacrifice someone for the sake of some plan, some 'master plan' as she had said. But the way she said it, it was a duty, something forced. The whole idea made me sick to my stomach.

Something eeked out, these pitiful noises from my pitiful mouth; half growl, part moan, looking out and around me like he too would pop out of thin air -I needed to get my priorities in order; He wouldn't be re-appearing here, he said that he'd be coming back to the Priests house. It couldn't have been the first time since a demon had gotten the better of him. I didn't know the exact way it all worked, just that when he faked his death the first time at the mansion, he told me they'd be expecting him back at the Priest's house in two days. Sitting here, lamenting, fixed nothing.

"I'm really, really sorry." I remarked to that patch of grass, once laden with angelic blood, turning about face militarily. I picked the pike handle and head up with a heavy sigh, gathering to my feet. I did screw up. Maybe this was time I needed to make things better, though; as long as I tried to fix my mistakes, that had to count for something, right?

The Ford roared to life in the distance, the Priest was getting ready to leave.

Immediately, I began to run towards it without another thought about leaving this family behind. Times were good, life was fun and enjoyable. I at least owed him an explanation, and an apology. Turning an eye to the sky I sneered, running full out towards the car, watching the van pull onto the lazy suburban street. Right behind it, I chased the van all the way to the highway, giving up on my pursuit and leaping to sit on the back of it instead. Determination grew more and more powerful, dead-set on making everything right that could possibly be right by the time he revived himself back at the home. My time here had been good, and it was my duty now to repay my debt. The sun began to rise by the time we pulled into the driveway.

Back at home I started right away, squeezing myself through the door frames to go back into the basement, keeping my bulky body parts close to me, not to break anything, wreck anything like a vicious little statue. What could I do? The whiteboard caught my eyes, snagging it from the wall and placing it at my feet.

After about twenty minutes of serious contemplation, I had a nifty little list going.

-Fix the pike

- Fix anything I'd wrecked in the house

- Try to write out an apology.

Fixing the pike was my biggest chore; the metal was all bent over itself, wearing a few new holes, dented and just short of being an unrecognizable mess. I couldn't go to the workshop; no amount of clothing could cover up my brutish aspects now.

So I set to it; I tried bending the pike back into shape using my strange little hands, the metal cutting into my fingers like it was made to, stubborn to bend, fold, move or re-form at all. Tossed to the side I moved onto the pike handle, gnawing at the frayed end until it was practically flat. It wouldn't win any beauty contests, no sir, but it didn't look so bad. Satisfied, I placed it aside, going to work on generally cleaning around.

I tried this once before, about a month into my stay here...

"What are you doing?" Raziel was reading something, looking up from the side of his book as I came down the stairs with a bottle of cleaner and some paper towels.

"Cleaning." I said dutifully, feeling the need to do something on my long, drawn out bouts of standing around and staring at the wall. The fun I had, oh man, but still, it got boring. So instead of feeling like a leech, I could try and help out a little bit. Forgetting for a moment that what I said sounded like nothing I wagged the cleaning bottle around in the air, pretend-wiping it for the full experience. The angel slowly began to shake his head at me, baffled. "We don't make anything, any mess here. There's nothing to clean."

"There's got to be something." I bit my upper lip, sneering to and from the things in the room; something had to be dirty. Something had to be cleaned; Raziel laughed, sitting up.

"There's NOTHING to clean. The Priest gets a woman to dust in here every Sunday while we're at church, and she cleans anything else that needs it." He shook his head again, sitting back down, "Go read a book or something."

"I've read your books" I said curtly, still spying for dirt, "The non-religious ones are boring and tactical, and the rest are so religious they'd burn off any normal person's fingers mid-sentence. And I'm not saying that just because, I'm legitimately critiquing them like any other book."

"You're talky today." He said, not listening for obvious reasons.

"Gah, I know, I'm bored out of my mind." I relented, walking to the tiny window of the basement, the small rectangle leading to the outside world. It remained closed most of the time because it was a stupid pointless window, and that it was also rusty and semi-broken. Taking a finger and pushing against it I got it to open, pulling away and letting it swing in an annoying series of screechy, obnoxious arcs. Slowly looking towards Raziel he already had that dead, cold stare, threatening me from the comfort of the couch. I pushed it open again, finding his face now at a more extreme degree of annoyance. I laughed, slowly closing it without the noise pestering us both. "Touchy."

"Go dig around in the old toy closet if you need something to do. Second floor, next to the bedroom."

"We have a TOY closet?! And you're just telling me about this NOW?" I cracked a laugh, racing upstairs with boundless energy that could power the building. He muttered something as I left; I didn't care. There were little nooks and crannies all over this building, little treasure coves of hidden fun in my theological doom here. The toy closet didn't disappoint. Mostly full of board games wearing enough dust to keep a person warm, they looked used and old, practically pointless. Interesting, to say the least.

I stuck my head deeper into the closet, scanning the boxes for something interesting, looking at the ones I'd never heard of before, painted plastic figures and an extremely retro style all over the place, like they'd been here for years and years, untouched. Leaning against the wall I opened one up, filing through various cards and trying to make sense of it.

"These used to be for the kids that'd come over for Sunday school." I dropped the box out in surprise, spilling cards and dice everywhere. I didn't even realize he was there; I huffed for a moment before squatting and trying to pick up the pieces.

"I thought you had precious books to read." I muttered under my breath, embarrassed while ruffling the cards in my hand back into order. He continued to stand there, watch me pick up pieces until I spread my hand out at the rest of the mess all around me. "Feel free to help!" It was a clear enough message; he leaned down and helped me put the rest of the game back into the box.

"Don't you get sick of talking to yourself?" He said as I looked up, picking the game from the floor and filing it back into the closet.

"Sometimes." I sighed, looking around at the other titles. "It's pretty isolating." I shrugged, digging deeper.

"But you're a smart guy; you figure it out most of the time." I looked farther into the closet, seeing something lumpy and colorful towards the back. There was no way to tell what it was, so I reached back blindly for it, "Though it doesn't help me when you're being a pain in the ass, that's the worst."

"Pain in the ass, that's the worst." The toy squawked from my hand as I pulled it into the light, shaking out the little bits of dust. A parrot! A…fake standing parrot on a faker wooden branch. With a laugh I shook it, the parrot repeating what sounded like a disjointed horse running on pavement; flapping its one working wing while doing so. I leaned a little closer, inspecting how it worked.

"Well, that's interesting." I turned to Raziel. "What does wacky talking Polly teach kids? Why is this here?"

"Interesting, Polly teaches kids." The parrot repeated as it was suddenly yanked from my hands by the angel, who stared at it like the parrot was preaching winning lotto numbers.

"Ugh, God that's creepy." I muttered.

"I could hear that…"

"Hear that, hear that."

"Yeah, so can everyone."

"Can everyone, can everyone." The bird certainly took its duty seriously; it was already starting to get annoying. I rubbed the bridge of my nose before suddenly snapping to attention. Hear that… hear me? Though the repeat parrot? Its golden plastic eyes were suddenly shoved in my face, parrot hanging over me like a recording microphone. After it finished singing its broken horse song over again from being moved, I cautiously spoke.

"Marco…"

"Marco, Marco"

"Polo!" Raziel brought it back closer to him, the two of us staring at one another for a second before it became a mad dash for the basement. God bless the crappy toys of yesteryear!

The bird garbled nonsensically the entire run through the kitchen; Raziel led the way with me close behind, making the last turn to go down the stairs. Unfortunately; ghosts stop caring about walls and don't have to have spatial awareness, it slips your mind. As ghosts exist, they pass to and from one room to the other with no need to use the door, make sure it's unlocked, so on and so forth. Same can't be said for anything you carry, any real, physical thing; sometimes, you forget those rules, you overlook that what you have may in your hands.

This time, we overlooked that the repeat parrot was a fairly large, clunky thing. Understandably, Raziel practically beat the thing into the wall on the last turn, arms loose at his sides, the momentum of the run swung the toy hard, right into the drywall. Hard enough that it cracked the base, hard enough that it broke away from the base, tumbling in a strange, short arc. We were both excited enough that we didn't realize this in time, and that as he went to practically leap down the stairs, he inadvertently punted the repeat parrot across the basement and into the wall, smashing it, and knocking over a ceramic plate in the process, smashing that as well.

Our glee dropped clear of our faces as we both stopped at the bottom of the stairs, hollowly looking at the repeat parrot and the carnage that surrounded it. Not a word was spoken from either side as we slowly turned to one another, then back to the scene. I forgot who exactly cracked first, but we burst out laughing knowing full well that a stupid repeating parrot would never work anyways. Laughing that it was a one in a million shot, that it was so very unfortunate; but laughing together spoke leagues more for an experience then any toy could.

I smiled, remembering how I actually got to clean something that day, how we joked about that for days afterwards as I cleaned the basement now, all demonic and scaly and oversized. The sun was just setting, the end of day one without an angel, a sort of trial run on my own. It dawned on me how silent everything was, how eerie this basement became with no real activity as I tried to fill it, going back to fix the pike head again. I began to gnawing it back into shape like I had done for the handle without much luck, but I did manage to make it look a little less like a jumbled mess and more like the scalding weapon of pain and torture I'd come to know. Holding it in my hands it struck me; with the weapon broken and disfigured like this, was I stuck in this body? I had figured that the pike would fix itself for some reason when he got back; that he'd take it with him and just appear back like his holy armor did. It didn't. With all the dents in it from before, how old and rustic it looked, it wasn't a part of him, it had to mean I'd be...

"No..." I began to shake, began to tremble, "No no no no no!" I could put up with a lot, but being stuck like this for the rest of my time? I knew that soul was beneath this layer, that I wasn't some evil dinosaur from Hell, that I was more- but stuck in this body for eternity?

You can fly, you can fight like this- my body tried to reassure me, tried to help, to cope. I didn't want to fly, I didn't care all the crap I could do like this, I wanted to be myself, wanted to be what I actually was, not think that showing off in some powerful demon body was enough to make me happy. This... this form was not 'happy' this form was 'dealing with it'. It was a monster, plain and simple. I didn't have the knowledge to know how to escape this body, I didn't have the awareness, the expertise to shift forms on my own.

Staring at the pike a little differently, I suddenly went to work like my sanity depended on it, slamming that metal into the ground to bend it, working though the night. I tried time after time to activate it like I had done once before, smacking myself on the back over and over and over again until the area was bruised and bloody (only for a bit, it'd heal nicely for me to start injuring myself all over again out of desperation). No luck. It was still a little misshapen, but any person who saw it pre-mauling, and saw it now post-mauling could tell it was the same weapon; just with a few extra wiggles in the middle of it, and an extra point that would snag on anything unlucky enough to catch it. The floor around me held little blood pools, where my bending and sharpening had hit me, where my fingers had sliced into it, where I tested it on my own arms to see if it was sharp enough. When I was done with it, the pike had become a sharp, crooked, nasty little thing.

Glaring with disdain at my own hands, worried that the rest of my life would be devoid of everything I grew to love as a regular human being, I suddenly heard a noise, a laugh, from upstairs. Tired and dismayed I laid the weapon on the ground, slowly and carefully sticking my head through the floor without even having to stand up.

In the middle of the main living room with the much larger TV, sat the Priest. He was staring at a chessboard, thinking hard at it like he was in the middle of a game. Looking at it myself, both sides were at start without a single piece moved, nothing out of place. I tilted my head a little, confused as the Priest only sat up taller, eyes narrowing.

"Neri... right?" He spoke as I suddenly ducked close back to the ground, just my eyes above the floorboards, spooked.

I didn't entirely know where I stood with the Priest- he was more or less the person I avoided, I didn't talk to, because of obvious reasons. He's got a literal guardian angel, he's the business side of their" Great Beyond" exorcising campaign- he's the guy that fills the gas in the car, while I sit and chat one-sidedly with Raziel. I knew he liked music, I assumed he used to have a body of people that attended a church before he went full time as an exorcist, and he stashed old, sometimes broken (or now broken) toys in a closet upstairs. All other things, clueless on. Just in the last twenty four hours, I'd learned more things about him than I had the previous four months, and I'd barely spoken to the man.

More than that, I couldn't actually talk to him, much like Raziel, and I couldn't even be seen by the guy. It took a while after I started joining them on their exorcist excursions for him to realize I was even there. I was the epitome of nothing to him. But from the few conversations I'd been apart of in the Transit about even existing...he wasn't pleased, but he didn't seem to care. I slowly raised my head back to table height, monstrous hands mid-level, ready to duck back down in case he had an entire case of holy water ready to throw.

"You've been working on something all day." He looked out and around him, not focusing on me specifically. My stomach flipped, nervous about what he was trying to do. Was he going to exorcise me himself? "I can tell because it sounds like Raziel is swinging the pike at a wall." I put my head back down to the floor below me, looking at the pike for a second. Guess it made sense that if he could hear and understand Raziel, he'd hear and know the sound the pike makes. The Priest laughed a little, sitting back in the chair as I brought my upper body more on the level. I guess I could try and talk to him, no sense in not giving it a shot, but I wasn't expecting much.

"If that's annoying, I'm sorry." I said softly. The Priest only laughed for a moment, shaking his head.

"I can't hear a word you're saying, only sounds like someone's left the TV on in another room." My head lowered a bit, depressed by another shining example of trying to stick the square peg in the round hole. I wonder occasionally what I'm trying to do with all this, where I'm trying to go in life. Why I keep trying so hard. He continued on.

"So, Neri is living in my house. I finally get a straight answer- Raziel has bizarre tastes." I ducked away a little more again- this couldn't be good. Did Raziel never tell him I was living here? What sort of strange lie had he made up? The Priest scratched the side of his nose, leaning back again.

"When we had your previous 'family' over to visit, I asked...uh... what's her name..." He snapped his fingers, looking around like the answer would be tucked into the corner of a room. I repeated" Katherine" about ten times over by the time he gave up "Kristen, I think, how she managed to communicate with you when her daughter wasn't around. She said she didn't. But before all that, she said you'd used a system of knocks." Raising my head a bit more, I kept my gaze even with the table as he suddenly rubbed his eyes, worn down by something.

"Our poor clients must feel like this, but one knock for yes, two for no, okay?" Worried a bit, I raised farther into the room, still apprehensive. With a careful claw, I tapped on the table once. The Priest jumped where he sat, leg hitting the side of the chessboard and nearly taking the whole thing out "OH! You actually are in here!" Snorting with a pulled back grin, I tapped on the table once more.

"Well...uh..good, yeah. I didn't ... know if you were actually listening, but okay. I wasn't just..." Laughing a little, I pulled my upper half to rest my elbows on the floor, roughly about the height I'd be if I stood there as a human being. "So... uh... you're a demon, then." The laughing slowed, burdened again just a bit. I tapped on the table. The Priest frowned.

"I see. That's unfortunate... but I appreciate the honesty." Deliberating for a second, he suddenly leaned forwards, taking his first move on the chessboard- he shook his head in disagreement with some thought not in the conversation, "I told Raziel not to get involved with demons; but here we are. He's got previous history of doing so, but I'm sure you've heard that story already." I stopped, waiting there, readying myself for some sort of backlash. The Priest only gave a small smile.

"Do you know what Raziel talks about the entire time when we're supposed to be praying in church?" I lowered my eyebrows, concerned- with a careful claw, I moved my knight up a bit, the Priest's eyes snapping to the action with a smile. He moved his next piece quickly before resting back in the chair, thinking. I tapped twice on the table.

"You." The Priest nodded like he was annoyed with the topic, but half meant. "He mostly talks about you." Sitting up a little taller, I looked the man square in the eyes, trying to read him. He looked a little conflicted, but pretty much at peace.

"That's not the best when we're supposed to be paying attention, but he rattles on and on about stuff that's happened, usually until I tell him to cut it out." The Priest laughed, delegating on a move, head resting on a hand.

Making my move, the Priest quickly brought his bishop into play, the two of us deliberating for a few turns, playing a regular game of chess. CorNering one of his knights, he suddenly sat back in his chair, contemplating.

"Did Raziel happen to tell you anything about when he started working with me here?" My eyes popped open, no longer caring about chess. I knocked twice on the table. The Priest snickered. "Figures as much, he's never been an open book." The man kept his eyes down, thinking as he talked.

"When I was in my mid twenties, I finally passed my last tests for becoming an Exorcist. I was three years later than everyone else, didn't really like the testing part of it- I didn't fail out of anything, I had another job on the side that took up my time." He made his move as I started contemplating mine; the Priest sat back, looking along the walls. "Our final test and the last event is receiving and accepting your angelic gift - and everyone else had gotten such talkative, happy and excited exorcist partners. My turn finally comes, and I get...' He moved his hands around a bit, face almost frustrated and disappointed. I watched closely, interested.

"Well I get the one that won't talk to me. I say 'Hello' I say 'I'm happy to meet you' and 'What's your name'" The Priest laughed, shaking his head, "Raziel just stands there, tells me his name, and says he's tired and wants to leave, then tries to walk off. He was the worst, he was literally the worst one there. I remember feeling like my whole career was doomed and I got the defective angel in the bunch." I laughed along with him, perplexed. He didn't strike me as that type of person now.

"He was always short-tempered about a lot of things. Hated demons. Always hated demons." The Priest grew quieter, dismayed as I held my claw above my piece, halted. "Only wanted to do work. Never interested in talking or socializing. He was roughly about my age when we first partnered together, but he acted like my grandfather did. It took a very long time for us to even become friends."

"It doesn't take an empathetic bond with a person to realize when they just don't care about themselves. That they've given up. That's been Raziel for the last thirty years." I held my chess piece for a second, thinking and sad. "It was Raziel's idea to have his place separate from mine, here. It's been his idea to keep to himself, even despite everything." Reading the frustration, the disappointment and worry in his eyes, it suddenly changed to something else, lifting into a smile. I slowly took my move, eyes intent on the Priest.

"But with you, well..." He grinned before shaking his head, almost disappointed in a far-off, hardly caring way. "You're good for him." I beamed, nearly dropping my piece onto the board as the Priest ruined the moment.

"I'm about 95% sure it's not a curse, but when you're friends with a person for most your life, and you see them act like this for so long, you just want to see them happy, to see them find their place." He shook his head.

"And I'm not sure what place that is, or what you even count for, but I know having you around makes him excited for the future, and excited to improve and see new things." The Priest moved one last time, suddenly spotting I'd been walled into a check. "So if you're wondering, that's why I've been okay to let you stay here, even though this goes against so...so many things."

I stopped, hardly knowing what to say. Why bring this up now? He could've gone on, not telling met his.

"Th...Thank you." I smiled. The Priest only kept his eyes to the board, a glint of conquest in his eyes as he took the last obvious move.

"Life can be unpredictable. So can death, I guess." I moved my king to the side one space as he countered me, folding his arms. Checkmate.

"But you'll need to get better at chess though to earn your keep." He laughed as I slowly tipped my king over. That was fine, I wasn't paying much attention to the actual chess game. I didn't know what to think, Raziel was just that big brother, sometimes antagonistic figure, right? The dis-sociate? The thought of making him happy warmed me, though. Made my heart fill with joy; until I remembered it was my fault he'd gotten killed. That weight was still sitting on my throat.

The Priest motioned to the board once more.

"Up for another game?" Least I wasn't so terrible a chess player.

I nodded at first, forgetting about communicating before knocking once more on the table. The Priest hesitated for a second, thinking on something with a smile as we both re-organized our sides, ready to start again. We played for a while more.

"It's almost time" The Priest suddenly said out of the blue, mid turn. I looked up, head snapping outside to see it already dark, the end of the second day. Already? I panicked, standing back up before realizing I was already standing in the basement. The Priest looked around, trying to find something, gaze narrowing towards the basement, "Yup, he's coming back." I frowned a little at him, unsure as I suddenly saw a whitish oval opened up alongside me, hanging in mid air. It spooked me, brightest white as it began to drift through the floorboards, heading into the basement. Squatting down and dropping back through the floor, there was another white circle about head-height, a ghostly opaque floating oval, the two not far from one another. I backed away from it, curling myself out of harms way; I'd never seen an angel re-enter this world, I just figure they flew in, landed like homesick seagulls, and that was that.

The ovals began to expand, pushing a little farther back; the one above me was getting closer and closer to the other, now just within eight or ten feet of one another. They stopped growing and shifting, staying in the exact middle of the basement, just to the side of the operating table I had once been tied to. I watched with extreme fascination before my brain began to kick at me again, began to remind me of the circumstances of his death, of how a lot of this was my fault, that looking like I was sorry at first glance might help my situation out.

Shaking nervously, I bowed my head down, almost looking like I wanted to play; my wings unfurled a bit to lie heavily on the ground. With one curious eye I watched the circles as they suddenly grew intensely bright, as the air around me began to whistle, as the light bleached out everything in the room. It sounded like an airplane ready to take off, of the wind whipping through the room, of everything drowning in noise as the ovals screeched in harmony.

The light suddenly blasted everything in the room, just the edges of corners recognizable as the angel-missile shot directly through the first circle like a well-placed arrow, vague bluish shape halting quickly at the second one. The air clapped in a sonic boom, wind whipping out everywhere in a quick gust, blowing things off the table, items from the shelves, knocking the cable box from the top of the TV. The room stayed lit in an intense white light as something else shot into the basement along with Raziel, something I figured was armor, or baggage of some sort. Just as instantly as it came, the sound returned, the light dropped dead from the oval as it tightened out of existence, papers floating about the room. So much for cleaning.

I suddenly remembered my regrets, bowing courteously, eyes clenched shut. Please don't be mad, please don't be mad.

My legs wiggled nervously, ashamed, afraid, unsure, and scared for what would happen, curled into the corner, pleading for mercy. I refused to look up, no matter how much I wanted to. I heard shuffling, metal clinking together, low mumbling before I was confronted quite directly.

"Well, Natalie, you sure look different than the last time I saw you." That voice. My eyes snapped open, mouth hanging limply as I finally looked around me, finding Gauzier and Raziel standing there, arms crossed. Natalie… the fake name I had been using. A little confused I looked down at my arms, still the same demonic beast I had been for the last few days. My eyes darted back to them, bewildered. "That's right, we can finally drop this whole charade now, you deceitful demonic scum."

I couldn't move, I couldn't act; my entire body was frozen with fear, shaking as I tried to understand. Play the role, play the role! Snapping forward quickly, I arched my back up best I could in this tiny space, tail whipping back and forth.

"Don't." Raziel said finally, voice hard and uncaring, cold. I dropped the act immediately, looking back and forth for some sort of clue.

"Oh God it does obey you, that's hilarious." Gauzier looked almost happy yet annoyed, arms crossed; both swords attached to his sides. His face, his mouth; was grinning. I don't think I'd ever actually see him grin so conceitedly, so pleased with himself that he was practically bursting at the seams with insidious joy. He knew- but for how long? What was he told?

Quickly turning to Raziel, something stuck out much more; the wings on his back weren't stripped stubs as they had been, they were quite a bit larger. Not as large as Gauzier's was, but definitely an improvement. He too held a weapon, a pike still, but the head was radically different; it looked like two diamonds joined at the sides, almost like a two-pronged fork, two barbs sticking out from the wood just below that. My blood went cold- the shape, completely different... They'd…he'd… sold me out. For a new set of wings and a new weapon, he ratted me out.

Twirling the new pike around once with a grin, he leveled it square at my head, face suddenly vacant.

"Leave." He said flatly, "Now."

21

"You've….you're joking, right?" I said breathlessly, trying to look around the new pike head, trying to reach his eyes as Raziel only readjusted, keeping the pike directly between us. "I - I'm so sorry for what happened, I feel terrible that it… I mean…" I backpedaled, forgetting my vocal stance with him once again, trying to make sense.

"Leave." He said coldly, walking slowly towards me, weapon outstretched "This is not a request, it's not a joke, and it's not a ploy. I don't want you hiding in the yard, I don't want you thinking everything's fine, I just want you to get the Hell out of my home, NOW!" His tone rattled the walls, clearly hearing his intent as I winced. Gauzier chuckled, leaning against the side wall and throughly enjoying the show. Something was wrong here, this was not all his decision; it couldn't be. The guy I knew, who I'd spent nearly four months with, this wasn't him. We'd grown so much closer than this.

"You should be so thankful you can leave at all." Gauzier said lightheartedly, "If it was my decision, I would've seshimi'd you the moment I got back here, cut into thousands of little pieces. That's the only way demons should exist. Especially one as deceitful as you, trying to corrupt what was one of our best exorcists in his heyday." My body suddenly went active, seething with anger.

"Stay out of this!" I snapped at him as he only chuckled, my attention full back to Raziel. "What happened to you? What did they do?" He remained tense, eyes cold and lifeless, flipping the pike in his hand edgily. It was so much like our first act, our first big lie, but with all the anger and frustration suddenly very real.

"Raziel's finally understood what you've been doing these past months, Natalie." Gauzier paced around behind him as Raziel kept the weapon leveled at me. "This was his idea, his own free will, isn't that right?"

Gauzier barked out.

I could see Raziel's eyes slightly flicker at the words 'free will', the same way they flickered when talking to Amber about being an exorcist, when the answer was being shuffled around to protect someone. The slightest hint of worry or opposition- but it was so minor, so quick.

"I just haven't had the courage to do this until now." He said coldly, laughing emptily as an afterthought. "It's going to be a beautiful thing to get back my life." I looked him straight in the eyes, reading the cold, apathetic glance and scrutinizing his face as that arrogant front was recycled over and over. After a few seconds of silence his look began to slip, trying everything to keep it up and shoving the pike against my throat. I've known him for some time, I knew what phrases he tended to use, and when he anxiously threw together whatever he could. The edge of the pike made tiny circles against my throat, shaking.

"Liar. You're lying!" I slumped down on all fours, neck curling up as my lips pulled back in a fearful hiss, quickly storming towards Gauzier and ignoring Raziel outright. That smarmy shit Gauzier, he was the cause of this; he had to be the cause of this change of heart in some way. The angel pulled himself from the wall, reaching behind his back and drawing out the swords defensively as the two of us bristled, face to face.

"Think what you want you dumb animal, but I'm only here to supervise, not direct your boy Raziel against his will, because despite all things, you're still a demon well above his rank." He used the sword like a baton, pointing behind me, "I'm here as assistance, not as director."

I only hissed more, barely noting how well our conversation lined up.

"You can understand me, can't you?" I said quickly, finding another deceitful smile as his eyes darted behind me, the only bit of warning I had before something impaled, not kindly, into my side. Instantly the air was taken away, bringing me to my knees as I furiously dragged my head over to find Raziel with pike sticking all the way into my ribs to the handle, aiming for my heart. Shocked. Gauzier wasn't controlling him, this really was on his own- no! No, still, still there had to be something else. Before I could think, Gauzier's sword sliced through half my skull, lobbing off half of my upper jaw and nose in one swing. Bellowing in pain, I rolled onto my back, pulling the pike from Raziel's hands as it remained lodged in my ribs; breathing was labored, lung punctured like I could never get a breath. Gauzier geared up for another shot, bringing the sword over his head.

"Stop. This is my fight, not yours. It's under control now." Raziel demanded of Gauzier as the angel let up, scouring at both me and him before letting out a distraught growl. The angel put the weapon away and slumped back against the wall in one smooth motion. He had control back- Gauzier was actually listening to him. Did Raziel out-rank him again?

I raggedly got to my feet, painfully cringing back hard to the ground as the pain rolled and swelled. Black clouds muffled my vision for a moment, smoke re-forming my missing snout as I slowly got to my feet, pike still buried deep in my flesh. This heavy body limped pitifully, facing Raziel once more, wheezing for air as I stood just in front of him now. My head bobbed wearily with each breath, feeling that pike nestled right into my ribcage, lung trying to heal around the blades.

"You are not welcome here anymore, do you understand that?" Raziel sneered like a victorious dolt, grabbing a hold of the pike and yanking it from my body. I let out a pained cry, stumbling forward for a moment, holding my side, body overcome with pain as the weapon made much more of a mess exiting my body than it did going in. Wheezing, limbs trembling, I slowly brought myself back up to his gaze, stubborn. He seemed about 80% as enthusiastic as before. "We're done with that stupid act, do you hear me? No more! Get out!"

The angel drove the weapon straight into my heart this time with this stupid, desperate look on his face like that'd be the final straw for me to leave. Like I couldn't feel the restraint and anxiety dripping off of him. I've seen him give his all, I've seen him give absolutely nothing. This was as close to a mask made of a paper plate with Raziel's face on it that you could get.

Looking down, following the pole back to Raziel, I could only feel, well, pain- but also a deep, deep sense of frustration and anger. I sat up taller, pole pulling from his hands as I let it remain in my chest. He couldn't hit my heart if he tried, that broke 15 minutes ago.

He wasn't doing this all entirely on his dime, it couldn't be that. But it left me with this vast, disappointed shadow that hung over me, a sick, aggravated sense of pity. I was a true friend. I'd always be a true friend. That's what he felt- I know that's how he felt about this. But again, like times in the past, he lets himself get convinced by a stiff breeze and a few words. He lets things like this control his life. Raziel gingerly reached up, pulling the pike from my heart, now about 40% as enthusiastic. I didn't react to it and just sat there, staring at him. He seemed equally as worried, just for a slip of a moment.

But it wasn't all that either. It couldn't be.

"What are you doing?! Stop playing around and drive the demon out!" Gauzier shouted, livid. Raziel's eyes were quick to him before back to me with the same amount of vigor.

"I AM!" The angel growled, exasperated. I saw the pike flash up before everything went dark- sharp, biting line against my neck, feeling something heavy hit the ground just in front of my feet, cutting my head off. I remained sitting, unmoved.

A second passed before I felt the same weapon right back into my chest, removed and reinserted again, and again, and again, and again, stabbing me over and over. Every time it hurt a little more, and every time it hit against the back of my ribcage knotted my stomach more into itself. He was goading me back to fight- that had to be it. Gauzier was trying to get me to lash out, just as Raziel was- but for entirely different purposes. It's easier to drive something out when you feel you hate each other. Easier to lash out at someone when it's in self defense.

My head reformed, looking down to watch him stab again and again, sweating profusely, limbs and stances completely forgotten, all his training and careful footwork thrown out the window. Same as I saw with Gauzier back at the cat demon's house, flustered and desperately trying to hard to do the right thing, to please the right people that it didn't matter who it took down.

"I hate every lying, hollow word you've ever said!" He was wheezing, gasping for air, still choppin' away at the ol' heart. "I hate every miserable, brainless thought you've ever rambled on. Everything would've been so much better if I never let you live!" Raziel gave a smile, eyes focused on his task and nowhere near looking at me.

"Get out! Get out of my house, get out of my basement, get out of my afterlife, and don't you dare think for a second that you will be missed!" His rant stopped for a moment, trying to gather steam, arm back, ready to strike again. "You think you're welcome here? You think you can fit in? You're a demon! You'll always be a de-!" The world stopped.

Leaning forward quickly, I pulled him into a tight hug. Tears brimmed on the edge of my nose, rolling down the long sides of my face as his tirade stopped dead in its tracks, holding him tightly. I didn't try to crush him and he didn't try to get away. Even Gauzier seemed a little shocked by the move; but I needed to say something, needed to at least let my sentiments known, to apologize, to reassure that despite what he heard, that my intentions were never evil, never against him. I hugged harder, just happy he survived after the encounter with the giant horse demon. The pike dropped to his side and the angel instantaneously went limp.

"It's okay." I whispered. It'd be so easy to lash out and react like they wanted, but the truth was I've never seen him this upset before. Even through the Mia escapades, even through him blurting out all his frustrations with his job or even him getting so angry he couldn't kill some stubborn demon that refused to die, had he been anywhere near this upset. Raziel remained lifeless as I gave him a couple quick, light pats on the back, sniffling. "Breathe." Like he could hear me, I felt him take a few ragged, distraught breaths.

Leaning back I finally saw his face as all the makeup and pomp was stripped away, the exact same feeling he had been in before, just without that paper mask. Raziel's eyes were wide, sad, looking down at my feet. His body was in mourning, wobbling and trembling like the pike had done before, just a couple key fingers on weapon like he was about to drop it on the ground. He didn't look up, the angel only closed his eyes, leaning until his forehead hit my chest.

He didn't say a word but I knew exactly how he felt.

"Raziel!" Gauzier roared out, angel's eyes split back open as steel suddenly pierced my back, both of Gauzier's swords tearing down alongside my spine, like he was trying to fillet me. I cried out in pain as both swords sunk into my spine, body spasming and thrashing side to side. Like someone turned off the lights, my body went down, no feeling below my neck.

"That's enough!" Raziel shouted quickly, tone waiving like he was startled, genuinely angry. I drooled and rolled my head on the ground, disoriented.

"That was not under control! Are you so blind you don't see how easily manipulated you are by this lying beast?" He gave a little laugh, beyond outraged. "This is exactly why I'm here, to assist so you can do your goddamn job!"

Raziel looked over at me, giving this broken, threadbare frown as he quickly yanked a sword out of my spine. I arched my back, grunting in pain as my head slipped back to the floor, beaten, bested, but slowly healing.

"Just give her a chance." The angel almost whispered, mumbling as Gauzier's head just about did a 180, snatching the sword from his hand in a rage.

"I'm sorry, what was that?" Gauzier stormed up to Raziel, appalled at me, appalled at him, appalled that one of two swords was not currently jammed in my spinal column. Woah... wait. "You want to try that again, Raziel? I was panicked for him- the fact that Gauzier didn't just flat out get him kicked for saying it once was incredible on it's own. The angel looked away, reorganizing himself.

"It's not trying to manipulate anything right now." He said quickly, deliberating his words, "She's just very confused."

"Confused?!" Gauzier scoffed, still swinging the bloodied sword around like a baton, "What did you say not five minutes ago, right before we came back down here? Where's all that resolve and determination now? It's a demon, Raziel! For God's sake! Why they haven't ripped out your wings for letting this thing live here, for lying..." He stopped quickly, shooting me a glare before saying any more.

"Get this Goddamn demon out of your home, now. That's a simple task, isn't it Raziel? One even you can follow, I bet!" I grumbled with a growl, shifting enough to speak.

"You barely deserve..." I wheezed, words thrown up sloppily, "To lick the bottom of his boot, let alone assume any sort of rank." Grinning tiredly, I huffed a short laugh at his expense. Gauzier's eyes went wide, lip curling in my direction as he ripped the other sword from my neck angrily, whipping it at my head, missing and sinking into the wall next to me instead.

"Aim next time." I insulted, spitting in his direction. "Spaz."

The angel looked like he would pop.

"St. Michaels. Now." He held the remaining sword to Raziel's throat threateningly, his tone skittish. "I say it, the demon leaves but can come back, but you say it, and it's locked a far enough radius away from you and this house for all eternity if it has any sense to leave. No demon would be stupid enough to stay. Do it. Now." My eyes darted to Raziel as he stared angrily at Gauzier, looking at me quickly before back to the sword pressing against his throat. The St. Michaels. The nuclear bomb of exorcisms, as he had put it… I trembled at the thought, struggling to move my unresponsive body.

"Do it, or I'll be forced to take greater measures against that thing, as well as you." Gauzier suddenly got emotional and angry in the blink of an eye, turning towards me with a grin. "Kick out this lying, treacherous beast that got you killed, and get yourself back on track. This is not a hard decision, Raziel!"

"Give me a moment… just… don't. I'll leave!" I looked desperately to Gauzier as he acted like I said nothing at all. He could hear me, but he was choosing not to translate.

The angels glared at one another as Raziel slowly put his hands together the same way Gauzier did back when. I pulled myself on all fours, swaying heavy, head darting to both of them.

"I said I'll leave!" My stomach was already dropping, body feeling heavy, weighted down. Gauzier only smiled at me politely, wandering a couple steps back and leaning back against the wall, hand pressed to it peculiarly as Raziel began to chant. I tried to run for the wall, dragging my legs tiredly, making my way for the window. My hand hit hard on the wall, solid, unforgiving, fingers suddenly tingling with the same sensation I had felt with the barrier Raziel had put up in the utility room. A trap… My head snapped back to Gauzier, standing behind Raziel, waving two fingers and knowing full well what he was doing, trapping me in here with a barrier so I couldn't escape the exorcism, and forcing Raziel to kill me off. That snake!

My hands began to feel heavy, like lead, acrid air bursting out from the middle of the room and starting to burn my demonic flesh. I looked to the ceiling, my escape route the first time, finding that charged as well. Why wasn't Raziel stopping? Couldn't he see I was trapped in here? Couldn't he figure out something was wrong? I mean, I was stubborn, but I knew that trying to sit through the granddaddy of exorcisms was a poor idea.

But his eyes were clenched shut, reciting the words to the St. Michaels at breakneck speed, trying to get it done as quickly as possible.

I started walking towards him, stopped immediately as the wind in the room gusted like a powerful storm, air almost aflame. My claws bit into the carpet desperately, body pitched forward.

"Raziel! Stop! The idiot's trapped me in here!" I yelled into the wind, sound beginning to die from the area as the air sparked with fire, a mix of red and blue flames. "Make him stop! I'll leave!" Gauzier only laughed, yelling out joyfully.

"You can complain all you want, he can't hear you!" The angel laughed, pushing himself harder against the wall. "It was never the intent to let you free! You may want to say your last precious goodbyes, Natalie!"

Lips pulled back suddenly, growling loud as I could in his direction as the wind picked up more, growing hotter and hotter as the entire room was being engulfed in flames only I saw. Bending down low, my skin began to burn away, smolder and pull back to reveal my demonic bones, before those too were quickly burned away. I watched my hand as the experience suddenly got painful, my human hands hidden away beneath the demonic exterior, gripping onto the carpet. Behind me the rest of my demonic body burned away in a swirl of black smoke, darting erratically to try and catch up to me, to beat the wind that blasted through the room in a horrible torrent of air and fire. With a dull roar, the demonic black energy finally burned away too, cracking the entire back wall and busting out the tiny window as it did.

I tried to find Raziel through the fire and flames, gripping the carpet with everything I had as the spiritfire blew overhead, as I was slowly burning away. I had always survived, always managed to pull through these things, these attempts to kill me. My head bent low, I begged and pleaded, prayed. Squinting, I could see my hands begin to burn away as well, black and charred, my hair going along with it. Crying out in pain, I pushed myself against the ground more, breath short, pained, shaking in terror.

"Raziel!!" I shouted, body ripping from the carpet as the wind grew too strong, throwing me into the back wall. My spine twinged with the barrier, the front of me stuck to take most of the damage as I quickly eroded away, toggling with consciousness. Desperately, painfully, I screamed for him, over and over, trying to reach the angel, trying to get him to stop, to save myself just in the nick of time. He never heard me, body pinned helplessly as I was about to be thoroughly ripped from this world.

Just as I felt it was all over, as I felt my own soul begin to erode away; there was a crack behind me. The painful shock flickered and shut down for just a split second - my body suddenly darted through the barrier, rocketing outside. My smoldering, tumbling mix of bones and muscle shot through two houses, arching low, hitting the ground once and jumbling to a stop two streets over, in the middle of the road. With half a working eye and half an arm my bones finally rested, staring straight upwards, stare right into the sky, fighting to stay awake with a single thought.

He was holding back, all these months.

Heaving and gagging as just bits of a disassembled body, something blocked my path overhead, something large, black, dripping with blood. The big cat smiled, all four slits of eye closing smugly.

"Why, Hello there."

I only stared because I had to, mind trying to piece itself back together, body trying to heal as fast as it could, the bones slowly forming over themselves, the skin re-moisturizing from the black charred mess that stunk like spoiled bacon.

"Ttthhh!" I managed to say, tongue hitting the exposed skeletal parts of my upper jaw; most of my face was gone. I didn't even have anything below my ribcage, let alone a bottom jaw.

"You look in the need of some help, my queen." The demon said politely, sitting down. Now with enough muscle to furrow my eyebrows, I gave a sort of wary look.

"Thhhh." I looked down to vaguely see my jawbone coming after me, rolling quickly through the grass of the house I lay in front of. Shuddering, it crawled onto my side, scooting itself over my chest and jumping excitedly back into place. Muscles quickly snapped over the sides of them, stretching across the rest of my face, across my teeth, puckering up to finally form a mouth. The cat demon looked at me expectantly as I glanced over at it, stretching out my new lips. "Help would be appreciated."

The demon nudged at my shoulder, pushing me into a sit, using my one available arm to prop myself up as the rest of my body restored itself.

"You're alive..." I nodded my head at nothing, vacant, tired. "I thought you were tied to the house."

"As I said before, I can kill who I please and I can go where I please." It said happily, even as its tone was nothing but worried and concerned. This had to be more then a coincidence, with all the demons in the world, how the cat-demon I helped before would be so conveniently right there, one of the friendly, intelligent demonic faces I knew.

"Did you save me?" I questioned, using my newly reformed left hand to pat the cat-demon on the head. My feet were still missing; that, and the rest of the demonic dinosaur beast.

"I may have had a hand in it, yes." It was careful of its words, deliberating what it said and how it was said to me, just as the other demonic version of myself, or whatever the Hell she was, did. I stopped patting. There was a strangely familiar feeling about this moment.

"Who are you, really?" The big cat only smiled.

"A very old friend of yours." My jaw hung open a little bit, more confused then anything else. I stumbled on my words.

"Do you have a name? I feel terrible that if we're 'very old friends',

I can't seem to remember you." I felt stupid, felt out of touch of things. The last bits of my foot came back together, whole as a human once again. The cat swayed its head a little, grinning and chuckling.

"You wouldn't. Try not to bother yourself too much with that, I don't mind the repeating introductions." It sat on its haunches, placing one paw to its chest royally. "I am Palug, Cath Palug, at your service, my queen." I scoffed for a moment.

"Sure... Yeah. Why not." I got to my knees, standing up shakily on refurbished legs. The cat was there to help brace me up. "Was not expecting... whew. What a day." I muttered, looking back to the…cath… Palug as it suddenly leaned closer, smelling me, its eyes flaring and squinting rapidly like nostrils.

"You're very odd like this." It almost giggled. "Like a bad joke." Gaping at the beast, I didn't know whether to laugh with it or be offended. I ended up giving it an uncertain sort of nod, scanning around for someone else to validate how awkward and strange this conversation was.

"I feel like a bad joke." I relented as the cat demon…Palug… glared elsewhere, bristling in the direction of the Priest's house.

"We need to leave now." It said shortly, biting around my midsection and darting away at an incredible speed, plunging directly into one house's basement, into the dark. Unable to see where I was and what was going on, the demon's shadow hunkered by the window, obscuring the only light source. "Where is the Colus?"

"Co-loo…who?" I cracked a paranoid laugh. Palug didn't reciprocate, glowing vent-like eyes darting to me quickly and groaning in annoyance.

"The…red and white flying dinosaur demon …" My eyes snapped open. My other form? It had a name?

"Um…uh… it… sizzled, and disappeared with the exorcism." I babbled. Colus. Yeah, that sounded like nothing but gibberish to me. I really was all kinds of useless.

"The Colus does not disappear." The cat laughed haughtily like the very idea was preposterous; suddenly freezing up on something outside. "The angels are looking for you, tracking you" I grumbled, seeing them a distance away, scouring the area where I had rolled to a stop.

"They can go fuck themselves for a while." Leaning closer, I tried to hear what they were saying. Raziel was standing there, looking around the area, shrugging and keeping his arms crossed, while Gauzier did a lot of pointing and shouting. "Can you tell what they're saying?" The cat nodded quickly.

"…What do you mean, where did it go, that…." The cat stopped repeating for my sake, skipping over what I could only assume was a line of cursing, "'demon needs to perish.' 'I don't feel anything out here, there's nothing, she's just dead.'" My body suddenly froze up, remembering my chase in the Priest's house; how Raziel had spilled about being able to track any spirit he's tethered himself to, past or present.

"He knows where we are, he can track me down." I hissed out in a panic. Palug's eyes were all over me in an instant. "Oh God he knows exactly where I am right now."

"What? How is that possible!? That's not the plan!"

"Yeah, well, he…sorta…tethered to me when we escaped from helping you out." Gah, what was it with this 'plan' shit again? The cat glared at me, expecting answers, "I didn't know it at the time, and I didn't agree to it! It just happened!" The cat lowered all four eyebrows, slowly panning back to the window, like it was disappointed in me.

"He's not looking over here." Palug said, trying to figure things out, "He's deliberately looking everywhere but over here. I asked back then if he was a nice angel, and you said no. Why is he helping you now?" Remaining silent, feeling ashamed, I only watched out the window as the two of them argued. More correctly, that Gauzier was shouting at Raziel, and he wasn't saying much back.

"That's the same angel from the house, isn't it?" The cat moved onto the next question, growling as it referenced Gauzier. The two of us peered from the basement windows like hidden enemy spies.

"His superior, yes. I think."

"He's got a mouth on him. I don't want to really repeat what he's saying for you, but he's angry." Palug looked back to the outside world, "Short and sweet, he does not like you." I rolled my eyes.

"I'm not surprised, Gauzier made that point pretty clear ten minutes ago."

"Maybe he---they're leaving."

Something suddenly hoisted me up, pushing me farther from the floor, head hitting the ceiling, my balance shifting more to rest on four legs instead of two in the darkness. I re-arranged myself to crouch down. I knew what this was.

"I guess it really doesn't disappear." I said softly, my voice now back in the body of the Colus, or whatever it was. Demonic dog-dinosaur fit better to me; 'Colus' sounded like a high-priced novelty drink. I peered outside a little easier, watching the two angels start walking back towards the house, Gauzier just ahead of Raziel, scanning the houses nearby quickly. As Raziel passed next to us, his eye shifted in my direction, dragging on the exact spot where we hid, knowing full well where we were. He said nothing, made no other notion than that, eyes shifting back to Gauzier before looking away. It was another full minute before either of us took a breath.

"Do you think he'll try and track you down?" Palug sounded generally confused, asking a little more urgently. I sighed, shaking my head a little.

"No. He wouldn't; pretending I'm dead may be the best thing he's done for me." It came out a lot more depressed then I meant it to, feeling stupid for sitting amongst fellow demons and lamenting over an angel that had tried to kill me on many different occasions. The cat-demon nuzzled the side of my head.

"So you did manage to make a friend." Palug said honestly, not a hint of hatred or anger behind those words. I laughed half-heartedly. The cat's head nodded against the moonlight. "I don't understand your need to make strange friends. But we should get going; we need to meet up with some others."

"Others?" We both exited outside, standing as two demonic beasts, roughly the same eye-level and a refreshing change. Palug was just a bit longer then I, though; it's long stringy tail flicking back and forth as it walked slowly ahead of me.

"We're meeting up with more allies to back up the Fallen." I jogged a few steps to catch up with it.

"The fallen angels? We work with them? Wouldn't they hate us?" My body was nimble as ever, keeping pace easily. "Who set that all up?"

"That would be Excelsis Nona; she's busy attending other things, so we're making due without her for the time being. We need as much support as possible right now, and you can help us."

"Well, alright, how can I help?" I muttered under my breath; head turned back towards the Priest's house as it panned out of view, obscured by three rows of houses now.

"Well, you can give energy to the rest to fight" He said quickly as the conversation dropped off to silence. My heart felt heavy, guilty, saddened. That chapter of my afterlife was quickly disappearing, quickly fading away, dwindling to nothing. All the work I'd put in to make that friendship, to get that connection with another person, thrown right out the window for the chance to walk away from it. Least it didn't end in a completely violent bloodbath like I had joked it would. Least I had that, I guess.

"What do you call yourself?"

"Hmm?" I turned back to Palug, perking back to the conversation. "My name, you mean? Wouldn't you know that, old chum?" I crooked one eye at the cat, giving it a sort of lopsided glare. It only laughed.

"The one angel referred to a Natalie, would that be you?"

"Neri. Natalie's just a fake name." My shoulder sunk in a little more as I walked, stance broadening out; I was dead tired and I think I had the right to be.

"Neri. It's a lovely name." Palug suddenly went into a jog without me, darting ahead. "Come along Neri, we've got work to do." Letting out a tired breath I loped to catch up, eventually taking to the air, away from the Priest and away from Raziel.

22

"It may be best not to say much. Demons here are mostly a mix of human and fallen angels; they don't expect intelligent conversation from a larger demon like you, Neri." Palug and I sauntered through the neighborhood; heading up to what I was told was the local, makeshift home base. "More then that, they might be a little…edgy if you tell them you've been exorcising demons for nearly half a year."

"You don't think I can still make friends?" I laughed, stretching out my wings just a bit.

"I know you can, I just want to make clear that if you tell other demons what you've been doing, I can't promise you'll be able to stay at this house. "Our travels took roughly an hour, landing a few times to walk with the cat demon for some much needed background information.

" Yeah... I understand."

The Avilla Demonic War, first started by some angel named Avilla and her best buds in the middle ages, was something that had been going on for thousands and thousands of years. At times, demons took reign, and at others, the angels did. It was a war souls fought because they could, not because they knew why, and the reasons were pretty primal; demons hated angels, angels hated demons, when a group larger than four on each side got together and duked it out, whomever won claimed it as a major victory and wrote it down in whatever journal they kept track of things in. Since neither side really communicated with the other, both sides were constantly winning and perpetuated this war, like bloody recreational games. As Raziel had said some time back, we didn't wipe out massive quantities of their numbers; they didn't do the same for us.

Recently, that was not the case; demons and ghosts were executed in high numbers, Palug said. There were fewer acceptances; more demand of knowledge of what a haunting was really about in the human world, more exorcisms, and more violent house cleansing nowadays, in comparison with the usual blessing done on a house years ago. It was the difference between asking nicely, and shooting the demon in the back of the head, then asking it to leave. Tactics had changed, and the demons were pissed and blamed the angels for everything, while the angels blamed us for dirtying their shoes, for mud being so wet, for nighttime. Basically.

In the past, the collections of the demons were small, loose groups of conveniently located haunted houses in close proximity, where word spread underground amongst some sort of demonic lounge room, and small uprisings would take place. More recently, under the direction of their Excelsis Nona demon; powerful, self-perpetuating demons would patrol known haunted areas, looking for willing soldiers. These soldiers would latch onto them like little soul-power strips, and transport them back to the safe houses. Palug briefly explained that there were few soul-powering demons around, the angels knew this and targeted them first; if you've got no demon to help fuel the others, the uprising dies. Both myself and Palug were self-powered, valued additions to this group of rebels, just outsides the property now, a lone, cold, run down shanty of a place, obviously condemned and vacant.

"How is it again we power the others?" I said tiredly, having a hard time taking in all this information. Palug took a deep breath.

"The amount of life-cycles we've gone through, the souls we've consumed leads us to develop our own stability in the world, which in turn can help stabilize others." I chalked my ability to power others up to the demon that consumed me; all that black carpet ever did was eat souls, no wonder. It laughed a little, nodding towards the house, "C'mon, let's get inside before the sun comes up."

"Why, are you going to burst into flames?" I joked as Palug rolled a growl at me.

"It blinds me. That's reason enough." I paused, offset. I just figured everyone else had the same tolerance I did.

"Is that how it works for everyone?" I followed obediently, feeling stupid once again. I really knew jack squat about my own kind.

"We all have our different settings, different reactions to this world we inhabit. Some can take the sun, some can't. Here we go!" We stepped into the house together, expecting some sort of madhouse of entertainment, a rush of applause for the cat-demon bringing back another fighter, someone else to help the cause. It was empty. The half-dilapidated stairs noted that something may be going on in the basement, but it was a sad welcome party. Palug glanced around, cutting out a short whistle as a demon, a man in a hoodie with a long, deep scar across his forehead, poked his head out.

"We're home, and I've got reinforcements!" Palug nodded over to me as I grinned a little. Oh yeah, take it in, big bad dinosaur's here to help.

The man seemed less than impressed.

"What do you want, a parade?" He slipped back underneath the stairs, grumbling to himself as I looked a little vacantly to the cat demon. Even without eyes, you could tell it was thoroughly annoyed, it's growling escalating steadily. The head popped back up through the ground, grinning. "Relax Pug, chill."

"It's Palug."

"Pug's easier to say. Congrats on bringing home a…" The man looked at me, tilting his head a little, "Lizard….dog…thing" My head drooped, feeling more like another rivet in the metal instead of a gem. Not like I was looking forward to being treated like royalty or anything harebrained like that.

"Her name is Neri." Palug noted to me as I nodded, sitting down, "She's an Outlet, like myself." An outlet must be those power-strip demons it mentioned before; the man seemed more impressed with that.

"Oh, well. That'll make your job easier, Pug. Neri." He nodded, slipping back through the floor as Palug shook his head at the site, sitting down tiredly.

"I don't know about you, but I'm exhausted. Feel free to roam around, we've got twelve other spirits in this household, all of which shouldn't cause you any trouble." It said it with a sort of laugh, walking tiredly over to the other room and flopping down and leaving me to stare by the door like an uninvited guest.

I took a few cautious steps forward, light glittering through a few spotty holes in the roof, showing off the dust that collected in this place. In the physical world, it was just an abandoned house, two stories with a full basement; but like this, it was littered with souls, wandering entities that were fortunate to gather in one place. Palug had said in our walk to this place how much harder it was to find well-meaning, eager to fight souls, that the area seemed to tiring down. Souls weren't something to be picked up as they pleased, there was a pretty short time frame of a few years in which one could persuade the other to join us, after then they started getting harder to convince. Either stuck in their ways, haunting where they died, or having the isolation drive them to madness. A depressing thought. Strutting through the house, I noted the handiwork, noted the little details to the house that perked my curious mind.

"Oh, well, look at that." A voice said off to the left, standing around in the kitchen area. I jumped a little, "We recruited a dinosaur bird." A man stood against the kitchen wall, leaning close to a woman who looked like she'd rather get a sandwich then pay any attention to this spirit. I regarded them; the man had two small protruding horns from the top of his head, hair cut in a sort of wavy, laid-back Mohawk. The horns continued from his neck, lining down his back and stopping short of his hips. No stereotypical demonic tail, pitchfork, hokey expression of evil and gloom, but he didn't have a shirt on. He didn't seem to care about shirts at all. The woman took a look at me, back to the man before back to me.

"Don't pay this idiot incubus any mind. He's about as suave as a can of corn and about as dangerous as one too." She got right in the demon's face, pushing him backwards easily, laughing. The man tried to speak through her fingers.

"Oh, so that's how you wanna play it, eh?" He craned his head around, grinning, following the woman as she came closer to me. She seemed normal, dressed in a long, white, half-torn nightgown, fingers elongated, and eyes hazily half-awake. You couldn't help but feel a little wary of her, like she was masking something. The woman looked me up and down, tilting her head off to the side and trying to look at the other sides. Watching her, I posed a little bit, stretching out a back leg with a smirk.

"Well, looks like you're good to fight, we always need-Tolstier, I said no!" She suddenly screeched at the incubus behind her, putting up one of her hands like she was looking to smack him upside the face. The demon jumped a little, looking at both of us before cursing to himself, wandering off. The woman shook her head a little, grumbling under her breath, "Why he chooses me, of all people, I'll never know." I smiled quickly, watching after the demon as he fell through the floor.

"Got a name?" She said, glaring closer at my eyes. I pulled back a little. "You can speak, can't you?"

"Neri." I laughed nervously, sitting down. The woman nodded. "Sorry, It's all a bit much right now."

"Kayalin" She smiled unevenly, both of us stuck in awkward conversation. "And don't worry about it, we were all there once." Smiling a bit more, I tried all the standard ice-breakers.

"So, 12 spirits reside here? Any heads up on anyone?" Peeking through the floorboards of the upper floor, I caught sight of someone looking down on me, scurrying away from their spot as our eyes met. I scoffed a little.

"We're all pretty benign. Tolstier may be one of the worse ones, but we're all good spirits, more or less." The woman, Kayalin, laughed, "We've got our designated enemies, but thankfully that's not each other." I grinned, kind of missing the ridiculous calm of the Priest's house. I was tired. I was not in the best mood. I wanted to meet people, to at least seem interested in what I was doing, but I felt like loose end after loose end dangled elsewhere; everywhere but here.

"Most of the demons or human-remnant spirits stick around in the house during the day, like right now, but the fallen angels all sit in their cheer squad in the backyard, soaking up the sun like they need it to survive." She pointed to her left nonchalantly as I perked up.

"Fallen angels? Really?" The woman tilted an eyebrow at me,

faintly suspicious.

"Yeah...Why, what's a fresh demon like yourself getting all excited for those feather-heads outside?" I flashed a quick grin at the woman, eyes darting about like I wasn't concealing some big, annoying secret. I'd gotten to know a number of the exorcists about, and heard stories through them of the fallen angels in the area. But none of the exorcists ever knew what happened to them, or if they were still around.

"I don't know, just find them interesting."

"Revenge, eh? Well, most of the angels outside are assumably the nice ones, not the real dickhead angels like we know they can be. Though they don't talk to us often. Don't think you'll be finding your exorcist outside, sorry." She pointed to the sealing mark burned into my back. "Looks like you've had quite the time with that one, though." My stomach instantly flopped around, trying to figure the most non-demon exorcising angle I could. Something popped into my mind.

"I had particular issues with one exorcist, fought and lost a number of times, yeah" I coughed awkwardly; face stagnant on a half-grin. "Well, thanks for the advice, Kayalin, I'm gonna continue to look around." She nodded as I left the conversation.

I walked steadily parallel to the outside wall, skirting the far wall of the home, finding some little pitch black dog-demon digging at the ground, growling at nothing, jumping quickly to dive onto prey that just wasn't there. Shaking my head, I passed through the outside wall and into the backyard, where my mind had wandered since it was mentioned.

The sun was exceedingly bright; I squinted my eyes against it, wishing for a moment that the goggles on the back of my head actually moved and did something, be some sort of protection against this morning light. There was laughing coming from the backyard, putting my head down so my hair would block out a bit of the sunshine, I saw a group of figures at the back of the lot, sitting underneath the trees. I wasn't sure how they'd react to me; they seemed to still distance themselves from the occupants inside, like they were too good to associate with demons. Taking a few slow steps forward, I heard their conversation stop dead, that I had been spotted.

"You confused or something, demon?" One of the fallen angels called out to me as I stopped in my tracks, unsure what to do. There was more subtle conversation, whispering to one another as I began to be the object of attention. Squinting through the light I could see there were four or five of them sitting there, a mix of men and women. Nervously, I pulled back my lips in that same awkward smile I had done years ago, few teeth poking out here and there. The person who called to me laughed lightly, baffled. "Are you new here?"

She was asking questions like she expected me to actually answer. I cautiously raised my voice, testing if that angelic divide language barrier was a problem.

"I am." I took a few steps closer, still a ways out.

"Do you know who we are?" The woman called again, tone wavering curiously. Apparently it wasn't.

"The fallen angels, if I'm not mistaken." The group of them began to talk more amongst themselves, only the words 'educated' and 'dinosaur' I managed to hear from them. Damn right I was educated. Polite, too. My pace turned to a regular walk, less like the stalking motion I had done earlier.

"You're awfully ballsy to walk straight out here in the middle of the day." One of the men in the group said, closer now. I opened my eyes wide to the sunlight.

"Light doesn't bother me. I actually used to like taking naps at noon." I don't know what I was trying to accomplish, we both seemed pretty edgy about one another; I had met those jackass angels that haunted my nightmares. Reassuring myself that these angels were the ones thrown out, the sympathizers, I calmed down a bit.

"I was talking about walking towards a bunch of angels." The man's tone grew a little more serious, as I broke from the sunlight and underneath the same shade as the rest of them, getting a much clearer look. It was like a pow-wow, as Kayalin had said. The four of them sat underneath the trees in a circle, somewhat relaxed, two men and two women. The man addressing me was dark-haired, olive-skinned, wingless. Actually, all of them were wingless, their arms thin, weight light, and generally anemic looking. The other man in the group was a sort of pastel blond with a light scruffy beard going on, picking at the stuff underneath his shoes. None of them really looked like a threat.

"Eh, I'm not scared of you guys." I tried to be friendly, but not too much of a kiss ass. They'd be way more suspicious if I did that. One of the angel's scoffed.

"Aren't you colorful." The man said again, eyes watching me closely.

"Oh… uh… thanks." I looked down at myself, smiling back to them awkwardly. "So you guys can understand me, that's cool!" I instantly felt like an idiot as not a single person in the circle seemed to care. Part of me wanted to spill my guts, pop out of this form and swap exorcism war stories. Other part, the logical, socially aware part, let me know that sitting here and not saying much was my best guess to getting anything done, and to be considered anything but a threat. Maybe complimenting someone would help me out; I opened my mouth to speak.

"Listen, I can see from your little sealing mark there that you've had run-ins with angels, so before you go thinking anything ignorant, we had nothing to do with it." The man sat down a little more comfortably as he recited this like it was ingrained into his memory. I looked to my pike-shaped scar with a shallow laugh, about to speak up before being interrupted again.

"With Raziel, it looks like." The other angel only shook his head, grabbing a stick and poking it into the ground. I held my breath, about to desperately explain myself before he kept talking. "That must've been fun."

"Ehg, well..."

"Who?" The one woman asked, unfamiliar as the man answered.

"He's this high-strung Secare exorcist a few towns over, gets killed a lot. Goofy looking weapon." The angel looked up, eyes sharp and wary as he wiggled some fingers at my scar. "Surprised they sent him against you, he must've really pissed someone off." Lots of stuff to pick through and think about for later as I only sputtered and blurted something out.

"I was... a surprise." That worked. That'd fit my fiction. Not untrue either.

"You know him?" The woman asked the fallen guy more questions, derailing my conversation.

"Nah. But I've heard stories about him, and the stupid looking pike he's got."

I had to get back on track.

"Anyways, no I didn't think of saying anything dumb like that." I looked at them as their heads perked up. "I just came out here to say hi. What's your name?" I asked the skeptical man politely as he just stared at me, looking to the other people in the circle like it was a big joke. There were two women as well in the group, a slightly older, Hispanic woman who had first called out to me; the stereotypical perfectly-wavy angelic hair-floof, arms propped behind her as she looked around the group. The other woman was a blonde and seemed annoyed, quiet, uninterested. After a minute of skeptical staring, the man relinquished his name.

"Azol" He looked away, easing down. He pointed to the other members of the pow-wow, starting with the black-haired woman, to the blond man and finally the blonde woman. "That's Saya, Marc, and Ibe" I nodded as he said this, scanning over this group for any hint of a clue, besides that they really weren't that interested to know me. Angelic introductions done, I picked up.

"Neri. I'm an outlet...thing." I laughed nervously as no one even raised their head about it, perked up, or gave a damn. The awkwardness was starting to choke me out. I tried to wrap up, "Well, just wanted to say hi, it was nice to meet you." Nodding quickly I turned from them, heading back inside. Twenty feet away, they suddenly laughed with one another, no doubt at my expense. Lowering my head a little I picked up the pace, heading inside and feeling more out of place than I ever had before.

Darting through the kitchen door, Palug was standing there, watching me, off put.

"Have fun outside?" He asked a little condescendingly, head

snapping quickly to the left to give a quick hiss to a spirit, half hiding behind the edge of a wall. The spirit ducked away out of sight. I laughed hollowly.

"I don't think they like me very much." My smile faded, "Is that the usual thing?"

"Usually, they don't talk to anyone." Palug turned from the door, noting me to follow him into the other room. "There's a real divide in this place, Neri. No doubt you can feel it."

"I don't mean to sound like an ass, but I kinda figured." I mentioned back to the front of the house. "We had the whole history lesson on the way over about how demons and angels hate one another. Color me surprised that doesn't magically change." Shrugging, I looked back outside to them in the yard, looking over towards my window, doing the exact same thing.

"I suppose." Palug gave another quick motion to something on the other side of the room like an annoyed parent. The angels caught sight of me peering out the window, quickly turning back to their circle with shoulders hunched.

"Things have been difficult for the last year, especially." I slumped to the ground tiredly, scooting my legs underneath me.

"Since your super Nona person left?" I questioned haphazardly, hearing the tiniest scratching noises just a room over, attention half to the matter at hand.

"No, no, she's been gone for nearly fifteen years." My head shot back up.

"Fifteen years? Doing what?" Outraged, I glared at the cat beast, shaking my head.

"Well I mean she has other parts of the world to attend to, she can't stick around the USA forever." The cat shook his head, surprised I was annoyed. For some reason that didn't really dawn on me that their leader was just 'leader-ing' elsewhere.

"Oh."

"We all pitch in and try to do our best." He stated innocently as I only frowned. "Anyways, with what little troops we do have, there's still petty conflict. So I was hoping you might be able to help."

I was getting a little annoyed with him, and with the careful way he spoke about things. Something irked the back of my mind, plagued my thoughts with frustration.

"Let me guess, you want me to schmooze up to the angels and try and get them buddy - buddy with the demons in this place, right?" I could feel the anger perforate my words, bubble through. Palug nodded happily.

"Yes, that's exactly right. Since you've got previous experience."

"Oh, well, since I've been stuck with some idiot for a few months, I'm the automatic expert all of a sudden?"

Palug's face went flat, grinning suddenly like it was a gut reaction.

"I thought he was your friend."

"Still an idiot, though." I gritted my teeth together a little more as that scratching sound returned, driving my frustration higher. "Listen, I appreciate the help earlier, ol' buddy, but it's starting to annoy me the way you're hiding information. You know a lot, don't you? Palug's smile vanished.

"I know enough."

"Which is more than I do. You told me to try and ignore it, but you know what, that's getting really hard with all this substantial crap going on, you understand?" I rose to my feet angrily, tail twitching around out of instinct as I bristled tiredly against my supposed friend. "Why is it everyone keeps this from me? What is this big, goddamn "Master Plan" that you and that other demon keep talking about!?" The cat-demon's eyes were nearly closed, perking up quickly.

"Cempe?"

My eyes furrowed a little lower.

"Is that the me-demon thing's name?" My voice was barely above a baseline, so very annoyed and angered by the dawdling in the conversation alone.

"It's not a… you demon. It's a completely separate entity. A different person. But that's her name." My glare remained un-changed, still waiting on the other answers, never to be received, tail still flicking about. Palug stared at me for a little longer, before closing its eyes and looking away. "There's good reason you don't know what you do, Neri."

"Because it's a big inside joke to screw around with my head? Or are we keeping hush hush because your army's lead by an idiot?" I growled as the cat returned.

"Hey!" He paused, held back by what he could say and still kiss the ass of this leader from 15 years away. "That's not true!"

"Then what is true?" I muttered from the side of my mouth, hearing the scratching noises on the back of the wall once more, tipping me over the edge. "For fucks, sake, WHAT?"

Snapping back to the wall I drove my hand through it, grasping onto the spirit and ripping them through the wall, expecting someone snooping on me, the snooping demon, or the annoying as Hell spying demon. I got a child instead. A kid; couldn't be over eight years old, grasping him tightly around the wrist. Instantly my attack stopped cold as he stared at me, completely terrified.

"That's Jonas. He likes dinosaurs." Palug said flatly as I continued to hold him there and feeling all degrees of stupid. Another kid suddenly ran into the room behind me, a carbon-copy of the same child, twins. My head flopped around at the two of them.

"Give him back!" The one kid yelled at me as the air around me erupted in light, a sweltering cloud of explosive fiery goodness rushing up by my face; instantly I dropped the kid, scrambling away from the smoke and fire with my butt hitting against the wall. As the smoke cleared they were both gone, sounds of feet darting up the half-broken staircase behind me in the entranceway. Palug remained as he was, tail switching back and forth in his own brand of annoyance.

"They've wanted to meet you since you came in here, but they're afraid the beasts in this house will hurt them. Thank God you showed them how relaxed and polite we can be." There was no smiling this time, no support, no hints of joy in his tone, nothing but frustration at dealing with a person like myself, demanding answers to questions I wasn't supposed to know.

"They threw FIRE at me!" I said a little defensively, calming down. The sounds all together vanished, muting back to the solemnly quiet house.

"It wasn't real. They're illusionists." The cat demon got from its place, walking a step and a half closer and sitting down once more. "I know you're frustrated. I know things may be getting to you, but you don't know these things for a reason."

I lowered my head. I would not be getting answers today.

"Why? Why can't I know the whole thing now and cut out the waiting? What do I possibly have to gain from not knowing everything?"

Palug smiled, reminiscing on something.

"Enjoy bliss for a while. It's not an IF you'll know, it's when. Enjoy your time until then." I stared at him wide eyed, a little spooked.

"What'd I do?" The cat demon cut a laugh quickly, nuzzling my head once more. I wasn't reciprocating the cat's version of a pat on the back. The woman in white watched the two of us from the wall, resting comfortable in a lean. Palug perked up, bowing to her.

"My queen, how are we today?" I suddenly sat up straight.

"I thought I was your queen!" I spat out, before realizing I sounded like a pouting two year old. Palug laughed.

"It's a common, respectful greeting." The cat demon bowed again, "All female spirits are greeted as such, if they're polite." I sat hard against the wall, feeling my only lead, politely, go darting right out the window. That explained a few things, at least. There was a little bit of relief in knowing I wasn't in charge of anything important; didn't help me pinpoint just what or who I was, though. Kayalin noted our conversation's end, speaking up.

"Having a little spat, are we?" She said expectantly as I felt the conversation direct away from what I needed to know.

"Hey. Palug. Let me ask you one last thing." I sat back on my haunches, bowing my head a little respectfully and letting my hair sway back and forth, speaking out sheepishly. "Me and "him" you know… we didn't know each other or anything before, did we? We weren't like…

married or something, right?"

I don't know why I thought he'd tell me, or why he'd be the authority to know. I swear we sat in silence for a full minute before either one of us even so much as breathe or made a sound. This was broken by Palug's uproarious laughing, a fearful sound that scared both myself and the woman in white at first. He slumped over to his side, laughing and rolling about a little bit, nudging Kayalin a little and trying to get her to join. She looked at me a little funny, laughing half-heartedly while her eyes darted around with no idea why she was doing it.

"Was that some sort of inside joke?" She leaned over to me, whispering as the cat demon continued on. Feeling deflated, I twitched one part of my lip in a very half-hearted sneer.

"Apparently." Snorting, I watched him as he stopped, trying to gather himself from the delirious puddle of laugher he became. Palug looked at me for a second, rolling over to the one side and snickering some more.

"Oh, I'm so glad you're here." He grinned, sighing heavily like he was holding back the laughs. I nodded emptily; still isolated, even like this. But the place was starting to feel like a strange sort of home.

23

I learned practically squat over the next three weeks. My days were dedicated to sitting around by the angels, fake sleeping in the sun, listening to their unrelentingly boring conversations about how the day was, how it'd be tomorrow, from sun up to sun down. Repeat the next day. They knew I was listening in, so they kept everything torturingly generic. No matter how much I smiled, they wouldn't so much as talk about how much they hated anything. Everything was good. Everything was pretty, and fine, and the weather was fantastic, and my God I wanted to bash my head against the wall after the second day.

I got relief from my duties when Palug and I went perusing for new souls, new recruits. It was pretty slim; he and I kept pestering this one stubborn ghost of an old man living a few blocks away. He was a vicious little thing; anytime we got near, he'd come darting out of the house, heading straight for us, kitchen knife in hand. Palug and I were smart enough to stay on the other side of the property line as he's stop just short, cursing and ranting and promising us all sorts of unfortunate events. He was intent on staying, but mentally dwindled away in these last ten years of ghostdom to a gibbering, cursing mess. Still, with no other immediate leads in the area, we couldn't help but try, each and every day. We found out a week ago that the old man had been exorcised from the property, another casualty in this war. Even though he was a crazy, murderous old coot, Palug and I kept our mouths shut walking past the house out of respect. I wonder if Raziel was to blame.

Not once did I run into him in that time, though something peculiar would happen at night every now and then. I'd get these annoying twinges of emotion, blips of anger, or rage, or something I'd even consider sadness, just half a second of it. It reminded me of the very first actual thing I'd remembered, besides eyes, of feeling stretched out, of feeling tied

269

to everything around me like a giant web before it shimmered away back into numbness. Now and then I'd wake up, sit up straight and tall, my head pounding like it was trying to rip apart from itself, and it'd all just smooth back into normalcy, each and every time. Weirdest of it all was sitting there, quiet and reflective, and feeling that tiny compass in your head move, feel it shift back and forth so slowly, of my tether to the angel Raziel. I could point him out; find him in a drop of a hat, even more when the needle shifted, when he and the Priest, assumably, were on the move. He got pretty close, enough that it made me wonder if I was being missed, or if I was needed. No, no he wouldn't do that. I was dead to him.

I couldn't even begin to explain the paranoia of my trust, I questioned it constantly. He could point me out to all the other angels, more dangerously, the Cherubs that I was told were the worst of them all, higher then Gauzier and Raziel combined. They were dangerous, four-winged battle monsters, tracking down the groups of demons like bloodhounds. Or Piranha; it depended who you spoke to. Palug, of course, laughed at the mention of them; no help, really. I laughed a little at first too, having the imagery of large, angry angel-babies hunting like giant battle-bots, but it passed with time.

When I wasn't ghost-scouting, or laying around like a giant lump of demon by the angels, I spent my time amongst the others inside. They really were a good group as Kayalin had said. That first day, I had met eleven of the twelve (now thirteen with myself included) demons in the house, the last being this large, practically dead demon in the basement where most of the spirits attached to; the boys attached to the Black Dog spirit, the other little back-up soul powering device. It explained why everyone else was so tired, so exhausted most of the time; they couldn't help but reflect the mood of their base, the giant demon in the bottom of the house; so black that it was hard to define. Palug filled me in that it was a large, coiled and fattened snake, a 'naga' named Manasa. She didn't move much and preferred to stay in the dark depths of the basement, taking up most of the lowest level of the house. I felt bad for it staying there like it was imprisoned, but it did make things reliably convenient.

Besides Palug, I spoke most often with Kayalin, the woman in white. We seemed somewhat close in age, we could relate to one another, even though I wasn't sure she realized I was anything but a big, rambling outlet spirit. I guarded, most importantly. I was good at that. Guarded and napped about. None of the other demons in the house kept a schedule like that, none of them slept. Palug from time to time would doze off, but always be a breath away from full mental awareness, venty eyes popping open like a squeezed plastic baggie. He was essentially the den-mother for the entire house, angels and demons alike; the demons treated him like a guardian, like a savior. The angels treated him like a maid. It wasn't a good relationship, but it was more than most of the demons had with the angels outside, who were often from the bits of honest conversation I heard, scared of the others inside. They had this stigma about the bad spirits, that they were one of them, but they weren't at the same time. Angels, no matter the position, didn't want to be associated as being bad spirits; though they were a little too involved in themselves to see that the demons were crabby at best. But not evil.

It almost seemed like everyone was wrapped up in their own little worlds, their little fantasy of how they saw life after death. I was starting to see how everything, really, was a plain, middle ground; not black and white, good and evil - kind of felt like we were all just kidding ourselves.

Palug spent most of his time there at the house, or with me. Every now and then he'd leave off, dart out at strange little hours and not say where he went, and be gone for a solid twenty minutes. I was never invited on these outings, claiming that this motley group of spirits needed someone to watch over them, lest the Cherubs come down and bust all our heads. I did my best to try and follow what he told me, that hidden friend of mine, and ignore the inadequacies around me, try and enjoy my time here instead of fretting about it. You never really squash that doubt, though, no matter how often its told to you.

My life now was full of rhythm, full of the gentle ebb and flow of the days as they passed, as my mind slowly turned away from what it had been, to what I was dedicated to now. I enjoyed my time there at that house, but it always felt like something was unresolved, that certain actions never fell away, never ceased to pester the back of my mind. The short list; of where I came from, where I'd be going, why the angel'd turn on me after our time there, why large, threatening, impossible demons, the… Cempe, would haunt my steps. I hadn't seen her for my entire stay here, not that I was complaining. I hated her for what she did, for tearing Raziel in half.

We set out one day in particular, Palug and I, not getting any hints of new ghosts, of any spirits to recruit in a part of our neighborhood full of more industrialized buildings, enjoying the peace of a quiet evening, walking and talking like we normally did. He and I did seem to get along quite nicely, a similar view on things, happy to talk about whatever wasn't my own past, it seemed. I'd been accepted with the rest of the demons in the house, they were all fine with talking to me and didn't ask questions, didn't prod into my life. With Palug, though, it really was like talking with a family relative of mine, someone close- even if he was a large, off and on bleeding demonic tiger cat. It'd strike me randomly how strange my life was.

Passing in front of an old, dilapidated church and back towards the house; this conversation felt particularly relaxed. I spoke up on something that had been nagging me for a long time as I held on their stained glass windows of the Heavenly feathered figures watching over us both.

271

"Let me ask you something, If I can." I watched my front feet as I plodded heavily on my hybrid demonic hands, avoiding his vented gaze. "When I first met you in that old womans house, were you actually a resident spirit there?" The big cat laughed, as he always did.

"I lived there for about six months before you and the angel arrived. Fought a lot of exorcists, I must say, before you finally showed up." His tone pulled back a little, hushed, almost reminiscent in a loving way.

"You were waiting for me?" I turned to him, keeping my head low. This was something I had suspected for a while, that his involvement with that exorcism was a little staged, that it was a part of this infamous 'plan'. The cat looked in my direction before nodding slightly.

"I knew you were in the area, that it was a matter of time before we'd meet up again."

"Why didn't you tell me we were friends then, hm?" I felt like I was almost lecturing him, scolding him. "Considering your first way of saying hello was trying to take off my head." There was still a bit of a twitching fuse on this subject. The cat held his head a little higher, taking in a deep breath.

"You wouldn't have believed me. I could see how terrified you were the first time you saw me, trying to declare our acquaintanceship at that time seemed like a poor idea." It was my turn to laugh.

"I didn't know if you were going to eat me, you were the first other demon I'd had contact with. I didn't know anything about this side of the playing card, you know?" I scanned the area as a car suddenly burst through both of us, our energy and spiritual forms buckled out and swept back together painfully for a second as we gathered our bearings. Gritting my teeth, and shaking my head out, I picked up where I left off. "It worked out though, I considered us pals then." My tone suddenly picked up rather girly as I grinned to the night air.

"Did you consider us BFF's at that time, Palug?"

"Yes, your heart still seemed in the right place, my dear." My course changed direction quickly, nudging him playfully in the shoulder as we walked together alongside the street. I could see why we were friends, if that whole back story was actually true.

"So." I calmed down, serious once more, "If you were there at that old woman's house, who watched over the spirits here at this house?" Palug turned to me a little quicker, eyes resting on my face.

"Cempe did." I stopped walking.

"The other me-she demon?" The cat almost bellowed in annoyance.

"It's not you in any way, it's just another demon. I swear." His pace pulled away from me as I remained still. The cat noticed my halt and slowly swept his front half around to a stop. "She was very helpful and did a great job keeping guard."

My head flopped side to side in frustration and a sort of childlike annoyance.

"What is she to us, really? You can't consider her on our side, do you? She killed off Raziel, not to mention tried to bump me off whenever it was convenient, or I was in her way."

"She can be a little…overbearing sometimes, but she's a good soul."

"A good soul. You've got to be kidding me." I took a step away, shaking my head with more gusto this time. "All she's ever done is terrorize me and injure anyone around me, why would anyone consider that a good soul in any way?" Palug walked slowly back towards me, keeping his head low.

"You don't mean that." I remained staring at him, eyes a little wide, recanting it. Why wouldn't I mean it, it was a fair and honest opinion on what I'd experienced.

"I'm fairly sure I do!" The cat was just in front of me now, head butting lightly on my neck, like he was mourning the dear, departed respect I'd lost for Cempe, the angry wall busting horse-dinosaur demon. He spoke, just above a hushed grumble.

"She's watching out for you. Just like I am. Please don't speak ill of her… Neri." I had all but closed my eyes until he stumbled on my name. Watching out for me? Cempe was watching out for me? Well, I mean, she had mentioned babysitting, it fit, but something about her watching out for me really shook me. Made me nervous. I decided to avoid the Cempe topic altogether, to fall back into line.

"You're watching out for me?" I said cautiously, my smile soft and heartfelt. I knew I could take care of myself, but knowing that someone was blatantly trying to guard me was a change of pace. Palug kept his head down, but I could see him smiling from the edges of his face.

"Maybe." He pulled away a little, looking up at me.

"That's not very cat-like of you. It's rather doggish." I laughed, a giggle, actually. Palug grinned.

"I don't have to be cat-like, you know." He protested, raising his eyebrows as he sat up a little straighter. I found myself giggling more, in this body they came out like little, high-pitched half-roars. God how I hated this form sometimes. If my face wasn't already red, I would've been flustered. Embarrassed, I nudged him hard in the shoulder once more, setting off back down the street with a full grin.

"C'mon, let's go." I set off at a little jog, the Cath Palug following close behind. My mind was a flutter with questions, starting to wonder on just who this beast was. Maybe more importantly, if he was trying to imply he had other forms then this one. I laughed a little more before I suddenly stopped cold in my tracks. Palug loped a little past me, stopping quickly as my face was troubled and confused, scanning the area. The tether, I could feel it. More importantly, I could feel it move significantly.

"What is it?" Palug was concerned, coming closer to me with a great amount of worry to his tone. "What's wrong?"

My head snapped back and forth, trying to make sense of it. The tether felt like a compass, with the needle moving ever so slightly but still keeping the same direction most of the time. Now, it felt like the compass itself was spinning around, that my due North was arcing just in front of me. Raziel; he wasn't far at all, a mile away at most.

"The angel, Raziel, he's close by." I said in a bit of a panic. Palug suddenly reared back to his hind legs, heaving back to bring his massive torso into a stand high above me.

"Is he going for the house? Where is he?" He looked around, eyes flaring and closing quickly, trying to find him. Loping quickly to the street I could see the van dart past, two blocks away; that brightly painted ghost mocking us from a distance.

"There!" I yelled out, suddenly darting towards him and the van. Palug wasn't far behind." He's not going for the house, but he's not far from it!" Not far didn't even cover it, the angel was three houses away from our local central base of the entire, fifteen mile area. I stretched out my gait, gaining speed; Palug was faster.

"Listen, Neri, I hate to say this…" I cut him off.

"I know. Protecting the base is first and foremost. If he gets wise to where we're hiding…." I gasped for air as we rounded the corner, seeing the van parked in the driveway, already empty. "We'll need to defend it, no matter the cost."

"Right, even if that means the worst."

"I know. I can do it." I grumbled under my breath, flaring my wings open once to take to the air, to land on the roof. Looking over my shoulder, Palug gave a nod before heading inside the house as well. With little grace, I flopped through the ceiling, stopping in a teenager's bedroom. A spacious teenagers bedroom; no people in immediate sight.

The covers were folded neatly, the books all arranged, angsty posters hung from the wall. Picture perfect room, except that the entire thing was preserved like a museum, no clothes on the floor, like the room was uninhabited in every way except for the things that were placed in it. I shuddered, skin suddenly cold as a figure blocked the light of the hallway. My head snapped to it, finding a 15 year old kid standing there, mouth agape and staring straight into my eyes. Neither of us made a move as I tried to figure out if he could see me or not, or if this human kid was often traumatized by the sight of his own room. I tilted my head slightly; it was enough to set him off.

"Aaaaaahhhhh!" He screamed, backing from the room and running out of view, voice trailing as the wall blocked the sound. Like a wild predator I was fast after him, my head sticking from the room to watch him dart down the hallway, still screaming. The wounded fish instantly attracted all the sharks in the building, that familiar face clomping into the room below the lofty hallway, ready for the attack. Raziel's glare suddenly vanished as our eyes met.

"Neri?" He said quickly as Palug rushed in behind him, catching him off guard and clamoring up the steps. The angel threw himself backwards out of the way, almost dropping his weapon, forgetting the mission at hand. "Cat demon?" Palug ignored him, speaking up to me instead.

"There was a wake going on in the first floor, this child doesn't know he's deceased." He got to the top, still hearing the whimpering and shrieking the room over in the master bedroom. "We've got to reach this child before the angel exorcises him off." Palug stared at me for a moment before darting into the room, moving forward slowly like he was stalking him. Raziel just kept looking between the both of us, supremely confused, waiting for me to make a move. I stared for a second before remembering 'how much better it'd be for both of us to pretend we never met', of the things he'd said. Lowering my eyebrows a little, I walked calmly through the hallway, eyes kept straight ahead of me, ignoring him. It hurt.

"Hey! Neri! It's me!" He called out. I grumbled under my breath without falter. No kidding- here's that pretending it never happened thing in progress, right here. Passing the angel on the first floor, I stuck my head into the master bedroom, finding Palug curled up, trying to be as non threatening as possible while he talked sweetly to the spirit of the teenager. It was obviously not taking this well, pressed against the wall next to the closet, he was fidgeting around for something amidst the clothes.

"You need to relax, child. We're not here to hurt you."

"Yeah?" The kid said cockily, pulling out a baseball bat from the closet and brandishing it in our general direction, "Is that why there's a bunch of damn monsters here in my house?" The bat wiggled from his grip, passing through his hand and dropping hard to the floor. The kid pulled back on his arm quickly, staring at it.

"God, what's going on…" He hissed in a panic, arms folded tight to his body. "What do you things want with me?" He yelled out quickly, tears starting to crowd the corners of his eyes.

"We're here to help you" Palug said calmly. This didn't help.

"Help me with WHAT? What do you monsters need to help me with, huh? What could you-" I interrupted sharply.

"Hey, got a name?" I barked out, drawing his attention quickly; he jumped a little before calming down, looking over to me before back down at his hand and the baseball bat at his feet. I could hear Raziel coming up the stairs.

"Peter" The teen said quietly, using the sleeve of his shirt to wipe his face quickly. "What, you here to help me too?" He cracked out, voice shaky and rocked with emotion.

"Depends on what you choose, Peter." I meant to say more, but

I felt something just behind me, the pike nudging me in the back from
the angel at the top of the stairs, looking politely to get past me and Palug
crammed in the doorway. With a sort of low, flat glare, I flopped my
wings open, closing off this section of the hallway in a rush of red, white
and yellow feathers. My head hung a little lower, off-put by seeing him
altogether. I didn't need this.

"Choose what?" The kid calmed down a little more, still wiping his
eyes. I was feeling very blunt.

"If you'd like to come with us, or if you'd like to let the angel here
to exorcise you from this house."

"Exorcise why would you…" His red, bloodshot eyes grew
impossibly wide, staring at his hands. "No…nononono, this is a joke!
A…a… a dream!" I scoffed.

"That'd make things easier. But no, I'm afraid that's true and
you're dead as dirt." Palug suddenly shot a glare at me, like I was being too
insensitive, too harsh. "It's true!" I backtracked, feeling something push on
my wing, trying to get through. The Saint Michaels barrier singed feathers
and burned my back, a bubble of protection around Raziel as you could tell
he instantly backed off. I grumbled, starting to lose my temper.

"Listen. It's a lot to take in right now, but we're scant on time here.
You come with us, we can help you, find you a new home; or you can go
with the angel, which I'm pretty sure he's going to slice you in half and
you'd probably end up with us anyways. Either way, this life is over, and it's
time to start the next leg of this wacky little marathon." The kid just looked
at me, wide-eyed as Palug shook his head a little.

"We need to work on your spiritual social skills, Neri."

"I'd be all poetic and lovey about this moment, but I can't hold
off Raziel for much longer." I turned to the kid sarcastically. "Sorry, but
facts are facts." Just as I finished that, something sliced neatly through
the armpit of my right wing, the entire thing slumping to the ground and
disappearing in a rush of black smoke. Raziel pushed past me not kindly,
muttering under his breath as we lined up.

"Looks like you found yourself some friends." He shoved himself
into the room, significantly larger wings smacking me in the face as the
barrier pushed me a good five feet from the entrance, burning my skin in a
familiar manner. Palug was strangely unaffected as Raziel took a few casual
steps towards the kid in the corner like they were old friends. "So, hi there."

The teenager instantly tried to grab for the baseball bat again,
succeeding in holding onto it for just a half second. The bat flipped in the
air out of his grip, landing softly onto the bed beside him while we all
ducked a little.

"What do you want? Are you trying to exerci-exorcise me?" The
teenager babbled at wit's end, barely keeping it together, barely registering
anything at all. Raziel stopped quickly, holding his hands up like he was

hostage before turning around to glare at me flatly.

"Thanks; you spooked him." He grumbled, even though he kinda looked like this was one big joke, like he completely forgot what happened almost a month ago. Like we were still good pals. A little off guard, I growled low, loud enough for everyone in the room to hear it.

"Like I'm lying." I pushed myself farther into the room; Raziel was on the left of me, Palug to the right, the teenager in the farthest corner away. Now it just became a race on who could entice the spirit first, like a crappy carnival game. Raziel looked at the two of us, shaking his head before lowering his hands and walking nonchalantly towards the kid.

"I'm not going to exorcise you, you're still a good spirit right now. It's just due to the circumstance of your death that you haven't passed on just yet." He coughed, trying to be serious, trying to push away the strange vibe of this moment. "But I can help you go into purgatory, where I'm sure you'll get into Heaven just fine." Palug turned to me, whispering.

"Why isn't he going to exorcise him?" I cocked my head a little.

"I think he might've gotten a new job. Along with a new weapon and new wings at my expense." Raziel turned behind him to glare at me a little as we spoke to one another, attention back to the ghost of the young adult in front of him. Still good at picking up the tiniest hint of sarcasm.

"Why should I go with you, why are there monsters here?" He leaned down a little bit like he was going to grab for the bat once more, crumpling against the wall instead and sliding to the floor. "What do you things want with me? Please, can't I just stay with my family?" The room fell to silence, hearing those words echo'd by myself in the past and crippling my enthusiasm. The nerve struck unusually deep.

"Well, because you uh... can't. It doesn't work out well." Raziel muttered, as awkward and off his step as I was. My skin felt cold, shaking my head back and forth, desperately trying to figure out why I was even trying to get this obviously distraught person on our side.

"Death isn't meant to be a showdown like this." I spoke softly as my own realization pressed on my throat, letting out a bewildered wheeze. "We're here to give you options to…help…to…" I stopped, finding my logic fall short. Why were we here, really? We couldn't offer anything but an eternity of fighting, of time still spent on earth, just amongst friends so your brain doesn't dwindle away. The angel offered life, really. Heaven.

"We're here to see if you'd like to join with us, we always need good souls to back up our cause." Palug spoke of it like a fallen brother, like a triumphant, glorious grunt. It was war, plain and simple. There was no glorious cause. I sat up a little straighter, really looking at what was going on here; we were trying to con a kid into ignoring his chance at everlasting life, to stay and suffer.

"But what if I don't want to leave? If I just want to stay here…" The kid started looking over to us, hopeful and desperately trying to grasp onto some idea. My eyes widened. "Do these things let me stay here?" Spooked, I looked quickly back to Palug as you could see him weighing the outcomes of lying to a panicked, miserable child. My head snapped to Raziel, who looked just as unsure and panicked, furrowing his brows the tiniest bit. My alliance buckled.

"No, no... just..." I sidled a bit closer to Raziel and Peter as you could see the angel tense up. Putting out a hand, I lowered my head, looking at no one.

"Go with him, okay? We're uh..." I looked back to Palug as all four vents were wide open, confused as he looked back to the angel. "I made a mistake, we're really here for people with no chance. You have a chance. You should take it."

"Neri!" Palug said, shocked. I looked back to my demonic brethren.

"I can't, Palug. I... we can't. We can't!" Looking back to Raziel and Peter, I gave a sort of bewildered, dumb smile before scooting backwards like submissive doormat, miserable and confused. "Just go with the angel. He's your best option here. Just do that. I'm sorry."

"Neri!" Palug hissed as I inevitably bumped into him, backing from the room. "What? Why are we leaving?"

"Because I'm not going to force an innocent child to be a demon!" I hissed back angrily, beside myself. Realizing everything was silent and tense, I tried again.

"I'm sorry for any confusion. Sorry about that. Good luck." Awkwardly shifting towards the door, I kept talking. "Right. Right. Um... Bye. Sorry."

Palug's head darted back and forth between the two of us as I turned towards the wall, passing through that. With a short wing beat, I was to the roof, looking around me like there was an answer drifting about, that there was reason to go back inside and try to convince a child that Hell was better than Heaven. Nothing made sense anymore.

"Neri! Why are we abandoning our chance to save another soldier?" Palug pulled himself onto the roof as well, eyes vented in alarm. I kept my wings outstretched, flapping them lightly, not enough to pull me from the ground, but enough to move my limbs around a bit. I scoffed.

"Save? What are we saving him from? What are we supposed to offer him, Palug? Hey kid, come enjoy Hell, it's dank, and dark, and half the time you've gotta worry about some monster sneaking behind you and gobbling you whole. Face it, where we live, it sucks." The cat demon acted like I had just slapped his mother.

"WHAT?"

"It does! This kid's got the chance to get into Heaven, where we obviously aren't able to go for a reason. Real life, that living, breathing, actual life, they get the world around us. Angels and all good people and controversially good dogs, they get Heaven, from what I understand is a shining beacon of all that's good and lovely and pine-scented. But us?" I huffed tiredly, knocking my head against their chimney, "We're the bad folk. We get the shadows. The darkness. We haunt people's dream's - we wade on their conscious, we terrify them. Why would we try and convert others to that willingly?" Something erupted through the roof of the house, a single solitary pillar of light, ascending quickly into the darkness, cutting the night. After moment, it was gone; you could feel the energy sweep away from this house, as the ghost had been ascended, raised, whatever. Palug watched it as well, turning back to me.

"I understand my place in life, I know what I am. Why are you trying to convert regular good, honest people over where they don't belong?"

"That's not how things are, Neri." He said under his breath, struggling for the words he could actually say to me, that weren't taboo or forbidden, lest they jog my memory. "The angels are not 'good people', I can promise you that. They're not right."

I shook my head once more, fed up.

"Yeah? How do you know what's right?" I pushed a little bit more, frustrated. I knew he had the right answer, and I knew he couldn't tell me. "You wanna educate me in that aspect? Change things up a bit? I mean, if you want to inform me how I'm wrong, please, absolutely, go ahead." The Cath Palug growled a little more, only flexing his claws a little, quietly repeating himself.

"That's...not how it is."

"Well, that's exactly what I see. I don't know any better!" My own voice began to crack, just as Raziel popped his head through the roof. Palug and I both froze, slowly turning back towards him. I kept my eyes lowered, miserable.

"Neri?" He called for me as I slowly swung my head around, completely empty on sympathy or anything but a completely trodden spirit, shifting a little closer to the edge. He could see we were arguing, he knew what I had done. The angel tapped on the shingles of the roof for a moment, trying to figure what to say. He smiled honestly for a second as that sentiment faded, looking once to Palug as the demon cat glared as much as he physically could. Looking back towards me, he played around with the grit on the roof, nervous, anxious. Remnants of the tether laid it out perfectly. "I'm really glad you're okay."

I stared at him, breath getting shorter and shorter, belting out a distressed and unhappy little whine jumping from the roof, wings outstretched. Felt like I was about to bust into tears. Why'd he have to say that?

Pity, pity, pity; it was the last thing I needed from anyone.

24

I flew for a while, aimed nowhere specific. The sun rose on another day, cascaded into the sky like it always did; lighting the land below it, the earth above it, everything in between but myself and anyone else who happened to exist in this little shoddy plane of existence. I don't know what I was looking for, or what ditching a fellow demon in the middle of a fight would accomplish. It was probably one of the very few honestly true times that I wanted nothing better than to be left alone. I wasn't looking for Raziel to follow me and try and make me feel better, or to have my every move watched by Palug. I needed time to figure out where I stood, not have people obtusely take my hand and spin me their greatest riddle for me. They saw me as a child. A joke.

I swooped lazily between the clouds, head upwards, looking. Trying to see Heaven for myself, a glint, a glistening; just something to reassure me that it existed, that the ultimate version of all that was good and wholesome and lovely and white, was there. Squinting, searching and scanning the clouds I saw nothing, empty sky like it always was. With the winds biting out of the northwest, cold and bitter; choking, I fell towards the ground, landing in some little, obscure graveyard at least ten miles from where I took off from. My landing was gummy, arms and legs worn out from the hours of constant exercise as I took a few extra steps, folding my wings close to my body. Watching them until they disappeared as a distortion of light at best, my eyes wandered from my back to the area around me; it was an old cemetery. Some of the stones were just washed out white rocks, a few grave markers nearly sideways from the trees planted at their base 300 years ago. Completely serene, quiet, reflective. Ironic that I'd find a graveyard most peaceful considering what happened, but they really did plant them at prime locations.

Scanning, the trees above me were about to drop their leaves, the last bit of vibrant color still plaguing them in chunky bits throughout the branches. Dainty walking through, I took a seat at the base of one of the largest trees, folding my legs and arms close to my body with my wings half-wrapped around me for warmth. Leaves crackled in the air as a fine, slow snow began to fall, began to cover the world around me.

With a deep sigh I looked around, appreciating the quiet, the peace, leaning heavily against a tall, grand maple or oak of some sort. The snow twinkled on the leaves, serene and astounding. I felt nothing but envy.

Despite feeling like crap, I smiled a little, nestling against the tree, appreciating the well groomed grass, pruned trees and paid landscaping. Everything was dangled right in front of my nose like a child, taunting me and giving these hollow pretexts that this is what I should've been doing. Why bother being concerned WHY it's not the greatest idea to convince some poor kid to abandon family and friends in Heaven. Come join our side. That sure makes a whole lot of sense. Who in the right mind would recruit to this?

There had to be a reason I was like this, a purpose, something more than dumb luck. I could be ignorant, I could turn my head away at a few things, but the others, they were asking me to be just plain blind. I couldn't do it. Either I, or the demon that got me out of Hell did something worth being sent to Hell for. Though considering I was a whole lot of myself before the demon ever came around, and I was still in Hell, it was pretty obvious who the bad person was. I'm pretty sure I lured the garbage disposal for souls away from it's post to ride to freedom in the world above.

I smacked my head against the tree a little.

"I'm not pretending that I'm an angel." Leaning forward, I tried to talk through the problem aloud. The others, the innocent ones, they didn't do anything. They were completely blame-free, guiltless. That kid was left behind on a technicality; probably a suicide of some sort- still, he gets through. He gets in like he should. But what reason was there for me to try and convince him otherwise? It was like being given the choice between sitting on a golden throne, or sitting on a pile of cow manure. Which one is the obvious choice? Why was that so hard for other people to understand?

"Maybe it's worth it to try and get on the Angel's side, if that's what's right. There's probably a good reason angels are trying to wipe us off the map." The air around me cooled, flecks of snow drifting about hazily as all grew quiet once more. I settled down, taking a lot of heavy, uncomfortable breaths. Something needed to make sense, there had to be reason amidst this annoying, amnesia fog, hidden somewhere.

I was so tired. So drawn out. Wary, exhausted. This blindness, this ignorance of my own personal effects around me, it had to stop.

"You're an idiot." Someone spoke quickly as I jumped, sliding off to the side, scrambling to get to my feet. The sound had come directly behind me, another reptilian demonic head snaking around with a heavy grin— the Cempe or whatever she was called, sitting just on the other side, mimicking me. Instantly the hair bristled on my spine; confused for a second; she was roughly the same size as I was, not twenty-something feet tall, towering and angry and belligerent. But still angry, even at a mere 8 or 9 ft tall, like I was. She looked around the base of the tree, furrowing her eyebrows at my reaction and shaking her head while my voice bubbled in a low rumble, "This is only proving it, idiot."

"W…what are you doing here, Cempe?" I huffed out, looking around like I had flown into an ambush. The demon grinned.

"Ah, so your little bundle of questions is slowly unraveling for you that you get to know my name. I guess that's progress in some way." She laughed at my expense, settling down. "I conveniently picked the same graveyard, out of ALL the ones in this area to lounge about and talk to bones— I'm following you, what does it look like I'm doing?" The demon rolled into a sit, awkward limbs trying to get traction on the ground.

"Why?" Growling, she mimicked me.

"Because you're a whiny angsty baby that if I had a sweater big enough, would need your mittens pinned to your shirt." She looked away, voice angry and low, "You're a traitorous liability that can't be trusted." I choked on a cough.

"Traitorous?" Was all I could think to reply to, beyond mad.

"Yeah. Traitorous. Remember your little morality game? Lofting yourself up on that high horse?" Bristling more, she looked around the area for a moment, "Speaking of, are we harboring today? King idiot around?"

"It's just me this time, no friends to eat or attack." I spit it out like an insult. Cempe was not fazed.

"Shame. I'm losing my step, then." She lightened up, eyes to the grass next to the tree as the demon began to try and pick at the bark, generally bored. Her eyes dragged from the ground to glare straight at me, groaning, waiting for me to calm down, to relax. It wasn't happening. "Oh, for shit's sake, I'm not going to do anything, you can drop this angry monster business right now so I can help you out." My defensive pose slowly eased, slowly went to a shade less of petulant fear as I sat down, my body far from the tree.

"How could you possibly help me?" I grumbled cautiously, watching her as she dug her little wrist-horns into the grass, marking up the sod and the tree root unfortunate to pop out above the dirt. Cempe chuckled.

"Well, since I know everything and every part of what's going on, and you're stuck with Trivial Pursuit knowledge at best, I can maybe fill in a little of your empty head. Maybe then you'll stop with this constant bitching and moaning." The demon turned to look at me dead in the eye as my teeth were already pulled back in a growl.

"Why would you help me out, after all you've done?" Cempe scoffed.

"That's WHY I help, idiot." I felt outraged, felt like my privacy was being assaulted, that this demon knew so much about me when the longest we' known each other was barely the blink of an eye. I opened my mouth to say something, but she caught the sentence first. "You feel helpless. Trapped. Bewildered and lost in the great grand world of the unknown afterlife with one demon trying to help while another just constantly tortures your tiny, misunderstood soul. So we run away to get our head straight, fill our mind with answers that just aren't there, and worry those who care about us in a selfish haze. How am I doing so far?"

She smiled as my jaw hung open, breath of air I planned to use for my comeback just tumbling out as a sort of half gasping grunt. The dinosaur-horse thing grunted in return, mocking me.

"You think you know me?" I growled out, outraged, rocked off my base. Cempe leaned a little farther from the tree, tongue hanging from her mouth lewdly, taunting me on. In a flash I was at that tree, lunging out, trying to take a chunk out of her, a little tidbit of revenge for the grief she'd caused. I didn't care what Palug said, this monster was nothing but a thorn in my side.

Sailing at her she leaned from the tree, smacking me hard across the back as I missed her, as my teeth grazed the air just inches away. In a plume of smoke I dropped to the ground, tumbled in the grass until I rolled to a stop, body half crunched over itself. I saw my human toes far over my head; I wiggled them, now back in my regular body once again.

"I think I know you pretty well. Sit down and shut up you twit. You might learn something for once." Tilting back to my feet I stood from the grass, taking a few steps away from the demon; my teeth bit into my lip.

"What did I do, hm? You wanna be helpful? Tell me what I did!" I barked at the demon as she sat there, rolling her eyes at me. I wanted rest, wanted a little free time, not confrontation and more arguments. "I mean, there's gotta be some cause that I'm like this, so what did I do, huh?" Cempe cut a seething growl.

"Oh, that's an easy one; you've killed many, many…many angels. It's pretty much your job."

"What?"

"One of the best!"

"You're lying!" I spit out, outraged and taking a step forward.

"Why would I lie about that? It's a good thing! Like a good batting average." Cempe leaned forwards, eyes focused dead on my face. "It's true, and you know it to be. Stop kidding yourself already, demon. You're here for a reason."

"But... but why... how am I in Hell in the first place?"

"Oh, that. I don't know, you were a shitty person or something, what do I care." She raised a claw up, "But if you ever have an angel that's way too into your demon matters, you tend to fix it." My skin was loose and clammy, insides pumped with ice water as I stood there, shaking, trying to pretend they had me mistaken. I covered my mouth in horror as my legs suddenly stopped working, wouldn't move as I fell back, sitting down quite forcefully onto the grass. My conscious prayed it was a lie, that it had to be a lie, that I was still a good person. I'd never do that. Not willingly, at least.

It wasn't a lie. I could feel it in my heart. That sick, heavy, dead feeling that always lingered, that crept into my dreams, that clung to the edges of myself… it was true. I felt hollow.

"See, now we've got you seated and we can talk like normal people." Cempe laughed, relaxing back a little into the crook of the tree. She opened her mouth to say something else, tone dabbling for a second as she obviously saw I was upset. "Hey! Hey! Everyone kills the angels, they're cannon fodder! They die, they go back up there, get a pep talk, come back down for round two and we all dance again and again. Plus, they're assholes that deserve to be smacked around."

"It doesn't matter!" I spit out, rubbing my eyes. I deserved it; the time I thought I was just some good spirit wandering around in a bad one, that it all didn't apply to me…I really was a monster. No better then the rest. All this time.

Pulling at my hair, head down, my body went weak. The wind around me picked up, whistling, the world as distraught as I was. No matter how good I tried to be, I was never going to be anything more than what I was.

Neither of us said anything, the damage done. I tiredly pulled my legs closer to my chest, heaving for breath, mouth numb and head light, about to pass out.

"Relax. C'mon. Breathe." I heard real concern in the monstrous demon's tone, feeling regretful her chiding pushed me too far. I could barely hear her. "Well, actually, no, don't breathe so fast. That's half the problem."

I seethed through my teeth, trying to stop hyperventilating and not doing so well. Tears were streaming down my face as I looked up slightly, shaking.

"Oh, Jesus. C'mon." Cempe looked outright panicked now, "I mean, you're a demon, but at least you're really good at being a demon!" Letting out a miserable, retaliatory wheeze, I put my head back down, worse. My head got lighter and lighter, verging on passing out. Wheeze, cry, wheeeeeze, cry, wheeeeeeze...

"Okay, you're freaking me out because you're getting white like a piece of bird shit." The demon, looked around, holding up one hand, eyes tracking elsewhere. "Let me just see which one is...ah, there you are." I looked up just a moment, head swooning back and forth, vision starting to fade out.

"Yes? Okay? Very sad, sure sucks to be killing angels, you're giving me a headache annnndd-" Her dinosaur fist clenched shut as I no longer had any emotions, or any reaction, like a giant sponge suddenly removing all my issues in a single second. Wadded up like a tangled ball of tape, I only tipped over to the side, frumping against the ground, unsure what had happened. "There we go! I'm on a schedule here, okay? Angst on your own time." She opened her hand back up and I suddenly felt like myself again, if I had been transplanted from a time where everything was great and happy and I wasn't sobbing in the fetal position a few moments ago.

"Tether?" I coughed out, surprised and still very miserable.

"Look at all the interesting stuff you know about now." The demon said flatly. "How do you think I know where you're at?"

Wiping my eyes, I sat back up, head down and still shaking badly- the demon's eyes were on me for a few moments, taking a long, deep dismissive sigh.

"Listen. Whatever you've done, it's been with reason. Never unnecessary; a last resort; my God you try and reason everything to death first. As far as demons go, you're a role model." I leaned away from the beast. "Even with the amount of bloodshed; stop, you know, beating yourself up over it. Angels aren't worth the time." Cempe dug a little where she stood, slowly ambling off to the side, looking to leave. With a few confused and struggling steps, I followed.

"You sure you're talking to the right person?" I demanding haphazardly, empty on the inside. The demon chuckled.

"I ask that same question every time I see you. Yes. There's no mistaken identity here, Neri." The demon huffed a little as an afterthought, walking away at a much steadier pace. I loped after her, arms still folded defensively, uneasy to speak up.

"Why... what is the reason to try and convert people to this side?" It came out childish, abashed, unprofessional. The demon stopped where it stood, mouth crooked to the side in thought. "I mean, if you're the all knowing source around here." She looked back at me quickly, grinning that same toothy half-grin that my other form did, one eye squinted as an answer was arranged and prepared for me, no doubt covered in riddles and puzzles that'd take me a lifetime to figure out.

"Because words like evil, Hell, and Heaven, are just words."

"They... are you saying Hell and Heaven don't exist?" I tried to grasp hold of the meaning, tried to own complete understanding.

"No, no, I didn't say that. They exist; you've seen one of the three. They just exist differently each way they're spoken about. They're words. Concepts." The demon stared at me, looking to see that recognition, the understanding, the great ah ha! moment. After a solid minute, I felt her give up; I understood, just on the surface, that the meaning was tangible, but I didn't quite get the whole message. Cempe saw this.

"Your idea of Heaven is not my idea. My idea of Hell is not yours. Everyone's ideas are different. So who's to say what's right and what's wrong? Get it?" My lips pulled back a little, before dropping back to a frown. I didn't get it. Cempe groaned, thinking for a moment before looking back to me.

"I'm not bothered by your fantastic angel killing stats; you... obviously are, but why do you think that is?" Looking away, I muttered something like a despondent child.

"Because I have morals?" Cempe scoffed.

"Hurtful. I'll simplify it down so even a selfish baby like you can understand. It's bad because someone told you it's bad. But is it actually bad?

"Are you seriously asking if killing someone is bad?" I dropped my shoulders, more aggravated than ever. "Doesn't literally every religion frown on that?" Cempe grinned, turning her head about.

"Okay, that's a bad example. Demons. Someone told you demons are bad. But are they?" The monster looked around, "You've met both good and bad angels, as you've met perfectly honest and friendly demons. You don't think it's unfair that other nice, non-murdering demons are treated miserably? You think you're the only demon trying to be as nice as they can?"

"What are you saying?" I whispered, things starting to click more into place.

"We're not converting people to our side, we're giving a voice to people that everyone considers a lost cause." The demon tilted her head off to the side a bit, "I mean, that might entail a lot of angel killing, but that's more a consequence."

After a moment, I gave a sort of bereft shake of my head. I'd rather have morals.

"What would you have done?" I stopped, looking away with a frown like I'd rather not ask this demon questions, but I'd jump through hoops to just know anything. "With the kid at that house? And trying to convert him to our side instead of-"

"I know. What part of 'I'm entirely aware of what's going on' don't you get?" I scoffed.

"Fine, entirely aware one, what would you have done?" She seemed to sit for a moment, thinking on it.

"He seem like a nice kid?" Cempe asked as I gave a nod, "Look like he could throw a punch?" I sort of shrugged, confused.

"He threatened us with a baseball bat." The demon gave a smile, nodding with a full grin.

"That's fantastic. I would've pit him against the angel in a bare knuckle brawl and bet on the winners." She nodded, deciding this would've been the route she took, something completely backwards and morally rotten. About to chew her out in frustration, she suddenly spoke again. "I'm joking. Ease off there, crabbypants. We demons like to make jokes, as a form of communication to one another in something called hu-mor." Annoyed, I looked away.

"Yes, I understand." Figuring she wouldn't answer my question since she was the black hole of sympathy, Cempe replied.

"I would've let the angel have him." Surprised, I looked back.

"Why's Palug so set on converting everyone, then?" I followed up.

"Palug has personal investments in these types of affairs, he's not entirely the best mark of accuracy for what you should do. Especially concerning angels. Not a fan."

The demon grinned, nodding once before turning back to the sky around us, wings unfurling from seemingly nowhere, just like mine did. Except mine were this big, feathery, thin things, like a swallows'; hers, they were like crooked leathery flaps, the 'bone' of the wing looked like a stalactite, like they were made of poorly carved rock, the same tick-marks from her body going down them as well. At the end of the wing the bone divided into two, branching off where a reasonable hand would be to make two wickedly curved points. She crouched, ready to launch herself into the air.

"What are you?" I questioned, dumbfounded as the demon paused.

"Baby, I'm the same thing you are." Cempe took to the air, flapping once or twice before folding her wings completely, diving into the ground, back to the Hell below us. As the last bit of her tail sunk into the earth the black smoke gathered around my feet, twisting artistically around my body until it rose high in the air, waiting. With an annoyed sigh it snapped shut, forming and defining itself until my demonic body was back into play, standing there just as annoyed as my human form had been. Shaking myself out I looked fully demonic, ready for battle.

I felt like burying myself.

Looking around, worn down, frustrated, I took to the sky as well, to the clouds, setting off back for home with words swimming in my head. Concepts. Ideas. How they were just words. I knew of a group of people who were full of them, who needed a firmer push of acceptance, who were going to tell me many more words and paragraphs that didn't include how nice and pretty and beautiful their day was. I don't know what came over me, a sort of blasé determination, of a receded sense of individuality, of uniqueness. Tried not to think about it, tried not to pull it together enough to discover more disappointing and alarming truths; I planned on trying a little self control. Planned on letting my heart go a little colder, remove the emotion from my conquest here best as possible, and that started with avoiding the angel Raziel first and foremost.

Flapping hard with the wind I sailed back towards home, back to the clan of demons I resided with. Maybe it really was where I fit in best, where my place and purpose was at. Angel killer. Grunting, I dropped a little from the sky, wings swinging around harder to push me back into the air. What would ever be a good reason for that, I couldn't stop myself from wondering. There was an ominous feeling to how it was said, that even though I still desperately clung to the idea of being a Present, Praesens soul, that my other two soul counterparts were not going to be happy reunions, pleasant things. Maybe I was the only sane on in the bunch, the reasonable one, if my other two soul-counterparts were still around to exist, they were crazy and bloodthirsty things.

I shook my head out, heading back for home. It was all very disorientating.

After an hour of lazy scouting, I found the house, the backyard, the angelic pow-wow as it always was. It was a little later in the day, almost time for them to migrate indoors, sit around and snicker and laugh there. I intended on progressive, helpful discussion. Dropping out of the sky into the middle of their circle may have been a poor way to start it. I just didn't care anymore, though. The group yelled out of shock, scrambling backwards as I folded my wings closed, eyes tiredly half-open, half-caring what was being said about me, what judgments were made. Snorting, I spoke tiredly, glumly as my tail twitched around.

"I'm gonna need some answers, and I'm sick of playing stupid and ignorant to get them. So we're going to try the direct approach." The angels looked to one another, faces angry and feathers ruffled.

"We don't have to tell you anything, demon!" Azol said, the loudmouth dark-haired olive-skinned one from before. I huffed again.

"And you haven't. Congratulations. Now if we're ever going to be able to help one another, I need you all to stop being little babies out here and try to do something helpful, for once." They looked shocked, unable to speak up, to form a good comeback of any brand. This tactic would either ruin the entire house, or unite them. At this point, I didn't really care which happened. "There had to be a reason you were cast out, and I'm sure it was something dangerous like talking to the wrong church denomination, or sleeping in on a Sunday. So what was it?"

"I don't appreciate the tone you're taking with us, you should be glad we're even here!" The one woman, Saya, stayed close to the others, arms crossed in annoyance.

"I appreciate the support you've given us so far, from what I've observed, of sitting your depressed asses out here all day and talking about the good times, or the nice things, or the endless list of crap that has nothing to do with helping us at all!" I lowered my head a little, bristling for no really solid reason. "I know things must be hard, that you're conflicted about trusting anything but what you know, but we're getting nowhere, helping no one with you all out here secluding yourselves off. Usually, I will not hurt you. I will do my best to take care of you, to watch over you, to protect you. But this…” I motioned with my one hand, the loose circle around me that I was currently disturbing.

“This helps no one. The more we figure out about your falling, the more we can understand why things are happening the way they are. So start talking.” I looked around the group as they went silent, cautiously eying one another and simultaneously giving me death-glares at the same time. Rumbling unhappily, something broke my angry little tirade, interrupting me.

“She means well. We really do want your help, your support.” Palug was standing behind me, lurking in the shadows not far off. The angels all turned to him, startled, before back to me. Azol spoke up again, self proclaimed leader of them.

“We only follow the Excelsis Nona.” He said stubbornly, leaning farther away. I just about lost it.

“The dumb bitch isn’t here!” I shrieked, walking closer to him, singling him out. “I think you’ll do just fine!” I bit just behind his neck and grabbed cloth, lunging into the sky with my first hostage here, flapping my wings hard to bolt, straight up, straight into their precious Heavens. He shrieked, turned and twisted around to try and pull his shirt from my teeth. With my jaws clenched tight, parts began go shear off; in one fluid movement I snatched him by an arm and a leg, half his body dangling precariously above the house below us. We weren’t far up, but far enough that if I so dropped him, we’d be down one fallen angel.

“You dammed beasts!” He tried to throw a punch at me as I hovered mid-air, swinging his body around to throw off the aim. Part of me was actually giddy, actually feeling like I took back a slice of my own life-pie, that I wasn’t doing something under direction of another, or because it was expected of me. Sure, this might wind up a terrible decision and scare them all off, but it was my terrible decision. Not one pre-planned for me. Coughing out a laugh I flicked him into the air, grabbing onto just one leg this time as he dangled, head pointed straight for the ground. “Wh…what do you want from me?!”

“I wanna help you, dammit!” I shook his one leg in emphasis as he gasped, looking back to the ground.

“You call this help?!”

“You’re being stupid and stubborn, I’m helping in the sense that I’m trying to give you a kick in the ass like you deserve!” I laughed as I said it, emotionally thrown in full reverse as the words dropped like heavy stones, as I realized just how much of a carbon copy it was of what Cempe had said to me. My wings whirled around again, slowed by time, a little by fear. Holding on tightly as the world came back to speed, I groaned out, shaking my head and trying to continue on. My decision, new words were needed. "I want there to be mutual help in this household, I just want it to be okay for everyone to talk with everyone, for you all to feel safe and fine in the house, while the house-mates can feel like they can talk to you. That starts with trust, no matter how stupid that seems coming from a demon dangling you above the house itself."

Azol quieted down, arms still wind milling to get a view of the ground, before the side of an eye peered out to look at me. I could faintly hear the others shouting up at me, angry and threatening. I was already easing closer to the ground.

"Why do you want to know the reasons for our falling, then?" He glared up at me before swinging back to look at the ground, as the roof shingles were quickly surfacing to meet us, not twenty feet away. "You're not going to drop me, are you?"

"You keep swinging around like that and I can't make that promise" I smirked as I said it, flapping hard to make the landing a soft one, lowering quite slowly now. Gingerly, his hands skimmed over the top of the shingles, dropping down just a bit more. With both hands firm against the shingles I let go, Azol doing a sort of hand-stand for a second before flipping to his feet. I folded my wings, landing hard on the roof, one foot slipping through.

"It's common ground. Common hatred if you want to be blunt. Informational hatred if you want to be honest." The fallen angel looked over the side of the roof and giving a short wave that everything was fine, before turning back to me. "We're not stupid, you're not stupid, and you know that there's an annoying little divide going on when there doesn't have to be." He picked at his half torn shirt, the sleeve of it down by his wrist, thinking it over.

"You really could've just said that first" His tone was still defensive, but softer then I'd ever heard it. I gurgled a little.

"It's been a stressful day." Azol walked a little on the roof, brushing off his arm as I waited patiently for an answer.

"You can understand why we're hesitant on this, can't you?" I knew the answer to this one.

"Because you have heard the same sayings, day after day, beat into your head that demons are not to be trusted, that they'll charm you right into damnation." I heard Azol laugh and I nodded while he did, "I've heard that same spiel before, I know we're not the most darling things around, physically or socially."

"It's not that. You think we're new at this too?" Azol sat on the edge of the roof, contemplating jumping down instead of having this conversation with me. I furrowed my brows, sitting down a little tighter, a little more insecure on the edge of the roof unsure how to go about it. It was Kayalin herself who said that these angels had been around for some time, I guess it shouldn't come as a surprise to me.

"I apologize, but I am. Still, I can pick out an obvious snag when I see one. If you're all trying to fight back, to get back at the damned skies or something then, you know, we have to put our heads together. I hate to sound all after-school special like that, but it really is true." Fading, fading, melting away, I could practically see my confidence slide off the roof in a goopy puddle.

"It's not getting back at the skies. It's a matter of honor, first and foremost." He said, staring out at the land around us. "It's not that they kick us out of their paradise, it's that they persecute all we knew or related with, that we associated with at any point in time. They take a small bump in the road and dig it into our own grave and drag down all those around us. So actually fulfilling the lies they made up with demons, it never sits well."

"How small does this bump have to be?" I questioned, seeing how far I could push these newfound limits.

"If it's enough for them to question your motives, and it's enough to get you convicted and kicked." He kept his hands behind his back, walking a bit from the edge of the roof like a wounded politician. "It doesn't take much, but the embellished things they tell your closest friends and any surrounding relatives, it's enough to drive you mad." I snorted, disgusted, sick in my heart before stopping to consider their emotions.

"Is that the same story for the others?"

"There's variation. I backed a demon rebellion, while Ibe only helped another fallen angel." My eyebrows jumped from my head, shocked to say the least. Azol saw this and laughed. "Then again, that was a very long time ago in the 1700's." I frowned, guilty, the kidnapper.

"Let's go." I walked closer to him as he hopped onto my back. Grumbling under my breath that I was not a rented birthday pony to be ridden around on, we leapt from the roof. "Whenever you want to talk the details with me, or Palug, we'll be willing to listen. Don't feel pressured beyond that, understand?"

He cackled somewhere behind me.

"You have had previous angel experience, haven't you?" I began to wheel my wings around, trying for a soft landing.

"It's a little boggling how emotionally scarred you all are. Heaven's starting to sound like a real damn downer." I hit the ground, letting him off to a small mob of angry spirits and an unhappy cat/tiger demon. He brushed himself off, picking again at the frayed shirt.

"Only for those employed by it." He walked back into his group of angels, and me with mine, of Palug now joined with Kayalin and the small black dog. Split separate ways, no doubt each side was more then inquisitive on what had happened, how the crazy demon abducted one of the angels and dangled him by his foot for answers.

"What happened?!" Palug screeched at me, Kayalin and the dog following behind him in tow. I walked raggedly towards the house, all sorts of worn out and drained.

"Issues. We all have lots of issues." He stormed closer to catch up, angry still, about to chew me out. I didn't blame him. "They'll talk with us." He suddenly stopped, emotion changing drastically.

"That's great!" He stopped happily, looking back to the angelic group before calling out to me. "Did you have a nice day's rest?"

"Found out I apparently kill angels for a living. So that's something." I stopped, muttering low to Palug as he shuddered to an immediate stop, voice suddenly much less friendly than it had been.

"Who told you that?" Turning my head a bit, I looked the cat demon in his venty eyes.

"Who do you think?" The boys surged from the house, meeting me at the door to latch onto each one of my wings. "We had a nice long conversation in the cemetery." He looked back and forth, once back to Kayalin, panicking. I turned away, walking inside. Didn't seem like that was part of the plan.

I grunted tiredly, slumping into one tired mess, children climbing over me like a jungle gym.

25

"Are you coming?" Kayalin called out at the bottom of the stairs, voice just barely reaching me as I slept like a lump in the attic. The faint traces of the sunset were still visible through the hole in the roof, something that had fallen away with my heavy landing some two months ago. The angels still hadn't really talked with us since, but I was keeping to my word. I also gave up trying to spy on them like an idiot, just left them alone; the result seemed to be good. The angels spent more time inside, demons more time outside; there was a noticeable increase of co-mingling. For example, the touch football game going on outside right now.

Don't get me wrong it sounded like a Hell of a lot of fun, and I was dying to play, but I wasn't touch football material. The sounds of laughter and fun outside made the house seem far more lively and full like this, getting flashbacks of spending time with Amber and Katherine. I gave a sigh.

So the dog and I slept in the attic like good animals, laying about, enjoying some peace and quiet as the sun had long past set on this day. I could hear the fat little thing growling in its sleep that only raised more questions, being an insomniac with the rest of them.

"Get your big scaly ass down here!" Kayalin tried again. "I know you can hear me!"

I grumbled under my breath happily, re-adjusting my head, my one lip half on the floor comfortably. It was stressful trying to unite this house, trying to get two unwilling sides to agree with one another on more than a united hatred for whatever did them wrong. Like I had been doing nearly a year ago, it presented itself to me like a puzzle, full of pieces that claimed to be black and white, but really meshed to an even shade of gray. These challenges, these puzzles, this struggle here, I relished it. Loved it. The longer I stayed here, analyzed how these people fit with one another, what made them tick, the better I got at solving this intricate, strange problem of meshing them together.

Our relentless searching of the haunted houses in the area, and of the recently deceased/possible haunted houses had grown larger, a bigger radius that definitely encroached on regular Raziel territory; though I hadn't seen him, or Cempe for a few months. Not like the imagery of this season was helping much on my quest to put him in the back of my mind, to try and forget him.

But everywhere Palug and I walked, we'd see little Christmas angels, little annoying reminders of the very basic understanding humankind had. At first, seeing them was a little depressing, but now, I just found it outright annoying. I wasn't sure if it was before Christmas, or if everyone and their aunt were just too lazy to take the decorations down, but it was rainy, blisteringly cold from time to time, general winter weather. Demons used me like a portable heater.

Something kicked at my nose, not the first time, but nearly the same. Tiredly, my eyes wandered up to Kayalin, who pulled her leg back, threatening to kick me again.

"Why don't I just paint a bulls-eye on that thing, take the guesswork out." I pulled to my feet, stretching, yawning out loud.

"Why aren't you watching the game?"

"Personal grudge against football." I muttered.

"What?"

"I won't be able to participate." I shook myself out.

"Then participate, you sissy!" She jammed her hand half inside my face, grabbing me by the nostril. Instantly, I was on my feet.

"Ah! Agh, jeez, hold on!" I tried to pull away but she clung on tight, scoffing at me sarcastically. "I'm too big and it'd be an unfair advantage!"

"What, you don't think we can take you down?"

"Do I think the team with the two small children and a black dog spirit can take me down? No." I tried to get a footing, pushing ahead with limbs tangling to keep my nose hairs getting ripped from my face. "Alright, alright, fine, I'll watch." I relented as she let go, pretty much at the door anyways.

"Good. Glad you reconsidered." Kayalin laughed, exiting through the back door to the game being held just beyond it. "We're all getting a little cold out here, come help us all out." Gritting my teeth, I followed just behind.

This all came about by finding a loose football not a few doors down, so of course we stole it. Then, it became a game of wits, trying to convince a sizable team to go come together, angels and demons mixed. Breaking through to the outdoor world they lined up, teams picked, trying to get a handle on throwing the ball around evenly (this came easier to some more than others) as Kayalin entered back into the game, hands up, asking to receive the ball. Only Palug stood on the sidelines, same problem I had, but smiling on the entire thing, enjoying the comradery.

Our previous issues had long been sorted out. I more or less asked if what I was told was true, he gave a very nervous, somewhat disappointed shrug, and that was that. Being" really good at killing angels" sat in my stomach like a rock, but I was at least somewhat more at peace with knowing my shortcomings instead of pretending they didn't exist. Beh.

I sat beside the tiger-cat.

"This is your doing, you know." He said, nodding as I sat down.

"That's a good thing, right?" I chuckled, as the cat nodded more feverishly.

"It's very good. They haven't cooperated like this in years." He dawdled his tone, "It's football, but it's still cooperation. Beats pointless squabbling any day of the week. Things have been a bit of a mess, it's nice to see them less of a mess."

"I'm glad my more favorable skills can be helpful." I edged that previous anxiety and anger as Palug quickly looked to me, shaking his head. I don't think Cempe was supposed to tell me what she did, based on Palug's reaction. He'd spent some time out and away from the house talking with demonic horse-monster a few nights later, returning back after twenty minutes in an aggravated huff, fur poofed out to max irritation. I left that the Hell alone, pretending to be asleep.

"You're very helpful. Stop saying that." He looked back to the game, brows furrowing. "It's just been strained for a while."

"Since your Nona person left?" My tone lowered a little as the cat nodded. I wanted to know more about my apparent leader, pretty far behind the others now. Palug seemed relaxed enough. I looked to the backyard as well, "How long has she been away?" Palug frowned, thinking.

"I think it's been about 15- 16 years now." He shrugged, "The Excelsis runs Hell's battles, so she's been attending issues elsewhere. We get by well enough on our own." Looking over to him, he matched my actions.

"Generally."

"Generally, yes."

They referred to her like a God, like the unborn holy super-mother of all things demonic; it wasn't often that she came up in conversation, but when it did, they, demons and fallen angels alike pretty much kissed her ass. I didn't trust it.

"So, what does" The Excelsis' do?"

There was sarcasm; I didn't intend on sarcasm, but I guess my annoyance with the ass-kissery had shown through a bit. Palug turned from the game to face me, no longer smiling.

"She is our commander, leads our side of the war, one of the very few demons who has the capacity to wander both Heaven and Hell. Even with that ability, she resolves to stay on earth, to lead the fallen and downtrodden demons to glory."

"That's a noble mission statement." I snarked, tail twitching behind me. "How does she wander Heaven and Hell?" I figured if nothing else, I could get filled in.

"We don't really know how, we just know she can." He said it like a confident answer as I only shook my head.

"Another one of life's mysteries, huh?" Palug snickered. "Is she a fallen angel, maybe?"

"I doubt it." He said quickly, growing quiet, hints of loneliness as he said it. Turning to him, I leaned a little closer.

"You ever meet her in person?"

"Once, but it was a long time ago. She was busy running a rebellion, so I didn't really say more than a few yes's and no's."

"You still respect her after just a few yes's and no's?" He laughed.

"It's hard to not like the Excelsis." I gave a sort of dismissive harrumph without thinking. Maybe time spent with the angels jaded me, Gauzier had made a vague statement about the demon's leader some time back, calling it this 'brainless, vicious monster'. While the people here had proved that good and honest demons existed, I guess I was just stuck thinking them bad until they proved otherwise. I just assumed the leader would be some sort of snarling, slobbering behemoth; or that there wasn't a system in place at all. But then talking with Cempe counteracted that. I didn't know what to believe. Palug spoke up. "You don't think so?"

"I don't know, everyone just seems to uniformly like 'The Excelsis', but they never really say why. It sounds like really low-grade brainwashing for someone that hasn't been around for most of these demons to see, right?" I lowered my tone, nearly whispering as I had Palug's full attention. "I don't mean to sound harsh, but I can't imagine the life expectancy for a demon to be that great. Bigger demons like us are more resilient, but for most who lose an arm and never grow it back, how can they have warm memories of someone they've never met?"

Palug only kept staring at me, not saying a word. I shrugged a few more times.

"It's just kinda cult-y sounding, that's all I'm saying."

"I suppose that's true." He relented, uncomfortable, "But they have stories, and demons all have an expectation to be cordial to our fallen ally friends. This is a mindset set forth by our commander."

The tiger-cat stretched out, ruffling his shoulders.

"It would be just as easy for the Excelsis to trample all over Heaven and destroy everything there, but she doesn't. We're not like the Angels."

Giving a warm smile, I suddenly stopped.

"That's nice and all but, uh…" I pointed to myself, letting out a heavy whine, "Angel-killer extrordinare here says that's optimistic garbage." Palug's ears went flat, back hunched.

"I can't believe she told you that." The cat let out a distraught growl, about to say something more before hesitating, thinking on it for a moment. Slitty eyes tracking around, he focused on the game once more. "You can think of yourself like a police officer, at best. You enforce a boundary, you don't just go in and kill a bunch of angels." The cat's tail whipped around like mad behind us, pissed.

Thinking, I turned a little to him.

"What's the Excelsis look like?" Palug's eye vents suddenly lit up, happy to prattle on about his hobnobbing with demonic royalty at the drop of a hat.

"Tall. Very tall. Long wooden face, big silk ears. Very dignified. She's got a very furrowed, direct stare." He closed two of four vent eyes, looking thoughtfully to the side, "Sorta like moose antlers for horns, and claws for feet." I squinted along with him, not quite getting a mental image, picturing some sort of doll-ish, rabbit monster.

"Human?" I tipped in as Palug responded, almost sad.

"We were all once human." Off-put, someone suddenly called my name from the middle of the huddle before I could ask about the odd statement.

"Neri! Get your fat ass in here and help out!"

"Piss off! I'm too big!" I leaned from the sidelines to bark out my insults. The group laughed, their attention turning to Palug, the unsuspecting cat-demon.

"How about you? We need a good running back here!" Kayalin called out as I laughed at the idea. He was bigger than I was! With a short laugh, I was about to call back and insult her eyesight when the cat spoke up for me; his tone anxious and excited like he had been waiting for his name to be called to be put in the game.

"Hold on!" Palug suddenly got to his feet, turning to me excitedly. "Care to keep watch while I play?"

"What?" I questioned, half laughing, trying to figure this as a joke or not. "Uh…yeah, sure, I can do that."

"Great!" He stood there for a second, looking back to the game as I swear I saw him shimmer for a second, lose a little of his opacity before the cat-demon suddenly dropped his form, something like water falling away instantly. A man, a pretty much normal man except a few back horn-like overhangs like the demonic body he just popped out from, stood there. A human Palug. A Tall, dark-haired, darker-complexion'd remnant of a mixed Hispanic background, human Palug stood there. Needless to say, I was a little shocked. More so when he turned to me and grinned, running onto the field. "Thanks!"

"WH-What the Hell!" I shouted after him, tilting my head at the whole ordeal. That bastard did have a human form! I'd been living here for this long, and that was the first I'd ever seen. Ever. "Why didn't you tell me you could do this?"

"You never asked!" He called and waved again, grinning like
a happy-go-lucky fool. He didn't look over the age of thirty, dressed in
casual, church-going attire. Nice clothes. In my human form, I looked a
little like a modern Romani of sorts, but him, he looked respectable. You
could see the deep red scar down his chest the same as in his demonic
form, squinting against the light, even this low in the day. It must be a
rather weak form, unable to do much; I guess it made sense, with the
months of constant guarding and keeping watch, jumping around to this
form would be reckless. Dangerous.

Both fallen angel-women hooted for him as he ran into the game,
Kayalin giving a sort of fan girlish scream as he joined their team. Even I
was stuck smiling at him, mouth agape, half confused and half tickled pink
that this had been hidden here. Certainly would've helped my case on why
becoming a demon was a good thing. I laughed out loud, shaking my head
around a little as the game resumed. I couldn't stop grinning.

I sat on the sidelines as my shock slowly subdued, as I calmed
down, enjoying the nice night, the fruit of my hard work play and dance
before me. It was humbling, and like I suspected lying about in the attic,
it was a smidgen depressing as well. I wanted to play, I wished to have
fun, but didn't know my way out of this body more than I knew how it all
worked. I guess things just became a very poignant reminder of where I
was, and who I was. Sighing, I tried to put it out of my mind, just enjoying
the game in front of me.

Sitting there, third quarter in, something caught my attention. A
smell, sweet and lovely like dried flowers-nothing I mingled with smelled
sweet and lovely at any time of the day. Rising to my feet I scanned the
area, the smell growing stronger and stronger, trying to find it, walking
plainly onto the playing field just as their last play came to an end.
Someone gave a joking insult at my expense, my focus breaking the punch
line as the fierce, concerned snarl on my face wouldn't go away. The football
game stopped altogether, more people perking up to the same smell I was.

"Neri, what is it?" Palug walked from the middle of game play,
heading straight for me. "What do you smell?" I smirked for half a second,
pinpointing back to whatever it was, stench growing stronger and stronger.

"Flowers?" I scanned some more as Palug's eyes grew huge, head
snapping back to everyone else.

"INSIDE!" He yelled out, running back towards them, "
CHERUB!"

"What!?" I took a step back as the beast burst onto the scene,
heavy built body taking out two of the trees at the back of the property.
It was enormous! Like a giant white owl of sorts, red eyes like tiny little

buttons on its face, surrounded by snow-white plumage that fanned into a crest above its head. The talons were a blood red, along with the beak-like nose on it, edges serrated heavily. The cherub flapped both sets of its enormous wingspan, probably at least three times my own, hovering over us all, looking down as it decided which one to pick off first. It was pandemonium, most spirits immediately headed for the indoors, while a few, like the Black dog spirit and Palug, didn't move an inch.

"Neri! You have to keep it busy!" He shouted out, trying to help the others inside." I can't do anything like this; keep it away from the house!" I dawdled, looking at the giant bird as it picked a victim, landing massively atop Tolstier, the Incubus and one of the first spirits I had met in this household.

"Shit shit shit shit shit!" I took off running, stretching out my wings in the process and taking flight, quick and low into the air. My legs still scrambled beneath me, back flexing and tightening like I was swimming through the world, working hard as I could to get there in time, to save Tolstier, to be a help. It wasn't enough; the bird leaned down quickly and ripped the guy in half, spraying the area around us with demonic bits and chunks. I stumbled as the bird ate him practically whole, leaving a leg behind like an unwanted memento. "No!" Crashing into the ground just in front of the raptor, I feared it, quivered, afraid of the hideous holy beast.

The bird tilted it's head back and swallowed the last bit of the Incubus, feet stamping on the ground happily, excited and giddy as I tripped up, frozen in fear. The Cherub flapped both sets of wings at me once, trying to push me away, display how big and fierce it was, take your pick. I couldn't move.

"Neri! C'mon! Get it!" Palug called behind me, the black dog and me the only three spirits outside with the Cherub, the only targets left. "You're strong enough to, you can do it!" I spit out a sort of nervous, sideways laugh. I could handle a lot, I could fight back against most, but this thing, this ridiculously oversized owl of death, it scared the Hell out of me. The bird screeched at me, almost laughing, setting its sights on the noisy one in the bunch, Palug.

"Dammit!" The man spit out, taking a few steps back before outright bolting away from the house, out into the field. The bird followed, taking back into the air, judging me to be no threat. As it turned its back, as that unforgiving, rotting stare left me, I eased up once more, snapping back to attention, back to reality. Go, idiot!

"Palug!" I leapt from the ground, straining hard to gain lost distance, to catch up. The bird flew in slow, predictable wing beats, moseying along at a rather snail-like pace after the man, playing with its food. Banking sharply above the chase I gained speed, gained momentum and ferocity, urging my body to go as fast as physically possible. It responded, worked hard as it could as I went into a dive, aiming for the shoulder of the giant bird, aimed to clip one of the beast's wings off. I wasn't too late! I hadn't waited too long, I could still save this situation, still be of help! Pumping harder and harder I gained more speed than I ever had, more energy, faster faster faster!

Aimed perfectly at the shoulder, mouth open, things began to blur, began to distort and pull at the very fabric of the world around me. I felt that life-canvas tearing as I began to travel through things, seeing all sides of that bird's wing just for a second as I disappeared from the air around me, suddenly popping up on the other side, exactly below the bird, never once hitting it. With all the momentum of before redirected to where I was now, I smashed into the ground hard, tumbling over myself and sliding to a stop. The bird was completely fine, my attack, my rush had pushed through something, had thrown me past the target altogether. My head pounded, ached painfully like something was trying to escape out the back of my head. Palug ran past me, eyebrows furrowing as he did.

"Neri? He called once, focusing back to running for his afterlife, the bird not far from him now. Groaning as the feathers rushed past me once again, I ran. Running was still safe; running wasn't teleporting dangerously through the air around me like a reckless idiot. In a few strides I caught up, leaping forward to latch onto the bird's ankle, teeth hitting flesh and sinking in deeply. It only pumped its wings harder, pulling me off the ground in continued pursuit of the cat-man-tiger demon. Palug turned behind him as the bird screamed out in frustration, my body swinging around, stripping the ankle of whatever flesh was around it. "Flap, Neri!"

Gurgling, I opened my wings up; getting whatever spread I could to pump opposite the Cherub, both of us working hard to beat out the other. Snorting, I worked harder, pulling my head back like I was trying to pull in a massive fish; a giant white, feathery cherub. It became a sort of stalemate, the only thing keeping us together was my bite, jaws locked tightly onto the cherub, thankfully something tangible, something easy to bite that wasn't a mix of shadows. With all our force going outward and not upwards we dropped to the ground, cherub crashing chest-first into the dirt, taking out another tree as it did so.

There was cheering, something that stopped pretty quickly as the cherub's kicked its foot and me out in front of it, other talon pressed onto my head and pried me from its ankle. I tore skin and flesh as I was kicked off, rolling backwards to hop back to my feet, panting heavily as those fresh wounds started healing, wings tiredly out to the side. Barely aware that Palug got behind me, the bird flipped back to its feet, limping heavily on the one chewed up leg, back on the attack. White wintery wings flared out, lighting up the evening, the Cherub's tiny little mouth opening wide, wider than it should be, stretching out almost to the back of its head, screeching out impossibly loud. Palug covered his ears, the dog yelping out painfully, but I stayed resilient, returning the flashy display, flaring out my own wings and bellowing as loud as I could possibly do. Two monsters, opposites from Heaven and Hell, screamed at one another, bristling; the true dividing line in this world.

Neither of us made a move; the cherub stayed put, and I stayed at the brunt of the attack, wings spread out protectively, keeping this holy entity from the dammed spirits inside, fluffed like a spooked cat.

"Run. Go inside and do whatever you need to do." I spoke quietly from my back teeth, eyes locked cold onto the cherub as it chirped angrily, stamping about a little, getting impatient. Palug ran off, attracting the bird's attention for a second, head darting upwards, watching him go. I growled out viciously again, gaining the focus once more, flaring my wings open and stamping towards the bird, a universal animalistic challenge. "Right here, right here, c'mon, I'm your opponent here." Taunting under my breath, the bird made the first move.

Lunging out with those thrashing claws I jumped back, finding myself suddenly pinned beneath them from the chest down, lightning fast. I scratched and bit as much as I could as the bird accepted it, leaning over fatefully to disembowel me, just as it did to Tolstier. Pressing myself against the ground it got closer and closer, beak hovering just above my neck now, mouth zipping open. No longer did it smell like dried flowers, but stunk of rotten meat, of putrid filth, of halitosis. I gagged, smile zipping across my lips.

"Stupid neck-less bird!" I spit out quickly, using my long and quite handy neck to lunge from the ground like a striking snake, latching on just below the bird's mouth. It screeched in surprise, pulling back out of shock and pulling me from beneath its death grip with only a few julienning slices. Gritting my one eye closed I grabbed hold of the bird, finding nothing but feathers, feathers, and more feathers. With one last jerk I fell from the cherub, a ham-sized chunk of throat ripped out in the process. I spit it off to the side, opening my wings quickly to lunge back, aiming. The bird reeled back, suspecting my move, taking to the air. I followed.

"Bring it close to the house!" Palug shouted from porch, repeating it over and over until I heard and understood. "Trust me!" He reassured as I shrugged, pushing harder and leaping onto the bird mid-flight, latching onto the lower left wing, finding bones amidst a flurry of rushing feathers. The bird screamed out loud, hovering with three good wings, spinning slightly. What came next was no real surprise; these days I was getting harder and harder to surprise- the bird latched onto my back end, from my ribs down, teeth ripping deeply into each side. Sharp as metal it bit down further as I did the same to it's wing, stubbornly tightening my grip until it was practically concrete.

"Let go!" The beast screeched at me, voice distraught and pained, wavering somewhere between masculine and feminine. I snarled in response, biting down harder as the cherub laughed at my expense. "Take that wing and I've got three others, demon! You can't kill me this way!" The two of us meandered closer to the house lazily, my wings flapping tiredly to help push us there.

"I won't be killing you-" I gargled between feathers, shaking my head a little more to dig my teeth in nice and snug. "Angelic reject!" The bird hissed at me angrily, biting down hard to snap my back just above my pelvis, yanking back as it shredded the skin and muscle away from this form; I could feel every bit, every sinew snapping, every burn and tear, every broken bone. But it worked, my body held together enough for the bird to inflict its own damage, force snapping and tearing away the one gigantic feathery wing from its own body; I only acted like an extension of rope. My body shuddered in excruciating pain, large wing dangling from my mouth.

The bird heaved in pain, screeching out a mix of screams and growls, seething painfully. It held onto me tight, opening its mouth a little more to get most of my back end like it intended to eat me. I couldn't think, couldn't reason or breathe correctly, knowing to hold onto that wing with all I had, knowing that I had done my job to get the owl close to the house. The rest was out of my control, it was up to fate.

"You stupid demons!" The bird shook me for good measure as I hung there limply, eyes flickering back to its bloodied face, the face laden with my own blood. It was the only time I thought of Cempe, thought of how she was doing a poor job of 'watching over me', letting me hang in the clutches of death like this. The cherub arched it's back, ripping off both of my wings for good measure; I pulled my neck back, moving its own wing out of the way from doing so. This was my prize. My wings could grow back; I wasn't seeing the same effect from the giant white owl of death. Blood trickled down my neck, cascading away onto the ground far away. I tiredly watched it go. "Bloodthirsty, simple minded fools." It laughed, staying in the same place, hovering in position. I tried to fight back, trying to say more. There was gurgling instead; thankfully, no words needed to be said.

Something ripped open the roof of the house, exploding outward from it; black, dense, impossibly large. Manasa. The giant snake in the basement that couldn't have moved more the a few inches each year, lunging out like an animal possessed, mouth wide, aimed straight for the cherub and I. The angelic being screeched in terror, promptly dropping me, wings reeling backwards, trying to counter, trying to bring those talons up to fight back. No use; Manasa was far too fast, hitting the bird right in the throat, a heavy, crushing sound as it grabbed tight. I fell, sound falling away, barely aware of the giant-animal fight happening just above me, regarding the ground as it rushed closer. There were no wings to slow my fall, nothing to break the energy I was building up, to break the speed I gathered. Cempe... useless thing. Protect me; my ass.

My eyes drifted shut, closed lazily, teeth still locked on the cherub wing as it skewed my fall, twisted me around. I breathed harder, bracing for the ground, flexing my hands a little, the first things that would touch the ground, first things to crumple and fold into a broken mess. I felt grass instead. Eyes snapping open, I found myself sitting politely on the ground, wing still in my teeth, no longer falling. My front legs shook, wobbling. Above me, Manasa and the Cherub broke apart, the snake deeply scratched up, the cherub a striped mix of red and white. Screeching once more it turned away, bolting from the house, flapping unevenly until it was enveloped in darkness.

"Neri!" Palug called, racing out the door as my head tiredly turned back to him, mouth still full of white feathers. With a wary, painful smile, I spit the thing out, my arms buckling to rest on the sides, head dropping towards the earth. Palug grabbed both sides of my jaw before I hit the ground, hoisting my face back up to chest level. "You did a great job! Proud of you!" I stared at nothing, half at his waist and half the grass behind him, body exhausted, unable to focus. Grinning, slightly, I could feel the energy gathering back, feel myself slowly healing.

"Got you a souvenir." Coughing, I shifted my front legs to rest as they should, wondering about my lower half. "Do… Is there…" I tried to raise my head to check out the damage as Palug's grip remained steady, keeping my head facing forwards.

"I'd give that a little while longer." He laughed, smacking the side of my face lightly. I looked up, eyes traveling with a grin to my lips, along his human body until I got to his face, faded remnants of shiny streaks barely visible with the pale light. He'd been crying. Instantly, my smile fell away.

"That's not for me, is it?" I could faintly feel my spine readjusting, healing and adding on by the moment. He only smiled a bit, unable to speak, suddenly pulling me close in a hug. "Aw, c'mon." I smiled, pushing on my own; he really was a friend. After a moment I could feel my knees, after another the bones to my feet came back to life as well, healing considerably quicker. I didn't want to pull away from him, happy just resting here. Content.

"I'm already feeling better." I grinned, sighing. Human Palug had a scent to him, more familiar then anything I'd ever remembered about our friendship. I could hear him laugh.

"But if I wasn't like this, I mean, I could've helped, I could've fought it off." He patted the top of my head as the bits of muscles reformed themselves, a painful step in the process. "You wouldn't have had to do that by yourself, it was asking a lot." I grit my teeth as the pain subdued.

"Nah, I wouldn't worry about it. I've been disemboweled like 4 times now." Flopping one of my numb, meaty wrists around, I gave a dismissive notion.

"That's a really awful statistic." He pat my head a few times. "Like, literally the worst thing I've heard."

"Sure is." I could feel bits of my tail now, the tips of my toes, all other wounds practically gone except for the parts I still missed. Reflecting, my tone grew low. "This wasn't part of the plan, was it?" My voice was soft as the cat smacked the back of my neck once with more gusto.

"No, no this was not." He cut an actual laugh, not one to cover insecurity, to cover worry or doubt. It was very real. "You might have a harder time convincing you're a regular demon this time. No one survives the Cherubs, and no one heals to tell about it." Palug said as I rose to my feet, head released to look behind me; the very last bits of my skin came back, tail unfurling until I was almost whole, adding and finishing up my body, good as new. With a large coughing yawn I shook myself out, flaring out my wings just as the black smoke rose to form them, looking over to Palug once before back to the cherubs wing.

"Didn't know Manasa had it in her." My mind suddenly reminded me of my peculiar landing, of heading straight for the ground and suddenly just being on it, no more damage done. What a day; my head still hung low, exhausted. Full of pep and energy from healing, but completely emptied on the will to do anything but sit here tiredly. This was not the end I was told, scaring off a cherub was not the same as killing it. "It'll be back, won't it?" I could feel Palug stare at my face before turning to the same direction I was, crossing his arms.

"We don't use her unless we really need it, she's our ace in the hole; and Manasa tends to make lots of holes." He wiped at his face before scratching the back of his head full of short black hair. "But yeah. This one'll probably bring reinforcements."

I looked to the roof, to the snake that lay tiredly on the remaining parts still intact, scales like black onyx, subtle hints of color, like polished metal. She was wounded badly, drips of demonic blood slowly oozing down to our level, black and viscous. My newly reformed glare scanned back to the night, back to the skies, back to the wrath we were destined to incur.

26

"I feel like singing a song, anyone else feel like singing a song?"
I rallied, verging exhaustion, trudging on. We'd found a new house.
Abandoned, hopeless little thing some mile and a half over, large, spacious
basement, abandoned due to water problems, a flood of some sort, multiple
levels, set aside in a far, strange end of an even more desolate block. No
doubt it smelled, festered with asbestos and mold, which, thankfully, were
not big health concerns on our list. No, our main health concern was the
army of death approaching our stronghold, of the Cherub's recurring
wrath.

We'd been staying in a temporary house for a month while we
searched out the perfect one. This meant everyone, demons and angels
alike, stayed inside all hours of the day, no matter the disagreements and
frustrations that arose. Worse than that, the standby house was cozy at
best. Cozy for a four person household maybe, so with 12 resident spirits
including a massive coiling snake, we were pretty much butt-to butt.
Everyone, even Manasa, was excited about this big move, the angels too.

The day after the big Cherub-Neri fight, we talked. That big, happy,
culminating moment of super-honesty of talking about what they knew,
about what they experienced, was talked about. More correctly, Azol told
us everything about the four living there, while the others just sat and
nodded a lot. A bit of a cop-out, but we had learned all about where they
came from and a bit about the system they worked on.

Angels all started from different points in their lives, not unlike
the death cycle itself. It was a job they willingly took, willingly signed up
for, not unlike the mortal Army. For their different reasons, they decided
to be an angel. Heaven apparently doesn't just sign you up, give you a pair
of wings and send you on your way, they go through a whole rigorous bout
of training, something that can last as long as they deem you unskilled

and under qualified. There's incredibly high standards, until you pass those standards, you don't get to leave training. Some give up and shame themselves as just being occupants of Heaven, while others graduate when they're ready, if they're sixteen or sixty. All angels graduate the same level; start a sort of training –internship with an already established angel that they're looking to become, probably where I fit in as the demon exorcist Natalie. Aka, guardian angels mentor wannabe guardian angels; exorcists mentor other exorcists, so on and so forth.

After this long bout of secondary training, something that can last another twenty years or so, they take ANOTHER test to pass to become" established" . If they trained as exorcists, they're assigned a newly ordained Priest looking to do the same thing. That partnership lasts as long as the human's life does, then repeats until the angel itself, dies. Azol explained their lifespan as a sort of flexible thing; they're able to control how fast or slow they age, but they always do age. When that timer is up, when they're far too old to really function as any part of anything, Heaven or human, they get sent off to go spend more time on earth, to be born again. Then, when they die from that lifetime, they can start the process all over again; but if they're a high enough rank, higher than any of the fallen angels with us now, they have the option of just picking up where they left off. Some of them see this as a favoritism, it's apparently a rather touchy subject with any angel, if they're good enough to keep the knowledge of the training that they worked so hard to gain. Others see the rebirth thing as a fresh slate, as an opportunity to experience the good and bad all over again in a sort of sublime way. The ability to be reborn was something prized, something guarded. Only those in Heaven were able to get that chance. But for a fallen angel, there is no chance of re-birth, just a finalized death, the real punch line of the sentence- though if the angel decides to age incredibly slowly, they can stretch out their torment almost as long as they'd like.

As they got to how an angel falls and what happens when they do, the entire group got a little weepy. Conviction was as different and touchy as the person condemning it wanted it to be. Some had their wings ripped off for talking non-threateningly to a demon, even if the conversation itself was pointless, stupid. It implied that the angel was sympathizing with the demon. Azol was kicked out for starting up a rebellion against his own kind, sympathizing with a group of demons residing in one house who made him question his actions, and eventually lead him to rebel against his superiors, feeling like he was lied to. Saya was kicked out for supporting Azol in his rebellion; Ibe helped out a friend who had recently fallen, gave them advice and guided them to find others of their kind. Marc was kicked for asking too many questions, raising awareness and confusion amongst his peers that his superiors couldn't answer.

If they were convicted of 'fraternizing with the enemy' as it was so popularly called, they were sentenced to one of three things; they could fall, they could be booted back to cadet/whatever low position that applied, or they could be given a 'do-over', aka go get reborn no matter your age and try this whole brainwashing thing all over again. As I suspected, they were told practically nothing about our existence, except that we were the ultimate evil. Death and destruction incarnate. In their opinion, Heaven was trying to keep the message under wraps that each and every demon was different, that some demons, yes, were evil, but it hardly represented the entire mass of us. It upheld what they were taught as humans, oddly, through religion, and what was accepted as normal; they wanted the exorcisms to be fast, quick, no questions, wanted the slayings to be second nature, to not consider a demon differently than one does a tough stain.

"That's why we try and convert them to our side" Palug spoke stubbornly, mentally affected by the things we had heard that day, sickened and frustrated by what we learned. "To pull them out of that continuous circle of hatred." I had to say, it didn't come so much to me as a shock, and a few times in the conversation, I had to feign more disgust then I had, just to not seem out of place, to fit in. Oddly enough, it made sense to me, both sides of it; maybe it was coming from that I myself had thought the same, that I had learned of both sides of that coin, and could understand the falter of understanding.

"It makes sense, though." I pulled him away from the group, speaking softly. "From living with Raziel for so long, honestly, it makes sense. I don't know if there's much at fault here." Palug looked a little outraged, a little taken back that I wasn't weeping and crying and cursing the Heavens for their damnation any longer. Maybe I had grown up.

"What was that?" Azol called from the group as I spoke a little too audibly. Head snapping to Palug, he shook his head no just a bit, that no, that was not the part of my past to be telling the fallen angels and demons in this house. I bit my lip, wanting to spew, wanting to honest. Stumbling, I made up a sort of half-truth.

"From what I had observed some time ago, I can support that there is a grave misunderstanding between angels and demons, one that is not the fault of either side." Saya and Ibe whispered frantically behind Azol, the 'leader' turning around and quieting them down.

"That's rather perceptive." I chuckled hollowly, trying to glaze this whole blip in understanding over with humor.

"I'm freakin' ghost, I've got nothing better to do then analyze the world around me." From there, the talks continued until sides split apart, knowing more about the other then when we first walked in. Palug and I were pretty happy, fulfilled and satisfied with breaking down that barrier, learning much about our collective enemies. They didn't know better. That was the gist of what I learned there, that no one really knew all sides of this ordeal, no matter how much you think you might. Each decision was reflected by what you had been told to do in some respect, the angels attacked us because they were told to and the demons attacked the angels because they were supposed to. Resolution was just a word.

Things had changed massively in this past month, the people once open and willing to listen to anything I said, where I thought they'd be grateful I defended them all from the giant cherub, wouldn't talk to me. They had grown afraid of me, the sight of a healing demon was apparently a bad omen. Palug remained exactly as he had been, right by my side, keeping me company. Nowadays, he was one of the few I actually talked to on a daily basis, while everyone, demons and angels alike, left me alone. I tried to break the tension, tried to start more football games, tried to bring them all together. Nothing worked. I was regarded with respect, but the same type of respect one gives a vicious pit-bull in their backyard; I was a watchdog, nothing more, certainly not a family pet.

"Do they hate me?" I spoke out of the blue, sitting in the drafty, terrible cold on the roof in the middle of the night, watching the snow cascade peacefully. The sky was a muddy reddish color, our halfway house closer to a larger town in the area, light pollution disturbing the natural light given at this hour of night. Palug rested his head on his paws, fully demonic again, lower half of his body still in the attic.

"They don't hate you. They respect you."

"They'd respect me more if they'd actually talk to me. I feel like I'm getting isolated, shoved away." The cat-readjusted his head, tilting it farther off to the side, exhausted. Both of us had taken up being the outlets for most of the spirits in the house, giving Manasa the time to heal up on her own. I could support 4 of the spirits, while Palug handled 3, and the black dog took care of the twins. I had no excess energy really for myself, sleeping and napping a majority of each day.

"Honestly?" Palug started, tone half-settled that he didn't care what I learned. I nodded, stretching out my back legs.

"That'd be a nice change of pace, sure." I burbled a scoff, shifting my head to watch him as he spoke.

"They're nervous. You kind of pissed off a Cherub, which knows your scent, and it's going to try and track you down, especially after what you did."

"Oh, well, goodie. I made another friend." We both laughed as he continued on.

"You can handle those things, but the rest of us, well; we're not as strong as you. Not that we don't have the utmost faith that you can take down a full sized cherub on your own, with or without Manasa's help, but it's suspenseful waiting for it to happen, the calm before the storm."

"If I leave…will that keep you all out of danger?" I could see the trend in this. Palug shook his head.

"It'll still go after you, then go after us. It's got Manasa's scent, remember? Cherubs are a little ruthless like that." I nodded, laying my head back on the roof, tiredly mulling it over. They said that moving to a new house, to changing locations would give them some more time, but it started to seem like they really needed their leader to come back from her little excursion, from wherever she'd disappeared off to. My eyes slid closed, falling asleep in the new sun of a rising day.

So we walked today, walked along this open road in the middle of the night, massive snake slithering tiredly between all of us as I supported only three spirits this round, a few of the angels and demons able to connect back with Manasa. We trudged on like wary little soldiers, not even a quarter mile from the halfway house, already exhausted. I tried my best to raise their hopes, tried to break the tension that my presence there was a ticking time bomb of fun and excitement. They had all, in their own ways, told me they were grateful I had fended off the Cherub, had let me know that I was still appreciated, no matter how isolating it felt. Palug lead the pack, plodding slowly down the street, both kids riding on his back like a giant, misshapen merry-go-round horse. Kayalin followed behind me, angels on the opposite side of the giant snake. It was a worried, anxious little march, but I did my best to keep strong, to keep positive. This, unlike my tether with the angel, did not reflect on my spiritual passengers. Looking around that my song invite had been turned down, that the group was more focused on trudging on, I quieted back down, exhausted.

Something hit my heart. Struck me dead on, punched me hard in the chest. I stopped instantly, limbs frozen in pain as it grabbed at my heart tightly, squeezing it. Struggling, my feet shuffled beneath me as I lurched forward, gurgling.

"C'mon, keep up the pace there Neri." Kayalin meandered around me as I gagged for air, body wracked with pain and making tiny, straining sounds. She grazed over my face as I remained still, eyes wide open, unable to do a thing but stand and shudder in pain. Double-taking, she stopped too. "Hey, uh, you alright?" Kayalin signaled up to Palug, who stopped the procession cold. My teeth zipped back in a snarl, gritting and trying hard to get around the blinding pain. What was it? No one was doing this; there was no one around me, no hint of Cherub, no scent of dried flowers. We were completely fine, but my heart, it felt like a human hand was grabbing it, ice cold, squeezing it tightly inside my own chest. Closing my eyes I gurgled some more, drooling, neck bunching up, arms knotting over themselves.

"Neri!" Something smacked my head as the pain suddenly stopped, slowly ebbing away, receding like it never happened. Gasping for air I stumbled forward, head darting around, bewildered. Kayalin and Palug were both right beside me, the rest of the group looking back with concern. The woman in white snapped in my face, trying to focus my darting, panicked glance as I rested back to her face. "What the Hell was that?"

"I don't know…" I closed one eye, hand to my chest, "Is it possible for me to have a heart attack?" Palug shook his head no, head darting back to the group and back to me, worried. Just as the pain had finally ebbed away, something new took hold, absolute panic. Like I was suddenly thrown into the middle of a war-zone without the action, without a reasonable cause, without any notion whatsoever, something called out to me. Told me to run. Told me to escape, to fly, to get away, to go somewhere I had never been. It took every bit of my resolve to stay put, but I started nervously jumping from foot to foot, head snapping around, wary for the cause of my attack. I bucked nervously like a skittish horse, Kayalin and Palug both taking a step away.

"The Hell's wrong with you now?" She said in a bit of a panic herself, one of the spirits tied to me. Jittering, I settled on all four feet again, juking from side to side, almost bouncing.

"You don't feel that?" I said quickly, freaking out, "Something's screwing around with me." I was starting to panic the others in the group, the cherub fighter was tweaking out, was losing it. Palug stared me dead in the face, eyes furrowing as he turned to Kayalin quickly.

"Tether to Manasa, now." He said directly, wandering to the other spirits that were linked with me as well. I could barely control myself; barely keep reigns on this surge in power, this absolute panic that screamed at me to leave, screamed for me to run away. Why haven't you left yet? RUN! Go! Leave, now! I closed my eyes and shook my head, trying to fight back. Couldn't leave these spirits here, couldn't just run away like this. My body was showing me a direction, pointing out a way, but my mind was the only thing still keeping me here, tiredly trying to fight off the attack. One by one, they all detached from me, just giving more energy to this delusional fear and panic. He knew something was up, knew more than I did about what was going on.

Just as instantly, it stopped, my insane rocking back and forth stopped cold, stamping once to a halt. Looking around desperately for an answer it hit me again, the pain, worse than before. I tilted forward, slamming into the ground, front forearms twitching and grabbing at nothing beneath my chest. This time the pain spread away from my heart, radiated though my veins. This definitely scared everyone else, I could hear it as my neck bunched up, grunting and gritting my teeth in extreme pain. Palug ushered the others on, moved them forward, giving me space. Whining, writhing on the ground my body pushed forward, something I didn't control; it was heading somewhere on its own. I was being lured. Controlled.

Fingers twitching manically, my back legs still remained upright, stance spread wide, gripping onto the ground like I was going to fall from it. Slowly, so slowly, the pain began to let off, began to subside as I panted hard, snorting dirt away from my face as my eyes slowly opened back up. Scrambling, I got back to my feet as Palug stood just in front of me, no hint of a smile on him.

"You know which way to go, don't you?" He asked as I swayed to my feet, that extreme sense of fear starting to take hold once again, a vicious, tiring cycle of pain and panic. Barely holding on, I nodded my head quickly before darting around, looking at the area around me. Nearly behind me and slightly off to the left, there might as well have been a neon red sign, painted in the stars, showing me the way to go. The cat demon nodded at me, taking a step away. "Then go. We'll be okay."

Before Palug even got to the second letter of Okay, before that Y had left his mouth, I was already gone. In a rush of feathers, I practically erupted from the scene, taking flight into the sky, blindly being led away from my duties, away from my makeshift family of demons and angels. Fast as I could manage, I kept a lid on the speed at a certain pace, pulled back from going all out, lest I start darting around faster than I could feel, start teleporting past the space around me, instead of flying through it. This did not make the other, more agitated parts of my mind happy. Go faster! Do it! Quicker! Get there in time! In which I had to plead out, had to try and reason. No, I didn't like when that happened, couldn't control where I was popping up, couldn't manage it. My insides warred like bickering children, half of me, so aggressive, so agitated, the part that was trying to take control of my body, while the other half listened, but tried doing things its own way, tried to be reasonable.

Go! Life depends on it!

Shaking my head and roaring out angrily, I pushed myself faster, pushed past that brink of safe flying and skipping through space. I began to blur once again, life began to shred at its seams, began to tear some more, my head pounding intensely as I skipped like a stone through the sky, impossibly fast. My internal compass, the one tied to the angel Raziel, spun, out of control. It couldn't tell me where I was headed, where he was, what anything around me could possibly be. Whatever this drive was, whatever this unbelievable pull was, it wasn't coming from him.

The line pulled farther apart, skipping over greater distances. I didn't know how far I traveled with each jump; I didn't even know where I was going. Pain, quick and aching began to claw at my heart once more, though not enough to slow me down, not enough to be anything but a bother. It knew I was coming, whatever it was, knew I wasn't far now. Flapping hard once more, I broke through space altogether, shooting myself the final great distance away from my last appearance. Popping back into reality my internal compass pointed straight down, aimed straight for this large, lit up, high school auditorium. Exhausted and stunned it lured me in, pulled me closer and closer, quicker, faster. I darted straight for it; full-on charged the building, racing to cross that finish line. I was almost there! Barely, I noticed the parking lot dotted with cars in the middle of the night, room lit up like class was in session. It made no difference, with one last wing beat, I rocketed through the paned window glass, ripping out metal bars and concrete supports as I did so, as I dropped in through the ceiling, as I crashed heavy on the ground, possessed.

There was a light. A person, sitting in the middle of the gym, radiated this light; it had been calling to me. Slowly, cautiously, I took a few steps closer, being pulled to her though great demand, blocking out all others but this person, this woman. She sat in the middle, legs pulled to her chest, hands clutching over her head, pulling at her hair. Like a whip, the urge to get here vanished, the pull and demand to rush just in time fell away. Blinking, I could hear the world around me once again, finding the entire gym littered with angels. There had to be at least fifteen of them there, the cars in the parking lot; this was a big demon to exorcise, a difficult, impossible demon; it's the only one that would've demanded such attention. But she just sat there, contained to herself, wedged in a ball. How could that be dangerous?

One angel braced herself, gripping her weapon tightly, charging full on at the glowing demon; quick on the draw the woman opened up, swiping a hand generally at her direction. A thin ring of black smoke, like a rope, sliced this angel clean in half; as her back was turned, another angel charged at her, the woman continued her fluid motion and used this demonic rope, this black string to cut him into thirds. As those angels fell dead and scattered away, she sat there, glow dimming for a moment enough to see her face. My heart stopped beating.

It was me. My face. She… the woman, it was me, sitting there.

"You!" Someone called from across the gym, someone familiar. Squinting, I saw Gauzier and Raziel both standing there, completely dumbfounded about what was going on. "You're supposed to be dead!" The squabbling turned away from me, Gauzier practically screaming at Raziel, ignoring the more obvious problem in front of them. I took some steps closer, a few angels in front of me yelling things, threatening me; I didn't really care what. I could only see myself sitting there, this demand, this pull to get closer, to see it with my own eyes. It was me. My soul; a part of me I was missing.

I pushed through them, the angels in front of me, not caring what wounds I took, what damage was inflicted. Like in a haze, in a strict drive to re-join with my other part, I ambled towards her, smiling, ever so softly. She continued to fight, sitting there, always keeping an eye on my progress, until I standing just outside of her twirling circle, just away from the ribbon weapon that skirted about protectively.

I hesitated, just for a moment; this is what I wanted, right? What was going to happen If I did this? Would I be that angel-killer as Cempe had said; that ruthless, demonic presence? I mean, Raziel had said it, if I was split up, there must've been a reason for it, and it usually wasn't good.

"You can do this!" Raziel shouted from the edge, "Go!" Gauzier's voice escalated just after him, barely noticing the two of them fighting amongst one another. The other me put their arms to each side, head turning slowly towards me as I took a step forward, through the whip-like circle of death. My first step was demonic, while my second step was human, edge of the whip-circle stripping away my brutish other form, leaving my old self, my own, mostly human self, to stand in that circle with my other half. I looked at my human hands, as a dull roar came from behind me, seeing the dinosaur demon turn into a blackish mist, the Colus; hesitating for a second before joining in and mixing about with the other half of the black thread that circled the two of us.

Sound stopped, life vanished outside this circle, the light intensifying drastically; she looked so depressed, so unhappy, so worn and frail. My skin felt like it was electric, vibrating with energy as I took another step closer, body suddenly working on its own, as this conscious bit of myself practically stood by and watched. I watched myself stand just over the other me, tears in her eyes, suddenly shifting to her knees on the same level. As the two spirits knelt there, the light began to intensify, the energy buzzed louder and louder; leaning over, I took my old self and pulled them into a hug, joining us. She spoke out, the last words said as a duality of the same confused, disrupted soul.

"Finally."

The other me grabbed back, hugging close as well. The two facets of our same soul began to blur, as the room bent and churned, unable to see anything outside our protective bubble, unable to feel anything but lines blurring, of our souls syncing back together, of it all sliding back into familiarity. My head began to pound once again, something ripping open the back of my head, alarming me; the room began to spin, faster and faster, dipping and twisting, ripping apart. My soul latched on, etched it, while another part of me began to slide away, grasping at nothing as the rest of me spun. That energy was being used up, that panicking rushing drive being put to work as I began to pull away from it all, as it felt like half of my Praesens soul attached with the woman sitting there, and half was being thrown away. Tighter they spun, closer together as I gripped the very outsides. Something went wrong; a very much self-aware part of me was getting tossed away, thrown out. I felt less of what was happening to my body, grew more aware of the room, spinning, spinning, until suddenly, it was one.

My conscious bit of soul shot out like a cannon from the circle, crashing into the plastic bleachers, leaving a Neri-sized dent as I slumped to the ground, completely stunned. What the Hell happened?! Uninjured, unhurt, I shot a glance back to the middle of the gym, back to where my other slice had sat, still glowing impossibly bright. Just in front of me was Raziel, both him and Gauzier stopping their fight at the sound, turning back to watch the fireworks. Neither of them seemed to notice I was sitting just behind them.

"This is your fault, you demon-loving hack!" Gauzier suddenly pushed Raziel away, trying to slice him open like a fresh fish, but he managed to get just out of reach. "You let them join back together! Do you even know what you've done?" Raziel countered his stab, smacking the sword off to the side with the new and improved pike.

"She can be reasoned with, just give it a chance!" I strained, getting to my feet, feeling a little neglected besides being all around confused and disorientated. "It looks bad, but she's not trying to hurt anyone!"

The words took me back, stopping me for a moment.

"You can answer to me right here." I spit low at Gauzier as he and Raziel continued fighting, ignoring me. They braced close together before Raziel threw him off, the older angel stumbling backwards, stumbling right through and past my own body like it was nothing. In the exact same way the physical things did to a regular spirit, normal spirits were passing through me. I jumped back, eyes wide. What in the...

Suddenly, in a great finale, the light burst away, falling, calming down to a normal range. The angels in the gym looked to the female figure in the middle, MY female figure in the middle as she sat there, reclined back, eyes closed, head down. Even sitting, you could tell she...I...we... were already a lot taller. Bigger. The goggles on our head, those immovable, stubborn things, had broken, glass shattered by the three foot long black spike-like horns popping out from them. No wonder I was having headaches.

From her back, instead of wispy hints of black bars of some sort, those gaseous things that disappeared with the slightest touch through them grew black spines, six of them, rising and falling as she breathed. Her ears were slightly elongated enough to where it was noticeable, and her big toe held a sort of darkish nail, verging on the sort of slicing, killing claw that raptors have. I stood in complete awe of myself, as most of the others in the room did too.

"You've screwed us all." Gauzier gasped at Raziel, pushing him back as the exorcist was shocked, dumbfounded. As the two of them stared at the newly completed me, I passed another hand through Gauzier's arm, the angel jumping just a little bit. He brushed away where I had passed through him, looking quickly over his shoulder at me, then back to the demon in the middle. Like humans to ghosts, I could still be felt, I still existed. Maybe not in the same plane of existence as everyone else, but I was still alive; what a relief! That only left one big, unresolved spiky-headed demon of a question.

"Well well well!" The demon, myself in my voice, spoke up in plain English. Her eyes snapped open, electric green, pupils dilated and tiny. They darted about the room, seeing who was still around, what her situation was, just what was really going on; as she passed by where I stood her eyes lingered longer, smiling quickly, heinously. Any blood I assumed to have, went cold. This was not me. Not all of me, at least. I didn't quite know what she'd do, without my sane reasonable part behind the helm of that body… Oh no.

"I'm so glad you all came out for my big get-together!" She chuckled, gathering her feet she slowly stood up, arm shooting out to the side where her rotating mess of black strings solidified, turned into the paddle weapon, exactly how it always was in my hands. Egh, the bad puns; it really was a horrible beast.

She was at least seven feet tall, the weapon in her hands, while on the big side, looked a lot more reasonable. The new Neri checked the grip of the handle, swinging it around like she'd been training with the thing her entire life. Scanning the angels, her dead-eyed flat glare sized them all up, turning her back to crack it, readying herself for battle. No no no, this was all wrong! These motley bits of me, this was the angel killer, this is what people feared.

I darted into the circle immediately before anything happened, raced up alongside myself, towering more than two feet above me, pleading, begging. She could see me, I know she could.

"Hey! Stop!" Slowing just in front of her she watched me, no longer smiling, just simply annoyed. "You …don't…gah, what are you doing?" She tilted her head at me just a bit, longer hair sliding alongside my shoulder and smirking.

"Emotion comes later. Business comes now. Get out of the way of progress." She placed one giant foot up by my face, pushing me back in a gentle kick towards Raziel, continuing to shuffle about in a circle, ready to attack. "Who wants to dance first?"

"Oh God, Neri." He whispered under his breath, just behind me. I frowned. My thoughts exactly.

27

We didn't wait long. The first angel slowly inched up to the circle with cautious, determined moves; Neri's eyes snapped to him. She bared her teeth like some feral animal, even from where I stood; you could see they were more primal, pointier, lurching forwards and sizing her opponent up as the demon slowly lurched side to side.

Shaking my head, I tried to make sense of it all, tried to rationalize it out; I stumbled, a major flaw in my reasoning— I couldn't. I couldn't… actually wrap my head around the idea. It felt like half my brain was missing, that I was incomplete, that 'reasoning things out' was not my primary directive. It dawned on me how afraid I was, how paranoid and scared, how empathetic I felt for everyone else besides me. I still remembered everything I had done, who I was and where I had come from, I could still see and related the things around me. But beyond worrying about everyone else and emotionally fretting away, I couldn't think of anything else. It was like hitting a wall. Everything was overwhelming and miserable.

"The….the… God dammit…the…" I struggled, trying to remember the three different souls, the names of them, something not tied emotionally. I knew them, I could practically hear the names, but my mind wouldn't bring them up. Frustrated, I pounded my hand against the floor. The other. I was one of the other now. That was the best I could do.

Neri stopped, charging forwards with the paddle weapon towards the angel, slamming into his shoulder and pushing the man back a couple yards in force alone. His face quickly switched to full terror, scrambling to regain his footing as she swung the weapon down on his head, spikes from the middle of it crushing him into nothing as the physical lights shook in the building. I felt like I would throw up. Every single angel instantly knew they were very much in the wrong place, the atmosphere flopping from a mobbish mentality to roughly seven foot tall train wreck on the hunt. Panic.

Pulling away she sized up the next one, the first angel's dust cascading from her weapon like steam. Ruthless. Absolutely ruthless, I was paralyzed with fear. The worst of the worst. The truly evil. I felt for each and every angel she/I killed that day as I watched that nightmare scramble around in my body; a predator, a wolf among sheep. This was who I actually was, it felt like that icy hand was still squeezing my heart, pained.

"Should we reason with her now? While she's taking the time to scrape Talec from her weapon?!" Gauzier yelled behind me, sword clanking heavily on part of Raziel's armor. "Do you have any idea what you've done? Anything at all?" Raziel drove the wooden end of the pike into Gauzier's face, knocking him on his ass as he instantly looked back to the demon. The lights shook once more as Raziel winced, aghast.

"She can be reasoned with… she's just... Just...Neri!" He called out to her as she sliced another angel in half, busy and enthralled in killed the entire group of them off. Her head snapped around, focusing on him in an impolite, unreasonable manner as even Raziel took a step back, afraid.

"What? NO. DON'T do that!" I screeched, leaping from my spot, my hands trying to cover his mouth, trying to get him to shut up before he got himself killed.

"Neri...please...don't...don't do this!" He seemed to wilt where he stood as Neri only focused on him like a weak animal, smiling from across the gym. I desperately tried to put my hand over his mouth over and over to get him to shut up.

"It was nothing! Pay him no mind!" I shouted out to her, hand half-passing through Raziel's head as my existence was faulty, at best. I looked back to him as his eyes furrowed at his own mouth, putting a hand up to it, confused. He called again.

"Neri!" I looked back to him and her before trying to smack him on the forehead, hand going through his head as my emotional body switched to anger.

"Shut up!" I smacked him again; this time he definitely felt it, there was definite connection. Raziel jumped back as the larger Neri laughed, fighting against the next angel, simply using her strength to clock him in the side of the head with the weapon. Her attention focused to everyone else again, thank God.

Raziel looked around frantically, squinting, searching out for me in this strange, parallel dimension I was sitting in.

"Neri…s?" He almost laughed as he said it, distracted, side turned to Gauzier as the bastard got to his feet. The swords went high over his head, slashing down on an unsuspecting Raziel, cutting off his left hand, cleaving it just below the elbow. The weapon went flying as his dismembered hand evaporated to dust, clattering to the ground; I shrieked in surprise. He staggered back, clutching at his bloody stump of an arm, no longer worrying about whether or not there were multiple Neri's about, just concerned with Gauzier, the dishonest, insane little angel who laughed so heartily at taking down one of his own. Raziel fell back as the blood continued to pour out, evaporating away to dust before it hit the ground like a broken hourglass. Gauzier brought the one sword up to his throat, gloating.

"You've done nothing but protect...this... this MONSTER." He gasped, furious; one hand pointed back to the demon as she was starting to run low on angels to destroy. "And look. Just look! Look what you've done! Is this what you wanted!?" Gauzier seemed genuine for a moment, sweating, exhausted and just overall scared.

"Th...There's something wrong..." Raziel wheezed, trying to stop the blood from his stump best he could with his other hand. The angel started saying something else as Gauzier interrupted.

"What's WRONG is that you harbored a powerful demon, lied to everyone and you're surprised this is how it ended?" He took the sword away for a moment, aggravated and furious for a moment as he collected himself, sword right back to Raziel as the angel grit his teeth, seething.

"What's wrong is that the most fitting end to your career is letting this monstrosity rip you limb from limb, like you deserve!" He pushed a little on the sword as Raziel pulled back, "Instead of the merciful end I'm give you now. Raz." Gauzier spit the word out, driving up my anger.

"They can't overlook this treachery any more, there's no more promotions for the Hell you've caused." He paused, smirking at Raziel as he pushed himself a little farther away, one eye closed in pain. "You should start begging and pleading now, warm up for it when you get back upstairs, because I promise you, these are the last free moments of your life." My anger rose quickly, much faster than it ever had before, bubbling to the top. Without thinking about it, without hesitation, I reached down and grabbed the pike like it was made for me.

"Finally…" Gauzier raised the sword triumphantly, aiming it straight for Raziel's throat again, teasing the blade just out of reach, "We can start to fix your mistakes."

Whipping the weapon around, I smashed the new pike into the back of his head. Gauzier hit the ground like a stone slab, knocked out cold as his swords spun across the floor. I struggled with the weapon as the end flipped out of my hands, tumbling and hitting against the side of the bleachers a hefty distance away. Raziel watched Gauzier hit the ground, looked back to the weapon, then back to him. The angel was surrounded in his own blood and dust; I heard Neri call out in a challenge, taking down another person off to the side, eyes wild before she bounced back into the fight. What was this, really? It couldn't be real.

I rushed to his side. Angels didn't heal like I did; they bled to death;

that's what he said so long ago; something easy to bring up, something that emotionally scared me back then. Raziel's breath was short, in an immense amount of pain, but he still smiled, just for a second.

"I could see you, just a little bit, right when you hit him." He spoke out in front of him, incoherent from the lost of blood. I grabbed his arm, trying to hold the blood in as it passed right through my hands. I needed something to stop the bleeding; something to clot it, or wrap it up until something could be figured out. There was no taking him to the hospital, nothing to do besides whatever angelic first aid I knew, which was a blank as the rest of my mind.

"I'm so sorry." I muttered, trying to think of something else, trying to figure out some way to help him, while my whole being was focused on the utter horror happening in the rest of the gym. I had to help. Focus on helping.

My eyes rested on my own wraps, the ones that covered my feet, bandage like things that I had no real excuse to wear them; quickly I unwrapped the left foot, last layer peeling away to a gruesome sight. My ankles, where my first tether had taken hold in the first house, the chains that were linked behind my Achilles tendon, were ripped out. The tendon was still there, but my ankles had this massive, gaping hole that nearly went through to the front. Unwrapping the entire thing, my hamstrings were burned, ripped up and scarred, with more scar tissue then regular skin there anymore. Signing in annoyance for a second, I ignored it, taking the bandaged wrap and starting to dress Raziel's wound. His stump. It was a desperate, half-thought out move, but it worked. The blood stopped. Mine started. It leaked out my ankle-holes, spread all over the ground in no time flat. It didn't hurt.

"You... got it to stop." Raziel said, spacey, holding up his stump arm and shaking it about a little. Growing more tired, wearier, I flopped against the bleachers as well, sitting next to him and watching the tragedy.

The gym was a war-zone; bits of armor and weapons strewn all over it, arcs of dust-blood splattered in decorative streaks up and down the walls. She still worked on, swinging that paddle weapon around, chasing the angels who didn't want to face her, mowing them down, just a couple left. I couldn't watch; I covered my eyes, looking to the ground, sobbing out of distraught for them. This was me. This is what I was. Ruthless, terrifying. The worst. Everything I feared. I could only sit and watch, wait until she finally came over to us... then what? Would she take me down along with Raziel? I was unnecessary. The extra. I covered my head, crying out between my knees, a wreck.

"I knew there was something else here." Gauzier groaned back to life, hands still gripping the back of his head in pain; the pike! I tried to get to my feet, ankle rolling and crunching beneath me, sending me back to hit the bleachers again with an audible sound in their realm. This time, they both heard it. Gauzier suddenly focused on me like he could stare straight into my eyes. "Got you!"

The sword suddenly glowed red with a quick command, sweltering and smoking at the blade.

The angel drove the sword into the bleacher just a breath away, missing; the fire leaned right where I sat, right where I was unable to leave from, pinpointing me down. With the second blade ready, Gauzier steadied it just from my face. Something snapped.

"Neri!" I called out to myself, loud enough for anyone in my realm, or everyone else's realm to hear it. Gauzier stopped, eyes darting to Raziel, before back to where I was sitting, grinning again quickly. Something whistled, distant at first.

"Oh, you're just hel-" The paddle weapon erupted through him, throwing both him and the weapon into the bleachers inches from where Raziel sat, and straight through me. The entire structure whined, shaking from its wheels to slam into the back wall before setting on the floor once more. Raziel's eyes went huge- still groggy and sick, but very much awake at that moment, looking over where I was at before back to Gauzier's body a few feet behind him now, slumping down from leaning against the bleachers.

The angel's top and bottom half separated, rolling onto the ground, obliterated as I looked down, seeing the weapon's end through me, as well. Waiting for some sort of instantaneous death, I moved a little side to side, eventually shimmying from the one side without a scratch. Both Raziel and I stared at the weapon, following its trajectory back to the Super-Neri, who stood there with her arm outstretched exactly where she had thrown the paddle weapon like a giant underhanded dart. The demon snarled.

"Any objections to that?" She asked generally in my direction, scanning the room for any more angels; he'd been the last one, the last before Raziel at least.

We both shook our heads unanimously. Neri's eyes swept left and right, searching out for any being, living or dead with a seething, malicious smile. The spines on her back were all flared out, knuckles nearly dragging on the ground, weapon in her grasp as it tore and gouged out the laminated flooring of the gym. Feeling like we were witnessing a monsters in the middle of murderous ecstasy, the smile quickly fell, standing a little higher, eyes suddenly focused while her wacky elongated demon ears moved this way and that, searching.

Satisfied with something, she let out a sort of tired huff, standing up tall and normal. In the middle of bits of armor and destroyed weapons, arcs of angelic blood the demon yawned, reaching high over her head to stretch and roll her shoulders. Neri seemed tired. Scratching her elbow for a second as the spines dropped along her back. She had fish eyes. Flat, lifeless, not a lick of humanity in there. The type of eyes stereotypical monsters have. Her lifeless eyes turned back to us, walking quickly our way. There was no light to them, I really was the worse of the worst, gallivanting towards us. Panic set in, a blend of my own. I had to stop her- I couldn't let this take down Raziel too.

"And lastly, you." She looked to Raziel as he turned his head where I sat and perked up in alarm.

"Hey, hey, wait a second! I'm a friend, remember?" He tried to jog her memory, but Neri would not be stopped, walking plainly up just before him. She leaned over, hand outstretched to pick him up, to kill him off as a grand finale. I was too dumbstruck to do anything, it all was happening so fast. Something sparked, crackling over Raziel like a clear bubble pumped full of electricity. A barrier!

"The St. Michaels, eh?" She pulled her hand away, wiggling her fingers with a scoff before the demon grinned. "I forgot! Got any good excuses for selling me out and nearly exorcising me off, pal?" He only moved away more, looking around for an exit.

There was no emotion to this monster, no worry or concern for what transpired around us. A good batting average, that killing so many angels was like a good batting average is what Cempe had said. I couldn't get that out of my head. She stood back up, walking the short step over to her paddle weapon, half of Gauzier's body still on top of it. With both hands, she pulled it from the wall, tilting the flat side to dump his ashes off onto the ground, shaking it out. I found my voice.

"Don't kill him, he means well, you know he does!" I pleaded, crawling towards her. Neri only grinned, using both hands to flip the weapon around to the handle, the end of it suddenly popping open like a grabbing hand, stretching its clawed fingers out wide.

"How well was that? He tries to kill off the demon that does nothing but show him mercy, and you want to say he means well? Ha!" Her face went blank, concentrating, eyes flickering with life, just for a second. Something in my own body began to spark, began to twitch in response; my hand grabbed at my heart. Not this again. I gritted my teeth, kneeling on the ground.

"I... shouldn't have done that." Raziel sputtered, nervous and frustrated. "You're right, that... was really bad." The angel looked around, keeping his head down. Neri snarled.

"Don't apologize to me, I've spent most my time here in the gym." The demon growled, hovering a hand over my ghostly form as I looked to it, unsure, "Apologize to this general area, not the floor." Raziel looked up at her, confused before looking over at the best approximation of where I sat. He gave this sick, remorseful expression, ashamed of himself before looking at me, best he could.

"I'm sorry. Really."

Neri dropped the paddle weapon a little, softening her stance and looking worn. Empathizing only lasted momentarily as she suddenly thought it was a good time to make a joke.

"See, push a little and you get results." With one hand making an example out of Raziel, she turned towards me like we were having a learning moment. I snarled.

"YOU MURDERED A ROOM FULL OF PEOPLE." I screeched, nearly foaming at the mouth. Neri only scoffed.

"This is why we separated Angry Sad Neri from Business Neri." The demon only rolled her eyes, muttering before brightening back up to the task at hand with an enthusiastic clap, "Alright, it's time to move on!" The demon gave a hearty laugh, weapon high over her head.

"Wait! No no no no!" Raziel scrambled backwards, petrified. Her eyes flared open.

"There!" The demon drove the paddle weapon down at him, cracking into the St. Michaels barrier in the small, rotating weak point that circled him, the only place a weapon of this caliber could cut such a stubbornly tough barrier.

Wait, what?

The barrier fell like a shower of glass, the energy rushing away from the three of us. Raziel opened his eyes again as Neri was sitting back on her feet, kneeling and letting the weapon dissolve away, making no other moves, non aggressive and reasonable. I too began to breathe again, confused. Why wasn't she killing him?

"That's it?" He said cautiously, looking around for validation. Neri snorted.

"Why, would you like me to kill you? I don't think that'd bode real well for you at the moment." She questioned, chuckling. I couldn't help but gawk at my own complicated relationship, the conversation my body was having on its own.

It suddenly hit me again; I cringed, heart beating out of my body, racing wildly, out of control and in immense pain. As I managed to open an eye, I saw her doing the same thing, a hand to her face.

"Egh, not yet, give me another minute here."

"I'm not the one controlling it!" I wheezed at her as the pain subsided.

"Neither of us are, idiot!" She smacked me in the head lightly, shaking it before turning back to a fairly perturbed Raziel. "We're running low on time. Sorry." Neri's hand shot out before he could say anything, grabbing at his stump of an arm and pulling it towards her forcefully.

"Hey! What are you doing?" He tried pulling back, tried to recoil from the situation. She said nothing, pulling off my invisible wrap and tossing it aside. Instantly, the blood began to wheeze from the wound, splattering on her clothes as well as mine. "Hey!" We both said in unison.

"Be silent." She said quietly, bringing her thumb to her mouth and biting a chunk out of it. Without any more warning then that she drove it deep into his arm, creating only more wounds, grabbing it and keeping it still as both he and I started freaking out, struggling to pull away from the demon. He couldn't escape her grip, she was like dense rock, not even human. His thrashing couldn't even get her to move the tiniest bit, so incredibly strong.

"What the Hell are you doing!?" I smacked at her hand as those cold, wary eyes sliced over to me. With just a twitch of her lip, just the inkling of a smile, my heart began to pound once more, like it was trying to break free, trying to rip out of my chest. The larger Neri did the same, closing both her eyes painfully as our two hearts skipped and struggled, trying to beat in sync, starting to meld.

There came a torrent of wind, suction, forcing me right towards my own body, drawing me in. She pulled her thumb out of Raziel's arm, the angel taking it back, turning his body away, hurt and confused.

"W-what is this? Why did you…Just what the Hell are you?" Raziel looked to his stump quickly and completely oblivious that my larger body was trying to absorb the smaller one. I flipped around, grabbing on the floor, whatever I could, trying to keep myself from getting sucked inside. Would I lose this consciousness? Would my other self completely lock me away like the demon did when I first escaped? "You killed them all off, everyone, you…this isn't you."

"Of course it's me." Both Neri's said it, my mouth and voice working on its own. Bewildered, I slapped a hand over my lips, looking back quickly as the wind only picked up, drawing me in faster, my legs already partially gone. No no no, I didn't want to be a part of that monster, I didn't want to lose what I was, what I had made myself. My slide into my own body was going faster now. "Angels are just…reset…not dead. I'm just….new… and improved…" Larger Neri leaned over, struggling to cope with the absorption, my mind starting to stumble up, to get confused. I was seeing double, half of her vision, half of mine.

"How do I know you're not just going to kill me like you did the others? Why did you kill... everyone?!" He turned about to face me from two perspectives, anger and pose suddenly dropping as he knew something was wrong. Neri laughed shortly, coughing. No no no no no! "Neri...?"

"I solved a problem! Go ahead and check my work!" She said in one last burst, as the last bits of myself struggled to stay apart, as the double vision came together for a second, as everything suddenly went dark.

The farthest reaches of the gym perked up, a soft, slow wind from all edges, wafting closer to me, as all energy in the room sparked to life, winding closer. I could feel myself sit up straighter, not a sound to my ears, craning my head back. The last scraps of my soul, the part developed after

I had emerged, that learned from what it had gone through and even stood alone dissolved away, melded in with the rest of me. That emotion came back with each heavy heartbeat, taking the helm as the energy got closer, pulled every bit of me together, swirling about like a key. It was almost done. Finally. My mind sparked with experience, with flashes of the lives I had lived, of everything from my past, all swirling together, becoming one. The energy was just outside me now as it culminated, as I re-emerged, as my body became whole, once again.

That last rush drew in, bringing back the sounds, the humanity, the wisdom and personality of myself, all sides of it, all factions, of a particular angel shouting my adopted name, over and over. It all collided together, screaming at me, gathering into one solid soul. My fluttering eyes suddenly snapped open, staring straight up as I was one. Solid. Whole.

Me.

You could almost hear a bell chime with the occasion.

"Gk!" I spasmed, completed body falling off to the side and crumpling onto the gym floor. I was still me, in a sort of weird, halved and rejoined way. The part that had been outside my body was co-mingling nicely, not afraid, or panicked, or scared, just sitting around where It should be, settling in. I didn't have time to consider how each angelic death would have affected me; I just needed to get things done. That part would've just impeded everything; so I left it for last, separated it out to guard the angel, in a sense. My past… augh, I knew my past now, and my future soul, responsible for knowing all about what I did after death each time was still missing. I couldn't really figure what I was, I just knew that my whole story of being around for X amount of recent years was a complete crock of crap. Complete. Not only had I been around that amount of years, but maybe thousands before it. My past was like a large, black door at the back of my mind; sure, I could enter right through it, but with all the shit happening around me now, that might open more cans of worms then I had time for. But the Praesens soul, all parts of it, was the one that ran the show. Like I was sitting around in a fancy SUV, one I'd owned for years, but was finally looking in the glove compartment and reading those little tidbits you never really discovered. It was a lot like that.

A spark! An electrical shock of sorts jarred me back from wanting to get some sleep- there was a waning, drowning sound, not unlike a car alarm, came to my ears as my eyes opened groggily. I saw Raziel there, hand withdrawing, saying my name to a beat you could almost dance to. My fingers and toes twitched, making sure everything worked, that everything was in order. He stopped repeating my name, fearful eyes schooching away from me as my hand tiredly pushed me back on my butt, legs out in front of me, sitting up straight. Propping my hands back, I let my head hang low, trying to get my bearings. Wind whistled in through the broken window I'd made, a serene, beautiful peace with this gym entirely quiet. I cringed a little at the measures I had to take in securing this peace.

"Neri?" Raziel called out, confused, verging panic.

"Mm?" Slowly opening my eyes, I wiggled my hand and grasped it into a fist. The nails were a little darker then they should've been, almost a gray. Not quite claws, but definitely not quite regular human fingernails. My toes wiggled a distance off, that one blackish nail on my big toe was especially sharp, I smirked a little, wiggling them more. My body. At least I wasn't ridiculously short any longer.

"Isss that you?"

"Mmm-hmmm." I heard him scraping around a little as my eyes shot open. The wound! Did it work? "Your hand!" I stared straight at him, sitting up a little too quickly. The blood rushed to my head, heavy horns making my head tilt off to the side. He sat there by my feet, so much smaller than I ever remembered, my perspective almost the same as if I was standing up; the angel was grasping and closing his left hand, completely healed, reformed and right as rain. Demonic blood laced with corpsy angelic dust still circled us both.

"Ah, I'm glad it worked." I had a vague grasp of what I'd done, this sort of necessary thing; since angels heal like hemophiliacs, I'd given him a dose of my own blood, at least to regenerate his hand. Wasn't sure how long that healing would actually last for, but eventually it'd fade away. Better than any crappy foot-bandage would've worked. If he died now, if he went to Heaven, they'd cut him down; 'falling' would be the least of his troubles. I brought a hand up to my head, feeling my horns. Massive things; made sleeping on your back all but impossible. I smiled. "Very glad."

"Why are you crying then?" He questioned as I felt my mind get punched into gear, actually awaken, alarmed. I brought a hand to my cheek, wiping at my own eyes. They were wet.

"I don't know." Something pounded on the back of my mind, on the past-back door, begging to be let in, to be acknowledged, pulling away my focus. You need to check something; my past soul asked politely of me, showing me an image of the same blue eyes that had driven me nuts, that I thought belonged to Raziel, sparkling clear. The eyes had two small freckles inside of them, just to the left of the pupil; but this image was from a younger eye, larger, wider then what was on the angel, innocent and tormented eyes. These were the originals…the direct source of where that thought had come from, always plaguing me. I had to know. Like a woman possessed, I leaned forward, rolling to my knees, reaching out for him, reaching out for that final answer.

"W—what are you doing?" He pulled away from my hands, head smacking back against the bleacher. "Neri?"

"Just stay still for a second, relax." I grabbed the side of his head gently, pulling it towards me like I was fortune-telling with a bowl full of sticks. With his head firmly in my clutches, I used my one thumb to pull back the eyelid, peering at that eye. No freckles. Something kicked at my brain; it's the other one. Feeling stupid, I switched sides, pulling back the other eyelid with no apparent care or respect of personal space. The eye darted back and forth wildly, finally looking up at me, resting for just a second. In that split second, that dash of time, the two eyes, the one from my past and the one I held right now, lined up perfectly.

I knew him. And I knew exactly where from.

"Can…you let go of my head? Please? Neri?" He tried to keep under control, tried to understand as I suddenly realized that I was inspecting his head like a rotten coconut. I let go immediately, kicking myself back away from the angel. The tears wouldn't stop, they flowed more than ever now, dripping onto my new pants and streaking down my shirt. I knew him. I knew exactly where from.

That past-door ominously knocked, over and over as I mentally stood in front of it, opening that door slowly, afraid. It was dark; taking a few slow steps inside my own past I stood there, meek and tiny as the lights turned on, as this grand auditorium of memories flashed back into existence. Around me, people stood like an elaborate chorus house, lives I had lived, standing there watching down on me. Hundreds of them. They didn't say a word as I walked farther in, completely surrounded by all of my past lives, the women I had been through the ages.

Just as it started getting eerie one voice suddenly sang out, young and sweet, voice full of emotion, of experience, of life. She spoke no actual words, but it ran though my head, the story, the life that I was tied to that had those blue eyes in it, all coming back to me. Even in the recesses of my mind, standing there, listening to that song, I cried.

"I said, what are you?!" Raziel was shouting at me as I sat there, beside myself. Not literally. He was upset, he'd been shouting at me for the last five minutes, angry now, he had the right to be. Shaking my head a little, I began to remember more subtle things, names and places, instead of just emotion tied to this important story.

"Please…just…hold on…" I waived a hand at him, trying to sort the information out as he stood there, pike shifting uneasily in his hands.

"No, no, you've got yourself all put together here; I think it's about time for a few answers. What are you?" He demanded this time. His name…his actual, human name, it was just on the tip of my tongue, almost there, I almost knew it all. "You don't die, you regret killing animals, but you're suddenly fine with killing everyone in this room but me, so what is it?" He flashed the pike close to my face, more scared than angry.

"What is this? What are you?!" He took a half step back, looking to the massacred remains strewn bout the gym. "I mean…all of them, you

326

never would've…" He frowned again, bringing the pike back up to my face.

"What is going on? Just tell me what's going on!" Raziel suddenly begged, "Anything! Please!"

"C——Ch…" I stumbled, stuttering, eyes closed, desperate to bring it all back.

"Neri!" He shouted like I wasn't paying attention.

"Give me a minute…Ch… chr…" I snapped my fingers, fumbling over it, those last bits falling together.

"No more time! Answers!" He shouted as I slapped at my head, teetering on the edge of my own past, on the big, final answer. Name! Name!

"Chris…Christopher! Please!" It snapped together as I belted the name like a final answer. "1634! I knew I remembered you!" I pointed at him with both hands as his face completely blanked; I grinned like mad woman. That was the correct answer.

"Ha!" It felt incredible, that answer, all these years! I gasped, grinning, finally getting it off my chest, finally remembering, breathing hard. I saw his boots, watched him take a half step back, dropping the pike in absolute horror, speechless. Those same, familiar eyes were almost dots in his head.

I couldn't stop grinning, despite it all. Finally.

28

1633—Newcastle upon Tyne, England

My name was Joan. At least this time around it was; In 1633, I was 10 years old. My father was a wealthy lawman with a strict hand, my mother a robust, strong and able bodied woman. They raised eight children; I had six older brothers, one younger sister. We lived a good life far from the wretches of peasant living; my father had made sure of it.

For a while my mother made certain to home school us, judging the local school house to much too mixed for her tastes, for her refinery. When times grew tougher, when my father's dignity came into question and doubts passed about the town, my mother had to occupy more of her time with paid work; she was a brilliant seamstress, sewing any thought or idea into an amazing work of design. We tried to use my older brothers to help teach the lessons, but with my father out of the house most days, and my mother busy with herself, nothing was ever taught. This was also the time they blamed when I learned my brashness; my harsh, blunt way of speaking that was 'rather unbecoming of such a fine woman as myself.' I spoke like the men did, cursed like the men did, and frightened my schoolmates when I finally made my entrance at the local school. Not that I wasn't polite or respectful, I was the eternal optimist. But my manner of speaking was pretty terrible by anyone's standards.

So we started attending school, my sister and I. She was a soft spoken, easy going thing; she fit in perfectly. I couldn't make a friend to save my soul. I tried, over and over, trying to schmooze in with the other kids, trying to win myself over a chum, a pal, a something. I would not be deterred; eventually, someone would crack. Someone would appreciate me for how I was, I was upbeat through each rejection, taking a long sigh and turning about, trying to pinpoint someone else to prey on each lunchtime break.

Bored one day in particular, I wandered away from the teacher, squatting about in a patch of daisies. Some girls I knew who sat in front of me talked not twenty feet away, more than likely about how the weird girl was off sitting in a patch of flowers; I stood with a smile instantly, tossing back the flower I held and walking up to them like we were old friends. Without hesitation you could see them tense up, turn their backs away from me just a bit, forced to talk to me out of polite mannerism.

"Prithee, Why dost thou tarry…"

I stopped narrating, turning to Raziel, lip curled back.

"Can I just… paraphrase this? 'Ye olde English', it ye olde sucks. Trying to remember after all this time, it's going to give ye-olde ulcer." I scratched the back of my head, straightening up and looking at the angel, his eyes still wide and panicked, bug- eyed. "Also, do you realize that we're actually talking to one another?"

The eyes darted up to my face just once as he threw his hands partially in the air, completely exasperated and nerves fried, face back to the ground. I lingered for a second, grinning again (still excited in getting this whole thing right), going back to the story." I'll paraphrase."

"I say, why are you sitting in that flower patch?" The girls giggled to themselves, throwing in the double-meaning words that implied I was socially backwards for doing so.

"I like how it smells." I said simply, dusting off my period-appropriate ruffled shoulders and fixing my period appropriate hair. The girls laughed some more.

"It probably smells better than that barn you were raised behind!" They laughed outright at me as I stared at them politely smiling back, face never flickering or giving in to their insults.

"Would you like to come over and play sometime?" I invited, taking a step closer. The laughing stopped as both girls took a step away.

"For the last time, no!" They turned their backs to me, rushing off, heading back towards the comfort and safety of the teacher's careful eyes. One girl stopped suddenly, looking over her back. "I think I know of someone who would, though." The other girl stopped as well, furious whispering going on between the two of them, ending with more hilarious snickering. I perked up to their conversation, seeing if this was the opening I was waiting for, if this was something beyond childish teasing. The two girls rushed closer to me, the shorter one pointing far out in the field, the very edge of the schoolyard limits at the small, crumpled figure sitting at the base of a tree.

"Him?" I questioned incredulously that they'd think he'd want to talk to me. The shortest, scrappiest, nastiest person in the entire schoolyard; he fought with the other boys constantly. The rumors that flew about him; that he was raised by the dogs of the streets, that he'd routinely find sick children to beat up, that half the bruises he got were self inflicted, half from his father, that he used to stone pigeons for fun; all sorts of bogus, ridiculous things. His name was Christopher.

I scratched my head as the two girls backed me up, urging me to over there to talk to him. Mulling it over, I suddenly snared them both by the wrists." That sounds like a fantastic idea!" I pulled them towards him, still a good fifty yards out as they suddenly bucked and thrashed about, desperate to stay out of his sight, showing their true sentiments. Letting go, I continued towards him, walking flatly in his direction, destined to show them wrong, set on at least trying to talk with him, something a lot of people feared. Pfft. Schoolyard politics.

The closer I got, the smaller he seemed, legs pulled tightly to his chest; he was covered in bruises like the rumors spoke, scratches and cuts as well. It was at least every other day when you'd hear about a fight with Christopher involved, with blurry origins on just who started what. Teachers lectured him day in and day out and he'd just stand there, eyes glazed over, ignoring it. Sent to the back of the classroom or sitting at the very front, it didn't matter. He was one of the more hated people in this school than I was, I mean, I was just obnoxious. Maybe trying to talk with him, to make friends was a natural move. He had his head pulled into his knees, hunched in a sort of fetal position with his back against the tree. Christopher didn't hear me coming, only noticed that I cast a shadow over him. I spoke as he slowly unraveled.

"Hey. Are you sick?"

"What?" He gave me a sort of look, a sort of 'what the Hell's wrong with you' look. No worries, I was used to that sort of glance. Leaning over, I grabbed his wrist, hoisting the thin stick of a boy up onto his feet easily. His hair was a darker sort of auburn, bushy eyebrows popped up in surprise. I was at least four inches taller than him; it didn't say much, I was taller than a lot of my classmates. It added to the oddity factor. But I pulled Christopher to his feet, the boy's eyes wide, blue; startled, but not angry. Not at first, at least. I peered into them, leaning closer.

"Did you know you've got freckles in your eye?" I squinted at him. He used his free hand to cover his one eye, looking away. "You don't look ill. Why are you sitting all the way out here?"

I let go of him as he rubbed his wrists, glaring at me. My smile didn't falter, turning a supposed-to be intimidating glare into something of confusion, looking around like I was playing a joke on him. I didn't stop, elaborating instead, turning my back on him and opening my arms to the schoolyard.

"There's a lot better places than sitting out here! You can see all the way to the market if you climb to the top of…" I looked back behind me, finding him gone, Christopher trudging out away from me, out to the complete opposite side of the play area. I didn't follow.

The next day, I tried again. This time, I didn't even bother going through an introduction or making my presence known, I just sat at the same tree he did on the far side before he even got there. After some time I heard him coming along, sitting down where he sat before, sighing a lot and grumbling under his breath. Remaining extremely quiet, I put my head around the side where he was, making the boy jump.

"So do you like to sit out here by yourself?" Christopher grabbed at the ground, turning towards me.

"It's none of your business!" I leaned away a little, smile ebbing. He continued staring at me, both of us just glaring at one another, trying to over-nice or over-intimidate the other to leaving. After a moment, I smiled again, sitting back against the tree. I could hear him get frustrated on the other side, sitting back as well.

"It's not. But still, I'd like to know, if you'll tell me." I yawned and stretched out, looking out over the landscape. Christopher didn't answer; he still sat there, but he didn't run off. Relaxing back against the tree, I tried to figure why anyone would sit here, day after day, secluding themselves. It wasn't the best view, just a hill in the distance with some grass on it, a few trees and general scrub brush. If anything, where we sat was a kind of reminder how trapped you were in this town, like the world ended over the hills.

"You can leave, you know." Christopher finally spoke up, voice low and annoyed. I cracked a quick chuckle, closing my eyes and staying put.

"Oh, I know I can, but I've got no reason to." The two of us were at a sort of stalemate; Christopher didn't want to leave because he apparently claimed this tree in a property agreement I wasn't aware of, and I didn't want to leave because I finally found someone that put up with me in a sort of way.

It was an entire week that he didn't say a word to me; he'd just give an over-dramatic sigh in annoyance every time I sat in the same spot, against that same tree at the edge of the schoolyard. He wouldn't look at me in class, wouldn't acknowledge me any other time beyond sounding like he was in a great deal of pain every day that I came back. I ignored it. I sat in complete silence, never saying a word as he never said a word to me for our thirty minute class break.

That next week, he practically stormed to the spot, grumbling and muttering under his breath the entire way; looking around the tree, there was a new set of developing bruises on his arm he held gingerly, glaring at me for a second before sitting down heavily. I bit my lip, wanting to ask the obvious question but kept my mouth shut, turning back around, my hair-bow crumpling against the tree like it always did. He sighed a lot more, clearing his throat, nervously trying to say something. I leaned over in anticipation, as soon as my face was clear to him; he got annoyed in no time flat.

"What is it you want!?" He shrieked at me, finally breaking the code of sighing and grunts of annoyance. I gave a sort of smirk.

"I don't want anything."

"Why do you keep coming out here, then?" He looked around, not unlike a modern-day version of himself did, trying to find another person to validate an oddity for him.

"I like talking to you."

"Well I don't like talking to you! We don't even talk!" He was spitting out anything to try and get me to leave, to push me away. I only sat there, listening, not leaving, not taking offense and annoying him further. "They don't like you, you know"

"Yeah? So?"

"They say that you're crazy." He was trying to find a weak point in my armor of confidence. School politics was not the way to get to it. I smirked.

"And?"

"And uncivilized." I smiled and shrugged, driving him off the deep end, "Doesn't that bother you!?"

"Should it?" I questioned, faintly aware that our arguing was drawing a crowd, that it was alerting the other children in the area.

"Yes!" He screeched, shaking his head a little." It should!" I kind of shrugged, turning back against the tree.

" Does it bother you?" He suddenly stumbled over his words, huffing a lot an struggling for some sort of comeback. "It sounds like that bothers you." The boy was trying to gather all his outrage in a little bundle to throw back, but I didn't give him the chance. It mattered enough to him that he'd bring it up, that he'd remember it. And without him having to say a word, I made him admit that he didn't completely hate me. I'd picked up more than a few tactics from my father.

"It doesn't bother me." I answered finally; the boy huffed in annoyance some more, but I cut him off, "They can think what they'd like, no matter how wrong or impolite it might be. They're still wrong." He was leaning over, watching me, looking at me as I spoke like I needed to take the short wagon to school. I laughed, my eyes to him.

"Everyone says those kinds of things about each other; no one can get away from it." Christopher suddenly sat straight up.

"What do they say about me?"

I leaned farther back against the tree, counting on my fingers.

"You're mean, violent, raised by dogs and like to start fights, carry the black death and hate everyone. You know, stupid generic stuff like that."

There was a sort of scuffling sound, I thought he had kicked something on the other side of the tree; leaning over, he had an arm to his face, trying to cover that he was crying. Instantly, my front dropped, my thick skin thinned out. I couldn't stand to see him cry.

"I'm sorry! Please don't cry!" He switched arms before just putting both hands over his face and leaning forwards, letting out this high-pitched wheezing sound. Like planned choreography, a few of the more annoying kids, the kids Christopher usually fought with were right there to kick him when he was down, there to take advantage of the situation. They walked up to him, already laughing.

"It's rather appropriate your time is best spent with the girls, you weak mongrel." The lead boy got the others to start on him, spouting things like they'd get fleas from him, why he bother coming to school, etc and so forth.

I turned to Christopher, barely hearing his breath getting shorter, his teeth pulling back, gearing up to strike out. I watched their pompous, arrogant attacks, using a sort of mob mentality to pick on someone they were intimidated by. Hell, half the insults being slung were poorly-thought out mish-mashes of regular curse words. My eyes narrowed. Switching back to the kids in front of us, snorting in annoyance, I acted first.

Wailing out in a long, drawn out cry like an obnoxious bugle, I anxiously shifted closer to Christopher, grabbing a hold of the sleeve of his shirt, wailing out again. It instantly stopped all the teasing, the kids acting as they should when a woman's wailing in panic as I started spurting out as much bullshit story I could think of.

"Ohhh Christopher, you were so brave!" I started out, burying my head in his shoulder, something I had to lean over to do, "Don't cry to protect my dignity, you scared off the terrible Grisbane all by yourself, you should be a hero! I was just so scared, so afraid, I'm just so beside myself in terror, don't cry to cover my womanly inadequacies!" I bawled, openly crying my heart out.

Raziel raised his head up, glaring at me, no longer in a state of complete horror. I stopped.

"It was something along those lines. Don't look at me like that."

As I continued sobbing, I secretly dug my own fingers at my arm, scratching three deep lines across my upper shoulder. Raising an eye up, I scoped out how well my story had worked. It didn't have to be fool proof,

I just had to raise doubts, had to make them question. As soon as that happens, the details, they don't really matter. Everyone was dead silent as I waited for that one kid, that one idiot to turn the tide. Christopher as well; his face was red, staring at me in utter confusion, arms still up by his face and hidden from the rest of the children's views.

"The…what?" It came from the back as I jumped at the opportunity, leaping to my feet with a complete turnaround of emotion.

"You haven't heard the legend of the demon hound with the forty eyes that lives in the far reaches of these hills?" I called out like a great prophet, speaking to them all." It sneaks in when your backs are turned, devours children, pulls them away into the hills and you're never seen again. It almost got me!" I spun on my heels, brandishing the scratches up my own arm. I turned slightly towards Christopher, pointing at him.

"He's been sitting here, guarding us all from the Grisbane, keeping watch. If he wasn't here… I'd…" I held an arm up to my face, sobbing deeply again. I could see Christopher continuing to watch me closely, eyebrows furrowing in a sort of bewildered concern, looking back to the other children before back to me. Sucking up my tears I leaned back, eyes red, puffy. You don't live in a family of eight without knowing how to cry on command.

"And after all that, for you to say such things…" I got faux-weepy again, putting the boy on the spot and praying he got the idea, "Christopher, do they even deserve to know the secret of how you've been keeping the Grisbane at bay?" His eyes got wide as I turned my back on the rest of the kids, holding a hand out and waiting for an answer. Christopher looked to me quickly, before back to them, and back to me as I raised my eyebrows once, face twitching. His eyes flickered, unsure.

"….No?" I grinned quickly once, eyes flaring a little, trying to get him to elaborate. He suddenly furrowed his eyebrows, crossing his arms, " They don't." I couldn't be happier. Instantly I turned back around, angry and belligerent as I was infamously known to be.

"Alright, you heard him, beat it you lily skinned scoundrels! Hopefully the Grisbane visits you in your sleep, tears your throat out and leaves you for the birds!" I stomped towards them, hands out, shooing them away like mice. They looked at one another, slowly dispersing, the crowds settling away. "Shoo! Get, you pig faced simpletons!"

"Job well done on rescuing a loon, Christopher." One of the boys said in passing, the rest of them sort of grumbling under their breath, creating a general displeasure at my behavior once again. But their focus was no longer the small, scrappy boy sitting behind me. He wiped at his face one last time, clearing up, looking around in a bit of daze as I scared off the last of them, class lunch break ending as the teacher rang the bell, calling us back inside. Christopher stood up, brushing a hand through his hair, nervous.

"Thanks." He said quickly, looking around for any of the remaining kids and awkward as all get out. I smiled, rubbing my arm a little, looking around and seeing if everything was clear. We needed to go somewhere, just he and I.

"We're not done." I wiped my crocodile tears away and fixed my bow. "Follow me."

The two of us crossed the town, heading away from it and ignoring the fact that we should've still been in school. He didn't question dropping everything and leaving, it was probably a good move anyway considering things were still tense for both him and I with the other kids. We finally reached the limits, the base of one of the larger hills bordering our town, pausing at the bottom before starting the trek up it.

"Isn't our teacher going to be mad?"

"Probably – It's not much farther." I kept a steady pace, working hard to get up the steep incline; Christopher struggled more with it, wheezing and gasping, sickly-sounding. I paused, a little concerned as he went straight past me, pushing on. With a bit of a chuckle I followed, the two of us reaching the top of the hill in no time.

"What's up here?" He said, glancing around, already sounding annoyed that he made the arduous journey up the hill for no cash prize at the end. I pointed behind us, pointed at the town in the valley, where we came from.

"What do you see?" I questioned, sitting down like an old sage. Christopher looked at me, then back to the town, shrugging.

"Our town?"

"Bigger than that!" I put my hands up the air.

"Our town with some hills?"

"Bigger, bigger!" I almost shouted it, voice dead in the open air. Christopher looked around, trying to see the point, trying to figure out the visual thing we came here to see, shaking his head and shrugging.

"I don't know, I give up. Sky?" I stood up quickly, almost jumping into the air.

"It's everything else!" I beamed as he turned to me like I was a dimwit. Snarking, I elaborated on. "What people think of you, or me, matters only in that tiny part of town. Right there. That's the only place where Robert Folton, the-kid-who-picks-his-nose's stupid name calling means anything. But look! Think of everything else where that doesn't matter, all the other towns that exist and it matters in just that one little spot. It's nothing. It's not important." He turned back to the landscape, raising his eyebrows just a little.

"Hm." I watched his face, made sure he got it, turning back to the town that rolled beneath us.

"That's what we came here to see."

It seemed like it got through, seemed to make a difference. He got in less fights, nothing really stopped, but the fights did ease up a lot. He also didn't mind that I sat by the tree with him each and every day; he never said much, but he'd listen to whatever I was babbling about, which was more than anyone besides family ever did. It was a very happy little era.

"Then winter came along. You got sick…" I turned vaguely at him, the story dawning on me, unraveling as the words came to my mouth. "Really sick. Your family was a lower social rank then mine; they couldn't afford the same good, healthy food. All of a sudden, you just weren't at school anymore." My lip kinda twitched as I said it, wanting to laugh, but feeling that emotional wrath starting to weigh on me. Raziel was turned away, still listening, hand on his head and elbow on his knees, hunched over. His fingers etched around the metal headband he wore.

"A few of our classmates actually let me know."

"He's sick." The one boy said, looking at the grass before looking to the empty tree, now known as the Grisbane tree. I didn't see him the classroom, using this time to snoop around for some answers why.

"Yeah, really sick with the disease." The other chimed in.

"What disease?"

"THE disease." Like that helped to narrow it down.

I tilted my head, looking a little baffled, a little at lost what to do as I rubbed my arms for warmth. Scanning about I tightened my gaze, storming up to the schoolhouse, the teacher sitting on the back porch, watching all the kids in their various activities. Sneaking around her I got into the schoolroom, walking up to the teacher's desk and looking for a directory of sorts, finding out where Christopher lived. Memorizing the sector I grabbed my things, leaving out the front, setting out to track him down. Being sick, he'd get behind in his classes, be left out. I wouldn't have it.

Christopher lived on the poor end of town, the part my mother and father both warned me about. It wasn't a bad neighborhood exactly, with old timey crimes of sorts happening but it was pretty filthy, it lacked some of the commodities of my own area like clean water. It held a lot of danger to a young, unwed girl such as me, a thought that chased my mind as I pushed on, book under my arms and a bag of leeches in the other hand. Trudging along, I finally saw a familiar face, sleeping just inside one of the shanties in the middle of the neighborhood.

"Hey!" I shouted, running up to stand just outside of the entrance. His eyes popped open, scared, wary and into confusion as he saw me standing there. He looked terrible; his cheeks were puffed out bad, generally looking pale and anemic even more so than usual. A rag next to the bed was speckled in blood.

"Joan?" He questioned, looking around a little before back to me. "Why are you here?" Nervously, I held up the bag of leeches, still dripping with pond water.

"I brought leeches!" He instantly looked a lot sicker, shying away.

"Aren't those expensive?" He rolled over in his cot, facing more towards me. I kicked off my shoes, soggy dress dragging on the ground

"Not if you catch them yourself." I raised the bag up, "They're supposed to suck out the bad blood that's making you sick. It's worth a shot at least." I turned back to him, dancing around the elephant in the room with a sort of ease; internally I was freaking out.

"Gah, your cheeks are puffy." I pulled two leeches out, placing them on his face, "I'm gonna put two on your puffy cheeks." As I decked the small boy out in a menagerie of squirming, bloodsucking leeches, his father entered into the room behind me. I almost dropped the bag.

"Christopher, who's this?" He pointed at me as I froze in fear.

"Someone from school" He said quickly, averting his eyes away from his dad. The man looked over the two of us, skeptical. With my one free hand I reached back, pulling forward the schoolbooks quickly.

"The teacher sent me to read up on the lessons for the day." I smiled, cowering. I wasn't a fan of adults; not that my own parents weren't wonderful in their own way, but over and over, they had warned me about what the lower class would do, given the chance. Left things open ended on just what they meant, but I wasn't completely without prejudice, it was something I'd grown up with. "Sir."

"Aren't you Harold's daughter?" The man said, a little confused. I nodded quickly

"Hmm." He turned away from the room, muttering under his breath. Christopher looked up, genuinely surprised.

"The politician?" I grumbled immediately; I was not the type who liked to be known for their father's accomplishments. But everyone in town knew of him; it might've been half the reason I was so tolerated.

"That's the one- So today, we learned about the regency." I propped the text up on my legs, leaning back against the cot so he could see the book as well.

"Did the teacher really send you?" He questioned, moving more over to look. I bust out laughing.

"Hell no" The teacher cared about her pupils, but they'd never take that much care of their students. I put down the book, looking over him, "Are the leeches working?" He pulled a hand out from underneath the covers, trying to tug one from his face.

"I don't think so."

"Damn these archaic forms of health care!" I shook a fist to the sky.

"You did not say that." He said quickly, back still turned to me. I stopped shaking my fist in the modern time, hands slapping to my knees; it was the first thing he'd said since I started. Part of me worried he actually fell asleep, turned away like that. The other part wondered if my retelling here was doing nothing but anger and frustrate him in ye-olde torment.
"Eck, fine."

So I spent the next three weeks there. I'd wait and hope he'd come to class so I wouldn't have to duck out, dodging the questions both my parents and my teacher asked; I blamed the other; Had to stay late to help the teacher out, had to duck out early and head home to help out my folks. It worked for about two weeks.

Christopher seemed quiet and withdrawn, but I could tell when I walked in, how he'd perk up and listen as much as he could before eventually falling asleep, that he expected me to be there. Each day, you could see him getting worse, see him wasting away. He wasn't recovering. His family couldn't afford doctors, just whatever wacky form of treatment I brought in, which may or may not have ever matched the actual disease he had. If he had knocked out particularly early, I'd help out with whatever chores he may have had, his father resilient to let me work at first, but eventually taking some pride in having the upper class work for the lower.

I stayed late one day in particular, finally heading home at nearly dusk. My house was a fifteen minute journey away on foot, but this time I ran, knowing I was late, knowing I'd face some music for this. As I entered the back door of my father's home, he was right there waiting for me.

The best he got out of me was that I was elsewhere than school. I didn't tell him I was visiting a sick boy in the lower class section, didn't tell him where some of his stolen money had gone to, wouldn't say a word beyond that yes, indeed, I had gone elsewhere. It was my first truly stubborn and obstinate act of rebellion. He threatened with pulling me out of school, with keeping me basically tied up and locked here in the house. I begged and pleaded, cried and fought for the right to stay. I won, but not without a painful reminder to keep my mind where it needed to be, the first time he'd struck me. None of it stopped me for a second to keep returning there, each and every day without falter. I wasn't sure how much longer Christopher would be around.

It was by my sister's graces that I wasn't completely hung by my heels for it; she told my mother that I was off visiting a sick friend of mine, that I was safe and well. She never told my father this, as by a stroke of good luck he would be away for the next month altogether.

One day, the fourth week in, I arrived there as I always did, and he was on his feet. I practically leapt to the entrance, excited that he was feeling better. But as he turned to me, as those gaunt, pale eyes came upon me, I knew this was not that case. Struggling for words, I reached out to help him stand; he pulled away weakly, leaning against the wall.

"Let's go, I'm sick of the inside of this house." He immediately started walking out the door, blanket wrapped tightly around his body to keep warm.

"Hey, yeah, okay, let's go!" I said enthusiastically, my face in utter horror when he wasn't looking. I remained precariously cautious, waiting for him to fall over or just outright pass out. He didn't. He coughed and wheezed and struggled, but he didn't fail, not once. After a block of extreme caution, I sided up next to him.

"So, where are we going?" His dead, flat glare was focused just ahead of him, heading out of town; I knew where we were going. I still thought it polite to ask. Gagging for air, he pushed on.

"Up." His pace went a little faster, fast even for me to keep up. I kept quiet, mind internally panicking; I wanted to believe this was a good sign, that this was a step into recovery, that he was on the mend. Reaching the bottom of the hill we first went up over a month and a half ago, he stopped, leaning back just a little, sizing it up.

"We don't have to go up to the t—" I offered as Christopher suddenly grunted, eyes furrowed in extreme determination, marching up the hill with more vigor he had done the first time, "Jesus Christ!" I loped after him, trying to reason, to calm him down. But just one look in his eyes, icy haze of the blue they once were, I knew he wouldn't, not until he killed himself in the process. It must've been something decided, a wish from more than just five minutes ago. Biting my lip, I followed stubbornly, standing right behind him.

The pace didn't last long, his gasping got more erratic, more strained as he made it to the halfway mark. Christopher slowed to a stutter of the original speed; without a word I put my hands to his fevered back, pushing, continuing the pace. If he wanted to see the top, God dammit, he'd see the top. Damn the consequences. He shuffled, feet still working, forward momentum provided by myself. In twice the time it took to get halfway, we finally made it to the top, both of us falling over, strained, gasping for air.

"You okay?" I asked, sitting down and fixing my hair. I saw him nod, pulling the blanket closer to him, wrapping up tight. I looked onto the land, desolate, dreary one that it was as in the middle of winter, but it still held a view, still brought everything in perspective like it always did. The two of us sat there in silence for at least twenty minutes; I didn't want to spoil this for him, didn't want to chintz it up with morals and stories and folklore that'd make him feel better. For one of the few times in my lives, nothing said was better; it was Christopher that broke the silence.

"Do you believe in Heaven?" I grabbed the grass nervously with the question. My family was not religious.

"Well, of course." I lied, sitting closer to him, "Where this is no hurt, no pain, where you get to fly around as angels and do whatever you'd like, live forever, never be forgotten. It's paradise. Who wouldn't believe in that?" My words hung in the air without response.

Feeling like I said the wrong thing, I went on.

"Why, don't you?" I joked, leaning over to push his shoulder gently. He tumbled forward, barely conscious, barely hanging on. "Christopher!" I shrieked, instantly trying to pick him up, trying to carry him back down the hill; after a few steps I tripped on the edge of the blanket and went down hard, slamming into the ground. Doing my best to shield him we began tumbling, tossing and turning down that hill, shoulder slamming into the ground, face hitting hard as we rolled to a stop, my knees bloody and scraped up, nose broken. Christopher popped loose, his crumpled body flung farther down the hill, the blanket breaking free. I could see the massive sores on his back, still see him breathing, there was still hope.

Gasping for air I stumbled to my feet and covered him, scrambling down the hill and into town, shouting and calling for help at the top of my lungs. I got the attention of a carriage driver, parked and waiting for someone, the two of us retrieving Christopher and running through town, racing back for his house. When we got there his parents practically sprung from the door, cradling him and placing him gently in the cot, the same one he had been in for a month.

"Found 'm halfway up the south hill with her." The man said, backing away from the home, demonizing me in the process. They glared at me, shrieking at the top of their lungs.

"What was he doing out there?!" I was bent over, bowing before them, pleading for forgiveness, saying I was sorry, over and over again. His father brought a hand up to strike me, to hit me like I deserved when his mother stopped him, noting angrily how I was nobility, that he couldn't hit me unless they'd incur the wrath of my father. His dad kept the hand raised, bit his lip as he looked back to his son and tearing up. The hand turned to a point, straight out the door. "Get out! You've done enough damage!" My eyes pulled back in fear. I couldn't leave, not at the end like this, not after I'd been keeping care, working hard to make this last month the best it could be.

"No, please…just…" I stuttered, struck. It couldn't end like this. His father started nudging me with his feet, slowly pushing me forcibly out of his house as I was desperate to keep my eyes on my friend. "Please!"

I saw him sort of list and roll a little bit, determined voice suddenly breaking over the chaos.

"Let her…stay!" He shouted, coughing badly as I pushed my way around his father and sat next to his cot.

"Christopher!" I choked out, watching him as his breath got shorter, more tormented, fighting to stay alive. He gripped the blanket in pain.

"You said… no one gets forgotten." He coughed some more, taking shallow breaths. I nodded quickly as he turned to me, blue eyes wide open, that same moment that would torment me for years to come. "Don't forget me, okay?" I started shaking my head, heart hurting terribly.

"Never! I won't forget ever!" I leaned over him, mind recording this all. Christopher smiled, the first I had ever seen in the months we had been friends, heartfelt and honest like a pure moment of enlightenment.

"Good. I'm glad." He closed his eyes, turning away from me. His breaths grew more calm, more relaxed, breathing lighter, slower, quieter until they finally stopped. Mine stopped too, waiting for the next one, waiting for it all to be okay, to turn out. I've had friends die on me in the past, even in that lifetime. It was a part of life, it was the constant reminder how fragile everything could be, in a time period where a disease or a sickness was a death sentence. You numb to it, in some degree. I gagged a little, still trying to keep from breathing, waiting for him to join me, holding my breath.

This? I wasn't numb to this. Fighting, struggling, I had to take a breath, I had to gasp for air. He didn't. Bending down low I sobbed out loud, crumpling.

I sat there, eyes wide as that song ended, as the door closed once again, as the world around me began to turn. My head snapped over to Raziel, back still turned, then back out in front of me, face streaked in tears.

"…Oh." I leaned forward, wiping my eyes. It didn't hit me until it was all out there, until the story wrapped up and it really was just the two of us sitting there in the auditorium, amongst the wreckage I had caused. My stomach twisted into a knot, ashamed and alarmed on just what damage my story had done, "Listen, I'm sorry, I should've used a little more discretion, it just bubbled out…" He raised a hand quickly, stopping me from saying any more.

"Don't… apologize, alright?" His voice was ragged, more distraught than anything; I didn't blame him. "You're the last person who should be apologizing." I folded my legs underneath me, keeping quiet. He went back into a sort of thinking pose, larger wings flopped on the floor.

"I treated you like crap, that whole time. You do not get to apologize for anything." He pulled at his hair, half his armor strewn about in disappointment, just the sparkly shin-guard boots remaining. His tone lowered to nothing, burbling under his breath, "Why did you put up with that?" Digging for words, I came up short, mouth flopping open with the best I could string together.

"You were a good guy beneath it all, just frustrated with what you had to put up with. I saw that from the first day." I used my one toe-claw to scratch at my other foot. "It's not fair to just sit there and watch someone live like that."

"This from the demon." He didn't mean it as an insult, but you could tell he regret saying it, trying to grab onto those words as they already left; face turning enough to me that you could tell he was still pretty upset. The angel turned back, away from me, leaning over more like I was. "This….was for you."

I glanced up, tilting my head a little. "What was?"

"This!" He pointed to himself, raising the weapon for a second and finishing off with a fluff of his wings, "You took care of me, protected me, and helped every way you possibly could…" He threw his headband across the floor in frustration.

"I wanted to return the favor. If not to you, then to someone else. I wanted to be as helpful, at least somewhere. With the stupid Grisbane thing you made up, an exorcist seemed like the right thing to do." He put a hand back to his face, leaning off kilter. I was moved, eyes watering up again. All I'd ever wanted in the lives I had lived was to make a difference, to influence people for the better. "I tried to find you for a long time, checked every day. I heard there was an epidemic there a few years later, killed a lot of people off. I waited for you; what happened?"

I scrunched closer to him, just sitting alongside, long pair of legs sticking out far in front of me.

"I survived." I chuckled lightly, voice drooping all of a sudden, "Typhoid got my sister, too. That whole…that was Typhoid, by the way. No, I managed to live through all sorts of disease waves and died of a miscarriage at 26." Raziel shot up surprised, voice cracking.

"You got married?!" It wasn't the best conversation, but it brought a little relief from the heaviness of the topic at hand. You could see his face was still red; he had been crying, his back turned like that before. My own face wasn't much better.

"Married at 17, had three kids- almost. I guess." He looked hurt, a little off-put that I seemed to continue my life with no real snag that I'd witnessed my best friend die painfully over the course of a month. I smirked emptily, "My personality died that day too; I gave up. Spent a lot of years without saying a word to anyone. My father had me married off, trying to bring me happiness; but I was just…not the same after that." I got to my knees, walking over wobbly to the headband across the floor and standing just in front of it. For me. That had all been for me. Picking it up, I inspected the thing in my hands.

"Four hundred years. Never forgot once." I could feel myself starting to blubber under the weight of time and emotion. I turned around as he still sat there, wiping his own face a few more times, using the headband to visually punctuate my words, "That's why your recent death bothered me as much as it did. Reminded me of the first one."

He got from where he stood, ambling slowly towards me like he was ashamed of himself. Fumbling with the headband a few more times, I reached out to him with it when he was close enough. Raziel put a hand to it, tiredly pushing it out of the way. The angel ignored the offering and hugged me tightly, wrapping his arms around my shoulders.

"I'm sorry, and thank you. For everything." He said plainly as I lost it, leaning over and returning the gesture. Stoic facades didn't last long as we both started crying again out of joy, him a lot softer then I. "Finally."

I choked up a little, laughing.

"My sentiments exactly." I was overjoyed and fulfilled as a person on many different levels, that enormous burden off my shoulders for good. Looking at the headband still in my hands, I shoved it on his head like an impromptu crown. "This means you're going to stop trying to kill me, right?"

The angel laughed while the demon cried tears of happiness.

29

"So I don't know, and I'm not sure." I said quickly, standing up and looking over the destruction that was this room. Raziel stopped for a moment, looking up. My guts felt like rocks, regret and shame still feeling about the same it felt before. Maybe I wasn't a completely heartless monster.

"Hm?"

"You were asking before, who was I and what was going on, yeah?" He paused across the room, probably worried this held some implication that I was mad at being shouted at. God help me I would've done the same thing, really. "I don't know. I hold rank somewhere." The angel took a couple steps forward, about to step on another piece of armor before catching himself, stepping around it instead.

"I'm apparently something of an enforcer, or a police officer. Based on Gauzier talking about 'freeing a powerful demon' that seems about in line." I gave a nonchalant shrug, feeling like I was on the verge of tears already as I tried to play it off as something that wasn't THAT big of a deal. The angelic armor of everyone else surrounded us both like a beach full of seashells, scatted and splintered across the auditorium, some stuck into physical objects, some sticking out of walls. I don't know who started the process of trying to pile them into the middle, but it felt like a slow return to action, a nice 'relaxing' way to get myself back up to speed.

I was more complete now, but I still felt sick, out of it, my head still hurt, my stomach was twisting in knots, and I couldn't just run from this. I can't imagine how Raziel felt, picking up the debris caused by his benevolent caregiver friend. I was a pretty shitty consolation prize.

"How'd you find that out?" He asked cautiously, like this was some secret I had to keep safe now that I was definitively on a side. I gave a smirk.

"Got cornered by Cempe in a graveyard. She told me I'm 'really good at killing angels like a good batting average'."

"Jesus." Raziel muttered as I was happy someone else finally had the same reaction I did.

"Right? How awful is that?" Laughing a bit, I looked to him again for answers. He seemed to be on the same page, no longer guarded about keeping secrets or what have you. "You ever heard of a Cempe? She and I are apparently the same type of...thing." Raziel shook his head.

"I'm afraid not, no." A huff, I let my head hang for a moment. "That's the... big ...horse demon, right?" I nodded.

"I think I need a drink." I rubbed my eyes again, back to wandering the auditorium, picking up bits of armor and whatever else was around. Thank God the blood evaporated away like they did or this place would probably just be coated in it. I stopped. "Hey...uh… my eyes, they're not flat anymore, are they?"

The angel squinted, "They're normal."

"Good, they're creepy and frightening without the…" I mumbled into silence, twisting one piece of angelic armor that was re purposed inside out, middle of it ripped barren by what I sure hoped was the paddle weapon's spike. What a mess. "Oh and also, I'm formally recanting my previous statement of you being old."

"Oh yeah? Why's that?" He was back on the other side, gathering things up as well.

"Because I am much, much older than you." He stopped.

"How old?"

"I'm having a hard time pinning down my first life-kinda old. Like pre-organized culture old." I could hear him stop moving.

"How many lives have you lived?" He seemed taken back.

"Enough to add a symposium of them on the back of my head." I muttered, speaking up, "Lots. Honestly, I don't know. I guess I could take a head count, though it might take a while. But I never lived past 28, not once."

"Well, I can still be old, but you can just be… ungodly old." I cricked back a smile.

"Yeah, thanks for that."

"So with the whole… you know." He pointed between himself and me, alluding to the emotional asskicking both of us had just been through. I knew where he was going with this.

"400 years, man. Don't you even dare start assuming it was anything less than what it was." I continued to point at him, raising an eyebrow as we both just stared at each other. I had to look away.

"Ugh, you're grossing me out." I lamented as he scoffed.

"What? Why?"

"You're like... YOU. You look like you!" It was weird seeing him now, he looked like a grown-up Christopher would, you could see that exact lineage. It brought up questions about myself, if I was this mix of people, these…hundreds of people, how'd I manage what I looked like now? From what I remembered of Joan, from five to twenty five, she and I might look like distant relatives in the best lighting conditions.

"Sorry?" Raziel laughed, somewhat off-put.

"No, like, you look like you should. I can see that direct lineage and it's weirding me out." Rolling my shoulder I caught him just shaking his head at me, still off-put. Giving a dramatic scoff I tried again. "I remember what you used to look like, and I know what you look like now, and they're just relative. The same. I've got two memories and they line up and it's really squicking me out for some reason."

"I can't help that! Who am I supposed to look like?" We both laughed.

"Okay, like me for example; I know I don't look like Joan. It was obviously a past life/ different life type of thing, but imagine I did still look like her, and I was just older and told that story."

"Or, imagine someone you didn't figure could be that person, telling a story perfectly, and you realize it's been that person the whole time." He shot back, voice flat.

"Good point."

"I kinda figured, anyways." He said, inspecting someone's armor, severely dented. I stood straight up, ears moving back just a hint. "You've said a few suspicious things, but I didn't think there was any way it could be true."

"How?" My ears perked forward, fingers close behind to track the movement manually. Egh, it was like I was half dog with these damn things; they seemed regular human shaped, a little longer, but they moved back and forth like little emotional detectors. I made a face at it, focusing back to Raziel, mind lighting up, "With Cempe?"

"Yeah, with the whole switching body — thing. I thought at first it was turning you into different people, but they all looked just a little like the other… you. Is your name still Neri?" I almost burst out laughing.

"I don't know if it's ever actually been Neri. I might've named myself that. But at this point, yeah, that's probably best. I'M at least Neri - I've got a few hundred names to call me by if you ever get bored of it though." Different people; she'd been flipping through my past lives. If that was the case though you'd think I'd remember a few of them, think I'd have memory of it if they were…hiding, or whatever they were doing in my body to be recalled like that. Still as I was now, as I was obviously much more demonic looking, much taller, much more of 'myself' I suppose, I still didn't know squat about what I was supposed to be doing. Just that it was important; that I held rank somewhere. It worried me, as it probably should.

"We're sticking with Raziel, right?" I had to ask back; I had no problem with calling him Christopher, no matter how strange and odd it felt. He nodded back, larger wings flopping around awkwardly as he did so. I frowned.

"I have to ask or it's going to drive me nuts; when you went back, they knew all about our ruse, didn't they?" He slowed his collecting, taking a few sighs.

"They knew. Apparently they knew for a while."

"For how long?"

"Gauzier figured it out off the bat. He's an idiot, but even for that first meeting he was being especially pigheaded about, well, considering that my brand new unregistered apprentice might be the demon." The angel shook his head, "That's what was so aggravating, he's dumb, but he's not that dumb. I guess he was waiting for me to get killed before ratting me out."

"He knew?" I stopped, throughly confused. Raziel gave a disbelieving nod, still walking about. "Why didn't he do anything?" There was a grin, shaking his head for a bit before looking up.

"Because he was expecting you to kill me off or destroy my life." Raziel laughed, "You should've seen how furious he was when he heard I got a promotion, they had to drag him out of the room."

I gave a quick laugh, settling to an uneasy silence. Isolating and ruining his life was this gym 3 hours ago. I dumped the rest of the armor in a pile, apologizing to it quickly before walking towards him. That long. They were toying with us, all that time, those months of pretending. They knew, even then.

"They were desperate for any information." My clawed hands scratched my head as I felt extremely out of place, like a lone dandelion growing in a pristine yard. "They didn't even care that I ...um... harbored you for a while, they just wanted specifics on what you were doing."

I stood there for a moment, tone empty and forlorn.

"Did you tell them?" I muttered as he looked elsewhere.

"You didn't do anything wrong, you did work of 3 exorcists as one person so I figured the most they'd get out of it is that not all demons are bad." Raziel dropped one more chest plate into the pile. "They didn't seem to appreciate it, either way."

"I think I burned through all the good will in one sitting, anyway." I scratched the back of my mutant neck with animalistic hands. "If I keep pulling stunts like this, I deserve that ire." Raziel shook his head, sounding instantly nervous.

"But... but you're not... driven... to do those things, right?" God, this was the conversation we had to have, if best pal Neri was driven to murder angels out of instinct. My skin went clammy and cold.

"No. N... no I don't want to do that ever again." I wilted, shaking where I stood. It'd be easy to flip it around and complain that he's treating this situation like it was in the beginning, assuming that was something I had to do. But honestly I had to ask myself this question long before he did.

I kicked at the pile, immediately regretting desecrating their remains all the more, cursing under my breath. It was like I couldn't help it, like it was ingrained into me. Didn't mean that parts of me didn't fight and kick the whole way about it, that at least made me feel a little better.

"So you agree to come back to wipe me out, they don't give you the chop and get you a new set of wings in the process, eh?" Raziel practically shot into the air, back to how I remembered it. I hid a smile, happy to be off the topic.

"Hey, wait a minute! I didn't 'wipe you out', I let you go! You're the one that sat there and took that damage!" I just stood there, face scrunched up. "The wind, that was my own special touch to the St. Michaels to try and push your stubborn ass out of there." My ears went back again.

"That wind hurt the most!"

"It does if you stick around!" I paused, shaking my head.

"Gauzier sealed me in. I relish the friendship, don't get me wrong, but I'm not stupid enough to stick around for a St. Michaels. Palug got me out."

"Who?"

"First house taxidermied bleeding cat thing."

"Oh." We both stood over the pile, mentally annoyed as we saw fit. "They did give me back a few of my duties; I hate to say you're right about that. I wasn't given much of a choice; but I didn't mean to kill you, or even to get as close as I did."

"Well, I didn't mean you to get caught up in all of this." I crouched down by the pile, sick and worn on the inside. I saw who I really was; that didn't make things much better. "And I certainly didn't mean to alienate you from everyone you know. Or kill all your friends today." Muttering, I could hear him smirk.

"They weren't my friends." Lip scrunching up, I looked back down.

"They're fine though, right? Fine-ish?" Raziel didn't say anything for a moment, so I kept on, "Like, Heaven's got to have some sort of 'no-pain' contingency plan if someone dies as an angel, right?" Silence.

I peered out from the space near my shoulders for an answer as Raziel made an assortment awkward, 'unsure how to break the news' faces, face crinkled up, eyes darting around. That was answer enough.

"AggghhGod!" I bellowed, hanging my head more.

"I mean, if anything they died...quickly?" Giving a dead, unenthusiastic stare from the corner of my arms I watched him gingerly try to explain they probably felt every bit of pain every second they were alive. "So it was at least... quick."

"Egh, maan. How is that fair?"

Walking a little closer, he only shrugged.

"Well they're not trying to encourage you to keep getting yourself killed."

"I guess, but Jesus." I looked at the clawed hand partially in my vision, running my thumb along the sharpened, more animalistic edge. Raziel suddenly pointed at something, not as worn down by my little spaz out.

"Can I touch your horns?" He asked, inquisitive. Letting out a sigh, I nodded, putting my head back down as the angel prodded my extremely demonic acquisitions, digging his nails in at my horns. "Can you hear this?"

"It's reverberating a little, yeah." Raziel switched to my back spines, mushing them around. Smirking I raised them full up, splaying out the little membrane between them as he was quick to jab at that, too.

"Ugh." He muttered as I snickered, happy to talk about light topics. "Does that hurt?"

"No, they're just...there." I scratched the base of my head horns before resting against my hand. "These did, though. I've been having headaches for weeks."

"Must've been a seal with your goggles, makes sense why you couldn't take them off-- here, lower your head for a second. Or wait, no, look up." Trying to follow his instruction, something fresh and painful shocked my system for a moment as the angel tugged hard at my horns. Like a tack in the bottom of your foot, something cheap pulled loose, Raziel careful to keep the end of the horns pointed away for safety reasons. Half a shattered goggle lens dropped to the floor next to me as he carefully sidled up on the other side, using his new pike to dig and pry the other side out.

"Thank you." I said quietly as Christopher only nodded, concentrating on freeing my other horn like a collar embedded into my skull. I felt happy he was helping me and he seemed genuinely at ease with himself. Whether that was to ignore everything else or he was just genuinely happy to help pry plastic bits out of my horns, it felt like the best type of nod to the situation without outright apologizing or trying to pry for answers. "What happens if you go back now, after all this?" I already knew the answer.

"Bad, bad things." Still, he tried to laugh about it. Even though his afterlife was mangled and broken up as it was, he tried to make a joke at its expense. The flimsy goggle half was tiny in my monstrous, oversized demonic hands, a toy sized reminder that there was no going back to how things were.

"Hm." I relented, a little more pestered then I had been. His exorcist career was over, congratulations to the demon on dragging down another angel. This was different, wasn't it? What this all was, it had to be different then every other story I've heard, of demons luring the poor, innocent angels away from the light. It had to be different. I had to be different.

Right?

"I can fix this." I stated like my last will, folding my arms stubbornly.

"Neri, c'mon." Raziel was not impressed. Mimicking him from earlier, I raised my hand up quickly. The angel dropped the other shattered goggle half over two fingers.

"I'll fix it." Something told me I could. Some crazy notion in my head said, yes, this is possible, go ahead and say it. I was not going to be responsible for another soul dragged down with my terrible, probably correct reputation. "Christo-Raz, I will fix it."

My tired glance outside instantly kicked my over-serious facade clean off as I saw the light starting to return…dawn? Like this? Head whipping around, I searched for a clock, none in the gym here. With a giddy little squeal I darted out for the hallway, crouching under the door in a rush, nails scrabbling on the floor. Clock, clock, what time was it? Part of me knew I had already passed my usual return time, that I hadn't returned to being that dinosaur-demon like I normally did. Was I done with that cycle? Was I free from the constant pain each night? Scrambling through the hall, the rest of my mind was bubbling, wondering if that form had changed as this one did.

"Neri!" Raziel called after me, far behind my extensive loping distance, my stride length. In the hallway, though the barred cage surrounding the clock of the public high school, I saw the time was 6:42 am.

"Aah!" I yelped happily out of shock, jumping up in the air and putting a hole in the ceiling, horns jabbing into the concrete in the process, panels crashing down and busting over my head. "Ah! Damn…long-ass horns…" I clutched at my face, shaking my head out just in time for Raziel to come around the corner.

"What is it?!' He said in alarm, parts of his armor under his arm with the new pike in his hand. I pointed at the clock, too excited for words as he stuttered, confused, one eye almost closed. "Yeah, it sure is almost seven o-clock. Oh… OH!" He grinned, dropping his armor. I hopped around, back hunched, the two of us doing a sort of lame happy dance.

Something crashed as I bent my head lower, eye turned to see what damage I had caused now, sound crunching again as I was nowhere near the ceiling tiles; I could smell something, just barely, wafting aroma of a scent killing my happy dance effectively as it should. Flowers; dried flowers. With one hand on the top of Raziel's head, I got him to stop jumping around immediately like an impatient mom with a 5 year old.

"What? What is it?" He looked around, freezing up as another crunch was heard, coming from the gym behind us. "Whaaat…"

"Cherub" I crept slowly towards the gym, Raziel's face mimicking that of his former life, the pale, gaunt, 'vomiting for a month' face. On hands and knees I edged closer, hearing the cherub chewing through the hole I made earlier, struggling, bricks falling to the floor.

"Why is there a cherub here!?" He hissed as I snuck my head around the corner and finding my favorite white and red three-winged cherub, head butting into the last side of the wall in hopes to knock it out.

"I took off one of its wings a month back trying to protect the others."

"You what?! What others?! Wait you took off a WING?" He was reaching low-volume hysterics. I frowned quickly.

"Game face, Raziel!" The hysterics dropped.

"Right… right." Something whistled, an ominous sound before a bright white and red head exploded from the door frame, screeching out in a horrible roar, missing us by horrible inches. "Aah!" He yelled out. I didn't blame him, my game face was the same face as my 'get the Hell out of here face'.

"Shit!" I grabbed the angel behind the collar, running as fast as I could hunched over, horns still ripping up all the ceiling tiles above my path and leaving a trail of debris behind me like breadcrumbs. The bird screeched again, pushing hard to pull itself through the hallway, chasing us with a respectable speed, wrecking the hallway and expanding it as it passed. It was about 6 ft high, maybe 15 ft wide; still the bird was managing to get through. Well, that wasn't right. "Cherubs, can they control how big they are?" I swung my arm around, setting Raziel up to run all on his own.

"To a degree." He took right to it, bolting past me, "He's probably at his smallest now, he gets bigger!"

"I know! I've seen him bigger-aaghh, this way!" I grabbed onto him again, scrambling into the side-hall as the bird blew past us. Its roar of frustration echoed our hallway as the talons ripped up the carpet mid-stop, the sounds of the metal twisting and bending as it made a circle to attack again. "This might be the first time I wished I had that other body again!" The ceilings were higher here as I stretched my neck back to where it was supposed to be. Raziel smacked my arm.

"I can help with that!" He suddenly darted a completely different angle, wings flapping like mad and going though the walls, heading outside. Eyes wide, I talked to the air.

"Alright, go for it!" I said, a little uneased. Uneased more as the hallway stopped dead here. Leaning back I slid to a stop, bird coming up just behind me, stopping too. My weapon was still in the gym, practically unarmed except for my horns and wacky little toe-claw.

'Call to it', Something said. 'Call to it, it'll listen'. Eyes darting in panic, I tried to think of its name, all cool weapons have cool names; none of my past lives knew the answer. An auditorium of shrugging. The bird eyed me hungrily, mouth opening larger, zipping back, ready to take me down. Call to it, idiot!

"Heeeyy weapon!" I shouted, voice shaky and sounding all brands of dumb calling a weapon, weapon. It worked though, the light dimmed a bit around me, paddle weapon collected like the same black mist that would cover me, focused just on my hand. Falling away it was all there, a little more red, white and yellow then I remembered before it's color settled on a deep, darkened red. The pieces fell into place. "Co…lus?" The bird lunged forward, no longer patient as I figured the grand mystery of the paddle weapon. I braced the back of it, bird's beak stopping on the sides, hitting hard. The cherub pulled back, screaming at me.

No matter how much I tried to deny it, how I tried to think otherwise, how I tried to reason my way around these types of conflicts, something in me really did love a good fight. Loved the thrill of battle, of the raw energy, the raw power, the dangerous aspect of it. One that enjoyed life, but enjoyed fighting for it more, enjoyed proving myself worthy to live it. Grinning ear to ear, maybe I deserved this life more then I'd like to think. Maybe that part of it all was okay. The merciless killing of everyone in the room, obviously not.

Lunging out for my face the bird struck again, pushing the weapon into its beak, I leaned from the side. Cherub tongue wiggled at me, trying to reach me; I was quick to step on it, putting all my weight as I felt it beneath my toes, kicking the weapon, handle first, knocking it in the head. Pulling back on my hand the weapon propped back up, raising it over my head to club the holy owl good. Anticipating my move the bird chomped around my feet, carrying and pressing me into the wall behind us, the two of us busting through and into another part of the school. Spitting out a laugh I flipped and hopped back to my feet, leaning forward, ready to go again.

"You're smaller then you were last time, demon, you might as well put that weapon aside, you're no match for me!" The cherub cackled at me as I stood there looking to the Colus weapon, nodding.

"You're right. I don't need this." I gave the weapon a toss, apologizing to it quickly before standing there, ready to fight bare-handed, egging the bid of death on. "C'mon chickadee, let's dance."

The bird coiled its neck, growing to fill the class room as that mouth unzipped the whole head and down onto the neck, whitish hook-like teeth spread the entire route. I wiggled my fingers, shifted the position of my foot the tiniest bit as that horrible stench began to fill the room, the dried flower smell all but a memory. My eyes were quick, body extremely on edge, waiting for that movement, waiting to react. The birds eyes suddenly shrank in it's head, on the move! Striking out I shifted, head blowing past me, snapping at nothing. As the head began to retreat back

I grabbed hold of its cheek fluff, shoving the bird's head into the wall. The cherub snapped at me as I latched onto its nostril with one hand, bird suddenly thrashing and bucking around, trying to grab some part of me. I dodged it, head snapping just alongside me as both hands grabbed a nostril each; bird surging back through the class wall, through the brick and into the other adjoining hallway. It flipped and writhed, trying to throw me from it; I laughed, thoroughly enjoying myself as we came back to a level plane.

Toes digging into the carpet I held tight, straining to push the cherub back, to show that raw strength, to test my limits a little more. The bird dug in with both sets of wings trying to push me forward, my toe-claws dug in tight as we stalemated. At least at this size, the cherub and I were roughly equals.

"Neri!" Raziel called partially from the wall, my eyes dragging over to him as he pulled the impossible from behind his back, the pike. The first one; restored, shiny, perfect and just as it once was without a horrible metal snag in sight. My eyes lit up like Christmas day.

"You fixed it!" I eased up from the fight just a hair as the cherub pushed forward, shoving me a good six feet back as I restored my grip on the beast once more. "Maybe…I can…gawk at it later." Bent down low I pushed with all my might, gaining a foot on the beast.

"Not that, this!" He suddenly darted behind me, my back exposed. Eyes opening wide in alarm I looked to my shoulder, seeing the very edges of the first seal still in this body; the scar followed me around, used so often those months. "If this got you out before, maybe this will get you back into the other body!" He grinned confidently, swinging the pike back around over his head, as it always had been. Glancing sharply to the Colus weapon still a classroom back, I swiveled my head around back to him, lips pulled back in preemptive pain.

"Wait wait, I don't think that'll…"

THWAK!

He put all his force into it, put all his dedication and apologies into it, pike smacking me hard against the back, slapping flesh like a high-dive belly flop. I didn't have to look to know there'd be a sweltering red mark from his bout of enthusiasm. I scrunched my face up in pain, holding a breath like I didn't know what to do with it.

"Gaaaahhhdd…" My eyes started watering, twitching in the definition of pain. Raziel kept it to my back, hopefully withdrawing into himself, hopefully understanding that those rules were not the same as before.

"Maybe I didn't line it up enough." He said softly, pulling the weapon from my back to try again.

"No! No, no, oh God, no!" I shuffled away from him, shimmying

off to the side and taking the snarling cherub's head with it." That doesn't
work anymore." I tried laughing; tears of pain rolling down my cheeks. The
cherub, happy and gleeful creature it was, took advantage of my wandering
attention, thrusting forward, knocking me into Raziel. The angel flipped
over my back, hand grabbing onto my horns as my face was jerked
downwards, smashed against the cherub's beak. My body rose up with the
force, feet leaving the carpet as all stops were thrown out, cherub of death
free to do what it wanted with both of us attached.

It burst through walls, rolling in a circle and throwing us around
before shooting straight up, into the second floor. Still, he held on, and I
held on, both of us stuck to take the damage. In a sort of bewildered state, I
laughed.

"Are you having fun?" I called out to him, face squished trying
to talk. The cherub spun again and threw us into two more walls, both
reinforced cinder block facades.

"Not really!" He called back. I didn't know what he was bitching
about; I was taking the brunt of the damage, skin ripping apart only to
come back together, just in time for the next wall. Scanning behind me to
the wall before us, I calculated, legs jabbing out quickly to hold us up, the
ride coming to an abrupt halt.

"Grab onto the bird!"

"What? Where?"

"A part that doesn't have teeth!" My body ached, losing strength.
Impressive strength that it was, but I wasn't infallible. I felt the pressure
release from my horns as I snapped my head back up to face the Cherub,
Raziel grabbing desperately just above it's one eye as the bird hissed at us,
mouth drawing open, zipping back. My feet began to shake.

"Should've done this before!" Raziel swung a leg back, punting
the Cherub in the eye with his pointy metal boots. I grinned; those things
were so damn handy. The owl began to thrash about, knocking out the wall
along side us, one that edged the same gym we had started from, high up,
falling. It dove for the ground, blood leaking from the one closed eye. "Let
go!" He called, suddenly behind me. I relinquished my grip as the angel
caught me by the foot, flapping desperately with those new wings.

Panting for breath I watched it fall, crashing into the gym floor,
thrashing about and trying to sooth its eye. With a deep breath I looked
back to Raziel, relieved.

"I'm so glad you're on my side" My back throbbed in response,
"M—most of the time."

"I'll drop you."

I laughed, focus back to the ground below me as we hovered there.
It was growing; visibly larger in this bigger arena, craning its head back and
sizing up to lunge for a strike.

"Pitch and fold 'em!" I yelled to the angel.

"What?" He paused, eyes flickering, unsure. Bringing my hands way over my head I swung around, flipping back and grabbing onto his legs, scrambling awkwardly over his back. "Whah, what are you doing?!" His arms flailed about as I grabbed a hold, shoving the one wing lower than the other.

"I have more practice with these!" I yelled out as a flurry of feathers careened past us, missing by shear inches to tangle amongst the rafters. One cherub wing smacked us away, throwing us both into the wall and falling apart. Arching my back, I called to my weapon. "Colus!"

Raziel was already regaining control as I pitched towards the ground, hurtling at it. Not a second later that black string came about again, winding and forming into the paddle weapon; under great stress I slammed it into the wall, spikes first, ripping out cinder block as the floor was practically beneath me. Zigzagging and stumbling around I slowed, hitting the ground rather hard but without injury, weapon still in my hand. The Cherub flared its wings at me from the air, growing to its full size, the size I had seen in the first time and now again in bitter reminder. I bolted to the other end of the gym away from Raziel, the bird's hungry eye focused on me with no error. Looking to the weapon in my hand I frowned, pulling it close.

"Uh…go!' I said, shaking it about, trying to get that form back, the same form that protected me regardless how I chose to fight with it, as weapon, or as a demon. I needed that demon form now, needed that other protection. "C'mon, please, help me out again, Colus." I pleaded to it, stroking a hand alongside the flat side. To my delight, the weapon began to shimmer, began to melt from my hands as the cherub crashed down, screaming.

"Annoying demon!" It screamed at me, all three wings taking up most of the gym space. Completely evaporated from my hands, the black smoke began to skirt by my feet, began to follow me as I backtracked like I was on fire. There was a lot more smoke, streaming away from me as I only chuckled in response, glare snapping to the Cherub.

"I'm sorry; this is just going to get a lot more annoying." I saw Raziel land in a far corner, safe as the smoke streamed above my head, rising far into the gym air, twice the distance it did before. With a smirk it snapped closed, rising, forming, pushing into that demon form once more. Finally, I was starting to get the gist of this process, starting to figure things out for myself. I couldn't stop smiling.

I lurched forward, hands smacking onto the ground as the gym shook with my presence. As I opened my eyes, I could tell I was bigger. My perspective was double that I had just been, staring at the middle of the Cherub's chest, instead of from far below it. The smoke wafted away, revealing the same demonic form as before, just with horns. And double its sizes; so instead of being some 7 ft by 15 ft thing, I was some 15 ft by 32 ft thing. Roughly. I scanned my body over once as the cherub screeched out, backing up. You couldn't help but smile. My tail whipped around, sizing up how to take down this bird as we were both confined in the gym. Being shorter, I had more area to play in, more room to fight; the odds were falling in my favor. I hunched my back, snarling.

"Get it!" Raziel called from the corner; I tilted my head cockily; I could do that. Opening my wings I surged towards it; at least I meant to. My wingspan hit both sides of the gym as I was only surging against my own outstretched bones; bone won, my wings only working to wedge me back as I was. With a sickening lurched my head flopped back as I was thrown back into a sit, throat wide open; the cherub took the opportunity. Without a second of consideration its mouth was locked around my throat, throwing us both into the first and second floors of the school bordering the gym.

"Dammit!" I gurgled out, trying to jab my clawed toes into the bird, to slice him without having to use my teeth; only to find I was just toeing the bird in the side, that this form lacked such details. I was too damn big! The agility, the benefit I had being able to dodge these attacks, to be able to maneuver, that was gone. This form wasn't a much of a blessing as it had been one time. Growling, snarling, I clawed the best I could with my hands, ripping out chunks of bird feathers. The cherub only laughed, tightening its grip, bones starting to snap. Without my head getting cut off, without the chance to regenerate, I was stuck with the full effect of the attack, of the blood rushing to my face, of my windpipe slowly crushing, trying to suffocate me. This thing knew how to attack my type now.

Something scampered up my spine, dug in with the pike once or twice to help itself up before standing there, braced on my one shoulder blade. Pupil wandering down I only saw the top of his head, gray hair waving about as he reared back, stabbing the bird in the mouth in the parts that clamped down behind my neck, exposed. The bird began to try and shake my neck, tried to continue that grasp as he stabbed, over and over, breaking through the top of its mouth once with a familiar sight- the old pike. The hook-like top of it switched directions as he pulled with everything he had, ripping out a big chunk of the bird's inner nostrils. Writhing in pain the bird's grip snapped away; I slumped down to the floor, breathing hard. Raziel stood perched like the good side of my conscious, the angel on my shoulder as my eyes panned to him. He was looking quite proud of himself, cherub thrashing around dramatically behind him as he only raised his eyebrows. I scrunched my face up.

"Not a word." I grumbled low, grateful for his help. The bird flipped back to its feet, tongue jabbing through the hole broken through by the pike, licking it. Its eyes zipped to tiny dots, mouth flaring wide open, screaming at the top of its lungs. Lights dropped from the ceiling as everything shook, vibrating with rage, tearing this high school apart at the seams. Before I knew better I was swinging my head low, horribly low, culminating roar bellowing out as my head craned back, growing louder until it drowned out the Cherubs. Pushing harder, the roar topped it, shaking the building more, cracking some of the supporting walls and beams lining the gym as my neck went straight back like a howling wolf, jaws snapping shut as I drew near the end of my breath. The gym continued to rattle, echoing, car alarms sounding from the parking lot; eyes locked to the Cherub as it stood there, worried with itself. Fear didn't last long.

With a little hop it screeched again, barreling full out towards me not phased in the least. Muscles bunching up I tore into the ground, charging like a blind bull; I had to take another stance, a different view; be creative with how I used this body; I had brute force, but half the grace I once did. The bird flapped its wings once to build speed, legs hopping and stomping on the ground as the two of us were headed dead on, straight for one another. Made me wish the horns were pointed forwards, actually useful— wait!

"Hold on!" I shouted to Raziel as he gripped the hair along my spine, in the crook of my neck. With one last push I pointed straight at the cherub, bringing my arms around for that final strike, only to shift them nearly diagonal, pushing away at a straight angle, away from the bird; we missed hitting each other, but I wasn't done. I flapped open my one wing as it hit against the wall, ricocheting me from the side as I arched my back, throwing my head around, horns first. Like I was attempting a backwards flip my entire body came around after my head, tail swinging out to push me all the more from the wall, arms sticking straight up in the air. I aimed best I could, horns connecting with something hard, breaking through and pummeling to a series of crunching, broken stops, through the cherub's skull and into the gym floor concrete.

Panting hard I waited for movement from the bird, waited for my strike to go completely haywire, for those wings to start swinging around and clawing up my back as I was practically laying against it, back arched to keep from crushing Raziel, face pinned down by my horns as my legs kept my whole body in a sort of back-horn stand. Something moved around by my shoulder, angel dropping to the ground. He whistled as I remained stuck like that, unsure.

"Did I get it?" I questioned, trying to position my body a way for my hands to reach…anything, stuck pawing at the air.

"You got it." He said flatly, walking partially into my field of vision, sickened, disturbed and a little dazed, "Got it… uh, right through the head with both horns. That's what you were trying for, weren't you?"

"I was just trying to hit it!" My legs gave out from under me as I sat down on my butt, hands able to push off the floor, trying to get my horns out of the cherub's head. They wouldn't budge. "Isn't it going to evaporate away?!" I shrieked, legs swinging back and forth as I tried again and again to pull my horns from the wreckage.

With a sickening, dull crunch, my head pulled out of the cherub's face, snapping forwards with bits of meat, feathers, blood and brains caking the back of my head and hair. I made the mistake of curiously looking at it, this pummeled mash of blood and brains and something of an eye, jaw crushed into the top half; I gagged.

"Well that's one way to make a point!" Raziel joked, still sickened and trying to make light that I had pretty much polished off an army of highly trained exorcists and a holy Cherub. I didn't laugh back, hanging my head low, hair flopping down in front of my eyes, covered in blood. With a weary little shake I splattered blood across the walls, making this all worse. It had been fun. It had been exhilarating to fight, to pit myself against the enemy. Not this part, though. My head hung a little lower.

"I only killed it because it'd go after the others if I didn't. This… was just shortening that wait." I couldn't believe what I was saying, exactly what …part of me had said that I didn't quite understand before, "It's just business, and not the part I enjoy." Raziel's tone shifted dramatically.

"Hey, no, I mean, I get it, I'm just saying." I gave another shake, hunched tiredly like a dejected, ashamed animal. Thoughts coursed through my head, bits of information here and there.

"Starting to get the feeling this happens a lot." I said, disconnected from myself as I turned to look back to Raziel. "How do you break a routine that's practically ingrained into your soul?" Squinting I looked to the windows, still early in the day, over-thinking it all. It was on odd time to get philosophical- frowning, I suddenly doubled back, biting gingerly around the bird's twisted, broken neck and heading outside.

"C'mon. I need your rebellious angel-ness to help me with something"

So we buried it. Buried the cherub and threw in the parts of the angels from earlier. I didn't actually dig an enormous, thirty-something long grave, just helped push it underneath the dirt. After we'd done that it dawned on me that this was directly behind a high school It was a minor detail. Raziel said a few sarcastically tinged words and as I stood there, still squatting the demon form. There should be respect at least somewhere.

30

After an awkward pause, he finally spoke up, raising the old pike a little into the air.

"So, are you stuck like that again?"

"Hm?" I turned to him behind the high school, in front of the massive grave site that was entirely my doing, lounging about in the fifteen-something foot tall demonic dinosaur form. I'd almost forgotten; form melting at my request, smoke flowing away peacefully and not shot out of it like my exits had always been. After a moment I was back on my human feet, last bits of black smoke blowing away with the wind, back to the world around me until I wanted to call for them again. "No, no, I've got that all under control now. I appreciate the disfiguring scar you gave me for it, though."

I turned away from the grave site, turning back to look at the school and shaking my head. I was starting to think being a nonphysical being was more of a blessing then a burden; as a real, traceable person, I'd be sued countless times, over and over, living a life of shame, the social pariah of the town, paying lawyers to cover each court cost… the newspapers, agh, media would never let me out of their sights, insurance companies wouldn't touch me…

"How's that work?" Raziel asked, breaking my rambling thoughts. My eyes popped open, eager with knowledge that I had and someone who wanted to hear about it as the two of us strode around the building, working our way to the front.

"Oh! Right!" I held my hand out, summoning the weapon back again in no time flat. This whole thing was getting easier and easier, an accepted and very welcomed change from the pain in the assery I'd been through earlier. Holding it out in one hand I demonstrated it like a saleswoman. "This is called the Colus."

"Yeah, I heard you shouting for it earlier. Did you name it?" I flipped the weapon over, inspecting it with a bit of sneer like there'd be a brand name hidden along the blade somewhere.

"I don't know. I think it's just the thing's name." He shrugged as I continued on. "This only popped up as I was human-ish. Did you notice that it never came about when the demon body was there?"

"I'm not that observant." He said flatly, a little skeptical.

"Well, either way, it's because it's the same thing." Raziel stopped, propping up an eyebrow like I was sputtering gibberish, swinging it around. I tried to explain, "It protects me, either way. As a weapon like this or when I get to ride alongside and control the mondo version."

"It's both?" He leaned closer, inspecting it." You think it'll protect anyone, or just you?" Pursing my lips at the question, I flipped the handle towards him.

"I don't know, give it a shot." His eyes darted to me cautiously, hands just over the grip. He wanted to, his actions were practically screaming it, eying the damn thing since I fought him with it back at the house after the great football escapade. The angel was hesitating. "What?"

"You're the one who survives things she shouldn't, not me." You could hear him backing out of it, sizing up possibilities and trying to worm away from touching the handle, no matter how much he wanted to. "There's all sorts of warning bells and whistles going off in my head, telling me not to touch this thing." Smirking I began to pull the handle away, shrugging my shoulders. I could respect that.

"Then again..." He said with a sort of deviousness, a sort of aching want to disobey, to cause mischief. By the time I had just turned my head to see, to just catch him as he latched onto the Colus's handle with both hands, he was already shaking. Vibrating was a better word for it. Shaking back and forth at a very high frequency, where I could almost see two of him at one point was even more accurate. My eyes bugged out of my head as he suddenly shot away, not just launching from the area, leaving like someone kicked him, but rocketing directly away from me, going at least five or six hundred miles an hour; just—gone, speck of an angel arcing into the sky.

"Shit!" I panicked, jumping into the large demon form without a second notion, tearing after him as I raced after a disappearing speck. Flapping hard, he wouldn't be hard to find, branches cracked apart, leaves disturbed or missing completely, an area of land, forest, homes, light poles, you name it, they were either broken, cracked, or entirely blown apart and pointing upwards slowly towards the sky. Pushing faster and faster I followed the line of destruction until it began to point back towards the ground, nearing the end of the trail as I hoped, over and over and over again that my blood would help him out; It was the only reason I really offered him to hold it, some stupid, senseless part of me thought that with a bit of my blood in the circulation, Colus would be okay with him as well, maybe offer more protection for both of us. That was not the case.

Something shiny caught my eye, wedged at the top of a light pole, golden, pointy and hunched over like a dead caterpillar, one of the shin guards with a bit of dust still blowing out from the toes. Must've torn off a leg in the process, hitting that. I picked the armor up, continuing along for another few minutes until I found the other, a little more banged up. We had to be at least five miles from the high school at this point, an absolutely massive shot. The path was nearly back at the ground now, nearly over as it headed into some woods. Stretching my head up, I didn't see an exit wound from this area; he had to be inside.

I brought my wings around, landing just inside with both shin guards in my hands, shifting them to my mouth as I hurried along, following the plants torn aside, the new trail made through the worst of thickets. On my way I found a shoulder-guard, reassuring me that I was still on the right path. I dissolved back to my human form, gathering up the bits of armor as I finally had the arms to do so, trotting hurriedly along the path until I saw him, body wedged half inside a tree. He was a wreck, missing legs below the knees, part of one arm and most of the other hand, half his chest and other various wounds torn from his body. The only bit of armor on him was the other shoulder-cap and the headband, now around his neck. Wings were nowhere to be found; completely removed. Raziel's eyes were wide as humanly possible, one hand grasping the side of the tree, still shaking; though I wasn't sure it was due to the weapon this time. With a deep sigh of relief, I walked towards him slowly, almost mockingly.

"I saw... everything" He said in complete shock, eyes darting back and forth.

"Easy there Nostradamus." I plopped the armor down, shaking my head a little in shock myself. "Try to relax."

"Why am I still alive?" He said groggily, moving his leg-stumps around; there was no blood in the area, no blood anywhere around him whatsoever. Raziel was still healing the same I was, though at a much slower rate, something alarming. His eyes followed me as I stood next to him, tsking, shaking my head some more. "I'm out of range from the Priest, too. What is this?"

I sat down cross legged beside him, arm propped up on my knee.

"Temporary independence, provided by my blood from earlier."

"Oh." He kinda left it at that, few of the fingers on his one hand beginning to twitch back to life. "This is what you go through each time?" I nodded a little, propping my head up with my hand. This day had been exhausting and these constant form shifts wore me down quickly.

"It was like touching pure energy" Raziel babbled out, rolling his head a little on the trunk of the tree, still bewildered: he watched his hand closely as they healed at a snail's pace, dragging out this renewal process into a painful ordeal. "Like licking your finger and jamming it into the sun. I don't know how you're able to even touch the damn thing." He huffed a painful chuckle.

"It sounds stupid, but it wasn't evil energy. It was just like….yow!" He was trying to rationalize it all out as I gave a sort of halfway stare at the guy. "It didn't hurt. My flight here, that's what hurt."

"You shot away from me like you had rockets strapped to your back." I cackled softly, shaking my head some more. "Was it worth it? Did you have fun doing the wrong thing for once? Breaking all the rules o' angel of mischief?" The angel laughed at the rhetorical question; it turned to a cough, then to a sort of wheeze of pain.

"Not if it hurts this badly." My ears swept back; He'd only healed a few digits on his fingers more; this was taking an extraordinarily long time. I frowned, thinking.

Energy. Ghosts had to have that energy to even exist; the angel's tethered to a human Priest for that energy, just like the demons would to an outlet soul, like me, a source as a demon. The large demon had plenty of energy as a loose, somewhat collected being. Parts were able to fall off and regenerate in no time, like my wings did, like my head had that one time. The Colus was a being of energy; how I was able to power the others, that was established- so it only made sense that as a weapon, as a much smaller, collected, solid thing, that energy was only intensified. If energy was the driving force, if it was the link to this world, that also made the Colus a being of healing, as well. My eyes popped open.

"Oh!" I said in great realization, holding my hand out for the Colus to join again, forming that colossal paddle weapon once more. Raziel's broken body practically jumped to attention, to worry.

"Hey, I've had enough of that today. I don't even want to think about touching that thing ever again." I ignored him, setting the weapon on the ground with one hand braced against it, concentrating on how to get this to work on a tolerable level. "Neri? You're doing that thing where you're fiddling with something I don't know and not responding and it's a little unnerving." I cracked a quick smile.

"The Colus is a spirit of energy, what others call an outlet, one that's able to power those around it as a sort of mini base. Like a whole busload of available Priests can attach a busload of angels, except the Colus is that bus. You were right, it's just energy. A lot of it. And if a spirit needs this energy, then an excess of it should provide enough to heal." I grabbed hold of the weapon's handle with my right hand, left hand poised like an instrument of death, held out and away. "I think it'll work. You should be able to heal fine on your own, but I'm not sure how long that'll take. That, and since I'm actually mentally in control this time, I'm asking your permission and not just grabbing at your head like a loon."

Raziel continued to furrow his eyebrows at me, nodding and

shrugging a little as I finished. I continued to stare at him, waiting for actual words and not grunts and whistles. We'd moved past that. Sighing, he gave a more definitive answer.

"Yes, fine, you have my permission. Just don't kill me."

"I'll try not to" I lowered my hand slowly to his hand, hovering just over the two fingers that were actually there, two still missing. Delicately, daintily, my finger skimmed on just the top of it as it sparked, jolting him. The bones for the other two fingers were suddenly there, nasty whitish things as both our eyes jumped in surprised. It worked!

"Does it hurt?" I asked, retching a little as the nasty whitish bones twitched on their own.

"It doesn't feel good."

Slipping in a quick grin I touched the hand again, muscle stretching immediately over it, and with three more little jolts, the hand was good as new. Raziel sort of gasped at it, stretching the hand out, flexing it; it even looked like the rest of his body had started to heal as well just with those bits. "Ready to go for broke?" I questioned with a bit of a snicker, spinning the weapon in my hand a little and readjusting on the grip.

"I love broke." Raziel looked uncertainly between the weapon and me, closing his eyes tightly. "Do it!" Without another second to reconsider, to think this dangerous decision over like responsible people do I grabbed onto his forehead, shock transferring through me, diffusing the full charge. His head instantly tried pulling away teeth gritting together; I couldn't imagine how it felt, but it worked. His other arm was forming back in record time, muscle and bone forming and healing, racing to the end. I held on, despite that it was pretty much pulling the energy from me, that it was painful to him and me at the same time; but it was working. Soon the other hand was completely healed; just in time to wretch back and express the pain he was in. Looking down to his legs, it was almost healed to his feet, deep chunks of his chest filling in and zipping back to regular skin. Raziel shuffled his legs back and forth, toes almost there, almost done.

"Not yet, wings too!" He shouted, leaning forward, both hands grabbing on the tree roots face and eyes still closed. Taking another quick breath I held on as those weird little chicken wings, stumps on his back suddenly sprouted, fluffing back out to the classic Raziel I knew, the small, flightless things. After another second holding on, they jumped to the ones he had recently, the bigger ones. Out of curiosity, I strained, holding on a little longer, knees beginning to buckle; the wings were growing, still, spreading out a little farther as they suddenly jumped to something bigger, beautiful and fancy. What the…

"That's enough!" He yelled, but I was too distracted to register it. Something opened above his head, a whitish circle, a halo. The circle started tiny like a halo yamaka, growing and adding rings instantly, growing brighter, more diverse with thicker and thinner rings. It was dazzling; terrifyingly dazzling. Suddenly the halo pulsed, flashing brighter then the sun, blinding and charging at me, smacking me away. Like a great wall of light the force detached us, sending me head over heels once, landing on my butt, world blacked out, weapon torn from my grip as I lay there, dazed. I couldn't see, couldn't hear anything, panting for breath.

After a few confused moments of utter silence something jabbed at my forehead, grabbed at my horns; prodded my face quizzically. Swiping a hand out in front of me I found something, grabbing onto it, mushing it around. Another hand. Grasping it in a handshake I pulled it closer, pinching the forearm it belonged to; Raziel. I used the other hand to wave ahead of it, above it, finding his face by accidentally jamming my fingers in his eyes; there was another hand in the way for a moment as the handshake tried to pull away; I kept my grip, finding the top of his head, then swiping above it. Nothing. All the while my hearing and vision was returning slowly, worn down with the massive energy pumped into the angel to speed up his healing. Annoyed with only seeing vague shadows and hearing what sounded like bubbling water, I called the Colus back to my hand, vision and hearing popping back in a startling rush as it healed me. Letting go of Raziel's hand he stood over me, bending his knees enthusiastically, same as he had always been, no larger wings, no blindingly bright halo. Giving the Colus a light toss, the weapon unraveled into a mess of black strings before disappearing as I coughed and gagged in surprise.

"You know, I think I broke my nose some time back, and it fixed that too." He was strutting about excitedly, full of energy, bouncing on new limbs. "Fixed everything!" He held his arms over his head, wings extended, obviously in a good mood. Heaving for breath I remained on the ground, giving a slight smile and nod before focusing back on healing up for myself.

"The halo, the wings…what was that?" I gasped, not recovering so fast. Even my energy reserves were pretty exhausted on all aspects. The angel finally noticed this, stopping his grand prancing as I didn't just pop right to my feet, giddy and happy; the process seemed to work really well, but it was Hell on your body, took twice the amount of energy to heal half the area. It was like I had just resurrected two or three people.

"They were my originals." He said, a little saddened but still giddy with healing goodness. I closed one eye, trying to recant the first conversation, where he had called it 'being clipped and booted'. "You healed past what I'm allowed to have. They fell off as soon as you let go." He dropped one long, massively white feather just in front of me, at least three feet long.

"They were incredible." I said tiredly, sitting back on my bottom and holding the one feather up, running it past my fingers, the area was scattered with them. I felt like slumping into a nap, right here where I sat. "What about the halo?"

"Oh, that annoying thing just pops up every now and then. It's supposed to help protect, like a security alarm of some sort, but honestly I think it's just for show. Probably popped up because of the energy surge." He laughed it off; wiggling his toes like it was commonplace, no big deal, "Man, even my ankles don't hurt anymore."

My head slowly rose, squinting one eye at the peculiar angel, the strangely opposed, cursing angel that once wanted my head for a mantel piece, that used to step on my nose, throw water in my face at any chance, that ran away with a practically unknown demon instead of staying with a pain in the ass boss he once taught. Of the exorcist who was doing this to fulfill a past-life need to help others, who through corruption, through hardship, crappy job after crappy job, managed to be a good guy, true to his word. I just kept staring at him, shaking my head more and more before openly laughing, lungs pumping. Raziel stopped, a little confused.

"You…. You're a complex guy, aren't you?" I spit out awkwardly as he suddenly grinned, offering a hand and pulling me to my feet.

"I think I pale in comparison, body snatcher." We both walked towards the tree, reminiscent of hundreds of years ago.

"It's not snatching if they're all mine. It's more like soul-hoarding." I said stubbornly, legs practically crumpling beneath me as I leaned back against the tree; instantly my horns and spines stopped me, forcing me to sort of side up next to it, prop my head against it instead of laying back.

The sun peeked through the leaves overhead; vaguely looking to the path he had torn though the brush, shaking my head a little more. What a day. What a weird world I existed in. We both sat in silence, enjoying the peace we knew wouldn't last. My eyes were half-open, looking through the bottoms of my eyelids with a short smile.

"I think it's your turn to tell a story." I said softly, body half-asleep and trying to recuperate. The white feathers rustled as he turned slightly towards me, guffawing.

"Why, you're out of stories to tell?"

"All my stories end with my own horrible, untimely death, they're not really pick-me-ups."

"Oh. Uh, I'm not much of a storyteller."

"Well, don't Hansel and Gretel me to death then, tell it how it was."

"Hm, well." He twitched a little, trying to figure a way to start the story. "After all…that from before, I woke up in a field, like a white wheat field. There's no real transition, no long dark tunnel that's just not true. It's like you step from one half to the other, and you're just kinda there. There's people waking near me, crying, freaking out; they all kind of stop when you get the chance to look around. There's nothing really on the horizon, no giant fluffy clouds, it's all just white."

"Pine scented?" I mumbled.

"Pine what?" He stopped, turning back and squinting for a second. "Slanted?"

"Never mind, I'm being silly, continue on."

Raziel hesitated before leaning back and pointing at nothing, reliving his memory.

"So you finally see this thing, even whiter, farther off. It's the only thing around, like a giant city of some sort. You start walking, finding more and more people popping up around you, it's kinda creepy. It starts dawning on you how very dead you are, how you've left everyone behind. Someone greets you at the entrance, leads each and every person down a long road with little shops, homes, that sort all around and they give you the information you need. They don't bug you for a week, let you get settled in." You could tell he was getting bored with his story already, growing tired of it.

"Which life was it for you? You said you've been doing this for nearly 400 years, so I take it you haven't jumped back into the life-pool recently, have you?" Raziel turned to me as I passively expressed that I knew more about this then I let on, that I had been learning.

"That was my second life. No, I haven't gone back." He scratched his head nervously, "The first life I lived was… a really long time ago, I don't remember much of it. Just that I was married when I got out of it; we both died together somehow, so we didn't lose one another on the way up, and decided that we'd stick together for comfort's sake." The angel laughed.

"Because, let's face it, marriage after death's kinda pointless." He signaled generally around his hips as my eyes popped open, glaring at him. I shook my head.

"You must be fighting them off with a bat." I grumbled, " Continue on."

"So that all kinda fell through. She got mixed in with demons or something, got kicked out. I was practicing to be a guardian of sorts, and they gave me the ultimatum of either living another life as a do-over, or getting my wings clipped and keeping me on the short route. I wasn't terribly far in my training, I hadn't really gotten anywhere, so I chose another life." He turned over his shoulder to look at me, squinting, "What do you mean, fighting them off with a bat?"

I feigned sleeping before cackling softly. "So that life was the one in the 1630's, then."

"Yeah…" He leaned away, sitting back against the tree once more, "When I was done with that I went back to trying to be an exorcist this time from when I was roughly 10ish to when I was roughly 16 ish. Graduated at the top of my class, got right to work, did a great job at it, they even let me start teaching some of the classes; take a few apprentices at a time. They boosted me through the lower ranking demons, until a point I was able to handle some nasty stuff. Worse than you!"

My eyes snapped open, glancing to him with a grumble.

"You get what I mean."

"What happened, then?" I said shortly, shifting a little more to rest.

"My wife apparently did something horrible, even though we hadn't spoken in such a long time, and I had no idea where she was, they pulled me into the mess, ruined all the good effort and work I had done, and took everything from me with barely an explanation. I still don't really know what I've done." You could hear his voice tensing up, "They acted like it was out of mercy, that I should be grateful for them only ruining me, and everything I had worked for. But I was stupid, figured I could work back up to that level, worked to get better, but it never improved. They pretty much shut me out and I kinda gave up, stopped giving a damn. I mean, they had me exorcising family pets, for God's sake! That's the crap they had me doing, after a point where given the chance, I could probably take down a cherub on my own." Raziel turned to me, eyes wild and angry.

"Even this round, I got some duties back, but they were different and unrelated. Even those weren't all that above basic training."

"So you get this call for an annoying demon in a house by a graveyard." I tried to re-direct his attention as the anger fell away, corking up an eyebrow and falling back to the tree.

"Figure it sounds like a challenge, sounds like actual fun. I didn't put a lot of faith into the report being real, people over-embellish their stories so much that anything that's 'ten feet all' is usually around 2 ft tall. But I hoped it was something tough, that if I manage to exorcise it, I can get a little recognition back." His tone rose enough to tell he was smiling.

"But the thing proves to be a pain in the ass and acts completely strange, and it's left me questioning if I've even got the ability to fight something bigger than a Labrador anymore, so I reluctantly try to push it off on my boss after the thing just won't die. He goes on and thinks it's a nice woman, forcing me to pretend she's my assistant, while the whole time I'm going 'oh shit, oh shit, oh shit this has gotten way out of hand'." He and I were both laughing, relaxed and finally open with one another. I sat more upright.

"And here we are" I said, settling down; our laughing suddenly began to echo around us, another source. He and I both stopped as we heard it, the other voice doing a sort of half-laugh before shutting up as well. There was something else here. I rubbed the bridge of my nose; why was it that just as everything was going fine, that everything was well that we'd have a visitor. Something to bust up the party. "Maybe if we just keep laughing, we can ignore it and it'll go away." I said flatly as the voice suddenly gave an over-indulgent HA on its own; I could hear something big moving through the forest, a familiar toothy, pointy necked face soon broke the line of trees. Cempe. Again. I growled, even in my human form.

"Keep going! What an enthralling pair of storytellers you are, I'm learning so much!" She said sarcastically as I saw the side of Raziel suddenly jump up against the tree, stuck to it. She pushed her massive head through the last bit of brush, standing roughly the same size I had graduated to; I knew she could go bigger. More parts of my brain were flashing her as a familiar face, while the old bits of my soul were still hanging onto that previous hatred, that disgust.

"Not you again." His head leaned slightly in my direction, "Cente, right?"

"See-em-pay. Cempe." I corrected, getting to my feet, paddle weapon already in hand. "What do you want, Cempe?" The beast suddenly sat down, hand outstretched my way.

"Well, look at you!" She grinned, delicately pinching my one arm to bring it out to the side as my glare never changed, "We're finally starting to look more like yourself, not some weak little human analog fakie you were doing earlier." My eyebrows rose up, smacking her hand away with the Colus.

"Starting to?" Raziel said behind me, confused and a little shocked. "There's more?" I turned my head a little towards him, shrugging in disbelief.

"I think I'm edition two of three, to be honest." His face suddenly went wide bug-eyed, shifting farther away from me as I found Cempe making faces at him, flashing her teeth and leaning from over my shoulder. With a human hand to her face I pushed it away, bracing the weapon like I intended to fight her like this. "Why don't you just cut the shit, Cempe, talk to me one on one and stop scaring the people that have already had to suffer through your undivided love." I was acting on instinct, not entirely knowing what I was talking about, but if she had said before that we were the same type of demon, the she too must have a human form.

"Do you see the way she talks to me?" Cempe laughed, trying to reason with the angel for a second, eyes snapping back to me quickly. "You sure that's a wise idea?"

"I've got nothing to hide." I said tersely as the demon only laughed once, loud, snorting back to a normalcy as my eyes got a little wider, reconsidering, "Nothing I knowingly know I have to hide."

"That's better." Cempe pointed a clawed hand over my shoulder, "Tell anyone about this and I'll kill you seven ways before you breathe a word after 'Cempe', got it?" Raziel moved from where he stood.

"Who am I going to tell?" He shouted back, taking a few steps more behind me then out in the open as Cempe began to melt, similar smoke falling away from the beast. She dwindled down to my size, my height, black smoke wafting away with the wind to reveal her human form. Roughly my size in most regards, except for the same lengthy horn still on her head, this time sticking out from her left temple, just above her ear. It was a tall, notched thing, tick-marks all up and down it; her face was older than mine but not by much, nose-ring accompanying her face, lower bit of her ear lobes stretched and distended, marked up and pierced in various places. She was dressed in a sort of formal attire, a mix of strange fashions and half-armor, useful and useless.

I shuffled away from her as she stood there almost proudly, entire body covered in tick marks, horns jutting from each wrist and ankle, face held in a grin. Her hair was short, black-ish brown, spiked up and a bit to the side in a faux-hawk, two dots below each eye, and tick marks running down her forehead and her nose, across her lips. We both glared at her. The air of supreme arrogance let up slightly as the moments passed.

"Well, don't all jump and say something at the same time now." She took a step towards me as I took one back, hand still braced on the weapon, terrified. We didn't look that different. We looked like relatives. Family. The demon suddenly grabbed my one horn, rattling around my head, "When is this annoying game going to be done with?! Tell me, oh brilliant mastermind!" She glared straight in my eyes squinting, trying to define something in them that just wasn't there.

"Are you two related?" Raziel spoke up behind me, cuing into the same sort of weird circumstances. Cempe let my head go, spinning me around to buddy up next to me, arm around my neck as I acted more like a doll than a person.

"Why, can you tell who got our mother's chin?" She tilted my head slightly off to the side, eyes still wide in shock. She let go, bringing up her fingers to quote, "'Neri' here got more of our father's brutish strength. Everyone can still tell we're still sisters though."

"Sisters?!" My trance finally snapped as I pushed her away, scrambling like Cempe herself was made of death. Raziel repeated it somewhere behind me, both of us in a state of shock. "This is news to me too; we're nothing alike!" I threw whatever obstacle in the way, whatever notion I could use to slow her down. We were exactly alike; I knew it. But saying out loud, I tried to think otherwise. Cempe only leaned back against the tree.

"'Nothing ali-' Who are you trying to kid? You're better at killing the masses off than I am, I'll give you that. But I'm good at what I do." She looked up, eyes cold, "Neri's better at making convoluted, annoying plans of death and rebirth. Gets fixated on something she can't fix, never lets it go. She's got you all wrapped up in this one, Christopher." I could feel Raziel's glare shift quickly to me as my ears shot for the floor.

"The comradery, the result, it's all planned thanks to ol' Neri here." Cempe's grin split wide, watching me squirm. "Christopher's a nobody' she mewls, 'maybe if you leave me some brainless idiot he'll feel sorry for me and I can help.'" She took a couple slow steps away as Raziel was looking constantly to and away from me as I froze like a deer in headlights.

"And if he gets too close or something goes wrong, I give you permission to fix it. Kill him. Snap him in half or something, whatever.'" She stopped walking, giving as heartless and as black of a stare as she can, arms out to her sides. "Boy it's nice to be honest with each other, isn't it?"

"Hey, well, anyways, water under the bridge, right? There's an armada of cherubs on the way. Obviously that's your problem, not mine." Cempe made a pantomime of ripping a sheet of paper in half, like a torn contract fell at her feet. "I'm free of this. Done. Fix your own mistakes from here on out."

I could feel the hair stand up on my arms, so far beyond miserable and sick and angry all at once as Cempe began to leave, taking steps backwards like stairs were embedded into the ground, back to Hell.

Turning to look at Raziel for a moment, he looked furious. This time, he didn't bother to look at me, just gave a fed up, frustrated stare that I was terrified to break into the conversation.

"OH! Jeez, I nearly forgot!" Cempe's head rose above the dirt, rolling her hand like she forgot something minute. "Neri's a demon queen and she's known it since day one." Giving another genuine smile to absolutely ruin everything I had, she gave a wink.

"I thought that was a term of endearment!" I sputtered like a pathetic childish liar.

"Oh. It's not. See you on the other side!" Job completed, she slipped into the earth.

The wind spoke only of dried flowers.

31

"So." Raziel started, verging on utter terror. My head snapped around to him, bewildered. Well, now I had absolutely nothing to hide in any sense of that word. I wanted to figure this all out on my own, wanted to make sure what was true and what wasn't before coming forward with this information. Breaking that trust, that flimsy, finally established open trust, it looked bad. Really bad. Felt awful too. "Gonna try to be… you know… understanding this, best I can. Feels like I swallowed glass but, uh, sure what's your side of this?"

"Raziel, I'm… she's… I don't know. We can figure this out later." I relented, jumping into the demon form. "We gotta leave, right now."

"You're the uh…'Demon queen'?" You could hear him getting angry that my answers were not the apologetic type. I held a hand out to him as he kept his arms crossed tightly, eyebrows quickly falling down his face as I was far more interested in leaving and not dying than explaining myself. The cherub's cry could be heard in the distance, they weren't far at all now- out seeped an uneasy whine. Rushed and panicked, I spit out the best that could explain the situation.

"You know more than I do at this point!" Flustered, my eyes were stuck to the skies as it was far easier to look there than face the truth fuming in front of me.

"You could've told me!" Shaking, I kept my head up, looking for cherubs before an errant thought struck me that avoiding my problems got me in this situation in the first place. I bit my lip and looked down. Raziel was beyond furious, but more than anything he just looked worried.

"I started this life in shackles. I had to escape from Hell, a 'demon queen' doesn't make any Goddamn sense!" Shaking my head, I came up with as many excuses I could fill my mouth with. "I didn't want you to get in trouble knowing that…" Stopping, I bit my lip harder to break myself

371

from lying all the goddamn time.

Breathing hard for a couple seconds, I spat it out.

"I was scared. I heard her say it, figured she was lying, plugged my fingers in my ears and hoped for the best." Looking Raziel dead in the eyes as I said it, he lingered before his eyes darted away, disgusted.

"Is screwing with my life some sort of game to you?" I watched those angry eyes dart around for an answer, for something honest to latch onto in a torrent of chaos. Watched as they tried to define something that still wasn't there. I buckled.

"It might be true. I don't know." My breath remained short, shaking and afraid. It was tiny and confused in this massive, dinosaur-like body as I huddled near the ground, shrilling of birds slightly louder then before. "I really hope it isn't. But today's been pretty eye-opening and yeah, I wouldn't be surprised if the 'demon queen' is really that bad." I felt broken, shaking and ashamed the same way I had been before his return, before I had gotten kicked out. Silence.

A voice sneered behind me, head still just poking out of the dirt.

"You should really apologize to the boy." Cempe said, arms folding and watching this all unravel like a nasty little spy behind me, popped out of the ground up to her waist. Gritting my teeth I kicked her square in the face, her head knocking back with a laugh as she zipped back underneath the soil like it was no big deal. I snarled at her escape before realizing the words were terribly good advice.

"I am sorry. For what that's worth." I spit out. I jumped a little as something was already climbing up my one arm, trying to get to my back.

"Just go." He said flatly, grabbing onto the hair along my spine, reluctant and despondent. We could work it out later, figure things out, but for now you didn't have to tell me twice to leave. I noticed the ominous shadow above us, wingtips shading across the clearing, dripping onto the trees as it grew in size. Three of the five cherubs suddenly spotted us in the small clearance of brush, screeching out their find. Feet splayed out wide I watched with a wary eye like petrified prey as that shadow covered the entire clearing, sun and light gone. Wham! One hit the ground just beside me as I churned, twisted from the attack to take to the sky.

We erupted from the brush, exploding from the forest as my lumbering tail scraped off a few little trees behind me, tumbling across traffic on the first road we passed, in the middle of some town. Flapping fast as I could I shot away from there, low to the ground, wingtips dragging on the asphalt as it came around. Two of the cherubs dove after me at the same height, claws outstretched. I banked left and right, evading them as they hit the ground, quick to follow as I pivoted upwards, aiming for the clouds. There may not be another time to try and talk this out; these cherubs were devoutly fast, all bearing the same white, four winged bodies as the first one did, sporting different compilations of bird heads, slight variance. This wasn't going to end well, I could take one cherub head on, but five, it was the bloodbath I originally promised. Taking my eye off from where I was going, I turned my head enough to see him still sitting there, holding on tightly.

With a piercing scream another dropped from the sky, landing directly on my right wing and throwing me off course, claws ripping out feathers. With a surge in stamina I shoved towards it, knocking the bird away, struggling to keep altitude; I switched to a dive, giving my body time to heal. There was a team of Cherub heads right behind us, flapping into the dive; I hissed at them, facing back towards the front and opening up my healed wings, banking sharply, ground roaring beneath us. Arching my back I flapped faster, straining, pushing myself to tear and swing around, doubling back. They saw it coming; charging almost sideways to meet the two of us, closing the gap. Hissing out in anger I swung my tail around, wings shaking, throwing my body to switch directions yet again, back on the escape.

Focusing back in front of me, focusing on trying to get away, I flapped to my body's limit, pushing until the lines began to blur again as life began to pull and sway. I shot towards the sun.

It was a beautiful day, streaming clouds drifting like islands in the sun as they pulled against the earth, changing, never the same minute to minute. Just I as I was about to skip across the sky, make real progress in our escape, as things were starting to look up, it hit. The cherub's claws sunk into my head, latching onto both jaw horns and diving towards the ground, spinning me around. My face looked to the ground, chin to the sky. My body spasmed, spinning and throwing itself out of rhythm as limbs went everywhere; more cherubs latched onto me, pulling, ripping, cutting me down. Thrashing around, I tried to fight back as my head hung there, pierced through by the cherub's talons. In my short-sightedness, in my selfish thoughts of my own survival, I saw Raziel in the claws of the farthest cherub, soaring away, heading for the sky. That's when I saw I had lost.

Do not let up with a fight! My brain was screaming at me, pushing me on. It is never done, never finished, never this simple, fight!

All other cherubs pulled away, leaving the lone attacker still perched to my skull. Rumbling from deep within I flapped my wings, twisting my head in its grip, pulling harder still. Soon the bird began to twist as well, flying skewed, claws tugging, dragging across my skin and loosing grip. Screeching, over and over I kept at it, fighting back until my head suddenly popped free from its wicked claws, blood dripping alongside my face as I fought for control, to keep my promise to fix everything. There, above me, the flock of cherubs dwindled in size as I lost sight on which held the angel. I only tried harder to follow; my broken wings slowly stabilized me, slowly fixed themselves, slowly coming back into play.

Something struck me again, punching me towards the ground just as I started to recover. Same cherub, same game; this one must've been left behind to keep me away, to keep my attention down and around here, with a little luck kill me off to where I was no longer a problem.

"Really starting to hate you guys." I wheezed out, exasperated as the cherub's claws went for my wings this time. What was I doing? What part of me actually through that I'd get away from five cherubs? I arched my back, reaching, trying to grab it and fight back, missing, fatiguing. With one last look to the sky, Raziel was all but a dot, now. I had lost. My wings began to flap slower as the cherub dug into my back, ripping apart my skin, picking at the wings an all bones around it.

"Pathetic!" Part of me suddenly screamed in an outer conscious tone that I never heard before. It kicked me out of the driver's seat of this body rather violently, pushing me aside. I tried to move a hand, tried to turn and look somewhere, head fixed, moved by another. I was a passenger, all over again, trapped inside my own body.

In its control, my body suddenly flew on its own, bucking, thrashing, fighting the cherub on our back. My head craned back, ripping into the belly-lining of the bird, prying the claws apart and out of its grasp as I was quick on my stomach, facing straight up. The cherub screeched out in confusion as my head lunged, teeth sinking deep into the throat of the bird, ripping it apart with a merciless scream. With a few rotating flaps I broke its neck, tossing the carcass back to the earth unwittingly chasing right below us. My body crashed into the ground, bouncing from the bird and tumbling through the street, taking out signs, lights, poles and knocked out the wall to a restaurant in the process.

As I was still internally getting my thoughts back together from the crash, I found myself already back in the sky, wings flopping past their points, broken and disabled. I was using them anyways. The pilot was lining more accurately towards the group of cherubs, dust on the horizon, flapping harder, gaining speed with little nuances that I hadn't learned. The distance began to close, the dots began to reappear. Internally, I sat back, trying to find the reason, feeling around gingerly, searching all consciousness for the answer. With the rest of my mind lit in regular business florescent lighting, with everything defined perfectly, able to scan over the other factions of my brain, the past, the various present-es, there was darkness. Shadow. In those shadows, in that unopened, closed off half, someone was working furiously, flying that demon. It wasn't me.

Knocking back to reality, I could see them now, all five of the cherubs heading straight away from the ground, flying directly up into nothing. As we got closer, as we could practically see the angel once more, the cherubs began to evaporate, began to disappear from the area, to fade away with their cargo in hand, ascending.

"No you don't!" My pilot said, the dark-lit sections speaking, again.

I knew that voice!

"You!" I spoke internally as my wings began to fade away, as I began to fade with the rest of them, chasing them into whatever realm we were headed to. The voice ignored me as I struggled to reason it all- this thing, it wasn't someone else, it couldn't be; that left one frustratingly obvious option. "Are you my future soul?" It didn't say anything, but I noticed I was flapping just a little slower, a little more confused. Just like that, it disappeared, not only did the light remain off, but the whole wall closed down, unable to sense anything. Pointing straight up, half translucent; my body was suddenly mine again. My wings tore from my back, arms began disintegrating as the darkness of my presence was getting stripped away, as legs and spine-hair fell away in chunks, falling behind me. With the Colus stripped away to my bare human soul, I headed into that nothingness; skin and bones of this form disappearing into that great, proverbial white light of the afterlife; Heaven.

"Move it!" Something shook me indignantly, back and forth, back and forth. Sputtering, coughing for air, my body slowly stirred under my own control, slowly waking up in what I thought would be white wheat fields and great grand glory. I saw darkness. Dingy, terrible, prison-y darkness, there was a winged figure standing above me. Confused, I tried to see his face.

"R-Raziel?" I coughed again, only to get a swift jolt in the back of the head, struck. I lifted my arms to shield my head from it, finding my hands tied behind my back, feet bound together. Instantly, I went on the sarcastic defensive; I'd played this game before. "I take it you're not Raziel." You could hear his angel getting annoyed, fed up as I only tried to curl tighter into a ball, to protect myself. Where the Hell was I, exactly?

"Demon Nona, I order you to get up!" He called again as my eyes snapped wide open, brain on all sorts of alarms.

"What did you call me?" A joke- it had to be a joke, a prank. Like a frustrated little snake I writhed around, trying to get a better glance of what this all was. Nona? I wasn't Nona. I could take a lot of blame, a lot of criticism and the brunt of most damage, but I was not hopping on that train. "Where am I?" Switching sides, I could see the entrance, now. Half a story up there was a barred gate, I myself was squirming in a sort of dirt pit at the bottom of it. Even from down here, face to the ground, I could tell there were other people up there, watching me, looking down and gawking with a stupid sense of…I don't know, mischief and fascination. Like a zoo exhibit. And even from here, you could see that sort of ultra-white light, that Heavenly glow. I'd made it alright, I wasn't on earth, but I'd gotten my ass captured so fast that I wasn't conscious to enjoy it.

"Demon Nona, get up!" The guardian angel of sorts bashed me again with the wooden stick, aiming for my head this time. Eyes darting to where he stood I brought down my tied feet, jabbing him with the dark blackish nails I was growing to love; I drew blood. In valid response he drew a lot more, striking me over and over, knocking my senses loose enough to forget for a moment they were trying to charge me with grossly mistaken crimes. The angel finally let up, keeping the pole to just behind my head, pressing hard. "Now, Get up."

Coughing, bloodied, I gasped for air.

"You're impeding that process." I slurred, in no real mood to cooperate. Over and over through my head I kept up the same words- oh Hell no. I was not going to be that scapegoat this time- I'd play along with lesser issues, but this? This fragrant diaper of trouble? No, Hell no. With persistent determination and quickly growing used to the random pointless attacks from my guardian here; I got to my feet, face against the wall.

"Demon Nona's ready for transport." The one angel called to the other, his face a leaner variety with a nasty scowl to it, eyebrows like terrible unwaxed Greek legs. He was the taller variety, looked like he pushed around a lot of people in his day, the angriest, burliest angel they could find, just for me. That had to be why they thought I was Nona, up here like this, unchanged. Demon-y as ever, I was up in Heaven, no doubt about it, amongst the angels still. Palug had mentioned about this Nona-person being able to walk both Heaven and Hell. That had to be it. Please, that had to be it.

With two other angels joining me they pushed me up the stairs, these tiny, thinner then my foot, stairs and out of this little cage. From there I only managed to get a vague grasp of exactly where I was; in that town that Raziel had described, I was somewhere along the side of it, near a wall. There was a tiny outside window that I gawked at while I could, a break from the people lining the hallways as I passed, whispering, glaring at me, shouting less then Heavenly polite things. It was a spire of some sort, a dungeon and probably the grimiest place in the wide world of Heaven by far. After shoving me down embarrassing corridor after corridor, prancing me around like a tragic trick pony, I was led into a small room, small enough that I couldn't stand up straight in it. After twenty minutes of isolation and boredom, a person entered; wingless, arms on him like ripened hams. I could tell this wouldn't end well.

"We've been waiting a long time for this, Nona." The...detective, I guess you could call him, started, already with a bad taste in my mouth. "Many, many, many years for this day; and you bring yourself to us. It's almost sweet of you. Got a lot of people up here in a panic, not often we get visits from demons."

"Like that gives you probable cause to charge me with her crimes." I said curtly, ears going back. The angel paused; looking around for a moment before continuing on like nothing was said at all.

"If you'd like, we can just talk about these recent charges, if you're looking to keep your waiting time short." I tucked my head a little lower against the wall. "Or we can talk about what you've done to our good friend Raziel."

"I haven't done anything to him." I hissed out, lip curling back.

"But you have spent the last year and a half filling his head with lies and corrupting him, haven't you?" The detective almost laughed, ignoring my comments; there had to be an agenda to this. "Why do you both think you have to be mean to corrupt someone?" He laughed harder, throwing the file onto the table, stuffed with papers and reports. I squinted, unsure.

"How do you think angels were tempted to fall in the past?" He flipped the top of the file up a bit, looking at the contents for a moment before staring me dead in the eye, "I mean, barring the demonic royalty angle, this is the most cut and dry case I've seen all day."

"I haven't done anything to him!" I shouted louder, panicked. It couldn't be so simple. I wasn't trying to corrupt anyone, I was just... I was just trying to...

"We wouldn't be having this conversation if that was true." He leaned closer, sneering. "'Excelsis' Nona." It felt like the wind was kicked from me.

I stuttered for some retort, struggling; the angel cut me off, chuckling as he walked about the room. His eyes were filled with a disgust and hatred, a sick, viscous distaste for everything that I was.

"The way I see it, prior to your insidious abduction of his duties, he was one of the best. After you latched onto his soul like a blood-lusting tick, he's suddenly in the same predicament you are a few rooms over." He flipped his papers around noisily, dramatic as the rest of them. "Only seems to be one factor in that change, and that's you."

I kept my eyes tight on the man, remaining silent. I knew better. Raziel was the one to say how they'd been keeping him at this bottom grade level for so long, the slanderous mix of lies and half-truths to spin this story best they could. I kept quiet.

"You know, I had a great grandfather up here who used to talk of you, of your last great attack on us all. How you nearly tore apart Heaven and only succeeding in taking one particular, unfortunate man's soul. You like to keep things consistent, don't you?" My head rose just a bit, confused. Someone else? "Thankfully, I don't think we've seen you since. Raziel gave a rather detailed report on you some months back after your exploits with Decima, but I've heard you found another group and kept our Cherubs busy down below, gearing up for another little get-together, are we?"

My soul was starting to panic; there was far too much accurate information at hand here for it all to be bullshit, for it all just to be circumstantial. But no, Palug had said 15 years, I'd only be around for about four and a half, now. It wasn't adding up.

"Silly of me to ask, but there wouldn't happen to be a chance of you telling us where this next party of yours is going to be?" I snarled, snapping to refusal quickly.

"Not a chance."

"I figured." The man only smiled back as I was joined by two more people; my guard from before and his burliest best friend. "You're younger then any of us really realized. Then again, not surprised that you're the best they've got, some inept teenager, stepping around carefully and hoping everyone doesn't realize what an incompetent idiot you are. I gotta say, this all makes a lot more sense now." He folded his thin, pointless file as the detective stood up to leave.

"Your execution is planned alongside Raziel's little ceremony tomorrow morning, figured it was only appropriate. We're practically advertising for it now, lots of interest in residents seeing our annoying demonic visitor, much less the great execution of the great 'Excelsis Nona.'"

"What if I'm not her?" I held down as much fear as I could, trying hard to not crack under stress. The man's hand was on the door.

"Well, we've got tabs on your sister Decima, and Aisa is the only one of the three that knows better than to stupidly hand herself over like this. Doesn't leave a lot of names on the list, Nona." The man smirked with supreme satisfaction; my bones slid into my toes as he closed the door, numbing myself off.

After a ridiculously brutal round of one-sided interrogation; they assaulted and cut off my horns to jagged nubs only a few inches long. They didn't grow back. Each angel took one as a souvenir, gave a few more punches, and let me rest. I told them nothing, only curling up into myself, mentally tormented with questions that I didn't bother feeling anything for anymore. They tossed me back to the holding cell where I fell to the bottom, bones, cuts and bruises quickly healing, Left me with a lot of time that night, a lot of ambling, strange, confused thoughts. Why was I here? Why was I even allowed to be here? Why was every one trying to pin me as some grand demon leader? I wasn't good with the others, I mean, I tried to be and wound up screwing us over worse. Some big, impressive demon; I wasn't impressive. I was willowy, ill-tempered from time to time, I regretted enough to cloud my judgment and made selfish decision after selfish decision; these were all terrible characteristics in a person, worse for a leader. But that figure. That...expert flier from earlier, that thing. It'd been there all along; like a nasty little parasite leeching onto my life, it'd been there, hiding like a sadistic little joke.

"Was that you, Nona?" I asked aloud, chewing on the insides of my cheek nervously. "You what they're after? Have fun squatting in my head all this time, you royal pain in the ass?" My head bent low with a slow side to side motion, scraping my jagged horns against the wall in frustration.

"You frustrating waste of time, you spineless piece of shit! Take responsibility for what you've done!" I suddenly belted out, smacking my head hard against the wall. It wasn't enough; there were no sounds, no responses, even though I knew full well that side heard me, that it knew of what I was saying. The side remained stubbornly closed off, in hiding. All this time, when I had been figuring on being some lone soul, some one part of three, I was almost already whole. With the addition of the past soul… I kicked the rocks in front of me out of frustration, pounding my feet against the ground like a spoiled child. No one votes for a leader throwing a tantrum.

The rest of the night was spent in silence, head bent low, mourning whatever part of me was still trying to hold together what the other part was so determined to screw up.

It was early morning when I was pulled to my feet, half hunched over my knees, distraught and unwound. I didn't bother looking to them when they kicked me around for good measure, didn't listen to the words they said rallied for my head on a pike, leading me down to the outside world. It was built in white, streets littered with people; some angels, some regular folk. Everything was tuned out, volume muted, shut off from what was happening; it looked like a parade. People clung to whatever edge of curb they could find that lined my execution route, children gathered in packs, parents in groups. There was a distinct bunch that followed me as I was led, hands cuffed behind my back like I was heading off to jail with my two burly guards making sure I didn't get out of line. The sky was white, the buildings were hues of white, and the ground was barely gray. Any other time and any other circumstances, I would've enjoyed what I was seeing, that I was getting my vision of Heaven, right here.

I couldn't feel anything anymore. I hadn't slept, bound and tied the entire time, left to my thoughts and only my thoughts. At the end I was no better than the beginning, only confusing myself more, only running in circles and tormenting myself. I hated this. I hated me. I hated…that.

If this was all true, then I hated her most of all.

My parade route pointed to the middle of the town, to a giant Stonehenge-like group of rocks all centered on a middle altar. In there dual fires burned, one red, one blue. No guesses on who got which. Just as I pulled away from the crowds, as I emerged to take my punishment that Raziel, being led in much the same fashion, made his appearance from an adjoining road, with his own guard in tow. He looked about the same, completely worn down, exhausted, but noticeably more bruised, more battered; whatever healing effect my blood had, whatever I had done, wore off. His eyes rose to meet mine as our paths went side by side, slowly ambling up towards the sacrificial altar, hazy bluish pools of annoyance flashing away to look back to his feet. I hunched a little more, dismayed. Even at the end, even in the finale of things, I had still managed to make it all so much worse by being here, by trying to help.

"Why are you here?" Raziel said softly, muttering almost incoherently. Something kicked hard at the back of my shins as I was forced to my knees, forced to bow in front of the tribune of angels standing there. There were four of them, two helpers, one main older guy, and one I never hoped to ever see in my various lives, Gauzier. I almost laughed when both Raziel and I made the same disagreeable sound of annoyance and disgust. The little ceremony started, some bible verses, some grand yelling about heresy and gross negligence of duties. I wasn't paying attention.

"I'm not going to let you take the fall for this." One of my guards suddenly jabbed me in the back of the head, trying to keep me quiet; I shot a cold glare his way and continued on. "It wasn't just your decision."

"But it was my decision here, in my world. You've got your punishment back down in Hell, but you're taking both, now."

"That might not be entirely true." The grand orator announced my grand title, the Excelesis Demon Nona. I cringed, keeping my eyes closed. "Because of that."

"Like they haven't been beating that into my head for the last sixteen hours of interrogation or anything; I know, alright?" Raziel's guard was starting to get annoyed with the chatter as well, grumbling his displeasure as the angel ignored him, "Whatever that is, just…whatever. I don't care anymore. But you still could've gotten away."

I smiled, just slightly, bending my head a little lower. Even with whatever I actually was, whatever my final fate was, he was still concerned for me. It was a greater compliment then I could ever properly receive.

"I couldn't." I burbled out, shaking my head a little.

"Why not?"

"Because letting you take the blame for this one alone would be a worse punishment than whatever they do to me here." I said more audibly as my guards hit me again, hard enough to bleed. My head snapped towards them, "You try that again, I'd like to see you try that again. For God's sake, I got like a minute left of life here, just let me fucking talk!"

The ceremony suddenly stopped at my outburst, hushed crowds suddenly bubbling with arrogant, insulting blips of anger. I fumbled with my Heavenly handcuffs, trying to shake them loose.

"They're going to kick me out. But they're gonna just…kill you."

"I'd like to see them try." I grinned for just a second, still fumbling with my handcuffs.

"You're something else." Raziel shook his head at me, looking back to the orators as they started up again; you could tell they were almost over, that the time was nearly here. "I think you'd make a great leader." I stopped picking at my own locks, confused; He wasn't joking, he was honestly serious. Frowning quickly, I turned to the altar before looking back to him.

"I'll fix this. I swear to you that I will." I couldn't let this all end like this, I had to make things right. "If I do get the chance to talk with my future soul, I'm gonna bitch her out to start, I promise." Raziel began shaking his head back and forth, almost laughing with his eyes fixed down, blood in his teeth.

"You don't get it, do you? I don't want you to fix it." He turned to me, grinning for a second as his eyes suddenly darted back to the procession ahead of us. "I have a say in this too, despite what you may have planned. This is okay. It's a long time coming." All I could do was stare as my eyes went wide and a strange little smile appeared on my face.

The fire, the determination, the vitality of who I was slowly swept back, refilling; I didn't have words for him, nothing that could express that kind of deep gratitude, that reassurance. Twitching, struggling for words, I didn't have them, looking around for some way to reciprocate. I had to. I just had to. Gauzier was the way.

"If this does end, we're not going to do it on a sad note." I decided, biting my lip. Knocking my elbows towards each other I popped loose one of the shackles, suddenly on my feet, heading straight for the angel we both loved to hate. With all four of them turned away and my burly guards slow on the job, the crowd was the one who let them know something had gone wrong as their cries of terror escalated. I only took two steps; the rest practically lined itself up for me; how Gauzier turned and lined his jaw up just so. How I had my grip already tightened, already leaning back, how my punch square across his fat head sent the angel twisting over his own feet, toppling right where he stood.

My hand ached. No one dared move as I rubbed my arm, chains jingling in the silence only ruined by Gauzier's half conscious moaning. My mission done, I raised the one half chained arm behind my back where it was, standing contraposto, like I was waiting for the bus.

"Alright, chain me back up, I'm done now." I said, cockily eying the crowd. Both guards tackled me into the concrete with one putting a knee to my face, making sure I was as uncomfortable as possible. Leaning back I could see Raziel, alarmed, but generally smiling. That's all I was looking for, that's what I wanted to give back. "Happy Falling, Raziel!" I called out to him, partially through the guard angel's hamstring.

"It was still wrong!" He responded to the frenzy of people, more jumping on me to keep me subdued. I wasn't going anywhere; it's only then when I saw they weren't doing this to fight back, they were doing this to pin me where I lay. Admits the chaos the lead orator was moving quick for Raziel, the guards propping him back, pinning back his arms. He didn't fight it. The smile was all but a memory as there was no emotion to his face, no fight. Acceptance.

With two short words of speech the orator braced the weapon back, lunging forwards and piercing Raziel right in the heart, blade glowing red. I just about lost it as my view was obscured, as other people jumped on top of this pile already struggling to keep my angry soul at bay. As they should; I fought, shoved and struggled to keep watch, to fight for him. He stayed very still, head slightly back with his face tormented in pain.

"Raziel!" I called out, using my legs to kick like mad, no longer caring who I injured and who was in the way. I swung my head back and forth, grateful for my jagged nubs of horns that kept people from interfering with my view. Not again, God, not again. Blood began to soak down his shirt as the angel's face twitched, finally going blank, shutting down. His definition began to blur. "Raziel!" I called again, elbowing a woman and one of the guards in the face, kneeing and kicking and throwing a fit, trying to see. Raziel was leaning forward, slumping over the weapon; through a hazy mix of one soul and the other, I could still see someone pulling away underneath. As the angel leaned further onto the sword and away from where he sat, another person was coming more into view, gaining strength. I froze, confused as someone tried to push my head away unsuccessfully. Without warning, the two forms suddenly snapped away from each other, the fully winged semi muscular exorcist angel Raziel dead on the sword and almost transparent, and what looked like a much scrawnier, wingless, regular looking Raziel left behind, dazed and confused.

"Raziel?" My struggling stopped as this remaining Raziel looked over himself, trying to catch his bearings. That wouldn't be possible. Our eyes met for just a second.

"It is finished." The orator said as the last bits of the exorcist angel Raziel drifted away, dissolved to nothing. "You, dammed soul; I cast thee out." And like that, with just those words, he fell through the stone, floored facade of Heaven, gone. The crowd began to cheer, riotous for blood, for results. My eyes scanned frantically, panicking.

"We now take the arduous task of exorcising what most of you have only heard stories about." I ignored his words, searching for him; that tie, I couldn't feel where he was; I didn't know. My mind called out frantically, addressing a silent crowd that may never hear me. Please. Please, if anyone can hear me, please keep him safe, please watch over him, please don't let anything happen. It's the last favor I'll ever request. They were bringing me to my feet, willingly standing me up as the orator was walking closer to me, sword lit in a different flame, flanked by a sore, angry Gauzier.

"We know this doesn't quite work on you." He dipped a finger onto the blade, wiping the blue fire-goo off on my arm. It burned and hissed for a second, tearing into my muscles as I grit my teeth in pain, but it stopped there, going out and leaving a deep blue stain. Gauzier took the sword from the orator, smacking the flat side of the blade on my forehead once as the noxious mess began to bubble and burn like caustic acid, streaking down across my nose. He repeated the action with both arms, once on the back, once on the hips, each hand and one on each foot as I fought to keep him away, fought to show any real pain in his actions. "So we're going to give you a taste of real, live Hell, since you're such a fan." His tone was almost insidious, lathering up the sword one last time to smear it across my heart, burning and eating into my skin on contact. He suddenly put the sword point up at my heart, using small bits of force to slowly and painfully slide it into place. I couldn't help but whimper, cry out in pain, trying to fight back, but my whole body shook in pain, rattled from the outside in.

"Never show your face again." Gauzier thrust the rest of the sword into my heart, the blue bits of fire igniting like a powder keg; every inch of my body perked up like something pinched it tight and ripped it all different directions, all at once. With one last scream my body was torn apart in a million different ways, blasting my soul apart with a million tiny bombs. Noise, confusion, pain; everything went black.

32

It began again like the end of a film, the notion of reality, of a dream, flashing over and over and over again, my eyelids shuddering, tracking, back and forth in a closed off, darkened world. As my eyes stopped twitching, my head started, nodding slightly, over and over, off to the side. Fight. Fight it. There was a noisy voice in my head, kicking at me in the softest way, tired as well, compensated.

As I felt myself drifting back to sleep, falling back away, I twitched my fingers. The forefinger and thumb brushed on something soft and warm, pleasing texture and feel, good quality fabric. The fingers twitched again to the same rhythm, my heart. Grating the fabric between my fingers, I suddenly realized it on my neck, felt it on my other hand; with a wiggle of my toes, felt my feet covered in the same thing. A bed; I was lying down. Dragging my hand up, pulling it tiredly towards me, I smacked my own face, rubbing the bridge of my nose. I'd made it; another attempt to kill me off, even blowing up into a million different directions, and I still managed to- I stopped, alarmed, pinching my nose once more. There was more loose skin, more give to the bridge of my nose. Running down my nose, it was much larger, much bigger and more bulbous at the end. This was not my face.

Underneath my hand I could feel my mouth open as my lungs came back with a passion, gasping in air through a long stream of short breaths. I coughed; a wheezing, pathetic sound. At the relentless drive of my mind, with constant pushing, I managed to open my eyes. That action got considerably easier by what I saw, a wrinkled, pruned hand hovering over me, ready to strike. With my eyelids tempting to slink into my own head I stared at it, waiting for it to strike, for it to attack. It waited. Narrowing my eyes a little I tried to move my hand again, move my pointer finger. This old, decrepit hand did the same. As those fingers soon began to wiggle back and forth with my prodding, as I realized they were my own, that I controlled them, I knew something was very wrong. There came a screeching sound, a shriek that almost scared me; the sound of my own audible panic as another wrinkly old hand came up to join its brethren. They were thin, bony hands, blue veins attacking it like a coordinated army over the top, finger nails yellowed, worn down. I suddenly realized everything behind those hands was a blur, a medley of colors melding into one. My eyes darted about the room, trying to understand. Next to me on a bed stand were a pair of glasses; I cautiously put them on.

I was in what looked like a hospital bed, rails up on the side and locking me in. I saw the clear tube racing down from a medical tower at the side and right into my nose. Twitching my lips a little I could feel it there, clamping on with the same desperate measure I was in, wishing that this all around me was an elaborate, terrible dream. My arms told the same story, veiny, old, wrinkled and not mine, with an annoyed tug I pulled the covers down as my body was thin, stick- like joke of what I once was, an old person's body disheveled in a sort of backless nightgown. What the Hell was this?

"Emalee!" Someone screeched from the door, leaning against it like a mom, watching their child do something remarkable. Half-naked, I just stared back, confused and bewildered. "Well look at you, are we having a good day?" Eyes wide, I looked to the woman, looked behind me a little and back to her, more confused than the fact I was an old biddy right now.

"You…can see me, right?" My voice was rough, dry as I tried pulling it off like a joke. I was practically shaking in fear. She could see me. I know she did. If I was visible, I wasn't dead. If I wasn't dead, what the Hell was going on? What had they done to me?

"Of course I do, Emalee." The woman came closer, a woman all of about twenty three or twenty four. My panic began to rise, began to take precedence.

"Where am I?" The woman's face fell a little bit, reaching to the side of my bed and lowering the one arm rail, dismantling part of my adult crib.

"Well Emalee, we're in Palm Shades Assisted Living. You know that." That was it. Just…done. I almost leapt from the bed, hospital gown half open with my medical tower zipping behind me. I hurt. Each step was like my body mashing together, a struggle to just keep each leg moving; knees popping, ankles cracking, I dashed through the door, medical tower toppling behind me at the threshold and ripping the oxygen from my nose. Like a wild horse I worked this body the best I could, standing for a second in the hallway, zipping down one way as my attendant shouted behind me, racing to keep up. A dream, please, just be a dream. But with each painful step, passing the other tenants who all saw me too, with each foot closer to the outside world, I knew it to be real, true.

I made it to the lobby; the entryway looked a little like a convenience store mixed with a hospital, double doors guarding me from the outside that swayed with palm trees and white gravel landscaping. Pressing a weak hand against the glass I wheezed, body struggling for breath, straining as a grainy image of a figure stood in front of me. It was an old woman with large nose, face like a basset hound and thick glasses that made her eyes bigger then they should've been. She was extremely thin, arms weakly shaking to keep her propped against that glass; as I turned my head, my reflection following me. A body. They'd trapped me in a body. A body in a retirement home in Florida, none the less. An old body of some poor old woman named Emalee.

Something struck me, head popping up as I looked to the reception area, already nervous. The woman there smiled at me politely, a look that turned to confusion as I snatched the day calendar from her desk. I almost dropped it in shock, flipping through a few days to make sure it was true. Four years. This was four years after Heaven. Four years had passed, that I'd been asleep, away, nonexistent. Four years, opposite side of the country; I felt like I was very late to the game; my lip curled back to a snarl.

"You dirty sons of bitches!" I roared out in a foreign voice, tossing the calendar to the floor and stomping for the exit. They couldn't keep me here, they think they can kill me off, shove me away in a little spiritual corner, they've got another thing coming! I would not be held back like this, I was not going to sit around and pull on the sideline. I stormed up to the door and pressed against it, weak, thin, anemic arms only shaking as I put more pressure to it. Locked. A physical being's worst enemy. "God Damn you!" I shoved my hand against it more forcefully, made it hurt.

"Emalee, Emalee, calm down!" My caretaker behind me was standing there, my tower in hand; palms open like they tried to corner an enemy. Growing frustrated, I pushed again, throwing myself backwards from the glass doors. Trapped. Stuck. Four years. Four, long years. Four years without contact, four years alone. Raziel, Palug and the others, they had to think I was dead, gone, evaporated. That I didn't care, that I'd abandoned them. I felt myself begin to cry.

"I just wanna go home." I turned towards her, pushing vainly against the door once more before tossing back and knocking into the front desk. My lungs were burning, my body hurt, my bones ached. You could see the girl sympathized, that real, honest to God regret was there as she came closer, waiving off the two men behind her.

"I know you do, honey." She patted my shoulder, handing me the oxygen to put halfway up my nose and around my ears. "But we need to keep a close eye on you here; we're able to care for you." I wiped my face, beyond myself, doubting. What if this whole previous part had been just a dream? What if I was only some person going through mental delusions? That I was just slowly dying with a brain wandering the line of reality and fiction, playing make-believe; I snorted through my plastic nose ring and pulled my glasses up a little higher, hand wandering through my thin, whitish hair.

"I've got charts, right? Can I see them please?" I requested nervously, leaning down and picking up the calendar from the floor, handing it back to the receptionist. The girl looked at me for a second, cocking an eyebrow up before nodding enthusiastically.

"Yes, of course, they're your property." She handed me a clipboard; I needed to know if this was some slowly progressing disease, or something more. Scanning over the first page I saw" my" name, some important little details. Emalee Herring. 72 years old, admitted over a year ago. Alzheimer's. I sighed, cringing, flipping to the orderly notes, probably the most reassuring and helpful things on there. This body had been practically bedridden for two days now, careful notes about the lessening vocabulary, how Emalee here was due to be put on life support today if the condition hadn't changed and she was still on her way to becoming a vegetable.

There was a problem with medication yesterday, a lapse in coverage due to new medication that was to be started today. I gave a sort of angry smirk, tossing the charts on the front counter and just shaking my head in a very non-elderly move." Go figure" I said angrily, watching, pining for the outside. All that time I wanted to feel the breeze, wanted to exist in the world outside. Here I was, trapped inside. Trapped in here. Trapped in Florida, for God's sake.

"So we're feeling spry today, aren't we?" She said to get me to laugh, to lighten up. I only lay my head against the glass, ignoring her and in my own little world.

I did a system check, my name I had been going by was Neri, some people were calling me Nona; I could recall the past-life amphitheater on my head, but everything was condensed down, kept simple. Things ran a little slower, but for squatting in someone else's body, I knew who I was. More accurately, I knew who I was if this brain wasn't completely screwed over by Alzheimer's and the resulting dementia. I groaned out loud, looking about; it was a pretty busy place, a few other seniors were sitting by, watching outside as well. The sun was still trying to rise, still peaking over the horizon. Nothing but palms, modest temperature, clean air and a busy roads were in front of this place. I didn't get any of it. Gauzier had said a real life Hell, I guess this was it.

"Well, since you're up, why don't we try and get you something to eat, maybe a nice hot bath? After that, we could see about getting you some outside time, if you're still up to it." If my teeth weren't still anchored in my head, I would've spit them out. Food. Food? …Hot bath? I hadn't had either in…ever. At least not this cycle." Are we hungry today? Manage to get something down?" My head slowly turned to her with the utmost joy and bizarre flip of emotions, almost all thought lost on my desperate need to get back home. Maybe that was partly due to the elderly body I was using like a coat. Food.

"I think I can manage that." I followed her away from the door like a lost baby duck, tugging along my air-tower. With that promise, I'd follow her off the cliff if need be- as long as there was food promised at the bottom. It wasn't progressive, wasn't helpful to my situation, but if I could give a big FU to Gauzier for actually enjoying a part of my punishment, it was still helpful in that way. Down like this, I could still fight back. I needed to collect my thoughts, I needed a plan first.

She sat me down, amongst the rest of them sitting at their two or three people tables, spaced out, half mentally aware, half not. It was like a memorial, like a moment of silence for absolutely nothing, everyone just sitting there as a zombie. The walls were lined with inspirational posters, pictures of kittens and scenes full of flowers with a dedicated section in the corner to children's finger-painting; at least I hoped it was children's finger-painting. Things were generally painted in rosy colors, upbeat tones of yellow and blue. This is what it's like, I thought, bending and clenching my hands as they snapped and clicked, stiff and painful things; this is what it's like to be old. In all the lives I'd lived, all the times I had been a part of the great chain again and again, I never made it to this stage. Never lived past my late twenties, something striking me down each and every time, some terrible measure of death. Clenching my hands again I frowned. It sucks; old sucks. Now I knew.

The bowl hit down in front of me, a custard cup halfway filled with a yellowish, sweet smelling slop. Sticking a finger in it and putting it cautiously in my mouth… it… I…the clouds parted, the sunshine and birds and love and wonderful all came pouring in accompanied by rainbows and hoards of purring kittens. This body was ravenously hungry, I was ravenously craving the sense of taste; in under a minute that thing was licked clean.

"You've always been a big fan of Applesauce, Emalee." The social worker said enthusiastically as I pulled the cup away from my face, peering into it. Applesauce never tasted so good in my various lives. Looking up to her hopeful face, I put the cup down dignified, sliding it with two fingers back to her.

"Can I have some more?" I perked up suddenly, little nuances of perks coming back to me, that since this was real life, and I was real life, that she was here to serve me, I could really ask her to do anything for me. Least, that's the understanding I had. "Can I actually come with to see what you've got?"

"Absolutely!" She said, gleeful. The woman didn't get up from where she was, she didn't move as her eyes slowly dropped back to the table, hinting. I followed her glance to the pills laid out on a napkin, a handful of colorful pharmaceuticals. I froze. They'd missed a medication yesterday; what if that was the reason I was actually conscious, actually around? What if the lack of medication was my only existence? My eyes darted nervously to her, back to them, poking them with my finger. I had no idea what any of these were; a rough understanding of various different pills, but in practice, I didn't know pain killers from pancreatic suppressants. "If you take your medication, we can go shopping for whatever you'd like to eat."

"What's the chance in you telling me what they are?" I gave a brief smile; they wouldn't tell me. I've heard of the horrors that happen in retirement homes, the negligence, the brutal beatings that these old fogies get for barely stepping out of line. Not her, she seemed nice, but still, they would probably give me some fluff answers and hope I didn't look into it.

"Well." The nurse spread the pills apart, pointing to them as she explained, "These are simple painkillers, this one is Namenda to regulate glutamate, Razadyne, Exelon, Aricept and finally Cognex. They keep your brain active so you can do things for longer." I nodded as she read off the names, getting a little less anxious. Confused, too; everyone here was painstakingly nice. Well lit, well-cared for, understanding folk. Made me wonder just how this woman managed to end up in such a good place. How I managed to end up in such a good place. Still, if I was here due to a glitch, then I'd keep riding this glitch, with or without painkillers to help with my old-person aches.

"Well thank you, um, darling." I added on for effect, throwing back the pills into my mouth. Without a pause I pinned them with my tongue to the roof of my mouth as I drank the water, gagging and choking that I hadn't drank water in an impoverishly long time either. As I made a scene with my coughing and hacking on misplaced water I spit a few into my hand, jammed a few up my own nasal cavity, the rest under my tongue.

"Do you need help?" The woman asked, leaning forwards. I waved her off.

"Got it. Got it. Let's go shopping." I said happily, standing from the table, showing off my teeth and opening my mouth. All gone. She nodded slowly, helping me unnecessarily to the rest of my extravagant meal. I spit the pills out in a napkin a few minutes later.

I must've set a record, stuffing my poor old lady body to the brim with all types of retirement home food, kiltered back as my caregiver only scribbled a plethora of notes as the last two people in the cafeteria. Things right now were difficult despite how wonderfully great eating again had been; I had to figure out a way out of this body, had to get across the country to the west coast, back to trying to fight against the angels. I had to find Raziel. Picking my teeth, I stopped at the thought; pleading, begging and calling desperately, I begged whomever could hear, begged for help. Four years; spirits always started to lose it after two. It'd been so long; it felt like something that happened yesterday. It felt like my heart was going to drop into my toes with regret, with guilt. The social worker saw the worry on my face.

"Are you alright, Emalee? You did have quite a meal." I looked to her quickly, flashing a hollow grin before leaning against the table, conflicted.

"Worrying about an old friend of mine, I suppose." I scoped out the one window I could see where I sat. "Left on less then pleasant circumstances, I guess I'm just fretting about him."

"I suggest you write him a letter, since we're on a good day. Maybe it'll settle your mind." A letter, that was a fantastic idea; it honestly was. The Priest could find it, read it out for him if he was still there; I didn't know where he was settled at, if Palug had managed to pick him up and look after him, nothing. My worry subsided a little. I bet if nothing else, Palug's been watching over him, trying to convert on our side. Maybe things weren't so bad, so hopeless, he had a great sense on finding new souls.

She looked back to her charts as I actually bothered to look at her name tag, find out my own social worker's name. Beth. Well, now I knew.

"You're having a very good day, aren't you?" She smiled, looking up. I almost felt like bragging.

"Considering, I think you could say that." I scratched my thin, white hair, pulling one bit of it out in distaste. I missed my regular body. Senseless but healthy.

"We're glad to see you on your feet, spry as ever. Shall we get you a hot bath?" And just like that, again, all the troubles just melted away. Though I found out my definition of a hot bath, and the retirement home's definition were drastically different. I pretty much just sat there naked while someone just scrubbed me with a sponge that stunk of old flesh. I got the full picture of this body as my bathing assistant kept asking me questions, trying to lighten the mood, but I just sat there, arms stubbornly covering my breasts, legs crossed as well as I stared like I was in a coma in front of me. Not an experience I was looking forward to repeating. But the food. The food was still good, not to mention I still had the outdoors to visit.

I asked to go outside, starting with some simple requests. After I was ignored time and time again, my requests became pleas, before becoming short, angry demands. I got the same answer; we're not having outside time now, we'll do it in a bit, we'll see what we can do until we got to the final answer of 'Maybe tomorrow.' By that time, it was already dark; by that time, they were already putting us to bed at eight o'clock as I stared out that front room window, growing more anxious. Gathering some supplies to write a couple letters, I dragged the little tray table to my bed, light perched over my shoulder. At least I could let others know where I was, that I was okay.

Trying to not seem like a nut, or a demon trapped in an elderly Alzheimer's woman, I figured disguising the name and location a bit were good ploys. They'd prescribe me a whole new rainbow of medications if I was writing to the dead spirits. Far as I could tell, my existence here might be a fluke, an unplanned twist that worked in my favor. There were no other voices in my head, no angry old woman demanding her body back, this body was practically empty, mind shriveled away to nothing. Best I could tell, her mind was pretty much gone, mine had either taken over, or was working the bits of her mind that kept the body alive. Maybe I'd been in her mind for the entire four years. Maybe this was my one and only chance to exist, due to a fluke in medication. I grumbled angrily underneath my breath, debating what to write; I needed to talk with both groups, but I didn't know where Palug was at. I had no idea. I wrote to Raziel instead.

"Dear Christopher;

I hope you're well. No guesses for how awful I feel in regards to your departure; despite if it's wanted or not. I've been forcibly vacationed in Florida this entire time. It only seems like I've come around recently, more accurately earlier this morning due to a lucky flaw at Palm Shades Assisted Living Facility."

I kinda looked back on the message; it wasn't saying shit. It wasn't getting anything across besides that I was daintily dodging big, obvious statements that I needed to say. What would a possibly mentally-starved spirit want to see? To hear? I tried to channel my inner frustration, my worries and doubts from when it felt like the world was pitted against me, when I felt like I had nothing. It wasn't hard. Lip trembling, I started again.

Keep strong. I write this letter on a vague hope you've stayed with the Priest, that you haven't been kicked or moved elsewhere. Remember the good things, keep your mind working, do puzzles; if you haven't any, make them. I can't bear to think of you compromised any farther then you already are; they sure did a number, eh?

I've been looking into an early release, but with the moderate to serious Alzheimer's I've been told to have, this is looking unlikely. I'm not sure what to do.

I will come back. I'll do everything in my power to return, count on it. This isn't over.

Regards, Aunt Neri."

Writing it all down, trying to sum up the shit I'd gone through; I needed to leave. Damn the food, damn the outside, damn the body. I needed a way out, needed to get back to things, especially if I was supposed to be more important than some dire demon. I yawned, leaning back from the tray, addressing and sealing it up.

In the morning the letter was already gone, mailed for me.

I slept in past eight thirty, solemnly enjoying my resting sleep like I always did. It was nine o'clock when I had my caregiver come to my bedside, gently shaking me awake.

"Emalee, you've got a visitor!" Beth said happily as my eyes were suddenly open, confused- they couldn't have gotten here that quickly, the letters couldn't have been all but a town over, let alone if they had made it past the front desk. I ran a hand through my thin hair, sitting up a little more and giving a sort of lopsided look. "It's your daughter!"

"Mom! You're doing so well!" Another woman was at the door, early fifties, thin like myself, generally happy to see me. Pangs of guilt coursed through this sickly elderly body like lightning as the woman ran up to me, hugging. "I'd heard of your recent progress, this is so great!" Oh, God. I smiled warmly as my stare gave away that I had no idea who they were, or what was really going on. I'd be disappointing one very excited daughter of mine.

"I'm very glad you're here." I said softly, hugging back and trying to fib best I could. At least I could try and act like a respectable person.

"You better, its taken forever to track you down" The woman hissed in my ear quickly as my eyes snapped open, darting at her suspiciously. Track me down? This was not my daughter; not unless I'd dumped her in the forest and was hiding from her. No, no, this was not as it seemed. She grinned nicely to the nurse and looked back to me, "Well, get dressed mom, we'll take a nice walk outside. You still love the outside world, don't you?" The nurse perked up.

"She wouldn't stop talking about it yesterday, that'll work out perfectly for you, Emalee!" I smiled a little and nodded, glaring in paranoia at the both of them. "Well, we'll let you dress yourself Emalee, you've earned it. Come on outside when you're done." The nurse left first as my 'daughter' stayed behind just for a moment.

"Lighten up, 'mom', you're acting like I'm here to finish you off." The woman laughed, watching down the hall after Beth left. I knew something was off with her!

"Who are you, really?" I almost growled it, hand held behind me to keep my gown in order. The woman's smile switched from a sort of gloating, hiding sneer to one that was quite a bit more relaxed and light.

"Just having a little fun with you, relax you wrinkled demonic fart." She left the room, laughing a bit and heading back to the waiting room as I only gawked. I dressed myself and practically ran after her, medical tower zigzagging in tow.

I couldn't speak. Couldn't do anything but stand there and take it all in, the wind, the breeze, the heat from the sun and the world around me. Me and my 'daughter' were sitting outside now in the shade, enjoying the fresh air, the life that I was excluded from so often. I would've sprawled out on the grass if people wouldn't figure me dead. It was incredibly relaxing, so beautifully serene, even with the sounds of the city spoiling it around us. The gentle sway of the wind through my hair, the smell of the ocean not terribly far off, I couldn't properly enjoy what I was feeling because it felt like new. The blaring car horn not far off snapped me back to reality, back to my paranoid, confusing meeting I was having with my 'daughter' .

"Do you want a few more minutes, Nona?" The woman said gently, appreciating the outdoors, but not to the same level I was. My head was almost hanging off the back of the bench in deep relaxation. Even that word wasn't enough to snap me completely back to that seriousness. I pulled my head up towards my body, propping an elbow to lay my face against my hand.

"You're not my daughter, are you? If you are, there's a terrible bout of coincidences happening and your mom does not approve." The other woman laughed and wrapped me in a tight hug immediately, adjusting her seat on the bench.

"You're still the same, Nona. That's a relief. No one's heard hide or hair of you in years." I opened my eyes tiredly as it felt like I didn't know whether to hug back or to pull away. Considering all the crap I'd been through, I hugged back as we broke apart.

"It's luck that I'm around right now." I sat up a little more, hands on my lap. God that breeze was perfect. "Thank the good nurses at 'Palm shades assisted living' for screwing up."

"Let's just cut to the chase, we don't have much time." The woman watched as a person passed a little close to us, stopping the conversation until he was out of earshot. "We need you dead."

"Come again?"

"You need to get out of that body as soon as possible; the way they have you bound is incredibly tight, so nothing short of a violent death with a lot of movement can get you out- even then it's going to hurt like Hell." She could obviously see my shock at what she was implying, so she continued on. "No exorcism can get you out of there, a peaceful death's even worse; you're tied so closely with the body that you'd have to go through the whole death cycle in Hell that you know takes years. We don't have that time; they need you now, its absolute slaughter going on in the war as they're taking advantage of your absence."

"You want me to kill off this woman? I don't want to kill the living like that!" The woman let out an agonized breath.

"It's not the most ideal plan, but you're needed, Nona." Alright, now that word was starting to chaff. "If you don't manage to get out of it, you'll start forgetting. That nasty little Alzheimer's that Emalee has will start going after your memory, your functions. They're counting on your to stay in that body, to keep you out of the way for a few more years as they wipe every one of us out." She put a hand on my shoulder, sympathetically looking me square in the eye with a look I could almost remember, something that was still visible between two estranged bodies.

"You know we all try living our afterlives with the utmost care and respect for those around us, it's what makes us who we are. But you have to realize when sacrifices need to be made, when the greater good comes to mind. I hate asking you for what you don't like, but I do it because I think of others, I think of their well-being." She suddenly stopped, flopping her hand, cutting the air. "Wait, are you still…the…uh…"

"Yep. Though I think regular Nona's squandering away in here somewhere." I rumbled flatly as the woman smacked my back, laughing. It stung.

"Oh, this probably doesn't make a lick of sense to you then, you don't even know who I am!" She extended a hand out like a formal greeting. "I'm your sister, Aisa."

<h1 style="text-align:center">33</h1>

"The sensible one" I said a little non-sensibly. Aisa; it was the first time I really considered what that angelic detective had mentioned, that far too regular for consequential information as it stared at me with a bit of wonder before shaking her head with a cockeyed smile.

"Well, this isn't my actual body, but I guess you could say that, yes." She looked around before getting up and helping me to my feet awkwardly.

"We're sisters?" I questioned, gripping her hands tightly, more in the deep depths of apathy at this point in time instead of flipping out that I'd met another one of my extended family.

"Well, yeah. You, Nona, are the youngest, Cempe's the middle, and I'm the oldest." I clenched my hands with immense senior strength. She dropped out of the grip and took my elbow instead like a caring daughter would, help me along. Bells, explosives and firecrackers barraged my feeble mind.

"Cempe!" I almost cracked a hip spinning back towards her, nearly toppling off the sidewalk. Cempe was not the 'Decima' that the detective had said. Aisa only gave me a sort of laugh, sitting me back down on a new bench, slightly closer to the entryway of the retirement home.

"Oh, I know you've met Cempe."

"Yeah, yeah, I have, many times- who is Decima?" I was starting to panic.

"Same person." Aisa sat down next to me again, looking back out around us with a more developed sense of awareness, of some sort of memorable appreciation, that just mentioning the shenanigans that Cempe has put me through was something fond. Her eyes suddenly switched back to me as I begged for more information; that look of hazy loving goodness faded more into concern as my brain was obviously not processing this information. "She hates that name, so she sticks with the Decempedia's name of Cempe as a shortcut." I smiled, softly, nodding with my mouth slightly ajar, brain steaming and sizzling in confusion. Aisa re-adjusted her seat, getting a little closer.

"Okay, so, you know the Colus, right?" I nodded, I could still understand that, "Well the Colus protects you the same way the Decempedia protects Cempe—-or...Decima. Same deal. The Colus is your Distaff, while the Decempedia's the measuring rod. Just trust me on this one; you understand your own mythology, don't you?" My lip only twitched a little in response as I shook my head. I wished people would stop assuming I knew things.

"Ah, right, that's Cempe. Well, go look up your own name, that'll be fun- try not to swear too loud when you do." She laughed again, helping me back up as I felt my brain close to bursting, "C'mon Nona, buck up."

"I... why would this...why..." My mouth flapped open and closed, gasping for reasoning and a little compassion at dropping the bomb on an old lady like myself. Aisa only moved me along a little slower, staring straight at me like she wanted to help, but instead got a bigger kick out of watching me flounder.

"This is strange, talking to you like this. You could almost pass as an old woman with the face you've got on now." I wanted to smack her, if only I was fast enough, a big part of me was pulling to do that. I only hobbled where she directed me before I stopped, gaining my direction and footing once more, "Don't worry, I won't tell your others about this. Not good for the image, I know." My face scrunched up, waving my hand in front of my face like I had to clear the bad air, the misunderstanding.

"If I'm all so important, why are you putting me back in there?" The laughing stopped.

"Because it's still your choice. I can't make this decision for you, only you can. People are going to need your help anywhere, Nona. You'll have to choose who you help and who you leave. There will always be consequences, and I think leaving you in this home will help you come to terms with that." She walked me in through the first set of doors as I fought for precious question time from the first spirit willing to give me answers, no matter how confusing they seemed to me now. "That and you're a bit compromised until you get everything all set straight in there. Your binding is interfering with that as I can tell." She pointed at my forehead as I grabbed her hand, trying to grasp something solid.

"So it's really true? I really am this horrible demon leader?" I spat out choppily as Aisa suddenly stopped, grabbing me firmly by the shoulders and propping me up taller.

"As your sister, it's my honor and duty to respect you, no matter who you are, or what you do." She pulled me into a tight hug, one that probably bruised my elder body just a bit, "But I would not bother with you if you were some 'horrible demon leader'. I would not be trying to track you down for four years and come down to Florida, searching for you, even though admittedly, I am here a lot. I would not give you a second of my time if I thought of anything less than greatness from you. It's about time you acted like it though; this humble bullshit's going to drive us both nuts." She smacked my shoulders heartily, leading me up to the front desk, signing me back in and turning back around as I struggled for reasoning.

"Good luck, Emalee. I know you'll make the right decision, no matter what it may be." She gave a smirk, face dropping to a sneer as she pointed straight at me. "Your daughter loves you very much, so don't you dare think otherwise." I waved a little as she left me standing in the entryway of the assisted living facility, the isolated demon Nona.

Apparently.

"Did you have a good visit with your daughter?" Beth, my caregiver was right next to me again. I couldn't speak, couldn't…fathom anything. It was like the world stopped, seized, twitched and jiggled at the same time, that life around me grew distant, faded. That there was no one but myself in that instant, that there was no other living soul capable of sitting in just that moment, in just that time. People were affirming my worries for me. Acknowledging what I was trying to chalk up to someone else's problems. There were mine, and mine only. Beth pulled my arm slightly, pulling me away from the door, turning me on her power, her will, doing things for me. It was taking me back from the outside world, from the problems I knew existed, that I was ignoring and into this comfort, this subtle shield of ignorance I could choose to play, that I could continue to be led around, directed by others. Something in me began to harden.

"Yeah… yeah I did, thanks." I said shortly, placing my hand over hers and pulling it away with a gentle touch. "It's left me a lot of things to think about, is there a way we can move our lunch date to one of these window tables here? Been a long time since a clear day, and I plan to at least watch as much of it as possible. Would that be okay?" Both the front desk receptionist and Beth were a little pulled away, a little wary that the severe Alzheimer's patient was stringing out long, complex sentences.

"Well, I'm not sure, Emalee, we eat in the dining room, they don't appreciate it when we get food on the tables out here, if we make a mess."

"Then I'll be exceedingly careful. I just need a break, and I'm sure you do too, a switch in routine. We'll be in plain view of all the others, it's not like I'm asking to sit down in the middle of the highway." I tried using an old-lady smile, a sort of sweet-old grandmotherly approach to goad my way to get what I wanted. "We're never sure how many good days I've got, right? Why can't I spend the good ones having a good time?" Beth continued to look at me, finally putting up her hands and relinquishing her authority with a sort of despondent grin.

"Alright, we'll have lunch out here, but if anyone asks you, we're having a conference with food, okay?" I gave a quick nod as we started to leave for the cafeteria.

"Also, while we're at it, do we have any mythology books?" I questioned with a nervous smile, pushing my luck all the more.

"What do you believe happens after death?" I asked her out of the blue after we had eaten most of our food, talked into exhaustion about most of the boring, plain stuff and small banter like weather, rain, and current events. My mind was completely elsewhere, trying to rationalize this all out, trying to make sense of it. In this position, with the ability to understand more than just what was around me, I almost figured it my duty to interview anyone with more than three polite words to their name. My caregiver seemed like a pretty bright type, she was starting to catch onto my great pill hiding place, seemed like a good candidate. I saw a lot of myself in her, too.

The social worker gave me a strange look, shaking her head.

"Well, Heaven of course." I nodded back, looking outside, eyes concise, thinking, tiny; they had a mythology book but the arts and crafts student teacher had it at the moment, trying to put together a craft session that involved an intricate mythological back story and a tiny twirled tissue paper flower. At Beth's request, she'd be bringing it to us any moment now. Each moment dragged despondently behind the last.

"Seems like the polite response to make, you know? Telling someone else you fear they'll just rot in the ground, well, it's not courteous. It won't make you many friends." The worker only watched me, curious as I elaborated. "I told that exact same response to someone else myself, even when I wasn't sure. It's a nice thought, though. A nice sentiment."

"You don't believe in Heaven anymore?" She said worriedly as she sipped her drink, putting down her clipboard. My lip pulled back in a crooked smile, a very un old lady-like move.

"I think I kinda have to." I chuckled, switching hands, "You just wonder what might happen if you say nothing, though. That if you seriously believe life after death's just blackness, if that's all that person will see. Like if that person actually believes nothing will happen, or if they fall back on that old reassurance, that something's always there at the end, that there's always more." I shrugged my shoulders a little, watching some little chipmunk run across the gravel path, enjoying his little world that wasn't tied up in some blue-colored entryway paved with children's hand prints and fake flowers.

"That's a very interesting thought, Emalee." The social worker leaned back from her chair, scratching the side of her head. "A little depressing, though." I suddenly cackled out loud.

"It is, isn't it? Nothing like a serious bout of Alzheimer's to shake you up and consider your own life. Speaking of—" I sat up a little as the woman with my mythology book was coming down the hall, "Do you

know what a Distaff is?" I questioned; I knew it oddly from the Joan
tale, from my mother who mentioned it once or twice in passing as a
seamstress. It was something with sewing. Beth suddenly sat up as I took
the book from the woman, thanking her. It was a heavy thing in more than
one way, weighing terribly on my thin, bony arms and not only on my
mind.

"You know, that's so weird, I actually do. I've taken a few clothing
design classes where it was mentioned."

"Yeah?" I questioned, subtly noting our conversation getting more
relaxed, how two people roughly the same age would talk with one another.
"What's it do?"

"It spins threads. Like, takes the unwoven material and pulls it
through to be wound on the spindle." I flipped to the back, trying to find
'Nona'- no luck. No matches. Threads. The images of the Colus weapon
came to mind, how it unraveled, unspun itself and rejoined that way. My
veins were starting to run cold.

"Could you draw me a picture of it?" I said shakily, flipping
through the Mythology book randomly, hoping something would jog my
memory, pop right up. There was nothing listed in the index under Colus
either, driving my frustration.

" I'm not much of an artist" The woman waved a hand as I
practically slammed down the napkin her way, handing the caretaker a
pen.

"If you could, please, it's very important." I said earnestly as I
looked through the book, decrepit fingers withdrawing as I forgot I was
squatting in this elderly body, just for a moment. Flipping the pages, I
headed for S. Sisters. Sisters always seemed to be an ominous word. Beth
gave me a worried look, pausing. I must've looked like a nut, now. "I want
to do it the way you're supposed to, the original way, and I don't want those
damn youngins jilting me on what I need." I elaborated lamely. I was a
piss-poor old woman, and I think everyone around me knew it.

"Well, okay, it looks a little like this." She drew a plain rectangle,
quick little jagged notches and a long handle. The pills jammed in my nose
almost shot onto the table. Dabbing one old, infirm finger down on the
napkin I pulled it towards me and made the notches a little deeper, and
added more of a point to the top.

"Fuck me sideways." I muttered out loud, making my caregiver
sit up like on a seat of hypodermic needles. I couldn't breathe, even with
the air being forced under my nose; I was looking at a rough picture of the
Colus weapon laid out in front of me. Wait a second. "You said it's used
for spinning thread, right?" Beth nodded; Aisa said that the Decempedia
was about measuring... so if I spun the thread, and she measured it... My
eyes popped wider then my coke bottle glasses could handle, hands already
flipping furiously in the book to F.

There, right towards the top of the book, partially lit in sunlight from the window sat the little paragraph of all knowing answers. Fates. More accurately, the sisters of- Clotho, Lachesis, and Atropos; My eyes practically ate the page where it lay. Beth was asking something, questioning me more, but I pretty much blocked all parts of this world out except for me and that book.

'The Fates', or Moirae, were a group of three women attributed with choosing one's destiny; Clotho, the weaver spun the thread of life, Lachesis measured the thread, and Atropos, sometimes known as Aisa, cut it, determining how one dies. The Moirae were even feared by the Gods, sometimes referred to Roman mythology as Nona, Decima and Morta.' I continued to stare at it, looking up slightly to Beth with my petrified death-face, then back to the book. Right there. Nona, Decima/Cempe, and Aisa. As my eyes burned some minutes later, I blinked, staring all the more.

They really should've put Nona in the index, it was right there.

"Are you okay, Emalee?" My breath was shallow, spaced out; lip twitching as I tried to smile, as parts of me tried to move on, to continue this charade. Even with Aisa/ Grand mistress of Death's warning I wanted to scream, swear, throw a drinking fountain through the window and run away to sweet freedom. Something began to kick at the back of my head, pushing me back towards the earth I was falling away from. "I said, do you need me to get some help for you?" Beth was almost standing up, readying herself at my unresponsive behavior. My thoughts snapped back together.

"Nope, noooope, I'm okay." I said in exasperation, shutting the book quickly with an inane laugh "You know how these old texts like to anger up the blood" I shoved the book away from myself, running a shaking hand through my hair in a cruel reminder where I was and what I was doing. Beth sat back down, cleaning up her seat a little as my brain skipped on empty. If this was a joke, it was an intensely dedicated one. I looked up to my caregiver, someone who might actually have to carry me back to my room for once.

"Let me ask you something, if I might." I twiddled my thumbs nervously, looking outside, pining for it like a stress reliever. "If lived your life unaware you were secretly in some big position of power, how would you cope with that?" The caregiver gave me a sort of confused look, helping me to my feet. For the first time, I actually felt like an old woman, a bit weak in the legs, breath short, brain frazzled. Gathering up my dishes, we started to walk back to the cafeteria.

"Well, I guess it'd depend if I was looking for that reassuring answer or not." She gave me a hearty tap on the shoulder, "Or if I was just looking for something happy to fall back on." Beth didn't say a word more about it, didn't give me an answer beyond that, beyond a regurgitation of what I had said earlier. This had to be horribly funny to someone other than myself.

I pretty much had the rest of the day to mull it over; there was an optional reading class I could go to, something called 'finding the internet' class that I chose to ignore, and my caregiver was giving me a lot more freedom, more personal space. I was told to have a doctor's appointment tomorrow since my 'good days' were sticking around, no doubt due to avoiding eating any of the medication they gave me. Made me wonder what would happen if I did, though.

I sat at that window alone and away from the others, leaning back and watching the outside world, at the people that passed, the plants swaying with the wind, the hummingbirds that visited the bright red strawberry feeder hung from the tree; and here I was, sitting in some old woman's body, stagnantly recycling the air that had been recycled for me. Things were passing me by, always moving, always changing, shifting, growing and learning. Maybe I should consider myself lucky to keep experiencing it, again and again as a demon, reliving those lives, those small things I enjoyed so much. A fate; now that just seemed ridiculous; an old, forgotten myth and I was pretty sure to have learned time and time again in class of the old witches who sat around cutting lengths of string. Some stupid archaic fairy tale. Outdated. Why in the Hell would I be one of them? How did I manage to get stuck with that job?

It didn't feel wrong, though. That's what worried me most. It wasn't like it disagreed with me, that it was an elaborate hoax, that it didn't fit. It did fit. I liked kids. The damn Colus was made out of threads. I mean, Raziel had said that there must've been an important reason I was split up, that I was someone of importance. Possibly. Well, leading a whole gaggle of rebelling demons and angels, Hell, yeah, I'd call that an important reason. But if that was true, if Heaven had segmented my soul like this, it still didn't make sense why I woke up in Hell, why Nona was apparently squatting in my body from day one, that they would've just killed me off. I tapped my face, and looked at the poor people around me, at these folk cooped up inside, limited, segmented off themselves.

Nudging my chair a little closer to the window I laid my face against the glass, taking a soft breath of over-oxygenated air, at least enjoying that much of what I had. It was just my wacky ass body that was causing me stress right now, and the thought that my friends and comrades were all chopped to bits because of what I'd done, because of their association with" The great Excelsis Nona." What bullshit.

"It's a title, nothing more." Someone said in front of me as my glance snapped to the empty seat, now occupied by the demonic version of myself I knew, but short like the first form. I almost popped an artery as she held up her hands, "Easy there Betty May, I'm just an extension of your thoughts, a kinda figment of your imagination. I'm still stuck there with you. It'll just make things easier to work out if you can see it eye-to eye." My worried glare didn't let up as I only began to frown, looking around a little. It was a pretty impressive figment, almost looked whole; but as I leaned a little to the side, things got hazier, like she was a special screen I could only see from one angle.

"You're not the one responsible for the bad puns, are you?" I kept my voice low. Miffed, insulted that it was the first question I asked my more popular self, she looked away over her shoulder, temper steeped in frustration with having to deal with me.

"You try and come up with something witty with half a brain, it's not easy." I leaned a little closer, staring at her quizzically. She only glanced back, doing the same thing, "God, we're so old…" I got flashes of the other perspective, of looking at myself from the outside in. Considering, I leaned back.

"So you're the great Nona?" I tilted my head a little with a sneer before trying to look like I was glancing out the window instead of talking to a bare seat. She did something that surprised me, looking more frustrated then proud of that, acting the same way I used to do when someone mentioned my father as the great politician of the town. A title way over my head, a title I didn't want to associate with. Something given, not earned. Nona stared at me a little as my thoughts wrapped up, pointing a finger at me enthusiastically.

"That. Exactly that." My face pulled back a little; she was in my head, no surprises she'd be reading my thoughts. The demon went on, "It's just a title. The only thing it's good for is intimidating your enemies. I've built up that reputation for the benefit of the others, not for myself. Publicity."

"You're not toting that around? How many others get to be the all-powerful Clotho/Nona/ Superweaver?" It seemed like I was just antagonizing her now, picking and peeling any bits away that I could. The demon only mimicked my glance, looking out the window as well.

"No. You're talking about it like it's a curse, it's not. It's a duty. It's a massive amount of responsibility with the actual influence to change the world around you." She looked back to me, "That's what it really boils down to."

"What makes you think I'd be any good at doing that? I can barely keep up commitments in my own life, let alone everyone else's." I said a little louder, elderly teeth gritting against one another, Nona gave a sort of exasperated sigh of annoyance. "It sounds….tiring, difficult."

"Why do you think I vacation as often as I do? Why do you think you have so many past lives?" She stared at me straight on, more excited as her emotions suddenly slipped up, calming down. "In everything I've done, in all the wars I've helped with, fights I've waged, people I've met living and dead, you know what still tops as the best thing?" I shook my head.

"I don't know, applesauce?" I said flatly. Nona squinted a little, shaking her head.

"This." She pointed around her as I almost laughed, her face growing more troubled, switching the finger to point outside. "Well, not so much this retirement home, but that. The outside world, the lives and interaction of other people." I could feel her enthusiasm influencing me as she couldn't help but continue on.

"All the things about life, all the aspects of it, the complicated relationship, the good times, the bad times, down to things like fine cheese, a soft breeze, a warm day, fresh cut grass, for God's sake! They're all these amazing sublime feelings and emotions and love and danger and… everything. Even down to inclement weather, violent crimes, mudslides, taxes, anything horrible and bad and dangerous, they only really make you sit back and enjoy this world when things are good. These lives, all the subtleties, the brilliant exquisite parts that make you wonder if everything's just a beautiful, complex dream; that's what I live for."

I couldn't seem to find my eyebrows, wedged so high up on my head as Nona slowly smiled, looking back to me.

"This job, it weighs you down, it crushes those feelings, that life in you, impairs your judgment and makes you see the world from the only pair of eyes you've got. That doesn't make a good person or a good leader. That's why you've got so many lives under your belt, a fresh view on things, a new start to appreciate and accept life all over again. That maybe, if we're lucky enough, we'll be around long enough to truly value a small sliver of the whole life experience."

My eyes were practically bugging out of my head as each word made sense to me, made me relax, ease up a tiny smidgen more as we both stared a little at each other. She seemed like the farthest thing one would expect from a demon leader, not so understandably evil as I'd figured from the outside view. Nona tweaked her head a little bit, squinting.

"You've got to get that whole good and bad side of things out of your head. I hate to quote my idiot sister, but she's right; they're just words. Erase the meaning of good and bad and you're seeing the world exactly as it is."

"You have to understand how hard that is for me to do." I shook my head a little; I wanted to smile, I wanted to digest the whole thing and be okay with it. I wanted to understand it fully. I wanted to know. I stopped, rubbing parts of my face nervously, "That whole…. 15 year thing…"

"A lie, Palug's good at that; good at least at frosting over the truth."

"Ah." I guess I should've been more excited, more enthusiastic, it was an awful lot to understand, to digest and respect. I felt like I needed another good four years to sleep this off. "What about this whole plan thing?" My soul dropped back down to earth instead of fluttering away as Nona's smile fell just a bit, looking off to the side.

"Originally, I wanted to try something new, wanted to push myself to really develop my own concept, my own idea of self. Working in a system again and again grinds off your edges, you know? I wanted to try that raw, basic life once more, from a new angle."

"And that's me? What… am I just…" I dabbled, coughing on it, feeling the whole bottom idea of self fall from underneath me, like I was a formulated thing, not original, created out of necessity.

"Well, yeah, pretty much." She gabbed on as I rubbed my temples, face pained in fictitious agony.

"How long can I ignore this talk ever happened?" I said kinda incredulously; my stomach felt like it was grating on the sides of my ribs, like my heart was shaking, dying and afraid as I was. Nona stared me straight in the eyes, squishing her face up.

"You couldn't ignore this if you tried and you know it." God… dammit. I leaned back at her, hissing angrily.

"I'm not ready for this kinda shit!" The woman a table over looked at me suddenly, appalled. She could blow it out her ass for all I cared, internal rambling with the thing piggybacking on my conscious seemed like a more pressing matter. Nona gave me the same flat stare I gave everyone else, a true duplicate of myself.

"Sit down before you break a hip."

I slowly eased back on my heels, slowly sat back in my chair, pulling that medical tower closer to me for good measure. We didn't say a word to each other for at least five minutes, angrily venting while I stared out the window. I couldn't manage a group if they paid me, couldn't lead my way out of a paper bag. My thoughts stopped, belligerent tirade halting. That sentiment was blatantly disputed by one person, the only person to my knowledge that actually had any faith in me, besides Aisa. I stopped, eyes darting back to my fictitious figment as she looked back to me in mirror image.

"How does Raziel come into play with this?" I saw her ears go back at the mentioning.

"You know it as well as I do what that friendship meant. I heard he wasn't doing so well; I wanted to understand more what they have to go through, their side of this all." Her face perked up, "Which you did great on, so…" Her excited tone fell as I kept glaring at her, not sharing the same feeling. I didn't want to hear that I had knowingly screwed around with his life, that all of his problems really were chalked up to me. The nervousness was clear on her face now as the exalted demon leader twiddled her thumbs anxiously.

"I wanted to help a friend." She summed up as I scoffed.

"Yeah? How do you think we did on that one?" There was an awkward silence as I relented a little. The guilt collectively shared between the two of us was probably enough to power this building and a block and a half beyond it.

Sighing a little more, I hung my head and let up. "What was

planned?"

"Learn the angel's system, rediscover just what I become on my own. Palug and Cempe where there to guard me on my quest to do this, and they've done a fantastic job whether you agree or not with it." Something itched beneath my skin, bugging me.

"What wasn't planned?" I grumbled lowly, cocking an eyebrow up as a woman passed close by us; Nona and I both watched her with careful eyes.

"The rest of it." Nona said with a laugh. "This wasn't planned. Getting captured wasn't planned; Raziel's willing falling, definitely not planned. People still have free will against whatever we may figure, you know, we can't plan everything." I laughed out sarcastically, startling myself.

"This was not my doing! Free will my ass!" I slapped a hand over my mouth, sitting back down quickly as Nona only put a palm to her face. I scoped over the entire lobby of people, not a single person looked elsewhere but at my ranting self. "Sorry, sorry uh… TV infomercial and all." I called out to everyone and pointed to the TV. Our time to talk had just been cut short; they'd be shipping me off to bed pronto now. The demon bent down, hissing out like people could hear her.

"It was. Don't go thinking I'm some great puppet master or something. I'm just the part responsible for the whole Nona mess. Life after death; you're just you." I frowned. "Palug was there to make sure you had somewhere to go when the angels exorcised you, Cempe was there to guide you to your own past soul, and to finding Raziel. And to a few other things. God dammit I owe her big." She dawdled on a sort of tangent, looking around and spotting Beth marching down the hallway.

"So, are we going to…rejoin…or…activate or something?"

"No, no there's a time and place for that. It certainly isn't the retirement home, not like this." She sat up a little straighter. "It's up to you what happens now. Either staying here in this body for the rest of its natural life and stay out of the system, or get out of the body and jumping back into the fight, eventually things would be okay either way. This is entirely your decision this time, you run this show. Congratulations on the promotion." Beth stood just next to me now, looking out the window.

"That's a very pretty sunset we have." She said slowly, placing a hand on my shoulder, "Are we alright, Emalee?"

I held that grimace and quickly nodded, looking back to Nona. The seat was empty once more; visit over, just like that. Back to my own power, back to that light in my head turning off, the future soul going back into hibernation as I scanned for activity, for more help. Nothing. Done.

"I'm…something." I muttered low, trying to smile, nothing but a cracked and fragmented thing. I looked back to the sky, nodding again and taking a lot of short, strange breaths. My decision. I highly doubted that.

After another bath, another round of gorging, I sat there reclining back in bed, focusing. It was easy to get trapped in this cycle, this regimented, scheduled cycle of eating, bathing, eating, sitting around and sleep by seven thirty at night. As Aisa had said, people needed me. I was always needed. I needed to leave, that really needed no extra thought. Like I was that enthralled with little things like eating and hot water. Why Neri, you can choose to save a friend, or take baths and sit outside. What do you do? C'mon, seriously. Also, if you do stick around, you'll wither away like an Alzheimer's patient yourself. The decision wasn't hard.

What I was held up on was killing a person's life off. I was pinned to this annoying body, but it still had its own soul inside, one that I have been staving off the chance to explain itself, to have a say in the matter. As I had told Raziel before, I always felt much worse sitting something out, letting everything happen, to have others suffer my consequences. My stomach bunched into a knot at the thought; these previously unconscious four years was the era of others suffering for my consequences.

No longer. That was done. I wouldn't sit by another moment longer then I had to. That started with pill I had taken an hour ago, one of my daily medications, responsible for driving my brain, the one I had been avoiding that kept Emalee Herring here at bay. I only took half my regular medication worth; I didn't want to go back to being that stain of an idea, that pushed back and limited section of life they'd trapped me in for four years. I sat back in bed, watching the TV and keeping my senses open to that actual old woman coming back to life. I had no idea what I was in for. I didn't plan it being much fun. I'd certainly be pissed if there was someone else controlling my body round the clock. Not that our situations were entirely different at this moment, come to think about it.

There was a rustling at first, a sort of restlessness that perked up as something only I could hear. Turning my head this way and that, I made sure it wasn't from something else. The rusting came again, this time with a little murmuring, a little uneasiness. God how I wished I could just rip myself out of this body without having to resort to this. Internally, I was standing around in plain view, presumably my hands behind my back nervously as that old woman slowly came back to life, slowly took form once more.

"Wh....what?" She said audibly in my own ears, inside my head. She tried to move her arms, my fingers twitching, grabbing on tighter to the blanket as her consciousness woke up.

"Emalee Herring, am I right?" I tried to be nice, tried to be polite for the soul snatching her body right now, taking control and not giving it back. Facts were facts though; she'd been circling the drain when the medication was forgotten, there was a very good chance that if she got full control of this body again, she'd keel right over. In the days I'd been in control, I'd actually been putting on a little bit of weight.

"Who…. What?" She tried moving her arms again, fingers twitching a little more across the blanket. I kept stern control of the situation. Still felt like shit doing it, though.

"Listen, time's short. You know your situation, don't you?" I questioned gently, trying to guide her smoothly through this, try to make the process more natural. It felt like she finally saw me, finally recognized me.

"You again!?" She screeched in my head, practically making my glasses rattle on my face. "Demon, get out of my body!"

34

I was afraid of this. Instantly this meeting became an all-out tactical body-war.

"Listen! Listen to me Emalee!" My hands were jerking back and forth like I was having a seizure. Thank God I hadn't taken more than half! The old soul thrashed back and forth, fighting with every inch of its being as my hands grabbed tightly to the hospital bed sides; she started to work the feet instead, kicking like I was marching in place and pulling the covers from our body.

"Stop that, we'll be cold!" I let go of one hand and grabbed the blanket back up, fingers shifting back and forth as I tried to keep my voice under a dull shout so I wouldn't alert the night attendants. I could feel her starting to tire out, starting to wear down already. She seemed fragile, even mentally.

"Get! Get get get get get out of my head!"

"I'm trying!" I fought back, trying to focus; it felt like my brain was starting to wander, starting to daze about like it forgot what it was doing. "I never wanted to be here, this wasn't my choice!" She wasn't listening, still trying to fight back for control of her body, pulling angrily at the strings without much result.

"I told you before to get out, you bloody demon!" She focused her attention on me internally now, at that fictitious meeting of two souls in one body plane. I tried to redirect the conversation her way.

"When did you first say that?" I questioned as my hands came back under my control more, as this old body came back to rest. My breathing was frantic, even with the oxygen on.

"Years ago." Her anger suddenly skyrocketed again, "Why are you still here? Why won't you leave?"

"Dammit, I said I was trying to!" I pushed back, stealing some mental awareness from her and getting more control of the situation. She was difficult, no doubt about that. I still needed to reason with her, still needed to fix things. "I'm trapped in your body, glued to it. If I could leave right now, I would, you've got nothing I want and I've got no intentions to harm you…. Not originally, at least." I could feel her calm down, start to break down that she couldn't fight me back entirely this time. Years. She was the one keeping me shoved away; no doubt she'd be this strong-willed.

"Wh…. What happened?" Her tone was much softer yet still very angry.

"Let me just… lay everything out for you." God knows I hated that long, slow reveal process of my own. I eased up a little, fingers and legs no longer shaking and kicking on their own. "I need to get out of your body. Nothing will get me out of your body, except if we end this little soul-transaction here. If I give you back control of your body, you'll go into respiratory failure and die in a few days anyways. I'm sorry. I'm… really sorry for this, I'd never take a life of someone like you unless it was absolutely necessary. Either way this life is done, your death is very close at hand."

The old woman quieted down, withdrawing into herself. After a few seconds of silence, she started these short, angry huffs.

"Well… that's… that can't be true. I'm not listening to demons!" She said stubbornly, gearing up to fight more for her body, for round two. She was a scrappy thing, I had to admit.

"Listen to me, will you? There's something that happens to a person, that they know their close to death." Fighting for civility in the oddest place, I was drawing on personal experiences now, not talking like I was directing the situation in a very leader-y way. "A realization, a dawn of understanding, an acceptance of death. Are you telling me you haven't been experiencing this? You're in a home; this was never a recreational visit for you. You had to of figured this would happen."

She shut up entirely now, no sounds, no hints of it. For a second I almost through I was alone again.

"I've never had to suffer through Alzheimer's myself; I can't say I know what you're going through. But I didn't wake you up to just tease your soul before I killed us off. I'm offering an opportunity." Still no response, no result as I just went on, "Is there anything you'd like to do? I can get you there, I'll keep taking these annoying little white pills so you'll be able to experience it, be able to see it without just dwindling away in this retirement home. Anything at all?"

"I want you to leave"

"I already said I've tried, I can't. I'm stuck here, you're stuck with me. Considering all the demons to get tagged with, I'm probably the friendliest." I shook my head a little, both actually and internally. "I want to make things right, want to honor your spirit, want to give something to you even if this whole circumstance sucks." There was more silence, pausing. I retracted a little from my own mind, leaning back against the bed and twiddling my fingers. She stopped trying to steal control, just silent, almost hovering around. I knew she was there, it felt like someone was standing there next to me, breathing over my shoulder. I continued to wait patiently, ready to fight an old dying woman for control of her own body. This was pretty low.

Twenty minutes passed. I could tell because the tough-stain infomercial on my TV had a fantastically annoying clock in the upper right-hand corner. It felt like they were yelling at me, screeching in high pitched salesmen voices to get out. Get out now. Just use this cleaner, and your stains will GET OUT. As I contemplated defending myself against the TV, Emalee spoke up again, quietly at first.

"Anything?" She considered, finally.

"Anything at all. Even if I don't particularly agree with it, you at least deserve what you like."

"I wanna go to church, I want to get ice cream and go to the beach."

"Yeah, that… well." I paused like I was going to renege on my deal. Church? "Okay, that sounds like a nice change from the retirement home setting, we'll make a full day of it tomorrow." Church. Maybe she was hoping I'd burst into flames when I got in there. In fact, I think she was counting on that. I turned off the TV, trying to get some rest. She fought for a while longer, trying to catch me off guard, trying to gain back control as I sat there, fighting her. I had to keep that control, that restraint, like grudgingly keeping an old woman from herself for my own needs. My eyes watched the TV, did my best to ignore what I was doing. It was terrible. After a few hours the struggle started to die down, started to ease up until finally she faded away like I had years ago. With shallow, regulated breaths of air, I relaxed, slumping tiredly into the bed. Hopefully by this time tomorrow, I'd be free. I could 'get out'. What a sentiment.

I awoke all on my own, greeted my own caregiver as she came to wake me up for breakfast and enjoyed about twenty minutes of retirement-home serenity. With breakfast I took that same white pill, still half of the medication, keeping the rest for later. Each one lasted about two to three hours of her consciousness and my impaired control. By the time I was finishing my breakfast I could hear her start to move again; I preemptively grabbed onto the chair, alerting my care worker Beth as I tried to smile through it, pass it off as nothing but indigestion.

Which really wasn't too far off.

"Oh, you're still here." The old woman said crabbily, suddenly noticing the caregiver sitting right there. "Beth! Beth! Beth, help me!"

"She can't hear you." I said tiredly in my own head, one eye closed as this Beth-chanting was giving me a headache. "I'm not doing it purposely, it's just fact and she can't hear you think words at her in your head." Emalee quieted down, grumbling softly.

"Beth, Can we go to church today?" I said blatantly as the woman sat up a little, laughing quietly.

"It's Tuesday! Church here is on Sunday silly." If they could, my ears would've shot back.

"…but they still have church services on a Tuesday, don't they?" I questioned like I'd explode if I didn't get to one pronto. Maybe in a way that was true.

"In town they've got some later services, but we've got a doctor's appointment today, check on your progress."

"Did you eat all this food?" I had to check for a second who said it, Beth's lips remaining closed. Internal dialogue.

"Yep. I don't get the opportunity to eat often." I said quickly mentally, before switching to an audible tone. This internal / external speech was going to drive me nuts. "Ah, that's too bad." I said quickly, immediately plotting alternate means of escape. It was a building, it was real and solid and fallible. I could get through it. At least three or four of my past lives knew their own ways to do it.

"You're going to get me sick from eating all this food!" The woman bitched some more.

"Low on the list of concerns right now." I said flatly, ignoring her, bidding my caregiver farewell and heading back to my room, practically storming the hallway, shuffling as fast as my elderly little body could go. What had I got myself into?

"So I'll have to stick around with you until Sunday then." I stopped mid-step, body cold, eyes flaring wide, looking around me for a moment, looking to the gown I was in, to my wrinkled old hands, the waves of elderly here and there, to the poor florescent lighting and scenery not unlike a slow-motion zombie movie.

"Oh Hell no!" I said hotly, darting into my room, dressing myself in record time and sneezing out the rest of the pills at the wall before I was ready to go. Down the hall was a door that the employees used for smoking off to the side of the building, and as soon as everyone else was in their rooms dressing after eating breakfast, it'd be busy. Charging down there like I was on a mission, one attendant was just about to leave, just about to out there for a smoke. The door swung wide open as I almost jogged, body and bones jostling around painfully, trying to catch it in time. No luck, the door was in full momentum now, coming back to lock me out, to lock me in with this angry old woman, to keep me here for another week.

Loosening my Berber-like slip-on shoe with the next step I punted the thing at the door, aiming, wedging it in the space left as it close. In another moment I was there, putting the shoe back on, finger slipping the medical tape over the locking mechanism and turning away to let the door close naturally. It hit the frame, bouncing a little, resting closed. With the lock pinned back I just had to wait for everyone finish with their smoke break and leave this place once and for all.

"We're going to get in trouble." She said cautiously as I gasped for breath, lungs working overtime. I turned on myself internally, wondering if there was a way to make a fictitious internal face of annoyance.

"I think that's the least of our problems now." I said quickly as the door opened, turning my face away like I was talking to the elderly woman sitting in the hall behind me. She stared at nothing, completely vacant, but it worked; the two workers passed me, laughing about something as I was immediately out that door, out into freedom. The door snapped closed behind me; already smiling with the outside world. With the oxygen tank underneath my arm and slip on shoes underneath my feet, I broke out of the greatest trap I'd ever been in, Palm Shades Assisted Living.

After twenty minutes of internal bickering, and another five minutes of a lengthy explanation why Emalee Herring only went to this one church instead of the other before she was too sick to leave assisted living at all, we were standing outside the Catholic church. It was a tall, extravagant building, well taken care of with an extravagant amount of stained glass. The sign on the door beckoned me inside, both sides of the marquee plastering a few different bible verses to goad me into it. There were few cars in the parking lot, well groomed landscaping outside of it with a sidewalk cracked and jagged leading up to the front from the sidewalk. Cautiously I went up to the door, prying my evil, insidious demonic fingers underneath the handle. It all rang out like a bad idea.

"Oh, here, let me get that for you." Someone behind me spoke up, making my old bones jump as they grabbed the other door and opened it for me. I looked to them as they gave a smile, nodding me to go inside, to take that leap of non-faith, to crap on what even Raziel suggested I never do. Well, I still felt fine walking up to it, curiously peeking inside, taking slow, painful, tentative steps. With a foot inside the door I held my breath, sending the oxygen machine to start compressing more air, turning on noisily. Determined, I took a few more steps in the building.

I almost thought others could hear the anguish and annoyance Emalee put off that I had no problem entering into the building, that I hadn't burst into flames as I took wary steps inside. A little frigid, but it was pretty comfortable, no problem stepping in, taking a look around, craning my neck back to watch the fans spin slowly near the ceiling of the pitched and stained mahogany of the Catholic church.

It was breathtaking, from the colors of light filtering through to the solemn peaceful atmosphere, just the air of respect asked for coming in there; I couldn't help but smile in wonderment. People's beliefs had lead them to build this fantastic wooden sacrament of their faith, a determination that wasn't found much nowadays.

"Is there going to be a service or something we should wait for?" I said internally to the old woman who was still griping that I hadn't jumped out of her body, that I had no problem, as a demon, getting into this church. It was actually rather pleasant in a surfaced way, the type of place I wouldn't mind taking a rest, kicking up my feet and enjoying the serenity. I was probably all types of blasphemous saying that one to both sides. Ah well.

"No. You missed the service earlier; there should be one at five, though." My eyes shot open in alarm, reading my giant-text wristwatch. Ten in the morning. I was all for granting last wishes, last regards, but I was not going to put up with sitting at a church for seven hours. Taking one last cautionary look around I pushed forwards, making the woman screech in my head, "What are you doing?"

"Bringing you up to the front so you can say some words or something, we're going to do the other stuff and come back at five. Is that okay?" I felt like I was coaching a child, like I was debating and delegating responsibilities, duties and times where it was and was not okay to do certain things. I just had to keep pushing on, keep reminding myself that I was killing this woman off, that I was stealing the last bits of bedridden life from her, that I was trying to equalize the wrongs I'd be committing. I tried a different approach, "I was thinking we could get some ice cream and sit by the beach while we wait."

"What, not a fan of the church, demon?" I could hear her hold it over my head; hear her trying to use it like an advantage. "If it's too much for you, feel free to leave." I looked back to the ceiling, glancing around.

"I actually think it's pretty neat in here. Human or not, sitting in one place for seven hours is a poor way to spend your last day." Moving forwards I got to the front of the church, to the last pew before the…altar or whatever it's called. Didn't want to assume, so I took a few steps back, sitting in the second to the front pew. Everything smelled like old perfume. "Alright, uh, go for it, I'll hang out and try not to pester your prayers."

The old woman grumbled a little longer, starting a very quiet, very soft prayer; I tried to stay out of it, looking around and noticing the little things in the church, the handiwork on the stained glass, the soft, sweet smell of incense, that like this, didn't burn or horribly tear up my nose like it did as a demon. I sat back a little farther in the pew, watching the clouds through the two clear, regular windows at the front of the church. It was so quiet, so relaxing, very ominous feel to the whole situation, but it felt like I was sitting around at a friend's house, that sort of natural ease.

Smiling I leaned back a little more, resting my eyes and taking in the soft sounds and slight wafting breeze that circulated. Part of me laughed, snickered that I was enjoying this as much as I did. I inadvertently heard more of Emalee's prayer, bits of it; praying for deliverance, praying for peace, praying for strength in the great test she was enduring. It was a great test for both of us; I opened my eyes again, looking to the people around me, all praying for something, all sending their wishes on a whim, giving their concerns to someone else, taking the burden from their heavy thoughts.

Maybe a little prayer wasn't a completely ridiculous idea; there was a praying pad of some sort beneath the footrests; opening it up I shifted myself down, head almost slipping past the back of the pew in front of me. I had troubles, I had worries. If there was even a sliver of a chance that this worked in any way, form, or idea, I had to take it. It couldn't hurt to loosen my burden, at least mentally just a bit.

"Listen… uh…God." I started out, breath almost invisible, knees cracking, "I know we're probably on opposite sides and all like this, that what I'm doing is probably very wrong. So don't listen to this for me then, listen for my friends, for the people whom I've hurt in any way, for the people that need that care and hope that I just couldn't provide before, or in my absence. Seems like everyone need protection, needs that reassurance, the hope that someone else can take care of it. I guess talking to you like this voids my stubbornness to always be that person for everyone else." I could hear the woman's prayer let up, going quiet as I continued on.

"Please keep watch over my friends. Keep an eye on Raziel, make sure he doesn't waste away to nothing, if he hasn't already. Watch them until I can get there and take proper responsibility for my actions. They deserve the utmost respect; I'm the one that deserves their torment, that wrath. So… yeah, if you could, I'll try not to count it as a strike you've stuck me in some unfortunate old woman…. Uh, thanks." I unclasped my hands, sitting back on the pew. I guess the human part of me still craved that responsibility thrown elsewhere, hoped that someone else could help me out. It was probably a pretty pointless prayer. Shrugging, I looked around some more, realizing the woman had stopped talking or saying anything altogether.

"Hey, you still around? You haven't faded out, have you?" It was getting close to that time when the medication was letting up.

"No, I'm still okay."

"Ready to go?" I questioned as I felt her nod, or give the general yes command. Nodding once I got to my feet, gathering up my stuff and leaving the Catholic Church on my own accord.

"Oh God, this is fantastic." I practically shoved the whole ice cream cone in my mouth; elderly teeth buzzing in pain and cold. I ignored it, diving in. We hadn't eaten anything since the breakfast that morning, something that my young adult body craved that constant energy, that food, that need to eat like a lawnmower. Emalee was still pretty full, but she wasn't bickering and complaining that was pushing her body too far, that I wasn't acting elderly enough. We went to a specific ice cream parlor close to the beach, just a few blocks down away from us; I could see it there, guarded by one slow side road and one busier four lane road. The edge of the horizon seemed to slide to nowhere, shimmering glistening water like a field of white noise.

"Who is Raziel?" The old woman asked internally as she seemed to grow distant, more far away from the situation. She hadn't been raising as much of a fuss since we left, little questions here and there but generally nice and quiet. It was a relaxing change; I was actually enjoying the things around me now.

"Friend of mine." I said shortly, wondering where this was going. I took another bite of ice cream, some kind of pecan shortbread specialty flavor. It was better than a thousand applesauces rolled into a chocolate crepe; I was in my own little version of Heaven right now.

"Is that whom you need to get back to?" Her words were short, deliberate. I stopped eating, tongue hanging slightly outside of my mouth. The ice cream dripped a little over my hand as I set it down, dredging up my frustration all over again.

"Him and a few others, I left things a mess." I laughed out loud sarcastically, woefully, "They have to think I'm dead."

"You spoke a lot of him whenever you first… got here, or however you want to call it."

"I did?" I slowly began to eat again, sucking down the ice cream like a vacuum.

"Mm hmm. Over and over and over again until I finally told you to shut up. Then there was just nothing. You didn't make another sound for years and years, for the first few years I could tell you were still there, never saying anything; but when I started taking the medication, it was like you disappeared completely." She went on, still wary but much more at ease. More relaxed, confident of herself as I started gnawing on the cone, finishing it off.

"Again, I really apologize for this. I've never actually possessed anyone before. I don't plan on making this a regular thing." We both sort of quieted down, wiping my hands off with the napkin as another soft breeze came through, making me smile just so. "Emalee, I don't know how you stand that place."

"Church?"

I gaffed, "No, the retirement home. They never let you enjoy this part, stick you inside most days. From what I know of retirement homes, it seems like a nice one, though still. I guess that's just an immature perspective; since I've never actually grown old before." Maybe it was from living in the world without senses that it made me over-appreciate simple things I normally couldn't; like Butter-Pecan ice cream or an ocean breeze, that while a person has that opportunity to enjoy it, to willingly avoid it - sounded more wasteful than anything else.

"I've had my life to enjoy; that kind of peace is best for me." I nodded physically to no one, agreeing. Didn't make sense to me, but I could at least understand it.

"Well, let's go to the beach." I said after a moment, more regretful that she wasn't so terrible an old woman, that she seemed to have her stuff in order. Maybe I should've taken a colder approach to it, distance myself physically, you know, don't befriend the lobster, just cook it. I guess half of me really wanted to feel the full weight of my actions, to remind me. On cracking knees I stood myself up, throwing away the ice cream parlor garbage.

There was an annoying tap on the back of my head, I thought it came from the past life auditorium at first, but after a few more knocks, more prodding, I realized it was from my favorite hallucination, favorite figment of imagination.

"Hey, hey!" She popped in like a nosy friend, interrupting my thoughts, whispering internally. "Maybe you should stick around in this woman's body."

"What? Why?" My attention to the world around me waned, a little offset that not only was I squatting in some elderly woman's head, but there was an even more elder voice in that sub-section that was squatting there. This whole thing was so damn confusing sometimes.

"I can't be sure, but they might've damaged the Colus. They tried something like this once before, it feels a little like it, but different, either way, it made getting around in that body a living Hell. Stick around in the meat suit and you can actually get to where you need to be."

"What? How would they do that?" I paused at the quiet side street, focusing more on my surroundings. "She's not going to agree to that, she wants me out."

"I do want you out, but I'd be willing to help if you need more time." Emalee perked up, joining our internal conference.

"See, she's okay with it!" Nona said happily. "Trust me, on your own right now is not a good thing.

"It's like one big annoying headache" I muttered out loud, standing alongside the 4 lane road, the only thing separating us from the beach. I could smell the water, see it ripple against the sand, full of umbrellas, white sands, families playing around, having fun. The sun was highest in the sky now, a sweltering, wonderful heat.

"There's more than one of you?" Emalee questioned fretfully, trying to sound like multiple demons in one person's consciousness was a common thing.

"Technically, no; but technically yes. Something like that." I said internally, finding myself growing more frustrated, feeling like our time was getting wasted, that if the old woman was coming with us, what was the point in doing all these things for her now? Why couldn't it wait, why couldn't we get to traveling back home, back where real danger was, and not just the danger of a sunburn or bedsores? Snorting absentmindedly once I started walking, crossing the street. Three steps into it I realized I was walking through cross traffic's green light.

Four steps is when the semi-truck realized this too. There was no chance, no possible chance. Our entire motley collage of Tresillo souls was blindsided at fifty two miles an hour.

Emalee's body and all physicality of our ties, it all snapped, cracked, broke away as our two souls were torn apart, dead on the front of the semi. The rest of the truck breezed through my soul, screeching, skittering to a stop as I, Neri/Nona stood where I was, arm still outstretched mid-walk in pure shock. The man exited the truck cab wailing, screeching, beside himself at hitting the old woman blindly crossing the street. I just stood there in complete surprise, taking a brief look at the massive holes in my hands, feet, legs, heart, all the places where that blue-flame goo had been applied. Just like that damn repeat parrot, I couldn't be trusted with something breakable.

"Son of a bitch." I gasped airily in my own voice, own body, head leaning back to look into the sky as the sun whirled past, with faint bits of black smoke as my body cracked back, crumpling under the Floridian sun.

When I awoke, it was night. At least it wasn't raining.

"Well, they definitely improved on the whole punishment." I could hear myself say just over my head as each lazy eye struggled to focus, brain struggled to come to terms with the real life and the life I'd just brutally walked in front of a speeding semi . White. White down my nose, white on the arm that I lay my head against. White everywhere, a white Colus. Nona was there again, projecting herself to point and ridicule me." If you didn't want the old woman to come with, you should've just said so." She laughed sarcastically, cruelly. Why were all my other souls such jackasses?

"Shut up." I grumbled through my demonic dinosaur mouth again. At least, that's what I tried to say. All that burbled out was something like "Grrherbler." Nona's face dropped.

"Open your mouth, fluffy. This might be bad." I tiredly picked my head from the ground, letting my bottom jaw hang, looking around. There was no semi-off to the left of me, nothing but a long, eerie red smear left on the pavement. Nona was bending down to peer into my mouth as my eyes couldn't leave that new bloody stain, even as she was obviously disturbed by what she saw. "Dammit!" She paced away a step or two, tapping her chin as I was left to gawk at my body; or whatever you could consider left of the Colus body. Everything was white. My head, my hair, my arms legs, body, everything. Worse, it was pure white, and fluffy. Like…fur. No wings. No nails on my hands or feet, tail half what it normally was. I got a mental picture that I was something more goat-looking this time with the same stupid dinosaur head.

"Your teeth, too, they're like stubs. Not to mention they've disabled your ability to speak." Inspecting my teeth with my tongue, I gave a panicked look to Nona, hopping to my feet. I was shorter then her, standing on all fours, I was at least three feet shorter then I normally was, maybe the size of a large dog. Generally, I was the size of a person hunched over scooting around on hands and knees like an idiot.

"What? Why? What the Hell is this?" I babbled through my half-speech, rambling tone unbroken and loose, sounding like nothing but incoherent gibberish. Nona just kept shaking her head at me, trying to reason it out; fine, while she did that I was free to panic as I please, finding myself jittery, zapped of all energy. I had none. That's that they'd taken, that energy, they'd crippled the Colus.

35

"Oh God…oh God" I ran like a desperate little thing, bolting straight north. Just keep heading north; go straight north until it the ocean faded away, then go northwest without another thought. Just…north, keep going north. That was the way back to my unresolved issues, the way back home.

I killed her. My steps pushed faster in a panic.

"Would you hold on a second? Maybe we can figure this damn thing out!" Nona bitched as I coughed and wheezed, exhausted already. They'd sealed all the energy the Colus had, that black smoke only able to barely give another form, completely useless and white and tiny as it was. I didn't have that boundless energy, I couldn't fly, I couldn't…skip frantically through space like I once could. I was just one little disabled dog/goat demon, running flat out on my own power. I was not as athletically fit as I thought. Everything was just wrong.

"You figure it out, you're the one with the time, let me just run!" The two of us were bickering and fighting like children inside this frantic brain, both wanting the opposite. Nona wanted to stop and figure it out, wanted to 'visit' people to help us, little detours that were days out of the way. Every damn interstate exit had a quaint little story behind it, someone that could tell us a grand old tale or some shit along those lines. I wanted to go home; straight home. No detours, no rest. I'd sat out of the way for far too long. We compromised by screeching at each other and getting nothing resolved. I do want to mention that I was winning, being nearly fifty miles north of what we once were.

They were trying to hide me, trying to disguise me. That's what she'd said, that the angels had disfigured the Colus enough that even my closest friends wouldn't properly recognize it. It looked wrong, it sounded wrong, and it stunk just like the cherubs did. Which in itself, was not the worst of the evils. But In a world full of fluffy, whitish Heavenly angel-like things, a white fluffy demon fits right in. They were ruining the only thing I could rely on, breaking down the very thing that gave me that power, that ability to fight back. They'd taken everything now and left me with a little four-legged wingless goat-like creature that had stepped right out of a bad children's movie with jagged, broken horns. My hands pulsed and throbbed, feet constantly picking up, putting down; I ran full out without a thought. Blisters cracked and busted, nails starting to wear down to nubs- I'd wear them to the bones if I had to. Through trees, through homes, through whatever was in the way, I ran.

"Just try and be reasonable! If we just head a little east, there's someone that might help us!"

"We don't head east, we go north! I don't care if there's a" maybe someone" two hundred miles east, there's a gaggle of" Oh my God Help Me!" 2500 miles west!" I heard the demon sigh heavily.

"It won't be the same protection as before."

"I don't care!" I pushed on, mind swimming in mental torment; they'd secluded me; I couldn't touch anything, couldn't grasp onto a train to help me, couldn't hop on a plane to take me back home. They were wishing for me to give up, to admit defeat and stay secluded and pushed away from where I needed to be. They couldn't keep me away like this; gritting my teeth, I was surprised they thought they could. "I respect the Hell out of you; don't take this as a threat. But I'm needed. Figure it out on your own, you're the great plan-maker."

"Hey!" She suddenly grew a lot louder in my head, knocking away any doubts that I may or may not just be yelling at myself in my thoughts. There was definitely a separate sort of consciousness happening as it suddenly grew a lot harder to see straight. "I didn't plan for this, didn't expect it. I'm just as worried as you are; I'm just trying to be a little more rational about it instead of rushing off like a madwoman." My pace was starting to get strange, more wobbling back and forth as I crossed a great field, plowed low. Checking back to the stars I adjusted my path, biting deep and bolting off once more.

"How do I know you're not that madness? That you're not just my own little insanity creeping up on me?" My body suddenly locked up with that last word, hands grabbing onto the other mid-stride and sending me tumbling over and over through the field as I got a face full of thicket. The dust settled.

"For God's sake." Only my back legs were my own, still pushing my face slowly through the dirt. With something like a slap on the head they stopped working as well, taken over by the fictitious part of my mind, no longer in my control. I gasped for air; twitching and struggling for breath on my side as the reeds and plants around me soared overhead into the sky. "Get a hold of yourself you impatient pain in my ass!"

"Our ass; it's… your…fault…" I managed to wheeze in distaste as it suddenly felt like someone was sitting on my chest. I gagged.

"Don't you dare try and blame this all on me!" Her voice spoke like it stood next to me, not echoing in the recesses of my mind. "Life is not that convenient and you know it!"

"You…distracted me… your plan…" I growled feebly, turned into a sort of squeal of breath after that weight switched from my chest to my throat.

"You walked in front of a Semi!" That was all she said; it sounded like she meant to say more, that there was more to it. The weight eased slightly from my throat.

"Your plan?" I questioned again, empty, dead and goopy on the inside. I didn't like feeling like this. A sick, sad little part of me coughed up a laugh, "Still your fault."

"That's it." Nona suddenly took all control from me, body frozen in time mentally and spiritually. The demon body gave out a little wheeze, "You think this is a game? You think I'm fucking around with you? You don't get it, do you? I hate to pull rank here, but do you know what I've been through? Lifetimes of this shit. Take this day, stretch it out for a thousand years, and repeat until its pretty much commonplace. That's been my life." She pressed harder.

"Yes. Admittedly, not the best plan. Don't you think I know this?" Her control let up quite a bit as I gasped for air. "The consequences, both good and bad, made it worth it. If I hadn't done this, you wouldn't be there. Wouldn't exist. Raziel would still be miserable in his crappy exorcism job, Amber would've never had you as a friend, nothing would have changed, the list goes on and on"

"You're just gonna absorb me later, what does my consciousness matter to you?" I spat out angrily, the main glaring marker of frustration that really had been plaguing the back of my mind. The idea of just being someone's notched tab in a plan sat with me like a small pile of rocks. Nona grumbled audibly.

"I'm not absorbing you, you're absorbing me…Which then you'll be me, so it's more like a compromise, I guess." The demon leader started over flatly, "I'm not going to be murdering your 'you-ness'."

I gargled out in annoyance, looking around quickly with my head back down on the earth. I couldn't fight what essentially was me, even if she spoke in overly-poetic riddles. "…seriously?" I chewed on it for another moment, easing some of the spitting anger away.

"I am being quite serious." The control suddenly washed back into my hands…paws… whitish finger nubs as the demon let go, showing her own exhaustion for what was happening. It felt like a deflating parachute on my back, heavy and sluggishly pinned to this outer form as I gained all control, as I became the dominant spirit once again. I rolled my piggish goat body into a tired sit, still catching up on my breath. "Even though I know this'll end up okay in the end, with all that's going on now, I am scared. I know that things will be okay either way, but I still worry for them all. I'm not trying to work against you, I'm not some all-plotting superbeing, Hell, I've been supplying whatever energy I've got to you to help, I'm just…scared. Get it? We're all just very human, more than anyone else really knows." There was a long pause, the sound of the wind whipping by overhead, the sound of utter silence and awkwardness refined and boiled down to a musty paste.

"I don't get it." I hung my head low. "I understand what I know. That's not something I understand. I'm surrounded by giant snakes and cats and angels and dinosaur…dragon…goat things all day, calling us all very human, it's foreign." I got back to my feet, swaying back and forth with exhaustion. I wanted it all to be over.

"In your next bout of plans, maybe figure on letting the spirit know a little more. I feel like I'm still being excluded from everything, that I'm some sort of worn-down, dilapidated thing. Broken, but everyone still expects miracles out of nothing." My legs suddenly started moving on their own, pushing into a light jog. I wasn't controlling it, I was a passenger this time, like I only rode along, conserving energy.

"Welcome to the way everyone feels. That's not just you." Her voice was a lot louder, like I was only the figment of reality, that she was the main spirit in control. "We all go through our lives asking this, demanding answers to questions that may not have them, we… mess things up, get things wrong, miss turns and end up where we never wanted to be. It only makes us realize that when we do manage to get things right, when things do work out, how much better it is because of it. If our entire lives were spent doing everything right, we'd be wrong. But knowing what we go through sucks, knowing we screwed this thing or the other up, that's how we know when it's right."

"You and your sister subscribe to the same magazines, I see." I said softly, feeling myself get tired, sleepy. The disabled Colus's pace grew a little quicker as Nona let out an annoyed grunt.

"Get some rest, I'll take over for now."

"We're going northwest, right?" I said uneasily, forcefully. The demon almost laughed.

"Yes, we're going north, go to sleep." She shut me out, punting me into an uneasy, nervous induced sleep, forcing me back. After a moment of stubborn rebellion, my mind drifted away.

I was there, suddenly; standing in front of that same house, the Priest's home that I knew but different still. It was a little like Amber's home, a little like the Priests home, even a little like the first mansion I'd taken to fight with Raziel, instead of against him. Everything around me was white in this dream, bleached out and unimportant, details growing more defined as it came up the composite houses' front stoop. It had little nuances I remembered; how the mailbox always had a sort of lean to it even after we'd had the thing repaired and replaced, how the front of the house was more worn by the sun then the one side.

It had traits with Amber's home as well, how the light reflected off the porch on rainy days, how the knots in the wood seemed to make a short little face. Standing around completely human I looked up to that house, trying to find the sun, trying to find the world outside it. There was none, fingers drooping over my brow as I dropped my hand down back to my side. The grass ensnared my feet, bloody ankles and toes wrapped beneath the soil, glued down.

My mouth opened to call to them, to speak out, to reach to these spirits I'd abandoned and considered me dead. Nothing. No sound. No squeaks, no chirps, nothing, dead silence. Frustrated, angered I pulled at my feet, tried to get closer, reaching out for that goal just a breath away, trying to move. Struggling, reaching out, leaning for something. I stopped; looking down my chest I suddenly saw a long pole sticking out from my heart, blood red coloring seeping out in all areas of the space, down my shirt, across the air, down to the ground; looking up I saw Raziel standing there, face determined, bitter, violent and uncaring. He looked war-torn, battered, beaten up and worn down, those eyes glaring at me like two icy shades of gray. The color from the rest of the landscape suddenly sucked away, dripping from the sides of the dream to get pulled back into the house. It was like the universe was dying alongside me.

"Stupid demon." He said shortly, pushing the pike just a little farther into my heart. He ignored my pleas, my repeating chant of 'no, please, don't, please Raziel, it's me' that I mouthed to the air. My body was growing dimmer, weaker as I reached out for those hands, reached out for any bit of compassion, for the trust I'd worked so hard to earn after everything. He only leaned away from me as I reached out for him, lip snarling back. "Typical demon." He said again, pushing the pike again, hard enough for the end to rip open from my back, wedged on my ribs. Twisting painfully my hands fell back down, falling from the side of pike to lie limply there, shaking my head slowly. No, no… not this time, not typical. I wouldn't be that. I was still something else.

Coughing and struggling, I leaned back up, pike still driven deep into my heart. Reaching out desperately I was suddenly in my annoying demon form, thick, bulbous hands reaching. I pushed on; I didn't care which form I had to take; leaning to take his hand I could tell they were suddenly a bit darker, more of a caramel color as it was Palug that stood there now, attacking me; his face was just as hard, as stern and unforgiving. The two people I'd let down most. Gritting my teeth I still strained, still reached out for him.

"Please…" my voice barely cracked, shattered. He only leaned away, face falling to pure sadness, pure regret.

"We needed you." He let go of the pike, taking an abhorred step away. "Trusted you!" I lunged out, trying to follow, trying to explain; each of my arms and legs was tied, tethered to the white, blank canvas of life around me. I cried out, again and again; it did no help, slowly pulled away from the dream, slowly having that peace dangled away from me. I got violent, shoving, tugging and struggling as hard as I could to pull those strings away, those anchors. Palug only walked back to that house, that composite, shutting the door without a second thought, without regret.

"No!" My voice went audible, screaming out, "Come back, please!" The house was sliding out of view now, minimizing and scaling back. The farther I got away the more faded it became, erasing into the background. Soon, the only things I could see were those little nuances, that crooked mailbox or shiny deck before they too erased out of memory.

"No! No!" I shouted again and again, fighting against those binds, those stakes. Thrashing. My one hand suddenly pulled up more, followed by the other, body rocketing from the dream as I leapt to my feet. "No!"

I stumbled, tottering around for a second as I got my bearings, breathing hard on the verge of tears. I heard birds as I perked up to the life around me; wheat- the regular kind, with a forest of some sort just across this small, four-lane highway - what a horrible dream. They were never predictable, came and went just to torment me that little bit more; I figured Nona was the cause of them before, but I didn't know now. Taking a few more deep breaths I noticed a harsh division of sun and shade; there was a sign casting a shadow just behind me with the cool morning air, sun just peaking over the horizon, taking a few worn, sore steps away I read it out loud.

"Welcome to Mississippi, It's like coming home." I would've been happier, would've been more excited, it was a fantastic first day of traveling. My hands were still shaking from the dream, mind still in torment. "Yeah, I wish."

"If you manage to keep a pace of 25 miles an hour, for a whole day, that's 600 miles." There was a tiny, worn, broken and disheveled voice in the back of my head; I barely recognized it as Nona's. "3000 miles, give or take to get back home. No detours. 5 days. Easy." I looked down to my demonic little goat hands, all scraped up, white tinged with blood from constant breaking and re-healing. At least I could still heal like that. My head hung low, ashamed.

"Thank you." I said softly, emotionally kicked around, beaten blindly to a nervous little lump.

"Good. Now get going and don't bother me." I felt her bit of consciousness snap away, receding back, resting up and leaving me utterly alone, just like I wanted, I guess. I stood there for a moment, chewing on the numbers, trying to get my head straight as I sat half in the darkness of the billboard, half in the sun of a new day. I looked back.

Home, the board was saying, go home. I couldn't agree more.

Through the next three days we ran in alternating shifts; I ran the day while Nona ran the night. When one wasn't in control, they were sleeping, a few short words about anything of importance in-between, but a lot of free time to think, to get things under control. I guess I was starting to see more of the other perspective, starting to understand why a person in that position would be as stressed. I never really understood the full experience, I think; one of those moments where you have to be there, that you have to be in those shoes. Trying to empathize with something I thought was fictional, well, wasn't easy. I couldn't go 'Well, sure Nona, I understand what it's like to be ye-olde Goddess of….strings and life and birth and all that.' If we were both here, who was busy cutting up the strings of life and all the business? Wouldn't there have been a noticeable birthing rate drop or something? Maybe some real difference in the world if we were oh-so important?

It seems like forever, running. Seemed like the earth was rotating to push you away, run you in place. Days shortened to a small blips of memory when the sun was low behind you, lighting your path all the way, high overhead and an hour of sunset right before you. It raced away, mocking you for going so slow, just like the cars did, just like the planes overhead, just like the train racing alongside. So slow; but we didn't let up, didn't stop. Through rain, fog, cold, sun, storms; across plains, hills, over rivers a mile wide, there wasn't much besides rambling worry and that desire to be there, to take responsibility.

After an assumed 1800 miles of running, of three and a half days of mindless panic and worry, the world began to turn up at us, physically barricade up from the ground; mountains. My sore, aching hands and feet stumbled to a stop as they were on the horizon, jagged, vague shapes in the distance that looked like a glorious mirage. I couldn't believe it. It dawned on me how much my effort was actually working, how much closer we were, despite the consequences, despite the Heavenly choir fighting against us. For the first time in a long time I smiled, racing forwards, faster than before. We weren't far! Don't lose hope yet!

As night drew near my tiny goat-like demon dinosaur body was practically racing alongside them, heading north, pushing away the crops in front of me, darting around the loose, scraggly trees dawdling at the bottom of the mountains. With the sun pushing through the mountain tops I had a better gauge of my travel, better understood just how fast I was going, how each action I took was beneficial, was bringing me closer. I couldn't help but smile as I panted hard, working my body and soul to its very limits. I couldn't care, I felt like crying, felt like breaking down out of sheer joy at our progress as I loped alongside those tall, impervious things.

"Well, we reached the Rockies, eh?" Nona was waking up, groggily coming back to squat in my mind as my half remained at the controls. "Alright, shove off, my turn."

My loping got just a little higher, almost bounding along.

"Not quite yet, I wanna enjoy this part." The demon pulled away from trying to take control, letting me be as I weaved around the passing street, bounding through the fence on the other side and back alongside my race with the earth.

"Alright, fine, I could use a little more rest anyways." She reclined back, aware of what I was doing, but more just hanging out in the back, critiquing my style. I used the time to get a few questions that had been pestering me as of late.

"Do you actually do any of that spinning, cutting and measuring Moirae stuff anymore?" I heard her laugh out.

"Nope. Not once."

"Did you do any of it?"

"No." My smile dropped, confused as I dodged around a car on an adjacent road, running back into the fields.

"The hell do you do, then?" The ominous little leader voice in my head only kept laughing like a big joyful joke.

"Nothing! We're a figurehead! We fight this side of the war while the other side fights us, even though in the long run it doesn't matter. Aisa and Cempe tend to stay on that line; we're more in charge of rallying the troops, getting everyone together for recreational war games." I kept running, half ignoring her. "I told you, we're a name, nothing more. It's not a name, then a bunch of ribbon cutting ceremonies or something, just a name, something to be feared by our enemies."

"I think you've jumped into deep end." I said softly, grumbling. "You can't expect me to hear that little soliloquy before on how wonderful life is, then assume scaring everyone around you is your way of showing it."

Nona's riotous little laughter died down, mentally giving me a sort of playful shove.

"Go back in your little goldfish memory, what have you heard about 'Nona' before you realized that's you? Was it anything bad? Even once? No. You've got people that look up to you, who regard you as a great asset, a good leader. That wouldn't be true if you were a colossal asshole to everyone."

"Why does the whole upstairs kingdom want us dead, then?"

"They don't. They want us out of the way, sidelined in this fight so they could wipe the demon presence off the earth completely, like they're trying to renew it. They occasionally make pushes like this." I could hear her voice tense up, frustrated, "Like that'll actually DO anything besides kill off people who don't deserve it. Listen, Neri, basically what we do is inspire the others, lead, include, bring together otherwise troubled souls who need that kind of bonding, need that experience, so that maybe the next time they go through that life cycle they'll have a better existence to live for." I stopped dead in my tracks, panting hard at the bottom of one of the softer looking mountains.

"Next time? Are you telling me demons go through that life cycle when they die? They go through rebirth too?" I'd been assuming that when demons and fallen angels died, they just fizzled out of existence, disappeared from everything. The fallen had told me how preciously guarded that ability was to die and live again and again. I took a few more cautionary steps, figuring it out on my own, "How many people know that?"

"Very few do. Mostly because dead demons don't come back as they were, they don't die and just become the same thing over again, the soul divides, splits up. The bits of their own souls are segmented, combined with fragments of others, re-joined and renewed in a new life. Basically, they're fodder for combination into a new soul. Our real hope is that the new soul lives a better quality of life."

"Wait, wait, so if that was true, then we're technically all fighting bits of ourselves, that some demons might've been angels some previous life, and vice versa then."

"A middle shade of gray." She smiled in her tone as I suddenly felt sucked into my own feet, withdrawn back, trying to grasp the magnitude of everything being said. That means that… geez.

"But… why shouldn't everyone else know this? That'd stop all this fighting, stop… everything."

"Exactly. Then life after death just becomes one annoying blank map of purgatory. You think a few souls without something to do for a few years get crazy. Imagine that being everyone. That's no fun." She took back a bit more control, trying to take the reins from me. "You'll get it eventually, skippy."

"I feel small." I said, shocked, taken back. "And sick." Nona laughed again.

"Welcome to the great all-knowing other side. Now get some rest." I let go of that control, felt myself drifting in more ways then one, sliding, floating away as a notion, as an idea. There had to be more to this all then just that, then just the illusion of order. Had to.

I tried to find comfort in this, somewhere. There was none.

There were no dreams that night.

Time began to pass faster; It took us an extra four days just to get through the rocky mountains, stubborn things standing like the angels themselves, barricading, keeping us away. I don't think there was a single moment where I missed those wings more, having to ascend and descend the same mountain again and again until you weren't sure if what you trod on was the same patch of land ten minutes ago. Snow-crested peaks were everywhere, land torqued and bubbled from the earth itself, darting high into the sky as you could only sit at the base, gawk at it. The scenery was amazing, despite our constant paranoia and worrying bouts of insanity, these lush, rolling hills dotted with cactus, shrubbery, clusters of trees and grazing cattle. It forced us to slow down, take more notice of things.

At some point we made it into Wyoming, the bottom part of the state stacked with mountain after rolling mountain, a little easier to take. It was Hell. Arduous, difficult traveling, disheartening as that distance gauge was irrelevant here, that it was pointless trying to see how fast you were traveling by citing just one mountain. There were hundreds of mountains. But eventually, slowly and surely, winding through the valleys with my eyes to the sky, we made it through. The land, green as ever began to stretch out, began to buck and kick with more grace, settling down to rolling, grassy hills. Traversable things. With yet another obstacle evaded, conquered, it only powered me more to pick up the pace now that we were practically a stone's throw away… under a thousand miles left.

This body was a wreck already; we had to scale back how much we ran as the paw pads on our feet weren't healing anymore. At least weren't healing correctly; they were mashed and calloused things, each of this demon's legs splashed in blood, reddish brown streaks splattered across like we'd wandered through mud. The stamina, the ability to push it was receding back greatly, instead of running all hours of the day, we rested four or five times for a half hour to an hour each. Nona had to keep reassuring me that if we didn't give this body a little rest and ran it to death like I was pushing to do; we'd be set pretty much back to the beginning, taking years, not days to talk with our lost friends and allies. Patience.

"What is the Colus, exactly?" I questioned one dusk in particular, body resting and heaving for breath near the top of a ridge, looking at the land as it spread below us in the western part of Utah. The deity-but-not-a-deity grumbled a little, extremely tired and probably not much in the mood to take up the next shift.

"Latin for Distaff."

"Yeah, yeah, I get that part already, hardy-har, it's a descriptive sewing element and a weapon, very clever." We'd grown closer; that's already an odd statement, but I felt like I could relate and understand that part of myself a little more now. "But is it a different spirit, a helper demon or something?"

"If it's got sentience, you're asking? If what we're doing is pretty much the same as what you were doing to the old woman?" She shrugged my shoulders for me. "I guess you could consider it like a vessel, if that's what you're aiming for. It's not sentient, it can't stand alone, and it's just fancy, personalized energy. Personification of wishes and hopes from thousands of years ago- you know, made of old sacrifices and love, back when the Greco-roman religion had actual followers. Belief is a powerful thing."

I looked out over the landscape as the world cooled in a shade of bluish grays, darkening, preparing for the night. Even now, I could see quite a few stars, slightly turned from when this little journey began.

"Why weren't we recognized, then?" I said softly, trying to get the Colus's tattered body to get back to its feet, shaky and uncertain things. "If I'm this familiar face, why was I practically unknown back at the house, and with the other demons?"

"I don't use that form all that often; people wanna be led by a person, by a recognizable figure, not some massive dinosaur demon. I only used it before in really dire situations, which that was, God, hundreds of hundreds of years ago. Most of the demons aren't around for that long, so our existence becomes fiction. C'mon babe, time to go to work." She pulled the Colus up all the way, shifting back and forth on wary, broken and damaged limbs. "Even then, a key understanding in leading others is knowing when to show your face and when not to." Nona set off, down the hill and into the scrub brush of Utah, heading Northwest. I stayed awake, watching out of the corners of my own eyes, looking upwards. It might be one of the last skies I looked under as me.

"Do you think Raziel will be the same?" I could feel the demon cringe up, touchy.

"I don't know, Neri. Originally, I'd say yes, but four years is a long time alone. You know him better than I do." I thought back to how resilient the guy was; of the times he'd thrown a hissy fit for not getting his way, at the small changes that used to make him go off the handle. For the first few months I'd known the guy I thought he might've been mentally unbalanced. But after what he'd said in Heaven, after telling me he liked how things had turned out, that he was okay with me being whatever I turned out to be; my anxiety only pushed farther. I couldn't lose that, the progression. My heart hurt.

"Just…hurry." I said those last words before slipping back to sleep, to another night of paranoid thoughts and dreams that ripped my confidence to shreds.

Two more days passed until that great moment; Nona awoke me early, shoving me awake mentally as I slowly realized where we stood alongside that highway, looking to the sign laid out before us in a sky streaked in pale grayish blues with the dawn of the next day. We both grinned, demon grinning as well in response, standing in front of the "Welcome to Washington" sign.

Even as the tattered Colus bled from its nose, worn absolutely thin, struggling for breath, I felt close to bursting. Early the morning of the tenth day of constant running, of tracking across the entire country on feet alone, I set out, breaking into that first stride along the highway, into the great state of Washington, back home. Please, please, let it all be okay.

36

Stop. Stop. Stop. Each stride I took in the waning light of the sunset was the Colus itself fighting against me, begging and pleading to ease up. I couldn't. This close, just these last few miles away, I just couldn't. One doesn't run for 10 days and just start walking those last few bits, doesn't stop so close to the end. Blood matted the fur around my nose, matted it under my eyes, matted like a fresh kill beneath my lips and burbled down my neck as my stubborn soul fought on.

"Neri! Please!" Nona was trying to keep the Colus together like a heap of loose parts, using all her energy to do so. "If they've survived this long, another few hours won't kill them!"

"You don't know that!" Dammit, she was right. Groaning out loud in a pitiful little bay, I began to slow down, heavy feet dragging and scraping underneath me as I plodded stubbornly along, marching forwards instead. A few hours back there'd been a spike, a little surge in direction; it wasn't the tether but it wasn't far from it, it was more like an untold tie, a sort of empathetic bond to Palug. Nona convinced me we were to visit him first, that if we managed to convince him who we were, he could help us reason with Raziel; the two of them were roughly 7 miles apart from the other. She said he'd know if there was a way out of this tie, he'd have the expertise to help us out. She didn't say why or how.

The Colus was heaving blood, coughing and spitting it out in a fine mist as we trudged along. My bones were a slurry of material; each step painfully grated them together, crushing them further. This body was worn painfully thin.

"What if he doesn't figure out who we are?" I asked Nona stubbornly, angrily placing each paw forward, gritting in pain. "What if he tries to kill us? We're too weak to do anything but just sit there and get the shit beaten out of us"

431

"He won't." She said stubbornly, chest suddenly aching in terrible heartburn. It took me by surprise. "I'm sure he'll know a way that we can get the Colus back to normal, at least long enough for this all to resolve out. We just need this damn seal to crack, then I can do the rest." Too tired to put up any more of a fit, too annoyed and too frustrated to care, I only marched on as I was directed, as I was told, heading towards that vague, waning direction. It was a pleasant evening, peaceful as far as I cared to tell. As we grew closer to that spot, that area I'd abandoned them at, when the overwhelming sense of panic and pain got the better of me four years ago, I got a real sense of how long I'd been asleep.

The neighborhood was built up, new stores I'd never seen, they'd widened the road, took out trees. Some of the new trees were much bigger, some unchanged, the street that had been recently paved was a dull gray, cracked and worn. We'd scoped this place out for hours him and I, carefully searching the other parts of this half-abandoned subdivision, if they'd be finishing it soon, if the funding was gone, looking through the records at the building manager's office. Back four years ago, over fourteen hundred days, it looked bleak. The office had been deserted the three times we visited before moving out, the lights darkened and machinery unmoved. But seeing the new houses being put up now, that our tether-like link was so close, they were glaringly in the open, living right amongst the rest of the suburbanites. This was not a good sign.

My footsteps were slow, methodical, plodding through bloody paw prints behind me. The sun was nearly gone now, nearly parted, leaving me the blindingly white thing in an area of darkness, head swaying tiredly back and forth. I needed rest, needed a reprieve from this insane journey, from this body so very weak and worn. My heart began to ache along with hers, beating strangely, longing for something, desperate trying to drive me closer to him and to the house as it rose into view, no lights on, the darkest house on the block. There were cars at the two houses next door, signs of good living and children's toys strewn about the yard. They were active places that could tell their own stories, signs of life everywhere but that house, the one with the blue tarp covering the top. My heart dropped.

"How do we convince them it's us?" I whispered to Nona softly, continuing on; she didn't answer. Tilted forwards my bloodied paws dragged those last few feet, as our cross-country mission of discovering ourselves by bumming around the states came to an end. I was afraid we'd bust in and scare the Hell out of everyone, that our unknown presence could be cause for alarm and cause a scene. No, thankfully, it was much more stressful than that.

Before I even set a second foot down something came darting out from the side, a long, black shadow of a creature, scars racing up and down its face like patterned stripes. I immediately stopped, taking a few

steps away as Manasa kept on the attack, darting back and forth to rear
back, hood flaring out, twitchy with energy and impressive speed. I froze.
Following closely after her was Kayalin, tired and worn down, armed
with a sort of short sword-like weapon and keeping tucked tightly next to
Manasa. Palug was after that, pink-ish scars scraped across his shoulder
and back, head kept low, spine raised. He looked just as exhausted and torn
as I was.

"Well. They're sending the scraps now, I gotta say. Maybe this is a
good sign." Kayalin said tiredly, putting the sword more over her shoulder
and looking to Palug. The cat demon glared at me, eye-vents opening and
closing quickly, trying to read what was going on.

"Palug! It's me! Please!" I called out best I could, eyes darting back
and forth between him and Manasa as she was coiling back, gearing up
to strike at me. That black tongue zipped in and out; wait…was that it?
Was that all who was left? Where was Raziel? This body couldn't sense any
others inside, couldn't tell if this was their regular defensive team, or if the
rest were all dead. The snake was just over me now, hungry eyes focused
without error as I began to shake. "Palug!" Limping tiredly I moved farther
away, giving a pitiful, desperate look to the cat-demon friend of mine,
letting out a low whine of urgency. Please. Please know me.

"This one's different." He said, calling out a little louder, "Manasa,
hold on." The snake's head snapped back to him before turning back to
me with a hiss, slowly receding some of her body back into the house,
precariously hung over his shoulder awaiting the command - this had to
be it, this had to be everyone; Aisa wasn't kidding when she said it'd been
a bloodbath. Why would they stay in the same house, then? If they were
all getting pared away; the angels knew where they were at, they were just
picking them off as they pleased, as they saw fit. The twins, the black dog,
the fallen angels - did that mean that Raziel was… no, he couldn't be.
Please no.

Palug took a few cautionary steps closer to me, bristling. "It reeks
like a Hayyoth, but it's almost like it's masking something, like there's
something else." My lips curled up slightly, shuddering with hope, with
promise. Yes, yes, c'mon, you've got it!

I stood up a little higher, hopping just a little closer. Please Palug,
please.

"You think it's here to send a message to us?" Kayalin scoffed,
following loosely behind, "It's half the size of the other fluffy lizard-ish
Neri-like demons they've been sending at us for weeks now." My eyes
opened wider.

"Bastards!" Nona hissed inside my head, speaking up finally.
"C'mon Paul, C'mon babe." She spoke without me, taking me by a slightest
degree more of surprise as the cat-demon was closer now, as my shaking
worsened. I couldn't help it.

"Maybe it's our great leader, I mean, it's got that same look of terror down, the 'oh sweet God don't kill me' look that Neri did." Kayalin stopped, halting on her words as the cat-demon winced, "Sorry about that, Palug." The demon ignored her, head lowering just a little more as he scanned me again, trying to figure out the great mystery. I gave a weak smile in the opposition of the circumstances, nodding forward at what Kayalin said as the words came out. But as he loomed over me, as his lips began to curl back in a snarl, I felt my chances just slip away, drifting out on the wind.

"She's been dead a while. They're just getting better at mimicking her, that's all. Try and break our spirits down to dust." Palug leaned back as I shook my head furiously no, trying to fight back, trying to state my case. He looked at me with extreme disgust only, searching my being one last time before turning away. "These bastards just won't let up on me." He said lowly as that look switched from a hardened, cold look and into severe remorse, just for a second before turning his back on us, heading towards the house in rejection. This wasn't the same Palug I knew, not a bit. It scared me.

"No, no, Paul, you're wrong!" My lips spoke for me, Nona taking control, shaking with sorrow, with worry as the demon mouth only spit out gibberish, gargled bits of language that flopped out like a mesh of nonsense, crying. "Please Paul, please, you know they can't kill me off!"

The cat demon stopped, head switching back to us, quickly, more doubt to his glare. He hesitated for what felt like eternity, trying to understand.

"If by some miracle that does happen to be my Nona, she'll understand why I can't help her right now, why taking her in puts the rest of us in danger." His glaze lingered for an extra second before shaking his head, lowly going back to Kayalin. She looked over his back, squinting at me as she looked back to him. "Damn them." He said shortly, heading back into the house, followed closely by Manasa. The world slipped back to as it had been. I sat there, a shadow of my own self, splinter of the pride and confidence I'd had. As Kayalin was the last to leave, to disappear from what I knew, I bayed out loud; a terrible, forlorn sound as long as my body could stand it.

Nona didn't speak as we left, as we finally turned away from our former group, the ones we led and protected. Slowly we headed towards Raziel, at least the place I figured him to go, where I hoped he'd be. She was a wreck, light sobs happening as breaks to the silence.

"Everything will be okay, eventually." I said softly, trying to repeat her own words, ignoring my own obvious hang ups. "He's okay, that's what matters most- when we get this all figured out, it'll be okay."

"He would've known how to fix this, Neri." She said stubbornly, cranky. "This should've been his type of work from before, and now even he doesn't recognize us. Paul's more levelheaded than Raziel ever was. What hope is there left?" I tucked my neck a little closer, coughing out another spray of blood, listening to the crickets on the wind, moon a mere slice of its full glory.

"He was the one we went after the last time, wasn't he? How the one angel spoke of us tearing apart Heaven for another, that was him, wasn't it?" I could feel her smile, just the tiniest bit, just the slightest warmth at the question. No need for an answer, really. The corners of my mouth tugged, just a little. We were the same reckless soul, over and over. The same breed of idiot. I wondered if my little soiree on my own just only proved how very 'myself' I was. That I'd always be. With a determined snort I picked up the pace, heading in the middle of the night towards Raziel, where I hoped he'd be. "It'll be okay." I said once more, straining into a loping jog.

It was bewildering. Palug, who had always been so collected, so warm and normal considering things, so supportive, in those four years had changed so greatly. That resilient spirit was crushed. Flattened. What would Raziel be? How would he be now, mind melting away those years of silence? I didn't care. I needed to see him, needed to protect, needed to make sure he was okay, even if he no longer recognized me.

If these Hayyoth things hadn't gotten him first. Four years. Sixteen seasons, waiting, sitting alone in silence, on his own. I hadn't been able to withstand two weeks.

With one last longing look I took off, breaking into a full run once more. Damn the consequences. Please. Please be okay.

It took four hours for seven miles. At a time where I could do that in less than one hour, my body was falling apart. With a heavy limp, with bloody tracks, with this vessel barely taking the steps, I swayed up that final street in the dark night like I was lost. My mind flashed back to the days I'd spend on the roof, watching the neighborhood, peacefully remarking on the things I saw, of the parts of life so new. I was broken. Busted. Beaten and trodden, ambling like a sick animal up that final street, the Priest's home in view.

The sign on the front door said it all; Foreclosed. The windows were boarded up in front, red paint warning over that, dim, dark. Cloaked in the blues from the sky, tinged in a slight orange haze, even from here it looked unwelcoming, cold. I didn't stop. I couldn't. Struggling, wheezing for breath I walked that same street, the street I once flew around like grand cavalry with Raziel attached, flying through the three houses at the end to try and out-wit Gauzier. The same street I called home, fought for, fought over, shot out from, dragged away from, exorcised. The leaves had all fallen away from the trees, nothing but barren, desolate landscape. I'd been too late, sensing nothing, no energy whatsoever, no signs of life. The thought stole my breath.

After a sigh, I kept on anyways.

On shaking, cracking limbs I stood in front of it, craning my head back to the roof, wishing I had my wings. Maybe I could die there, let this Colus body rest, get my re-do. It might take years, whatever it did to fix this situation once and for all. A silly notion, really. I had to accept it, accept that I'd been beaten, too reckless. Too stupid.

The mailbox was gone, smashed to bits, grass terribly overgrown. He hadn't gotten my letter. Tilting forwards, leaning forwards I walked up that familiar path, passing through the doorway to an empty house, water-damaged, mud tracked in from the animals.

"The St. Michaels is gone." Nona said softly, just as struck, as taken back at the sight. Everything was in ruins. Every part of it. Slashed marks up and down the walls, more graffiti, broken windows. I could see myself popping up though that part of the kitchen floor, could see myself running past with board games, running for my life from the football crazed angel. The hours I'd spend in the lounge room, enjoying the diversity of the music I was able to hear. The memories ran rampant in this house, projections of me enjoying life, dancing, socializing, sulking, fighting. My eyelids fluttered closed, shaking my head, trying to clear them away. I coughed out loud, dripping with more blood, shuffling over to the other staircase, brimming with memories, instances.

Taking slow, methodical steps down the stairs I could remember where Raziel accidentally punted the repeat parrot down them, how the back wall was cracked, and groundwater leaking into basement as it came into view, just as much in despair, just as wrecked. No sign of Raziel. In the place where he and I spent the most time, that basement, it looked just as neglected as the rest of it; someone had stolen the punching bag, just a chain remained. The TV was gone, the only bit of couch left was a small wad of stuffing. I could almost see Amber and I sitting by the torn bits of it, the windows so desperately cleaned scattered across the floor. Coughing again my vision was blurring, leaning my head heavy on the wall just to keep myself upright. One wary, wandering eye caught sight of the cot, still as it was, flipped over and wedged more against the side; it looked like animals had been sleeping against it, mesh bent the other way. I couldn't think of a more proper place to lay this weary body down for good, that rare bit of kindness I rightfully owned.

Paws dragging, rolling and leaving deep red prints wherever I went, I creaked that sorry body into that room, heaving for breath, shaking as I barely nudged the metal. I used to hate this room, used to detest having to be shut away and segmented off. But now, just being back to being submerged in these memories… My body took over, I finally collapsed, finally tipped over, finally lay down. Taking one last look around my head slipped to the floor, breath ragged, leaking blood pooling around my head in no time. I began to slip away. The canvas began to pull back, tighten, accept me once again.

We'll have to pick this up another time, Raziel. Palug. Please don't forget me.

Just as my breaths started to slow, just as I let go of control of this body, as Nona and I braced for that painful transition and the death of our vessel, there was a sound. A creak. A growl. My eyes fluttered, unable to move my head, view half of the other side of the room, half of the doorway. More sounds. More creaks. My breath got more rapid, still shallow, but more focused, more constant. I wanted to know what it was. The creaks continued, getting closer to me, just outside the room now. Honking for breath loudly, excited with a tinge of hope, I tried to get to my feet, tried to stand up, gritting the nubs of teeth I had. The will power fell away, strength was gone, nothing left. There was another growl, more low, more ominous and animalistic. Something was watching this house. Any glimmer of doubt that it might've been Raziel disappeared as the beast came into view, roughly 6 feet tall and probably 8 feet long. Fluffy; white. Looked a little like I had; it was these things; these impostors they were sending out to cover my return, to blend me with the rest of them by tearing down the remaining demons with what was essentially my form.

They looked a little like a dog mixed with Colus, white fluffy fur everywhere, but built exactly how I had been, little white horns jutting from its head. The face was fat and wide, insidious looking while definitely looking holy, at least sanctimonious. The patterns were blatant rip-offs of my own, faded reddish strips across its arms and legs, speckled and dotted long its back.

"Pitiful copy." I gritted through my teeth as bumbling speech, continuing to wheeze with each breath as the beast laid eyes on me, mouth upturning at the sight. You could see how it looked a little like I had, see that they were trying to impersonate me. Disgusting. The dog turned more into the room, nudging on the door frame with a grin, fur bristling, growling as it's lips revealed the full set of serrated, dinosaur-like shark teeth. It snapping out at me in the air, threatening, wary. I didn't move, couldn't raise my body up from the ground any longer. Drooling, growling, seething mess of holy leftovers, the dog bristled, hovering over my body; it's lips bristled and rattled, like it was speaking out, clicking, like it was calling for something to the air around it, whiskers moving around frantically.

What did it matter, really? I'd gotten here. I'd done my best to try and get back and help, I'd done everything right in my book. It was almost appropriate that this thing finish me off, start my journey all over again.

Small part of me smiled at the effort put in. They really hated my guts. It was pretty heartwarming.

The Hayyoth listed side to side, savoring the victory, nails clicking on the ground with distant pauses between the sound. The growl cut me like a knife, slowly ebbing and flowing as the beast breathed, lips curling up past the teeth, wrinkling onto its gums as the monster's eyes grew wider and wider. I could feel Nona's aggravation, her sort of childlike wonder and fascination scraped raw at having to deal with these impostors in routine, but actions and retaliation pinned to the ground as the Colus lay dying instead. I closed my eyes for a moment, bracing.

The growling stopped.

Eyes open, the Hayyoth paused, looking side to side for a moment as it's ears perked to something else, something far more dangerous. It's eyes rose, started to crane its head up, attention pulling towards the ceiling. In that split second transition, someone shot in through the kitchen floor- a blur, viciously fast.

"Gotcha!" The blur dove at the dog's neck suddenly as it yelped in surprise, figure of a man in a voice I knew, scrawny as all else tackling this six foot tall mish mash of parts in excitement. They tumbled into the next room, someone's head slamming into the door frame on the way out. In my dead-eyed vision I could only listen to what was going on, a lot of grunting, growling, shit being knocked around and broken farther than the paltry mess it already was. My breathing got faster, more ambitious, more dedicated. I had to know, I needed to see for myself. It couldn't be...

The whitish blob faded back into view with the dog, now missing an eye with its fur sullied, trying to throw the man from its back. The two of them scraped into the ceiling, hitting the door frame again with a bone mashing crunch before crashing down just alongside me with a rush of air, my eager pupil darted at them with as much surprise as I could afford to dedicate to it.

"You things are a real pain in the ass, but great exerci—" The voice stopped all of a sudden, head darting over the side of the white dog's neck. Raziel. Clear as day. His face scrunched up, disgusted.

"The hell?" He glared at me, squinting, trying to make sense of the situation as the dog pushed off with his feet, the two of them shooting into the wall behind us, solid dirt. He... h... my God. I couldn't die here. I couldn't give up. He was alive! Four years, a house in shambles, he actually looked better then when I had seen him last. Weakly, faintly, I could feel myself smile, russet tears sopping from my eyes. That bastard was still alive! My heaving breaths meandered into a sort of shallow, whooping laugh. He was okay; the fears, the regrets, the drive to get here, it wasn't in vain. Still alive.

Raziel and the Hayyoth popped up from beneath the staircase, darting across my vision once again; the ex- angel had a couple blades on him, one in hand and one in his mouth, rearing back to strike; as they got out of view there was a whooshing noise, a squeal of air, followed by a lot more struggling. Silence. Terrible, terrible silence. Gritting my teeth I managed to lamely drag my hands underneath me, body shaking, refusing to give up death. No. I would not be taken down this easily; I would not give into those selfish wishes any longer. Straining, working hard to pull my body back to its feet, I failed, limbs giving out just inches off the floor. I was in sorry shape, one I wasn't sure the Colus could recover from. Grumbling from the other room took my attention, crumpling back down.

"Been a while since they've sent me two at once." Gasping, tired, he strode back into the room, brandishing the knives made from his second pike blade. The weapon was laden with blood, stopping as he looked over me. "Though I consider you less than a half, at best." He…wasn't recognizing me, he was figuring me as just another angelic ripoff.

"Raziel…Raziel… please… it's me." I said, whispering vaguely as my eyes wandered away, urging language, good, understandable language to help me out, to speak, to get around these annoying limitations. Communicate. He didn't hear me, or he didn't care.

"Heaven's been working really hard to kill everyone else." He was more muttering and aggravated than trying to teach me a lesson, wiping the blades against the wall and checking to make sure they were still sharp. Raziel suddenly looked at me. "So how did you manage to get beaten up when the odds are so far in your favor?" There was hesitation for a moment before the exorcist shrugged his shoulders instead.

"I bet you ran into the demons down the road." Letting out a sort of resigned, unhappy huff, he got to his knees, scooting closer. "I'll have to check with them later, make sure they're okay." Watching his hand he grabbed me by the neck, slid a hand under one side and readjusted his grip as I whined, too weak to pull away.

"Well, I'll put you out of your misery then, you joke of a threat." No! No you idiot! The ex-angel leaned over, quickly grabbing one of my horn stumps and raising my head off of the ground like it was an everyday experience. Shifting hands he pulled the knife from the floor, concentrating. No! No! No, Dammit! My body wouldn't listen to me, wouldn't work, wouldn't function. How I was even still conscious was beyond me. Squinting his eyes, those same, familiar eyes, he began to press the blade against my neck, meaning to slit my throat in a humane way.

"Funny looking head on you." He said under his breath, turning my neck a little, trying to find the blue veins amidst fluffy hair. I tried pulling my head back, tried to get out of the way, feet twitching as they hovered over the ground. I was positive the Colus wouldn't survive a beheading when it was this frail. I couldn't much survive a cut, let alone trying to regrow a new head with the shavings of energy I once had. Teeth pulling back, mouth opening slightly, I pulled in the deepest breath I could, puffing my chest out. With all my force, all my willpower, I shot it out through my nose, that breath, spraying a bloody mist right in Raziel's eyes.

"Ah, dammit!" He dropped my head, leaning back and away from me, one arm trying to rub it away and clear his vision. My body hit feet-first, planted in a half-stand, half –sit, limbs shaking like wind-blown trees. But they held, just barely.

"That still only puts you back to half a threat, you little monster!" Raziel grumbled, setting the knife down for a second to ridicule my petty achievement. "What? You plan to leave or something? You're crippled, you stupid thing. Where are you going to go?" Where would I go? Nowhere. I was exactly where I wanted to be, not the best circumstances, but this is where I needed to be. I had to make him understand.

Taking slow, limping steps, I put one shaky, bloodied paw out ahead of me, very slowly dragging my back half those few inches towards him.

"What, so you want me to kill you off now?" He questioned dubiously, not moving but leaning farther back as I struggled, standing just before him. I could hear him gear up to say something, hand hovering over the knife on the floor, ready to strike back if need be. Grunting, pulling that last painful inch, I slowly dropped to my belly once more, tiredly laying my head on his lap, face off to the side, hissing painful breaths. Constantly, over and over, I spoke the same word again and again.

"Please." I continued silently, body in so much pain, please understand, please help, please, Raziel, I was so sorry. "Please…" The words were garbled like the rest of my speech, useless. We'd built an understanding on useless communication, though.

"You're sure affectionate." He was trying to scoot farther away, half baffled, half concerned as I struggled and gurgled with each breath. The angel looked around for help, for something to pry me off that wasn't his weapon or himself as his panic slowly began to fall, hearing him huff and complain for a couple seconds in. Then he stopped, leaning far back like he was about to fall over, then after a minute or two of silence, Raziel only sat there, suddenly just as tired and exhausted as I was. Looking up, he wasn't actually looking at me or this situation, he was just sitting there, quiet. Tired. Burnt out.

After a couple minutes of silence, I heard something shift next to me, eyes open as he raised a hand up, ready to strike back. But the hand hovered instead, letting out another sigh of resignation as it felt like he didn't want to deal with this, that he'd rather slit my throat no matter the implications and go about this with the same surgical accuracy that most exorcists are known for. With a frown, his hand caressed the side of my face instead, a gentle and compassionate trait that no matter the terrible jobs he had before, or the stuff he's had to deal with in surviving four years by himself, never left. He gave a dutiful smirk, holding my face with the slightest bit of pressure, clearing my bloody eyes with smile.

"We all have our bad days." He said quietly, switching to the other eye, almost in mirror to how I had back in the gym as a newly re-completed demon. Raziel ran his thumbs over the bridge of my nose, spotting a splinter and working to get it out as gently as possible. "Just don't tell anyone else about this, sound fair?" I was shocked. He'd become so much more of a rounded person, albeit accomplished Hayyoth killer.

Tears suddenly welled up as I broke down, staring back at him like that. This is the closest I'd get to that interaction again, the most I'd be able to communicate with him. It all felt so impossible and heavy for a moment, overwhelming me; he'd lost so much and he seemed almost happier.

The relaxed grin fell away, surprised and confused as Raziel tried to understand.

"I didn't know Hayyoth could cry." He whispered, picking at some dirt and blood by my nose, pointing my head back off to the side as if I made him uncomfortable. It was like being trapped behind bulletproof one way glass, next to the finish line of a race, unable to interact as you watch your friends and family look desperately for you. Pure agony. Raziel worked on getting rid of the crud by my eyes. "You're welcome to rest up here, if you pull through. But just remember that I didn't kill you off, so I'm just asking for you to return the courtesy, okay?"

I tried to nod, heaving being mistaken for struggling to breathe as he was worried, looking me over for a second.

"You're in terrible shape though." He shook his head, moving me around a bit to just pet me like a sick animal. If all I ever got from that delirious running was 15 seconds of interaction like this, it almost felt worth it. "Just don't call anymore Hayyoth here, okay?" He pat my head especially hard, tinged in sarcasm.

"Not what I figured I'd be doing today." Raziel muttered, sitting against the wall quietly, stroking my head like a family pet. Not what I figured my Saturday to be either.

I closed my eyes peacefully. Happy. If I could rest up and pull through this, then there should be some way to convince him who I am. If I survived. Raziel let out a peaceful breath as I did the same. We sat there for a couple minutes, just the sound of the house settling, the wind slowly blowing through the window in the next room; just peace and quiet.

A grumble, a sound as Raziel had his eyes open, looking to the cot thoughtfully.

"You know, you're not all that far off." He said nonchalantly, solving some doubts that he didn't remember me at all. "The other Hayyoth seem to just throw color and pattern around and hope something works. They've gotten better at it in the last few weeks, though." He stopped, thinking about something for a moment before going back to stroking my neck.

"Your head's about right, neck's too small, but you're stocky and kind of dense like she was." He turned me to face the ground more, demonstrating in a way that I'm sure he was still talking to himself for the most part, but using me like a helpful prop to run things over in his mind. "You're way too white, missing the goofy colored spine hair, but at least you've got the mark on the right si..." Raziel stopped. Opening an eye, he was staring right at my back, not moving, not doing anything, just glaring at me, before suddenly looking up and around, before back to my neck.

"W...weird looking stripes you've got here..." His voice faded to a whisper, frowning before putting a hand on the mark. "Uh..." He said, voice already drawing back, alarmed. The seal, the disfiguring scar- it must still be there, he could see it. Raziel started picking at my back, swooshing my fur to one side or the other. The other hand was suddenly there, looking through the discolored mark to my skin, leaning close and looking for himself. He readjusted me in the light that was left, looking one more time before leaving both hands across my back, sitting there. Glancing up at him, his eyes were tracking side to side a little, wide and panicked. I could feel myself start to smile. He knew.

Raziel started breathing through his nose an awful lot, almost mad as he suddenly looked back down, determined. Leaning close, he put one finger on the very edge, at the start of the seal. The finger followed the exact curves of the blade, opening an eye to see him intent on the mark, eyebrows furrowed. With each unnecessary loop, his hand shook more and more, eyes wider. About to trace the whole thing he stopped, glaring at me. The ex angel didn't move.

Tentative, cautious; the picking got more frantic, moving my body just a little, looking for something. Before I knew it he was propping open my one eye as it lazily rolled around, struggling to focus, staring into it. Looking into those same blue eyes, the ones that had once haunted my memories, that I feared, to see them click and understand one more time, I felt like dancing. He opened my mouth, checked my back, returning to my eyes as they teared up more, mouth slowly snaring back, giving a weak smile. He knew.

Raziel suddenly leaned back a little bit, putting his hands up over his mouth. His arms were full of goosebumps.

"Pl..." He choked, mouth opening and closing, gasping like a fish, his face began to contort up, almost disgusted, letting go of the word I wanted to hear like it was accidentally dropped.

"...Neri?"

My smile pulled back farther into a hearty grin, shuddering painfully.

"Holy shit!" He suddenly jumped to his feet, standing out and away from me as my head hit the floor. I groaned. "Hoooly shit, you're supposed to be dead!" He was pressed against the wall tightly, shuffling back and forth with his hands in his hair, completely taken back and surprised like I'd spontaneously combusted.

"Y...You can't...buh..." Raziel seethed, struggling to breathe normally. The angel gave a quick, delirious laugh before shoving his hands at his mouth, "EEh, you have to be kidding m..." He wandered towards the doorway like he was going to leave before doubling back around, shaking his head fervently.

"They looked for you for…ever! Why… what happened?" My one eye tried to follow him as he swirled around the room in a panic. Something heavy and dark welled up in my throat, pausing to cough out a pile of blood for a moment that was almost black. My legs rattled as I slumped back to the ground, feeling a bit better. It didn't look pleasant, though.

"Ah, Jesus! Shit! Hold on!" He suddenly bolted from the room, running into the other part of the basement, looking for something, leaving me by myself.

"Can the Colus heal back from this far?" I asked Nona tiredly.

"I'm not sure, Neri." I could feel her shaking her head at the situation as well, floor above me thumping around for a moment as Raziel ran about. "He's...I'm glad we know him." The Colus smiled a little, nodding out of nowhere, to no one.

"Yeah. He's a good guy." Raziel came down the stairs behind me, arms full of dirty, dusty bottles of random medicinal cures and old angelic remedies. He stood over me for a second, shaking his head some more.

"I can't believe you're actually here. It's been years. At least three years. More than that, maybe. I don't have a calendar, so I'm just guessing; where the Hell were you?" He sat back next to me, rummaging through the bottles, trying to see what'd work as I wearily leaned forward, dipping a finger in the blood strewn about and dragging it to a clear section of floor. With the best of my artistic abilities to both draw, and manage to put one finger out to do it, I drew a picture of Florida in my own blood, moving the finger down towards the bottom and tapping on the floor to get his attention.

"What is that, a hat?" He laughed quickly, peering at one bottle in particular and looking back to me. "They kick you into the Great Lakes or something?" I grumbled with that weak smile still on me. He was just the same, thank God. A little more talkative and jittery, but the same. Taking a long breath in, I tried to speak a little louder; just being around friends, being happier than I was, I was starting to feel a little better. A little more energized.

"Florida." I said at a regular tone, same gibberish, garbled language being heard. Raziel stopped, raising an eyebrow and leaned over his back, picking up one bottle in particular. His hand grabbed around my nose, pulling my head back and popping open my mouth.

"They haven't done this trick in years, lucky you." He grumbled, shoving the jar of whatever it was down my throat. Instantly my mouth was on fire, burning like a thousand hot peppers grated into my nose. My eyes twitched, shaking my head back and forth, coughing. It felt like I could shoot fire out of my mouth, like my teeth might get up and run away, like my throat was dissolving. Definitely felt a lot more awake; painful shit. "So let's try that again, where were you?"

"Aghe..geh… sayd….Florida…dammit." I spit out, the last few words actually sounding like I meant them to. My eyes went wide, both of them. Looking back to Raziel, the ex-angel grinned wholeheartedly as I tried to do the same. "Four years… two months… there was a calendar at the front desk." My words were weak, soft, but defiantly my own. His hands suddenly grabbed both sides of my head, pulling my limp upper torso into a tight hug. I struggled to return the motion, limbs twitching around.

"It's really you!" He said happily, my neck craned back at a weird angle. My body was still a mash of organs and broken bones and muscles, it was all pretty painful, but I was too happy to care. "God, Neri, I'm so glad you're here! I'm sorry I was going to cut your throat! Everyone thinks you're dead! What the hell happened!" Grinning, I tried to hug best I could before realizing he was expecting an answer.

"Old." He let me out gently, propping me up on the floor as I sat up, swaying hard side to side. With a stubborn cough I sat up taller, forcing myself to be as normal as I could. Definitely feeling better. "I was... they trapped me… glued me to her. Couldn't… wasn't conscious…they screwed up, that's..." I coughed again, gritting my teeth and shaking my head. No more time for thoughts of dying, not anymore.

"You seem..." The angel looked over to the pile of old blood on the ground before back to me, nervous in bringing it up like we don't talk about the giant pile of blood in the room. "Unwell." A smile.

"I am unwell." Focusing, I could do this, I could actually be helpful instead of disjointed and tired. "They bound me to a soul. She had medication that made me nothing. Walked in front of a truck. Not on purpose." Raziel leaned back, surprised.

"A soul?" Shaking his head he tried to pick apart the bits of information he could. "A truck?"

"Retirement home, Alzheimer's. Florida... I can't believe it's been four years, it feels like last week." Glancing up at him, I looked around at the state of the house, at the passage of time. "How...how did this happen?"

"This?" He motioned to the house as I only nodded, distraught. "I'm not an exorcist anymore, so the Priest had to move out. He left the basement as it was so I had a place to stay."

"That's nice of him but what happened to the rest of it?" The walls were scratched and dented, evidence of years of battling going on as the angel crossed his arms. Scars raced up and down them.

"Well they've been sending Hayyoth my way for years now, and eventually everything got busted up." Raziel pointed upwards with a nonchalant laugh, marginalizing the undoubted years of anguish and loneliness he'd endured. "I actually live on the roof now, most of my leftover stuff is there. It's not so bad. Florida, eh? How'd you manage to get all the way here?"

He was going through the full range of emotions, half annoyed and angry, to ending those annoyed and angry sentences with a smile. I never realized how much I missed this. My chin began to bobble.

"Ran."

"The entire way?" He said incredulously, eyebrows perched high on his forehead, threatening to merge with his hairline. I gave a weak smile, looking back to the floor. The ex-angel shook his head, "Yeah, that sounds like the sort of stupid shit you'd do. It's you alright, no question." He started to laugh, sitting farther back, still trying to take it in.

"I… didn't know what had happened to you. If you were dead, if you'd lost it… four years alone…that'd you'd forget." I tried to bite my lip, tried to hold it together, but I just couldn't. It was a strange mix of laughter, of smiling, of utter disabling relief as I wept, tears ruining the nice work he'd done cleaning up my some of the blood that collected by my eyes.

"Neri. Hey, stop looking at the floor for a second. Neri." I picked up my head as he held his hands out, looking around quizzically as a joke. "C'mon. I appreciate the vote of confidence, but I'm fine. I'm okay!" I only choked up more, gagging on words.

"I know, I'm happy… I swear." I shook my head a little more, half grinning and bawling at the same time. The angel scooted closer, hugging me again. I was still so utterly exhausted, still so broken down, but my spirit was happy. It compensated a lot of pain. Very happy. "I can't hug back in this stupid goat body." I coughed and laughed, wiggling my dumb goat hands around.

"Most people are saying you exploded." Raziel laughed and patted my back.

"I did! I did explode. They put some goopy crap on my body, I exploded, then it was 4 years later and I woke up in a bed in Florida." I looked to the side for a moment, squinting. "I don't know how that all works out either, but they're not wrong. Wait, who's they?" Raziel let me out of the hug, setting me back down as I sat there, disheveled. Shaking like a wet dog, I sat down with a huff.

"Other demons in the area. Heaven's been boasting about how they've killed you for good for years." My ears went back. Raziel looked aggravated as well, before flopping back to the happy side of things instead. "So what did they do? Why do you look like a goat dressing up as a Hayyoth for Halloween?" Laughing echoed in the room, not expecting his very honest opinion as I definitely missed talking with him. I leaned against his shoulder as we sat there in the room, backs against the wall.

"Apparently they've put a seal that doesn't let me access any energy besides what I have. Nona's on the other side of it, so she can't actually join back or do anything, unless we crack it somehow." I inspected a hoof-ish paw hand, twisting it over to the other side to show the messed up paw pads mushed from hours and hours of running. "The Colus apparently started as a series of animal sacrifices, usually goats, but the Hayyoth flavoring is Heaven's take on it. You wouldn't happen to have an idea how to crack this seal, would you?" Raziel looked surprised, thinking hard for a moment.

"Something with a lot of energy and a sharp point would probably do the trick. You're asking to pretty much do the same thing you did to the Saint Michaels barrier back at the high school." I could hear him gently saying he couldn't help in the middle of his words, "There's nothing like that here, but I'm sure we can figure something out." He hesitated for a moment before clearing his throat.

"So you're still... uh... learning about yourself?" Raziel squinted as I gave a laugh.

"Yeah, we've had hours of conversation on the way back here." I shrugged, motioning to something else like she was sitting next to me. "She's hanging out." The angel started to say something else, suddenly stopping and looking over to me with a sly grin.

"Did you fulfill your promises?" He almost whispered it, like we could get around talking about Nona without her knowing- he was talking about promising to bitch her out as soon as I could. Laughing, I started saying something, control suddenly snatched from me before I got a word out.

"She did." Nona's mood was much less jovial, but still not unhappy. Horrified, I shoved hard to get control back as Raziel seemed off-put and shocked. "I did. I d--- don't do that mid conversation, it's creepy." Growling under my breath, I looked back with as normal and as undisturbed grin as I could. Nona moved the Colus's arms to do a sort of shooing away, 'meh fine' type of motion. He gave a quick laugh before shaking his head, looking out into the other room.

"Can you walk?" Raziel spoke up as I was pretty comfortable slumping where I was. With a couple tries, I managed to get back to my feet, body swaying around, but definitely stronger and more put together than I had been. The Colus toddled around, exhausted.

"Sorta. I feel a little better, but it feels like I need a couple days of sleeping or recuperating to feel less like my bones are made of sand." I realized something, "No offense." Raziel gave a laugh.

"None taken, they're only made of dust when you're an angel, I'm legit now." He hoisted it like a compliment, also getting to his feet, picking up the swords from the ground and avoiding the blood pile. "It might be easier to rest up on the roof, I can carry you up there. Hayyoth tend to come in this way so we're not safe here." I nodded. Raziel leaned over to pick me up, stopping for a moment.

"I'm genuinely sorry for treating you like an animal though. And nearly killing you. Again." I scoffed.

"Don't be, it was nice." I said quickly as he hesitated. "Well obviously not the killing part, I mean..." A sound, something heavy in the next room. We both froze.

Then it came again, that most inconvenient, ominous sound, a creak of some sort, a light growl that swept through the house, breezed past the doorway, just for us. We both stopped, looking to the door frame. Raziel set me down gently, arming himself with the knife and tiptoeing towards the door frame.

"This has bad news, 'this is a trap' written all over it." I said flatly. He stepped around me, peering out from the room against the back wall.

"They've been sending them more and more frequently." He said softly, scrunching his face up, "They're just Hayyoth. Thankfully I've gotten good at taking them down on my own, I can handle it."

"They know I'm here, that other Hayyoth must've let them know." Internally, Nona affirmed this statement. He started to creep closer to the door, gripping the knife tighter.

"Raziel, please." I begged, starting to get anxious, worried. The ex-angel only turned to me, beaming just a bit.

"It'll be okay. I swear." He passed through the doorway, something sparking up immediately behind him. Barrier. Same barrier that had been there before, that had kept me locked in this room, that pinned me into this house when the St. Michaels was being said. Raziel noticed it too, eyes flaring behind him as the door warbled with the energy, visible and angry. "Dammit!" He said as I stated the same, head snapping quickly to the basement's main room. A raucous, audible growl escalated, harmonizing with more than one member as he almost shimmied on his feet, eyes going wide. Panic. Fear.

"Dammit!" He yelled again, darting away from the door as a whole pack of Hayyoth chased after him, growling, snorting, chasing him down as he bolted up the stairs.

"Raziel!" I shouted, dragging my worthless, broken self up to the door frame, trying to see him. The barrier flickered and sparked, kicking me forcefully away from it, hitting that back wall. Charged as well, it pushed me back to the middle, my senses and reasoning flickering and twitching. From far away, straight out of a horror movie, I could hear him yell, cry out in pain.

"Raziel!" I shouted back, trying desperately to kick myself out of my own little comfort box.

37

"Let me go!" I screeched, staggering back and forth like I was drunk. Listening, desperate to hear anything, I could just barely hear Raziel yell, somewhere alongside the house. Who's barrier was this? "Raziel!" My voice echoed off the barrier's walls as I panicked.

I coughed out hollowly, body still aching, sick. Hearing nothing but deafening silence, nothing but the ebb and flow of time, I seethed, head down, charging for the doorway. The barrier was hot, sending a sickening wave through my body made of embers and ashes. Connected for a moment it threw me backwards again into the wall, which kicked me into the middle of the room. One eye twitched, jumping back to my feet only to slide off to the side, disoriented. Coughing again I righted myself, head and nub horns to the barrier once again with the same result, battering my poor goat body.

I'd use the Colus for whatever it had left, whatever progress in healing I'd made. I'd fight in this slack body with every pained, goat-like breath I had left in me.

Shakily gathering to my feet, I shook the blood from my face running full steam at the barrier, thrust more violently around the room, blood trailing after me. My body was spasming, struggling and twitching, head aching once more. No energy. I shuddered to the ground.

Nona's voice was suddenly there, eagerly kicking at me, rooting me on.

"Wait, do it again! Get up! Keep doing it!" She said. About to whinge and protest, she cut me off. "He's counting on you! You want to help him? Get up!"

Taking a couple short, wheezing breaths in I shook my head. I couldn't let him down. I couldn't let myself be tired when he's spent years up on the roof believing I'd come back. I couldn't disappoint him like this.

Sliding my limbs underneath me I rose back to my feet, legs shaking, heart pumping. Glaring the barrier down like the punching bag, I let out an angry, frustrated snarl and took off towards it.

We hit. My horns connected against the barrier, resonating that crumbling, burning feeling as I pushed as hard as I could. Just as the barrier was about to shoot me away again, I grit my teeth and pushed harder. The barrier began to sing.

"A little more!"

I heard Raziel again, yelping out in pain. I bayed as loudly as possible, this tormented, struggling sound of desperation resonating within these tiny walls. I stayed up right against the barrier, feet kicking out from under me a few at a time, head buzzing, swirling and shocking violently while colored streaks of light darted in arcs from my head. I shoved against that barrier harder, pushing with everything I had until it felt like the energy would tear me in two.

"Wait….wait….." Nona's voice was growing softer, "Wait…wait wait…….almost….yes!" She laughed out loud as I suddenly responded; my vision doubling before coming together quickly. Energy pumped in my veins as I kept pushing, cracking the barrier and surging through.

My mind lit up, eyes going wide as the last bits of my soul melded together, shaking. Energy surged through my skin, flitted and darted about, desperately finding a place to be useful as I only cracked my head towards the rest of the basement; four Hayyoth stared blankly back at me. I gave a smile. It didn't seem to help things.

Smoke and dust swarmed my form, screaming through the cracks of the seal, pushing and fighting my way back to full size. There was a heavy thumping, my heart, stretching out, working as it originally did at the breadth it was made to be; growing as I did it pulled the very edges of myself, head suddenly into the place the operating table once stood. It felt like I was pumped full of energy, like every sinew, every base of myself awoke and was vibrantly alive. The rest of my horns shot back into existence with a painful jab, teeth grew sharp and lovely, white fur fell away like Christmas snow. I could feel myself rise up, bristling with energy, with power, with determination. Back and forth my eyes tracked, trying to understand, trying to make sense as my hands open and closed on their own. But I was solid once more; no part was unaccounted for, no vapor of an existence lurking around. Finally, it all snapped back into place.

I was gargantuan, I was unwieldy and strong. Energy was no longer rationed, doled out sparingly like a soup kitchen; it was a well, a river, an entire ocean at my disposal. I felt formless. I pushed through the floor, head somewhere near the Priest's bedroom, shoulder in the kitchen, tip of my tail far out by the street. The gangly teenage version of the Colus from before, I was easily twice that size, if not more.

The smoke fell away, red nose in view, higher than it had ever been by the ground, hunching just to see into the basement as I towered above it. The four Hayyoth in the living room remained frozen, senses picking up the other five outside attacking Raziel. I gave an enthusiastic smile, pulling back farther to bare my teeth as my growl shook the nails from the walls. The Hayyoth fought each other, scrambling out the backside of the house as I was happy to follow.

"Need something?" My head surged from the basement mud, catching three of the four hayyoth by their back ends, ripping them underground and burying them beneath the house in an instant. A sound, a panicked screech near the fence; my eyes focused tight on it, wings partially open, surging from the basement in an effort to help.

My spade-like horns broke through the ceiling of the basement as I charged full at the four hayyoth there, head low, pulling and tearing up the remnants of the couch, snagging and ripping the chain from the wall. With a smile I pushed hard with my back legs, gritting my teeth, I erupted through the side of the house, ripping the entire wall from the cement in the process. The house moaning out, tilting onto its side as I made my grand entrance back into the world. Tall enough to look into the third story windows, strong enough to hold it over my head; no kidding I was a force to be reckoned with.

They stopped for a moment, the Hayyoth instantly scattering from Raziel as his arms were bitten up and bleeding pretty badly. He looked to them for a moment before turning around, face aghast at both the house crumbling behind me and the massive sixty some-odd ft tall beast barreling towards him. I gave a very recognizable smirk, tightening my glare.

"Jump!" I shouted. Raziel gave a half assed and extremely unsure hop; I dipped one horn into the soil to catch the angel on the top of my head, darting forwards and eliminating the rest of the Hayyoth behind him in one move. Turning around, spitting them all back towards the house, the insides were immediately writhing and churning with more Hayyoth being produced on the spot. A huff, I swung my back end around, knocking a neighbor's chimney off behind me and taking out the last of the fences. For a moment I worried I'd headbutt the angel into the next zip code, but he righted himself, grabbing onto my hair desperately.

"Jesus Christ, tell me that's you!" He was out of breath, smell of blood strong on my nose.

"Right?" I said happily, prying him from my head like a pet spider as more and more Hayyoth dumped out from the wreckage of the basement, swarming towards us. Raziel tangled up in my claws, roughly about the size of a hamster to me now - but not one of those weirdly hairy ones, the little gray ones. "You alright?" He gave an incredulous laugh, looking back to the house quickly before back to me.

"Yeah! Yeah... There were more than I thought." He kept shaking his head, looking at me for a moment before instantly looking away. "Are you kidding me?"

"Barrier trick was a good idea. I tip my colossal stupid horns to you." I leaned back on my haunches. Raziel kept shaking his head, keeping an eye on the Hayyoth that spilled far into the yard, closer and closer to us here at the end. "You look like a blood sieve; remember when I said the Colus was a being of healing?" I smiled as he focused back at my eyes. I placed him up on my nose; he looked anxious and pale.

"Wait, no no no that felt like-" Focusing and snorting hard it looked like a turbine was placed underneath his feet, wind blowing all the blood and injuries right off in an instant. He stopped his explanation, looking over to his arms before down at his shirt. "How did that fix my clothes too?!" Two more quick turbines as he hopped in place for a moment, looking back over himself before back to me, angry.

"What was THAT? Don't just do things!" I gave a toothy grin.

"Writ of healing/ protection and transferring the tether from the house." Something tickled my tail as I didn't pay it any attention. "You could literally wander into the mass of Hayyoth and be unscratched."

"How do you know how to do these things?" He faked being pissed and unhappy as he had a big stupid grin on his face the whole time.

"Oh, I know how to do all sorts of things now, man."

Raziel suddenly stopped his jovial grin, worried and looking behind me.

"They're eating your tail." He inched up to the other side of my nose, looking down. "And your feet." I followed his glare, finding the Hayyoth all adorably trying to inflict damage and take chunks out of me, only to have it reform immediately after their teeth left. I tilted my head a little.

"Aww, let them have their fun. I'm about to commit a war crime anyways."

"Pardon?" I nudged Raziel back on my nose to a fairly safe spot just above my eyes like a pair of glasses.

"Your demon pals, which house do they live in?" He started asking a question before pointing out behind me. I followed his direction with my head.

"The grey roof about six houses away, why?"

"Just figuring which way to point." Before he could ask I took a massive breath, energy shredding the Hayyoth at my feet as I landed back on all fours. The inside of the basement seemed to spit and divide with Hayyoth, coming from the room, pulling from the walls, seeping from the sky out of thin air. There must've been twenty that popped up in a few seconds, joining the hundred or so all tangled up in each other snapping and wriggling like an angelic pile of live bait. "Keep your feet up, okay?"

"What? Why?"

The Hayyoth hissed and growled in a tone that was once mine; I'd outgrown them. My blood started to boil, watching my careful thought out form being bastardized, assembling from bits of fur and smoke, twisting and falling out of the air as they were thrown into existence as quick as possible. The house itself looked like a natural disaster had taken it, but new Hayyoths spawned from the utility room, spawned on what I was pretty sure was the roof, basically in places that meant a little more. It got to me, for some reason, like little bits of trash being sprinkled over an already crappy situation. I might've used a little more force than necessary because of it. It also felt good to remember what I could do.

I planted each foot wide, starting my head towards the ground, mouth open slightly as energy undulated in waves, like a shock from my nose and my tail alternating between both ends, building stronger and stronger. My skin began to darken, taking a deep breath as the wave suddenly sat at the very tip of my tail, slowly pushing forwards in a ring; the glow of my eyes began to brighten, spotting some light emitting from my nose and mouth as I focused on the pile of Hayyoth, some darting out, swiping towards me, some running away.

Twitching my lip I leaned forwards on my feet. Braced. Readied myself as that surge of energy collected, coursed through my veins, heading for the front, towards my head. Mouth wide open, a skinny, silent, errant bolt escaped a split second before a massive torrent of light and energy erupted forth before immediately being followed by this deafening, concussive thunder, heard from miles around. The energy continued, this torrent of light and strings blasted forth, ripping away any shadows, any darkness from the night in just that moment. The force pushed my head back, wings flipping open hundreds of feet into the air. My tail slammed into the ground, bracing myself as lines, extensions of my tongue best I could tell, erased the Hayyoth and most of the house in an instant, cutting up and destroying the little shits in wisps and curls of smoke. Smiling, Raziel suddenly kicked the ridge of my eyelid. I snapped my mouth shut, dropping back down onto all fours as the echoes and thunder slowly died out, ravaging the landscape for miles.

"Something wrong?" Coughing, shaking my head around a little with a smile I tried to focus on the angel. Both hands were up by his face, distraught and aghast.

"Y...yeh...phelw.." He mumbled as it dawned on me that he'd been living at this house for years. Years and years past just being stuck there waiting for me to get back, but for at least twenty whole, human years here on earth. New Hayyoth already began to form; not just by the fragmented remnants of the house, but in the yard, the house next door and farther down the street.

"I'm sorry if you... I mean that was your house, even if it was covered in Hayyoth." I nudged my head up a little, trying to get his attention as he was still fixated on the house corner left. "There might be some salvageable bits left we can ch-"

"You missed that part there." He said quickly, pointing out the roof with a ruthless grin, apparently happy to be free from the house. I hesitated. "Do it again, get rid of the last of it." A pause, a smile, shaking my head a little before taking another quick shot, lightning and rumbling rattling the hayyoth as they only looked over in horror.

Behind the lot stood a spread of littered bricks, bits of windows, bits of Hayyoth. Heaven knew where I was, and a handful of lookalikes was not the way they'd retaliate. It'd only been wave 1.

The sky echoed in chatter from the air all around us, a twitching, chattering, snapping assembly of these annoying sub-copies, flurrying back together. Hundreds of them; more, patterns only a second thought now as everything was a sickeningly pristine white. Every place I could see had these assembling beasts, florets of white fur gathering in driving masses, clamoring to come together fast enough. Pulling from dead air, from the ground, the sky, everywhere in between, they meant to just overrun us in these damn things. Taking some heavy breaths, I stopped to look around and assess the situation.

"How cool do you think your demon pals think you are right now?" I muttered, finding new hayyoth littering the ground like snow, none of them stupid enough to chew on my feet as I sat.

"Pretty cool." He laughed, finally reacting to what a house you've lived in for twenty+ years getting eradicated from the earth should feel like. "It's...gone, it's all gone. I don't have to stay here anymore." Both hands on his face, he still seemed pretty happy about it.

"You alright?"

"Yeah!... yeah." I figured if he wanted to extrapolate about being free from the house to me, he would. But if he was just happy for whichever reason he had, I wouldn't pry. He nodded once more, looking down. "Yeah." I gave a smile.

"So." I let my eyes fall, finally addressing the issue around us. "Hayyoth." Raziel nodded before remembering the snowfall of Hayyoth around us, head snapping down.

"OH... God, Neri, I didn't even know this many Hayyoth even existed." He stood on my nose, surveying the winter wonderland around us, of every literally square inch of visual sight being occupied by pissy, unhappy lizard dogs. I hesitated a moment at his words, nodding a little off to the side. I was happy to still be Neri to him.

"These new ones didn't even see what happened before so they're not smart enough to back off." I raised one hand, three Hayyoth latched on like leeches before dropping back into the writhing pile of angelic backup. "So how much do you hate Hayyoth?" About to say something else, he suddenly sneered.

"I mean, a lot."

"MMMM. Me too." Ruffling my shoulders I brought my wings back out, sweeping them around in front of me to make nearly a straight, continuous line on front of us, lowering it towards the ground as a few hayyoth were stupid enough to latch on as many more backed off, confused. "Snowplow?"

"Snowpl..." He looked to my wings before spinning around. I couldn't tell if he was happy or just disappointed in me. Or some strange combination of both. "Well, yeah." Happy.

"Get a little farther back." Sizing the Hayyoth up, I lowered my head a little, hunching so my wings nearly touched the ground, pumping my tail around to bounce back and forth, dancing.

"Grand finale of changes my ass." I heard Raziel gripe from my neck somewhere in disbelief. A laugh.

"READY?" The snarling, churning mass of Hayyoth began to gather, edging closer to my wing plow, a few biting down and ripping feathers longer than they were. I focused in.

"Ready!" We both gave respective thumbs up as living out the snowplow dream suddenly became very important to me, making accompanying snowplow engine sounds mixed with regular Moirae Colus roars.

"BBBRRRRRRRRRRRR" I screeched out, charging forward into the swarming masses, head, wings down as an incredibly effective snowplow would be. I had twenty or thirty suddenly on my wings, head and horns sweeping side to side as I pushed through, Hayyoth flipping and spinning over the top of my wings like a shower of confetti. They glittered and de-wisped, florets of hair losing form before slamming into the ground. The Hayyoth initially rushed at us, but with the cresting wave of hair and unflouret'd dead angelic beasts coming towards them they stopped, backing away and trying to get out of the path. But with the easily ten thousand Hayyoth surrounding us, there wasn't much of a place to go.

"Fen- FENCE!" Raziel shouted from the back of my neck, wings shuddering momentarily as I ripped out the neighbor's fence immediately followed by the other side of the same neighbor's fence. I pushed harder, speeding up to catch a good clump of Hayyoth, now cartwheeling over the sides of my wings like a waterfall.

"I am VERY LARGE, and it is VERY DIFFICULT to be polite!" I shouted over the dull roar of the beasts, a few getting sassy and latching onto a wingtip for a moment before being knocked off by the next Hayyoth in line.

"Not saying you should, but don't you have a human form?" Lunging forwards I took a colossal bite at a swelling of Hayyoth, getting bolder and bolder by the second that I wasn't necessarily killing them, just shoving them all around like a massive machine. Taking out five or six in a row got the Hayyoth back on the move.

"I do! I do. I actually never use this giant Colus form like what we're doing right now." Turning sharply I headed back towards familiar property, turning my head back to talk directly at him. "I didn't actually fix anything- I broke the seal, but it's not exactly gone. I can't get back into a normal form." Raziel's look snapped over my shoulder, hand up and mouth open to say something before it felt like something punched me hard in the back of the head.

It shoved my at my own neck where Raziel sat, getting a quick glimpse of him dropping off the side as the beast grabbed onto my head with two claws, stopping our snowplow efforts dead.

I couldn't see where he fell- my oversized self could easily crush him if I didn't have pinpoint accuracy on where he was. Getting an eye to the situation I saw the cherub's claws frame my vision, driving my head at the ground, taking out yet another part of the fence with a wing as my arms were tucked under my body, wings too spazzed out at the sides and too weak to hold myself and the weight of a cherub up. Eyes to the grass, I caught sight of Raziel in the last moments, right in front of me, right where my head was about to smash him into nothing against the ground because I got a little too cocky in playing stupid with a massive threat. Arms were too far way, legs still in mid-fall; I panicked and broke a promise.

"STOP" I screeched out as it cursed him mid-run like he was frozen solid, I tilted my head to the side and opened my mouth wide, teeth slamming into the ground just on both sides of him, Cherub grinding my head into the dirt. It remained perched with both feet on my head, taking little snippy bites at my back as I sighed a breath of relief, dropping the curse in an instant.

"GEH RAHEHHL N SHHRY." My head and teeth were still pinned down as I reorganized myself to retaliate, "Leh mehr jhrst geh hiss cotsutter a heece ah hy nine hen he hars to interrupt mid sentence!" Head from the ground I grabbed the bird by the throat to rip it off my head and slam it into the ground. Realizing this was yet another large, massive creature into the mix, I bit on the cherubs legs with my teeth, swinging around to chuck the cherub like a skipping stone halfway down the block. Seething, breathing hard, I watched it go.

"Sorry. I didn't have any options." I said again. Raziel seemed equally as stressed at the close call we just had. Shaking his head for a moment, he watched after the cherub and patting my wrist a couple times.

"Extenuating circumstances." He blurted out as I gave him a look for a moment. Keeping my glance on him for a moment, I slowly looked back up to the sky with immediate disapproval.

"There's another one coming." Scowling to the Hayyoth that were once again stupid enough to get close enough, I thought for some reason there'd be an end to the number of Hayyoth and now Cherubs they'd send at us.

"So what do we do? Can't we just leave?"

"Uhh, Sorta. I'm not sure I can move myself in this form somewhere farther than a couple blocks." Raziel shook his head, shouting up at me.

"After what you did before? You don't have enough energy to move yourself?"

"I do! I could try something stupid, but I'm not sure what the seal on the Colus is going to do. If you think of that little goat thing, I'm more or less that, still, but most of my energy is just surrounding outside of my own body." The cherub farther out spotted me, bringing it's head lower to flap flat out at me, narrowing my choices and conversation down. "I'm less collected and normal then I normally am, it might still work. But if we could thin them out a little and leave, that'd be better."

"A...alright. You take the cherubs and I'll take the Hayyoth?" He joked as I considered it, giving a nod.

"Works for me!" I sized up the cherub nearly on top of us, snarling and readying myself for a fight.

"Wait! Wait I don't have a weapon!" Squaring my haunches I leapt up, smacking the outstretched claws of the cherub off to the side and sinking my teeth in around it's neck. With one powerful flap I whipped my head around the other way, sending this cherub cartwheeling into the neighbors house, dazed. Landing on all four feet I stayed away from crushing Raziel, who was feebly kicking at a few of the Hayyoth coming up to attack. "You destroyed my other ones!"

"Egh. Okay. Hold on." Yanking a tooth out of my own head, I spun some thread of life up for a moment around one of the roots, mushing it with my hands to make a pretty rough, kinda chunky looking weapon that was more or less a hilt on a tooth about a foot and a half long. I presented the end of it to him for a moment as he eagerly took the slapdash weapon from me, face falling in disappointment. "There you go!"

"Ohhh. Uh. Th- Thank You." I stared at him for a moment before taking the weapon back away, sitting down properly to stop my fights, letting the Hayyoth chew on my tail as I actually reformed my own tooth into something that didn't look as crappy.

"Ungrateful baby." I muttered, looking up at him as I worked. You could tell he was giddy to get a new wacky weapon and could see through my mostly surface sarcasm. "You have a specific era of human development and caste that you'd like me to model this off of? Or is a goddamn 'sword' okay?"

"Sword's fine." Flattening the material, I refined it into something interesting and not total shit.

"Better?" His eyes lit up as he took the weapon from me, clearly happy.

"Yeah!" Taking a few practice swings at the Hayyoth that were getting ever closer, he suddenly stopped, looking at the hilt. "Could you make this blue?"

"NO." Taking a couple flaps from the ground I focused on the one cherub that was patiently waiting for us to stop bickering in the neighbor's backyard and the other cherubs coming in quick from the sky, "GOOD LUCK."

"Aren't they going to tear me limb from limb?" He called out behind me.

"You're protected!"

"Not against being crushed I wasn't!"

"I'm trying my best, Raziel!"

He charged forward, sword in hand into the first mess of Hayyoth as I set out after my quarry. I couldn't get over how much fun this was in the most basic of ways. After all this time of worrying, of fear, of anxiety and shame, this was nothing to be ashamed of. Unnatural in a humanistic way, my God, sure; but in this after-death race to be born again, to make a difference, to be a part of it, I practically lead the pack. A part of me mourned the loss of my sincere respect for every living and non-living thing, not that I lost it, precedence just took more importance in my life, in what I had to do, who I had to protect. But this, fighting against an unlimited mass of angelic beings who were shell-like beings with barely enough sentience to finish a paragraph, this was just plain fun.

Dodging around the cherub's first strike, I sunk my teeth into a wing as the cherub got a hold of one of my arms with both legs. Instead of this going anything like it had as just a fractured soul, I bit through the wing on my first pass, using my weight and momentum to swing up onto their shoulders and ripping the cherub diagonally out of the sky and back on my own wings in one motion.

Looking down over the rest of the demisilo rejects around me, I saw Raziel involved in another squirreling Hayyoth pile, not far away in the sea of white angelic weeds, fluffy white hair matched with angry, snarling eyes, wanting our blood. This was getting out of hand. They… this wouldn't end, they weren't hoping a few would do the job, this wasn't carefully planned; they were just sending as many as they could make with no regard for anyone else, trying to overwhelm us. I don't think" thinning out the pack' was even possible. We needed to leave.

Something suddenly plowed into my head, claws raking across my horns pitifully and throwing me off balance, knocking my face towards the ground again. This was a familiar feeling; snarling I whipped one wing out at it, knocking the cherub away, smack it into crowded air.

"Neri!" Raziel yelled out over the gurgling, growling masses, voice risen in worry. The cherub screamed, darting, all four wings flared out at me again, that madness, that insane need to kill to maim and take down

their prey. With one outstretched hand I smacked it's head away, lunging
deep and ripping out the whole lower vocal system in one swing like I had
done before. I scrambled onto its shoulders, scrambling to pull myself away
from the waves of angry she-clones of yesteryear.

Perched heavy on the dead cherub's back I launched from it,
flapping my wings once I let the cherub carcass drop away, diving towards
the only other confused, angry mass of violence. Aiming, calculating,
I could see him, still fighting with my slapdash weapon in hand. In a
sort of loose, hunched dive I flopped straight for him, putting my head
down, slamming back into the ground, arms at my side, crushing anyone
underneath me as I skidded those last few yards. I gave a sort of half-leap
to clear the rest of the distance, Hayyoth scrambling to get out of my way.
You could see that sort of questioning ridiculousness, that dubious look
of confusion in what the Hell I was trying to do in his eyes, belly-flopping
from the sky like that.

"CHANGED MY MIND." I bellowed, voice booming and massive,
"Get clear!"

Raziel shoved the last Hayyoth away from his arm, untouched by
anything, just for a moment as my slide came to a stop, as my nose softly
nudged into him, as the two of us evaporated from the scene in an instant,
transporting out of that Hellish mess. Gone.

Some seven hundred miles away we popped back into existence,
dropping out of thin air about four feet from the ground, thumping onto it
with a sickening crunch. Coughing, gagging and shaking my bloodied self
out, I tried to get to my feet, body giving out. This sickly, tortured whine
escaped as I saw Raziel laying there, about four or five feet away from my
nose, laying back with his arms flat to the ground. He wasn't breathing.
I forget if he needs to breathe - I get a little panicky when I see someone
clearly not and he just wasn't.

"We good?" I shot some air over his way as it ruffled his shirt and
nothing else. "Raziel?" A couple seconds of pause as I started getting up
to go and check on him; the angel suddenly popped to life, taking in a
huge gasp of air before rolling to his side and coughing. He kept at it as I
slumped back to the ground, watching with a lone eye.

"Mm. Yeah. I'm good." He rolled over onto his back, folding his
hands across his chest and laying there like he was contemplating taking a
nap. I gave a wary frown.

"Yah SURE? Because that sounded a lot like death." He kept his
eyes closed, raising his eyebrows the tiniest bit as his overly peaceful stage
act left me mystified.

"Yeah that hurt a lot." He started coughing again, shaking his head
with his eyes still closed.

"Oh. Sorry. Normally it doesn't, but also normally I'm not transporting four hundred times my weight so you know..." I let my eyelids droop, listening to the birds and the sun, in the dead middle of nowhere without a single problem for this exact second. It wasn't often I didn't have a single care so I had to take advantage of it when I had the chance. Both wings flopped heavy on the ground as the angel sat up like a pin.

"Grand finale my ass." Raziel muttered, giving a half-hearted kick at my nose. I huffed once in a laugh, body drained, exhausted. Man, what a day. Thankfully, they should be here any moment now, fix this situation for good, put things right. Stupid parts of me believed that everything was my own duty, that I was the only one to rely on . Not true, really; I knew my mistakes, knew my shortcomings, knew this had all been very informative, inspirational. It gave me back that drive I knew I lost, that deep found respect I lost so often. I wasn't a great leader. I wasn't close. But I tried; someone had to try.

There was a hum suddenly. Resonance.

Raziel shuffled around a little, picking up his head as the audible humming grew louder and louder. "Do…. Do we hide?"

"Nope. That's our bus. No hiding. Not anymore." I grumbled with a determined grin, trying to get to my feet, energy already replenishing. I managed to prop up my upper body as the ground in front of me began to glow, humming shaking the ground around us, fanning out. Raziel crouched behind my head, using me as a barrier.

"I want that engraved into stone." There was a voice just beneath the earth, glow illuminating more and more. "We'll make a mantel, and that'll be the only thing that hangs over it." My eyes narrowed as that impossibly long horn made it's appearance first, as her head poked above the surface, both of them, rising from the ground smoothly like any great zombie movie portrayed. They continued to rise from the soil, gripping their respective weapons like a great homecoming at their full human size, towering over Raziel easily; Cempe and Aisa. I grinned, happy to see them. Genuinely happy to see them.

"So, oh grand poobah, like I told you forever ago, we ready to end this annoying little mission of yours?" Cempe tossed her head a little with a grin, glare suddenly switching over to Raziel, spotting him duck down a little farther out of sight.. Aisa leaned back a little as Cempe jerked a thumb to him. "Still?"

"YEAH, still." I switched back to look at Raziel squatting alongside my neck. "Don't worry."

"You'd think the guy who got beaten up by pets would be the first one dead in this Hayyoth wave." Cempe muttered low enough I wasn't sure he heard it. Judging on the aggravated noises I heard next to my ear though I'm reasonably sure he did. "I mean even steel eyes Jacob got wiped out in this and he had steel eyes." I harmonized with Raziel, annoyed.

"Can you just focus on helping me out of this body?" The Colus body staggered to it's feet, wobbling heavily as I stumbled side to side for a second. "Ad lib on your own time, Cherubs and forty metric tons of Hayyoth are on their way and smartassery is just going to have to take a backseat right now." Letting out a curt, dutiful growl, I stood up as strong and as powerful as I could be. Cempe gave a mocking bow, jerking a thumb to Aisa.

"Har-dee har your way over to Aisa then, your mistake was thinking I could help you with something complex." She made a motion for Raziel as his body solidified, freezing in terror. "You should stand over here by me, It's safest here." Cempe didn't actually say anything threatening, but the color drained from his face as he quickly looked back to me for a clue. I motioned over to her myself.

"She's actually right." Taking another couple steps towards Aisa as she walked away from them both, farther out to the side, "Scary as that is." I muttered as Cempe spit out something insulted, tone muting to talk to Raziel, coaxing him over like a lost puppy.

Aisa took a few steps closer to me in her normal humanist glory. Two large horns sticking out the back of her head curled around by her face decorated in rings and bands; she was about ten years older then Cempe, who was about ten years older then myself sitting at the youngest of this group. We weren't really sisters, not by blood at least. Aisa was a little stockier then the rest of us, carrying that heavy, insidious weapon like I had to. Like half of a pair of cutting sheers, the edge was jagged and sharp, rust dancing about the blade as she herself was decorated in flowing, rusting fabric. By far the most responsible of us all; I assumed her age helped with that, though. Young as I was, I couldn't always be that old soul, I was still a teenager. Even with all our titles essentially being lies, there was a bit of truth to each one of us.

Aisa beckoned a finger for my head as she stood just below me.

"C'mere you behemoth." She laughed as I complied, still wheezing for breath. As my head got low enough, she slapped the side of it lightly like a pet horse. "Glad you decided to join us."

"Retirement's not for me." I said, coughing out as she brought that scissor half up to my head, lining for the strike, resting the notched blade between my eyes.

"This is going to hurt like Hell." Aisa said quietly.

"I know." I braced up for it, closing my eyes quickly. My eldest sister reared back, slowly, gearing up and saying a few words under her breath, starting the long chant. Maybe this was my deserved pain and torment that I had been looking for, my penance for screwing with Raziel's life so badly. But at least with this problem resolved, I could finally start fixing my own. What a long, exhausting road it's been. Aisa continued her chant as the Falx, her weapon's name, darkened farther and farther, patina nearing a deep black.

A voice chimed in, alarmed.

"Wait, what are you doing?" Raziel called out as I opened an eye to the interruption. Cempe swept the Decempedia in front him, keeping him back, all joking and humor gone from her face.
Raziel leaned forwards to shove it away, stopping cold like the devil himself kept him from it. His eyes darted back to me, then back to the measuring stick.

"Yeah, I wouldn't touch this one either, meathead" Cempe laughed, sneering as his hands wretched away shakily. I spoke up.

"Don't worry, Raziel. It's gonna look bad but I promise this actually works." Cempe rambled on some other fake lore, really getting a kick out of screwing around with the angel. Rolling out a throaty growl, Aisa put a hand to the side of my chin and directed me back towards her. She had this doofy grin on her face, keeping her voice low.

"He's terrified by everything, it's adorable." Aisa laughed, motioning to the Falx as it was ready to do it's terrible trick. "God help him when he gets to the difficult stuff." I groaned.

"Egh, don't remind me. Not looking forward to that." You could hear Cempe laugh raucously about something in the distance.

"Cempe's been especially cruel since she hasn't had you to beat up on. She's really quite happy you're back, I promise." I spit out something of a scoff. That didn't surprise me. "Ready?" I nodded. We needed to do this quick, I could feel those Heavenly eyes wandering our way; with all three of us gathered here? No kidding they'd pick up on that sort of activity. I was surprised we had as much time as we did, maybe all their attention directed back at the Priests house was slowing their reaction time.

Aisa began to mutter those words again, that old chant as the weapon was held all the way back over her head; the skies began to darken, the light began to wane, fade away as I put as much cushion between my actual self and the Colus. Sparks, glints of light began to collect on the blade, began to gather on the very edge of it. An ironic fact that with all that light and darkness talk all being a middle gray in reality, light was the only thing that could really cut through the darkness of the seal.

The light on the Falx grew brighter and brighter, bits of light and energy zipping to it, gathering and wedging together. The chant ended; stopped as the blade was all the way back, readied. With a twitched grin she swung the Falx in a quick arc, chopping straight into my own head, embedding itself into the Colus's forehead. I could feel the blade slice all the way through, painful edge spreading to a sort of warmth as it cut to my tail. Bright white light streaked over the entire body of the Colus as its skin grew dark, starting to pull away painfully. Like every hair on my body was aflame, like my skin was getting pulled away from the muscle, the feeling darted quickly to every inch of my body, the Colus nothing but a black shape edged with bleeding veins of light, vaguely what it had been.

Whirring, buzzing and spinning, the pull grew intense and almost unbearable, gritting my teeth. Aisa reared back the Falx again, slamming the blunt end of it into my forehead, breaking the barrier as it all leapt away in a heap of smoke, as the Colus was allowed to dissipate into the air naturally, as I was finally freed like a million pieces of heavy duty sticky tape were ripped from my skin in the same instant.

I sat down in the bare remnants of the Colus body as it dissolved away, falling again in a second to hit the ground in a much smaller, sturdier form, laying back against the ground like Raziel had been when we arrived. My head rested against the bottom of a tree like a pillow.

My eyes rolled around in my head, the last bits of smoke dissipated from the air as the world was blurry, hearing the Hayyoth in the far distance. My ears flitted back and forth; you could hear the air as it snapped and exploded with the things, replicated and seeping down like a snow. My panting, exhausted breathing slowed down, fell back to normal rhythm, eased back to what I had always known. Things began to clear up and brighten; spying an arm and a hand, not a blue spidery vein to be seen in the lot of them. With a grin I got my hands underneath me, pushing myself into a sort of sit.

I was tall. Obnoxiously tall. I was back in the clothes, the uniform I had made for myself at least a thousand years back. I could see the fur, not my own thankfully, that covered my upper bits, around the arm, the long strands of my hair streaming down from the side of my head across the front, adorned in a pair of golden rings, air woven around the hole in the middle. Jewelry on my neck, something fancy and golden, layered in numerous chains around my neck, obscuring the disfiguring Pike mark that Raziel gave me. I coughed, woozily trying to stand up, eyes rolling in my head as I stumbled back to my knees.

“You want to hurry this up? Something something ad lib forty tones of hayyoth etc. We don't have the time for this.” I could hear what sounded like a human hand against a Decempedia, slapping it for effect as she walked towards me. “Wrap it up!”

Looking from hand to hand, bending and clutching my fists for a moment I opened them back up, knowing what I needed to do. That ocean, that sea of power was all still there, perhaps even more so.

“For every moment that you're not up on those dumb lizard feet of yours, I’m gonna take loose swings at Raziel. Maybe then we can get to fixing your mess back below.” I crouched next to the tree, looking over my shoulder as she was swinging wildly around by the angel, but still plenty enough to scare the hell out of him. “Oop, it's getting closer!” She called over her back, not even looking at me to see if I was up or walking around. Cempe mostly did this for her own amusement.

One hand back to the tree, I braced myself into a stand, wobbly and uncoordinated, but on my feet. Raziel's eyes lit up, about to say something to the deity as I put a finger over my lips, keeping him quiet as he kept looking to me, to her, to the wildly swinging Decempedia, and back to me.

"Nearly hitting himmmm." She called again as I made a motion he should take a step out to the side for what I was about to do. Raziel got offended, pointing angrily to Cempe as she was limiting his ability to get away and he couldn't just take a jaunty walk away from my sister.

Spotting Raziel motioning back to me, she looked over her shoulder, happy.

"See, that wasn't so hard, was it?" Grip tightening on the tree behind me I ripped it from the ground, swinging it wide over my head to smash over Cempe in an instant. Raziel's abhorred glare switch from me to the tree, inches to his side as he scrambled over to Aisa, horrified by the whole lot of us.

"Nona..." Aisa's mothering voice came out, disapproving of the age old tradition of smashing your sister over the head with a live tree.

"A TREE, NONA?" Cempe popped up from the meaty tree innards, spitting out leaves and bark as she did so. "What are you, five?" I folded my hands, bowing over to Aisa for a moment.

"Thank you. Aisa. For helping me out." I smiled politely back to Raziel, then Cempe, facade falling mid-sentence. "Raziel, hello, hope everything's well. And thank you, Cempe, for being a reAL BALLBAG THE WHOLE TIME." I bellowed out at her as she zipped over to me, fifteen years of distance and emotional separation made up in an instant as this was the relationship I had with my sister.

"I'M not the ballbag YOU'RE the ballbag!" She shoved her face at me as I returned the favor, the two of us literally butting heads.

"Thanks bunches for telling me I kill angels mid-term, THAT sure was a lot of fun to deal with for ages!"

"You were annoying!"

"You, Me and Paul are gonna have SECRET PLAN TRAINING where we learn not to constantly bring up SECRET PLANS to the main component of that SECRET. PLAN. You Goddamn BALLBAG."

"Yeah, this is normal." I heard Aisa mutter. I hissed and spit at Cempe as we kept on our toes. Unfortunately we were the same height.

"Oh, you had no idea what was happening, it was fine!"

"No ide---" I fumed, struggling to gather my words. "Not the point!"

"It didn't even matter in the end, why are you so picky?" She turned her head to the side as I reached up, snapping her horn in a moment and hitting her with it.

"I was almost working for the ANGELS, you SHIT." Cempe snatched her horn from my hand, snarling.

"Almost?"

"Alright, alright. Break it up." Aisa walked between us as we foamed and snarled for a few moments more, huffing out as it felt good to finally strike back after how many years of frustration. Cempe was a fool if she wasn't expecting at least some aggravation to the things she screwed up. "These cherubs and hayyoth are extremely dumb but we're going to have to reschedule our little baby argument breaks until we figure this out, alright?"

"Fine..." I relented.

"I guess." Cempe hesitated for a moment, going back to trying to fix her busted horn back onto her head.

Aisa started walking to the edge of the field, motioning to me to come join her.

"How's it feel?" She gave a hearty smile.

"Foggy." I twisted to look at my pants, these knee-length parachute like things, at the jewelry around my neck. Turning back towards the front I nearly hit Aisa with my horns, these massive things; I was teetering around 9 feet tall while the horns, straightened out, were probably 6 feet + long. But they zigzagged instead, last segment crooked up at a forty five degree angle, wind whistling through the worn hole in both of them. Felt a little like someone was constantly pulling on my hair, hanging from it. I shook my head a little, trying to make a decent sentence. "Feels like nothing's missing, but there's only a candlelight on in the room, if that weird analogy makes sense to you." This was the voice I knew, this was where my other little halfie forms all lacked.

The two of us lovingly looked over the oncoming field of rushing Hayyoth, of Cherubs that dropped from the sky, of other winged goodies I hadn't danced with all joining in, all swirling about, just across these fields. They knew where we were. We knew where they were. Everyone was blisteringly out in the open. Blatantly exposed. For some reason, with my whole family here, it didn't bother me. Considered 'heavy hitters' to the rest of the demons, there really wasn't anything we couldn't take. Be it a thousand + cherubs, Hayyoth and Desigeias like this, or the entire holy army. We didn't come together often, they left most of the fighting up to me anyways. But all three of us here? It was a lot less of a problem that I was still sentimental enough to know would've been.

"Good to have you back." Aisa said again, cleaning off the Falx with her fingers.

"Good to be back" I rubbed the back of my head a little, stretching out, yawning. The field before us writhed with activity, pulsing towards us in jagged little heaps and gearing up like a torrent of bloodshed, of battle. Roaring out in defiance, in anger, the horde grew closer, more massive. Aisa and I both began to smile in sync.

"It's weird, isn't it?" Cempe's fingers dug into Raziel's shoulders, latched on like a parasitic leech as I turned around just in time to see him desperately trying to squirm out of her grip. Cempe could easily pick him up and toss him like a pebble across the state if need be and based on how little he moved trying to lurch out of her grasp, I think he was starting to understand this. I frowned, crossing my arms as his eyes desperately shot between us both, pleading for help. "She looked almost normal before, but now, eegh. I'm pretty sure she ate your friend Neri."

"Grow up, will you?" I spit out, lip twitching. "Can we pretend to be decent people for a second? Raziel's our guest. He's been through enough and doesn't need your bullshitting to be the Goddamn cherry of the day, alright?"

"You see? Back for five minutes and she's already ordering me around." She readjusted her grip to just get him with a loose arm around the neck. "I take it back, you can just rot it the conga line like the rest of 'em if you're gonna come out of this with a snippy attitude."

"You think that's snippy? I'll GIVE you snippy!" Conjuring up a swath of strings I let them hang ominously, tired and more than annoyed at her constant antics of being quite possibly the world's best antagonist. Tilting her head slightly to the side, she opened up her arm and let Raziel stumble back.

"Temper unbecoming of an Excelsis, am I right?" She nudged Raziel as he only looked over to me, looking just as tired and worn out as I was, slowly trying to shuffle out of her reach. "See, Raziel knows what's up."

"Ladies! Please! We have more important issues at hand here." Aisa barked out, equally as annoyed at our many disagreements that surfaced in regular day to day life. Cempe and I might be sisters but God knows we were entirely different people. Scowling, she got to her feet, coming up the hill to join us both as I mentioned out to the undulating field of Angelic beasts.

"Just trying to loosen up this annoying awkward situation with a little- God damn that's a lot of cherubs." Her face dropped, impressed and swinging the Decempedia over her shoulder like some ancient warrior.

"How should we go about this one?" Aisa looked around, stare stopping on me like I had answers, a little too emotionally drawn elsewhere to come up with something smart and useful.

"Nona takes care of it."

"What? C'mon." My arms swung down, heavy. "Do you guys know how tiring rebuilding a soul after running 250 hrs at least is? It's a lot."

"Why, don't you wanna show off what you can do to your special friend here? Make sure everything's in order?" She smacked my shoulder lightly, "C'mon, Heaven screws you over for half a decade and you're not looking to at least teach them a little something? Push back for our side? I think it'd be a fabulous moral booster for the poor schmuck demons getting their asses handed to them thanks to your little hiccup." She took a few knowing steps towards Raziel, who smartly tried to back away from her path.

Cempe's lanky body snatched him like no big problem, spinning him around as the thunderous roar of screeching holy birds and Neri rip offs was starting to grow loud. Shaking him a little by the shoulders, she crouched behind him with a doofy grin. It was probably the closest thing to excitement and appreciation I'd get from her on my big return.

"C'mon, don't you wanna see Nona do cool shit? Eh? Eh?" When neither Raziel nor my own expression matched what she was looking for as a response, her eyes hardened, squinting at me just a little harder. "Screw you, you owe me. Do it."

"I agree, Nona." Aisa said behind me, catching me off guard. The holy army of doom wasn't far at all, now, coming up the last few hills until they'd reach us. Rather polite of them to do it just from the one side, give me all this time to talk and sort things out in a respectable manner. I smiled quickly at the thought, shaking my head and turning back to Aisa as she explained, "Would send them quite the message."

"Alright, alright, fine." I said lowly, holding open my one hand for the Colus to pool and form into with no complications whatsoever. "I do this, you quit antagonizing Raziel."

"No." She glared at me, before switching to glare at Raziel. "He's far too impressionable and easy to confuse."

"Please stop shaking me." He said flatly, arms pinned to his sides, glaring back. Cempe's mood switched quickly, grabbing him around the shoulders again.

"See, this is far too fun to pass up." She shook him again, turning over to me. "They're not far now, sooner you get rid of them, sooner we get back underground." Sneering at her I slowly panned away, shaking the Colus out, now considerably smaller, more manageable, reaching out six feet instead of ten as it no longer stored my remaining energy.

"Fine. Christ. Give me some space." Aisa stood back by Cempe and Raziel, squatting behind me like they were waiting for a grand firework to go off, the grand finale. Grumbling, I tried remembering how it was done, tried getting the sequence all right in my head, trying to sort out the details. It'd been some time. "I'm doing this because I want to and not because I can't control myself, alright?" I pointed to Raziel first as he shrugged, then to Aisa and Cempe as they look confused.

Stepping onto that grass, overseeing them all below me, feeling the energy the battle, the familiar surroundings, it became second nature to me. Became natural. Muttering low I chanted the words under my breath, rotating the Colus twice on one side of my body, twice on the other side, looping in front. Even as the immature part of me was stumbling, struggling with it all, the rest knew quite well what it was doing. It's when

I stopped questioning. Stopped putting the blame elsewhere, stopped blaming the black carpet of Hell for getting me out, stopped blaming the angels for doing something that made me do one thing or the other. Yeah, unfortunately, I was responsible for a lot of this, and I was exactly who I was. I swung the Colus twice over my head, opening up my palms to let it spin freely, snatching the handle with my other hand it suddenly snapped straight up, left hand grasping the handle, right hand on the back of it, braced. As I stood in front of that squirming mass of angelic hosts ready to fight back against me and what I was associated with, as my vision was entirely mobbed in white; that's when I pretty much accepted my duty, my job, all that.

The last word bit into the air, Colus lighting up with that red energy, back growing intensely hot; I tightened my grip the holes as the Colus widened, glowing brighter. An intense beam of energy shot out from all seven holes, shoving the weapon against my braced arm and against my face as I struggled with it. My body skidded back a few feet, nails clicking into place as a beam of energy enveloping the whole area in white, stealing all definition from the land around us. Color began to erase away as it erupted out, sweeping across the land below us. The beam split up from one to two, two to four, four to sixteen, indefinitely, all becoming these thin, razor-like wires or strings that reached as far as the light would touch. The weapon grew heavier by the second, from something comparable to a gallon of milk in my hands, to something weighing hundreds, thousands of pounds. I struggled to keep it lofted up as the cherubs careened from the skies, cut in half with these supposed strings of life, the Hayyoth screeched and wailed, diced and cubed as the strings darted across the grounds, back and forth.

Twitching, digging deep I lofted it high over my head, supporting the Colus as the beam strengthened, broadening out. You could hear the wires whizzing through the air, long tearing ragged bits of sound. One eyes closed, one open, I could barely read the demolition happing before me, just seeing bits of things drop from the air, seeing the movement of the world around me grow to a halt.

The light began to flicker, starting to die out as the Colus dropped from my hands, slamming into the ground with a rattling shake. It left me standing there with a stance I could probably use to ride a horse, hands shaking, looking out in front of me, shocked and strangely okay with it, like a renewed sense of awe for something I'd done a thousand times. My knees quivered where I stood. Something grabbed my hand. Aisa.

"Alright, time to go." She said with a laugh, tugging me along to the ripped gash in the earth seeping with red light. I suddenly grew serious once more. With this window of opportunity to leave, we had to take it.

"Right. Let's go." I walked a little jaggedly towards the open. Cempe was trying to push Raziel into it, his hands clamored back, feet pointed straight towards the sky. Seeing my help coming around once more she let him fall, waving a hand at him and entering into the crevasse herself. Aisa was close behind; I climbed in after her, top half of my body still in the mortal world, resting on the edge of it. You could hear lingering cries of anguished from the army over the hill, of the second attack coming around quickly, retaliating. Frowning, I extended a hand to Raziel. "I don't deserve it, but trust me."

He looked at me, looked back to the cherub re-emergence, then back to the hole.

"Kinda a no-brainer with this one." He muttered, grabbing onto my hand quickly.

Without another second to hesitate I pulled the angel in, pulled him down, pulled him into Hell and damnation, just like they always said I would.

$$38$$

I figure I'm due for a little explanation.

So around a hundred years ago, for one reason or another, we had a sizeable battle. The terms were the same, and the reason was muddy as ever- it wasn't the largest battle I was a part of, and it certainly wasn't the smallest. Generic, middle of the road battle. Average. I lead this one as I often do at the leading edge of the attack in my formal garbs, same as what I normally wore, only I don on this large, fearsome looking wooden-like mask and attach some white to red silk to the holes in my horns. Demons wanna be lead by a respectable figure, and surprisingly, a bright-eyed 17-19 year old woman was not everyone's idea of fearsome. The mask keeps me somewhat aloof, mysterious; that usually scores better and gives some much needed privacy when I want it.

I had been informed beforehand that Raziel was in this battalion. Despite my soul-hopping, I do like to keep tabs on friends and family, make sure they're doing okay. It's a bit nosy, admittedly, but I had heard he'd gotten kicked out of his rank, that he was tumbling down the chain of command; and as both sides lined up that day for our grand little battle, I saw him on the very front lines. He didn't even look like he knew where he was – this was a bad, bad sign. The one s at the front are the battle fodder, they know how to hold a sword/pike, and they know how to die. Angels have that advantage of just ascending to Heaven instead of actually dying like the rest of us, but the statement remains.

The battle starts and I see him running straight for me. He doesn't know exactly who I am, just that I'm their grand leader, sticking out like a sore thumb at 9 ft tall. He's unaware that I was Joan. I do my best to run diagonally away from him, but he's charging straight for me. Grumbling in frustration that I am going to have to fight him, I stop, and the pike's instantly in the back of my leg; before I even think about kicking him around to get him out of the way, I stop on his face. Desperation is practically pouring out of the guy, completely out of his league and his mind. No fancy footwork, no legitimate plan of attack, he's just desperately trying to do something right. I knew him in his heyday, he is a good fighter- but this was like watching rock bottom chase after you in desperation and stab you in the calf- it was all sorts of wrong. I couldn't help but feel sorry for him.

Back into the seriousness of the battle, he pulled the pike from my calf in hopes to hit me one more time. His strikes are blatant and tactless, so I step out of the way easily. Before he gets the chance, I stepped onto the pike to crush it into the ground before he could connect again, using my one free foot to push him over and out of the way. I didn't want to fight him, and I didn't want to see him like this either. I just wanted our exchange to be done, I didn't want to be in this moment with him anymore. Raziel wasn't done.

"You, sick, sadistic empty shell of a soul!" He screeched after me from the ground, humiliated and off guard, he fought verbally instead. "Scabs on the world, why don't you things just die off already? It'd make life better for the rest of us!" I stopped where I stood, looking back at him one last time with a sickened sense of awe as the angel's mouth snapped shut. We lingered there for a second as war raged all around us, cries of triumph and anguish enveloping this moment as it paused. Not a word uttered, I frowned, struck worse than any real wound by any metaphysical sword or knife.

I couldn't help but think of him as that friend, whose trust I worked diligently for, screaming and screeching at me like he knew who I was, like he was angry at Joan. My brain willed me to move on, to step out of this moment, to leave it behind. I couldn't. Over and over was this incessant, running notion of 'That was your friend. That's what he thinks of you.' I hoped to forget about it, let the thought fade with time. It didn't.

That had been the catalyst for this entire Neri escapade.

Darkness, dankness, curtains of black smoke flanked by evil red lights; Hell was not a favorite of mine. I came here when necessary, hid here when I pissed off one too many people up top and led everyone to assume I spent a lot of my time here. I didn't. None of us really did. Sitting around in a dark corner was not the way to really live our lives, to enjoy that around us. For every year lived out up top, I spent maybe four days down here at the very most. Cempe was the only one who spent more time here, keeping up the image, keeping up this end of the business. She equated my need to not sit in eternal damnation as cowardice, of not sitting through the crappy part of this job like she did. It was a big reason we fought as often as we did, which only drove me to leave more often out of frustration. We understood one another enough though, considering, we were still pretty close. She wouldn't have helped me if she honestly hated me.

I didn't take care of the unfortunate souls wafting about Hell. Not one of us did. They were here on their own accord, their own thoughts of the evil in their existing lives, we didn't do a thing to recruit them or anything. They just showed up, despondent, empty, tortured souls. They parade around for a couple decades before they want something to change, before they would sometimes break out of their lines and make a trip up top. That's where I managed them, when they wanted out, when they wanted a change in their lives, I was the one to help lead them down that path. Help them fight back. When they died this round, it was my hope that fragmented apart, they'd have a better chance to have a better life. Some of these conga-ing souls had only been here for a few years. Some had been here for a millennia. Sometimes that's all you want to do, drift around aimlessly for a couple thousand years to get your head on straight.

Our goal was to give that downed spirit a purpose, a vigor back so when they eventually did fall, they felt accomplished.

After a particularly gruesome battle a little over a decade back, I remembered standing in one of the larger caverns that had been filled to the brim with demons before the attack. Now it had bits and remains of those demons, nearly all had been wiped out in one of the worse battles I had lead. Cempe wandered in as I stood there despondently, stuck mulling those same words Raziel had said, about being a sadistic, empty shell of a soul. I barely batted an eye at sending all of those demons out to fight; I barely cared that they didn't come back.

Cempe and Aisa didn't participate so much in the warfare as I did, and I could understand why. This was solely my duty, my burden. I knew that without the chance for something better, without that fuel for new souls to keep up this whole cycle, there'd be more problems than there already was. Chaos would reign with darkness far worse than my own brand.

"Heard your last attack really sucked. Glad you're down here to squat in hiding though, really appreciate the time we get to spend together" She laughed behind my back, stretching out and snickering at me. I turned to her slowly, face contorted and distraught. Her facade dropped its joking immediately, "And now I feel bad for saying that. Gearing up again for vacation time?" Vacation time= rebirth, at least Cempe's version of my time up top was called that. I shifted to my butt, sitting down heavily and overlooking the stereotypical Hellish cavern, scraggly and dripping with what I sure hoped was water. Everyone brought their own version of Hell when they came down here, open a new door and you're never quite sure what's going to be behind it. Kicking at the rocks overlying the edge, Cempe sat down along with me.

"Thinking of something different, something new." I said in a tiny, annoyed voice. This wasn't my political voice, it was the voice cobbled together from hundreds of others in jarring array. She looked at me, turning back to the empty cavern before shrugging.

"Lay it on me, whatcha got in mind?" I stopped my sniveling for a moment.

"Seriously? You're not going to ridicule me for leaving again?"

"Who said I wouldn't?" Cempe laughed, switching how she sat on the rock's edge, "It's getting a little damn dull in here, and your 'something new's are usually dangerous or exciting and usually end in an unnecessary bloodbath of sorts, or flipping Heaven upside down looking for someone. I'm up for it, opportunity is closing, so whatcha got?" I watched her eyes for a few seconds, caving in. If my sister was actually willing to do something, I should take the chance. It was still warm in Hell; it hadn't frozen over just yet.

"Segmenting" I said, wavering at first before my confidence came back just a bit, "Willingly."

"Why?" Her eyes hardened, "This isn't from that stupid thing Christopher said, is it?" I really had to stop telling my sister every damn thing that happened on a day to day basis. She knew Christopher by name as well. I'd almost forgotten that she'd been in that life with me, the Joan 1630's one, my amazingly soft-spoken, well liked and not a total pain in the ass sister. We didn't always reflect ourselves in each life; the environment and upbringing had an impact too.

"Maybe, but I've been wondering about it on my own."

"What, you want three Nona's running around? I don't wanna put up with the one that won't shut up about the famous dead people she knows." Her tone lowered, "What if something happens? We can hold down the fort for some time, but if you get yourself exorcised and killed off, that's going to cause problems and you know it."

"Then we'll dice sparingly." I said flatly, hand to my chin. "We cut the Postremo out, Present does the legwork and I konk out in back until need be. No early death, no hassle. I need a rest anyways." It was this future soul that kept me constantly alive, that made me incredibly hard to kill.

"Still leaves you a memory-less robot. Not to mention you'll re-meet Christopher like I know you're trying to do and probably rip the guy limb from limb." My ears went flat back, caught.

"Hey, I never really got that one resolved out, it's about time I worked around to it. He's just, I dunno, intense. Not the same. Got a stare to him like he wants my eyeballs pickled. I'm just not quite sure who exactly he is anymore." Cempe gave me a semi-upturned grin, shaking her head with a laugh. "I'm not afraid of him, okay?" I wasn't sure I believed this myself.

"How does Paul feel about all this? You two are still an item, aren't you?" She grinned again, propping her head to her knees. "What, you two got an open relationship now?"

"Oh my God." I groaned, getting to my feet as my sister laughed.

"Can we stick to the topic, Decima?" I lowered my voice as she stopped laughing instantly, scowling.

"Why do I have to be included on this train wreck?" We stopped bristling at one another.

"I need you to keep it on track. I need someone to make sure it doesn't get out of hand….whatever that may take." I cringed on the last part. Cempe immediately perked up turning to me with a grin; she could hear a 'do what you think is right' proposition a mile away. Her idea of right and my idea of right were vastly different things. "I'm setting rules, though."

That's essentially how it all started. We had checkpoints, rules, had time schedules to complete, left some things up to chance and scheduled the rest. Left just a few scraps of memories, cut away the rest of the past, set it aside. Not that it all didn't go just a bit horribly wrong, but Cempe did step up and take care of the unplanned parts, help and fix things to keep it generally smooth. Generally, it was a success.

Generally.

I snapped back to reality around me, as the three of us and Raziel all fell through that great black cravat, miles and miles of blackness, coasting down. The light above us closed into a tiny dot, fading until it resembled just a star. That's when Hell opened up beneath us, when that over-dramatized red light panned out to that same skeletal conga line as before, the stupid and half aware demons we put in charge to lazily circle around. I looked quickly to it, the four of us lit up a red haze, slipping back to darkness as we continued on. What was going through his head, I couldn't imagine. Lots of explaining left, I guess. Biggest thought in my head wasn't how he'd react, he'd get over it, but how much I could tell him. Knowing that everything around you is run on a hoax, well, doesn't sit well with most people, and certainly not those who spend their lives dedicated to that hoax.

This place was full of caverns, full of rooms decked out to whatever religious need it met, the various versions of everyone's Hell. Unofficially, my sisters and I were the ones to oversee everything, to overlord these domains. We never did, really, finding them just as eerie, as creepy as everyone else. My only job was to really fight the battles and help re-fuel the life pool; Cempe took care of our presence here; Aisa visited those who wanted a guide to death. Mystery revealed.

As we fell through these grounds, fell past the droves of wailing, moaning, screaming people, I closed my eyes. I hated it here.

Through the next flickering light we lost sight of Aisa, our feet hitting a fleshy, bouncy surface below us instantly, stopping our free fall. A massive, black, coasting demon of sorts, each wing was like a halved scissor, sharp edge glimmering in the little light we did have coming from the tendril of her forehead. Falx…err… Aisa in her little weaponry dinosaur form of her own, this pilot-fish looking personification of death.

Swinging off to the left, we dove into the next cavern, our official entranceway to our private section of this Hellish nightmare, the Hall of the Fates, officially. Surrounded in liquid lava, our little Hellish Styx, you could hear people wailing and shrieking like elevator music. Aisa swept around in a low, lazy circle, showing this place off. There were huge, colossal columns of carved rock with a pantheon of sorts that stretched up far over even our heads, a series of low, large steps leading up into the back darkness of our quarters, with a door Aisa could probably fly through. It was all exaggerated, all over-blown, out of proportion to give that belittling feeling, that air of superiority. Thankfully, we could personalize our rooms how we liked them, which mine was nothing like what was around us now.

There was a small crowd gathered; Aisa must be playing up to that, letting out a guttural roar and swinging wide in a showboating arc. Cempe gave me an annoyed shove in the shoulder; grinning plastically, trying to get me to play along. My frown didn't change as she hoped it would, not with everything on my mind. I looked away.

"Agh." Frustrated, her glare switched to Raziel. "We should've never brought you down here." She dawdled, looking around her before raising her tone to something more threatening.

"Don't think I've forgotten what you've done, angel!" She hissed at him. "My sister here might see something in you, but I sure don't." Gritting my teeth, I snapped back to her.

"Cut it out!" I snorted once, leaping from the Falx, arms wind milling to keep my balance. Over the heads of the others as they began to cheer, over the molten magma I fell, face tightened up, uncaring. I should be in a good mood, should be the cheerful and play this up. My big re-appearance into my realm, and all I could think about was Palug and Raziel. I furrowed my eyebrows, hitting the ground hard next to the dopey looking demon, an attendant of ours. Crowds cheered.

"Excelsis Nona!" It bowed next to me, taking me off guard. This. Forgot about this, still in Neri-mode. It was a fat, squat looking demon, horns jutting out from all sorts of crazy angles on his face. He and Cempe communicated regularly, though still outside our little knowledge circle, he was one of our top messengers that relayed information. Standing up taller, I gave him a faint grin, letting my face fall again, "Heard you struck quite the blow to a whole field of angels on your undercover infiltration of Heaven." Behind me, Cempe, Aisa and Raziel all landed a few steps back. As my lips twitched to say otherwise, Cempe suddenly jogged the few steps, hand around the back of my neck.

"Nona's infiltration plan worked as it was supposed to! Go up top right now and you'll find a whole field of angelic mulch with our signature on it, to send Heaven that message that we are not to be trifled with."

She laughed out loud, others laughing as well. I didn't share the same sentiment. "Behold the return of our great leader, back from the grips of the angels themselves with all their precious secrets!" She yelled out, riling up those in earshot. There was a grinding sound behind me suddenly.

"You did it on purpose?" Raziel suddenly shouted out, anger and frustration percolating over a respectable level. The cavern of demons quieted down as I spun to face him, trying to show him it was a ruse, trying to explain it was just for show. He didn't pick up on it, "I trusted you! You-" Aisa suddenly wrapped her hand around his mouth, silencing him before any more damage could be done, trying to calm him down. Cempe turned to me as Raziel struggled, trying to fight and get free, eyes flat. So much for considering me a good leader.

"This is why we don't have company." She hissed in my ear as I internally fought whether to go over and help him or leave him there to panic and flail about. The others around me began to mumble, converse as the word 'trust' bubbled and surfaced like breaching whales. Bewildered, my head snapped around to the other side, confused eyes watched me intently. I wasn't acting as I should, as I was known to be.

"Are you alright, Excelsis?" The helper-monkey asked again, as I lowered my head a little bit. I knew what I had to do. They wanted a fearless leader, I'd have to give it to them; I took a deep breath, glaring at Cempe quickly out of the corner of my eye before taking a slow breath.

"Only the foolish and the angels put their faith into trust, especially with a bloodthirsty demon such as I! I'm only loyal to my respected colleagues here!" I roared out in a laugh, arcing my back like some kind of maniacal arch-villain from a bad Saturday morning cartoon as I pointed to Raziel. "Pathetic Fallen scum! Now you'll heed the torture of a thousand burning waters for what you have done, for the demonic innocent you have slain, for the lives lost by your cruel hand! You live in my realm now, the realm of all demons, realm of the true inhabitants of this world; away from the soft, padded world of the angels! It's time you learn your place!" His eyes only zipped to little dots, eyebrow twitching as he leaned forwards, fighting all the more. My face remained unfaltering for a while, taking a few steps to put the crowd behind my back. He never was big on understanding sarcasm. Except that we was.

"Aisa! Take this lump of angelic trash out of my sight; imprison him in the crimson room! I'll deal with him when I'm done with my welcome party here." I grinned, eyes holding steady on him just for a second. As soon as he stopped looking everywhere but at me, I winked, once, quickly. Both of his eyebrows furrowed instantly, looking back to Aisa as she only pushed him on, starting to drag him in towards the building. I sauntered closer to the rest of my group, arms wide out. "Back amongst good company!" I shouted out, grinning, hands held open wide as they cheered.

"I'm sorry that I haven't got better news; that I'm here without warning. The angelic army's gathered up impressive numbers, trying to rid us all from their tainted, fractured system. They're eradicating us from the topside world. They've struck us deep, taken dear ones away from us." I watched as Aisa and Raziel went through the front entranceway, out of sight finally, taking a small breath to only power what I had left to say. "That's why we launch our counterattack exactly four days from now, on the cusp of night. We will not stand for their injustice, their hatred; we will not stand to watch another demon die! We are the darkness, we are the others, and we will make them know this!" I yelled out triumphantly, fist in the air as they erupted in cheering. Cempe was just behind me, grinning and nodding. I turned to the helper behind me.

"A...al..." I snapped my fingers a few times, trying to remember this thing's name.

"Alvo." Cempe said quietly.

"Alvo!" I said with enthusiasm, "Send the word out to recall everyone up top. They wanna think they've won; we'll give them that feeling. House them in the best accommodations that we've got and alert them that I'll come to talk in three days. Talk to Decima if there's any complication." The demon grinned like a proud young lad, nodding quickly.

"Yes, yes of course." I turned away from the helper, heading towards the inside, Cempe quick on my heels.

"See? Isn't this a better way to live?" She laughed a little, waving to the others alongside us as I practically stormed towards the entrance of our quarters.

"No. I keep telling you to stop pushing events like this on me." I threatened through gritted teeth, running up the stairs quickly, stone-faced. Heels spinning on the top step I raised a fist up one last time, gathering another cheer from the crowd, facing my loyal crowd. Oh yeah, I remembered why I spent so much time up top.

As soon as my back was turned towards the inside, all I wanted to do was relax. Even above trying to explain everything I could to Raziel, even above checking on Palug, I was utterly exhausted. From the run earlier in the day, from the mending of my various souls, fighting my ass off, no, I think I deserved a rest. Even if Raziel was there stabbing me in the eye every few seconds, I still needed sleep. My arms hung tiredly at my side as I crossed that threshold, of the doorway at least twenty feet over my head. The first room inside was just as extravagant as the rest of it seemed, keeping up that facade, just in case someone wandered in uninvited.

"Put the security barrier up." I said tiredly, rubbing my head and scratching the side of my face. I heard talking up ahead; Raziel. They were in the little red alcove, the four by six foot 'Crimson Room' that held a potted plant out of view from the main entrance. We had no crimson room, it's where we told the others to go when we wanted them out of the way, to be inside and not have to deal with our semi-egos; the two polar lives I lead in death.

"Ah, there she is!" Aisa said happily, give me a sort of faux bow as Raziel stood beside her, still obviously angry. I rolled my hand, trying to return the gesture. "Little overdone, but I think it'll do."

"It better." I said tiredly, rolling my sore shoulder. "Because I'm not going to bother to poke my head out until then, I'm exhausted." I looked down at my feet, wiggling my toes a little as I saw someone stand blatantly in front of me, arms folded. Frowning nervously, I slowly raised my gaze up as Raziel was there, annoyed as ever.

"So…what?" Still angry. "It's all true?"

"Well… uh…" I stood back up and away, swaying around like a lanky oak to find Cempe also trying to get my attention. She switched to a different language, the Castillan I once spoke as a common tongue; now reserved for talking around people we didn't want to talk to.

"Be very aware of what you tell him and what you shouldn't." She was talking about death after death as Raziel's head suddenly jumped to her, squinting and trying to understand. "Not that I doubt he could, but it ruins a person." I cleared my throat, sputtering a mix between English and Castillan at first before getting it right.

"How am I supposed to explain things without explaining them? He's not stupid." His head whipped around to me, eyes growing angry again.

"Get creative, or lie. Those are your options." She shook her head a little, looking down on him.

"Or just tell him the truth." I shot back.

"I'd really appreciate it if we can all talk the same language here, instead of talking over me." Before I could open my mouth, before I even thought to conjugate something up, Cempe caught it first. I knew she'd been waiting for a moment like this.

"I'd appreciate it if you could just sit down and shut up for a while, you pain in the ass." She turned full to him. "Wipe that constipated frown off your face while you're at it, Nona goes through all this to protect your whiny, bitchy baby ass with a lot of shit that could get us ALL in trouble, and I don't think you're the one to start demanding anything but 'please oh please don't beat the shit out of me like I deserve'! To answer your questions, yes, we are in Hell, yes, Nona's that Nona the Fate, and no, we're not going to hurt you unless you keep pulling shit like this. Got it?"

She took a few breaths, hands wringing Raziel's fictional neck in the air. Cempe gave him a few more glares before looking back to me, shaking her head. And with that, Raziel effectively shut up. There was a sketchy, wandering glance for someone to step in, to back him up, but he found silence, even from me. It wasn't that I hated the guy; it just needed to be said.

"C'mon, let's go." I beckoned a finger at Raziel, who continued to look rather scared of Cempe as she seethed in annoyance.

"I'd go with her if I was you." She threatened, curling her lip up. "She's your only friend down here."

"Aww, he's not that ba-" Aisa started, Cempe quickly slapping her arm in annoyance as she immediately stopped. I grinned, shaking my head and headed off with slow, ambling steps taking me farther down the hallway. I heard him join me after a moment in utterly awkward silence.

"You didn't have to call me scum." He said softly, worn down as well and breaking the silence. I didn't turn to face the ex-angel, scoffing emptily to the stale air. I hated this place.

"Better then scab." I said quietly. He stopped walking as I kept on with slow, lumbering steps.

"C'mon, that was a long time ago."

"I'm not holding it against you. I'm just very aware that until you knew anything else, that's your opinion of me." I looked a little over my back, giving a sideways smile laced with retrospective guilt. Raziel tried to back himself up.

"Well, how was I supposed to know that Nona and Joan were the same person?" Smirking and looking away, he kept talking, "I honestly thought 'Nona' was some sorta disfigured monster." I belted out a laugh.

"Good! That means my publicity stunts are working. I get a dramatic reduction of uprisings and shenanigans when people think that." I was having fun talking about politics when he sorta quieted down, not quite on that same page with me.

"So it's all true?" It was like he wanted to think differently, wanted me to go 'Aahh, gotcha!' Let the curtain go up, big studio audience laughing and clapping at this fantastic ruse. Instead he got me glaring at him, half an eyebrow raised as we stormed along to my corner of this compound. Raziel held his hand up by his sides. "I just didn't figure you as the violent type." He said it pretty quietly, but I caught it immediately, stopping the little atrium before my room.

"I'm not the violent type." I said quickly, doubling on my words as soon as they left. "Agh, well It's a job, it's not me, personally." It was almost comical how he had to crane his neck all the way back just to shout at me.

"How isn't it you? You just chopped up a field of cherubs and ordered some sort of big rebellion to wipe Heaven off the map!" He was struggling to understand, struggling to reason with it. "I mean, Jesus Christ, Neri! Or Nona… or…whoever the Hell you are now. How can you say that's not you?"

"Because it's not! I just…. God dammit, I feel like I'm scolding a child like this." I looked around, shedding off a few feet by suppressing

the future soul and dropping to the ground at a regular height. I looked
the same, but only stood around six feet tall, not nine. Raziel's somewhat
surprised eyes followed me as I continued on, unfazed by the atmosphere
change. "It's a duty, a job. Did you and all your angel-pals consider
themselves just one mind, one thought? No. It's not any different here." His
surprised and shocked look didn't change with my words at all, looking
towards the door quickly and pointing a hand to it.

"There are LAVA pools full of dead bodies in your front yard!"
I leaned against the walls, exhausted and propping myself against the
marble with relative ease. Staring back at him, he looked like he was on
the verge of throwing a tantrum. Seriously mentally disturbed by what
he saw around him; but that always seemed to be the case, even when we
had first teamed together up top, usually with stuff that honestly wasn't
that disturbing. But a corpse river, yeah, I could agree, this was honestly
unsettling. I snickered out of place, shaking my head with a hand to my
temple.

"I know, that's fucked up, isn't it? There's a reason I don't spend
any time here." Raziel's uneasiness softened a little, more confused than
anything else.

"And you're…just going to let it happen?" He said quickly.

"I don't really have a choice, I'm not doing any of this to them."

"But you're their Excelsis or whatever!" My ears went back as he fell
against the other part of the atrium, frustrated.

"You mean I should go out there, inspire every empty-headed
spirit to come fight for us? Fix their problems? I'm just one person, Raziel.
Regardless of how tall I get." He didn't say anything against it, so I assumed
that's what he meant. "They stay in that lava pool on their own until they're
ready to come out, change their lives and do something. I have zero effect
on their lives until then. Being the 'Excelsis' means I'm a figurehead, that's
all."

He wasn't coping with this well; screams of torture and death
resonated down this hallway like the sound oozed from the walls. I looked
back to my room before back to him.

"Are you still Neri?" He said as I only raised my head up, insulted.

"Yes, Raziel." He frowned and looked at a different wall.

"But are you really?" Frozen on his overtly philosophical questions,
I only grumbled.

"I understand you're saying this to make me really consider if
adding two whole sections of soul onto an base, memoryless and honestly
pretty impressionable and naive soul means I'm still the same person, and
depending on your definition of 'same' I guess I'm not." I folded my arms,
walking closer to him, "But if you want to think of it as the same soul that's
gone through the same things despite this, with the same consciousness
throughout, only more knowledgeable and no longer blabbering on how

she doesn't know stuff, then I am. I'm still the same person, Razzle. I could recite this whole thing back to you chronologically if you really want me to."

He shook his head a little and put up his hands with a faint smile, eyes back to the ground the next moment as another scream from the molten river outside echoed through our estate. Things quieted down a little as I slowly sided up next to him, mimicking him. He didn't look like he was doing well.

"When you thought I would make a good leader, you weren't honestly hoping for that, were you?" It was a soft spoken sentence lacking the desperation for a response, silence being my answer as he kept his head down, eyes averted. I let that hang in the air for a few moments, looking away as well. "That hurts."

"I was hoping for something better." He said after a time. I frowned instantly.

"Hey, it's this or the cherub army; those are your two choices." I spat out, insulted.

"For you, not me." I stopped, standing up straight awkwardly as he looked at his one arm, face just as worn down as my own, his face almost as ever-changing. Nudging a smile I rested more against the wall, looking around to this marble enclosure, this elaborate cage.

"I'm good at what I do, Raziel. My job is to find people without purpose or hope, with nothing left to their voice; I take that emptiness and give them something back. That's what makes me happy, no matter what disguises or fronts I have to hide that behind. I'm lucky to be an active part of life, to be able to actively shape it for masses of people around me. And to be a part of it for so long, it can't be judged in an afternoon, you know?" I couldn't tell who I was exactly talking about anymore, if I meant the world around me, or my influence on Raziel.

"It's complex?" He muttered unhappily.

"Very." I sided up next to him, resting against the marble stone.

"I'm a guide, a guardian, and not really much more than that. I'm just human, like everyone else." I smiled, trying to catch his eyes. "That's my highest honor. It certainly isn't wishing anything but the best for those around me, be it those burning alive in the pools outside, or the one standing in front of me now."

"And that's what you want?" He asked uncertainly, staring at that great big contradiction of what had just happened around us coming down here, and what I said now. Nodding, I spit out a quick laugh.

"C'mon let's go inside." I grabbed his hand, starting to pull him towards the unassuming door to my room. Raziel's eyes shot up at me.

"Why, what's in there?" He said it like the hounds of Hell were behind it, a strong sense of fear in his tone enough that it was almost bewildering, that I'd be leading him to his re-death after taking all this care to save him. I furrowed my eyebrows, sneering a little.

"This is where we eat the unborn and unbaptized fetuses to gather strength in the moonlight." I said flatly, pulling harder as he came away from the wall, "It's the only part of this underworld I enjoy." His gawking glare didn't change much, honestly considering my bullshit statement. Dropping his hand, I stood next to the door, pressing both palms against it.

"I was joking! Develop a sense of humor, Frankenstein, it's just my room." The door lit up quickly, sliding away to the pitch black hole of a space as we both gingerly stepped inside; you couldn't tell the walls from the floor, faint sound of running water and the musty smell of dirt as I scoured the wall for the switch blindly.

"You keep the electricity bill down, I see." He said sarcastically, the sound of something hollow resonated once like a drum. "Dammit!"

"Yeah, I wouldn't move around so much, hold on." I patted the mossy wall frantically, trying to find the lump. "Cempe's probably been in here, screwing around with my controls- Ah! Here it is!" A mushroom was just underneath my fingers as I held my one hand out, calling the Colus up. Pressing the weapon against the mushroom the energy was infectious, bio luminescent lines of mushrooms firing up, racing in planned patterns and lines across this cavern, lighting it dimly. The lines raced to the top until they sunk into the walls, lighting up the quartz at the top of the cavern, bluish green glow acting like a fictitious sky above us.
Glowing silk worms hung from the ceiling, thousands of them, a gentle, mesmerizing swaying group. There was no furniture in the room but just a series of flat comfy rocks coming out from the wall, different vantage points all gathering around the waterfall at the far end of my room; it was a massive space, big enough to hold at least two full grown Moirae protective spirits. Everything was almost covered in moss, best of all; you couldn't hear a single screaming voice of torment in here. I've tried.

"I designed it to act as much like the outside, even down here." I said quietly, smiling as the memories of building this place all came sweltering back. "Figurehead or not, I hate this place. That's why I stay up top most of the time. When I occasionally get trapped down here, this is where I stay. Unless, you know, I'm revolutionizing someplace."

"Mmn." Raziel kept looking straight up, taking a few steps farther in, still rubbing his head. I turned back to the Colus, setting it onto the ground, bracing the mushroom.

"Stay." I coached it like an obedient dog, taking a few cautious steps away before nodding that it wouldn't move or evaporate. It was nice to be in this room again.

"This is incredible."

"Thanks. Since I've remembered this place exists, I've been meaning to visit it again. At least I can get some rest."

"You're resting? Now?"

"Still the same collaborative person who ran some 250 hours straight." I turned back to him sarcastically, "I'm tired."

"Don't you have to run Hell or something?" He said it almost like he was worried about my response. That I'd sit up and go 'Oh, right!' And just zap him out of existence. I had an idea.

"Nah, I'm actually gonna bestow it upon you for the next five minutes, that sound okay?" I joked as you could see him stand up taller, frightened as I leaned over and poked him on the shoulder. "Alright, there you go, now you run Hell. Feel the cosmic power yet?" Eyes squinted nearly shut, you could tell he was bracing himself, scared. After a second or two, he began to relax.

"How about now?" I kept at it, giving a slow grin. Flipping his hands over and back, he frowned, looking back to me.

"I don't feel any different." Suddenly catching on to what I was doing, he looked back at me, not amused. "Oh. Right. Okay. I get your angle now. Clever." Laughing and heading towards the water, I motioned him to follow like a terrified stray. Again not a too far fetched description of the guy; his freaked-out glare was almost gone by now, running a finger along the glowing vine mushroom wall.

"So you remember or know everything now?" I stretched out next to the waterfall, horns resting a natural groove in the rocks and shifting a little onto my side. I nodded.

"All accounted for." I opened my eyes a little, looking to the ceiling, eyes furrowing, "Ask at your discretion. I don't want to keep anything from you, but there's a creepy amount of depth to what I know, if you get what I mean."

"Big picture stuff."

"Oh yeah."

"Ah." Was all he said, walking over to one of the lower rocks and sitting against it. What would he ask? There had to be a million questions pestering his mind, especially now. In his position, things like 'what the Hell just happened' would've been the forerunners of that list. He sat there, contemplating, looking around before finally speaking again. "Why do you go to sleep? I mean, whatever, but seriously, that's been bugging me practically since we met this last time, at least."

Frowning, I propped up on my elbows.

"That's what you're going to ask? Are you serious?" I couldn't help but laugh as he only shrugged indecisively.

"I've got other questions. That one just seemed relevant to the conversation."

"Raziel, we're both sitting in the central core of Hell, it's all kind of relevant to the conversation." I kept laughing, lying back down. "You know what, alright, fine; your wish is my command." Grumbling under my breath with a smile, I figured best to describe it in a way that wouldn't put anyone else to sleep in the process.

"It's personal preference." I grew more serious, reflective, "I like to start the day like I used to, parallel life enough to relate more with it by waking up and sleeping like everyone else. Being constantly awake is Hell, your brain never slows down. Give someone a few hours and a thousand past lives to bug you, you'll appreciate the time away from it."

"That's it?" He crept a little closer, wandering to sit more by the waterfall with me. I laughed once more, running a hand through the tiny waves rushing against the moss-covered rock.

"It's a chance to relive moments of life I fear I'm forgetting." I swished my hand about the water, "I worry there's a limit, a cap. That it's all in vain, no matter how much I want to remember and experience it all. I fear I'll forget something, someone. Dreams help." My tone grew vacant, distant, snapping back together with an uncertain grin as I blindly swung my arm around him.

"Hey, before I forget, let me do some quick surgery on you, okay?" Intentionally screwing around with his tentative views of this whole situation, Raziel only slowly turned to me, eyebrows furrowed. "It's not a big deal, it'll be quick. Trust me." He furrowed more.

"You a surgeon too?" He said flatly as I dragged my sorry butt up, sitting cross legged. I dropped out of full form and went as small as I could go, so it'd be somewhat less awkward and invasive that way.

"Something like that." I focused in, remember what he'd said before about me doing something and not saying anything, so I figured being apparent might help. "My area of expertise lately has been the division of souls and soul bits. Sometimes when we adapt a Postremo, we'll get remnant conditions that can latch on. They're called Malums. I named them." Raziel didn't quite get what I was trying to gently bring up.

"What are you saying?"

"You have problems regulating body heat, yeah?" Raziel suddenly looked shocked, like it was some sort of surprise he was consistently the temperature of a mostly refrigerated piece of bread. "I mean, not this lifetime, but I've died out in the cold before too- it's annoying, you feel like you're never quite warm. Of the Malums to get it's not the worst, but it's correctable. I can fix that for you, Raziel." A thought struck me.

"I mean, unless that's your thing. Sometimes people make it their thing. Labeling an issue, roping that into identity, that sort. Something people do."

"Bu... but how would you know how to fix that? Heaven's never had any answer for it, they said it's..." He stopped, knowing he was taking their side for a moment and looking like he remembered where he was at in the same breath. The ex angel spit out the rest hastily, like someone trying to get through a story as fast as they could, "It's not fixable, it's penance, it's to teach patience, pick one. A solid no, though. And no, it's not 'my thing'." I gave a laugh.

"Raziel I don't know how to tell you this, but here on the hip side of town we fix our problems. Not saying that Heaven is intentionally letting people Malum it up for patience sake, but I'm just saying, if you'd like to stop being the temperature of a mostly busted refrigerator all the time, let me know." I loosely grabbed his shoulders, rustling him a little in an effort for him to relax. "It's not a big deal, literally will take maybe a minute."

He sat there, looking around for a little bit before shrugging, giving some general consent.

"You've done this before, right?"

"Plenty of times!" I shook his shoulders a little more, slipping in as quick and as unnoticeable as possible. I was still sitting there, talking, but also navigating the sometimes complex, twisted labyrinth of another person's soul while still cracking jokes. "And it's only gone... catastrophically once. Decent..." I removed the Malum, immediately separating myself from him as professional and as courteous a manner as I could.

"Decent odds. How do you feel?" Raziel wobbled where he sat for a moment, looking himself over, confused.

"The same." He gave me an almost disappointed scoff. "Did you do anything?" Breathing on my claws I only got to my feet, popping back to full form.

"Yup, we're all done, hold on a moment." Snapping my fingers I suddenly made the waterfall warm and welcoming like a nice tropical getaway, winds tepid, but not too hot. Pushed the earth in a bit to make a shallow, kiddie pool-esque type of divot that I'd mend later, pulling my hands a bit farther apart, gave it some naturally draining grooves to the side and made it a bit deeper. This realm was my clay, this room especially so.

It was about time I spruced my dank waterfall hovel up, letting the silk worm lights brighten a little, letting a few other lush, tropical plants spring from he cracks in the rock. Moss covered more of the walls, a few different strands popped up adding some new color to the area as I surveyed my work, caught up in the intense world of home horticulture. It already seemed much cheerier in here, happy with the changes as I waved my hand at him.

"Alright, give it a shot."

Raziel was alarmed with all the room changes for a moment, looking around and surveying the new 'pool' with a tinge of apprehension. Looking back to me I waved him along again, looking back to the walls and judging how I felt about this new aesthetic.

The sound of the waterfall suddenly changed, like it was hitting a duffel bag, water spraying from the middle as I turned to find out what went wrong. Raziel lay face down in the water like he decided to nap there, his back legs still sticking out.

"Neri do good?" I called out as he didn't move for a couple seconds, dragging one hand up to give a thumbs up, arm immediately back in the water after that as he slowly dragged himself entirely into the waterfall, huddled like a rock. Grinning, I felt pretty happy, making a couple motions and deepening the shallow hole farther down so he could fetal position there easily. The angel suddenly scrambled for the surface.

"Hey, uh, could you, um..." He started as I laughed, jacking up the temperature by about ten degrees before he could finish. He immediately slipped back underwater with two thumbs up this time as I walked towards the walls, pruning and futzing around with the room a bit more.

"Ah huh. Not trying to overwhelm you. Let me know if that's too pedestrian I'll turn it into a tributary of Styx if I need to." Raziel didn't move or do anything but try to catch up on 350+ years of being uneasy and cold.

Felt good to help people.

39

We talked for some time; Raziel never asked about any of the" big picture stuff." We talked about the weird subtleties of what had happened in the past, little unimportant things, like I was the leader on a very quick, brief sightseeing tour of Hell. Where are the demons? Welp, they're about. How old was the Estate? Very. Etc.

No matter, with Palug's return I'd be explaining a lot more whether he was okay with it or not.

We migrated over to the wall, sitting on top of an especially cushy rock, moss and soft grass and plants dense over the whole top of it. It jutted out from the wall, plenty of space to sit, lounge about, play cards and just talk and converse. I wanted to keep it light, keep things happy and uneventful.

Sitting therein we both enjoyed the rest from constant movement, from the over-stressing situations I managed to get into on a fairly predictable basis. Listening to the gentle waterfall, to the solitude of all the perks of a Japanese sand garden with half the lighting; it was a soothing, unwinding moment of peace and ease.

"How you doing? Good?" I asked again, feeling like an anxious host desperately trying to impress her guest. I mean I fixed his brain and literally put him in the best possible place I could figure in Hell, but it didn't feel like enough. I was very aware of everything and it was getting to me and I just had to beat that thought into, through, and past his head that even Hell didn't have to mean what it normally does. That he wasn't here to be penalized for being my friend, that everything was definitely fine and not a problem and he wouldn't figure out this whole place was as hollow as a bag of straws.

Raziel paused, looked up, shook his head before looking back to his cards.

"Yes. Fine. Still." He shuffled one card along, trying to decide what he'd place down. My gaze was leveled at the top of his head like a laser.

"It's not weird or anything, right?" He paused. It felt like my heart would scrambled out of my throat. Why pause. Why stop. What was wrong. "You'd TELL me if it was weird, right?" He remained paused, twiddling his fingers on the back of the card for a moment. It was weird. Oh no.

"It's a little weird." He muttered, keeping his head down.

"EGH, NO. WHY. WHAT DID I DO."

"Nothing! It's fine!" He looked up, before quickly looking back down as it only made me that much more worried. "The whole thing is weird. Lots of it."

"What?! What do you mean, 'lots of it'." I put my cards down for a split second before holding them back up to my chest. "Is there anything I can fix?"

"Stop...asking that! You're creeping me out asking that. It's Hell, what could you possibly fix?"

"EVERYTHING." I wheezed desperately, eyes flared wide as Raziel recoiled. Looking between either pupil he seemed horrified, slowly easing back to normal and finally putting his cards down.

"Alright. I... I guess it's kinda weird with the... being really tall part." I already had myself suppressed to the smallest I could go, which was still about 6 ft tall not including the horns. Figuring he knew me as Neri, I quickly dropped 8-9 inches in height, and put myself back in those original clothes. Raziel stopped talking, watching skeptically.

"Better?"

"I... I don't know. I'm not sure." He muttered, putting both hands up for a moment as I only let out a long, constant wheeze. Raziel demanded the floor to speak.

"I mean, I guess when you talk about ruling Hell, it's one thing to talk and another thing to see it."

"I don't 'rule Hell', but continue." I said flatly.

"Just a lot of stuff has happened in such a short amount of time, I guess I'm used to things going a bit slower and this whole thing feels like a fever dream." Thinking, I nodded along with him. That was a fair point and the entire reason I was trying to take things at a snails pace despite the planning and orchestrating I needed to do about our upcoming attack. Couldn't just dump Raziel in the room and figure he'd entertain himself, then it'd make it into a recreational prison. "I might've figured the 'Demon Queen' or whichever had some power but I also figured it you probably didn't actually exist."

"You literally fought me!"

"I didn't know! I figured you were just some big demon in a mask!" I bust out laughing.

"Is that the metric on which you judge who to attack? Tall people?" I shook my head, looking back to my cards. "I don't know how to fix that."

"I guess I'm just saying it's weird and it's going to be weird, but I don't think you can fix it." He sat up, looking around for a moment before back to me. "But it's nice in here, and I appreciate you trying, and I didn't think Hell could be like this."

"Alright, well, that's appreciated." I gave a smile, looking over my surroundings again with a sense of pride and peace.

Our peace never tends to last long.

As if on cue, my stomach hurt. It was a dull, anxious sort of pain, far away and subtle at first. I tried to shake the notion off, tried to chalk it up to other matters until I saw Raziel doing the same thing, coughing into his closed fist with his other hand to his stomach. I sat straight up, watching him as the pain dulled away for a moment before brightening back up in a horrible little jolt. Raziel coughed again, frowning in sync and trying to pass it off as nothing, like I was.

"What's wrong?" I questioned intently, putting down my cards. Raziel shook his head like it was no pain whatsoever, grinning for a second and waving his hand.

"Nothing, feels like indigestion" He looked up, eyes locking tightly together as that wave of pain hit us both. "Or…like someone's… driving a knife in my chest." This couldn't be some tether problem, if he and I were both feeling it. Oh no. There was a knock at my door, something rushed.

"Nona, open up, we've got problems!"

"Great. Whelp, peace over, you win, time to go." I grabbed Raziel by the wrist, leaping towards the door; the smoke was already wafting by my ankles as we bust through the threshold, storming past Cempe with her hand raised, ready to knock again. She scrambled up next to me as I popped back into full form, the full nine feet tall, dragging Raziel along like a child. A wave of pain hit us both again, stumbling my walk just for a moment.

"Paul?" I looked to Cempe as the fate nodded quickly, all joking aside, serious. Looking back ahead of me, I picked up the pace. "Sounds like the Fleur Du Lis; we're both getting sympathy pains."

"Sympathy pains? You call this a sympathy pain?" Raziel said behind me, tugging back quickly, "Who's Paul?" Looking back he pulled his one hand away with the stain of blood on his fingers, red spot just above the heart on his shirt. Cempe and I both stopped instantly, looking to one another.

"You didn't TELL him?" She practically ripped off my ear.

"He didn't wanna know big picture stuff!" I elbowed Cempe in the ribs, "It was better to enjoy some peace and acclimate." I looked to Raziel, frowning at the blood on his shirt. It was a dirty trick, a dirty foul little trick that meant one thing.

"You want me to come with?" She offered, looking once to Raziel and shaking her head in disgust. I shook my head no.

"We can handle this- but be on standby, just in case this goes sideways." Another sharp pain in my stomach made us both stop, retching for a moment as panic and worry crept up in my mind. "We gotta go!"

I snagged Raziel again and jumped into a run, turning back as we exited out the far door, back amongst the lava pools and dead river corpses. Without a crowd to appease, only the helper-monkey stood there, confused as I dragged my previous victim along gingerly.

"Nona, what is-" He pointed to Raziel and back to me as I let go of the ex-angel.

"Paul's Continuum." I said quickly, fixing my gloves and craning my head back, "Colus!" Algo…or whatever his name was, immediately bowed to the angel out of respect. You could see the black smoke begin to swirl loosely around the lava platform in a broad tornado rushing towards me in a more skilled, artful way. I kept my eye on it, attention purposely focused elsewhere.

"Sorry for previously, Sir, I had no idea!" The demon smiled politely to him, perhaps even more jarring then the bow; Raziel's head snapped to me, and then back to him. The smoke slammed together from both sides, flaring and rushing out in full demonic majesty, wings unfurled, ready to launch in a hurry. Now in the body of the full-grown Colus I leapt from the platform, from the hall of fates, heading towards the surface in a mad dash. I could feel where he was, I could practically see Palug in my head, find him amongst this darkness. As those cross hairs lined up, something jabbed the side of my neck angrily.

"You know I'm going to ask what the hell is going on, right?!" Raziel shouted at my head, grasping desperately onto the fur along my spine. "Who is Paul, and why do the demons suddenly respect me instead of wanting my blood?" My flapping started to get faster, started to blur those lines once more, pointed straight up at the pinprick of light.

"You sure you wanna know? It's big picture stuff."

"Neri!"

"He's my other, my soulmate!" I turned my head to look Raziel in the eye as his face squished up in distaste. I ignored it. "They're attacking him up top with a particular weapon called the Fleur Du Lis, that's why we're both feeling the effects!"

"But what does that have to do with me? Why am I feeling it? I've never met the guy!" I turned back ahead of me for a moment, only to turn back. Sorry Raziel, this information was going to come out whether you were ready or not. I prayed he was ready, that he would understand eventually. I clenched my teeth.

"Because you two are the same person!" I shouted quickly as both our faces blurred out of existence, darting through the fabric of space with Raziel's panicked response wailing out behind us.

"Whaaaaaaaaaaaaaat!?"

Spain, 1278

This round, my name was Maienca. I lived in the principality of Asturias, the oldest Christian establishment on the Iberian Peninsula in the Northeast section of what today is Spain. This round, I did not live in the middle of wealth, did not have that security net to fall back on easy living; it was all wretched poor, day to day living for me. It also didn't help that I grew up stubbornly, that I grew up a bit of a shit. I've always been that kind of rebellious spirit no matter where I went. That didn't help things here. Previous to really meeting Paul, this round Pere, you could say I was a brat. I'd say that too.

It was my first life done for the sake of a break, smack dab in the middle of the Crusades. Prior to then, demons enjoyed a fairly relaxed lifestyle; we were a loose collection of enigmatic and unfortunate souls. My sisters and I still had small competition from one minor religion to the next, things weren't radically different or anything really, still had opposition, but it came to be more that we were just the dead after life, not the hideous evil creatures from the depths of Hell. There were still fights, but nothing on a scale seen in the Crusades. Souls desperate to continue that sanctimonious drive from life suddenly began conflict, arguments that began to result in fights, escalating to full uncontrollable warfare. Even with this push Heaven was on today, it absolutely paled in comparison. With so many getting wiped out, with this brand new idea of having to lead others into rebellion, I couldn't take the endless fighting, the burden; escaping up top. Leaving in turmoil, I happened to arrive in turmoil, having a consistently crappy attitude for the first 14 years of my life.

We lived in the heart of the town, admits the hustle and fuss of the market place. I stole, constantly. This life was also where I got my penchant for learning how to break open a lock, a natural talent to me in any of my future lives in existence, this natural sway for breaking into things. Sleight of hand tricks as well, come to think about it. Either way, I was a pain in the ass. Loud, annoying, I only quieted down for a reason. My parents could barely handle me, the only child they dared give birth to. We were Christian; I had to be if I wanted to keep my tongue. Or fingers. Or an arm. The crusades were rough.

So they sent me off to help in the Monastery on the outer limits of the town; there they tried to teach me the gift of shutting the Hell up during service, of doing what was asked of me, of trying to be civilized. I didn't take to it very well, feeling like I didn't fit into the situation, residual hatred and frustration from my demoning job outside of this life. With this rise of a new church, why the Hell would I help out? Their solution was pretty straightforward; I found myself reading a lot of biblical text, stuck in the room with the giant paper bible that was supposed to beam some sense into me. That too didn't work very well. I wasn't ill treated in the least; I was just tolerated as one does a headache; give it a quick fix and hope the situation resolves itself. I felt alone, isolated.

Instructed one day to read nearly a fourth of the whole book in one sitting, I found my eyes glazed over the text, juggling the knowledge of offhand Latin I knew, trying to read the intricately perfect handwriting on every day; I found myself looking for inking errors instead, sighing out the window. I had the attention span of a gnat; it was non-violent torture.

Fingers racing over the text, I stopped. Face scrunched up, I picked up the fringes of a tune, of a soft, sweet melody. Like something out of a dream, I suddenly heard music from the entryway, something far away- a lute… well, it was technically an Oud, but it was a type of lute. It was enchanting, wonderful and mystic; not one of the biblical hymns I knew, nothing religious in any take, just a common song you'd hear every now and then in the marketplace. The gall someone had to be playing that in here—standing like in a trance from the book I began to walk down the long hallway, smiling more out of confusion then pleasure. My feet edged down the way quickly, racing faster and faster to find that music, that sound. As the notes changed, I stopped; the sound was just the other side of the door; my head snaked around the edge, curious.

Inside that small room was a boy, roughly my age, sitting precariously over the lute, eyes furrowed, figuring out the notes he played as they came out. He was one of the 'junior monks' I suppose, in training, under just as much stress and expectations to learn these texts, and here he was, fiddling around with a lute. I wasn't a bold woman that time, I was shy despite being a pain in everyone's ass, wary of those around me; but I just found myself already walking into that room, drawn to him. It was like something I couldn't control, it wasn't an option to ignore this and go back to my own quarters. The boy jumped as I practically stood over him, smiling and laughing already.

"My apologies." he said quickly, hand over the strings of the lute like he intended to put it away. I stood, dumbfounded, forgetting how to smile and react as just being around him was an experience in itself.

"Please." I stumbled on my words, "Keep playing." The corners of my mouth tugged slightly, walking to the other side of the boy as he looked uncertainly to me, smiling once more and leaning back over the instrument. As he started playing once more, the way he played, it was like I could see through him, could feel that energy, that serene peace. It was something I didn't have, something foreign in these years. Staring at Pere was like seeing all facets of that tresillo soul, all at once, like experiencing the past, present, and future in one smile. Basically, I was struck.

"Maienca." I said out of the blue, no regard to spit out this kind of information at a proper time, like a break in the song, or when he might've asked for my name. Pere/Paul/Palug stopped, laughing again before shaking his head a little back and forth.

"Pere." he said quickly, eyes snapping up to me before back down to the instrument. He played without interruption for another hour, until his mentor came back and shooed me from his room.

There's a notion that people carry, that some romantic dunces believe that the entire purpose of life is to find the other half of yourself, to discover the other part of your existence. I had never been that type of person, I worked diligently to lead the others, I worked to fight back, I worked with half the thought that with all these lives lead, I actually would meet my other half. Knowing as much as I did, I figured a" soul mate' was just something made up by people, that it was just a word. But just sitting in that room not only awoke that type of love, that bond, but it jarred all factions of my soul. My past and future soul, left behind in Hell as a loose collection of thoughts, ideas, a churning mass of shapes and black, hazy forms; began to buzz with life. Life that I wasn't leading, that I wasn't in control of, those other parts knew something was going on. It definitely put Cempe and Aisa on alarm, almost in fear, watching non- choreographed parts of myself freak out, swimming with colors other then the same, dull, hazy gray. In my own existing life, it translated to some serious emotional heart fluttering. I just couldn't ignore that drive to see him, to meet with him again, to just be around him.

For seven months, while he was supposed to be studying up, supposed to be working towards his eventual move into the sanctimonious part of the monastery, while I was supposed to be having the love of God change my heart or else, we were inseparable. If I wasn't sneaking around to visit him, he was sneaking around to visit me. Obviously, being stupid half-adults, we were caught, over and over again, it was no secret what we were doing and our annoying young love was tolerated as much as I had been tolerated in the past. You hope it goes away. You hope it fades out; rests, disappears or some small argument tears that devotion apart. That never happened. And as we got closer to Pere's indoctrination, it began to cause more frustration and annoyance. They began to pressure him, pressure his devotion to the word, their tones changed towards him and me, this terrible bout of uncertainty.

Four days before he had to make up his mind, I found him standing just outside my doorway early one morning. Heaped over the wrinkled bible, asleep, I yawned and stretched out, smiling, already happy to see him. His face had been clouded with worry, he looked frightened and exasperated, an unusual scowl that pretty much dropped as our eyes met, back to that ever-dependent smile.

"We're going to leave." He said quickly in embrace, whispering over my shoulder, "I came here to find direction in life, and I have. But it's not with them." I couldn't speak, couldn't reply, holding him close. So we left. We walked out of that monastery with the unkind words at our back, with the stigma and shame nothing short of being exiled. We were so happy we just didn't care. I figured a happy, beautiful life lived with that other half was worth whatever years I could get out of it, that it was the only thing that mattered.

Most souls live their lives without knowledge of when it's their turn to pass on. Most of the time, it's not planned; neither me, Aisa, or Cempe have any real control over that life span of any other person beside our own. We know that we can't take too much time off, and generally, we plan on each life lived to be as long as our fictitious age demands it to be. That's why my lives all fizzled out before I was 28, why Cempe's never lived past 38 and why Aisa has never broken 50.

I wasn't supposed to live past twenty, this time around. Four years into our marriage, right on cue, I grew sick. I got a bug like everyone else around us and grew gravely ill. Just when it looked like I was due to pass on, like I was about to see the end of it and call it a day, I got better. It wasn't supposed to happen. I wasn't 'supposed' to live past that day, but I did. I fought against that planned death, struggled and practically ranted, somehow managed to break my own death date. It was the only time I had, and I honestly think it was because I didn't want to leave Pere, that I didn't want to split from him ever again. I wasn't being rational, Hell, love is never rational. But as far as I could control, as I could influence under my own power, I wouldn't leave. Not on my own terms.

Exactly a year after that first illness, I grew deathly sick again. I survived. A month later, diagnosed with the incurable ailment. Cured. Little odd occurrences started happening after that, life and 'the plan', ironically, trying to resolve itself, trying to make good. Trying to kill me off. I was shot with an arrow. I 'accidentally' fell down a steep rock face. Kicked in the face by a goat, part of our little meager house collapsed on me, I mean, I survived it all. Pere began to think the world was conspiring against us, but of course, he said it with a smile. Our life was in perpetual drama, surviving one thing and overcoming another; I managed to get three more somewhat good and often painful years out of that original sentence, until that fall of 1287.

Apparently seething with annoyance and frustration, it was Cempe that came to retrieve me. There was no rhythm to how the stray warring soldier came to our tiny little farming stand, how she managed to pick the time when Pere was traveling to town for supplies, how she knew just where to find me. The Fate inhabited and controlled the soldier body with about as much grace as a child does with a broken puppet. Stumbling up to our front entrance in a strange, jumbled mess, she didn't even bother trying to make up something believable.

"Enough of this, Nona, we're done playing around." I remembered the male soldier calling out an a strangely effeminate tone, eyes half-focused and half-closed. Pinned against the back wall I reached for whatever iron we had, bracing it in my hands like I had done it a thousand times before. It felt like the other parts of me were flaring up, were reacting to this, surrounding me, sentient on their own. Full of this uncontrollable need to protect this life, to keep guarding my health and survive yet another obstacle, to stay with Pere, I fought back. In that life, Maienca was never a fighter. Ever. Loud, yes, but never raised anything heavier than a sack of potatoes towards anything worse than an open fire. I guess that was a fairly ironic life, but fighting at that time was just something I seemed to understand, to know what was going on as I took my first two cautious steps outside the door, possessed.

The soldier stopped, shaking it's head and raising up a hand.

"I'm not even going to play this game with you." It snarled, hand grasping into a fist as lightning struck me dead. Cempe didn't even bother to ask or talk to me or do a damn thing besides overkill the heck out of Maienca.

Sprawled on the floor, without giving that obligatory five minutes to let my soul separate from the body, I suddenly popped to life, arms out, battle ready once more. Cempe was gingerly stepping out of the soldier's possession, poor guy confused and delirious from the five miles Cempe had stormed in anger to get to my isolated house. She gave me a dubious look, shaking her head back and forth as Maienca's soul was ready to kick her ass, as it didn't bother questioning anything else.

"Grow up." She said coldly, lip curled up at me.

"Grow up? You don't even know the meaning of the word!" I hissed back in not only the voice of Maienca, but of the hundreds of other women I had been previously, all lined up and harmonizing with the same anger, an auditorium fighting back. Cempe's eyes flared up before squinting to tiny things, taking just a few short steps to tower over me, still that fragment of human soul.

"That's such a stupid, childish thing to say." She put one giant foot on the top of my head, shoving my soul feet first into that Hellish slop below, just beneath that house. My soul; at least the rest of it. It was like molasses, like a choking, strangling feeling that burrowed through my ears, seeped into my skin, sunk into my brain and wormed around, struggling to find where it was supposed to go. Confused I thrashed around, trying to scream, trying to get away.

I remember being scared and uncertain as that black cloud of gelatinous smoke put back all bits of my soul in the right order, as I grew those extra inches, as I became life and life again, that same Nona with another life- notch on my belt. Stubbornly, suddenly, I was spit out, decked out in the horns, the gear, the clothing, the foot-wraps like I was now, everything just as it was supposed to be, just very confused.

There was no twenty minute slow-restart of the brain, there was no waiting time to get all my memories back in check, it was just like jumping back in where I left off, yet more relaxed, more laid back, more focused like how it was supposed to be. Sitting there, eyes wide on that cold hard ground of the inner workings of Hell, Cempe slowly descended alongside me, laughing and giggling like it was all one big joke.

"Thank the stars we've got you back, Nona, you were being completely ridiculous, trying to fight against us in that weak human form. Did you manage to learn more about Christianity?" Braced against the wall, she checked around her nonchalantly, waiting for an answer. I couldn't give one. She assumed all that work, all that love was just a human thing, a human fluke. That maybe as I was back to normal now, that'd disappear, it'd fade back to nothing and I could just resume doing the same work I was doing before. Those feelings…that drive and desire, if anything, it was intensified now. Dead. I was dead, separated. Slowly putting a hand to my heart, my breathing began to get fast, my eyes began to constrict back, I began to panic. Looking around frantically I looked back to the surface, breathing hard and without a word; I stumbled back on my feet. I couldn't stay here. I was dead. Gone. Separated from him. Breathing quickly and without a word I shot towards the surface, scrambling to get back to him. I left him. I was gone.

Cempe yelled out behind me, startled. "Nona!?"

Pushing, working, digging through that earth, I couldn't even figure to use the Colus to get there faster. Couldn't think of anything else. Pere please.

Light began to peek through my frantic digging, my struggling, my desperation. My teeth clenched together, faster, back to that life I had snapped apart from. My fingers were almost to that light…almost…there…

Already, I could hear him.

Busting through that last layer, that last bit, I pulled myself from the dirt anxiously. My eyes were immediately on Pere in that house, holding onto my lifeless Maienca body, cradling it. I couldn't move, hands shaking, half of me still submerged in the ceiling of Hell.

"No… no." Pere's frame shook from across the room, a slow, torn sobbing coming from the man who never seemed to stop smiling. "This… this can't be happening."

"Pere…Pere!" I shouted behind him, dead voice reaching and breezing past the man as nothing more than a static cry, inaudible. Tumbling through those last inches of dirt, my only thought was getting back to him, to keep being there. "Pere!" I shouted out, voice shutting down as something grabbed a hold of my ankle. Cempe.

"Nona, Gods, what's the matter with you? Get a hold of yourself!"

It was one of the first times I saw real fear on my sister's face, a bewildered, confused look. I thrashed to get away anyways as she clung tightly to my leg, "Nona! Stop it!"

"It's your fault!" I yelled out, wild eyes turning back to focus on her like the enemy. "You think I was fighting for no reason? That I was disobeying my sentence for fun? I found something to live for!" My voice escalated to a petrified screech.

"I found something better, more honest then all this, and you took me away from it!" Other foot secure on the floor, I yanked my sister through the dirt like a spoiled vegetable, the two of us bristling at one another amidst that tiny shanty of a room, heads scraping the ceiling. Wiping off her face, she kept her frame low.

"Snap out of it!" She darted for me, meaning to strike me upside the face. We locked hands.

"This isn't something to snap out of, Cempe!" It felt like the edges of my soul were frayed, unsteadied, hazy things as my strength was already waning, emotionally drained. "My life with him was more important than some stupid fictitious Fate duties, then this pointless fighting, it's more important than anything! Why can't you understand that? Why don't you get it?" Her face contorted instantly, putting in all her force to throw me back away, toss me across that room. I crashed against the table, breaking the poorly made thing in half as Pere suddenly jumped to his feet, startled. We all were. This hadn't happened before-not since the golden ages, never had we been able to affect anything in the physical realm until that very moment. Ignoring that fact, Cempe stood tall in the far end of the room, teeth clenched in anger.

"You stupid, selfish brat!" Cempe spit at me. Wood crumbled under my touch as I pulled my head from the wreckage. "You think this is all about you? The world's conspiring against you and whatever stupid love you've baked this time?" She looked as if she meant to say more, stuttering, confused. Turning back to Pere, then back to me, then back towards the wall, she held up her one arm up by her face. It was the only time I could remember my sister shedding a tear.

"You disgust me, you know that? Go ahead! Have fun! Watch him fall apart, watch him suffer, watch him move on without you and die like all the rest, you worthless, scrap of a human being!" And she was gone. Silent.

My eyes slowly panned across the room, holding my head tiredly, seeing my dead body out of the corner of my eye. Clenching my eyes shut, I turned away. Shuffling my legs off the side of the splintered table I tried to collect myself, tried to make sense of this stubborn refusal to get back into the swing of things. It scared me too; I almost wanted to forget it all, to move on, but this bond with him, it wouldn't let me. Burbling out a quiet groan of dismay, I pulled my knees closer, keeping my head low. What a mess. My own dead, flat eyes glared at me, accusing. Hurt. What now?

There was a buzzing sound, a warbling static, white noise as I could feel myself waiver, skin wiggling. It was a horrible little feeling; sitting up immediately I threw myself back against the table, horns scraping and propping my head up. It was Pere standing in front of me, his hand outstretched, face wrinkled, trying to understand. Slowly, he leaned forward, following my movements like I was as visible as anything else. This wasn't real. Pere was as normal as anyone else in this world and anyone before it, not since that Golden Era had we actually made contact with anyone. People just didn't believe in us anymore; our influence was a dead and forgotten thing, but maybe with my other half… he was staring straight into my eyes, locked to me as he continued to lean forwards, hand outstretched.

Looking down to my own hands I looked back to him, sniffling and holding the one hand up. He stopped, looking to it, then back to me, once over to the body and back to the hand, cracking the faint bearings of a smile.

"Maienca?" He asked uncertainly, hand hovering just a few inches away from mine. "Please, if that's somehow you…" Loose smile on my face as well, I leaned forward, grabbing for his hand; I could see the hair stand up on his arm instantly as he jumped, choking out a disbelieving smile. He explained it later that it was like seeing me but not, knowing I was there without so much as a few hazy details. He took it as a sign from God. Unable to really tell him otherwise, unable to speak to him, I could only stand alongside him, continue to be by his side. That's how we lived out the rest of his days.

Once my corpse was buried and laid to rest, I'd rarely leave that house. It was a sort of imprisonment that I didn't mind, I had to stay with him to almost guard him. I couldn't talk to him; he couldn't understand a word said, I was only able to vaguely influence any dreams that were open for influence, which wasn't often. But he knew I was still there, and it kept him happy. He'd talk to me, tell me about his day, things happening around town.

I knew the recesses of Hell quite well; I knew that it wasn't my favorite place to go, so the trade-off was something I could tolerate. My sister Cempe didn't speak to me again for those fourteen years that Pere had left, Aisa visited on occasion, gently trying to persuade me to come back with the rest of them, but I refused. Time spent here seemed to be the only thing that mattered, I had no wishes to leave him.

Driven by these thoughts that God had somewhat spared his wife, had granted that small favor that allowed me to stick around by him even after death, he went back to the religious side of things. Disqualified as a practicing Christian minister of the times, he became a type of healer, read from scripture, taught the lessons on his own. That went on for nearly seven years, until he was informed that the religious take on the afterlife left behind was not a kind thing, that spirits roaming about were always evil. He didn't believe it.

Soon his life began to wind down; a few years of general solitude with him, Pere eventually succumbed to a disease himself, one of the first very short, quick waves of the Plague back in 1301. I waited patiently, grasping at his hand, unable to help or reassuring him that this was all for the better; that we'd be together finally, that it was a happy time, try and keep positive. His breathing was pained and erratic, speaking out to me in delusional, half-thought out words. It was always just something natural for me to be there with him, especially now with this important transition. But with the fall of his last breath, we inadvertently split ways. Separated. He went to Heaven, a good soul.

The cursed demon Nona waited, left behind.

Confused and bewildered, I watched that beam of light take his ascended soul, shooting out a painful bit of energy that burned my hand entwined with his. The area grew dark, lifeless, left only with a corpse and nothing more than that. Panicking, I immediately tried to follow it, bolting from the house and leaping high into those skies with the Colus I had ignored for almost 14 years. The flimsy house tether snapped. My wings were heavy and uncoordinated, Pere's light fading from view into absolute nothingness. Letting out a couple strained breathes, I looked for it. For this "Heaven." Nothing.

Higher, then?

Gritting my teeth I shot higher and higher, the sky cooling into a darker, rich hue. We never flew this high, there was never a reason for it. Air was sparse and cold; my wings began to blur and tilt as my sight grew dizzy, far and distant from the earth. I pushed into the stratosphere, reaching for it, reaching for the moon, letting wishes and delirium fill my head. The race paused, the light was gone, fourteen years wasted in the span of a minute. Lost. Nothing. There was nothing here.

I fell back down. Nothing. Nothing was up there.

I looked for their Heaven, tore this world apart for answers; days, nights, searching, fighting, crying, desperate. It HAD to be there, he had to go somewhere, had to exist. Nothing but blue, vacant skies as my will would falter, fall back to earth. The notion, 'It couldn't be possible" possessed me to keep up the search, to keep trying for many long hours at a time. No luck.

After twenty years, I realized Heaven was a state of mind; a feeling and an understanding, not as a physical place you could travel to; the breath of that idea unlocked many new things, took what was physical and real and changed it. Once more I tore into the Heavens, flying and racing up for the clouds, looking for it. My hand brushed something real, like the clouds themselves were moldable, physical objects to me as I latched on tight to that feeling, throwing myself at it like I had nothing to lose. Without warning, I slipped through.

Head-first I crashed into the fields, Colus form stripped from me as I scrambled in like a fox into a chicken coop. There wasn't any confusion if I was supposed to be there, for my first unintentional raid people were well aware the giant horned demon woman wasn't to be trusted. People began screaming and streaming into their town in droves. Back to my feet I stood well above them all, not helping my situation as I had more important things on my mind.

"Pere!" I called out, like he never set foot beyond the fields, waiting patiently until I ruined everything. Scouring the landscape, a tower stood farther out, the closest and most important looking building in the entirety of Heaven. "Pere?"

I didn't know what had happened to him, yelling out for him, storming across those fluffy white clouds of paradise like I was looking to have it demolished. My time spent with him in the mortal realm taught me civility, grace, taught me how to act like a real person; but with time spent away, with twenty years of desperation under my belt, I really could care less how upset people up here became with my presence.

Stomping around the pedestrian streets there were very few warrior-grade angels around; their tactic at the time was keeping most of those around on earth. Scanning each face quickly I headed for the tower, calling for him desperately as people treated me like a human tornado. Snarling, charging my way down the main road, something hit me like a golden arrow. Stopped, foot up mid- run, my head snapped around to a particular face which rang familiar. Pere, now angelically named 'Paul' stood there, just as shocked. He had been practicing healing tactics like most of his life, looking for a way to heal me into Heaven. I came to him first, seeing his face more youthful, more classic, that beacon of understanding in the ongoing panic and chaos. Everything was just as it was, even after all those years apart. Nothing was lost.

A slow, warm smile spread to both of our faces as I ran to him, crowd of people dispersing behind Pere in an instant. We hugged, both of us readjusting as we sobbed like babies in the streets of Heaven while not a single person had an idea what to do.

"How did you get here?" I remember him asking as I pulled back a little to see him, all teeth and smiles.

"I don't know! I... it was an accident?" We laughed for a moment as I spotted something new. "You have wings! Look at that! Boyyy Pere I might be some variety of terrible beast!" The angel gave a laugh, putting both hands on my face.

"I know... it's okay. We'll figure that out later."

We left Heaven on our own terms without any more violence than that. The story must've evolved on its own, how I ripped the skies apart and beat up Heaven on the way just to tear one soul from the glorious light, sinking my claws in deep on an unfortunate man. There wasn't a routine of 'falling' yet, no ceremony with this segment of the religion still rather new. So we just left. All three souls each. Scared the living Hell out of people and dove out of Heaven.

But it was clear that things had changed, back underground and back in Hell. Pere felt like he was being slowly strangled, slowly burned and ripped apart as a full angel hanging out underground. We panicked, my sisters as well, desperately trying to figure out a way to stop it as he was wailing and smoking in an obvious amount of torturous pain.

It was my idea to pare the soul away, the future soul he earned in Heaven, but I didn't really know what I was doing. I knew how to do it, I'd done it on myself in the past, but I did a pretty poor job on Pere, and it's haunted me every day since. I blinded him to natural sunlight, gave him these sloppy, slapdash scars, threw everything I considered the future soul into the life pool to solve the problem in a panic. Paul took to demoning easier than anyone I've ever seen, and we've spent our times together since. But your mind wanders to just what becomes of that future soul, sent back a little unorthodoxly into life once more just as it was, what it evolves to.

Enter Raziel, that last angelic third of Paul.

Electricity coursed through my veins. I had to reach him in time; with Raziel grasping tighter at the top of my shoulders, he was feeling it too; that drain, those sympathy pains.

Paul knew as much as I did about this life, he was generally immune to most unkind deaths like myself if he kept his spirits up, kept his faith in what was pretty much indefinable in the first place. It's not a great system, but it's one that works. His faith must've been shaken. Broken. After enough angels tell you how very dead your other half is, how they finally kill the unkill-able, his faith must've waned, must've doubted. Worse than that, he might've done this on purpose, accepted a new death. His soul would be segmented, dispersed, scattered.

Narrowing my eyes I pushed just that tiniest bit faster. Please, hold on.

40

The two of us blinked across the earth like a skipping stone towards Paul. I knew where he was. I knew the ground he had walked on last. I could pin him down within an inch of his quickly fading life. I gave everything I had, taking hit after hit of energy as I traveled, battle ready, in this jumbled form of muscle and pissed off demon. I had to save him, had to fight back like it was expected of me. I had to make that difference to the person closest to my heart; the soulmate who may have lost all hope in me.

Even in the tormented disruption of our souls, as it was ripped from one bit of land to the next, Raziel still found time to berate me mercilessly.

"Same…" We skipped again, reappearing ten miles away, "Person!?" He punched angrily at my neck before we left again, not far now.

"We'll get this all…" We hopped again, surging back into existence, "…settled later!" I shouted, pumping my wings faster, snarl already on my face. The pain in my heart was growing, sharp little veins shaking, shuddering before branching out further. I missed a wing beat, stuttering on my efforts as I could feel his life nearing the end. Paul, don't give up!

Tilting my head down a little more, leaning forward another ten degrees, putting every last ounce of excess energy to get there in time, we made that last final skip across the earth as the fabric of reality tore apart.

Twitching, flashing, pulsing to life, we were suddenly there.

Immediately, it was a sea of Cherubs. Varied bird heads turned to us instantly as we popped into existence, gasping, exhausted, panicked. The trail of blood told the story, Gauzier standing alongside the crimson path that led right into the Cherubs mouth. Paul, in the gullet of the bird, quickly dying away. Something in me snapped. There was no contemplation, no thoughtful tactic put into this one.

"Off!" Writhing in a loop I dumped Raziel from my back, both hands gripping the earth to give me that last stretch of speed like a dart aimed for the guilty Cherub, my jaws open all the way. Teeth ripped deep around his neck and gullet as I practically bowled the Cherub over, closing down and separating the entire mouthful from the rest of the body. Dainty enough to not injure Paul any further I twisted and shook my head back and forth like an enraged alligator, like a primordial beast as the cherub scratched, screamed and struggled to get away. In a second the others were atop me, tearing chunks out of this demon body, scratching deep grooves across my face, blinding me in a thrashing flurry of claws and beaks. I shook my head back and forth to only pull harder, ripping out a hole in that Cherub and tossing the whole bloody mess over my head and high into the air. Shaking to get away from the ravenous Cherubs I leapt out of that form, body breaking through the black smoke. I could see Paul, tumbling from the bloody mess, face pale, gaunt, minutes from fading away, from true death.

I reached for him, craning back as he fell back towards the earth. Paul's eyes were closed, shirt soaked in his own blood. Beaks and claws thrashed below me, all grabbing, trying to hit and tear me away, raking deep lines across my skin. My attention was nothing but Paul as the sounds all ebbed away, as the cherub's arterial spray etched over the sky in festive lines, as my hands were just out of reach of Palug, of Pere, of Paul. C'mon, c'mon, get it together!

Groaning out loud I pushed off a feathery white cherub head, stretched back farther as my fingernails just grazed his bloodied clothes, that last sliver of an inch as the very top of my pointer finger snagged around the fold of his clothing. A spark; just a snapshot of a smile before I pulled closer, flipping him and I both around and away from the forest of angry, snapping beaks. Arcing through the air I landed on my feet, followed closely by Paul's body, straining my nine foot tall frame just the tiniest bit. Securely in my arms I leapt back, over and over, dodging from the beaks and feathers as they screamed after me, teeth flurrying just where I had been before as we skipped in reverse. Heads and beaks smashed into the ground in an advancing wave as they snapped and grazed toes and limbs; snippets of putrid breath just out of reach. One cherub tripped up, giving me that moment to turn on my heels, bolting straight back for Raziel as he was almost done picking himself from the ground. His demeanor changed with the wave of death coursing behind me, rushing, anxious bird heads all snapping at the silk tied to my horns like bait.

"Run!" I shouted out though the mask as he dawdled just a moment, looking behind him to begin that bolt alongside me. Leaning over I put him under an arm, running like someone stealing a pig as I dashed, getting just a few steps farther before something stopped me cold. A cherub bit onto the silk on my horns; both Raziel and Paul went skittering on as the feathered hoard enveloped me in an instant. Foot to the ground I threw a quick Thread of Life up around me, slicing into the group of cherubs as they backed away, just a tiny breath as I pulled out the Colus weapon to fight back fully.

"Wait! Hold up, wait a moment!" Gauzier called out somewhere a few leagues deep in birds, voice reaching over the squabbling mess. "We're not putting this to rest so easily, fall aside!" Each one of them stopped like trained dogs, pulling themselves away from the three of us to leave a wide concourse of interrogation to the Master of Ceremonies to this circus. He strode like royalty, like a beloved master of all things feathery, taking his sweet time to get to me, Raziel, and Paul, still picking ourselves up from the mess. Obviously Gauzier had adapted a new job in these last four years.

Looking quickly behind me, I hissed out to Raziel under my breath.

"Everyone okay?" I saw him nod as he kept looking between me and Paul. I couldn't show more concern for Paul beyond this, or they'd know to attack him to get to me any time he set foot up on the earth. Looking quickly to Gauzier, he was flipping and rotating the Fleur Du Lis, dilly dallying his way over here. We'd run pretty far by human standards and he was really milking the situation for all it had.

"I'm okay, him... I don't know." I could hear the angel shake Paul a little, gingerly trying to get him to wake up. Least that way he could fix his own wounds and I wouldn't have to do any energy draining resurrections. Especially not like this. "He's in really bad shape, Neri."

"I know. Uh..." I pulled up my mask just a bit, enough for Raziel to see my actual face beneath it. "I'm afraid I'm going to need you to trust me again. Paul's not going to last much longer without it and I might have to do something drastic if he goes critical." Raziel frowned, turning back to the front of us.

"How drastic?"

"About as drastic as it gets. If he gets to the point where me helping him would kill him, I'm gonna have to find alternatives. And... uh, that's you." Raziel kept quiet, fuming and uncomfortable about the many layers of half truths I had to tell. His tone went lower, throughly annoyed.

"Are there any other ridiculous truths you're keeping from me?" I let out a long breath.

"Right now? You want to do this right now?" I hissed back as Gauzier made some benign note about talking without him, or some guff like that. He was still decently far off and had a whole swarm of cherubs to get through first. I cracked, needing his cooperation.

"You lost your job because you were my friend. They weren't punishing you for you wife's crimes, they were punishing you because you were my friend in our life. People associated with me are kept in lower positions, because they're paranoid I'm going to gain an influential foothold in Heaven." Raziel's eyes went wide, slowly swiveling back to me.

I tensed up, lowering the mask back over my face as he did. "They were still the ones who took that to a ridiculous degree of punishment! I mea, it's their…..I'm sorry." In his shoes, I wouldn't give me the time of day, much less trust me for anything else.

"Seriously!?" He screeched, making Gauzier stop for a moment and the cherubs turn to his seat on the ground. I made a quick motion to keep his volume down because the last thing we needed right now was airing laundry in front of Gauzier of all people. It didn't help the situation.

"I could NOT CARE LESS." He bellowed, fairly upset. "How long have you known about this? Years?"

Frowning, I rolled my eyes.

"Th…Three hours? Maybe? If tha-" Paul began coughing, sputtering out weakly as things took a turn for the worse. His breathing whistled, lungs probably punctured from the Fleur Du Lis. Making a frantic whine, I looked back to Raziel for his approval.

"Fine! Just go ahead. I've apparently done nothing on my own without your 'help', so yeah, fine, go ahead and do what you need to do." Gauzier stopped, confused, looking back to me as Raziel kept looking straight forward, arms folded tight in annoyance. I shifted a little farther away. No matter how much he might've said he wanted this lifestyle, my input was far too much. I realized I had a certain knack for wanting to control a situation, that I couldn't just let something BE if I thought I could help out. Which was the problem, I always thought I could help out. So I meddled a lot. I lowered my ears a little.

All was quiet as he snapped up again.

"You're not going to tell me you're my damn mother or something, are you?" I crinkled my face up.

"Nah, that'd be weird." I said quickly, as he turned to me just a moment, tilting back away and muttering beneath his breath.

"And this isn't?" He pointed to himself, Paul and then me. I winced a little.

"No, I mean this is weird too." Something interrupted me.

"Hello Raziel. You look like Hell!" Gauzier waited for a second before howling out a laugh, obnoxiously loud. He was getting far too much humor out of this situation. I took a few steps back, next to Raziel and Paul as I kept the weapon brandished at him.

"You sir, had a simple command to wipe this thing out before it got out of hand. Kill off the demon. You failed. When we could've had a seven year break from this monster, you didn't kill it off. Why you were put up with for so long, why they didn't eradicate your soul on the spot still boggles my mind." His glare was dead serious on Raziel as they bristled, eyes snapping to me just for a moment as I raised the Colus up, figuring I could get in a sneaky strike while he rambled on for his own means.

"Don't even bother, Nona. Kill me and all these cherubs rip you limb from limb. Use that little light show of yours, and everyone here dies, including your beloved damnation. Die like a demon with some thought of dignity for once, if you even know what it is." I kept quiet, flipping the Colus around in my grip.

"Nona, Nona Nona, always full of surprises, aren't we? You'd think you'd have everyone gunning for your head with the chaos you've caused. With the…leisurely walks you take in our sanctuary, defiling the world around you." I kept my glare tight on him, mouth shut. Gauzier switched to Raziel, pointing the dagger his way as I quickly glanced back at Paul. "But again and again you seem to fool simple folk into doing your bidding for you." I kept quiet, fuming.

"You think you know anything about this wor-" A sound stopped us all; Paul was gagging for breath, paler than ever now, heart starting to give out and die. We all heard it, Gauzier stopping while Raziel turned to face him; I growled again. I couldn't put this off any longer, with such poor timing, I couldn't just let Paul die and pretend this wasn't a problem. They already knew he was a way to get to me, so I was protecting absolutely nothing. Paul gagged for one last breath, stopping. No time to wait or explain.

Flipping the Colus in my grip one last time I slammed it down at the ground and threw up a barrier of strings, shoving Gauzier out and away to give some distance, quickly picking the weapon back up to aim, pointed directly at Raziel's heart. I grabbed him around the neck, trying to steady him.

"I'm really sorry." I whispered, gritting my teeth and stabbing the angel with the Colus, closing my eyes as I did. I couldn't bear to look. A gagging noise, gasping, disbelief; I kept my head turned away, I knew what I was doing without having to watch it all happen. It was halving him, all over again, just like my body had done to Gauzier on autopilot in the gym, shearing someone completely in half. But this had a purpose to it, a trust that was needed. Something I was exploiting at the moment.

My heart beat quickly, suddenly rocketing in pace as the energy charged through the Colus, through Raziel, through those linked souls, to Paul. A wake-up call, a very violent, rather unorthodox, potentially dangerous wake-up call. I gurgled in pain, Raziel wheezed as Paul remained silent. I opened my eyes to the side, watching his body as Gauzier freaked out, yelling profanity while the Cherubs took a few steps away. Concentrating, finding that link, that connection, he couldn't be too far gone, not yet. Raziel was strong enough to go through this, Paul was too fragile.

Teeth clenched I pushed just a little harder, used a little more energy, trying to snake through that darkness of death, of the soul, it was suddenly there, like the tiniest fading ember of life. Charging more energy, pushing my body far past what would've been safe, I made that ember erupt into flame.

Paul immediately sat up, yelling, shrieking in pain as I quickly pulled the Colus from Raziel, keeping my hand on his head. I put every bit of my own energy into trying to heal him, to save him now from death, from his body falling apart from being cleaved in two. More gurgling, more grunting, my knees buckled, my hand holding onto the Colus fell to the ground as well, still gripping the weapon. Looking quickly over to Raziel he was almost through healing, hands wrapped around my wrist, trying to pull away, looking through this facade I needed to wear. Sealing up the energy I quickly pulled my hand away, trying to brace my weak body from collapsing on the ground.

Shaking, trying, I slid near the side of the barrier, gasping for breath.

My sides heaved, all poise, grace, and dignity gone, blood draining from all orifices on my head. Something awful welled up in the pit of my incorporeal stomach as I ripped the mask off, vomiting off to the side the biggest pool of blood I've ever seen. Gasping, struggling for air, I wearily looked over to Raziel, patting himself and making sure everything was alright. His eyes popped from his head, uneasy about the pool of my sick, and my much more frightening facade, face covered in blood.

I looked over to Paul, half-bracing himself up, moving. Alive. I would've cried if my tear ducts weren't oozing blood like a horror movie.

My head swung heavily over back to Gauzier, who stood much like anyone would witnessing that horrible little event.

"Suh... Surprrriiiise." I coughed out hoarsely, wiggling my wrists up a little from the ground, voice garbled and tired like I was drunk; my heart was beating erratically, body still twitching with residual damage, energy. If there was ever a time to attack me, now would be it. I couldn't let him die, though, needed to act at that moment, even then it was pushing that time limit, reaching far through death to even find his departing soul. I had cut it close, way too close. The barrier of strings broke apart, leaving everyone and anyone open to any attacks.

"Can you never do that again?" Raziel bellowed, just as surprised and freaked out. "Please?!" I coughed again with a meek smile.

"Nona?" Someone called out behind me, that familiar voice, what I had known and love all these hundreds of years, what I had fought for again and again. Whipping around to witness Paul with an arm over his head, desperate to see in the light. I shouldn't have shown weakness. Should not have even flinched that he had re-awoken, that he was okay, I was supposed to act like I didn't care, that I was just terribly dedicated to my crew. I just didn't care, now. Shuffling my tired legs just a bit I scooted closer to him, immediately wrapping my arms around him like nothing

else was real in that world. His voice eeked barely above a whisper, "I…
thought they'd gotten you."

"They wish!" I choked on a laugh quickly as the two of us held
tight, faces pressed next to one another. He was the only other soul I
clung to, that through those lives he was always there. Realizing that
I'd almost lost that, I held him closer. "Don't pull crap like that anytime
soon, alright?" I could feel Paul smiling, pulling tighter just a little bit. The
echoing gurgles of the Cherubs almost made for good background music.

"Leave them alone." A voice, Raziel's from behind my back. I
turned a little away to catch him standing guard behind us, between
Gauzier and myself, holding a hand out tiredly as the whole scene
remained on pause. Everyone just seemed tired, unwilling to fight. I'd
rebound, but it'd take a while longer after giving out pretty much all my
spare energy. Raziel had to be feeling like crap as well, Paul pretty much
immobile for at least the rest of the day. The only beings around with the
will to fight was the entire other side of the field.

"She just stabbed you and nearly killed you, I mean, you KNOW
what they are, right? Has all sense gone out the window here?" Gauzier
flashed the Fleur du Lis around a little more, exasperated like he was the
only one talking English. "Here's a refresher for you; She-" He pointed to
me as I shifted more onto my butt, taking the war-mask from the ground
and putting it over Paul's head so he could actually see something. He held
it gingerly.

"-is the demon responsible for pretty much every one of our
friend's deaths, commands those who threaten us day and night, who we
fight. She's the God-damn demon that started this war! She is one, if not
THE, top demon. Right there." Gauzier glared right into each eye as I sat
there, mouth shut. I wasn't necessarily all of those, but the more crap they
heaped on me, the more positive a sign it was. I was surprised, usually I
get quite a few more tags added on, but he knows his stuff. Obviously not
everything, though. "Are you that far removed? I mean, I can't believe I'm
asking for a rational decision out of you, Raziel, but seriously? If I figured
anyone who wanted this monster's blood spilled, it'd be you."

"Someone likes you." Paul leaned over, whispering next to me as I
cracked a brief laugh.

"He's a fan of my eyes, told me himself." The two of us laughed
with our out-of-place hyjinks as Raziel turned slightly back towards
me, giving the stink eye. I knew that look all too well, face blanking in
immediate 'I'll shut up' mode. "Sorry."

"I knew something was always a little off." He kept his stance wide,
almost in a sparring pose. "I'm not stupid. And that first time, yeah, I tried
doing my job." He shifted his feet a little, taking a quick glance back at us
before back to Gauzier.

"But, I don't know, for some reason it felt rehearsed. Haven't you been getting the feeling that there's something off here? You know, planned?" He turned back to me, obviously still angry with the various lies I've spouted, "What I don't get is that the usual punishment for what you've been doing is just death; non-existence. Especially for you. There in Heaven, it should've been worse, but they just imprison you in a body a couple hundred miles away. They pretty much let you go. I mean, you know that, right?" It was probably the only time I wish I hadn't given that mask away as my glance sort of blanked, eyes wide. I hate overly aware, super-conscious folk like this sometimes.

"I know that." I kept my head low. "They're also well aware I'm impossible to kill, though."

"But why didn't they try to?" Raziel turned a little more towards me. I tried opening my eyes wider at Gauzier, a sort of 'well, I'll tell you when he's not around' thought, but the fallen angel ignored it, only narrowing his glare just a little more. I really should've told him everything when I had the chance. Gauzier peeped up as well.

"I'd also like to know why Heaven expected you to get out of that little treatment." Both turned to me, I suddenly felt two feet tall. "We could've tried many more effective things. Or just prison. Or chop you up into pieces and keep the bottles at four different places around the earth"

"Jesus." I muttered, shocked at the low-down gruesomeness of his plan. "Bit harsh."

Raziel cleared his throat, rolling a hand that me derailing the conversation wasn't the answer he wanted to hear. I was afraid Raziel would leave if I told him everything, the whole truth was pretty rough. Notes for the future, lying was not a valid alternative.

"I've got friends." I spit out as a meager little answer. As both of them along with the whole boatload of cherubs behind them kept their piercing glare on me; I buckled a little, lowering my head off to the side more, "Lots of friends."

"Wait, so if I got fired, apparently for unknowingly being your friend in a life- " He spoke loudly to Gauzier simultaneously as a sort of school report on why he lost his job, "You somehow already have friends in a higher position that can decide the type of punishment you'll get?" Are you blackmailing people or something?" He scrunched his face up, confused. I shook my head.

"Alright, I'll be blunt. I'm not going to unravel everything while Dagger McGee here keeps wringing his weird, misshapen hands like Sherlock fucking Homes." I could feel Paul snicker next to me, keeping his head down with a smile. "I was more or less 'dead' for four years. You're mad I didn't get seven? God, how AWFUL. World's tiniest violin made of the dust from a thousand demons that Gauzier and his rag-tag group of cherubs slaughtered in my absence." They both remained quiet as I huffed and crabbed.

"See, even for that, I'd kill her off." Gauzier said plainly, shaking the little sword at me again and taking a few steps forward, "Why aren't you letting me kill this demonic witch again?"

"It's a one sided fight. They're both exhausted, it's not fair." Sitting like a tired little lump, I wiped some of the blood on my face off onto my arm. I felt like someone needed to hand me a wet-nap, or a napkin, or something. Gauzier didn't approve of the nonchalantness of the conversation.

"I'm not aiming for chivalry here, I'm aiming to kill that pathetic demon queen bitch off while I've got a chance!" Raziel kept his arm up in front of us, only agitating Gauzier more. "You don't think I'll go through you to do it? We're not friends, idiot, I couldn't give two shakes if you're dead or not. I just want that thing, and that thing, dead!"

Gauzier shoved at Raziel to get through him, stopped by him once more. With a nasty little snarl to his face he sliced his arm with the Fleur du Lis, using the opening to plunge the knife deep in his chest. Pulling it back out Raziel made some surprised huffing sounds, stumbling back towards me.

"C'mon, another step back." I coached like a worn, tired mother at her kid's soccer game. I used Paul as a handhold, shuffling myself up to almost catch Raziel as he stumbled into Paul and I. Slapping a hand on his back I healed his wounds instantly, trying to at least be helpful and not just the lying slanderous demon asshole role I was playing today. "See? Not a big deal. Just a punctured lung." Raziel only gave me a low stare, still deeply upset.

Looking down I realized I too had a spot of blood where the Fleur Du Lis was infamously known to attack all souls tied together. Paul spotted a matching decoration as well.

"God, I hate that thing so much." I grumbled, asking for the mask from Paul as he fumbled a bit, trying to get it off. "He needs this more than you, sorry."

I hefted it up to Raziel.

"If nothing else, it's a shield. The end's quite pointy, though."

"I don't fight with a shield, it's not my style." He hoisted the thing up, already facing back to Gauzier, gripping the strap gingerly with a disappointed shake. "Your blood is everywhere inside of it."

"Just block with it!" Gauzier rushed back at him, knife clunking off the wooden mask as I continued to shout useless advice, "It's effective against getting stabbed."

"Shut up, I know what you do with a shield!" He continued to parry Gauzier's attacks, deflecting them as they took small chunk after small chunk of wood from my war-mask's face. Watching the two of them fight, Paul sat closer to me, desperately trying to see through the broad daylight. Probably should invest in a pair of sunglasses, really. Grinning, I knocked my head at his softly.

"Aren't you proud of your little non-son?" Paul snuck his hand behind my back and patted the side of my head in a bit of feigned adoration. I laughed. Gauzier's head snapped to us, livid as Raziel took the opportunity to bring the war mask heavy down on his head, knocking him into a phase of compromised consciousness.

"Don't call me that." He squinted at both of us, shaking his head in disbelief, "I don't even know why I'm still helping you, I swear. This little system you've got going on here, still sucks. You're not off the hook." I stopped snickering. Gauzier didn't share the sentiments, boiling over the top with frustration that this tired group of demons and fallen angels, giving half a damn about this fight, was still winning.

"Attack! Get them! Kill them all!" He shouted to the birds around us, heads perking up as most of them were just beginning to fall asleep from inactivity. They ruffled amongst themselves as a hundred eyes all leveled at me, stamping, crying out, readying them for battle. There was no rest for the wicked.

"What's the chance I can get you to help me out here?" I hissed over to Paul as I slowly got to my feet, contemplating my options. This might be the perfect time to unveil my alternative reason for splitting myself up earlier in this whole crazy escapade. Finding and helping Raziel out was a big check on that to-do list, but I had other reasons, other thoughts and ideas. I was an experimenting idiot at heart.

"I can't feel anything below my knees and I'm entirely blind to everything around me, what does that factor into as a chance?"

"One to two percent at best. Alright, just sit tight then; I might need you to keep things together if this goes wrong." I tried wiping some of the blood from my face, dried and crusty like a thin sheet of paper, surveying around me. I could take them all out in the Colus, but that'd leave Raziel and Paul unprotected, and God knows that Gauzier's trying to wipe out this little triad by any means. I needed someone to guard Paul and Raziel, and someone to fight the Cherubs at the same time. I needed to be two places at once. I grumbled; if only I had sisters or something to help me when I needed it.

"If what goes wrong? Nona-" I grinned, ignoring him and trying to concentrate as he suddenly latched onto my free hand. "No no no, I'm not sitting through another plan like this, I just got you back, I'm not going to sit quietly if you get yourself killed! I love you, but you have to stop acting like some war-hero idiot! Use your head, for once!" Paul was seething in a strange twinge of personality; it wasn't completely unheard of, but a rare thing. With both hands on his face, I kissed him right on the top of his head, laughing as I did so.

"I'm glad to have you back." The Cherubs around us were tightening closer, snapping, lashing out within fifteen feet of us. "But if I didn't do something crazy before, you wouldn't be here. Crazy plannings the only thing that works!"

Eyes to the cherubs, I sent out a single strand, cutting and slicing into the birds closest to us, making the whole group back away. I hoped this worked. I hoped my planning had been worth it, seeing if the factions of your soul were able to function on their own, how they could still related to the whole Tresillo, how they acted when split. If I could manage to divide my past and future up and use the present soul as that link between the two, the applications in the future would be massive.

Eyes darting to the other half of the closing circle, there was no time like right now to give it a shot. I closed my eyes, mentally wandering that office space of souls, trying to find that dividing line. It might as well have been a thread on the floor, nothing obvious about it, practically invisible; I knew it was there. Aisa was a master at cleaving that line in half, her biggest attribute being incredibly keen on the matter. Not me, though.

Ignoring the growing, churning mess around us, the sounds of frivolous fighting that sounded like someone stabbing a fence over and over again, I found what I thought to be that line. With a deep breath I grabbed hold, flaring out the divide as that internal office space began to fall apart, began to separate. There was a heavy whirring noise that outdid the Cherubs snarl, like both halves of my brain were being shaken violently before it stopped just as quickly. Opening my eyes almost made me fall over, seeing with a different picture with each eye; my left eye was staring at myself, the somewhat-tall future version of me like it was supposed to. My right eye was staring at Joan.

"Son of a bitch!" We both said in unison, bringing the left hand up to rub our individual faces. I was hoping for a collaborative collection of past souls, maybe something that looked like the original Neri had, not a specific soul. The cherubs lashed out, not five feet away, their faces glaring at me hotly in confusion, feathered mouths twitching and shuddering. It'd have to do. Staring back at each other and trying to ignore the gawking around us, I tried to keep the directives short and sweet. Simple enough like patting your head and rubbing your stomach; something that my brain could almost work on its own.

"Get rid of the cherubs and keep them safe." We both sneered at one another, the future soul running at the Cherubs immediately, jumping into a sort of gimpy version of the full-blown Colus, yet smaller. With one directive running off on its own, the scenery around me began to sink in. No one was fighting, only Paul was frantically trying to see through the sunlight as the two of them were frozen, both a little off-put.

"That's your big plan?" Gauzier taunted me, laughing out loud as he lowered the Fleur du Lis. "Turn into a small child? The longer I'm around this all, the more of an incompetent leader you're turning out to be. Here I was worried there's some kind of elaborate plan at hand!" I walked slowly up to him, mouth clenched shut. Young child or not, I was very much still the same person, nothing to be trifled with. My eyes sketched over to Raziel's, stumbling up on my scheming plans. His eyes were huge. Not just widened in fear or alarm, just generally enormous. I leaned a little away from him, attention back to Gauzier with some rather appropriate laughing.

"I'm a collector of big plans, you think me coming on your glorious sanctuary was a fluke? An accident? You think I wasn't plotting for twenty years how to do it, just to find out the big magical secret was wishing on a God damn star or something?" My steps were slow and methodical, "What you think you know, what you understand about how things work? It's lifetimes behind what I'm discovering, down to experiments like this one; Think on your own for a second here; half of my soul's acting on its own without me having to control it. How to you think that'll play into these diabolical, harebrained master schemes of death and destruction the future, eh?" The black whipping rope suddenly ripped up beneath my feet, twirling about both Raziel and I.

I didn't like having to be the enemy here, I'd rather he just go away, to be honest. But that, it was all true, and you could tell by the way Gauzier's face all seemed to gather by his nose, the way his pupils constricted to pimples of what they had been, that it was the plain truth. I had him now. Grinning and taking a deep breath to continue on, there was a hand on my shoulder, suddenly dragging me back, away from Gauzier. My eyes popped open in surprise as the thread of life crumbled in confusion.

"Don't use that voice in that body." Raziel said, frowning like a disapproving teacher would. "It's not right."

"What are you doing? Raziel! I've got to kick his ass, it is long overdue! I can end this fight in a snap! A literal snap!" I hissed at him, shuffling my legs a little so it looked like I was leaving willingly. I don't even think the cherubs were fooled.

"You've already punched and tore the guy in half, there's nothing left to do. He doesn't get it. Just stay over here." He was pulling me back towards Paul who frantically tried to squint and see what was going on. Behind him, the other half of me was attacking another cherub; two more cherubs tore at the body as it evaporated into a black mist, only to re-join and bite into another. "I'm not going to watch you bastardize the form of someone I know just…don't. You're creeping me out."

"I'm still the same person, just like this for the time being!" I struggled some more as I could hear Gauzier laughing behind me. My quaint English accent wasn't helping things here. "It's my freaking job! Let me go!"

"No! You need to just-" He bit on his words, yanking me by the arm to give a half twirl away, next to Paul, "Just stay safe, okay? You owe me, and you know you do. Stay there." I stopped fighting, watching as he lingered for a moment, turning quickly to go back to squaring off with Gauzier.

"I saved you from death at least SI - SEVEN TIMES" I yelled at his back, still riled up with my childish, over-exasperated huffing.

"And how many of those were your fault?" He called, storming towards Gauzier.

"At least HALF!"

Why would he push me away, demand I stay safe, this was my fight! As soon as you give people that reason to think they know better, aka looking like a small, impressionable child, they don't take you seriously. That's half the reason I used the mask; not a lot of people were intimidated by a young face. Didn't matter how terrifying I could be.

I sat down in a huff next to Paul, my head just coming up to his shoulder as he could instantly tell the difference, that something was off.

"…Whaaaat…"

"I got sidelined." I grumbled, taking the bow from the back of my head and handing it to him like an impromptu visor. Behind us the Colus roared out happily as my vision flickered to half of the fight, rearing back to strike a practically dead Cherub with deep claw marks across its eyes. Blinking again, it switched back to Paul, giving me a rather skeptical look as I sat there like in time out. "I'm still working out the bugs in this, it could be really useful."

"How did we manage this then?" His tone wasn't angry, more just worn down, tired, and used to my comedic and reckless shenanigans by now. "I thought Joan made it to 26."

"She did. I can't really figure why I'm stuck at this age myself, the Praeteritum's not the best mark of accuracy, but it was the present soul I was interested in." I kept my voice low, a few skips away from Raziel and Gauzier as their fight carried them farther and farther out into the field. Not like it really mattered, but they were busy fighting one another again, and didn't need my obnoxious talking in the background.

"Why?"

"It's the only one of the three not tied to anything. It's malleable. Workable. No one knows about it because it doesn't exist in the same dimension of reality that we all do." Paul raised an eyebrow, eyes still nearly shut. With a smile I continued on, drawing a little diagram on the ground to help illustrate my point, "Life lives in the third dimension; we scoot along the fourth as spirits. People assume that just like life, that's the only place we exist is in that one dimension, but that's not true. For a short time separated from the PS and PO soul in the gym, I was in something completely separate as just a mix of present and past soul. That's when I figured out that the Present soul exists in the fifth dimension, where things are expressed as a fold in time. It's a dot that connects the past and future soul together." Paul didn't move a bit, staring at the dirt before staring back at me, then back to the dirt.

"Get it?"

"I'm working on it, maybe try a different way?" Behind us the Colus roared out again, tearing into a new cherub. One of the feathery beasts was falling towards us, massive white head gasping out its last breath just alongside. As the Colus, I pulled it away, working after my next victim before snapping back to sitting next to Paul.

"The fifth dimension is time travel; fastest point between two places isn't a line, it's a dot, the over-lapping of the start and the end into a singularity. The present soul is that dot, connects the past and future souls in a completely different plane." Thinking on it, something hit me. "I guess what I'm doing is about the same as a wormhole. I'm still very connected to the other half of me right now, except you can't see that connection."

"So how does that work out with splitting the soul up?"

"Stretch out the dot. Use it as a connecting segment between the two and deal with the headaches of trying to control two souls." I laughed, putting a hand to my temple. That was my theory, at least. For all I knew I had just screwed up my body's systems beyond repair and I'd suffer a cruel, agonizing death in a matter of minutes. I hoped not. Paul continued to shake his head with a disapproving frown half meant. He wasn't the one pushing me to take stupid risks like this, and wouldn't support them if they were dangerous or potentially life-threatening, which a lot of them were, but he'd remain there. Provide backup. Be a stable backbone. In this line of soul-hashing, of life so complex and segmented, that was precious.

If not for the anguishing torment beforehand, or the fact that I was sitting around in a 12 year olds body and both of us were beyond worn down and tired, this whole thing would be a much happier event. At the moment we were both having trouble just keeping our eyelids up, watching the show instead while chaos, bloodshed and ultimate cherub destruction happened like a moat around us. It was a far from romantic, and to be blunt it felt like Paul was frustrated to be there.

Raziel and Gauzier continued to fight, a series of short hits by Raziel with the end of the war-mask, while Gauzier tried desperately, over and over to try and stab him the Fleur du Lis. The mask was looking pretty beaten up, large chunks taken out of the face, especially gouging at the painted-on eyes as if on purpose. All the while they spat half-thought out insults at one another, concentrating too hard on the fight instead of the words coming out. Distanced away and able to hear the jumbled bits of speech as they were tossed around, it was like one long, winding insult just waiting to finish itself with a point. The most I heard was that there was a 'Stupid son of a jerk and you frilly little half-wit of a cherubs cousin's fat ass old man.'

They were both pretty good. A lot of the moves were the same but Raziel was right; you could tell Gauzier was getting flustered with no real progression in killing off the fallen angel, that his hits were getting desperate and wild and almost silly. His arms would start to swing around like it helped while both Paul and I could hear the labored breathing from where we sat. After another ten minutes or so with no real winner, Paul turned to me.

"Where's Cempe? She wouldn't miss a fight like this - something's wrong"

"She's on standby, but you're right. She should be here."

I put a hand to the earth. I tried to sink into it, tried to fall back underneath that ground into Hell for a quick check, because he was right; she'd never miss a scrap like this. My hand went about two inches underneath the soil and stopped, electricity buzzing up my arm as my eyes snapped open. There was a barrier hidden here, placed on purpose. Blinking once I switched to the eyes of the future soul, some quarter mile away, three different cherubs latched onto its back. Writhing and pulling away from them I dipped my toes into the earth, feeling the same shock. Blinking again I was next to Paul, already in alarm. Gauzier didn't have the strength to put up a barrier this large; it at least covered a quarter mile around us or so, but Cempe'd get around that. It had to be huge, massive; for all I knew it took up the entire state. Only one person could do that, the point to this mission to drag me out of Hell. As if on cue, the air began to hum and resonate as my blood went ice cold. I knew this person.

"Raziel!" I yelled out to him as the world began to scream, as the hum reached a piercing, deafening tone, erasing all other sound. I screamed again and again for him as my present soul began to retract, reeling in the other half of my body. I couldn't reach him. Raziel was looking around in alarm while Gauzier remained on the attack. He knew what this was, he planned for it. I'd need every bit of my energy and soul to fight him, to fight 'that' . He had to be 'that', there was no other explanation. The Colus was having a hard time moving, defining curves and lines blurring and fraying out like it'd fall apart; the resonance this barrier screeched at was almost the same I existed in.

"I HAVE TO GET HIM" I screeched out to Paul, lips just inches away from his ears; he gave a confused motion for a second that even right next to each other, he couldn't entirely understand me. Looking back to the fight in a panic I made a motion for him to stay where he was, nodding confidently before streaking out into the field. Short little legs carried me as fast as I could move in this form. I continued to scream his name, words evaporating from my mouth as they left, reaching nowhere.

Higher and higher the tone went to a blisteringly sharp note. All the cherubs left in the area stopped right where they were, dropping to the ground and writhing about. I had to stop, clutching at my head with both hands, trying to continue on. He wasn't far away; one hand to his head as

Gauzier remained attacking, more fervent than ever. Shaking back and forth for just a moment I loped a few paces more, back to a full out run as the sky around me dropped with balls of white and red feathers. The Colus stopped where it was, huddled in a suffering little mass of black energy, undefined and hazy at best. Apart, I couldn't cope with this so well; I had to get Christopher back by Paul, and had to rejoin and back with the Colus before It came about. There wasn't much time.

Through dazed and diagonal steps I came up next to him, latching onto his wrist and immediately trying to pull him away. His head snapped back at me, angry, mouth moving quickly as he shouted something, pulling his arm from me, pointing back at Paul and continuing to fight Gauzier. Shocked for a moment I only frowned more, grabbing his wrist again as it pulled him off center, a strike from the Fleur Du Lis skimming up from my war mask and plunging into his shoulder. I saw him gasp in pain and tilt to the side, turning a glaring eye in my direction as I stood there, the aggressor and the distraction all in one.

Frowning I yanked his wrist down and off to the side, hand to the shoulder and healing him instantly as he pulled away again, adamantly pointing to his shoulder for a moment, then to the big massive death circle churning farther out, back to Paul, over to the cherubs for some reason before back to Paul, yelling static the entire time. Glaring for a moment he focused back to Gauzier, ignoring me outright as even if I was a wee child, I was still a fairly competent wee child that knew slightly more about the situation. That's fine, he can be pissed all he want about how this turned out, but I wasn't so easily swayed I'd just let him continue to be distracted and wander his way into Gauzier's plan.

Letting out this inaudible gurgle of anger I locked up in a stance, jabbing him hard in the ribs with my tiny angry children fists. Raziel instantly danced off kilter, one eye closed and grabbing his side in pain. I latched on again to a wrist, trying to pull him towards Paul one last time, using the tether to scream "RUN RUN RUN" as much as I could, hoping that'd be enough for him to get the message. About to yank his wrist from my grasp a third time, I could see that hesitation, that mental debate, looking up to the spiraling quasar that was angelic death in just a few seconds flat.

Gauzier made another stab as Raziel brought up the shield to defend himself, motioning to him slightly that he needed to finish this fight, that it probably meant a lot to him to finally prove himself and work through those issues from many moons ago. The angel shook the Fleur du lis over his head a few times, shouting a lot of screaming angelic energy sounds towards both of us with the break, wind and dead cherub feathers all streaming together, pulled into this massive glowing aura. Like that was everything that counted in this world of his that was going to exist for just a few more seconds, he started pulling his hand away again, making that final decision that this is what he wanted instead of surviving. I frowned.

Free hand up; a wave of Strings of Life erupted from the ground, skewering Gauzier through forty or fifty times in an instant. I grasped my hand closed, eyes dead locked on Raziel that playing nice was wearing thin the tiniest bit as two more diagonal bunches of strings popped out from adjoining areas, rupturing through the angel all at once. Raziel looked to me, then back to Gauzier for a moment before back to me as I pulled my fist towards me a few inches, the strings mincing the angel through a thousand times over as his form instantly collapsed to dust. With one final hand out and pushing away I spread Gauzier flakes thin about thirty feet behind where he stood. Raziel's eyes were like saucers.

I let go of his wrist, pointing one more time towards Paul, figuring my display of power would get me whatever I wanted. Instead, Raziel only scolded me like a bad dog.

"NO." He mouthed, finger pointed at me like I should be ashamed of solving a problem. "THAT WAS MEAN." Shocked, I was about to start pantomiming up a storm in retaliation as the horrific angelic screeching sound suddenly began to wane.

"--u've g-- - be kidding m-------to ---ad you on!" The sound suddenly returned as I looked to the center, everything silent and calm, worn out.

"He's trying to goad you on." I spit out finally. "He's trying to get you killed and he's about to succeed." I growled, huffing for breath tiredly as being over the top was terribly exhausting. Contemplating fighting back, he left me with this soured, unhappy look before focusing on the circle instead.

"But it's gone, whatever that was." As he said it, as he jinxed our luck. A crack of lighting, a circle at least fifty feet wide about four hundred yards out suddenly slammed down at the earth, depressing a good five or six feet into the dirt. The air sizzled around the edges of the circle in anticipation, buzzing as the first wave of the exorcism let up, energy sucking towards that depression in the ground.

"It's landing! He's not leaving, he's just getting here!"

Raziel's head snapped back at me, his generally squinty and tiny eyes were back to being enormous. "Who?" Without time to answer I whistled to the Colus, black energy jumping into the sky, flying straight for me. Raziel took a few steps closer, head jumping from me, back to the landing site, and back to me.

"Who is it? Who's coming?"

"Your demon executioner extraordinaire. You know who it is." I pulled at his wrist again as the Colus was almost flying sideways, trying to avoid the draw of energy. Paul called out to us, waving us to get closer. We weren't far, maybe another two hundred yards or so, but we were past being out of time. Any second now that'd wave would come out, wipe out everything that wasn't protected, angels and demons alike. And they called me cruel. The Colus screamed right past me, jagged bits of energy desperately trying to hold as both parts of this soul was unstable right now. Cherubs cried out in anguish as they were pulled to that edge of the circle, as they crumpled down dead, as they tried to survive this attack. The drawing wind grew to hurricane force gales, Colus looping behind me, flapping with every bit of energy it had to bring us back together as it worked on its own strength, my heart already beating erratically, just behind me now. "Ready?" I called out, hopping quickly behind Raziel, hands to his back.

He looked quickly behind him, eyes widening as the messy bits of Colus stretched it's jaws wide, black smoke darting in delusional patterns like ancient text. The sun blotted out of my vision, darkening around me as I snarked, half smiled at my hands against his back; they were the same hands, same back, but it was an ironic little reminder of the time that had passed, that it was roughly 400 years ago.

"Well, this seems familiar." I laughed, blasted by a torrent of black energy and Colus not a second after that. In that same moment the draw of energy stopped, air completely still. Like high-strung wires being cut the sky seemed to rip apart, whirring and snapping as he rocketed at the earth; it was the same routine any angel did coming down from Heaven in the place of their choosing, but the scale difference was astounding. Raziel's return had ruffled some papers and knocked a few things off the shelf. This entrance would rip trees from the ground and kill everything not protected.

Churning, still developing back to what I was supposed to be inside the disorganized Colus mass, I could see the air ripple with the strike at first, the detonation cushion of air suddenly erupting into flame. Like a nuclear bomb it spread out on all sides, instantly vaporizing the Cherub drawn close to the circle. The rush from the Colus shoved Raziel up into the air, shot-putting the guy directly at Paul as the wave of flame was quickly rushing for us. Cherubs tried to flee the scene, crumpling dead and disintegrated as I pushed off with what I hoped was a foot, jumping after the fallen angel, body still sorting itself out. That wave was darting straight for us, not a second to lose, no time for error! Concentrating, my disjointed souls snapped back to one, reaching out cloaked in black smoke to pull together that gigantic paddle weapon, collecting to something malleable. Teeth clenched tightly I slammed it into the ground just in front of both Paul and Raziel, now landing, one hand grasping it tight enough to fall behind its protection as well, sliding out and to the side from momentum alone, scrambling with every fiber of my being to get back behind the Colus in time. Raziel started to roll slightly past as I snatched him up, shoving him back behind.

An explosion of light and heat streamed around the Colus, only our four foot wide patch of ground and the fifty feet behind it was spared, blistering torrent of heat burning all the grass around us, vaporizing the angels and cherubs left out in the elements, bits of them tumbling into nothing alongside us. Immediately after the first pulse of fire and despair there was a second, more forceful blast that shoved both me and the Colus backwards about three feet. I pushed hard to keep where I was, the black smoke finally clearing I could see I had made it back to the full sized me, the nine-foot tall wonder of awkward height difference, silently giving a little cheer that my plan, on most levels, had worked. But celebration could come later.

As the attack began to die down, I slumped behind the Colus, I checked them both to make sure they were okay, a few scrapes and burns, but they should count themselves so lucky to survive his attack. They'd been using them for years, but there was no master like the original. Both Paul and Raziel coughed, dusting themselves off as I stood up from the mess surveying the damage. He'd cleared out the entire field, not a cherub or angel left to be seen.

"Who is it? What is it?" Raziel peered from the side as the Heavenly welcoming glow had finally died off of him, standing on the hill ever so proud of his work. He was roughly my height, overbearingly tall for the occasion; his wings spread like two stretches of light yards and yards from his body, at least fifty feet out on a modest guess. He was pretty muscular, not bulky and lumpy but scrawnier, war-torn sort; he didn't wear a shirt. In the times I'd fought him, he never once wore a shirt, a pompous arrogant little shit who enjoyed showing off more than anyone else I'd come across. One hand held a sword he was almost obligated to bring it with, while the other was clenched tight, ready to fight. As that mystic glow of aura and angelic haze disappeared he grew more distinct, the blonde, loose curls hitting just above his shoulders, the devious look to his face. Raziel looked back at me, face almost star struck, shaking his head back and forth a little bit. It was awe. Fangirlism awe. "Is that…."

"Noooonnnaaa." He called out in a sort of sing-songy voice. I growled.

"Saint Michael the Archangel." I said flatly, grip tightening on the Colus, "The main course."

41

"Saint Michael? Like…THE Saint Michael?" He peered around the Colus once more with a daft sort of grin to his face. He was honest to God excited about this. Giddy.

"No, like Saint Steve. Yes, Saint Michael." I groaned, pulling the Colus from the ground as you could physically see Raziel remember he wasn't on our side, that he was our enemy, that this was our opposition. His face fell, looked over to Paul before looking back to me.

"Oh… oh, God, we're screwed."

"Thanks for the reassurance, Raziel." I took a few steps towards the archangel, switching the Colus to my other hand anxiously as the wind blew past.

"You've... you've fought him before, right?" He sounded like he was about to start laughing, desperate and intense at the same time. I paused, looking over my shoulder with a wink.

"Few times." Rolling my shoulders, I dropped the smile, getting serious. "I need you guys to stay out of the way, best you can, alright?" They both nodded peripherally, slinking back from me, Raziel hoisting Pere up by an arm to scoot him away.

Michael's wings folded, light and brightness receding over his back, steeping the man in an eerie, alien like-light, blocking out his features as an unintelligible mass. He was easily 200 yards away, if not more; but the Archangel was plenty fast. My steps were heel to toe, strafing away from ex angel & Co with my sights dead on Michael. Watch for movement. Anything at all.

There!

Michael's arm moved once to the side- in the next moment he was inches away as the Colus was braced between us, brought up with the spiked side outward to ram into the angel's body as his wings carried

520

him at the speed of light. He made this quiet, paned, guttural grunt, not expecting me to read his moves from so far out. I gave a smile.

"Not even a Hello?" I snarled, pushing hard with my shoulder into the angel, spikes impaling themselves deeper in his body. The archangel winced, brilliantly bright wings flashing up and blinding me as he kicked away, just for a moment. Two burned retina ghosts flanked my vision, kicking backwards from the fight as well to try and read his moves. Like Gauzier, Michael didn't like to dawdle and today was no exception.

In a single blink the sword came straight for my head, piercing through the hazy wisps of light, tip of the sword gleaming and bright as I threw my head to the side, blade catching on an ear. I dropped down and threw a punch at the breath of a figure next to me, Michael juked to the side as I caught a wedge of him regardless, fist sinking into pliable human flesh. With a foot out of nowhere, I was kicked hard upside the head, sent backwards as I rolled and jumped back to my feet, stumbling for a second and almost falling back one more time from momentum.

The dust cleared and the intricate patterns on his wings fading from my vision, we sized up, not far apart. Michael was between Raziel and myself, keeping absolutely quiet like the Archangel couldn't tell they were standing right there. Michael didn't even look at them, only shaking his head at me in disgust.

His wings shot out, cracks of lighting darting across the sky as he shot straight for me; I kicked backwards as hard as I could, away from the guys most importantly, but out farther into the field where I was less restricted by what I could do. I wasn't fast enough; Michael still sailed towards me as I leapt backwards at top speed. Tackling me with one arm he sunk the sword in with the other, taking me across the field and halfway down the block in a split second.

Two hands on the Colus I split it apart, short daggers in each hand as I went to work, parrying and driving them in anywhere I could as we coasted backwards. The Archangel shoved hard and drove my body partially into the ground; knees grabbing at one of his feet to lock him in place, forcing him into a somersault and flipping him over as I rode the angel like a toboggan, head submerged into the ground. That only lasted for a second as he kicked me away, up into the sky as I used my height advantage to whip both halves of the Colus into the fray, both open hands now summoning a tangle of strings from the ground itself, dicing and cutting into Michael like a cheap TV infomercial.

From the dust not just one sword, but about four swords followed in quick succession, using my hard to maneuver and wingless self stuck windmilling in the sky as a pincushion, each sword finding it's own isolated place to pierce through. Wind knocked from my sails I tumbled down, landing on my feet and quickly removing the weapons from my body, tossing them to the ground as Michael staggered to his feet, missing half of one wing and most of the other. With a snarl they both popped into full form, tucked back behind his body as the Angel was no worse for wear. With the swords out of my body I quickly healed back to full, lowering myself and readying for his next attack.

We were fighting in a somewhat deserted parking lot next to two adjoining large fields that were connected though a thin line of shrubbery. The boys were standing under what looked like a rusted out basketball hoop, pavement around them dried and cracked from wear and tear many years ago, the land left to fold back with mother earth, I suppose. Unkempt trees lined the road that ran alongside us, giving the perfect little battle area to settle our differences.

Taking a couple seconds to gasp for air, I watched to see what he'd do next, mimicking me and readying himself for an attack. His wings moved slightly back and forth, breathing hard; the closest I'd see him to being inconvenienced by me at all. With a sudden grin, he stood up tall, wings folded high above his head.

"Excelsis Nona! Good to see you!" Both hands up, he greeted me from forever off in the distance like I'd been invited to his party. "It's been a while!" I flashed a grin.

"Yeah! Sure has, Mike." I paused for a second, giving a pedantic roll of my hand like my hunched over stance was all part of an elaborate bow. Fingers slowly floating back towards the ground, I pressed the tiniest bit into the soil, mind distracted for just a moment as the angel's wings moved, in front of me in a blink. The concussive wind followed him a moment after that, hair and silk blown straight back as the angel didn't attack, only stood there to give my stomach time to fully crawl into my throat.

"Tired?" Michael said quietly head tilting a couple degrees to the side as my eyes grew, throwing myself backwards hard as I could, arms crossed in front of my body to protect me. Holyfire erupted from the ground in a spray far over my head blinding all vision as my entire view was blue, liquid arterial spray in a heated blue mist. A shadow, a form, the slightest hint I had projected itself on the smoke as I was nearly at the ground again- Michael surged through, sword drawn, golden blade adorned with jewels and paintings of himself piercing a monster through the skull, like something you'd hang up in a chintzy restaurant.

Foot to the ground I surged forward in full Colus form, monstrous cavern of a head not entirely caring where Michael's fancy picture sword stuck in, biting down hard on the wisp and getting something solid. I drove the toothpick of a man into the ground, running that smidgen of human being across the dirt until I felt something kick hard at me, lifting my head into the air and spitting him out just in front of me. The angel's face was more aggravated than alarmed, wings ground completely off, blonde mop head of hair spinning up and around to obscure his view.

Feeling my veins run hot, I shot off a full torrent of light and strings at the angel, paring and dicing him for the split second I had him in my cross hairs. New wings popped back out of nothing as he shot himself backwards, sputtering and stumbling to stand with the remaining limbs he had left. Light receded, halves of trees from an attack pointed slightly up kept it out of harm's way from Raziel and Pere, making sure to aim somewhere safe lest the worst happen.

"I'm a little tired, yeah." I dropped from the Colus to land in human fashion, followed up by grabbing hold of the weapon before it hit the ground. "Threw up a pile of blood about an hour back. Feeling better now, though, thank you."

"Glad to hear it." He said lowly. Sneer and a grin, the Archangel bolted straight for me once again across the field as we brought the two swords together once again, Colus and Fancy Picture Sword. It's probably got a real name. His eyes were an icy shade of gray, liquid silver sliding just above the edge of the Colus as I pushed back, stalemated against each other. Like fighting against the cherub it was like struggling against a brick wall as neither of us moved. Snarling, putting a leg further out for leverage, we were equally matched in strength to an annoying result. Michael spoke around the Colus like he was nonchalantly leaning against a wall.

"Spectators?" My grip slipped the tiniest bit as I shoved him back a few feet.

"Survivors." I kicked backwards, trying to navigate through this half-developed neighborhood.

Michael was dangerously fast, never letting up, swords at my neck as I kept skipping backwards, trying to figure my plan of attack. He had one dominant sword and a secondary, smaller sword he seemed to pull from nowhere. I couldn't catch him on a 'non dominant side', there wasn't really an aspect of weakness. Kicking a little less, he was suddenly face to face. I thrashed my head once to the side to fend off the one sword with a horn, throwing a wrist up to catch his hand and knock the other sword away. Matching his speed I cracked him in the jaw with my knee, jumping a half step back and into that perfect position, that fighting stance. With just a cocky smile over to Raziel, I punched the archangel directly in the face without a single flaw to it. My grin stopped suddenly as his sword cut off my one arm in a clean swipe.

"You ass." I snarled, swinging a leg around to hitch kick him from the side, archangel taken off guard. I was tired of running from this floppy headed deity. I darted off to the side, recalling the Colus to my other, non injured hand to chase after him, on the offensive. His wings flashed once, blinding me for a second as the archangel phased through the bluish haze, taking to the sky just over my head. It'd be nice if this was a clean, short fight, I was actually still pretty tired.

Launching into the Colus I surged from the ground after him, snapping the angel up like an errant crocodile taking down a heron and dragging him back to the ground. Michael sputtered for a moment, throwing something straight into my mouth as I dropped out of form, holyfire and shrapnel concussive behind me, blue fire and smoke surging past my head.

Back and forth I parried his sword blows, large paddle weapon cutting into the air with destructive little cracks. The Archangel went to stab me over the hilt, sword sliding right between my eyes. Thank God that's not where I kept the important things. Growling, I shoved the spiked Colus into his body while the end of the St. Michael sword popped out the back of my head, blood dripping down my back. We stalemated; the spikes on the front of the Colus rammed into the Archangel, his favorite sword lodged in my head. Eyes darting to one another we both withdrew at the same time, leaping backwards to gingerly hold a hand to our wounds. The Saint raised an eye through those blonde locks stubbornly.

"I won that."

"Bullshit." I tore into the ground towards him without delay, swinging the Colus to try and cleave him in two, archangel darting backwards with just barely a scratch across his stomach. He frowned again attacking with more energy, the slightest tinge of anger to his face while I did my best to evade the barrage of gleaming metal trying to dice me into bits. Tightening my grip on the distaff I pulled it closer, throwing as much excess energy I could to charge the weapon up, keeping my eyes focused on where he'd stab next.

Raziel suddenly spoke up alongside me with words inaudible and distracting. A searing pain alongside my head, I watched half my cheek and my left ear slide off to the ground and disappear in a fit of smoke. Raziel quieted down.

Attention full back to Michael I swept the weapon around to push him back away from me, cocking the Colus to rest just over my shoulder. The archangel looked almost confused.

"Giving up?" The glow of the Colus suddenly burst into full glory, steeping the area around me in a reddish haze.

"Something like that." I laughed as the strings and energy attack blew out at Michael from the four holes in the bottom of the Colus near the handle. It completely ripped through my right forearm, other hand behind my back to catch it rolling off my shoulder as it flickered back to neutral. I threw the weapon at the archangel without a moment to spare, knocking the guy back a few feet with more injuries. With everything I had I jumped high into the sky, away just as both of his swords cut the Colus into fourths, breezing through the weapon like it wasn't there. His glare shifted from the ground behind the weapon to me, out in the open, hopping around like some unlucky bullfrog. White streaks of lightning jutted out from all sides of his back, makeshift wings of pure energy shot him straight at me, swords gleaming against the sun as I could only windmill there like a sitting duck.

Michael tackled the wind right out of me, the two of us twisting and shooting far from the boys in an impressive arc across the empty lot behind the demon stronghold. Twisting, trying to break free, that bastard only kept laughing, rather pleased with himself. I got an arm free, cracking him in the head over and over with my elbow until he finally let me go; we both crashed not a second later, tumbling about in the semi-paved parking lot as I struggled to get my footing.

I wasn't making any serious advancements on this fight, evenly matched as I had to think of something new, or re purposing something old into something new. An idea struck me.

Michael made a stab for my torso, missing and grazing alongside as I kicked him up into the air away from me, twisting back onto my feet as I took up a quick stance, hands held up like I was dredging something out of the deep water. Strings erupted from the ground into his hand, holding it there for a second as he dropped his weapon, body healing around the cuts the strings would do as he went into a spin instead, disoriented. Raising my hands again and again, new strings erupted as trip lines across his landscape, shearing off a wing, taking a bit of arm as the Archangel tumbled.

New wings flashed up as I brought a hand down, cutting them off to keep him suspended in the sky as I stabbed him through, over and over, juggling his movements in the air as he was helpless to find purchase anywhere; his combat was almost entirely based on his wings, while I kept things versatile. I threw a smile.

The Archangel was unimpressed, anger flashing over his face as the sky went red, breaking all strings as soon as they came out of the ground, nulling my attacks. I knew what this was- A thought hit me, looking around to see where Raziel and Pere were currently standing, behind me about a football field away. Too close and directly in its path.

St. Michael recovered, landing squarely on his feet only to re-adjust the small golden glasses over his nose. Face falling from that gallant super-smugness to a look that regular people have, he opened those wings up wide, arching far behind him, over the parking lot, over most of the area, taking up quite a bit of the sky. Even from where I stood I could hear him start his own namesake, the great demon exorcist chant, supposed to incinerate anything with even a wisp of darkness and evil in its heart, and he was purposely aiming it at the lot of us.

A wave of fire rushed for me, blue to red, converting the area around me and behind me to an ember charred landscape for a half mile behind us. Letting out an angry growl, I put my hands in front of me, interlacing my fingers and bucking my elbows out to widen my protection as far as I could.

"Michael, YOU STUPID SHIT." The fire hit dead on as the first wave whipped past, burning up all that around me, starting to singe the bottoms of my hair, my eyebrows, encasing me in fire. I tried to slow my breathing down, tried to concentrate. If they stayed behind me, they should be fine. Glancing quick behind me the basketball hoop they stood under seemed uncharred as Pere had Raziel by the shoulders, steering him and himself slightly to the left or the right based on how the fires lapped behind my back. Gritting my teeth I pushed harder against the prayer, giving them more room for safety as the fires seeped into my skin, flaking my arms and face to take the brunt of the damage. I tried to see through the flames, eventually bending my head down and reciting my beliefs over and over. It's just fake fire. It can't hurt you.

Light flickered for a moment as the Saint Michael's prayer dispersed, broke out of it's bubble to rip across the sky and scar the clouds themselves. Face lost in shallow pain, I suddenly tensed up, spotting the area in front of me empty. Someone spoke behind me.

"What's the basic rule to fighting, Nona?" Whipping around, Michael stood next to Raziel and Pere, both stumbling back like he just appeared from thin air. "This isn't a spectator sport!" The Archangel drew both swords, holding them both up and over each guy's head. He wouldn't. Then again, this was St. Michael. As the light of his wings reflected off the swords, as the two men shot desperate looks my way, it was obviously clear that he wasn't screwing around.

Dammit!

My first breath pumped through human lungs, second a huff of air already in the Colus as that black smoke encased me, flapping my still-forming wings to shoot myself directly for the bastard. Concentrating, pushing hard, time seemed to slow down, seemed to distance the seconds as my wings pushed faster and faster. Pinpointed down to the very dust that surrounded the Archangel I made that last jump, ricocheting across that field in a heartbeat. Figuring myself clever I flashed to the right, then the left, his face moving ever so slowly in that quarter of a second as I dashed into appearance just behind him. Mouth open, ready to tackle him full on in this monstrous body, I spun quickly on my lizardish heels. I leaned to strike him, so close to winning; he was suddenly facing me, sword pointed directly at my core. And without much more prestige then that he sliced into my own hip bones, swords catching and jagging up to split me open like a trout.

Reset; cut into the very essence of my existence, of myself, I tumbled out of the Colus as that black smoke spun around angrily. I was back to being roughly Neri-sized once more, no goggles and six little nubs for horns as I fell onto the grass, arms already wrapped tightly around my midsection, trying to hold my own organs in.

"Still tactless as ever, Nona."

I would not be healing, would not be able to fight back, would not be even able to touch any of that demonic energy for at least seven minutes. In that time I'd be able to feel every pain, feel each ripped muscle. Every soul outside that system at least had one, a failsafe way that two of us could fight and still get a winner. Fighting a fight where everyone's terribly aware how fictitious everything is and it goes nowhere; it's even more pointless. But having a core made things equal. By all technicalities, I had just lost this fight in a massively disappointing way.

I shuddered and gurgled against the ground, body in shock. Paul ran up, crouching nearby, trying to help.

"Always the bleeding heart." St. Michael wiped the blood from the sword, muttering disappointedly under his breath the whole platter of gripes he had with my morals. "I was expecting more of a fight from you, Nona. I'm sorely let down." I gagged a little more in pain, opening my eyes to see both the guys not far away, looking seriously concerned for me and petrified of Michael in one kaleidoscope of terror.

"It's just a minor…setback." I coughed out, shoving spilled organs back into my own body as I sat up. My vision was hazy at best, blurred as my eyes rolled in my head.

"Ah. Well, if it's just a setback…" Michael said blandly, purposely dragging the sword on the ground in front of me as he passed with no fight whatsoever. Huffing a little more for breath I tucked my knees higher, blood spilling out from the sides of my lap to form my own little moat. The archangel laughed. "In the meantime, I suppose we can take a look at our spectators here. Having fun, kids?" He bent over Raziel and Paul, propping the glasses a little higher on his nose to get a good look at them.

"Leave 'em alone!" I shouted out, pulling off my own foot-wraps as even more blood began to ooze out. "They're not a part of this!"

"You made them a part of this by keeping them around!" Michael suddenly got angry, turning around to point that sword directly at my head. The golden sword glinted with the sun, bouncing off the fancy etched pictures along the blade; I stopped trying to wrap up my wounds, set on just deadpan glaring with all the energy I had left.

"They wouldn't BE here if you kept a better eye on your stores!" I grumbled, giving a weak motion to the Fleur du Lis, somewhere out on the field.

"I have an excellent record of my stores!" Michael huffed with just the faintest hint he probably had no idea of any of his weapons and they were stored in some variety of pine-scented underground box.

"Yeah? That why the Fleur Du Lis gave us a set of matching tattoos?" I shuffled the tiniest bit to try and stand up, collapsing back to the ground. "You think I throw up piles of blood for fun? You goddamn idiot." Watching the gears turn in his head, you could see the Archangel finally understood maybe I didn't bring random people here for fun and I was trying to defend an impossible situation.

"Ah, well, anyways, let's meet our viewers while we've got the time. I'm a simple man, Nona. It takes a lot to come down here and I expect at least a little entertainment!" I resumed wrapping up my torso like a bloody Christmas present as he grew bored at yelling at the top of my head.

His eyes moved to Raziel.

"You! I used to be your boss, didn't I?" I looked up to find Raziel almost at full panic, looking in terror at me, then back to Michael, then back to Paul and me once more. The undertones of being star-struck and fangirlism all but died away as Michael held that sword out just at Raziel, using it like a baton. The archangel snorted, suddenly barking out commands. "Answer me!"

"Yes sir!" Raziel saluted out of confusion as the Archangel turned back to me, laughing sarcastically.

"That's grand! So we've got a fractured, blind Dusillo and a Continnum who wouldn't know Heaven from hot sauce. Quite the team you've got there, Nona, you think you can train your family circus to stay home next time? Golly, glad they're here to play witness. That's…just fantastic." I slowly got to my feet, whimpering out once before trying to keep that tough facade on as Michael turned back to the grey-haired fallen angel, "So you're the one in the dark, eh? How's toiling going? Enjoying it?"

My face scrunched up at his teasing, throwing a rock to pass through the angel's back.

"That's enough!" I hobbled closer to the group of men, thoroughly annoyed. One particular trait Michael had was the ability to annoy the Hell out of anyone with any bit of knowledge that he knew more of then you. He was a show-off, an antagonizer of the highest degree. It was his job. "You want a fight, I'll give you a fight." I coughed again against my arm, trail of blood behind me defied my own will.

"But you leave them out of this. No wandering attacks, nothing. I can fight you better when my mind's not pre-occupied worrying about their safety, or what you might do in a dirty, underhanded move like before." I growled out, lowering my eyes; I could see the grass through my own ankle-wounds as Michael grumbled.

"You've already lost, Nona, We don't do mulligans here."

"What do you mean by the dark?" Raziel piped up with a voice as frustrated and foreboding as my mood. Not now, Raziel, don't bring this up now. I turned slightly to him, trying to relay that information, trying to emote the will for him to shut up. Michael always used demonstrations for his explanations, and I just couldn't bring more people back from the dead. The angel's eyes flared up as he could sense I was trying to cover this up too, growing angrier, "No, you're on probation for the crap you haven't told me. What dark? What are you talking about?" Michael towered just a little more, eager to give out this knowledge as I kept my mouth shut. Looking back to Paul, he only shrugged. Someone would tell him eventually.

"The boy's giving me an opening, Nona. I'm happy to fill him in on something you should've told him before." Sighing, I tightened the wrap around my stomach just a little bit.

"I did try to tell him, he wasn't interested in it." Wincing with my one wrap, I rambled on, "We talked about sleep cycles instead." Michael scoffed as Raziel spoke up again.

"WHAT. DARK." The Archangel looked back to him for a second, only using both hands to point out the problem even more and waiting on my word. Raziel looked at him in confusing, then to Pere, surprised this was the direction our fight was taking. I crumbled.

"Yes, fine. Go for it. Keep it to the point though, okay?" I kept my eyes averted, disappointed. "It's been a long day for everyone here."

I'd wanted to tell Raziel these great immortality secrets, wanted to tell him everything, give a little information with everything on how the demons and angels kept life in balance, how the afterlife worked. I had many other loved ones, people dear to me, I've tried to convince them too. Between having so many of those lives already fragmented, back into that life pool and unrecognizable to me now, and those completely ripped apart to find that everything was a hoax, I was scared to try anymore.

With everything I'd screwed up this far, with this re-joining of lives seeming like one big lie to him, I knew he wouldn't take it well. I had so many wonderful memories from this round that'd be tarnished, that I'd look back upon and cringe at how bad I had toyed with this poor guy's life. But we had to tell him. At least start down that honest path best we could.

"Hmm. Well." Michael put the sword into the ground, wing glow dying back to normal as he sought for the right words to say. "I've got a usual speech I give, but since we're short on time I'll skip to the good parts."

"You do this regularly?" I muttered as the Archangel turned to me, hushing me. Paul sat alongside, asking me if I was okay as I gave a weak nod.

"I'm telling a story right now, Nona. Shh." Raziel kept looking between the two of us, face furrowed in confusion that our battle would go on hold, just that easily.

"A long time ago, with Christianity being fairly new, we had our first Nona encounter when she suddenly appeared in Heaven, trying to get this guy here." The goldylocked angel pointed to Paul, as he raised his hand up once in attendance. "As soon as she got him, she left, and we tried to figure out what exactly happened, tracking down the demon who trampled across our Heaven."

"Trampled." I scoffed, rolling my eyes. "I knocked over a tree, I think. People were just surprised."

"Whichever." Michael rolled his hand, trying to get back on topic. "So we find this demon leading a band of loosely collected demons and spirits, and fight them because we figure if one demon can do it, soon we'll be overrun by demons knocking over trees and what have you."

"THAT's your reasoning? I apologized!" Michael stopped the story again, turning around to face me completely.

"You want to tell the story? How about you focus on your gut problems and I'll tell the story. That okay?" He turned to Raziel and held a hand to him. "Do YOU want to give this a shot?"

"I don't know what's going on!" He bayed, far more confused than when he started. The Archangel held his hands up for anyone else to speak up before dropping them, marching towards the end of the story with much less enthusiasm.

"So we start fighting them, they fight us for a hundred years or so before we realize it's not working. Half the time we're not meeting at the right areas, the other half we're meeting small bands of random demons who get destroyed by an army of thousands of angels. Morale goes way down for both sides."

Michael rolled his hands as Raziel continued to squint at him, confused.

"We know that these souls go to be reused, and that's helpful, you know? Well…YOU don't know, but it's what these little deaths are for." I slowly grumbled to something loud and angry, frustrated that this explanation was awful.

"We work together!" I shouted, breaking their miscommunication suddenly, "Mike and I both work to plan these outbreaks, these rebellions and wars. We plan how many people approximately should die. We plan them. All of this, it's orchestrated. Planned." Raziel slowly swiveled on his heels, turning his head just the tiniest bit as he took a half step forward.

"You…. What?" I kept my head lower as he struggled to understand, "Why?"

"Because demons need a chance for something better, and angels need demons to fight. If we opened the lines of communication, we'd have a world with no conflict, and aimless souls get destructive, reckless, and lose their minds." I quieted down, feeling the strength slowly return to me. Colus strings began to perk up from the ground and waft about. "Life needs those souls, and souls need a purpose."

"Why were you fighting then?" He said, taken back, shocked.

"We're deciding who is going to win the rebellion in two days." I grumbled, "We're actually pretty good friends."

"Awww, Nona, that means so much to me to hear you say that!" He feigned a heart-flutter, grinning as I bit my lip, kicking him in the leg.

"That doesn't mean you get permission to act like a little baby, threatening mid-fight and terrifying my friends. If we're going to let them know everything, there's no reason for your little 'har-dee-har badass' routine either. Your jackassing factors into a few hundred more demons to make the fight interesting." I pointed at him and sat up a little straighter, feeling relieved to have that burden off my back, "We're had a lot in common and eventually became friends. We tried telling the truth for a while, you remember that?"

"Egh. Do I ever." The archangel leaned against his sword, shaking his head. "Absolute chaos."

"Wait, so this... this is the guy, then?" Raziel's tone bit up, angry. He turned to the Archangel, appalled. "This is the 'lots of friends', friend?"

"I mean to be fair he's the only friend I've got up there, I haven't been up long enough to make friends with people that weren't related." I looked over to Michael. "I don't think those people much consider me their friends either." The Archangel shook his head, confused.

"I'm not sure what you're talking about."

"Keeping the penalties light. Your stupid old lady curse." Michael slapped a knee, cracking his head back in a laugh.

"Oh, that. Yeah."

"You've compensated her royally, right? She didn't deserve that." I gave a growl as he only put two hands up, waving me off like Emalee Herring's life was an afterthought.

"I'll look into it." Aggravated, I looked back to the group.

"You okay, Raziel?"

His eyes looked hollow, empty. His arms just hung there, dejected and confused, unable to even pull himself to anything but a slumped over mess as his eyes tracked back and forth. It looked like the guy was about to break down.

"So everything I've been fighting for…it's just fake?"

"It served its purpose. You felt accomplished doing it, right? That's all that matt-"

"That's NOT all that matters!" Raziel suddenly yelled at the Saint, taking a few angry steps forward. "The shit I was put through to get where I am, the blood, sweat and tears I put into my endeavors, everything I've done is fake! Why would I be okay with that?!" Michael took a few steps back, showing more fear than I had ever gotten out of him in battle. He turned to us.

"How am I supposed to live, knowing that now? What am I supposed to-" His glare locked up, turning away from me instantly, storming angrily towards the street. I lowered my face again, taking deep, saddened breaths. I hated being right. Hated it.

But I was not going to let this fall to pieces without a fight.

"Raziel!" I jumped to my feet, giving a quick nod to Michael and Paul as they nodded back. Hobbling in horrible, gut-jiggling steps I hopped after him, trying to catch up until I was practically at his back, breathing hard. "Please, Raziel."

"You stay away from me!" He twisted around with a demented,

delirious look in his eyes, "Just get the fuck away from me, haven't you done enough damage?!"

"I've apologized for that, just listen to me, please." I said softly, non confrontational. Even if we never spoke again, I needed him to understand the afterlife wasn't all fake. The system it revolved around, absolutely, but it was like advanced babysitting at best. This world did still matter. He didn't protest, so I kept talking, "People still matter in this realm, but the afterlife is only a step to better things." Raziel stopped, turning back to me with an accusing finger.

"You know how many of my friends you've sacrificed for 'better things'? How many of them believe in this cause with everything they have? They dedicate their goddamn lives to it and they die for nothing. Don't you DARE try and convince me that somehow people actually matter to you. The only ones who do matter are the assholes like you who get to control it!" He turned around, only to turn back and face me, "You people toy with everyone else's life, no wonder this all sounds so great and reasonable coming out of your mouth." I took a few deep breaths, keeping my head low. Something scratched frantically deep underground.

"People do matter in this life. Everyone does." It was as far as I got. I could see Raziel's feet turning back to me; see that exact stance to fight as he hopped on the balls of his feet. Through one more slow, deep breath I held it, immediate pain as Raziel punched me, right in the face. I could've believed that it wouldn't hurt, could've stuck to my morals that actual physical violence was pointless. I let up this time. I let it happen. My head moved back only slightly.

You could feel that tension leave the area suddenly, feel that shock, even from him to do such a thing. As his hand pulled back I kept my eyes closed, tears running down my face, mixing with the blood that gushed from my nose. Like his words, his doubt and confusion wasn't the theme song constantly running through my head; that I hadn't considered what a bull-headed position it was to have. I could understand why he'd feel this way. Taking another slow, deep breath, I snorted as much blood out my nose as I could. Raziel took a few steps back.

"Neri…I'm sorry." He stuttered as someone came rumbling up behind me, unable to stay on the sidelines any longer. Paul.

"That's enough. I'm not going to let you stand here and take this abuse from someone too stupid to pull his head out of his ass." Paul fumed. "Like an immature soul like yours knows better."

"Excuse me?" Raziel barked out, back on the defensive. "I've been a part of your little 'system' for almost four hundred years now. I think I have a right to be outraged at living a lie for so long!"

Paul growled.

"But you died when you were 10, and no matter what 'growing up' you do here in the afterlife, you're still that goddamn ignorant ten year old!" Raziel looked like he too had been punched in the face as I brought my hand up, wiping my nose, vision tinted red.

"Like we don't understand what we do, you don't think your little outbursts have ever come up before? The world needs new souls, and demonized souls need the ability to have a better life. Angels have the perks of living as long as they'd like, that if they do die on the battlefield, they go right back to Heaven and restart. Demons don't have that, so if anything, life is FAR more precious to us than a bratty child pretending to be a human being can ever understand!" I curled my lip.

"Paul!" Snarling, he ignored me and kept at it. That was too far.

"How precious, exactly? Ordering your friends to all die for a fictitious cause YOU made up, just how precious is that life?"

"We lament the death of our friends; we understand this need to find a better life than what they've got. We mourn those lost, but we know it needs to be done."

"That's even worse!" Raziel screeched out, "Speaking of, aren't you going to take back whatever bit of you that's me, or whatever the hell is going on here?" Paul's head snapped to him.

"Keep it. I want nothing to do with you and the excess remainder of my soul." There was venom on his tongue as it lightened up, just a bit, "We've grown to be different people anyways, it wouldn't work." Again, there was more scratching, more frantic tearing beneath the soil as I could feel the barrier St. Michaels had put up shudder. Raziel looked between both of us, shaking his head with disgust as he turned around immediately.

"Fuck this." He resumed storming off, pace much less frantic into more of an ambled confusion. The answer suddenly popped into my head, a way to make him understand, looking up to him as I could feel the stomach wound begin to heal. My seven minutes were up.

"Amber!" I called out after him as he stopped, giving a 'why do I give a damn' look over his shoulder. "You saved her from being a smear on the ground. You did, not me, not Paul, not Michael. If that isn't the meaning of this part of life mattering, I don't know what is." He turned back around to us, kinda of opening up his hands to flop by his sides.

"It's just one person."

"Avoiding the obvious response about the value of people's lives, alright, what about any of the people's houses we've exorcised demons from? You don't think that their lives were changed or affected by having their prayers answered? I'm sure any relationship either you or me has had concerning anyone else, that's all scripted too, right?" I turned back to Paul with a slowly confident smile, "The politics behind the afterlife are yes, entirely fake. But this life isn't about that." I took a few commanding steps forward, gaining my footing.

"We're only trying to give structure." I snorted out more blood, feeling the demonic energy begin to return as I slowly grew those inches back to my full body size, "Everyone needs something to believe in; we all make this afterlife." I gritted in a bit of pain as the horns behind my head began to grow once again.

"Our involvement here continues beliefs in life. If we didn't, the world just wouldn't work. The system we have set up continues that cycle, it fuels it." I shook my head out a little as I kept growing, beginning to tower over the fallen angel once more, hair falling back to my shoulders. "It is not perfect. It's not faultless and it's not honest. None of us think that what we do is the most pristine thing in this world. But considering the alternative, it's the best we've come up with. It's what works."

Shaking my arms out I cracked back into that full height, looking back to Michael and Paul for a moment as I fell back to a regular height suppressing that future soul, body renewed from the reset.

"The world before this was an unorganized mess of scattered souls claiming land until they faded away. Thousands and thousands of souls that disappeared forever. We've been working on this system every day since." I spoke softly, taking a few steps forwards to him; his face looked completely blank and empty, no fear, no anger, no hatred; but also no happiness or understanding. It looked like he had checked out, that he was trying to will his soul to leave the area through passive means. I felt for him.

"Plus, when you learn everything is malleable, you get to be a part of our cool insider club." Michael piped up as I immediately gave him a glare.

"Not helping."

Raziel didn't blink or breathe, just kept his eyes affixed to the ground, slowly twisting back and forth. I took a step closer.

"Listen, I'm sorry this couldn't all be something better. I just want to you to try and understand that it's not belittling your efforts." His eyes suddenly clicked back into focus, looking over me to the angels behind me, looking out over the half-developed land. His voice was hollow and sad.

"I don't understand." He looked back to me before his eyes jumped elsewhere, "This is your world, not mine."

My ears shot back in regret, in shock, holding a hand to my chest as I couldn't think of another word to say. I'd given it my best. I'd done everything in my power to try and help him out in life, to try and give him a sense of the world around me, to give him that perspective. It wasn't enough. I had to know when there was no more to say, that a decision was completely out of my hands. This, it couldn't be helped. I lowered my head in defeat.

"I'm sorry." I said softly as the ground began to shake apart, that barrier just beneath the ground suddenly cracking and dispersing away. Like a murderous bloody demon horse she rose from the ground, horns broken and chipped to thrust herself out of the earth, red eyes as wide and as crazy as I'd ever seen her. Cempe; bloodied and angry for getting trapped underground. Cempe, furiously trying to get through the barrier for the last half hour as she panted and heaved with unbridled rage, head whipping over to Raziel with a crazy little snarl. Even out of the path of destruction I could feel my veins grow cold.

"Michael, you asshole!" She looked past us both, back hunched with a wide stance ready to tear into anything that dare reply back. Her demon form melted back to human as she stormed past in the same position, heading straight for the archangel.

"Why Cempe, were you waiting to come up?" Michael spit a little arrogance at her, chiding the fate with as much sass as he dared. She pulled the Decempedia's weapon form out of thin air, cracking him upside the head with it and continued to push him on the retreat as the archangel just laughed and laughed. Watching the two of them squabble like long-lost lovers, Paul came up alongside me, arm over my shoulder.

"They'd make a fantastic, masochistic couple, and they don't even know it." I shook my head a little as he laughed. Turning back to make a similar remark to Raziel, I found him still walking out away from us, trying to leave in that dejected, unwanted way. Cempe saw this too.

"Oh no you don't, you little liability!" She rushed back into the demon form, charging straight at him like a wild beast possessed. Raziel eyes went wide as he suddenly began to bolt, running full out in terror. "I'll give you something to throw a punch at you insensitive prick!" Before I could say otherwise she snapped him up, diving straight into the ground, straight back to Hell. I didn't stop her.

42

"Let me out!" There was a dull thump at the very non-assuming door as Cempe only moved slightly, arms crossed with her back to the new, makeshift dungeon. We were back at home, back underground in our corner of Hell. With my loss to Michael, I was to only bring 3200 demons, while he was to bring a fruit medley of 5600 angels and angelic otherkin; I'd lose. For my big push back after all those others had been lost with my geriatric imprisonment, for that grand revolt into the middle ground of the world, I'd lose. I'd need better fighting techniques next time; I didn't always lose. "You stupid fakers, let me out!" Raziel bellowed like a spoiled teenager as my sister whipped around back to the door, easily frustrated by loud, irritating sounds and stupid insults.

"Trust me Christopher, the injuries I'll leave on you will be very, very real! Shut up!" Her eyes slid back to my direction, slumped against the wall with my arms folded. I perked to attention as she was curt and annoyed, "What did I tell you? You let some immature brat like him in, let him learn the truth about us, and now we've got to babysit him and keep him silent. Money doesn't work for this sort of thing, so can you please fix your accident?" She pointed at the door for emphasis as he threw himself against it again.

"We can't fix this." I said softly; contemplative, "I've been trying to 'fix this' for almost ten years now. It's a lesson in when to intervene, and when to butt out. We need to do the latter."

"Butt out? Have you lost your mind? What are we going to do? Let him tantrum himself to sleep, then just dump him in the woods and hopes he keeps his mouth shut?" Her shoulders dropped a little, worn out too. "You gave it your best shot, but some people don't function like we do. You know that. You tried. So take an active role in this, he's your problem!

Sighing, I lowered my head, scraping my horns against the wall while I thought.

My head was filled with the voice of St. Michael, talking with him earlier up top while both Cempe and Raziel had darted back underground. With the barrier lifted, with the fight over and the reset completed, the two of us were left standing around like an unofficial queue.

"So what is the fate of our associate? Get it?" He had asked, putting the two swords away and taking the Fleur du Lis with him while he was at it. Sneering, I shook my head.

"Never heard that one before. They do award the biggest wings to the smartest people, don't they?" Giving a sick, tired little grin, my eyes slowly swept back to look at the spot where they both went underground, staring at it in a far away sense of loss, just like I had when Cempe had snapped him in half the first time. The feeling was the same too; that everything was broken and shattered.

"There's options." I said slowly, taking a long, deep breath. "Lots of options that I don't want to use, other options he'd never go for, and lots more that are terribly depressing." I turned back to the Saint who was busy picking off dirt and debris from his arms. He almost smiled as I waited for him to speak up, jumping to conclusions all on his own.

"Are you looking for my input as a friend?" He said in this overly saccharine tone that he knows I hate. "Best friend Nona? BFN?"

"I don't know how anyone finds you scary." I mumbled, scoffing." I figure you deserve a say in this as well, since you've got your hands in this." There was an actual smile this time, almost a sort of wide-toothed gawking guffaw to accompany it as the saint practically giggled. "Yeah, it's pretty funny, I had to kill a real person to get back here. You've always got the wackiest ideas."

"Alright, alright, ease off there."

"Did you send hayyoth after Christopher?"

"It keeps people focused!"

"Did you TRAP ME in a room with a barrier while he nearly got torn limb from limb?" I pushed a bit farther, happy grin still on my face as I felt like I was two seconds from smacking him upside the head.

"Barrier solved the problem, didn't it?" Michael waved a hand. "They were weak Hayyoth! They couldn't tear a bag of dog food open if they tried."

"Don't you have a real job to do? I heard you had like...a giant office building or something in Heaven."

"Funny, because I hear you have some sort of giant Hell-estate where you're at all the time but here I find you road tripping across the country instead." He made a vague motion above him, "You should come visit sometime, I'm sure you'd like it." The archangel ribbed.

"Hard pass." I crossed my arms, getting back on topic. "But

what I'm saying is your people are putting it together. Raziel suspected something was up, but Gauzier's been crossing the angelic divide himself and basically had it figured out."

"And apparently stealing weapons from me as well." Michael shook his head, serious once again. "I'll take care of that."

I shook my head a little, snapping back to Cempe in front of me now, livid and angry at this problem on our hands while yelling at the door. I frowned. My problem to fix. Michael would fix his problems, I had my own to deal with. Fixing. Everyone seemed to need something fixed. Something started to gnaw at my brain, chewing up my thoughts and regurgitating them in the same mess I've always mulled over. What the Hell was a 'fix', anyhow? Blanket statements barely covered this at all.

"Here! This is how we should fix this!" She summoned the Decempedia to her hand, pretending to stab a fictitious Raziel and proceed to beat him to a bloody fictitious pulp. She looked to me for a reaction, for a laugh of some sort; it fell short, in no mood to joke. She craned her head back to the door, "You hear that? That's what we're going to do to you if you don't learn to shut your damn mouth!"

"You stupid monsters!" He shouted back, throwing himself back against the door a few more times as my frown pulled farther and farther back with each thump. Without discussing 'the plan' or figuring how to really 'fix' this problem, I walked towards the door, weaving around my sister to open it up between thumps. He was right there, shoulder out, ready to try and knock down the door, blindly throwing himself at the situation. Frowning again I grabbed a hold of his shoulder, taking him off-balance immediately as I just pushed him easily to the middle of the dungeon, shutting the door once more.

"Lock it." I called out to Cempe as metal slid into place. The dungeon was dim; a small off-shoot of a room that had at one point been rather pleasant, rosy and nice. Now it resembled a slimy slant of rock, volcanic cavern of a tiny lava flow of some sort. It was a pretty miserable place. Raziel looked confused, trying to find that ember of anger to keep this fit up.

"You! You're the last person I want to see right now, why would you…" He stopped, stuttering, looking back to the door and back to me, trying to figure this out, figure what my angle was; my catch. "Tell her to open it up, let me out." He demanded, pointing at me. I ignored him, letting go of his shoulder to look despondently at the walls, trying to find a place to sit down at, trying to gain a bit of perspective. Confused when I didn't answer back, he furrowed his eyebrows. He started to say something, pointing to the door as his hand hung around with no dialogue, unsure.

Sneering, Raziel looked back to the door.

"What'd you do to her?"

"Nothing! What'd you do?" Cempe yelled back, muddled.

Picking the back corner, I gathered my legs beneath me, sitting down quietly with my arms folded. The angel stood there, milling around for a moment, nervous.

"So what, you come back in here to try and convince me to become a demon like your boyfriend or something?" He laughed as he said it; I believe he was trying a very dry sort of joke, a light jab. I didn't laugh. I remained quiet, re-adjusting my back a little to put my head lower. Raziel's type of laugh quieted.

"What, you out of things to say?" His tone cut up a little sharply, "Or are you hiding more things I should know?" This too ended on a laugh, to try and convince me the meaning wasn't as harsh or as angry as it was said. I remained completely silent, no smile, head bent down, trying to absorb this situation best I could.

"Let's see, maybe this isn't Hell at all, it's Heaven?" He was just being flat-out condescending, now, "Oh! Or secretly you're renting from the devil?"

Raziel walked towards the door before stopping, snapping his fingers.

"Wait, no, I got it, Saint Michael's your dad, right?" He said sarcastically, tone dulling as he turned away from me, laughing like a pompous jackass, still confused and on edge. My ears snapped back in annoyance.

"You about done?" The laughing stopped as you could feel the tension skyrocket back up in a heartbeat.

"Or what? What are you trying to prove?" He shuffled around some more, unable to leave, unwilling to stay here. It raised other questions. "I don't want to talk to you. I don't want anything to do with any of this...Heaven and Hell tag team garbage." Mouthing off to the top of my head, I kept quiet. Raziel was intentionally pushing buttons, trying to get anything from me, anything at all. I gave nothing back.

"Do you feel sorry for me? Is that what this is about?" The angel took a step away, as distant and far from me as you could get in this ten foot squared room. "Or, are you just sitting here to show the others your great and fantastic mercy?" I opened my eyes, slowly scorching the land around him with the intense-death-like glare I sported as I sluggishly settled on his face. That arrogance evaporated as the fallen angel took a half step away.

"You seem like you're having fun, so let's make this more familiar." Raising a hand up I snapped my fingers, instantly back to how I first was as Neri- same clothes, same goggles, same height. The chiding assholish grin immediately dried up as Raziel's look poisoned.

"That's not fair."

"Please, if you're all for taking pot shots at me, shouldn't matter which variation of soul we go with." I slapped my knees for extra effect, welcoming further assholishness head on. His 'great and fantastic mercy' comment really stung. "No masks, no future souls that are pretty much masks in themselves. I'm all ears. C'mon. Keep 'em coming, Raziel." Both hands out to my side, Raziel remained dead quiet, like I thought he might. In his eyes, Nona wasn't me, and it gave him this weird courage to make his remarks hurt just that little bit extra. I also figured I might get through to him better this way.

Things remained silent for a few seconds more.

"I'm here to fix this." I looked Raziel square in the eyes.

"Fix…me?"

"No. Fix 'this.'" I shook my head out a little, eyes locked on an unimportant piece of wall. "Which means I'm supposed to kill you. You're my responsibility and my last loose end." Staring straight ahead, I slowly looked over to him as he took a step backwards. I was aware of the tension and fear in the air, the distrust that was almost palpable as a visible thing. Smirking, I switched to contemplating with one arm, leaning slightly off to the side to stare at the wall behind him as the fallen angel held his breath.

"Are you?"

We held our stances for a few moments, silent and anxious. Those two blue eyes switched frantically back and forth as I only looked to the far wall.

He broke after a while, head swiveling back.

"Bu- But Neri, you can't be serious, I'm your friend!"

"Well…" I tilted my head side to side, arms folded. "It'd clean everything up that I wouldn't have to worry about any negative consequences." Unfolding my arms and looking back to the man, he took a step back.

"But I'm not a tidy person." I muttered as he moved the tiniest bit, trying to understand in crystal clear terms what was about to happen. "So how about this: after I finish weaving strings of life for the continent of Asia, and after I eat the pile of unbaptized fetuses, I'll get right on it. A solid maybe." Raziel moved a little more, eyes squinting hard at me. I looked back to the angel.

"That means no. I'm screwing with you, no, I'm not going to kill you." I could hear him breathe again. I smiled at the awkwardness, grinned at the same social intrepidation that had always been there. Living around my sisters put everything into a bland universe, no chance for misinterpretation, no miscommunication since we all knew the same things, more or less the same type of people. Settling down I found him still not joking, still confused, wary, arms halfway to his stomach like he was ready to strike back if I changed my mind. Seeing that fear, that anger still there, it killed my elevated mood, folding my arms back to lean against the wall, calming down back where I started.

"I am genuinely sorry, Christopher." My insides were a spiraling mess of shrapnel, turbulent and heavy with frustration and regret. Keeping a straight face through that entire ruse was as much joking as I could put forth right now. Everything felt heavy and confusing and I wish I had a week or two to digest it. He looked up long enough for me to catch his eyes. "Really."

Milling around for a moment, he slid his back down on the wall, letting out a tired breath to sit across the way. Raziel fumbled with his hands for a moment, running a fingernail under his cuticles to scrape out any devil dirt. It felt like an eternity before he replied.

"I know." Okay. Good. That's progress in some way.

"I just wanted to help people. This was never a ploy or a game to screw with your life." He remained quiet, looking at the wall and unwilling to look over at me. I let out a sigh. "I just want you to know that."

"Why'd you do it? Honestly." The ex angel crossed his arms, keeping his head low. "Did you feel bad for me?" Thinking on it for a moment, I looked around the walls myself.

"Yeah." Stretching out against the back wall, I felt his eyes rest on me like his life was some sort of sacrificial feel-good task. That wasn't it. "You were getting punished for knowing me, without even actually knowing me. Fed you some garbage about being tied to someone's falling, I figured at the very worst if I told you the truth and you hated me, you'd at least know the truth and could sort things out yourself."

"And that was by posing as my assistant." He muttered as I laughed.

"No, God no, that wasn't supposed to work out at all like that." Grinning at just how skewed and twisted the plan had gotten, knowing my sisters were desperately trying to retrieve my innocent self and how they must've been freaking out for the last decade, it's a wonder it worked out at all. "That was exploratory. I figured you'd kill me and then I could assess just what I had to do from there. But I... didn't figure I'd be literally impossible to kill. So that's my mistake."

"This is all a lot to take in."

"It's gonna take time, Christopher."

I didn't want to nag or make him feel like he was an unwilling participant in a lecture.

"The door is open. You're free to leave or do whatever you'd like."

"I can?" He piped up, instantly back on his feet. I nodded.

"You told Cempe to lock it." Raziel looked to the door, "I heard it lock."

"Well, I'm telling you that I believe it's open." He started to say something else, walking hastily for the door to have the handle jiggle, and nothing more. Raziel scoffed sarcastically.

"Well, I believe it's still locked like I said." He said shortly, looking back like this was another dirty trick I'd planned ten years ago.

"And that's why it stays locked, because you believe it is." I shifted my seat just a bit, "But if you believe it's open, it will be open, it's not a real lock. You think we get a locksmith down here to open these things up if we forget the fictitious keys? You know, in Hell?" Raziel jiggled the handle again with no luck.

"Wouldn't telling me this jeopardize your security even more?" His voice went flat.

"I'm pretty secure in our resolve to how real our locks are for the rest of the house, but the weird lava tube prison in the back yard is fair game." Looking around to this dim, disgusting corner of Hell. "The afterlife is a battle of belief and will. That's the gist of it."

"I suppose this is your way to try and explain things? To, you know..." He wiggled his fingers around, patronizing how I spoke, "...get me to understand and accept this ridiculous afterlife scenario?" Raziel began vainly pulling on the door handle like a patron five minutes after a business closes.

"No, I've given up." The pulling stopped.

"Given up?" He turned his head a little, "On me?"

"I've given up controlling this situation. Blindly forcing one conclusion like this isn't an issue with many people involved is a step in the wrong direction and I'm not going to destroy someone's soul like a bag of trash that needs to be taken out." I folded my arms, trying to be as nicely standoffish as possible, "Ruthlessly dictating the results of how things are gonna work like you don't deserve a say isn't why I do this. I'm tired of trying to force the results I think people want, instead of listening."

I didn't like to admit that I'd screwed up, that I had nothing more to give, that this whole situation hurt more than it really should have. I was a wreck; I couldn't wrap my head around the idea that I tried everything that normally did work, and it turned out so badly. Felt especially bad that he put this trust in me for the last four years to make it back, and I put him in this situation immediately afterwards. Like the universe was trying it's damnedest to keep conflict in our friendship.

But I had to learn when to let go; I had to learn when free will was the only thing that anyone could count on; that it was the only thing people retained in life and death, that it was constant.

"So in that way, I give up." I mumbled.

Raziel turned more to me, almost disgusted, or revolted, shaking his head in disbelief.

"So that's it?"

"That's it." I picked at my toenails nervously, "That's my fix."

"What about those who want you to, you know, kill me?" I got defensive in a heartbeat.

"Fuck 'em. They got a problem with it, they can come to me.

There's no set way to go about this, so they can stuff their opinions in a sack if they don't like it. You tell me what you'd like to do from here on out, and I'll do my very best to help make it happen. That's my decision."

There was a moment of silence before the door suddenly clicked open, like the lock believability dissolved. I smiled as the angel leapt back, shocked at more than just the door opening up to a surprised Cempe on the outside. He pushed the door open a little farther, closing it as Cempe's angry face was just on the other side of it, cursing into the crack of the door. She pushed back hard as his foot braced against the bottom.

"She's letting me leave, so go away."

"What? You impertinent, immature little shit, she might let you get away, but I sure as Hell won't!" The door slammed shut, vicious scrabbling sounds and the desperate sounds of the lock holding its place. Part of me smiled, just a bit. "Open this up, right now! Dammit Nona, don't teach him how to lock doors!" I could hear him laugh, at least huff happily at the lock in a shade of disbelief that the crazy ramblings I had been spitting out were true, that it worked.

"Huh." He pulled his hands away from the lock as the door rattled again and again, an exasperated, annoyed growl penetrated through the thick walls; Cempe retreating.

The sounds dulled to nothing, to shallow breathing and occasional foot-scuffing, the awkwardness of this whole situation contained in a single room. My thoughts went back to my protest in the utility room of Raziel's quarters, how I had shut myself away in there, how I was content with hurting no one, how I wasn't bothering anyone in the first time since I came up top. Looking around me now, I could see myself doing the same thing; but this time my problem was right here in the room with me. I pulled my knees closer to my chest, thinking; making myself as tiny as I could get. Internally, I was an emotional little nightmare; the words 'fail fail fail' circulating around fast enough to spin their own current. I wanted this to be over, I wanted things to go back how they were, I wanted everyone to be happy and nothing more.

"I don't hate you, Neri."

My eyes popped open, the fail-tornado stopping as the only thing I could hear was the despondent echo of his words. My tight-wound self broke apart, letting go of my knees to turn to him as the angel was half facing the door, half facing me.

"Not to say I appreciate what you've put me through, but I don't hate you." He turned back towards the door, hand bracing on it softly, trying to be sneaky.

"We've been through too much anyways." I could hear the door lock slide jaggedly from the frame, opening this dungeon cellar carefully and silently. I scuffed up a laugh at that, taking those breaths, genuinely relieved. Raziel turned back with a smile before his face was back to the door, opening it up with no Cempe in sight. Cautiously scanning outside the door the fallen angel suddenly slipped out, gone from the dungeon without a second word to that. In that awkward silence, I pulled my knees back towards me. No more meddling, I had to stop. I could hear his footsteps grow farther away as I sat, bothering no one. Torturing no one. It was an isolated little stand.

My thoughts flashed back to Michael and I's conversation up top, debating the options I had in this matter. I started to walk back towards the portal down to Hell, the leftover hole from Cempe's jagged form when I stopped, toes digging a little into the ground nervously.

"I may need your help with this." They were fumbled, unimportant words, under spoken and out of place. St. Michael laughed more now, an audible, thundering thing that took me off guard.

"See, now I know you're going soft, asking for my help." He started quieting down as my mind was occupied in thought, trying to figure a way to resolve this out. "You care deeply about him, don't you?"

I stopped, sighing a bit and tossing my head left and right. I hated super observant people like this, no mystery left in the world with a gaggle of them around to point out every detail. I suppose I was one of them, though. Maybe that's what frustrated me, associating with versions of myself constantly. No variation.

"Yeah, I do." I finally relented. Hearing it out loud, I think it was news to me too.

"More than Paul?"

"Hey." Raziel's voice interrupted my thoughts, big, block-like head of his stuck back in the door, face scrunched up like the very world around him reeked to high Hell, "You coming?"

The two of us walked around Hell like some grand, fabled estate; I didn't say much, didn't give answers longer then two words while I pointed out and labeled the various attractions here around us. I didn't intend to sound despondent and uncaring, but I had no real idea how to handle this anymore. There was no place for Raziel here in Hell, go up top, and there's no place on earth where he wouldn't be hunted down and eradicated like the rest of us. With the grand ceremony of his falling, how big of a deal they all made that day, he wouldn't be welcomed there, either. He had no place to live; and in all my leagues of irony throughout the years, I was the one who took that all away from him, just as I had screamed at him, exorcised from Amber and Katherine's house. Karma had a way of biting people in that ass like that.

We stopped alongside Styx, regarding over the bubbling magma river like the clearest blue waters you'd ever seen. A partially disfigured face floated by, tongue-meat bubbling out of his eyes to mingle with the lava around him. I cringed.

"This is fake?" He asked, voice as disgusted as I felt, trying to shake off the nasty little surprises Hell had in store. I nodded, snapping a little more to attention as one of the jagged Hell birds swooped close overhead, screeching out loud enough to make my ears ring. We stood at the corner of the Moirae plot, which segmented most of the other chambers of Hell until detail all but erased from sight. "It's an, uh…expansive lie."

"Everyone's got their own Hells, so we try to cater accordingly. But see that one? The veeerry very far one out there?" I pointed as he came closer, squinting to a chamber of Hell easily two miles away. Raziel nodded. "That's empty. Everything past that point is empty."

"No one has any more ideas about Hell?" He tilted his head a bit, really straining to see if there were some birds or anything floating about down there. I shook my head.

"People have their own ideas, but they also know something's there to lord over them, be it Cempe, the devil, whichever. So if you can't see our house down there, people don't consider it 'Hell' anymore. They're finicky."

"So what if you put a second estate out there, would people just start showing up?" He said flatly, but starting to get the idea. I grinned, motioning out there.

"Yeah, it's pretty funny. Here, I'll show you." I jumped into the Monster Colus body, scooped him up and did a few quick tears in reality to the far end of the caverns, nearly out of sight. We popped up in a completely empty cavern flanked by the same smoky, red lights the prime part of Hell had, but less detailed and inspired. My claws sunk into the rock, twisting my head to look back down the cavern with Raziel sitting shotgun up by my horns. "Watch."

Everything remained silent for a moment as he looked around, disappointed before looking down on me that my heinous, insidious lines knew no bounds. No souls popped up, everything was as clear and empty as it was before. I tilted an eye back towards him, smirking.

"Call 'em over."

"What, like a dog?" He seemed mortified.

"Just anything, they don't care." Looking back to the souls I tried to figure why at least a couple didn't come with us as we flew out here.

"HHHHEEEEYY" Raziel shouted, screeching at the top of his lungs as I pulled my head in a little towards my body. "Sor-"

Before he could finish, two souls suddenly appeared, floating and twisting around in circles, lives devoid of lines to follow. They flitted about with their weird legless bodies and ribcages just as I had been, twirling and bumping into walls as Raziel watched what he had done.

"What are they doing?" The angel seemed almost sad or surprised.

"Free-styling. I forget you've got little baby lungs…" Drawing a deep breath I saw Raziel cover his hears, smartly understanding the terrible loud sound I was about to make in a sixty foot tall monster body. "HHHEEEY LOOK AT HOW MUCH FUN WE'RE HAVING OVER HERE!" I bellowed as forty or fifty souls arrived in an instant, all spiraling and floating about like jellyfish caught in a whirlpool. They bounced off of both of us as the angel tried to gently shoo the ribcages away, some spiraling like a top into further empty caverns down the way.

"No, I mean, why are they like this?" He watched after them, far more bothered and unhappy, just like I had been when I first saw these souls myself.

"OH... uh... they're lost, Raziel." I opened up my wings, gripping tight onto the cavern wall and pumping my flight muscles hard to shove the whole lot of them at least away, back towards their respective homes. "Sometimes the only thing a soul wants is to drift aimlessly, to think and improve themselves. See where they went wrong." I motioned to the lava pools of dead bodies, now thankfully far off.

"Sometimes people just want to suffer, live and wallow in the mistakes and problems they've made." Raziel gave a light scoff.

"You cater to both."

"Well, we cater to all. But for the most part if you're getting fancy with what you want, you think it's happening to you but you're just drifting about like these Lost like everyone else. Let's not get crazy here."

The angel remained staring at them, locked.

"Can you save them?"

"Eventually, everyone in here wakes up. In their own time, of course." One of the lost spiraled close as I gently grabbed it, holding it up by a rib as it's little arms windmilled around. "But they need to solve their own problems out first before they do. Sometimes people drift in here for ages. For most people it's about 3 years." I snickered, passing the lost off to Raziel like a football.

"And then?"

"They fight for us. Or they choose to go into the Life Pool." The Lost listed side to side, clearly uncomfortable with being held and grabbed. "You'd think more people would choose the Life Pool, but a surprising amount of them want to fight with us instead. About 70/30."

"You have access to the Life Pool here, then?" Raziel's voice went lower, "Instead of that being... you know, just a Heaven thing."

"Yeah, sorry, that might be a bit of a secret." I muttered as Raziel scoffed and choked on his own frustration. Changing the topic might help out here.

"Over the course of even a hundred years, the way this place changes based on ideas and stigmas is fascinating. You get a good movie that the world sees with its own idea of Hell, and this place starts flickering around like mad. Makes everything terribly unorganized and a bit of a mess. That's what Cempe keeps track of, tries to bring that order into whatever ploy comes by to mess everything up."

"When you figured this all out, what'd you do?" Smirking, I looked about like the answers were written on the walls.

"Sulked. Tried to fight back. Held it over people's head, then sat in a shame spiral for a couple decades being overwhelmed by something so much bigger than myself." I looked to the cavern wall across the way, swinging my tail into the side and gouging out the wall about seven or eight feet deep. With one wing beat I flew over there, dissolving and neatly dropping Raziel off on the cliff edge and myself in human form for a serene, isolated location, like a bench carved into stone up on a cliff's edge. "I use it to my advantage best I can, but I feel that I hide from it more then I really should. For some reason, I'm happy to be at that medium."

Unsurprised by my general shenanigans, Raziel shook his head and sat down, feet dangling over the edge. I joined him.

"Of hiding?"

"Ignorance is bliss." I looked over to the soul caverns, the same place I had escaped from. The rocks around it barely contained the ruddy red smoke wafting about, the demons flying in tight circles, the undulating, constant twisting line that went about infinitely. "Back at that time, I went into new lives often. I didn't like knowing what I did; I needed that ignorance, that break." Raziel turned his head a little at the millions and millions of lost, confused souls.

"How'd this all start, anyways?" I laughed as he clarified, "How'd you get this job?" Finally, those 'big picture' questions. It was a bit overdue.

"I found the afterlife was a series of people emptily wandering around, tying themselves to pieces of land until they eventually disappeared. Thousands and thousands of people just standing around. I wanted a more active afterlife then that. I wanted to do more." I spread my hand across the caverns like I could paint the landscape with my words.

"I was always curious on what happened to a person after death. When I did leave that life, I found other souls in death with the same ideas. Feeling like I knew more, or had a better grasp of the situation, they appointed me as leader. When a big enough gathering made this known to the world of the living, little myths and stories start popping up." I laughed again at the madness that this all came out sounding like.

"That's actually where the Colus came from; used the basic form of the goats and other animals sacrificed in my honor to manifest that energy into a sort of weapony—-distaff…thing." I suddenly looked back to Raziel; he still seemed interested, not letting this go off on deaf ears. I turned back to the river, "Over the years, I made modifications. Pushed my boundaries, tested limits." …Broke friendships, abandoned family…ran away from my home country… I frowned, continuing back on track.

"Worked hard to find the meaning in death; when this all came together, I finally did find that meaning; that life is better. That's where things count." My tone grew sad, almost, "Death's important, but that living, breathing life, that's center stage."

"Why don't you go back?" He said bluntly. I grinned.

"I do. Best medicine for an inflated ego." My smile fell away, "But I know that I have a job down here; I don't get to enjoy the full experience, just where I'm supposed to be in age; so I never lose who I am. That's the upside of things, but I don't get to see much of that life. That's why I spend all my time up-top as I can, generally being neglectful of my duties." We both kinda quieted down, staring off at opposing features.

I scanned over the massive expanse tiredly, distant. It was weird being so frank and blatant with someone about us all. While it was somewhat fun to explain and organize what you've been doing for the last 3500 years or so, it made me feel hollow and empty. Like the most I could amount to the backbreaking labor of shaping and working this massive space was the certain feelings I got out of it. I was proud, happy of what I'd done. But after such a long time, the only thing I could remember from it was feeling proud and happy.

"I'm... sorry about before." Raziel spoke up, obviously ashamed. "I don't cope with stress very well. But I should've never done that." I smiled, rubbing my nose a little for effect.

"It's alright. It's a pretty screwed up thing to go through." I nudged him with my elbow a little, trying to get him to lighten up. His gaze was locked on the ground, though.

"What he said about being an immature soul." Raziel looked up to me, "Is that true?" My ears fell a little lower.

"Yeah." Raziel immediately began to protest.

"So even though I've grown up through here, that I'm four hundred and some-odd years old-"

"It's not the same as growing up in the existing world. Hormones develop the brain more, mature the soul, I suppose." I could see him slump where he sat, "Dying before those have a chance to take effect leaves you immature."

"You're immature too."

"Oh, I'm not denying that, but it's a choice, not a condition." I immediately tried to recall my words as Raziel seemed to slump more and more. "There are worse things in this world, Raziel, try not to let it get to you." My words breezed right through him.

"So even with the hair..."

"Sorry."

"I don't suppose there's any way to fix that?" His voice was low, but immediately jumped up in tone, "I mean, a way that lets me keep living this life?"

"No, I'm afraid not. If you were somehow alive again and went through life normally, that'd fix it. But that's just not possible." I was fidgeting where I sat, trying so hard to keep my options under wraps, to keep what I had set up just in case he asked me. I wasn't going to meddle. I had to take that step away, had to allow people to make their own decisions, their own faults.

This anxiety practically led me to bouncing in my seat with a slightly delirious look on my face, trying not to blurt out what 'I think he should do.' No. No more. Had to let life be, had to keep my damn mouth shut. This obviously didn't fool the angel for a breath of a second.

"Why do I have the feeling that you do know how to fix this?" Raziel glared. My eyes shot farther open, before squinting, just barely, looking out directly in front of me. I felt like I was going to pop. "Why can I see you hiding this and doing a poor job of it? From whatever part of the tether that's left, it's like I'm hooked up to an addict." My mouth clenched tighter, shaking my head a little and refusing to spit it out.

"So you do know something!" He stood up, grabbing onto one of my horns and shaking my head around in frustration. "What is it?"

"I'm not going to meddle anymore!" I spit out as he only shook my horn more violently.

"This isn't God damn Scooby Doo, tell me what you know!"

"I'm not going to keep dictating your life!"

"Well, obviously you have options, so tell me what you know!" My neck was starting to get sore as I pulled away. "You told me you'd fix this!" That knife struck especially deep; I froze.

"Alright, alright, stop!" I waved my one hand up as he let go. I launched back into the Colus form from the cliff side, shooting us both back towards the estate to skid and jettison our human selves like a couple skipped stones. The black smoke dissolved into the air around me as I landed back on my somewhat-human feet, letting the rest of the energy spread out for a tasteful landing. My body was heavy to me, tired.

"Back inside?" He pointed to the grand column entrance some ways back. I nodded warily.

Raziel was right up to keep pace next to me in a sort of half-jog.

"What. IS. It." He hissed again, eyes locked on the side of my face; you could practically hear that will breaking.

"Rebirth" I said shortly, scowling at those around me and trying to make this peaceful offering as tense as possible. I was so very run-down by keeping up this ruse, far too much face-time for me to handle in such a crowded amount of time. I missed the outside world, badly. Raziel watched around us as well, keeping his voice low.

"But… that's Heaven-only. I know for sure that's JUST Heaven only." He watched my eyes intently as I said nothing more, only raising an eyebrow and tilting my head a little. His face blanked, leaning closer to shake his head, "Right?"

"I pulled some strings. Make a pun out of that and I'll end you."
"What's the catch?"

"Present soul only." I frowned just a little more, "That's the catch." I looked back to the Fate entrance, still a good eight or nine hundred yards away; my head snapped to those around me, gawking still as my trudging walk was panning into a public march. I needed damage control. Growling, I grabbed Raziel's head and shot us back into the base, past the barriers and into that first atrium gilded floor to ceiling with fictitious gold.

My skin tingled with residual energy, hands on my knees quickly to gasp for air. Raziel mimicked alongside, trying to recover enough to speak, half taken back if my wild assumptions understood anything.

"That's... how is that...?"

"It's not a redo. It's a restart." I tried to explain, "You wouldn't have any memories of this life, but you'd be the most 'you' possible." My gut felt like molten lead, sloshing around as it felt awful just to talk about.

"You'd be a new person, but it'd give you a chance to try again and life a full life without my interference."

My voice grew quiet again.

"That's the very best I can do." Just the thought of him forgetting everything I'd worked for on this mission was unbearable. It physically hurt to think about, and I couldn't understand why. Those were some of my greatest joys in this life; not the power, the fame, the influence I had to turn the tide as I generally saw fit; it wasn't the leadership responsibilities at all. It was having that connection with another person on a deeper level, being able to tell them anything without it being taboo, without being frowned upon. I tried to smile. It wasn't just like I was losing a friend; it was like I grew that bit more inhuman, insensitive to the world. I'd lost so many already.

"Nothing?" Raziel suddenly slumped heavily against the wall. I looked back at him as his eyes were wide and excited, not the exact response I was looking for. No. No more. No more meddling. I had to stick to that. If this made him happy, that should make me happy too. My plastic smile didn't change, corners of my mouth working hard to remain positive. His face suddenly clouded with worry, "What'd happen to the rest of me?"

"It'd become the skill set for someone else. Just like everyone else."

"From life to life, that personality is the undying constant. I know that first hand; you'd still be you. But everything else, memories, knowledge, so forth, would be gone." I muttered, leaning against the wall. "I mean you wouldn't be exactly you, environment has a big influence in how you're brought up, and it's not like you'd suddenly just snap to and still be the same person you are now. It's just an option. Like I said before, you're free to do what you want."

"I'll take it." He said without hesitation. My horns felt like they could slide off the back of my head.

"What?" I turned around to him, brooding lost momentarily by shock.

"It's the best option. I'll take it." He said a little more carefully, looking back to me as I couldn't figure what to do with myself, sliding a little on the wall before I stood back up straight. I couldn't believe this. "When can we do this? Can we go now?" My mouth flapped like an open door.

"You want to do this NOW?" My voice cracked as the angel shrugged, giddy for the prospects of going to die. Idiot! Do it for his happiness, not yours! Buck up! Keep it together! Like a squirming mass of eels, I tried my best to hold onto that facade. I should be good at it. I smiled. "I mean, sure! Yeah! We can go now. If you want." He nodded, looking around like he'd just won a free cruise.

"Cool! Yeah, absolutely. Let me just uh…get a few things. Stay here." I grinned, nodding excessively as I turned away from the atrium, walking calmly towards my room. My feet plodded rhythmically as I got farther away before my steps became more disorganized. I started stumbling, barely walking, going faster. I had to be happy, had to keep positive; this is what he wanted. Restraint in other's free will, I had to learn to let go. I had to be patient. Have that calm, collected mind. Had to be a leader, had to be strong. By the time I got to that door, one eye was twitching hard.

I ducked inside that pitch black room to the soft, soothing waterfall that calmed so many of my worries whenever they arose, quieting down my generally noisy, raucous soul. It was where I came to think, came to relax, came to unwind.

As the door slid closed, I broke down alongside it, sobbing out loud, wrecked cries that muffled to stale air with the soundproof door; just like I had designed it to do.

43

I sat alone in that dark room with my back pressed tightly to the rock, the disheveled heap of human emotion called Nona. There was nothing left to me, nothing to hide all plain as day and apparent as ever as I sobbed a little more, quieting down. I couldn't let this all go so easily; I couldn't ship my friends off to that great beyond of life at the snap of a finger like it was nothing, I couldn't lie to myself. I wanted to be selfish. I wanted to hold onto that idea that no, there was no clean escape, that his best chances were to stick around here; but I knew he wouldn't be happy. Maybe that's what I had to accept. Maybe that'd what I had forgotten; my greatest joy in life was helping those close to me, was interfering, to a point. I couldn't just sit by and watch life take effect, I had to direct it. Had to shape it, try and make it better.

I don't think there was a way to change my incessant meddling. If I didn't, I fell apart. To be needed, to need those around me, to fit into this fabric of after-life and direct those through smoothly, that was my mission. It's for his happiness, I reassured myself over and over, rubbing my eyes. I sat up a little taller. I wanted to be selfish; but I had to know when to let go. No goodbyes.

Lowering my head again I sniffled, running my hand over my eyes and nose to try and clear some of the tears away as I finally stopped crying. Speaking of ridiculous; here I sat. A wish waiting to be granted, a duty waiting to be performed, and I was taking a ten-minute sob-a-thon to work out my own personal issues. I wanted to be selfish; this conflict was all about what I wanted. My own selfish thoughts.

I stopped, lowering my head back towards the ground.

I wanted to be selfish, but I wanted his happiness more. Ultimately, that's what got me back to my feet. It's what got me moving past that door to my dark little sanctuary and back into the hallway, determined.

It's what moved me past that, kept me walking. By the time I got near the auditorium I had formed a thin, crispy layer of self-determination that acted like a buffer zone, muttering internally reassuring sentences to will my next steps, to go farther. But as soon as I saw him sitting there, generally looking around the room and acting bored, it started again. Broke. Like a grand pirouette I instantly turned my back to him as the tears cascaded down my face, horns ripping into the wall and making my smooth move all that more awkward. I couldn't stop. I wasn't audibly sobbing anymore, the tears just wouldn't stop coming. If I could shove the things back into my face, I would, but there was just no slowing this down.

"Neri?" Raziel called out behind me, obviously confused why I just had my back to the room for no solidly good reason. I straightened up, coughing a little to try and rid myself of that horrible sobbing voice, gargling around until I found the tone that lacked all warbling emotion. It came out sounding a lot like a robot.

"Ready to go?" I could hear him get up, walking closer, instantly suspicious. I crossed my arms a little tighter, freezing up. Not that I hadn't cried around the guy, but this was me, trying to be strong. As if my mental little fail-tornado wasn't validated before, it was sure working overtime now. "We should get going." He was all of a few feet back now, still stalking around me with somber steps, trying to catch a glimpse of my face. Instantly, an idea popped to mind as I reached over my head, pulling that war-mask from the air itself to slide over my face, to protect myself. It was a pretty pitiful cover-up by anyone's standards. Not to mention the only thing the mask did show was my eyes, the part that gave this ruse all away. I nudged the mask off-center with my thumb.

"You okay?" He asked, tilting his head a little to try and see through the battle-scarred mask as I nodded thoroughly, still weeping like an open wound. Guess I couldn't control every aspect of this life after all.

"Absolutely." I said with tethered pep, turning away from him to stand back in the grand auditorium. Twisting, stretching out my back, his stance hadn't shifted a bit. You could almost physically see him computing everything together, percolating on it. Neither of us said anything for a full minute, both standing, glaring at one another like the enemies we had been when this all started out, the terrible names we slung back and forth because neither of us really had a damn clue what was going on. In that way, we were united, I guess. In confusion and a hopeless sense of abandonment from what we had known, it's how we became friends, dissociates.

But standing like this now our friendship seemed just that tiniest bit farther away. I, stuck in some stupid battle garb in some grand, central palace forged on lies and half truths; while he stood opposite, stripped down to pretty much the bare essentials of the human soul. I raised my head just a little bit; collected tears on the inside of my mask suddenly rolled out, dripping audibly to the floor. I wasn't fooling anyone.

"Oh, well, that's good. For a second there I was starting to think you were crying. How silly." He said flatly, walking towards me with intentions for the door. The drip pattern changed as I followed his walk, watching him pass me by as he stopped, looking to some old relic off to the side. "I would've been honored." The crying ceased, just for a moment.

"Honored?" Why honored? In his shoes, all I would've felt was guilt. Shame. I had to keep that out of this situation, but honored, that would not be my first choice. Without provocation, the tears started again.

"I don't know." He shrugged his shoulders, taking a deep breath as he looked over the object nervously. "I'm just one guy. To find I really meant something to a person who's met a million of my type, it's endearing." I tried to smile, lips twitching back unevenly as I took another deep breath and lowered my head a little more, almost bowing at the fallen angel. Considering, it was more mature that anything I could've scrambled together at that moment. Ironic.

Like a slow, bitter reveal, I pulled the mask back, propping it over my face like a distended visor. The tears coursed more than ever now.

"They won't stop." I coughed out a jagged little laugh, sucking air back far too fast and heaving a little instead. I was a mess, plain and simple. "I'm trying. It's not working so well right now."

"Well, Why?" His tone dropped all hints of a joke, dead serious, "You said it yourself, I mean, you're always talking about how a new life is the best thing a person can do for themselves. If it wasn't for you, I wouldn't have that chance anymore. I should be thanking you, not having you cry for me." This didn't help my tears out much at all as I remained quiet, pensive.

"Neri. Hey." He snapped his fingers a little to try and get my attention, get me to see him eye to eye. "I'm not dying, I'm just going away. You know, vacation."

"Something's telling me this is goodbye." I finally spit out. There it was. This didn't feel like all the other 'see you laters' that I had said to other friends, other acquaintances. It felt like the end. Like death. Like goodbye. Stripped of his past soul, there'd be no memory of myself left there, no remainder of the childhood of Christopher, nothing. I'd be the only witness to that tale now, my memories the only thing that remained of it. Wiped clean. Gone. The end. Even though he would live on for himself this time, it was the end to another dear friendship, one step closer to being inhuman. The remnant, watching all your dear loved ones go on and pass you by. You weren't truly human, that next step closer to utter demonization and isolation from the rest.

Raziel suddenly burst out laughing; my head shot up fast enough to almost snap that war mask back over my face. It was an uproarious, loud, boisterous laugh that was completely out of place, startling even. I didn't know what to make of it, half confused, and half just plain insulted; this was a sensitive moment, Goddammit! He suddenly knocked his head against the wall on accident, sides shaking as it calmed down just enough to get words out.

"Like that's ever stopped you before!" He cracked out before laughing harder again. Remaining confused, the very ends of my mouth tried to tug back towards a smile as he continued on, "I know you, Neri. You wouldn't let this go without even trying." With my eyes back to the floor, I smirked just the tiniest bit more.

"I said I wasn't going to meddle. I mean it."

"Oh, bullshit." He laughed again, wiping the tears from his own eyes. "I wouldn't have agreed to it if I didn't think you would." Grinning a little heartier, I tilted my head just a bit.

"What do you exactly mean by that, Mr. Raziel?" I think he just gave me clearance to continue to meddle around, to pester, annoy, and bother my way into change in this new life. The angel grinned.

"Means whatever you want it to, Excelsis Nona." His excitement quieted down, fell back just a bit to a hush. "People are people. You seem to be the same person from one form to the other, even if you had yourself splintered, or whatever the Hell you did. Who's to say I won't be the same person? Hell, I might even be better!" Wanting to fully ride on that train of thought, I couldn't help but be honest.

"I've got a lot of experience being me, Raziel." With a soul like his, this upcoming life would be the main factor in how he turned out. The only reason I turned out the same time after time was because my praesens soul was beefed up with enough previous lives to make a bodybuilder weak with fear. For me, the chance of variation was minutely small. For him, it ranged around 93%, with a 100% chance of him never remembering me again. Shaking my head a little, I tried to clear these pessimistic thoughts.

"I guess there's only one way to find out." I said softly, leaning from the chair to stretch back onto my feet. I stared straight into his eyes. "Are you ready?" There was extra emphasis on 'are': are you still willing to do this? Are you prepared? Are you sure? Is there any doubt left?

He kept up that same doofy smile once, ready to answer energetically, ready to continue this bluff for a few sentences longer as he suddenly frowned at my gaze, growing serious, reply dulled down to the same muddied uncertainty I carried about.

"Yes. As ready as I'll ever be." Neither of us made a move, both stuck in our own thoughts, our own internal war with no escape as I kept nodding, breaking the gazing war occurring to look about the room. I closed my eyes, nodding.

So many memories of this same conversation, echoed through the ages. This palace had once been a gathering place of friends, who leave after their souls wear down; eroded away by years and years of the same screaming lawn outside, of the prison-haven I lived in. Eventually, they always go back into that pool; the demonic version where nothing is left intact, where your dearest friend from one life may become your enemy in the next. Where everything became the same middle gray, time and time and time again, and life began anew.

"…Are you?" My eyes opened back to him as he let the question hang in the air. Would he wait? Was he asking for time? A delay in this? I scanned over him visually; I could see the regret, the doubt himself, could see the question opening this decision up to me. The possibility he could stay, at least for a little longer. For my sake. Catching my breath, I stopped.

I wanted to be selfish.

"I want you to be happy." I said best I could, taking a few deep breaths. "And I know that happiness is found elsewhere for you." Human beings were tarnished. Imperfect; and I was one of them. I had my own wishes; yes, they were selfish, stubborn, rebelliously angry little noises, but ultimately I had to think for the greater good. For the big picture stuff. A small, battered smile crept to my face.

"I'm ready." I nodded, hand up by my face. I was no longer crying. Heroics aside, I may have simply run out of tears. "Let's go."

"I can take you to the surface if you need me to." There was a voice from the hallway, Cempe's head darting out from her doorway, listening in. Frowning and getting to my feet, I walked quickly over to the atrium's side, hearing another door close simultaneously as I did. Privacy was not a word commonly used around here. I turned back to Cempe with a sigh, looking back to Raziel before back to my sister.

"I'd appreciate that." I conceded as she rushed out from her room, following me back into the atrium with her eyes deviously glued to a slightly worried Raziel. She didn't utter a word; turning her head up to look away like she couldn't be bothered.

"Why can't you fly up there yourself?" I stopped next to him as Cempe went ahead, working to disarm the security barrier at the door. "Are you injured?"

"Exhausted. I've got no energy to fly anywhere, much less to the surface. Or Heaven for that matter."

"Wait, how are we going to get to Heaven, then?"

"Mike's got something set up for us." The face on Raziel almost washed all fears, regrets, shame and problems away in just that moment. I smiled, pushing my angst as far away as possible as the security barrier disappeared. "Yeah, I'd be scared too." Cempe pulled the Decempedia from the wall, letting it dissolve away with an almost perky look back on us both.

"Anywhere specific, or just up top?" She led the way as her own black smoke began to waft about, waiting for the signal.

"At the 3rd Nexus point, straight up." I rubbed my face as

immediately, it seemed like we were on Cempe's back. The fate lunged from
the steps to the Moirae temple in the weapon form, swooping low over
Alvo to surge upwards through the cavernous rock at a breakneck speed. I
sat a little closer to her spine; arm wrapped around one of the protruding
horns scathed with tick marks, shaking my head a little. She had to be
anxious to ship Raziel off as soon as she could. He raised his head, both
arms wrapped around a spine two vertebrae down.

"Is there a specific time we have to be there at, or something?"
He questioned, suddenly ducking low on her back as an outcropping rock
grazed close. Her wings were like a cross between a bat and a stalactite; not
the best for agility or speed, but could take far more damage than mine
ever could. I shook my head.

"I'm just excited to see you leave!" She craned her head back over
her shoulder, grinning with half-attached pieces of flesh dangling from
her jaws. Her wings busted through another stalactite, shuddering the
flight a little with a dip off to the side as we both braced for it. "Things can
finally go back to normal around here." Cempe mumbled to herself happily.
Something tapped my shoulder, speaking in as much of a hushed whisper
as possible.

"Why does she hate me so much?" Raziel's eyes darted to my
sister's head and back to me, trying to ask as stealthily as possible.
Unfortunately for him, horses have great hearing and he was fooling
absolutely nobody.

"You gave me Typhoid!" Cempe growled out, telling the end of
the story and just assuming everyone else would know what she meant
by fragmented bits and pieces of a much larger and more interesting tale.
Waiting to see if she'd do it herself, I filled in with a grumble.

"Cempe was in that same life with you and me. She was my older
sister. We try to pal up together in these lifetimes so we can keep an eye on
each other." Raziel and Cempe both simultaneously nodded as I spoke loud
enough for them to understand. "She's convinced me hanging out with
you for that month made me a carrier for Typhoid, as she got sick and died
about 5 months after you did." Raziel's eyes went wider.

"Oh!" He looked up towards Cempe as she lent us an eyebrow and
a discerning smirk, expecting an apology like Raziel had any capacity to
get or give Typhoid on purpose. Continuously, I shook my head no as she
ignored me. "Well I'm really sorry that happened." The fate turned back
ahead, already grinning.

"All your family had to do was not drink dirty poop water and we
all would've had a much better life. But no!" I could see the angel frown,
rolling his eyes. We exchanged similar fatigued glances as I tried to fix the
situation. "No, we lived in a time where half our town bathed in the same
toilet water in the streets!"

"Alright, Cempe, that's enough!" I barked as she started laughing.

I turned around to Raziel. "She has a hard time saying 'Thank You' or accepting apologies. Even if you don't give her ammunition to fight back with, she'll make some shit up."

"Right." He said flatly, readjusting his seat on her spine.

"I don't have to 'make shit up', I got to watch my sister dwindle away into a manic, catatonic mess for 16 years and being unable to do a goddamn thing!" She shouted again but with her words tipped in real anger and frustration. "You go through the same thing, stuck at arm's length away, dead, then talk to me about how a 'oopsie, sorry that happened' is good enough." Angered, I spoke out in real frustration.

"People don't choose to die of Typhoid, Cempe! Just like you don't get to choose if someone is at fault. It happened. It sucked. It's over. Move on with your life you don't get to blame someone and you don't get to have closure!" The beast spit out a guttural hiss, accidentally brushing the last of the cave stalactite before we headed straight up.

"Watch where you're flying!" I turned back towards Raziel, trying to mediate best I could. His eyes were locked at her back, picking at some of the scales and dust there.

"It's not your fault, Raziel." I said quietly as he looked up, sacked with guilt and worry. "Similar but much kinder advice; nothing we say today changes what happened. The whole town went through a wave of Typhoid right after you died." He paused, looked around, and peeped up at nearly a whisper.

"I am sorry."

I nodded.

"I know you are. She knows it too. Don't worry about it."

She remained quiet, pointed towards the speck of light piercing through that darkness, racing for it, until we made it back to the world that was more pine-scented and lovely than this one.

"Good luck." She said to me after she dumped us out, still in that demon form, eying the exit. I nodded, looking over to Raziel and back to Cempe. She followed my gaze, furrowing her eyes a little bit as I repeated the action, flaring my eyes up to try and make a point. Say something! Last chance to settle those differences; wish him good luck too, just something! Her eyes glazed over in understanding to half-slices of wary apathy. "Don't fuck up this opportunity, you're lucky to have it."

Cempe growled, dropping back into the world of Hell below us, leaving this area blissfully quiet. Taking long, deep breaths I looked around us, hands in my pockets to try and keep this iron will going. All the trees in the area were flattened; brushing against the earth like a great gust pushed them all over. Regarding behind me, the blast zone went on for a few hundred yards more, trees still standing upright like fringes on the end of the sky. Despite the destruction, it sure beat a lava river full of disrespectful corpses lolling about. I felt a little better coming back up to this level of earth, much more so then being stuck with bio luminescent lighting and a room that smelled like a compost heap on the best of days.

"We've got a little farther to walk, c'mon." I nodded at Raziel as he quickly nodded back, obviously nervous. I didn't blame him. Our time was coming short, so many precious questions at hand that I wished I was allowed more time to ask. I stuck with the important ones that would gnaw away at my soul if I never found them out. "Can I ask why?" I said calmly, taking large, slow, lumbering steps, still stuck at the full nine feet. Suppressing the future soul took energy that I just didn't have.

"What, you mean for the…" Raziel laughed, "Like I said, you talked so much about it."

"Respectfully? I call bullshit. What's the actual reason?" His joking tone subsided into silence. I decided to elaborate. "I know it's not just because you feel you can't fit in, or that this information is seriously THAT detrimental to your well-being that'd you'd try and forget it all. It sucks. We know it sucks, you know it sucks, but not enough to cause that bad of a crisis. I just can't figure definitively why you would do it." There had to be a reason; some of my previous friends had fallen into shambles finding out the truth; they weren't terribly sound in their expectations of life to begin with, though. He had it together more than that. I guess the real question I was asking did border those selfish lines of 'was it something I did?'

"I don't feel like I'm a part of this life anymore." He said quickly, finitely. "And I haven't felt like it for a very long time. Everyone talks of the lives they've led, the things they've done. I don't have that. There's a hazy reminder that I've lived once before, and the clearer memories from the 1630's, and even those have basically faded back to white for me. When we talked in the Gym, years ago, it felt like I knew the story, but it was the first time I heard it. But it feels like I'm fading away as a human being, that I've just become, I don't know."

"Outdated." I frowned a little, still keeping my head up. I knew this feeling well. Raziel nodded.

"Yeah."

"That's a good reason." I huffed out just above a whisper to where it almost sounded like I was disappointed it wasn't something easier that I could rationalize out and help with. "Everyone succumbs to that feeling eventually."

"Except you?"

"No, especially me." I cocked my head to the side like I was hit; this was once a deep sore for me, being called outdated, facing that the world I lived in now was not the one I started from. I overcame that centuries ago. "I'm old-hat from Greek mythology; I practically coined the term, Raziel."

"Then why do you stay around here?" He started backtracking, "I mean, if you feel that same horrible feeling, why don't you let it go?" I shrugged a little in alarm.

"You mean…. Game over?"

"Well, yeah, I guess." I paused, thinking it over. This too was something I'd mulled around until I pulled purpose from it, invented my own reassuring meaning until it fell out of the queue of things I worried about on a daily basis.

"People still need me. I can't be selfish and ignore that." My tone lowered. "Not to say I'm calling you selfish. You have all right to be." There was a long, drawn out, ominous silence before he spoke again.

"And you don't? Let's say people don't need you anymore, everything's in perfect harmony." I coughed out a nervous laugh at that as he stopped and shrugged, continuing on, "But what happens then?"

I turned back with all intention of a smart-ass remark, of a sarcastic view on the culture of the afterlife today, on pulling in all the common enemies one does about the view of the world. Blame the youth, blame violent games, blame anything with a hint of disregard to its morals like it was the epicenter of social decay. As I reached his face, as I looked into those same eyes I had to stand up to as a child, that I've faced time and time before with a benign wrath like no other, I blanked. Froze.

The joking thoughts all fluttered away with the wind, watched them carry off into the distant nothingness that I couldn't comprehend an answer. Nothing. My one ear flitted back as the moments began to turn awkward; I threw together whatever words were left lying about in cheap compensation for something meaningful.

"Guess I'm not sure" I tried to smile as I turned back ahead of us, to the clearing haloed by trees, marking the nexus point between the three worlds. Simply put, it was one of many railroad junction where the magnetic fields made ascension or descent easier; at least a couple hundred years ago. It was barely useful in this day and age, speaking of outdated. I cringed a little as Raziel kept up alongside.

"At least, thankfully, that'll probably never happen, right?" He blanketed his statements with speckles of laughter, unsure tone practically dripping onto the ground behind us. A perfect system where I wasn't needed? I'm sure he was right.

We walked to the center of the Nexus point silently; I gazed up into the sky as night was quickly approaching. Wind raced around the fallen tree trunks, blowing the grass around us like it intended to snap our souls away right here, like it was asking for us back. Trying to whisk us back into life, just like that. I used to wonder if that's how it all seemed to work in the very beginnings of our life, time long before the Greeks, long before organized culture, at the very steps of it all, souls drifting about aimlessly with no worries or fear, no stupid war to keep them pre-occupied, nothing. It was almost absurd how complicated we made this out to be. I shook my head just the tiniest bit.

"So…what's going to happen, exactly?" He pointed at his own head, "I'm not terribly sure how it worked out the first time, so it's pretty much still new to me."

"I'm not entirely sure. I don't get this treatment myself." I said quietly, faintest traces of whistling energy started to spark around us, "Here we go." The sparks snapped and sizzled in a few place as I stood still, Raziel's head whipping about to try and catch the energy as it happened. The sparks grew more common before linking into full-on lightening as it raced about us, suddenly angry and violent looking things. It was all quite intimidating, like we were about to be electrocuted into oblivious by a deviously planned trap. I took another deep breath.

"Is this going to hurt?" Raziel laughed sarcastically, eyes following the lightning as it raced about faster still.

"Immensely." I looked back to the sky as the lightning shot up higher and higher, nearly done with the preparations. I wasn't lying; it was not a pretty thing to demons like me; angels would tell me how much of a pleasant thing the transfer was. I didn't believe a word of it, must've hurt like Hell to everyone. I suddenly smiled, "Should we sing a song to ease the tension?"

"A song?" Raziel's voice was almost panicked, "What…like…some sorta chant to make this easier?"

"Something like that." I grinned, standing up straight like I was rehearsing for choir. The pathway was nearly completed, last bits of lightening streaking up in dangerous, angry patterns in the sky; I took a deep breath; it was something we sang as more of a joke, non-serious, "Earth be-looww us, drifting, falling, floooating weightless… calling, coming hooo—-!" The tunnel slammed into the ground around us before I could finish it, shooting the two poor, misguided souls like human bullets at the pearly gates themselves.

'-Oh-ome!" I coughed out, staggering back from my spot as my head swooned. I bent to my knees, hacking out a few more times as someone staggered drunkenly around me.

"Never…heard…that chant" Raziel said hoarsely as I almost groaned; only resorting to shaking my head blindly. My eyes tried hard to adjust in the light, to where we popped up at, if this ruse had worked or if I would be immediately thrown in jail like last time.

"New life might do you good, then." I squinted at the developing world around me; I could see Raziel's goofy ass eyebrows from here. "You alright?" I called out, taking a few more deep breaths to regulate myself on this ultra- pure air. So far no one had busted me over the head, so already my experience here was better than the last.

"Yeah…I'm…yeah." He was out of breath too, coughing before suddenly gasping in surprise, "What'd they do to you?" I stood up quickly, finding myself reach maybe up to his nose, just like when this had all first started out. Even before I had found anything else out, I grumbled in annoyance. I liked being tall.

At this point I also realized I was in a skirt.

"Goddammit Mike." I grumbled, brushing myself off; my ankles were healed and my scars were gone as well, all dolled up and respectful looking in a place where I was infamous to start trouble.

"They took away your horns, too." My hand was instantly at my head, running through my hair without interruption. I grinned; not that I hated the horns, but the same way where it's fun to feel a buzz-cut for hours on end, this was my version. The jaw-horns were gone as well. "Is this what you'd look like normally?" My eyes snapped back to him and this theory.

"No, it's just a repression of those aspects. I do believe I'm 'incognito'" I quoted with my fingers, eyes falling back down to my skirt. "The other version is normal, this version is not. People tend to get alarmed if I show up regularly. So it's half that and half Michael skewing this situation so he gets a laugh out of it. Which he's no doubt doing somewhere right now." I slowly went back to feeling my smooth jaw line, coughing out a few more times before I realized I was staring into a void of activity. I snapped back to attention, still awkward.

"So, uh…we're here." I gave an empathetic flail of my arms at the whole lot of bright scenery around us. I turned my head this way and that; in front of us was a large, elaborate walkway paved with white and barely off-white flowers, sketchy, lacy-looking tress stretching far into the sky to disappear with the clouds. It was mesmerizing, like a twisting string of ribbons forming dazzling shows. Shielding my eyes, I could almost get lost in the scenery around it. "Despite everything, it's really pretty beautiful." I said softly, already feeling more at ease. I kind of liked it here; maybe I should overturn it in violent battles more often.

"I think that's where we're supposed to go." He pointed behind me, at the large, white, technical building that stood alone. There were a few people here and there, some outside, some making that sacrifice indoors. "Looks like a hospital."

"Life and death do tend to mirror the other, that doesn't surprise me." I turned to the same direction, suddenly having this terrible pang of fear and nervousness at the time we had left. I think he was feeling this too.

"So do you have to go now?" He questioned with just a tinge of fear to his tone. I almost smiled.

"I didn't survive a stupid lightning tunnel to wimp out the first five minutes here. If what I hear is right, the inside works like a hospital too; they're not going to zap you back entering in those doors." I laughed nervously, pointing to the entrance where an old couple talked between the first and second doors as an example." I'll wait with you. Waiting's always the worst part anyways."

The inside was just like a regular hospital as well; we got in there and had no problem registering his name, in which we were told to sit and wait for the doctor, or 'after life specialist' to call when his turn was up. It felt like I was sitting on a bomb in these amazingly comfortable waiting-room chairs. The area was speckled with other people; mostly elderly couples sitting side by side, holding each other's hands and reassuring them of their soon-to-be passing love. I squinted, almost studying them; they made this departure look all too easy, I had to say I was a little amazed with the general tenacity of the crowd. Maybe this was the key in my understanding, that I lacked the maturity and insight of a person who lived life like it was their last. I frowned. I was finally seeing the side of Heaven I wanted to believe existed; the good, honest, and pure side that was hard to come by anymore.

I looked back to us, sitting side by side, but staring off in completely opposite directions. These people all had reassuring words to make this exit more natural, more special, I guess. They were giving that kindness back, dredging up stories and jokes that had happened in their lives, or here in Heaven to make the other laugh, to send them off with a smile. Basically, they were using all their mental resources, their experience to make this seamless, while I sat here using the group like research, studying the findings. I opened my mouth to say something just as the Specialist came through the door.

"Arthur?" He called out kindly, two nurses at his side. Both our heads watched as the old man stood up with a smile, whispering back to his wife and loved one, nodding a few times and leaving with the doctor like he'd come right back. My stare stayed with the wife who stood there, hands folded, praying silently, not a single tear shed. She bent her head a little lower, mouthing the words as she only smiled, looking to the outside walls. And like she hadn't just thrown away her hard-earned relationship she nodded to a few of the other couples before heading for the door. I was almost bewildered. Lingering there for a second, feeling that time frittering away, I turned back to Raziel, only to find him staring at me.

"So…what exactly do they do?" I hopped a little in speech, throwing my compliment barrage on the back burner while I answered this question. I'd start after that.

"Dice the present and the past soul, throw them into the pool." I rolled my hand quickly, trying to ease into this rather unsubtle act smoothly.

"So it's possible I'll get my memories back?" He questioned as I stopped again, feeling rushed.

"In some sense, you could, but the likelihood is next to infinitely impossible. Present and past souls dissolve at different rates, ensuring you don't get any repeat offenders. Past souls become natural skills/ talents, not remain as memories." I stopped, tilting my head a little, knowing these were the spotty remnants reincarnation theorists thrived on. "Not usually. So at the best case, you'd have the same skill set as before. But still none of the memories."

"Ah." He shut up for a second as I took that deep breath, ready to lay it on the line, "You sound like you studied this." I stopped again, growing frustrated.

"It was my original mission to find out over 3000 years ago; now, listen Raziel." I finally managed to start as the doctor came through the doors again.

"Christopher?" He called out as both our eyes popped open. No way. Not yet. I scanned behind me as no one else was standing up, looking to our faces expectantly. There was no time! Nothing!

"Y—yes?" He called back as the doctor extended a hand behind him warmly.

"It's your time, son." My eyes grew huge. No nonononono, not yet. I spoke up immediately, jittery.

"Any way to get a bump down on that list?" The doctor looked back down to his clipboard before glancing over at the receptionist and ending the visual tour with his two nurses.

"No, I'm afraid not. C'mon, time to go." He called again to Raziel as he stood up uncertainly, grinning as nervous as I'd even seen him. I stood up too.

"Ra—-" I stopped, glancing about, switching gears. "Christopher, wait, please, just a second." His turned about half to face me, looking at the other people around us before back to the doctor and finally back to me. I fumbled for a second with this added attention, feeling that weight slowly begin to crush the truth out of me, begin to dull away that nervousness. I had no other time, now.

"Don't let people push you around, don't let them sell you short of anything less than who you are; don't listen to naysayers who tell you can't do something; just live for yourself, do the best you can in this life, work hard to achieve all that's coming to you and steps after that." My tone only pushed faster and faster like I couldn't stop, "Insults hurt as much as you let them; life is too short to worry, too precious to forget, too essential to live without-the moment we forget this is the moment we truly die. So don't take everything to heart and never forget where you are and where you've come from, do your best I have faith in you and I know that you'll do great things!" I ended it practically shouting, gasping for air like an obnoxious fool. That was hardly tactful. Figure a lifespan as long as mine, I'd learn some tact. You'd think that would happen. Slowly looking back up, he seemed almost bowled over with the information.

"A—alright." He said in shock, like he was registering the information without anything to come back with. The doctor smiled awkwardly in my direction as he put his hand on Raziel's shoulder, trying to lead him into the other room. The fallen angel began to turn away.

"That was very helpful." The doctor nodded again as my face was left looking like I needed a paper bag and an answer, an actual retort to my compliment barrage. Raziel looked back to the door and back to me with a sort of urgency, an understanding of the time gone, of the end of this ride, of the true meaning of this event. His lips curled up in a snarly twinge of a laugh, face blanking in panic the next moment.

"H-Hold on a second." He spoke to the doctor, worming around between him and the nurses to stand just in front of me. Without a word his arms wrapped around me, pulling me close against him. "Thank you. I wouldn't have this opportunity without you, Neri. I wouldn't be here, wouldn't have done anything differently, still would've worked as a bargain basement exorcist for at least another fifty years or so. You've done absolutely nothing wrong, so stop acting like you have." He whispered as I remained pinned, unable to move. I'm not sure I would've.

"Besides." He patted the top of my head heavily, suddenly making this as 'little sister-ish' as possible, "You gotta keep your energy up to find me when I surface again, make sure I don't turn out to be a shit. I'm counting on you, Neri." This is why I hated being short.

"You could just try not to be a shit, that'd work too." I smiled a little, closing my eyes. A handful of instances all flashed by at the same time of this same situation, reversed, revisited, relived in previous lives. They were vivid bits of life, moments that stuck out when I was truly happy. Here again now, it all felt the same; I relaxed a little more. "To die will be an awfully big adventure." His hug stopped.

"Isn't that from Peter Pan?" He laughed, letting me go. I frowned, retracing it back, eyes popping open as I remembered that's exactly where I heard it from. God-damn Peter Pan. I'd been carrying that mantra around for almost ten years thinking it was some great insight of poet laureate, and it was from God-damn peter pan. I huffed out my distaste softly.

"Dammit." I said before an awkward laugh, rubbing the bridge of my nose as the doctor was behind us both again. His smile said warmth while his body language read like a bouncer. There was no time left, and our extension on that had run to an end. I bowed a little out of respect. "This is it, Christopher." I held strong with a steady smile; he returned the sentiment.

"Goodbye Neri." He said it like the word surprised him, nodding a few more times as I nervously scratched my head.

"No, no. I'll see you later. It's not goodbye." His eyes flared back open.

"Right! Yes! See you later, then." The angel nodded a few more times awkwardly as the doctor led him away with a gentle hand. I remained standing in front of that door as he soon fell out of sight, fading away into the other room, still looking back to me, grinning. I kept my smile up stubbornly as that last bit of gray hair disappeared, as I was the spirit standing awkwardly in front of a door I'd never pass through, the intersection into rebirth that I'd never cross, left to act like the guardian that I was supposed to. It was all so terribly depressing for just that moment, before a hand suddenly fell to my shoulder.

"I'm proud of you." I jumped at the voice, expecting Paul or Michael behind me with a guilty conscious, only to find one of the other women standing there instead. I looked back to her as she nodded and smiled, to her husband who did the same thing. "At such a young age, too." She complimented again. I smiled, taken back by the honest generosity and strength they were trying to lend me, trying to help. That in that brief, beautiful second, we were that middle gray. Equal.

Before I could utter a single thank you, I felt it. That same pull I had dashed through as a monster escaping Gauzier that first time, that net being pulled thin, stretching tight; the bond was breaking. The tether. My head whipped around back to the door; I wanted to bust through, I wanted to convince him otherwise, wanted to be selfish all over again. But the last smile he gave me made me stop; it was the exact same smile I'd seen while he was dying with typhoid in that cot, that raw, truthful, happy glint of soul that shined through despite everything, like true enlightenment. That alone kept me anchored where I was as it pulled tighter, reaching the breaking point. My ankles shook, wanting to move. He was happy. I couldn't replicate that.

Pulling in a deep breath, I held it once again, lowering my head with my hands folded down, eyes closed as my nerves struggled to remain calm, tried to stay put. That connecting line sang with tension, stubbornly holding on, as desperate as I felt. I had to let go. This was it.

Snap.

Just like that, it was done, broke away completely, gone. I felt that bond, that life, that soul flow away from this area, felt it pass on, felt it dissolve that tether into nothing. I nodded my head a little lower, purposely opening my mouth to let out that breath, to take in another, to move on with just the intention of a smile. It hurt; so much more than I expected it to.

I wanted to be selfish, but I made someone happy instead.

EPILOGUE

"I like the part after that."

I pulled my head up slowly, swimming in thoughts and emotions left from this memory. It was a rough time, a rocky little section of my very long-winded life as it should be; I took a deep breath and dredged up a lighthearted chuckle, turning back here in reality.

"You get a kick out of any part where I make an idiot of myself or I do something stupid." I said flatly, reclining more against the special chair with the notches purposely worn out of the back for me. Not that I could feel it anyways, but it was rather considerate. "Thankfully that's most parts of this story. Everyone's entertained."

"But tell that part." He glared at me intently with those same blue eyes as ever, "You have to tell that part."

"Alright, alright, easy there skippy." I fluttered my hands a little bit, tapping my cheek. "So as soon as that's all done, so is my contract with Michael. In the middle of this terribly sentimental scene full of emotion and great understanding, I popped back into the full 9 feet, and Aunt Neri's head goes through the ceiling in the middle of the rebirth hospital."

He laughed, pulling the covers over his face as I grinned, his enthusiasm was infectious. It was funny now after these years, funny in retrospect. Lord knows I cursed Michael a blue streak at the time for it.

"And THEN, all the nice people who had been the sparkling example of goodness and civility proceed to forget any of what they before and chase me out of Heaven on a rail like I've never been chased before." I pointed at him almost angrily, "You never know real wrath until you get a gaggle of geezers with nothing to lose behind you. Those suckers get angry." We both laughed as he sat up in bed, fighting off sleep like every good insomniac does.

"And then with the battle the next day?" He was leading this story on now; he knew all of it pretty well for someone his age, God knows this was at least the fourth time I'd told the whole thing all the way through, all forty-something sessions of it. Endearing to know he was paying attention but it only re-assured me that our story time sessions here would be drawing to a close before I gave the poor kid a complex, or I'd be toted to school as a show-and-tell object.

"For being massively out-numbered, we did pretty well." I yawned, stretching back over the top of the chair; it was nearly 2 am. His mom would be pissed if she wandered by now to still find her son awake. "We all fought very hard to turn the tide in that battle, managed to get the others on the run for a little bit. Considering, it was pretty good. Though we did still technically lose, but no one's really keeping track anyways." My focus faded as I stopped, looking to the plastic stars glued to the ceiling like I peered into the Heavens themselves, smirking. He rested back into bed to get comfortable as I rolled around a box in my hand, back and forth.

I'd gone back to the house to salvage this scrap of ghost metal years ago, surprisingly still in decent condition for being abandoned behind the high school. I held it up against the night-light, watching it refract the colors as they bent alongside it, distorted. All angelic-made metals seemed to do that. Maybe the metal was still around because it believed it would be okay, I don't know. My hand snapped closed around it.

"So, you're how old now, Ian?" I shoved the box back into my pocket and pointed to the clock. "It is the 18th now, so Happy Birthday."

"Eleven. I told you that yesterday, too."

"Right; you'll have to excuse me, I'm despicably old." I smirked, looking off distantly. He'd made it. Lasted longer than the last time, outlived his paltry record of 10 years without a hitch. I'd been the guardian for nearly seven of those years. He was still a good kid; different, but not unlike how he had been, still exhibited traits from his previous lives. For example, he had been getting picked on by stupid middle school brats recently and had been reprimanded for starting fights. These were all claimed as self defense, but his mom specially asked me to ease off the ancient battle war-stories. All epic battles of my past from then on had only been misunderstandings, fixed with both sides telling each other how their words hurt them. Then everyone, demons and angels, would shake hands and agree to disagree. He wasn't stupid; but the fights did ease off before they became any real sort of problem. Wasn't hard to see the kid still had a lot of fight in him, reassured me that things weren't so terribly different.

But he smiled. Often. Constantly; a drastic improvement from before. I couldn't help but smile back at that.

I didn't live at the house like I used to. I spent most days with Paul scouting the state for new recruits, popping in occasionally to give a hey to Cempe, and usually wandering back to this house around dusk. I was not a guard ghost, was not unwelcome or shunned in any way. I was just a welcomed guest that didn't have to knock to get in, respected and accepted Aunt Neri, and I loved that title. I could be the unrelated ghost-aunt. I could do that.

The standard soul takes roughly seven years to pop back into the life-stream, but Raziel's took nine. I didn't have to look very hard; Michael oversaw it and had a knack for the ironic, you had to be careful of what you said around the guy. So with all that talk about life being pointless and not meaning anything, it was no wonder the search ended where this all had began and kept winding back to.

"Did you ever find him again?" He blatantly asked as I slowly looked up. Our conversation normally didn't lead in this direction; I smiled in a far-off, reminiscent way. I could still see him there, could see the resemblance, the same stare, same grin; same spots in his eyes as well, still sitting with him. To Ian, these were stories about someone else, not about his past-life. That's how I'd keep it, too. I figure once he did pass on, if he did manage to remember these stories and find me, then the memories and legacy would be his. But a kid his age didn't need that kind of baggage. Life was still carefree.

"Nah. I figure eventually we'll see each other again, though. It's a small world." I ran a hand through my hair, fingers knocking against my horns as I looked about the room for a little while longer. It was average. Perfect. Normal. Car posters of foreign makes and models that I hadn't heard of in years, sports equipment, actual football gear, clutter all topped off with cutesy knick-knacks that his mom had put in here at some point in time. None of it screamed messed up, emotionally disturbed youth whatsoever. I should've been proud, I suppose. I was, don't get me wrong, it's exactly what he would've wanted. I'd fulfilled my request, stepped in when I thought I could help, lend an ear when it was needed.

But facts were facts; playing ghost nanny wasn't the same as actually being there. Wasn't the same as his actual mom. When he mentioned in passing that he'd rather have me for a mom than Amber, that was my bright red flag to leave. I'm a friend, not a parent. I had to know when to stick around and went to give that space. From my own sea of children that I've raised, that's always how I did it, let the kid decide for themselves what they wanted to be, how to shape their own lives, add input when asked and discipline when necessary. Generally, it took a lot of screwing up to find that out. That's what made life so much fun.

"So when are you coming back next?" He asked, fingers picking at the threads of his bed as I yawned once more, fingers stretching with the light of the door. Suddenly the light flickered; a vague shadow of someone else outside the room, pacing about. My blood went cold; busted. Time to go.

"This will be my last time for a while, Ian." I recoiled from the door, ears lowering in shame.

"What? Why?" He suddenly sat up, leaning a little more from the bed. My eyes dragged from the dampened light and back to the various rehashed souls of a friend and half.

"Got things to do, people to see." I chuckled, trying to play it off as a laugh. He wasn't laughing, "I've got to meet up with some even older friends, people I haven't seen in thousands of years. People I picked a fight with, but ran away from. I've got relatives to get in touch with, stuff I've put off for far too long."

"Will you be back next week?" His eyes were wide awake now, confused little saucers desperately reading my actions for answers. Something's never changed.

"I don't believe so." I tilted my head a little as you could see the unhappiness in his face, "But I'll do my best to pop in every now and then. Don't think I'm abandoning you; your mom and I keep in touch, so If I find out you're causing more trouble at school, I won't hesitate to come back and kick your butt. I'll pass the message onto Santa, as well."

"He's not real." He said sullenly as I got from the chair, kneeling close.

"Maybe. But then again, neither am I." Ian's face flipped to something indignant, baffled.

"You're real!" I raised my eyebrows.

"Maybe I'm not. Maybe I'm a ghostly figment of your imagination!" I laughed, getting back to my feet to flounce a bit about the room. "Oh no, time to call the wacky truck, we've got another one ready for the padded room!" I managed to get him to smile a little more, but not laugh, still rather frustrated, sitting there. The chuckling stopped.

"Buck up there kid. You're 11 now; you don't need me to babysit you anymore. Practically old enough to vote and buy cigarettes. That being said don't you dare start smoking." He kept quiet, arms folded as my jokes all missed the mark terribly. Letting out a heavy sigh, I sat back in that chair alongside his bed, leaning back on it a little bit. "You know we'll always be friends, right? I'm not going away." I stopped, almost groaning in the irony of it all.

"I'm just taking a little vacation." I tried to brighten back up, "It'll give you a little more freedom, maybe now you can have some fun with your friends that are afraid of ghosts. I have no fears that you'll do just fine without me, Ian."

"If I pray, will you hear it?" I froze like a block of ice. With hearing all these stories from my point of view, and without much exposure to the regular side of church, there was a conflict on just what he'd like to worship, to believe in. As backwards as it was, I'd rather he went with the church. Not that my own twelve-step program wasn't any good, but it was the more normal way to go, if that makes sense. It did teach morals, better to pray to the idea of a loving, vengeful God; at least have that as a basis of life and build yourself out of that. Plus, it was just kind of off-putting to be prayed to. I was a friend, not a pseudo-deity. At least not to him.

"Sure." I said after a moment. I couldn't say no. "I'll get your message somehow. But, for now, it's time for bed. I can hear your mother pacing about outside, you better get to sleep little man, before we're both in trouble." He frowned a little more before crawling back underneath the covers, mulling things over.

"Will you stay until I go to sleep?" I grinned, already propping up my feet.

"Of course." I pulled the box back from my pocket, holding it back up to the light. Ian/Raziel squinted at it, inching a little closer. "01This is my gift to you for your birthday, to keep you safe from harm and whatever might come your way while I'm gone. It'll protect you." I pried my fingers under it like I intended to open in, suddenly swinging the box back up by me as his face slid to disappointment once again.

"But only after you get some sleep. Real sleep. I don't want you to just close your eyes and pretend to sleep, I know the difference." He rolled his eyes at me, dropping back into bed like he was annoyingly magnetized to it. I smiled; the box contained a rounded out bit of the first pike, something I'd been carrying around as a sort of memento, a good luck charm. There was also his graduation medal he had showed me back so many years ago, his achievement from graduating the "angelic academy" the second round in a record amount of time. It was like the materialization of hard work, perseverance, and an unmistakable drive to be the very best. It felt right to give, something just for him. It was technically his anyways.

The room began to rest, quiet down once more as I hummed to myself, looking back into the plastic galaxy above me, deep in thought. Next time I went through this cycle, I'd have to get some of these stars for my own room.

"Where are you going?" He said quietly, shuffling a little more before settling back down.

"Greece." I leaned over, placing the box on his dresser carefully. "I'm hoping I've still got family there."

"They'll be happy to see you, right?" My lips twitched into a smile.

"Let's hope. I said some very terrible things to them that I'm not proud of." My smile dropped, easing back into the chair, "I'm going back to work things out, to apologize while I still can." It was almost that I could feel the worn wood of the chair, that I was almost actually there, sitting down with him. The distance between realities was depressingly vast, sometimes. He never seemed to mind it. Even first re-introducing myself back when he was just three or four years old, there was no notion of fear. No worry, never alarmed by me, even after he realized I was a ghost, a dead spirit. It was just natural.

I could hear his breathing begin to slow, body easing and relaxing, about to head off to sleep. I could tell he was utterly exhausted, forcing to stay awake, knowing this would be the end of our time together. Shaking my head a little, I recalled all the times I'd been in this same position, standing at the edge of the death of a friend. It was only sleep this time. There was always life after this night. I folded my hands, leaning farther back in the chair. I could feel myself start to doze off, this environment all terribly comfortable. So welcoming, as it had always been.

"Don't forget about me, okay Neri?" My eyes suddenly popped back open, looking back to the kid. He was already gone; asleep, at least. Head tilted slightly off to the side, breathing slow, normal, eyes peacefully closed. I remained in high alarm for a few seconds more, stifling an echoing laugh for these same words, from millennia to millennia, and the same ones I'd always repeat.

"I won't." I said softly, resting my hands against my stomach, "Not ever."

www.ingramcontent.com/pod-product-compliance
Lightning Source LLC
Chambersburg PA
CBHW082105090726
47910CB00009B/2598